SPIRE OF FOOLS

IN ALL JEST
BOOK THREE

D.E. KING

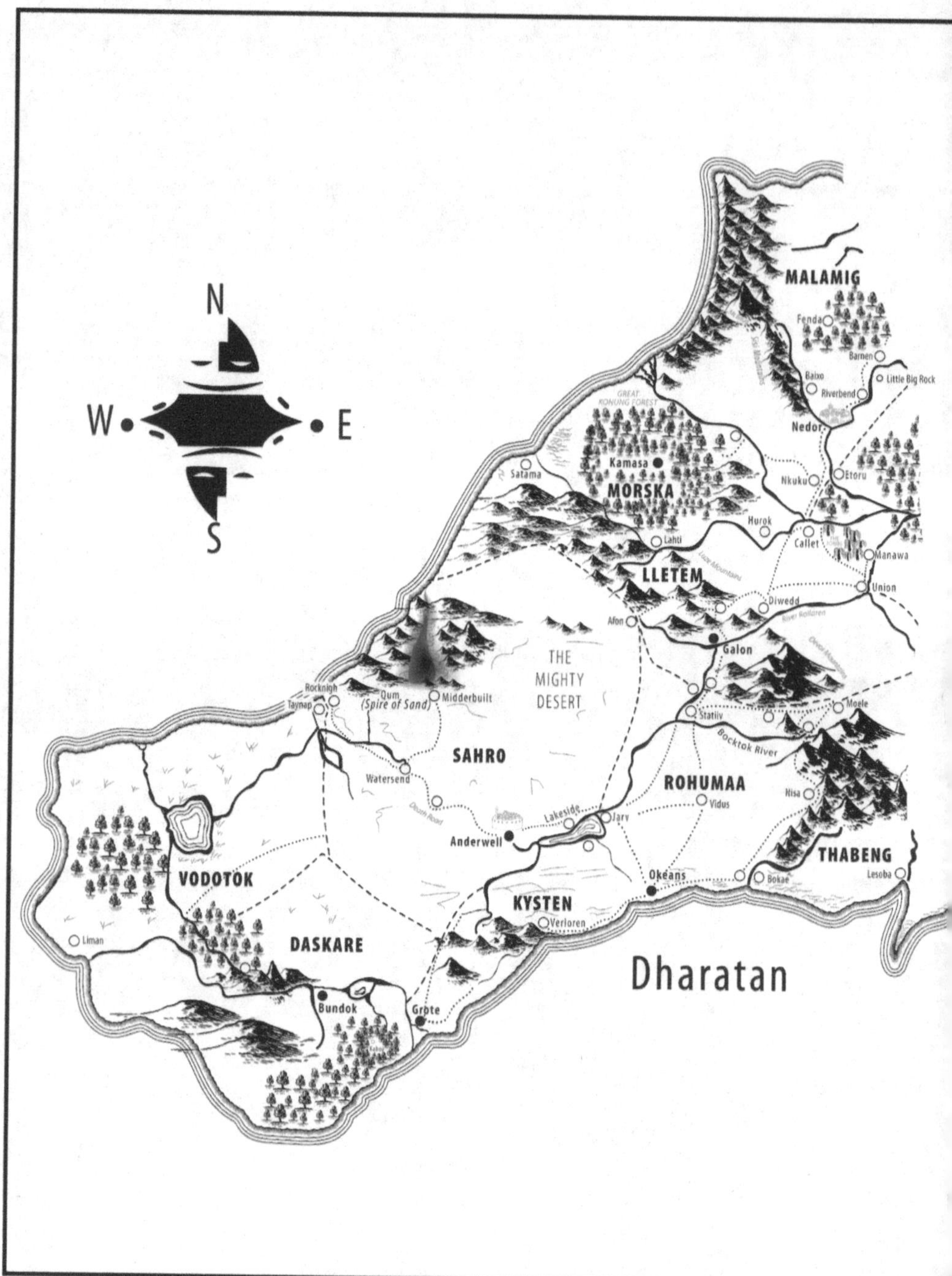

N
W
E
S
MALAMIG
Fenda
Barnen
Baixo
Little Big Rock
Riverbend
Nedor
GREAT KONUNG FOREST
Satama
Kamasa
MORSKA
Nkuku
Étoru
Hurok
Callet
Lahti
Manawa
LLETEM
Union
Afon
Diwedd
River Rolfaren
Galon
Rocknigh
Qum
(Spire of Sand)
Midderbuilt
THE MIGHTY DESERT
Moele
Taynap
Statiiv
Watersend
SAHRO
Bocktok River
Okum Road
ROHUMAA
Nisa
Vidus
Lakeside
THABENG
Liman
Jarv
Anderwell
Okeans
Bokae
Lesoba
VODOTOK
KYSTEN
DASKARE
Verloren
Bundok
Grote
Dharatan

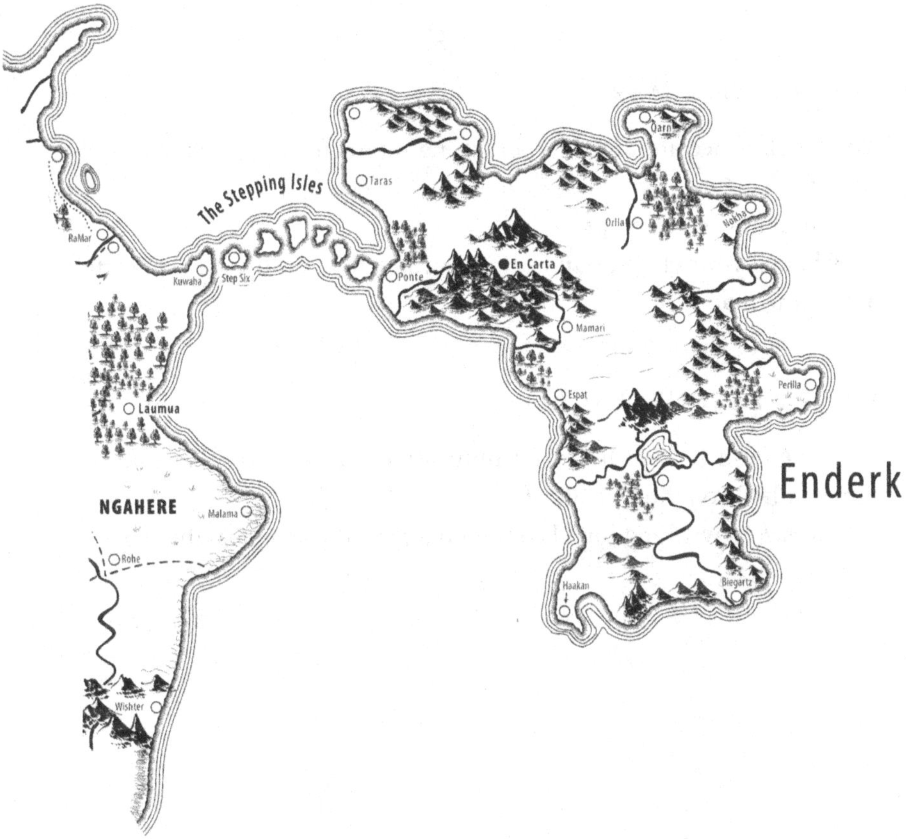

The Stepping Isles
Qarn
Taras
Orlla
Nokha
RaMar
Ponte
En Carta
Kuwaha
Step Six
Mamari
Laumua
Espat
Perilla
NGAHERE
Malama
Enderk
Rohe
Haakan
Biegartz
Wishter
Map of
Mid Scurra

INTERACTIVE MAP

INTERACTIVE MAP

This book is accompanied by an online interactive map, which can be found at

kingdarryl.com / maps.

Choose your chapter and see pins for where all the key characters are on the map.

WORLD RESOURCES

We have an extensive list of pronunciation guides and other information available on the website at

https:// www.kingdarryl.com / books / in-all-jest-series / the-world /

ARBERY

*P*eople knocking on the door was a new experience for Arbery. Unless it was someone not looking for bread, which she doubted, then those outside were getting bolder.

"What is it?" Dedrick walked in with another batch of the skimpy loaves that had become the norm now the wheat supply had run out.

"They're knocking on the door now."

"Best I stay here and watch over things then."

"No need, go back to what you're doing, there'll be more than knocking if we don't have enough of them things you call rolls."

"They're hardly loaves, are they? What else would you call them?"

Even the words between them had a terser edge recently as, pragmatic as they both were, even they couldn't get past what was happening around them. The wheat had run out over a month ago, despite the promises from the mayor. Now they baked with emmer.

At first Dedrick had refused it, but if nothing else he couldn't see people go hungry any more than she could. It was a harsher grain that made dense chewy bread.

But it was food, and Mals ate bread, it was the thing they lived off. Now even the emmer was running low. Because no one liked it, few grew it, which was fine when wheat was in plentiful supply, but not now.

The mayor had taken to rationing things and they got a single delivery each day, which was never enough. Word was that it was the same all over the realm, and even in others. Arbery had even heard of rioting or so the story went.

In theory the people outside were decent enough to let those who missed out the day before start at the front of the line. Now that everyone was suffering Arbery was seeing even that slip away.

"Off with you." Dedrick grinned and left the front of their small shop, heading back to where the baking ovens were.

Arbery took a breath, shook her shoulders out and headed to the door. She'd only just raised the bar when it pushed in on her with such a force that she stumbled backward, the bar still in her hands.

She tripped over her feet and landed on her backside with the wooden bar clipping her across her right ear causing her to cry out. Her eyes clouded over a bit, but she could see a group of men push their way in.

"Oi, stop that! We were first!"

Yelling began in the line but didn't deter the four men who pressed into the shop. Arbery saw them grab the bread on the counter, stuffing it into sacks they carried.

They'd already turned to leave when Dedrick rushed through the back hall.

"What's going on here? Arbery!"

Outside the shop those who'd been lined up had filled the doorway, those at the front being crushed by others behind, all desperate to know what was going on and not miss out on their ration.

Dedrick grabbed the closest of the men with his big meaty right hand and pulled him close. Before the man could do anything, his face was hit by Dedrick's other fist and he crumpled instantly.

The next of the robbers pulled a long knife out from its sheath and held it out at the baker. "Don't do anything stupid!"

His colleague closest to the door also drew a blade, waving it at the crowd in the door. Those closest to him were pushing to get out, while those behind were trying to see what was happening.

Arbery watched it all as though it was happening in slow motion, still shocked by being knocked over. Just as it felt like the robbers were trapped and done, the one at the door swiped his blade across the front of the woman nearest him.

Her dress sliced open over her abdomen, and blood began to pour from the cut. It wasn't very deep, but she screamed enough to halt the crush from behind.

Grasping her middle, she fell to her knees while others in the crowd began to scream. The group behind were frightened enough to stop pushing, and everyone was able to back out of the doorway.

Arbery looked at Dedrick. "No, Ded, it's not worth it!"

The man nearest him still waved his blade. Like all his companions, his head was covered in a knitted hood. In between them the fourth of the robbers lifted their punched accomplice upward as he began to come to.

"Let's go!"

They slow stepped their way out of the bakery shop waving their blades at the people watching on. Dedrick cautiously followed them.

"I'll find you, then you'll get what's yours."

The one who'd cut the woman held up his sack. "Already have, baker." His laugh was as much a sneer as anything else and once the four were free from the crowd they turned and ran, guiding the injured one as best they could.

Dedrick turned and knelt beside Arbery.

"Are you alright?"

"I'm fine, tend to Marjorie, she's more in need than me."

"There's blood on your head!" He looked horrified at what he was seeing.

"It's just a scratch. Help her first, Dedrick, she needs it more than me."

He turned and went to the crying woman who was sat against the wall nearest the door. "Go get help, you lot. Someone get guards, someone else a healer. Now!"

"What can I do?"

A man Arbery didn't recognise stood close to Dedrick. "Grab me a cloth... there's some behind the counter. We need to stop this."

Arbery got to her feet, feeling normal now apart from the throb on the side of her head. She wiped up the blood from where the wooden bar had cut her and walked toward the crowd gathered outside and shrugged

"I'm sorry, but they took it all."

A groan erupted from the group still there.

"Will she be alright?"

"Aye, she will but she'll need some care. There's nothing you can do to help now."

Slowly they all began to disperse, but not before checking for themselves through the doorway that the woman was still alive and there was no bread inside.

"There you go, you'll be okay until the healer gets here." Dedrick was trying to console the woman.

"Never seen the like of it, never." Arbery shook her head; the whole thing had her shocked.

The man who'd been helping Dedrick turned and pulled at a necklace under his tunic. On the end of the cord, he showed her a token with a jester's face carved on it the same as the small wooden version on the back wall behind the counter.

"So, you're not just a concerned citizen?"

"I'm not. And this is happening all over, Arbery."

"Robbing?"

"Yes, and more in some places. There's no wheat anywhere and people aren't happy about it."

"But this..." She pointed toward Marjorie.

"Desperate times cause some people to do desperate things."

"Surely it's not come to that? It's only bread for Thenis's sake."

He shrugged. "I've seen worse to be honest, bigger fights than this and it's not going to get easier for quite a while."

"You'd be wanting a room then?"

"No, that's not why I am here. Can we step out back?"

She looked at Dedrick.

"There's nothing you can help with here, love, I've got it covered."

"Okay." Arbery followed the stranger out to the back courtyard. It wasn't as friendly-looking as it had used to be. Nowadays they kept the back gate locked closed, except for when deliveries came.

The fence had been strengthened and raised as a deterrence to those wanting to break in, and Dedrick had begun to put spikes on the top of it.

Arbery had laughed at him, telling him it hadn't come to that, and yet, it had.

The wiry man turned and looked at her. "I'm Kalling."

"Arbery, but you know that. Why are you here?"

"Our… friends… would like your help."

"How so?"

"In the past you've spoken about doing more than just this." Kalling waved his hand in the direction of the two rooms that Arbery kept for people on the Circuit as Goran had called it. "Well, now that time has come."

Arbery thought she knew what he was asking, but didn't want to get too excited until he said it. Her heart had picked up its pace and she felt like it would jump out of her chest.

"As you've seen, things are changing. Not just about the wheat shortage either."

"Shortage… there's none to be found at all. Unless the rich are hoarding it to themselves!"

"They aren't. There's a lot more going on than what you know, but one thing that's true is it's all gone."

"All?"

"All."

"Okay. So how can I help?"

"My family, our friends, would like you to start running a discreet inn for us."

"An inn? There's none here for sale is there?"

"It's something new, Arbery. We took ownership of it some time ago, and we need it to be in place for us now."

"Okay."

"And we also need the Keeper. And I've been told that you're the perfect match for the role. You and your man."

"Really?" Arbery couldn't believe it. Just when she'd wondered how they'd survive if there was no bread at all, this comes along.

"Yes, Arbery, really."

"But what about here? We can't just abandon people when they need us the most."

"We've got that figured out as well. You'll just have to trust me."

2

KARPENMOR

Karpenmor stood stationary at the top of the marble stairs leading to the entrance to the subterranean temple complex. The iron door below was plain except for the image of a tall tree pressed into it.

In contrast the public temple above ground was ornate, expansive, and luxurious. Karpenmor didn't understand why Uksod still lived in quarters below ground when he could have chosen anywhere in the temple above that had light and fresh air.

When he reached the door he turned to his guard. "I'll be fine on my own. You can wait here."

The Vrah's face didn't change, but he nodded ever so slightly, before bracing himself into position. As the door closed behind him Karpenmor paused to appreciate being alone albeit briefly.

As he did every day when he came to visit Uksod he had to adjust to the stench of the caves.

The caves extended deep underground giving them a damp and musty smell, but what made it pungent and unbearable, at least to Karpenmor, was the smell from the bats that called the depths of the caverns their home.

The effluent and their natural stench had tainted the entire complex and he couldn't adjust to it the way the acolytes and priests seemed to be able to do.

As he began his walk the distant ever-present hum began to vibrate through him. Karpenmor had no knowledge of what it was or where it came from; it was deep and ever so slight, but there was no mistaking it.

It had been weeks since they'd found the priest collapsed and unconscious. Karpenmor had struggled to get much information from Trorn or others about why the old man was so sick.

All he knew was that no one was concerned he would die, and that he was just very weak.

He entered Uksod's room, glad to close the door behind him and take in the smells from within. The priest's room always had smouldering incense coming from a brass burner that hung on the side of the fireplace to his left.

A fire burned constantly keeping the outside chill at bay and providing some light for the chamber. Candles and several lanterns lined the walls, brightening it even more.

The high priest lay flat on his back, the bedcovers pulled high on his chest. His eyes were closed and from this distance Karpenmor couldn't see him breathe. Uksod's number two, Trorn, stood from a chair beside the bed when Karpenmor entered.

"Highness."

"Sit, Trorn. Any change?"

"None, Highness. Neither worse nor better."

"You're still adamant there's nothing a healer can do for him?"

"I am. What weakens him cannot be solved except by rest."

"For how long?"

"I cannot honestly say, Highness. The last time this occurred it was several weeks, but there's no way to tell if he is affected less or more than then."

"And nothing else you can tell me about what caused it?"

"As I have said before, Highness, there are some things within our order I cannot discuss. Even with you."

Karpenmor wondered how long that might stay true if he'd used force to push the priest further. Trorn wasn't anywhere as old as

Uksod, but neither was he a young man. Karpenmor doubted it would take much persuasion to learn what he was talking about.

He knew that Uksod wouldn't hesitate a moment to use such methods, but even thinking of them caused Karpenmor to cringe. That wasn't the way he wished to rule.

"My concern is about the cause, Trorn. You say that you know what it is, but not how to heal it. What if it is not what you think it is? What if it's something more sinister?"

"Sinister, Highness? What do you mean?"

Karpenmor hesitated. "Like my father, or a poison?"

"Ah. Your father was an illness of the mind, Highness, this is not that at all."

"You're sure?"

"While this is lasting longer than previous times, Highness, it mimics everything I've seen before."

"And he will recover?"

"Yes, Highness. While the healers can do little for him except make him comfortable, he is effectively just asleep."

"Asleep! The longest sleep ever."

"It's the best way to describe it. When his body is ready, he will wake up."

"I hope so, Trorn. He is needed, and soon."

The priest shrugged. Karpenmor knew they had had this conversation before and there was nothing new to add.

"Let us hope it is soon. You can leave me if you like, I'll stay and watch over him for a while."

It probably sounded more abrupt than Karpenmor intended, and he caught a momentary bristle in the other man, before the priest nodded and stood again. "If you need anything, please send for me."

"Of course."

Being alone in the chamber caused Karpenmor to ruminate. Nothing really came from him sitting and staring at the old man, but he knew that his desire to visit every day was due to his father's recent death.

Karpenmor regretted how little time he had spent with Schevenal before he'd passed. It had seemed pointless given his madness, but then the message and pendant he'd sent him at the end highlighted how little Karpenmor had really understood.

What did he mean in that final message? What would get him and who should Karpenmor watch out for?

Underneath it all his father had been alive and conscious of his surroundings, even if he couldn't say anything. And Karpenmor hadn't bothered to visit often at all.

Now Uksod was all that he had left of anyone resembling a family, and while the man lay comatose, he couldn't not come. He wouldn't repeat what he'd done before.

What was Trorn trying to hide about Uksod? Karpenmor still had concerns that it was his mind that was sick. Could there be a cause of the madness here within En Carta, that was being kept hidden?

Uksod had never fully explained what it was that had driven his father into the state he had been in, not in a way that made sense to Karpenmor.

Rather than it being a physical ailment that crippled his father's mind was it something external? Was it also affecting Uksod? *Will it affect me?*

He'd often worried that it was something that might be passed to him from his father just like his looks and build. So far, he'd not noticed anything changing, but it bothered him, nonetheless.

If it was an external cause, then he might still be exposed but could potentially avoid it. If only he knew what it was and how much Uksod knew?

There were so many things that only the High Priest knew of the distant past. He had lived a very long life, much longer than normal, which meant he knew things that no one else alive did.

Karpenmor had read plenty looking for answers about the amulet and the events surrounding his father's return from Dharatan. He hadn't found nearly enough to satisfy his search for answers, which only left him Uksod to learn the truth from.

You'd better recover, old man!

Getting answers from Uksod wouldn't be easy, he'd never been one to readily share information.

All the planning and timings around the enthronement Uksod had kept to himself as well, brushing off Karpenmor's concerns and questions.

While in theory Karpenmor was already the ruler, until the ceremony was completed his ascension was not official. His family had ruled Enderk for so many centuries there had been no talk of that changing.

It was the strongest of the Imperial Families that ruled over the realm, and as far back as Karpenmor had read it was the Family One that held that honor except for one time.

The Family One had taken power from Family Three, who it appeared had never recovered from that. They were still considered one of the lesser families.

Did the name of his family come from the fact they were the more powerful, or was it just a coincidence? Something else he didn't know the answer to. As Regent, Uksod had continued the rule of the family and ensured that the throne was there for Karpenmor to inherit.

He needed to remember that this frail old man had held off the other families on his behalf. Karpenmor wondered how many times the other families might have attempted to undermine that while he was still a child?

Uksod had told him that Lady Natillian's family was the second most powerful in the realm, and the most important to pay attention to, another thing he would need to understand more.

The priest knew the importance of the ascension to secure the throne, which made it even more important that it was completed. And yet there'd been some reluctance from the old man to even discuss it.

All that he could put it down to was that Uksod didn't want to give up the power he'd once had. As though he was clinging to the last vestiges of his remaining power. That was understandable to Karpenmor, and he did feel for the priest.

He needed to remember the sacrifices that Uksod had made so that the throne was now his to ascend to. Unless there was another reason?

Surely not?

He looked at the bed again, considering for the first time that maybe there was another reason for the delay.

Could he be waiting to help one of the others take control? What has he been promised in return?

The room suddenly seemed small and Karpenmor stood, pacing around it, constantly looking back at the old man asleep in the bed.

Asleep! Huh! There's more to this than I'm being told.

If there was a plot happening around him, then it wouldn't just be the head of the priests he'd need to worry about. Trorn would need to be party to it as well.

That would explain his reluctance to tell me anything.

Karpenmor stood over the body of the priest, the only movement the light rising and falling of his chest.

It would be so easy to end this now if it was true.

"The pillow would be enough to finish you off, old man."

Disgusted with himself, Karpenmor stepped away from the bed, and stood as far from the bed as the room allowed. That wasn't his way, it wasn't how he was going to rule.

Why would the priest wait all this time to finally act, when he could have replaced Karpenmor when he had no ability to stand up for himself? In all the years his father lived in the Amber Room, Uksod defended his rule to those outside wondering where their High Prince was.

It made no sense on the surface, but now the thought had formed in his head, Karpenmor couldn't put it aside completely.

I will have to pay more attention to everyone around me now. If there's any truth to this, I need to be ahead of it. Perhaps his illness will allow me to see that which I couldn't before.

There had been small things which on their own had annoyed Karpenmor but hadn't seemed more than him being impatient. Some of the palace staff were slow to react to his instructions or didn't appear to be in any rush to do as he wished.

He'd accepted that perhaps they were as unused to change as Uksod was. Karpenmor had found it hard enough to accept himself, needing to be the one making decisions rather than leaving them to Uksod or someone else.

Up until this new thought had crept into his head, Karpenmor had accepted it as part of the transition.

Unless...

The more he pondered it the more he recalled instances of those around him not being fully compliant. It was a subtle thing, as though they resented him taking it from Uksod, or was it that their loyalty was to Uksod?

Maybe I'm just being paranoid. Am I that insecure, that I need to believe he's ready to depose me, or worse? Maybe it's me that's the problem, perhaps I need to be more assertive.

Karpenmor knew he wasn't fully convinced about his own role. He thought he'd kept that hidden from others, but maybe that was one of those things people could detect without it being said.

Even more reason why the ascension needs to happen. I need to make it clear to all that the tide has turned, and things are not what they were before.

He looked over at the bed one last time, his perspective permanently altered about the man who lay there. Whether it was true or not, he knew what he had to do now.

There was nothing he could do here, or at least nothing he was prepared to do. That wouldn't be his style. He was smarter than that, he could make change his way, not with the closed fist Uksod and others used.

Despite the smell outside, Karpenmor was glad to leave Uksod's rooms and quickly headed back the way he'd come.

3

KARPENMOR

It was only a dozen steps to the top, but he always paused when he reached them, breathing in the normal air from the palace. The brightness took a moment to adjust to and he smiled as he looked around the wide hallway.

He liked living in the palace, and after his recent trip away found that he enjoyed the comforts his life brought him. All the more reason to make sure he was across any potential threats to his rule.

He laughed. If there was any attempt to overthrow him it would be by killing him, in which case he'd have no concern for rooms, fresh air or comfortable clothing.

Without the hum that filled the caves his ears began picking up the myriad familiar sounds of his palace.

"There you are, Highness."

Karpenmor turned to his assistant who appeared uptight.

"What's wrong, Aika? You knew where I was going."

"I did, Highness, but you were away longer than expected. Your next appointment is waiting."

"Remind me who that is?"

"Lady Natillian, Highness."

"Yes, of course. We shall go there now. Do we know what she wants?"

"No, Highness."

"You don't have to say 'Highness' after every word, Aika. We've discussed this before."

The young woman had begun working with Karpenmor once they'd arrived back from Ponte. With so many things to coordinate it had been a blessing. She was also the first person he'd appointed directly without Uksod or anyone else's involvement.

He didn't know much about her, something he would need to remedy, given how close she was to his daily activities. Hopefully the awkwardness she exhibited around him and in their exchanges highlighted her honesty. Having an assistant was still a little strange to him as well, but he hoped it would pass with time.

"Sorry…" She stopped herself.

The meeting chamber they approached was one of several that flanked the large main hall of the public palace on the ground floor where he conducted ceremonies and events that people could attend.

Smaller ornate rooms on either side were used for more intimate gatherings and meetings. The room chosen to hold Lady Natillian was considered the best of them all, each having a status attached to them. Leaders of the Imperial Families would always be greeted in this one unless a deliberate slight was intended.

The Leader of the Five Family was not alone when he entered the room. Her attendants, a guard and a young woman who appeared a few years his junior were with her.

"Highness," they all said, bowing their heads in respect, Lady Natillian's voice the loudest.

Uksod had always warned Karpenmor about his need to be cautious around the leaders of each Imperial Family, that their needs were not always in line with his.

Despite that he knew, he needed to get to know all of them better if he was to rule effectively, starting with this older woman.

"Lady Natillian, to what do I owe the pleasure?" Karpenmor took his seat and gestured to her to do the same. He couldn't help but look to the young woman on her right, something about her caught his attention.

She had the lightest-colored hair he had seen in some time, almost a gray tone to it, and green eyes that were noticeable even across the space between them. She was attractive to him at least, in a curious way.

He caught Lady Natillian watching his eyes and brought them back to look at the leader of Family Five.

"I wondered if there was any more certainty about the enthronement ceremony, Highness."

Karpenmor had only learned the full details about the timing of the enthronement ceremony recently.

Twice a year the sun was blocked from their view; Karpenmor did not fully understand it, but only once every few years was it completely blocked.

Known as the Tenebrosity this was the only time that the new High Prince could be enthroned. It had not been seen for nearly a full two years.

With Karpenmor having come of age and only one more eclipse to occur this year, the priests believed it would be the one. It was overdue and everyone now expected it to happen. Which is why all the Imperial Families had been advised to be in the capital for the enthronement.

"We are as certain as we can be. If we knew it for a fact it would be public knowledge."

"Of course, Highness."

The young woman brushed her hair off her face with her pale hand, and Karpenmor found himself drawn to look. A tattoo ran down the line of her forearm from her wrist toward her elbow, and a silver nose ring caught the light as her face turned.

He could feel his heart beating a little faster and nearly shook his head to clear it. *What is wrong with me?*

"And Uksod, Highness?"

That brought his attention fully back to the older woman. *Of course she would know. Who inside the staff does she pay for information? It could be Aika for all I know.*

"What do you mean?"

Lady Natillian smiled. He didn't like the look of it at all.

"Word is he is unwell, Highness. That he's been out of sight for some weeks."

Karpenmor knew there was little point in denying it but took his time in replying, a technique he had read about. *Let there be space between what is asked and the reply.* "Yes, he hasn't been his best, but nothing to be concerned about. He'll be fine to conduct the ceremony."

She looked at him without reply for as long as she could without it appearing strange. *Showing me she knows what I am doing.*

"I just wondered if he was well, Highness, no other reason."

I am not so sure that's all you mean. Why so much interest in Uksod?

She spoke again before he did. "Do you have word on when the other families will arrive?"

"Nothing specific, though I expect them imminently."

Another lengthy pause. "Let me say that their delay seems a little unusual. For something so important, families like ours thought it prudent to be here as early as possible."

What is she trying to say? There's another meaning in what she's trying to convey, if only I knew what that was.

"They do have much further to come than everyone else, Lady Natillian. I'm sure that there's no other reason behind it. May I say that your approach is noted and appreciated?"

Her smile this time was much more natural. Karpenmor's eyes drifted left to the young woman, again.

"Forgive me, Highness, I did not introduce my granddaughter." She turned to the young woman whose face had blushed slightly. "This is Bhoomi, the eldest daughter of my first-born son. She came to the capital to witness the enthronement and spend some time with her old grandmother."

Making yourself out to be old and weak, when of course you aren't. Bringing your granddaughter wasn't by accident, I assume this is how it all begins, the presenting of potential brides.

Karpenmor, stood, and smiled. "It is a pleasure to meet you, Bhoomi."

"Highness." She had risen with him; her voice was soft, and her mouth smiled ever so slightly as she looked at him.

"And are you enjoying your time in the capital, Bhoomi?"

"Yes, Highness. It is quite different to what I expected."

"So, it is your first time here then?"

Bhoomi nodded. Karpenmor felt like he could stare at her for hours but sat back in his chair and focused his eyes on the leader of the Five Family. If he wasn't mistaken her mouth had the slightest of smiles on it, which quickly disappeared when he looked back at her.

"Did you have more thoughts about the delays of the other families, my Lady?" He didn't want her to avoid that topic.

Another pause, her eyes never leaving him. "All I meant was that their trips are taking a lot longer than I expected, as if something was delaying them or they were in no particular hurry."

Karpenmor held her look. While Uksod had warned him that he needed to be cautious around her and the other family leaders, he also needed to form his own opinions about this woman.

She seems harmless enough, a little cunning but that's to be expected, perhaps having her on my side could help me in the future? Karpenmor was also a little tired of having to be on guard around everyone, all the time. He really did want to work with the people of his kingdom, not fight them.

"An interesting idea. So, hypothetically speaking what could be a cause of the delay?"

"It is not my job to speculate as to the ways of the other families, Highness."

"You have given it no thought at all?"

A subtle play on words but it was her that had begun the conversation. He knew, as she did, that she'd thought a lot about it.

"You mistake me, Highness, I have thought about it, but I do not know the actual reason for the delay, only that it seems a little strange."

This time it was Karpenmor that let his mouth turn a little up, just enough to let her register his thoughts.

"I appreciate your frankness, Lady Natillian, my question was only to seek your wise counsel."

She sat quietly while Karpenmor waited to see if there was anything she had to tell him.

"I am sure there's nothing to it, Highness."

Karpenmor took a moment before he replied. Perhaps she could help him for the benefit of both of them. "Maybe you could assist me with that, Lady Natillian?"

"I'm not sure I understand, Highness."

"If there was a reason behind it, I would be very appreciative to whoever helped me learn what it was."

This time she was the one to slow her response.

"I see."

"As you said before, maybe there is nothing behind it, but..." He let the idea hang.

"I will see what I can find out, Highness."

"Thank you. According to what our esteemed priests predict then this eclipse will be the Tenebrosity, and everyone will be able to get back to their usual business. Is there anything else?"

"No. Thank you for your hospitality, I was unsure how my visit would be received."

"I am not Uksod, Lady Natillian. Nor am I my father, either. It will take time for us to get to know each other, but I can advise that I prefer a direct conversation over any other."

"That is good to know, Highness."

Karpenmor's eyes moved back to Bhoomi, who was staring at him through the strands of hair that kept falling across her face. It took all his will to focus back on Lady Natillian before he stood and left the room.

4

LANI

Standing on the parapet of Anderwell's western wall, all Lani could see was desert. A gust of wind blew at her, forcing her to close her eyes.

Despite the sandblasting, as the residents called it, this was her favorite place in all of the city. Some days she could stand here in complete calm, not even a hint of a breeze, but on days like today, you needed to be covered from head to toe.

Lani loved staring out across the dunes, watching as the sand shifted over them. Initially all she had seen in the desert was a single yellowish color, but now she appreciated the depths and variations in color it held. It was easy to see where the red and orange stains of the walls throughout the city came from.

This is definitely not Barnen.

Not that Lani wanted to return to Barnen; her life had changed too much since she'd left there, running for her life carrying the amulet, Ashantha's mask and journal.

What she couldn't answer currently was where she did want to be. Despite how she was being looked after in Anderwell it didn't feel like the place Lani wanted to call home either.

She and Tillandra were engaged in a strange dance, uncertain of whether the other could be trusted, but still dependent on each other. All because of the amulet that was bonded to Lani.

She didn't think the older woman completely believed the prophecy was about Lani despite what was happening. If it was to be believed, then she had a role to play in saving Dharatan.

Looking out across the sands all Lani felt she could do was run away, not save anyone. She shook her head and scoffed at the very idea of her being special.

If she hadn't seen what the amulet did, and the magic these Jesters held, she'd think herself completely mad to even consider any of the prophecy real.

Lani watched more winds swirl across the dunes as the sun dropped further.

I need to be able to disconnect it from me. Until then I'm linked to it and these people, whether here or anywhere else.

She had no friends here, no one close, nor had she back in Barnen. There'd been the kin, but they had been more like her kids than friends. Odajeen was friendly to her, but it wasn't the same.

In reality she had no friends anywhere.

The sound of something scraping caught her attention, and she turned to see the older woman walking toward her. Odajeen had taken to using a stick, like Gizen did, allowing her to navigate the new surroundings more easily.

"What do you see, Lani?"

"The sea of sand, same as always, Odajeen."

"I do wish I could see it."

They stood in silence for a few minutes, Odajeen facing the same direction as Lani, unable to see what she could. It was something that Lani liked about Odajeen -- the woman had no need to speak.

"What bothers you, Lani?"

"I don't know what you mean."

"I can sense it in you. There's a turbulence stronger than these winds."

Lani said nothing, even though she knew the woman was right.

"Sorry for asking, I'm too nosey for my own good. Apart from the boys, you're as close as I have to any connections in this place."

"But you're from here… they're your people."

"They're not my people anymore. There's a connection between us, but my life is different. There's no coming back to be one of them, Lani. I am who I am."

"Does that bother you?"

Odajeen's laugh always sounded funny to Lani. It was part cackle and partly a deep manly laugh. "Only that I know something of the past now, but I don't have answers to why. Perhaps I'd be better off not knowing."

"I get that."

"So that's it?"

"What?"

"The thing inside you I can sense. You came here looking for answers, but you haven't found them."

"I guess."

"Perhaps your expectations weren't realistic."

"I was told I'd find them here."

"I understand. Of everyone I probably understand more."

"Because of your wiped memories?"

Odajeen nodded.

"Why did you come up here?"

"Sorry?"

"Well, it's not for the view."

Odajeen chuckled. "I wanted to ask a favor but now I am not so sure."

The old woman faced Lani; her all-white eyes locked in Lani's direction. If Odajeen could ever be described as staring at her, it was now. Lani couldn't bear to look at her missing eyes, so she let her vision focus across the older woman's shoulder, back along the wall.

"Ask."

"Are you sure?"

"I won't know until you ask, just do it."

They stood saying nothing, the sound of the wind filling the lack of words, until Odajeen finally began.

"I wanted you to use your skill to read my journal. Tillandra returned it to me, there's nothing they can do with it -- they can't read it. I want to know what happened, why I did what I did, and before that as well."

It didn't surprise Lani that Odajeen would want to know more about her forgotten years. Wanting to know about her own missing memories was the reason she'd come to Anderwell.

"What mask would I wear?"

"What do you mean?"

"All of the other journals that I've read, I've used the mask of the dead jester. I become them, or part of me does. That's how I can read their journals."

"I never considered that."

Lani could see the older woman's face drop.

"Where even is your mask?"

"I think it's still here." Odajeen tapped her forehead. "It has to be, right?"

Lani had seen what Ashantha's face looked like after he died and the mask came off, it was very distinct.

"I agree."

"It makes no sense. I was so certain that I should ask you… it was one of my feelings… that I should ask."

"There was no harm in asking, Odajeen. I just don't have any idea how we'd make it work. I can see why you want to know."

Inside Lani wanted to help, partly because Tillandra had told her not to, she didn't like being controlled. Also, if she couldn't help herself then the idea of helping another felt better than brooding all the time.

"I'm meant to avoid using my skill, at least for a while."

"Why's that?"

"I got sick from using it all the time with Tillandra. She said I'd drained my energy too much, not allowing enough time to replenish it after using the magic."

"And yet it was her that was asking you in the first place."

Lani nodded, before remembering the old woman couldn't see her. "Yes."

She looked toward the desert, staring at the dunes in the fading light. "I…" Lani stopped what she was going to say.

"What, Lani?"

"I feel bad saying this... but I feel like I'm being used. She lets me do it then warns me about doing too much. I think the only concern is that if I was harmed by it, they couldn't use it — me — anymore."

"Have you told Tillandra how you're feeling?"

"No."

"Maybe that's the best place to start. My instinct about you is you'll be able to read her reaction, Lani. You'll know if she's telling you the truth."

"I'm not so sure. And they've been doing so much for me, wouldn't that be ungrateful of me?"

"What have they done for you, Lani?"

"They house me and feed me, I'm safe here from those outsiders."

"Like you said, they benefit from that as well. You brought them the amulet; all they're doing is what they do for everyone they find on the road. I don't think you need to feel guilty about being fed, Lani. Not if what you say is true. I'm sorry."

"What for, Odajeen? It's not your fault, you're the one that has been trying to help me."

"I just asked you to use your skill for me, without thinking about the consequences for you."

"That's different."

"Is it, really? I asked for my benefit without thinking about what it means to you."

"It's not the same. Not to me. I understand why you would want to know. I came here trying to get my own answers... I know where you're coming from."

"You don't need to do it. I didn't know the cost you'd be bearing to do it. I only thought about my own desires, and... never mind, I'm sorry."

Lani stared as the sun set over the desert, leaving its bloody stain across the sands temporarily. While she'd questioned Odajeen's intentions when the woman had guided her toward Anderwell, she now felt she could trust what the blind woman told her.

"I don't suppose your feelings have told you how on Dharatan I could do it?"

"No, it was just a strong feeling to ask you to do it. The only thought I had was maybe it's like how we both touched the brooch and connected through that."

The experience that had happened when they'd touched the brooch her mother had left Lani still made her skin tingle. The memories of her mother being killed still brought on a tinge of sadness.

"I don't see how that would work. There was a connection in the brooch we didn't know about, but it was a separate thing, we both placed our hands on it. This would have to be different."

"I don't want to harm you. For all my belief in these strange feelings I get, there's no guarantee it's not just my wishful thinking."

"I'll think about it."

"Thank you."

The smell of burning oil from the torches drifted along the parapet, as guards finished off lighting those on the walkways. There wasn't much daylight left. Lani took one last look over the desert.

"The sun has gone now, let's walk back down." She took Odajeen's arm and turned her back toward the tower. "How are you finding being back here?"

Odajeen took her time answering.

"It is confronting. That's why I wanted to know. Being here raises questions but provides no answers. So I just have the pain of my loss, what I gave up, but no reason of why."

Lani didn't respond.

"Bringing you here was important; it was the only way to break the spell that kept me away from here. You gave me that, so I shouldn't want any more from you, but..."

"But?"

"It sounds ungrateful, but without answers I wish I had never learned of this place again. All I have is the pain that once I was part of this, once I was more than what I am now."

"I'm sorry."

"You misunderstand me, girl. I am still grateful for it; I need you to understand what drives me though. I was happy out on the road, doing what I did. I had my own sense of belonging and a place in the world. That has been upended now. I don't know what comes next."

Lani focused on guiding the older woman down the steps. She didn't speak again until they stepped out of the tower onto the road.

"The Lady in the Stone made it sound like they weren't expecting you to find your way here either. I don't think any of it is very clear."

"That doesn't help."

"I know, but we're all learning. I have no idea what it is I can do, or how. Tillandra can't explain it to me either. Their grasp on magic is limited to what they already know, but even she admits things are changing. What is it she called the change?"

"The Occultation."

"Yeah, that. She said there's more happening now than she's seen in her whole life. The fact the newcomers all arrived with special magic was a first for them. Usually, they have to coax out the skills from someone, but now they are showing up already with them."

"I can help, Lani, I can feel it, but I can't make any sense of it without my knowledge."

5

TILLANDRA

If I can't protect my own, I'm useless as a leader!

Tillandra put down her mug of chai, unable to swallow any more of it. She wasn't pitying herself; it was the standard she held herself to.

Despite what the goddess in the stone and everyone else said, she didn't feel equipped to be the leader of the Jesters. It didn't matter how many times someone called her Mother Folly, it still sat poorly on her tall shoulders.

Every morning since Kooka and Bea had brought Goran back to Anderwell she visited him in the dungeons.

If they couldn't save him from himself, and the other version of himself that he was fighting, he'd be the second of their court that she'd have lost since taking over as leader.

She'd made the final decision to send Ashantha to Enderk seeking more information on what they were up to. It was there he'd uncovered the amulet and tried to bring it back to them.

That action had led to his death at the hands of the Vrah and to the girl Lani getting the jewel and Ash's things. She was Tillandra's other major problem.

Her long legs hurried her toward the college, the morning chill

27

causing her to cross her arms across her chest. *Goran first, then I'll deal with the girl.*

Whether or not Goran had gone mad they didn't know. Right now, his alter, Zoran, was the dominant one. It had been more than a week since she'd last seen Goran.

The two of them were very different and Zoran had no alignment with the Jesters and their goals.

If Goran never comes back, does that mean we have to keep him locked away? Can I stomach that?

Her thoughts on the alternative were not much more palatable to Tillandra. Wiping his memories of everything to do with the Jesters and removing his magic would solve the issue of him being rogue, but that was a cruel option and one she had no power to inflict.

The only person she was aware of having had that done was Burgendetta, now known as Odajeen, and it was for very different reasons.

Killing was only allowed by one of the Court in self-defense. But Burgendetta had broken that rule back when she was the Mother Folly, prior to Ninarto.

The magic that gave them their powers took hers from her immediately, wiping her memories and had she not already been blind, would have taken her sight as well.

It was a harsh punishment, but Tillandra and all the Jesters knew of the consequences of such an action. Their role was to bring peace and not to kill for their own purposes.

The Court was not involved in that decision, and she had no idea whether the gods would allow such a thing. Which left them imprisoning Goran for the rest of his life.

If he wasn't himself, if his mind was broken but his skill was still active, he was too dangerous out in the world. Not only did he know about their entire organization and what they did, but they didn't know how far he might misuse his magic.

She hadn't given up on him, visiting every day and hoping to see a change. She always took the first time slot; it was easier to fit it in then before the many facets of her role took over her day.

Tillandra knew her enthusiasm was waning. The others in the

Court were ready to stop but she'd pushed them to continue. How much longer she could keep it up, she didn't know.

For all they tried, Goran hadn't improved at all. If anything, he was getting worse. His body looked weak and emaciated. He barely spoke and was dirty and unkempt.

Early on Beantic had to use her skill to subdue Zoran, but that wasn't necessary anymore. As the body faded before them, so too did his will, and his ability to influence others.

Is this where he'll live out his days? He can't go to the Broken Home, not with his ability still intact.

On the western side of the city, they had built a compound that housed anyone who had lost their minds. Some were brought to Anderwell like that already, while for others it happened over time.

Some students lost their minds while learning to use their powers. When that happened, their skill was lost as well. The difference for Goran was that his mind wasn't lost, it was under someone else's control. That made the Broken Home impractical to hold him.

I really should talk to the Lady in the Stone; it should be their decision on what must happen with him.

At the bottom of the stairs Tillandra knocked at the steel door. The guard inside walked over and looked through the grill.

"Good morning, Mother.

"Good morning, Hulfer."

"Coming in?"

She nodded and he unlocked the door before opening it inwards. Once she was inside, he locked it again and hung the keys beside it.

No keys were allowed close to the cells, and the guards stayed out in this anteroom far away from the reach of Goran's mind, despite how weak he had become.

If only Goran would take over again.

~

Tillandra sat at the table in the middle of the room. The chair was too small for her long legs, but it did a good enough job, even if her knees were up near her ears.

She looked around the semicircle of cage-styled cells; all but one was empty. Only those in the Court, and the guards, knew of their existence. She laughed.

Assuming that guards have never spoken of it. Probably the whole city knows they exist.

Today she struggled to sit here and be still. She had larger issues than him to attend to, time for this was running out. Something needed to change, and soon.

"But not yet."

Her voice filled the open space and the man on the cot stirred. A few moments later he raised a hand and rubbed at his eyes, before turning over from facing the wall of his cell. "Mother?"

The crackled voice was weak. She chose not to reply, not until she knew who it was she was speaking to. It wouldn't be the first time Zoran had tried to trick her.

Slowly the man swung himself upright, his long locks of hair flopping across his now heavily bearded face, before he swept it away. The mannerism was very Goran-like to Tillandra, even in the dim light of his cell the way he did it felt familiar to her.

He stood and walked clumsily toward the metal bars that made up the door to his cell. "It is you."

Tillandra smiled at him. "And it is you, or so it seems."

"He's winning, Tillandra, I don't get through often."

"Why are you letting him win?"

He stared at her curiously. "What do you mean?"

"You don't seem to be fighting."

"He's so strong..."

"Why have you given up on us, Goran?" It felt good to use his name out loud -- to him.

"Why have I given up on you?" His voice rose in pitch as he said it and his eyebrows disappeared up into the wild locks. "You gave up on me."

"No one has given up on you, Goran, we're here every day with you."

"You know what I mean." He waved his right hand around in a

circular motion. "Before. Using me as a courier at best, out on the Circuit. Never sharing what was going on in the Court."

"You knew it was only temporary."

"Was it?"

He shook his head back and forth like he was trying to shake something off.

"What's the matter?"

"He's coming. I get to feel it before it happens now. I can't beat him."

"You can and you must, Goran. We need you."

"I'm not sure why… anymore."

Tillandra felt his words cut her inside. It pained her to see him even if he was playing pity on her.

"It's not him that you need, but me." The change in voice was abrupt and Tillandra instinctively sat up straighter. "What does he have to offer? Nothing, he's weak and pathetic."

"Go back to sleep, you're not welcome here."

"It would seem neither of us are very welcome here. Look at the dreadful place you're holding me captive. Treating your own like this is an abomination."

"YOU are not one of our own."

"Get used to me, Tillandra, I'm not going anywhere." Zoran reached out for the wall with his left arm, bracing himself as though he was about to fall.

Tillandra watched as he seemed to be wrestling within himself. Despite his confidence, he didn't appear to be as dominant today as he proclaimed.

Seeing Goran's body so frail and struggling to stand she wanted to go in and help him but resisted the urge.

He grunted several times, deep internal sounds, and slid down to the floor. With great effort he crawled over to the cot that was his bed and dragged himself up onto it.

Tillandra wished Goran would come back for longer; she had questions to ask him, especially about what he'd done back in Nedor that had gotten him banished.

Perhaps it wasn't him at all, but Zoran? That would make a lot more sense. Did I make the right decision?

Her thinking was broken by the sound of keys in the door behind her. Turning, she saw Junther was here already for his turn. Tillandra couldn't believe her hour was up already. She walked over to meet her colleague.

"That was different."

"What?"

"For the first time Zoran was only out briefly and it was like Goran was able to shut him down again, or so it seemed."

"You're so hopeful, Mother."

Tillandra looked at him. She could see the lack of enthusiasm in him. "And you're so negative. Let's hope you don't end up needing us to believe in you, Junther, hey?"

She let the door bang closed behind her and left the dungeon, angry at Junther, and angry at herself. She still had no idea what to do.

6

———

LANI

little light from outside made its way under the shutter of her window. Normally Lani wouldn't notice it, but tonight she followed its journey into her room until it dissipated in the darkness within.

Sleep hadn't visited her so far and staring at the sliver of light wasn't going to help either. Instead of hypnotizing her it fueled her mind and the worries bouncing around in it.

It wasn't even that the thoughts were particularly concerning, they just wouldn't stop. Ever since her conversation with Odajeen her mind kept running through recent events.

On other days she'd been able to ignore it, but not tonight. Just talking with Odajeen about the masks had set her mind off. The idea of trying to do it intrigued her as well as worried her.

Putting on the masks affected her a lot more than just draining her energy. During the process her body changed dramatically. The most obvious change was that Lani's face and head transformed into the person whose mask she wore, but more happened than just that.

Sometimes one of her hands and even a whole arm changed into the person whose mask she wore. It had occurred to her that if she

33

kept the mask on for a much longer period her whole body could completely change.

A shiver ran down her back as she thought about it.

Would I be able to get back from that?

The last thing she wanted was to become Snibbo, the Jester whose mask she'd worn the most. His memories were bad enough. That was what she hadn't told Tillandra -- that she could do more than just read their journals.

When she was wearing a mask, it was as though she was in their mind, seeing as they saw. As she read passages from the journals it brought their memory of the event into her head.

She didn't need to read from the journal, she saw all of it, not just what they had written. But there was more: she could access all their memories, not just those written in the journal.

From the most mundane of things to what was written down, Lani could roll through moments from their past as if she had actually been there.

Now it wasn't just her own memories she had perfect recall of; all these new memories dropped into her own after she had taken the mask off. She had images and memories like Snibbo's permanently in her mind.

Lani tried to stop doing it when wearing a mask, but it was like when you bit the inside of your mouth, and you couldn't stop running your tongue across it. She was caught between the strangeness of being able to see events as if she were the one who had been there and capturing images she didn't want.

One of the oddest memories Lani had accessed was Ashantha's. She had used his mask to look back at their first meeting, and became fixated on looking at herself.

Over and over, she replayed the scenes just to stare at his memory of herself. Eventually she'd been forced to stop when the sadness of watching him die every time had set off one of her dark moods.

That didn't stop Lani looking at other memories though, she still needed to scratch that itch. She'd started probing Snibbo's memories and regretted it immediately.

The man had a voracious appetite for women and indulged them at any opportunity he could. Which meant trying to access his memories involved wading through his past physical experiences.

Even just thinking about what she had seen caused her to shudder. She understood what people did together but seeing it that way, through his eyes as a man, wasn't something she was ready to see, not then, not ever.

Lani rolled out of her bed, giving up on getting any sleep at all.

Maybe a walk will help clear my head.

She put on her boots and grabbed her coat and headed back to the wall. The climb up the stairs distracted her mind and the breeze caused her to shiver as she stood peering out into the darkness.

With no sun the desert was cold, something Lani still hadn't adjusted to. She pulled her coat tight around her body and tried to find peace in the stillness.

It didn't last long; the change of location definitely eased her thinking for a short while. Trying to not think about the masks caused the amulet to bubble to the top of her mind.

There was a spot somewhere in the back of her head that she could feel. Not like an ache, more like a hole. As though there was something missing.

For the last day and a bit Lani had locked the amulet away in the black box of Tillandra's. It was a short-term solution that allowed her to not have to carry it all day and night.

The box was very effective at cutting her off from the reach of the amulet, but at a cost. That cost had been Lani's health.

She had become dangerously weak and ill after they'd kept it locked away for just over a week. Since recovering, Tillandra had given her the box to manage her isolation from it.

Most of the time Lani was okay with just carrying the jewel, inside the black pouch. At those times, instead of the hole she could sense the slightest of touches from the jewel. She found that much easier to handle.

Thinking about the amulet always brought her down, so she let her mind wander back to Odajeen's request and what happened with the masks.

What happens to my mind when I wear them?

When she'd first arrived, the Jesters were horrified about her putting on Ash's mask. They had eventually told her why. For those not meant to wear a mask, placing one on their face would result in the wiping of their mind, or the breaking of it if nothing else.

Odajeen was a good example of what that did, and Lani had listened to what the Court had to say about Goran and their concerns for his state of mind.

Will that happen to me if I weaken myself from overuse?

Tillandra had explained about her need to protect her energy and not to do too much, but there was no real indication of how much was too much.

Would she only find out when it was too late? Would she be an empty mind wiped clean, or would the amulet take control of it, and she'd be wandering around doing its bidding?

At this point, she had more questions than answers. Lani had come to Anderwell looking to solve the questions of the amulet and her abilities, but they weren't here. Instead she just had more worries.

Like the stupid prophecy.

Lani had read parts of it in one of the books. Initially it had felt real and not just the ramblings of a crazed man, but so far they had been unable to find any other accounts.

Tillandra had decided they needed to use caution in accepting any of it as real, certainly without anything else that would confirm it was trustworthy.

Well at least that is what she'd said to Lani. The other Jesters hadn't been as convinced about its legitimacy but something about it had resonated with Lani.

She was unable to put it to rest easily, especially after the things she'd learned in Nkuku from the Watchers.

How could she be part of a prophecy? It made no sense. Why her? What could she do apart from these magic tricks?

Two sides of the same coin must face each other…

Was she one of the faces like it had read? If so, who then was the other, and what would happen when they faced each other? She didn't want to fight anyone.

So much of it read like riddles. Lani smiled as she remembered the seer she had met in Union, and the younger one in Nkuku. They spoke the way the prophecy had read.

Why did I not think of that before? Maybe one of them could make more sense of it? Was the writer one of their kind?

It was like a breeze had blown through her mind, clearing everything else away. She needed to hold onto this thought and discuss it with Tillandra.

Was there a seer in Anderwell? Or nearby?

Lani liked the idea of going back on the road to find another one and discuss it with them. Anything other than just wandering around the city every day waiting for something to happen.

She wanted an answer, any answer. Anything to make more sense out of all of this.

With this newfound clarity, Lani realized that there was a chance of finding answers in Odajeen's memories.

Being afraid of what might happen was causing her to be anxious about it, instead of seeing the opportunity that it was.

Odajeen was there when Lani was very young. The older woman had killed someone and lost all her memories. Why she had done that no one knew, but there was a possibility that the woman could fill in some of the many gaps in Lani's life.

Someone had to know why she was able to do these things, and why the amulet had bonded to her. They had to.

Maybe that person is Odajeen? I have to try, it might be my only chance to learn what I need. Perhaps that's why she's in my life, why we crossed paths.

Her mind felt much more settled now. Lani had a reason for what she was going to do today, even if she had no concept of how to do it. There may well be an answer that would help, and despite her fears being valid, she had to take the risk.

CARNUS

Carnus doubted he would ever get used to living in a city. The noise and smells still triggered his senses far too much compared to the forest where he had felt most at peace.

Even in Laumua he had never remained fully inside the city day-to-day. At any opportunity he'd made his way into the woods and soaked up the connection he felt there.

His eviction from the Tombs and banishment from Ngahere still hurt. He doubted that he would ever be able to forget or let it go.

In his own way being around Lani was the punishment that he needed to take. Just being banished was an empty feeling. It was as though he was bobbing around in an ocean with no place to land but unable to drown.

Seeing the girl like this kept his pain at the top of his mind. She was the cause of it and being around her reminded him how much he had failed.

If nothing else, he would follow her and protect her until it no longer made any sense. He still held onto a ridiculous hope that she might lead him to redemption.

What had he been told? One woman will free you from your shame, the other will not. If it wasn't his sister, then it had to be Lani.

He spent many days simply watching her as she moved about the city. So far, she'd shown no indication of leaving which had allowed him time to investigate other things.

When he could he trained with the city guards, keeping his skills sharp. He might not be one of the Protectors anymore but he would always be a warrior.

The streets of Anderwell were almost empty. It was the darkest part of the night when all but the crazy few were in bed. Carnus only needed a couple of hours' sleep each night and he usually took them just before dawn.

While others slept, he wandered every inch of the city and now knew most of the lanes and nooks that made up the strange place.

It was a big city with not all sections of it yet built out. He'd never seen a place where the walls were built so far out from what was needed, so the city could grow into them.

Every night he would at some point make his way to the tree out the back of the college. It called to him like the trees within the forests in Ngahere had.

Like magic, the spindly thing it had first been was now growing strongly upward, and its trunk was thickening. The boy Peka tended to it every day, laying his hands on it and spending hours by its side.

Whatever the boy was doing appealed to Carnus's love of the woods. He wanted to touch the tree as well but wasn't sure whether his exile included using that skill.

What punishment could be delivered to me through it?

As he walked toward the college a figure caught his attention moving swiftly down the roadway he had just entered. They were dressed completely in black, and his spine went cold.

One of them, here?

He couldn't tell if it really was one of the Vrah. Anyone could be decked out in a black outfit. Picking up his pace he stalked them on the opposite side of the road, remaining out of sight as much as he could.

They were heading toward the gardens but by a side route. There was nothing else in that direction. He didn't know what they were up to, but he knew it was very unusual.

Carnus lost sight of them several times as they turned down

multiple lanes and roads just catching a glimpse every so often. They entered the gardens and he slowed to catch his breath; whoever it was they could move very quickly.

Cautiously he snuck into the gardens half expecting a trap. Had they spotted him and led him here on purpose? No one was waiting for him when he crossed through the arch into the garden.

He couldn't see anyone. Carnus quickly stepped into the shadows pushing his back against the wall and let his eyes scan everything.

There was no one. If the person he had followed was here, they were hiding better than he had. It meant they would know he was here as well.

Carnus was prepared to wait them out, and let the dawn arrive in a few hours, exposing them wherever they were. He doubted they'd let that happen.

For now, he would have to be patient.

Out of the corner of his eye he saw movement on the wall across to his left. Carnus couldn't work out what it was at first.

It's a rope!

He looked upward and could see the rope being dragged up and over the edge of the wall. The person he had followed must have scaled it to the top and was now pulling it up.

If he could have reached the rope there was no way to grab hold and not let them know he was here, if they didn't already. He turned and slipped out of the garden, running as fast as his heavy build would let him toward steps that would get him up on the wall.

By the time he reached the spot above the garden the person who had climbed the wall was gone. Carnus stood at the outer edge of the wall and ran his hands over the rope that now was tied off on that side.

He could see where they had tied it off and dropped it over the outer wall. Carnus doubted he could have climbed as they had up one side and then down the other, certainly not at the pace they had.

If he had any doubts about the type of person he had seen, they were quickly disappearing. Looking across the land below there was nothing he could see in the dark.

If he'd been able to get there quicker, he might have seen what direction they were heading in, but they were long gone now.

Carnus had two choices. He could drop the rope so they couldn't get back in, most likely alerting them that it had been found, or he could leave it be, and go back to waiting to see who might come back.

That's if they come back tonight.

He doubted they would leave the rope there indefinitely; it would be very noticeable on the outer wall during daylight. From what he could work out they'd be back within the next two hours.

It would give them enough time to scale back up, move the rope and disappear back into the city. Except this time, he'd be here to watch them.

Carnus watched for a while longer, frustrated at losing his prey, but excited with what he'd discovered. And the idea of waiting to catch someone out gave him a purpose which he missed.

Looking one more time out across the landscape below the walls Carnus left and walked slowly back to the gardens to find a spot to wait.

Standing tightly behind the trunk of a date palm the figure in black watched the man up on the wall. He knew who he was, the Ngaherian warrior who had arrived with the girl that everyone was interested in.

He had been sloppy tonight getting seen. That wasn't acceptable and now his access back into the city was compromised.

The warrior might have considered removing the rope, or even dropping it, but chose not to. It meant he was more of a thinker than he appeared.

Without a doubt the man would be inside the walls watching for the climber to return, which couldn't happen now.

Very sloppy. I'll have to use an alternative option.

He'd spent too much time building his identity inside the city to have it compromised now. Not by a lump of a man like that one.

Perhaps I need to take care of him? Something to think on later.

Being extra cautious, the man waited another fifteen minutes before hurrying from tree trunk to tree trunk until he was a long distance from the walls.

Then he cut directly toward the desert. He had been hunting for the team he knew had to be out here, and tonight hoped to find them. He'd already eliminated most of the spots they could be holed up.

It would have been much easier if the priest had made their last contact. He was never able to be reached within the city walls, and now he knew why.

Useful information to share with the priest if he ever showed. Every full moon he left the city so they could speak, but it was never guaranteed the priest would contact him.

He'd decided to take matters into his own hands. He could lead them into the city and direct them to where the girl was living. First, he had to find them.

8

TILLANDRA

The fast walk back toward her office hadn't done anything to settle Tillandra's mood. Anyone watching would think she was heading to battle, such was the pace and grim look on her face.

When she reached the upper landing near her office, Tillandra was surprised to see one of the new arrivals, Gizen, waiting. It made her stop and check her words.

"Gizen, you're waiting for me?"

"Yes, Till… Mother. Sorry."

"Tillandra is my name, Gizen. There's no need to call me Mother, so nothing to apologize about."

"Everyone else seems to do it though."

"Habit… comfort… it's just a thing. Mother Folly is my position, not my name. Anyway, come into my office."

Tillandra led the way and waited until the younger woman was beside the chairs. If nothing else the younger woman had forced Tillandra to calm herself.

"Sit, please."

Tillandra sat beside her in the other armchair. "What can I do for you?"

"I have had another vision; it seems as though it's for you."

"For me?"

Gizen screwed up her face a little while she appeared to be rethinking her words. "Information for you."

The visions that this younger woman had were of great interest to Tillandra. There never seemed to be enough time to discuss how she received them, or any other details.

Her visions were always about things in the future, usually the near future. Vindisil was the only other person Tillandra had met that did that, but now that she was dead, Tillandra couldn't discuss them with her.

"Tell me more."

"It's about the man you have prisoner."

That surprised Tillandra. "Prisoner? What makes you think we have a prisoner?"

"I saw him. He is very thin and dirty, and his hair is all... messy, thick with beads in it. He's in a cell and you visit him."

"Ah. What else did you see?"

"I think Purple can help him."

Tillandra was perplexed. They'd seen Purple heal wounds and sores, but Goran's problems were different. "In what way?"

"My vision was of her sitting beside him with her hands on his head. He was smiling after she started."

"And?"

"That's it, all that I saw."

"The man you're talking about is one of our colleagues, and he has an internal sickness -- a sickness of the mind. I am not sure young Purple's skill could help such a thing."

"All I can tell you is what comes, Tillandra. That's what I saw."

Tillandra rubbed at the arm of the chair for a moment. "How is she doing?"

"Purple?"

"Yes."

"Okay. She is still confused about being here. She's young -- part of her feels she abandoned her family, but she enjoys being treated like everyone else here."

"That's a pretty typical experience for new arrivals. What about her skill?"

"What do you mean?"

"How does she feel now that she knows it's not normal, that she's special?"

"She's more confused about it now than she was. Before, she never really thought of it as special, it was a secret that she just used occasionally. Now it's a big deal to everyone and that is possibly part of why she is still to settle. She isn't used to such attention."

Tillandra nodded.

"And what of you?"

"Me?"

"How are you finding being here?"

"I'm here, that's all that matters. It's where I was told to be."

"Told?"

"My visions. First it was to meet Kooka which led me to Purple, but that was all just to get me to the boy."

"Peka?"

"Yes."

"And how is he?"

"Good. He seems to be happy here. He has settled to the place very easily."

"That's because of the tree."

Neither spoke for a minute.

"I'll think about what you have told me..." Tillandra wanted to discuss how Gizen understood her dreams but was interrupted by one of their couriers arriving at her door.

"Mother."

"Aster, you need me?"

"I have a message for you." He paused awkwardly. "Just you."

She nodded and turned to Gizen. "I'm sorry."

"I am done, thank you for seeing me."

"Thank you for telling me."

Once the younger woman had left the room, Aster came in. "I have this." He handed her a small silver tube, stopped with a cork.

"From?"

"Bundok, Mother. It was marked as red sky."

That caught Tillandra's attention. Red sky was the highest level of importance for a message. It told couriers that they couldn't wait to deliver it with other items, but that it had to be sent immediately.

"Who is it from?"

"One of the individuals on the Circuit, Mother. His name is Dylin, and he travels as a leather trader. He tends to loiter in inns and markets listening for any news and gossip he can pick up."

"Thank you, Aster. Why don't you go recover and I'll see if we need to send a reply?"

Tillandra sat at her desk, and gently prized the cork out of the tube. She pulled out the parchment inside and straightened it out on the desktop.

I have heard this from many sources in the city since I arrived. Something changed very recently. From what I have made out, three weather-beaten men arrived seeking an audience with King Ahn.

At first they were ignored, but the father kept up his demands and somehow forced his way into being seen. One rumor was he used magic to kill a guard, but I could not confirm that.

When he met the King, he gave him several gifts. This has been corroborated by multiple voices. The first was an old ring, something which set tongues alight. Word is it's his grandfather's, the lost king, Unx.

The ring hasn't been seen since his grandfather disappeared, eons ago, and the traveler could only say he found it in the desert. Some said he mentioned Sahro, others were not sure.

Of what I learned, the focus was always about the second gift, a beautiful orange jewel. Everyone seems to be drawn to it. It is some form of amulet, and the street gossip is that the King has never appeared better since he received it.

Gone is the rambling old man he had become, replaced by a focused man who wants to know more of where these things have come from. The King's more influential advisor, a priest named Fuling, has tapped into this.

They are looking toward Watersend, I know not why, only that's their aim. Everyone can see there are large numbers of soldiers being sent to the north toward our border. Their intent seems to be to push toward the desert and the city, but no one can tell me why.

Even in Bundok there are soldiers and knights everywhere. I have never been in a city preparing for war, but if there's a better way to describe the way it feels here, I cannot think of it.

⁓

Tillandra read the message twice, before setting it down on her desk and rubbing at her temples. That she'd previously made the decision to send soldiers to their border felt warranted even more now, and not just because of what had happened when she'd crossed the border carrying Peka.

She could only hope their preparations were enough to deter King Ahn. Somehow, she needed to understand his plans better; they needed someone closer to him.

Information was helpful, what you did with it was more important. The problem was she still only had part of the whole picture. Why on Dharatan was he targeting Watersend anyway?

The desert wasn't land anyone wanted, which meant he wanted to control the jewel trade, which would also require taking control of Midderbuilt. But she couldn't see that trade was enough motivation for what he was up to. The only other alternative was he was hunting for the Citadel Stone.

Why would he be? No one knows of it like we do, unless...

Everything Tillandra had read about the King said he was a fairly simplistic person. A brute in how he ruled but he'd never been particularly ambitious.

But the amulet had changed that — or was it his advisor, the priest? She re-read the note where it mentioned him.

Fuling. We need to find out more about this man, and what it is he's up to.

It was too coincidental that there was a religious compound now in Okeans. This priest was clearly a very strong influence and had bigger plans for the King. Not unusual, other realms were influenced by their religions, or controlled by them, but this wasn't normal in Daskare.

I've missed too many things by not having enough people in key places.

The entire purpose of their network was to feed information back to Anderwell, or at least members of the Court, so that they knew what was happening across Dharatan.

When it worked like now it was a powerful tool for them. The issue was when it didn't.

That's why I need senior people in and around each major trading center or capital.

Tillandra couldn't understand the significance of the ring. If it was the old ring of his ancestor, did it mean that old graveyards had become exposed somewhere in the desert?

Meaning treasure hunters had stumbled on this in the desert purely by chance. Why take them back to the King when they could sell them for a lot of money?

The amulet would have had some effect; Tillandra just wished she knew more about them.

I was warned more would be coming. If they are just buried somewhere, why can't they tell us where?

It was likely more would show up close by to where this one had been found. She needed to put someone to the task of finding out more about this, and where it had happened.

If King Ahn had the same thoughts, it wouldn't be hard for him to sneak small groups of people into Sahro. Their border was so large and encompassed so much barren sand, it was impossible to watch every-where at once.

How could someone just pick it up and not be harmed by it? Lani had said anyone that touched hers died instantly, but this one was different.

Tillandra stared at her open doorway, her mind drifting off a little, thinking about Lani.

The two of them had become somewhat addicted to her reading the journals, using the old masks.

Without any rest or using an animal to fuel it, Lani had exhausted her supply of strength and collapsed into unconsciousness for several days.

Tillandra should have known better. And yet, she'd encouraged the young woman, without pause as to the cost.

Since then, she'd avoided being around Lani, or asking her for help. Her sense of guilt was strong, mostly because she knew she'd do it again if it got her the information she wanted.

Tillandra needed to learn more from the past, if she was to navigate what was coming, but it wasn't the right thing to do, to harm this girl.

Despite the girl now being fully recovered, neither had returned to the work they were doing.

We need to get back to working on the journals, there's still so much we don't know. She's my best chance to learn more about this new amulet.

A new thought appeared in her mind.

Or maybe not, I could use the stones instead.

It would be a lot safer, and she had no qualms about that method at all. Whether or not she could get any sensible answers was the question. Tillandra stood, feeling a little better now that she'd decided to do something, rather than just pondering all the problems she had, and set off in the direction of the tower.

9

KARPENMOR

Three days had passed since the meeting with Lady Natillian, and he was more bothered now than he had been then. After replaying everything in his head many times he wasn't sure what it was that had prickled his concern.

She had been very respectful, he'd been polite enough and handled the meeting with her granddaughter as well as he should have.

It felt as though he had missed something that perhaps a more experienced person wouldn't have. Except he had no idea what that was.

Uksod had always been wary of her, and had often cautioned him about her — not in specifics, but it was memorable.

She was probably playing me like a lute, I just wish I knew what the tune was.

He knew that bringing Bhoomi had been deliberate and perhaps that was the only reason for her supposed concern about the ceremony and other families.

Even he wasn't naive enough to ignore the fact that many potential brides would be presented to him, each of the families hoping to lift their position through marriage into the ruling family.

Karpenmor was in no rush to get married. His mind was on the tasks ahead, but still the idea of seeing Bhoomi again was exciting.

The younger woman had been popping into his mind a lot since they'd met, and he couldn't control it. One minute he'd be doing a task or speaking with someone, the next he'd envisage her face and he would be completely distracted.

Karpenmor shook his head.

What's come over me?

A knock at his door broke his daydreaming.

"Enter."

Trorn walked into the room. "Highness."

"Trorn, I wasn't expecting you."

"There's been some change in Uksod's health."

Karpenmor waited for the priest to provide more detail.

"Twice now we've seen him open his eyes ever so slightly. The first I saw no point in reporting, however two seems more significant."

"You sure?"

"Yes, Highness. It appears to me, albeit I am no physick, that his body is recovering enough for him to try waking up. That's how I interpret it."

"Good, Trorn, that's good. I thank you for coming to see me about it."

"I will be a little busy for the next few days, so won't be watching over him, which is why I wanted to inform you myself. In case you were to go to see him."

"Busy?"

"Yes, I am meeting with the family priests, who have arrived to discuss the upcoming ceremony."

"What family priests?"

"Ah. Your Highness, one of our priests resides with each family. Uksod normally oversees their reports and provides them instruction, but for obvious reasons..."

Karpenmor rubbed the ball under his left thumb while he thought about what Trorn had just told him.

"And they are all here?"

"Yes, Highness."

"Even those from families Six and Seven?"

"Is that a problem, Highness?"

"Only that they made it here without problem, but the family heads are still a long way from arriving. Odd, don't you think?"

"I have not given it any thought, Highness."

He is very different from Uksod, that is for sure.

The man stood silently looking toward Karpenmor.

"Could you bring them to me, Trorn?"

He twisted his head, his face scrunching a little, as though confused.

"The two priests from the delayed families."

"Oh, sorry. Of Course. When would you like them to come?"

"As soon as they can, I'd like to ask them some questions."

Karpenmor watched the man hurry away before allowing himself a small smile.

Having people respond to his commands pleased him.

Another knock broke his train of thought.

"Yes?"

A courier entered, accompanied by a member of the Vrah.

"Highness, I bring a tube from the Mayor of Ponte." The young man seemed only old enough to be in service, his face not even carrying stubble for his days on the road.

Karpenmor nodded to him, and he came forward with the tube.

"Thank you, is that all?"

"Yes, Highness."

"Rest here overnight. If I have anything to send back, you'll be summoned."

The young man dipped his head before leaving, followed by the guard.

The stopper came out easily enough, Karpenmor wondering if the boy had opened it on his ride. He had been told by Uksod that couriers were always those who had never been taught to read to keep any messages secure, but that would be easy enough to fake.

～

Your Highness,

I send this notice of our completion of the bridge to Step Four successfully. As per your instructions in your visit here we had already built up enough supplies on Step Three to finish all the future bridges and work commenced immediately to move these to the western side of Island Four.

By the time this reaches your hand we will already have begun the next bridge across the narrower span to Step Five.

There was nothing else of importance in the remainder of the note and Karpenmor carried the message to his chair. It was encouraging news, those in Ponte were taking his instruction and proceeding at pace.

Getting the land bridge completed was very important to him. The original bridge's destruction during the reign of his father was a stain on his family's legacy.

Karpenmor saw the rebuild under his term as significant -- a new chapter. While his relationship with his late father was almost non-existent, he still wished to have Schevenal remembered better than he was now.

There was more to it than that. The armies they were building needed gold, and trade with Dharatan was needed to speed that up. Small amounts of trade happened now, but travel by boat was unreliable and couldn't scale.

No one had yet developed large enough boats that could cross the turbulent waters between the two continents, and half the numbers that set out were sunk.

Good news, very good news. Let's hope this eclipse that the priests told me about is a full one and my ascension will be completed.

When Trorn returned he was accompanied by two older priests, both wearing the same gray robes as Trorn; both their faces were cold.

"Highness, may I present Dellegan and Quirin." Trorn pointed to his right for the last name.

"Highness," the men spoke in unison.

"Thank you for coming. You attend a family each?"

Quirin spoke first. "Yes, Highness. I serve at the family Seven."

"And you, Six?"

"Yes, Highness." Dellegan's voice was noticeably deep.

Karpenmor stood and moved a little closer to the three men. "Perhaps you can enlighten me about something?"

"What is that, Highness?" Dellegan's words rambled together as he spoke.

"When would I expect your families to arrive in the capital?"

"I am not sure I can answer that accurately, Highness."

"Have you not just completed the same trip?"

"I have, Highness, but it was just myself and an aide. We traveled much more simply than the family."

"Were you with them at all?"

"At first, yes. I left them in time to make the meetings."

"How long ago was that?"

"Two weeks ago, Highness."

"I see. Surely you must have some idea on how long it might take, Dellegan?"

The priest's speech was even more hurried when he was being pressed. "At a guess, another three weeks or more."

"Three weeks!" Karpenmor was surprised.

"Just a guess, Highness." The priest's face had reddened a little from Karpenmor's outburst.

"What is your guess, Quirin?"

"Similar, Highness."

"Would you say that the potential Tenebrosity and enthronement ceremony are significant, Quirin?"

"Absolutely, Highness. Without question."

"So wouldn't you agree it might appear strange that your family might be cutting their arrival very close? That it's possible they might miss it?"

"I do not think they would miss it, Highness. I believe they will make it in time."

"Just surprising that other families have been here for weeks and your two might only make it a day or two before the event."

"There have been some obstacles, Highness."

"Such as?"

"While I was with them, we encountered a collapsed bridge which caused a significant delay. We had to travel nearly a week out of our way to get to one we could cross."

"Unusual?"

"Very. This bridge has stood for hundreds of years, Highness, but what could we do? It was one of the reasons I set out on my own so I could be here in time for the meetings."

"One of the reasons, Quirin?"

"A number of horses escaped mysteriously in the night from our camps and food disappeared."

"It sounds to me like there were external influences on you?"

"Perhaps. I cannot say, Highness, I left before any answers were found."

"The bridge affected my family as well, Highness, and we had similar events occur."

"I see."

Karpenmor turned away from the men and walked the room, contemplating what he'd just learned. It was the first he'd heard of it, and he had to wonder who was behind it all.

He turned back to them. "Thank you both, you're free to go now."

After they had left, Trorn spoke. "That is most concerning, Highness."

"What's that, Trorn? That there's interference or that I wasn't told of it until now?"

"I did not know either, Highness."

"I am not suggesting you did, Trorn, but nonetheless, I should know if someone seeks to delay them making it here. What would anyone have to gain from such a thing?"

"I do not know, Highness, sorry."

"Perhaps you might wish to put some thought to it. That is all for now!"

The abruptness of Karpenmor's tone appeared to catch Uksod's number two by surprise. It took him a moment to gather his thoughts and leave.

A small grin formed on Karpenmor's face.

He did like it when people jumped to his command.

Let's see if the person in my next meeting is getting used to taking my orders.

10

TILLANDRA

*H*er breathlessness had been getting worse over the last few weeks and Tillandra had to brace herself against the outer wall of the staircase while she waited for it to pass.

She could feel a burning pain in her chest that grew until she began coughing. Once the coughing subsided everything settled again and she carried on up to the top of the tower.

It had all started back in Okeans, when she'd been locked in the basement, although she hadn't realized it at the time. What was a tiny irritation in her chest had now become something more problematic.

Not that she had shared it with her colleagues. They didn't need to see her weak, what with everything else that was happening. Another cough formed deep down and by the time it had forced its way out, Tillandra's eyes had watered with the pain.

I'll be fine, it will soon pass.

She shook her head and stood tall, looking out across Anderwell to divert her thoughts. Below, the city was full of activity, people all in motion attending to their daily activities.

None of them knew about the decisions that had to be made on their behalf, or of the magic that protected them. All that the residents of Anderwell needed to know was that they were safe.

Looking out across the desert brought a small smile to her face. Tillandra loved the view that never ended, even on a cloudy day like today. The tower was higher than any of the walls making the sight unique, one which few got to see.

But it wasn't the view that she had battled the stairs for, and she turned to look at the pedestal in the center of the tower. On it, the circle of crystal stones pointed upward, the Mother Stone in the center slightly taller than the rest.

A dapple of sunlight had reached them and pierced several of the stones, reflecting mini rainbows across part of the tower ceiling.

Only a few of the closest within their society knew of the stones, and only the Court knew of the barrier they created, encircling the city.

Tillandra often wondered how it would have appeared to those who built this city, when the tower she stood in, and the four outer towers were marked so far away.

Each corner marked the outer circle of the barrier and were you to run a line from each in a semicircle you'd highlight the edge of the barrier.

That was the outer reach of the stones. Fueled by the Mother Stone, their protection extended to that line. As the year passed so too their power waned, the line shifting inwards ever so slightly, until it hardly reached the inner wall.

It was for this primary reason that Tillandra, or whoever was Mother Folly at the time, had to recharge the Mother Stone at Mount Qum. Untended, the power of the stones would diminish completely until they offered none of their magic to those within the city and would fail to keep out those of ill intent.

She didn't know the specifics of how it worked, but the knowledge has been passed onto her as it would be from her to whoever followed. So much of the magic in their lives they didn't know enough about.

Whether it was the Occultation which had obscured all past history for them, or the gods keeping the information from them, it didn't help them having to learn from trial and error.

Even something as important as the reason why she'd climbed up here today hadn't been told to her until after Lani had arrived in

Anderwell. Using the stones here to communicate with the Lady of the Stone was more than just useful, she should have known it sooner.

Tillandra was tired of stumbling around in the dark with what was being kept from them. She needed more knowledge, more understanding, so she could do her job better.

Tillandra placed her right hand on the outer ring of stones and her left on the Mother Stone. Instantly she could feel the vibration coming through them into her.

It was not as powerful as it was under Mount Qum, but more than enough to create that familiar sense of ease in her. All her anxiety seemed to slip away, and she felt calmer than she had in weeks.

Now what? Do I ask for Thenis to come, or will she turn up on her own?

"Both are the same thing, Tillandra."

"What?"

"I can detect you and you can call for me, none is better than the other."

"Okay."

"You're troubled?"

"Absolutely I am. There are so many things happening that we have little understanding of. Much of what would be helpful is either hidden or missing."

"There are reasons for that, Tillandra."

"It doesn't help me — us — do what we need to when we don't know what it is we're facing. Even simple things like speaking with you this way -- I could have done this before."

"There's a reason for that as well."

"I am all ears."

"As you and I speak now, so does the power of the stones weaken. Were this to be used every day, the protection of the city would last little more than a few months."

"That's useful to know."

"I understand, but before, there was less need. Circumstances have changed, which is why you have now been told."

"Is there more we should know now? When I look for answers they are either hidden or missing."

"That is our fault. You should understand that creating the Occultation

was no easy thing. That we were able to do it was a feat all of its own. Of course, there are things to it even we didn't understand."

"Oh great."

"Its job was to hide everything from your world, Tillandra, and it has been doing that. The side-effect is that 'everything' had been hidden, even the things we would have you know."

"Can't you just change that?"

"It's not something we can adjust. As it is, our hold over it is slipping. That which we call the Occultation is breaking and over time it will recede more."

"So, more things will come to light?"

"Yes, you will be able to learn more of the past... and more amulets will come."

"The one King Ahn has is the same as Lani's?"

"Yes, it was the one given to his ancestor, back when all of this happened."

"At the Great Fair?"

"Yes."

"I have been trying to learn more of that, but much of the history is missing or... still hidden."

"Like I said, it will come but it's not linear, things are unraveling in their own way."

"If the amulets were hidden, then it's not good that they are now being found, is it?"

"No, it is not."

"Can't you do something to stop them?"

"We did, the Occultation. But, like I said, we will not hold it forever. We cannot control how it recedes, all that we can do is to delay it as long as we can."

"Where are they coming from?"

"There are things that would I tell them to you, you could not hear, not yet at least."

Tillandra was getting more confused. "I don't understand."

"Think of the books you are reading, how you are seeing more things over time. It is like that. Parts are only visible now because the Occultation has disappeared in that area. Some of the things I could say to you would be

blocked from your understanding or hearing right now. In time you will learn much more, all of it."

"How long?"

"I do not know. We try to delay the inevitable, but we will not be able to stop it. When it is all gone, or close to that time, all the amulets will be free..." The words she was saying seemed to warble and go all fuzzy, until there was nothing.

"I cannot hear you."

There was a strange scratchy noise Tillandra could barely hear, then slowly the voice of the Lady became clearer again.

"... like I said before, some things you cannot hear. The Occultation will not last forever. When it is all gone, all of the amulets will be free."

"All? The records say there were eight of them."

"Yes."

"What happens when they are all free?"

"You have seen the prophecy?"

"There is some of it we've discovered. If they are all connected then they threaten you, is that correct?"

"More or less. They threaten the stone, not us directly. While Lani has one that cannot happen... unless."

"Unless?"

"Unless she is not one of us, not on our side."

"You mean she is one of them?"

"I mean nothing. Only that for the prophecy to occur, all of them must be present. If there is even one missing, then it cannot come to pass."

"She is on our side; I am sure of it. What makes you think otherwise?"

"I have no reason to think anything, I'm only telling you of the facts. It is bonded to her now but were she to be killed then it would seek out her replacement. Whether it is her that turns, or she is killed, her amulet is a risk."

"If we block her from it, she becomes very ill. I can't separate it from her. Do you know how?"

"We do not. The brooch does not bond like that to her, none of our stones behave like these amulets. Even though they came from the same hands."

"What does that mean?"

There was a pause, before the Lady answered, but Tillandra could sense she was running out of time.

"The men who were responsible for them both were brothers. Each was known as a Lapidarist. They carved the stones for use, but only they knew of the specifics."

"Knew?"

"There is only one still alive."

"Can he tell us?"

"He hasn't been seen for some time." The woman paused for a moment. *"You may have to make a hard choice, Tillandra."*

"Such as?"

"You may have to protect us all from Lani's amulet, no matter what."

"You mean put it in the box and let her suffer the consequences?"

"Perhaps. If it is the difference between them all connecting or not, then yes."

"I am not sure I could do that. It was killing her."

"If not her, then maybe everyone. Can you wear that cost?"

Tillandra had hoped that this conversation would put her mind at ease or provide solutions, but this wasn't going that way at all.

"You should be trying to collect as many as you can. The more you have then Lani's matters less, and you may never have to make that decision."

"How can I collect them? I didn't even know they existed until Lani turned up. I only heard of the second one once it was in King Ahn's hands."

"We will try to get you more information. The events are unfolding out of our control as well. If you can stop them falling into the hands of the descendants, then your odds improve."

"What do you mean?"

It felt to Tillandra as though the Lady was still speaking but no noise came to her. Then even that sensation went as well. Her awareness of the tower came back to her.

The figure was gone, without explanation, just another annoying thing for her to deal with. She wanted to be able to get all the answers she could, but there was always something stopping it.

How much did the stones deplete from such a session, Tillandra wondered? The Lady of the Stone hadn't said how often was too much to use them. The journey to Midderbuilt to recharge the Mother Stone was enough to do once per year, she did not have the time to have to do it more frequently.

Tillandra stood there with her hands connected to the power of the Citadel for a few moments longer. When she felt at ease again, she removed them and stepped back from the pedestal.

Immediately she could feel her anxiety creeping back in. There was no fix for what worried her, she had to make decisions. No stone, or anyone else, could fix that.

That was the burden she carried, and up until she was Mother no longer, she had little choice. One didn't step down from being Mother, you held the role until you died, or like Odajeen it was taken from you.

The older woman was the only Mother that had ever been stripped of the title, and here she was back in their lives, due to Lani. That question required some more contemplation as well.

She looked out across the city one more time before heading down to her office. There was work to be done.

11

LANI

She was still on the wall when dawn arrived. Lani was looking southeast this time down the river, which wound its narrow way toward Lake Phyrgian.

Despite not being able to see desert from this side of the city it still left its mark everywhere. Small clumps of sand gathered at the base of the trees protecting the small crop fields near to the water, a redness that tainted any structure, and a slight haze in the air.

Life clung to what little water the river provided, in stark contrast to the harsh land that lay to her back.

These few fields she could see was the only food, bar dates, Anderwell grew. Most goods came to Anderwell along the road that Lani had followed when she'd first arrived.

It amazed Lani how well this city survived in such a harsh environment, albeit that wouldn't happen if the caravans stopped.

The first of the traders coming from Lakeside, walking their wagons or mule trains appeared in the distance. It would still be an hour or so until they made it from the overnight camp to the city gates.

Lani could feel the anxiety about what she'd decided to do in her stomach. It shouldn't be bothering her as much as it was. If anything, reading those masks had more effect on her than she expected this would.

Not that it mattered, once she made her mind up typically, she followed through. And her and Odajeen already had a special connection through the blue brooch.

When Lani's mind block had been lifted, she'd discovered that much at least. Up until then the jewel had just been a memento, while now it meant so much more.

Her mother had given it to her as she died, the memories of which had only just been revealed to her. A tear formed in her eye and Lani switched thoughts, so as not to recall the vision.

There was more to the brooch, but no one could tell her what. Somehow it protected her from the amulet, or at least partially, and Lani wanted to know how and why.

She sighed and turned away from the edge of the parapet. It was time to get this done.

In for a toe, in for the whole foot.

Lani took her time walking down from the wall, and toward Odajeen's. When she turned into the roadway that the older woman's accommodation was on, Lani froze.

A chill ran down her arms and she twisted in all directions looking for danger but couldn't see any. The only people out in the city were the early-morning workers, and there were no thieves or thugs within Anderwell.

Stop being daft, girl. There's nothing to be scared about.

Wrapping her arms across her chest, Lani stepped forward toward Odajeen's. She realized her breathing had become shallow and sucked in several deep breaths to help her relax.

Outside the woman's boarding house Lani stood, staring at the wooden door, avoiding knocking. Part of her was against what she was planning to do, wanting her to turn and walk away.

It's just my mind, being stupid.

She knocked and waited. Her heart was beating faster in her chest, and she had to consciously maintain her breathing. It seemed to be an age before the door was answered by Irdan.

"Lani, it's early."

"Is she awake?"

He nodded; he'd never been a man of many words.

"I need to see her."

She followed him into the apartment where Odajeen was staying. The blind woman sat at the only table in the room.

"Lani, what is it?"

Her tongue felt dry and stuck to the roof of her mouth, even saying it was difficult. Lani waited until Irdan had left them alone.

"I will do it."

"Do?"

"Try what you asked me."

"Oh." Lani wasn't sure but it was almost as though the older woman's face brightened a little. "Are you sure?"

Lani nodded before remembering to speak. "Yes. And now, if we can. I need to get it done, or I won't."

"Come, sit and have some tea with me, you seem uptight."

"I don't want anything thanks," but she sat.

They sat quietly for a few minutes while the older woman sipped at the cup held in both hands. It always felt odd to Lani when they faced each other, and it was only herself that was actually seeing.

"You are sure?"

"Yes, but don't keep asking me, unless you want me to change my mind."

"I don't want you to feel forced by me or anyone else."

"I'm not, but that doesn't mean it's an easy thing to attempt. Are you okay to do it today?"

"Of course, I asked you, and if now is when you want to do it, then now is when I am ready."

Odajeen put her cup down on the table slowly and took her time before speaking again. "One thing though, girl, you must agree to."

Lani chest tightened a little. "What's that?"

"You cannot keep anything you learn from me. No matter what you might see or find, I need to know."

"What if it's bad?"

"What is bad, Lani? I don't want you to decide that for me. Would you prefer to not know about what happened to your mother? How she died?"

"No." Lani understood what the woman was saying.

"Then I want that from you also."

Odajeen slid a journal forward on the table.

"Tillandra gave this to me. It was my journal from when I was in the Court."

"Have they read it?"

"It is like all the other journals of the Jesters, Lani. Unreadable except by the one who wrote it, and you, when you wear their masks."

"I hope I can read yours, I'm just not sure how."

"Maybe it will help us, maybe it won't. One last question for you, girl."

Lani waited.

"Do you want to tell Tillandra, or one of the others about this before you try?"

Lani shook her head. "No. It's not up to her, only us."

They fell into silence, everything that needed to be said had been. Lani just stared at the journal, wondering if she'd be able to read it somehow.

"I'm coming to sit beside you."

"Okay."

Lani could hear the rapid breath of her companion, and as she took Odajeen's left hand with her right could feel her heart beating faster than normal. They were both anxious about what might happen despite the old woman's calming words.

With her left hand she picked up the journal and sat it on top of her knees. She couldn't read the inscription on the cover, so Lani clumsily opened the book single-handedly. Nothing happened, the scribble was just scribble.

"Anything?"

"No."

"Oh... well it was worth a try."

"I'm not done yet."

Lani flicked through random pages as best she could, but nothing changed, there was nothing in the book she could read, nor any images coming into her mind. It left her one other option.

"If you're still wearing a mask then I don't think holding your hand will do anything. I think I need to touch where it would be."

"It doesn't feel like I have a mask on, Lani."

"I know you can't see the others, but they don't look like they are wearing one either. Let me just try. I'm going to need you to lie down with your head in my lap so I can rest my hand on it."

"Okay."

Lani stood and guided Odajeen over to the sofa. She sat at one end and helped the woman lie down until her head was in Lani's lap. When she was settled Lani took a deep breath.

"Okay."

Another deep breath then as she exhaled, she placed her right hand onto Odajeen's forehead. There was something there, she could sense it.

It was subtle, a faint tingling in her hand, that let her know she'd found something. Lani closed her mind and could almost see the mask under her fingers.

She knew it was just a vision in her mind's eye but it was enough to confirm to her that Odajeen still wore her mask. Lani's finger was drawn to that spot at the top of the mask, when she wore them, that allowed her to remove it.

There was no actual hole there, just the impression of one, but nothing her hand could touch. She let her focus move toward it and felt it pulling at her.

Unlike wearing a mask, Lani couldn't connect to it the same. She sat back, frustrated.

"It's not working, Lani?"

"Something is, just let me sit with it..." She sounded cross at the older woman and stopped speaking. It wasn't her that Lani was frustrated with, it was herself, she didn't understand what to do.

There was something that she just couldn't reach, something she needed help with. A nudge, a different approach, or some extra magic.

She pulled out the jewels from the pocket inside her tunic and placed the pouch containing the amulet on the small table in front of them.

Holding the brooch in one hand she placed her other back on Odajeen's head. The feeling didn't change, so she moved the brooch and placed it between her hand and the older woman's head.

While she could sense something between her and the blue stone, it didn't help her get any closer to whatever was in that imaginary gap in the mask.

Lani opened her eyes and placed the brooch back in her chest pocket before looking at the pouch containing the amulet.

I shouldn't.

For all her desire to remove her bond to the stone no one knew how. Several times in the past she had connected to it consciously. Once she'd wandered off as if in a daze, and the other, she'd been able to tap into its magic to affect her captors.

Maybe it could reach in there? What harm can it do? Tillandra said the Derks shouldn't be able to find it here in Anderwell...

She had no other options. It was that or give up. Shrugging her shoulders, Lani leant forward and took the amulet, laying it on top of the pouch, before settling back with her hand on Odajeen's head.

As soon as she did so, everything felt different. It was as though part of herself had expanded and reached out to encompass Odajeen as well.

Everything felt muted and softer, as though she wasn't quite in her own body. She didn't really understand it.

As she looked down at the journal the cover now had words she could read.

This belongs to Burgendetta Mooz.

12

LANI

As Lani stared at the book cover, she could feel Odajeen's mind as well as her own. It was very different to the way it had worked with the masks Tillandra had given her and she was struggling to get a grasp on what was happening.

It was as though she was being sucked toward the other woman, as though the two minds were trying to merge. A warning shiver ran up her spine and Lani focused her will on stopping the movement.

By visualizing being pulled toward the woman Lani was able to fight against the power behind the sensation. It felt as though several men were pulling a rope tied around her, the effort to fight against it taking every drop of will she had.

Lani kept using the idea of her stepping her way back, even though they were the slowest steps she had ever taken, until she crossed an imaginary halfway point between their heads.

That allowed her more control, but she couldn't relax — whatever it was dragging at her was relentless.

She knew she should remove her hand and just let this go, every part of her was screaming at her to let go, but she couldn't. Lani knew she wouldn't ever do this again.

Her instincts had wanted her to leave this alone, but she'd fought against them, and now she was here she needed it to be worth something. This was a one-time deal to seek answers that possibly no one else knew.

Lani looked at the book cover and waited until she had the pull under some sort of automatic control. Then she used her other hand to flip the cover of Odajeen's journal open.

Sweat had already formed on her face, as she struggled with the two things. Whatever she was going to find out needed to be quick; she had no idea how long she could keep this up, it was much more taxing than what she'd done before.

She started at the back of the journal. It seemed the most logical place to begin, given that they both wanted to find out about what had happened to cause the wiping of Burgendetta's mind.

With the connection intact Lani was able to read everything in the book. Just as it did with the masks, she received more than merely the ability to read their words -- memories came as well, directly from Burgendetta's mind.

Unlike her previous work with the masks these memories were not visual, as the woman she was visiting in the past was still blind. Her memories were of smell, touch, and sound.

"She lives across from this building?" Burgendetta asked.

"Yes, Mother, she does," the man on her right answered.

"Why is she so important that I needed to be the one to come here?"

"There are things I would tell you if I could, but by the very nature of why they exist, I cannot."

Burgendetta shook her head.

"Why is it that more often than not, Hembleth, talking with you gives me a headache?"

"She's important, we think."

"You think? I thought you knew everything."

"There are things we know that you do not, but of the future, there's a limit to what we can tell. There is a prophecy..."

"Words no one wants to hear."

"... there's a prophecy that remains obscure. What it says is ambiguous in some parts, and recent events have made what we initially believed impossible."

"How so?"

"The girl's mother was someone we thought was important to the future of it."

"But now she's dead."

"Exactly."

"And so, you think that the girl might be her replacement?"

"Replacement? No. It might be that we should have thought of other possibilities than what we did. The girl was not alive at the time we got involved."

"How?"

"How?"

"How did you get involved?"

"We have... had, an ability to track the mother, and periodically would check in on her."

"It didn't help her in the end, did it?"

"When we discovered she had escaped Enderk, there was no expectation they would kill her. I believed they would recapture her and take her back."

"Escaped? Who was she a prisoner of?"

"The High Prince, but I cannot explain it all, there will be things I could put words to, but you'll be blocked from hearing them."

"If I didn't know how difficult you were already, I'd find that hard to believe. Most people would just say you weren't going to tell me."

"I'm serious. There are things that have been done, that you couldn't hear, see, or comprehend at this point in time."

"Because?"

"For the very reason they exist, so that knowledge of them cannot be shared."

Burgendetta rubbed her head again. She hated when he spoke in riddles like this.

"So they killed everyone but her, why didn't they kill her as well?"

"I don't think they knew she was there. Her mother buried her under herself when she died, it's likely the attackers thought everyone was dead."

"Okay."

"That and we don't think it was known she had another child."

"Another?"

"Can we focus back on the need for you to be here?"

Burgendetta knew he'd sidestepped that question; she filed it away as one to be followed up later.

"You were close by, and I need your help."

"Tell me what you need."

"She must stay alive, and it's your job to ensure she does."

"For how long?"

"As long as she needs to live."

"So, she's to come back with me?"

"I'm unsure on that."

"I can't stay here forever, Hembleth, you know that, so if you want her to be protected, then Anderwell is the place, for all the reasons you already know."

"I agree."

"Then why didn't you just say that?"

"Because there's things in the readings that make little sense to me at this moment, so I am unsure. On the surface you're correct."

"Who is looking after her now?"

"The new town captain, his name is Kyro."

"Why couldn't she just stay with him?"

"There's too much at stake, Burgendetta."

"Except you can't tell me what that means."

"No, I cannot."

"Great. Well at least our city is designed to take in strays. Is she one of us?"

"What do you mean?"

"One of the Broken?"

"In a way."

"More riddles?"

"Truthfully, I cannot tell. On the surface of things, it doesn't appear so, but there's something."

"Something?"

"I can't tell. Maybe if I spend more time with her, but that's what I don't have."

"What?"

"Time. I will be called away very soon, and I need you to do this for me."

Burgendetta shrugged her shoulders. It wasn't something she had planned for, but in the bigger scheme of things, that's what their job was. To protect those who couldn't protect themselves, and to keep the peace.

"Why are you so worried about her right now? If they don't know she existed, and they think everyone was killed, then shouldn't she be safe?"

"There was a survivor."

"I thought you said everyone but her was killed?"

"One of the attackers."

"Oh."

"He's a prisoner of this captain, Kyro, here in Barnen, so the sooner she's gone from here the better."

"Is he injured?"

"Yes, pretty seriously, from what I heard."

"So then how much danger is she really in?"

"Are you trying to get out of looking after her?"

"No! I'm just trying to understand the situation. If there's no one that knows about her, and this prisoner is badly injured, he'll probably die without anyone knowing anything else. Or am I missing something?"

"Unless his comrades decide to come back for him. Or others."

"Why would they do that?"

"I do not know if they would. They left him in the battle, but it doesn't mean that they won't try to recover him. Which just raises the chances of someone finding out."

"Surely they wouldn't attack this town? Derks aren't even meant to be here."

"This attack was very unusual. Don't trust anything about what's happened before. What I can tell you is that the future won't be like the past. It never is, but in this matter, things will be very different."

"You're worried about one bandit?"

"Assassin!"

"What?"

"He's an assassin. They are known as the Vrah, highly trained and with only one goal — complete their orders without failure."

"Except..."

"Yes, except in this case, there was failure. Hence why I believe there's a chance of the others coming back."

Burgendetta already knew she was going to do this thing. Despite the banter between them, they both knew she would follow his request. He was one of those that she and her colleagues served.

If they needed the girl protected, she and the rest of the Jesters would do everything they could to protect her.

"Who will introduce her to me?"

"I will, right now."

"That urgent?"

"I can't tell how quickly I'll need to go, and there's something I need to do to help you."

"What?"

"You'll find out."

She shook her head.

Hembleth led her by the arm downstairs and outside. The sounds of the roadway broke her reflection of everything he had just told her.

"The girl is still in shock, she will be upset when we approach her, but do not be concerned, I have a way to calm her."

"No doubt."

~

"Hello, it's Lani isn't it."

Burgendetta could sense another person in front of them, but there was no reply.

"It's okay, this is a friend of mine, her name is Burgendetta. She can't see. Do you understand?"

"Uh-huh."

The sound of the young girl's voice was uncertain and frightened.

"I met you with the guards outside of town. We spoke, do you remember?"

"Uh-huh."

"I looked after you, didn't I?"

Burgendetta heard no reply.

"I need you to do something for me." He must have turned to Burgendetta as his voice was now beside her left ear. "Hold out your hand, slowly, with your palm up."

Burgendetta did as he asked.

"Lani, I want you to put the blue stone in her hand... it's okay, she won't take it... just for a minute. You can keep your hand on it too. You will get to take it back, I promise. You trust me, don't you?"

"Uh-huh."

Burgendetta felt the small hand place something on her palm and then covered it. She felt the strong hands of Hembleth wrap around both their hands. A shock ran up her arm and she instinctively pulled back.

"It's okay. Don't be afraid, Lani, she just felt something. Did you feel something too?"

"Uh-huh."

"Good, it means you too are connected now."

"What does that mean, Hem?"

He took his hands away and the girl removed the stone. Burgendetta shook her hand before feeling over it with her other. She couldn't find anything wrong.

"What's that?"

"What?"

"I see a blue object moving over there." Burgendetta pointed in front of herself.

"You see blue?"

"Yes, an oval shape."

"Good."

"What?"

He didn't answer.

"Tell me!"

"I wasn't entirely sure it would work the way I intended."

"What did you do?"

"I linked the two of you to what is a small brooch. It has a special stone in it."

"How so?"

"How did I link you, or how is it special?"

She stared at where his voice was coming from. He was beginning to annoy her with his avoidance of her questions.

"Lani, it's okay, you can go and play now."

Burgendetta watched as the blue shape that she could see in the center of her forehead moved away from her. "It's moving."

"She's carrying it, you're seeing her movement."

"Why did you do that?"

"I told you that you will need to protect her, for the short term and that means you need to be able to see her."

"As if."

"This is the best I could do. When she's close enough to you, you'll be able to locate her by that blue vision. She's been told to keep it with her always."

"Will she?"

"I hope so, although I did a little more than just ask. Her mind will want to keep it close, it's not just for you to see her."

"What else?"

13

LANI

*L*ani felt as though a rope had been slung over her and she'd been pulled off a horse. The memory snapped shut and her mind lurched from the sudden change.

She opened her eyes to check on Odajeen but couldn't see anything. Raising her hands, she rubbed at her eyes but that didn't help. Everything was dark, darker than night.

"Odajeen?"

There was no reply. The space surrounding her was very different to the room she expected to be in. She was standing in the darkness, not sitting.

The old woman wasn't lying on her lap and Lani tried to fumble around to see if she could touch her but she couldn't. Neither of her hands touched anything.

What's happening? Where am I?

Lani felt her chest tightening, making it harder to breathe. She began to feel wobbly on her feet, so she knelt as though to sit on the floor, but her hands found nothing.

Desperately she reached out around herself, trying to locate the surface she stood on, but could find nothing. Her lack of breath worsened as her anxiety grew, causing her to feel wobbly.

The only noise she could hear was the sound of her heartbeat thudding in her ears. Growing stronger and faster the more she struggled to breathe. And then she passed out.

~

When she opened her eyes, Lani found herself still standing upright in the strange dark place. She wasn't sure but it didn't seem as dark. Either her eyes were adjusting or there was a hint of light behind it all.

The anxiety from earlier seemed to have settled. Her heart wasn't pounding, and her breathing seemed more normal. Had she fallen when she passed out? Lani felt her arms and legs, but everything seemed fine.

She seemed to be suspended in some strange place with nothing attached to her.

How can I stay upright if there's no floor and nothing holding me?

What little light there was didn't help her at all. In each direction there remained only the darkness, no shapes, nothing else to see, just never-ending darkness.

Nor was there any sound apart from her breath and her heart beating. Other than that, it was complete silence. Her stomach grumbled and it sounded like thunder rolling through the emptiness.

As she calmed herself, she tried to get a sense about the place — was it threatening or safe? Some sort of indication about where on Dharatan it was… if it was even on Dharatan?

She needed to backtrack and understand what had happened. Slowly she moved backward, trying to use the trick in her mind of seeing her past.

Lani had been sitting down with Odajeen's head in her lap. She had her hand placed on the older woman's forehead, in line with where the woman's mask should be.

She was reviewing her journal and memories… suddenly they came rushing back.

~

"What else, Hembleth?"

"It's an important stone, it will provide her with protection."

"Protection from what?"

"I cannot tell you that at this time."

She felt annoyed with him now. "So many secrets."

"Even if the words would leave my mouth, Burgendetta, you could not hear them."

"But why?"

~

Lani pushed back at the invasion in her head. *How can I see these memories without the journal? Without touching Odajeen?*

She checked around her and there was nothing to connect her to the old woman. Nothing. More deliberately this time, Lani focused on bringing the memory back.

~

"What's the plan?"

"The plan is that you and Kyro look after her and keep her safe. I have to go, I may be back soon, or not, but keep her safe, Burgendetta, much depends on it."

~

Just like she would with her own memories, Lani stopped it consciously. It was like using the masks of the dead jesters, but then it wasn't.

There was a difference and more importantly, Lani had no idea how she was accessing them or where she was. Somehow, she was still connected to the woman's mask.

I need to replay other times I've accessed a mask, to see if I can...

But she couldn't. She could only see, or remember, things that were at the top of her mind. As soon as she tried to dive into her stored memories, she hit a block.

What on Dharatan!

Lani tried again, and again, but she couldn't get to the place where she could normally see every moment of her past.

How can I not access my own mind? I can think like me, but not see the pictures of my own memories.

When she'd been younger, she'd just assumed everyone could do what she did. That it was normal to be able to picture-scan through memories and replay them like you were back there.

Other people had thought she was weird or making it up, in the end she stopped asking. It didn't stop her using it, and she'd probed her past as much as she could.

But there'd been a point where she couldn't go past, that had since been removed. Now she'd learned that had been placed on her by the gods, to protect her from the memories of her mother.

Is that what's happening now? Another block? Who did that?

The more she dwelled on it, the more her breathing shallowed, and her chest began to tighten. As much as she tried to control it she couldn't, the fear building in her mind was growing faster than she could calm herself.

She passed out again.

This time when Lani woke, she felt a chill run across her body. She felt scared. The feeling that it brought did nothing to help her maintain her calm, but it was involuntary.

Lani could tell there was nothing natural about wherever she was right now, and the sense of danger had grown. Lani knew she shouldn't be there.

As she ran her hands over her own body something felt amiss. She felt her shape, or what seemed like her shape, and clothes, but she couldn't see any of it.

The sensation just confirmed that whatever was happening wasn't right. She should not be here. The harder she tried to use the hint of light that broke the darkness the less she could see.

I'm imagining the light, there's nothing here but darkness.

Then it occurred to her what it was that she wasn't seeing.

I'm blind, that must be what this is!

The darkness was the blindness that Odajeen saw... or didn't see. As that realization hit, Lani pushed out her thoughts seeking her own memories again.

Nothing.

Next, she sought Odajeen's, and these came easily. Stopping, she sought her own again. Again she tried the older woman's and now she was able to see the truth.

I'm in her mind!

Knowing that there was a reason for her not being able to see, was helpful to Lani. It gave her a sense of control, as limited as it was.

How did it happen?

Lani knew she'd removed the amulet from the pouch which created the connection to Odajeen's mask and read her journal. As it worked with the other masks, she also became that person, at least a little bit.

Previously Lani's face changed into the face of the person whose mask she wore and sometimes a part of her body. But Odajeen was still alive... or had been.

How is this affecting her?

She hadn't become Odajeen... she was in her mind.

Was this what happened to normal people when they placed a mask on their face, why the Jesters had been so worried about Lani doing it?

Rather than having their mind wiped, did they end up in the mind of the person whose mask they wore? Lani had no idea; it didn't help her solve her problem.

Then it dawned on her, she wasn't in Odajeen's mind, she was in Burgendetta's. That was even stranger, and she had no idea if that mattered or not, maybe there was no real difference anyway.

I need to be sure.

She entered the woman's memories and found herself back in the spot where she'd left off. Pushing backward in time she let the objects of the woman's memories slide along a line, rushing past them, seeking distance from the spot she'd started.

Randomly she stopped it and entered the memory. It was not what she'd hoped for. Burgendetta was a young woman running from some-thing, or someone, stumbling in her darkness, but the feeling of fear was very clear to Lani.

She stopped, turning her mind in another direction, rushing forward in time. This time she let it keep going as long as she could, except it didn't go much past where she'd been at the beginning.

Then it hit a wall and stopped. Again, she tried to push through but ran into a barrier that wouldn't let her past. Lani slid slowly backward through the pool of Burgendetta's memories, until she found the spot she wanted.

Her hands were wrapped around something… A man's throat, Burgendetta was choking someone. The man thrashed against her arms, with one of his arms, trying to beat her grip free, but Lani could feel it as though she was there.

She could feel his breath slipping from him.

Lani jumped out of the memory; it was too much for her to face right now. She slapped her hands on her thighs and shook her hands out to try and break free of the thought.

It was a horrible experience to launch into without knowing what was happening prior — maybe the woman needed to do it… Lani half wanted to know and also didn't.

She pushed forward a little, somehow knowing there were few memories left. Now she heard a voice that seemed familiar.

"Mother, what have you done?"
It was Ashantha, he was there with me, he was there at the end.
Then everything went blank.

The barrier bumped into Lani again. This all felt very strange to her.

What she'd been told was that Burgendetta's memories had been wiped from her. But that wasn't true. They weren't wiped, they were blocked from her.

The mask she wore was blocking them, like a wall, that separated her past life and her current one. If not the mask itself, the magic that was behind it blocked the woman's memories from her, like Lani's had been.

But I don't have a mask on.

For no explicable reason, this knowledge mattered. Lani felt a sliver of hope, that it was just a barrier, something she had to find a way through. Back to where her body and mind were. Where she really was.

14

ODAJEEN

This doesn't feel right.

Odajeen relied on her instincts to survive. It was a harsh world when you were blind and old. Mostly she was ignored but not always. In Vidus she'd been brutally attacked, damaging her head.

When she had recovered, that was when Odajeen had sensed a change, she had been able to see memories that didn't make sense to her. Memories of actual sight, and other ones when she couldn't see but which didn't relate to her current life.

None of them made much sense and they were only fragments, but they had been enough to unsettle her. It seemed that the injury also allowed her to see Lani's brooch.

It had brought them together and she'd helped the girl get her to Anderwell, but she had been wanting to keep her from danger, not put her in its way.

There's something very wrong.

Lani's hand lay heavily on Odajeen's head. There was still a pulse within it, but it had a strange temperature to it. Neither warm nor cold. Odajeen wasn't sure what was wrong, but she could tell something was.

She moved the hand from her head and sat up, expecting Lani to respond, but she didn't. *What is it?*

Cautiously Odajeen placed her hands on Lani's head. Little by little she felt her way across her forehead, down over her eyebrows, stopping as she could feel Lani's eyes were open.

Odajeen felt around the eyes and nose. The eyes were most definitely open. Her mouth was closed but there was breath flowing through her nose. Softly but it was there, enough to give Odajeen some relief.

Maybe she's just in a vision or a trance? I should wait.

She felt Lani's hands, both now on her lap. Beside one of them she could feel the journal that Odajeen had given the girl. *Had she been able to read any of it?*

The girl's fingers lifted and fell straight back to where they had been. Likewise when Odajeen lifted one of her hands, it dropped heavily back into place.

Her concern kept growing. As much as she wanted to convince herself that Lani was in a dream state, she knew deep down that there was something else happening here.

She got to her feet, walking around the back of the sofa, and shuffled her way to the front door.

"Irdan, Irdan come quickly!"

The sound of his footsteps hurrying toward her should have put her at ease, but they did not.

"Odajeen, what's wrong?"

"Come in, there's a problem."

"What is it?"

"I need to explain something to you, but first I need you to check Lani."

"Check her how?"

"How does she look?"

"Strange."

"What does that mean?" Odajeen didn't feel better from his words.

"It's like she isn't there."

"You can see her body?"

"Of course!"

"How would I know, Irdan? You're treating me like I can see."

"Sorry. Her eyes are open, but it's as though no one is there. The colour is faded, or something."

"She's breathing though, isn't she?"

Odajeen could hear him move, but he took a few moments before he replied.

"I can feel breath on my hand when I put it under her nose."

"That's what I thought also. Her face?"

"Still, it looks pale, very pale the more I look at it. What has happened here?"

Odajeen didn't know what to say.

"Well?"

"We were trying something, but then it all felt different…"

He cut her off, his voice frightened. "What's that doing out on the table?"

"What, Irdan?"

"The amulet!"

"It's out?"

"Yes! It's sitting on the pouch on the table in front of her."

That's what I could feel, the wrongness that was wrapped up in what she was doing.

"That's very bad. It needs to be put back."

"I'm not touching it. I heard what it does."

"You want me to do it? If I mishandle it…"

"No, you're not touching it either. Someone else needs to do it."

Maybe we could use Lani's hand to do it?

The idea sounded okay but then she'd already tested the girl's hands and they were like lumps of dead meat. As much as she knew it was going to be unpleasant, they needed help.

What was done, was done.

"You're going to have to go get someone for me."

"Who?"

"Tillandra."

"Okay."

"Tell her that there's a very urgent reason she needs to come, but she should come alone -- for now."

"What if she doesn't come?"

"Tell her… tell her Lani's life depends on it. But only if she won't come."

"You're frightening me now, Odajeen."

"Be frightened, Irdan. I'm not joking. Now hurry."

"Consider me gone. But promise me you won't go near that… thing?"

"I won't."

Waiting for him to return seemed to take forever, minutes felt like hours. She ran through in her mind many ways of explaining what had happened, none sounding better than any other. This was bad and she knew it.

The door opened, and Odajeen heard two people enter, although neither said anything initially.

"She's over there."

"I can see, thanks. Perhaps you can leave us."

"Odajeen?" Irdan asked.

"It's fine, Irdan. Thank you."

Neither of the women spoke until the door was closed. Odanjeen could hear the tall woman come closer, her breathing hovering over Lani's body.

"So what's going on here, Odajeen?"

"Which part? What's happening right now or what we were doing?"

"All of it." Before Odajeen could answer, Mother Folly spoke again. "What's that doing out?"

"The amulet?"

"Yes!"

"I don't know. Irdan told me it was there, but… I do not know."

"It needs to be back in its pouch, or in the box."

"Yes, but who will do that? We all know not to touch it."

"Quickly, tell me everything, then I will have to work out how to get rid of it."

"She…" Odajeen swallowed and placed her hands on the back of the sofa to brace herself. "She tried to connect to my mask."

"Oh Thenis!"

"What?"

"What? What? You had her use her skill on you, and you're wondering why I am praying for a god's help?"

"She wanted to do it."

"Oh please. She would never have done it if you hadn't asked."

"Easy for you to say. You're not the one without any recollection of your past."

"That's a cop-out, Odajeen. You, of all people, should know better."

"How should I? I have no memory of before, before they took my mind. She knew how that feels. They… they took her memories too, but they gave them back to her."

Odajeen could feel the stare of Tillandra boring in on her. "She understood how that matters. I asked, sure, but I didn't push her to do it. Besides it was fanciful that it would work anyway."

"This is very bad, very bad. You…"

"You can blame me later, there'll be plenty of time for that. What's to be done about it?"

Tillandra laughed at her. "How on Dharatan am I meant to know? You think we've had a mask reader before? Her skill is unique, at least as far as I can tell, I've not been able to go over all the history we have yet – because…"

"What?"

"Because I pushed her too hard, and nearly harmed her."

She was silent for a minute.

"Has she spoken?"

"Not since we started. Nothing was happening for ages, she seemed almost ready to give up, then she leant forward and seemed to relax. But after a while that changed, she felt like… like she'd gone."

"Gone?"

"Her body is there, but I can't sense her."

Tillandra seemed to be standing in front of Lani, moving her, probably much like Odajeen had done herself.

"What's your man's name again?"

"Irdan."

Tillandra walked away from them to the door, which opened. "I think I might need your help, Irdan."

Odajeen could detect him coming into the room before the door closed again.

"I'm going to try and put that amulet back in its pouch."

"I won't touch it."

"I'm not asking you to! Just watch and warn me if you sense I'm getting close to touching it. Understood?"

"Okay."

The air in the room seemed to thicken and Odajeen felt just as on edge as Tillandra must have been. No one spoke, but she could sense some small movements in the area around the table.

Suddenly it was as if someone had lifted a fallen tree off her back. The room became lighter, and she heard Tillandra breathe deeply.

"Done. Lani? Can you hear me, Lani? Are you there?"

Tillandra's voice was calm and firm. Odajeen felt anything but that.

All her work to help the girl, getting her to Anderwell, was now at risk of being undone. She'd never wanted anything for it, knowing it had been the right thing to do was enough.

But it hadn't been enough though, had it? Fool woman! You wanted to know more, to know what you'd done. Best you'd left it all alone.

15

TILLANDRA

What a mess!

Of all the things Tillandra had thought could happen today, this was nowhere on the list. She stood looking at Lani across the room with her gut feeling tight and sick.

The vacant look on the young woman's face resembled some of those that lived in their Elder Gardens, the home for those who had lost their connection with the reality of this world. There they often sat with this exact look for days on end.

Is it permanent? That's the question.

"Explain it all to me, Odajeen, every detail."

As she listened to what the older woman said, she tried to grasp what Lani might have been thinking and trying. That she had taken the amulet out of the pouch was the most concerning thing of all.

The young woman also hadn't spoken to Odajeen either, so she had no idea if Lani had even been able to access her memories or read the journal.

"Thank you. How about you, how are you feeling?"

"Pretty stupid." Odajeen's face was pointed to the floor and her shoulders slumped.

"I meant physically."

"My head hurts, like I said just before."

"Can you explain it better? It might be important."

"It's not like a normal headache; trust me I've had plenty of them to know. There's a pressure there, like inside is too big for the space."

Tillandra pondered her words. "Like there's something extra in there?"

Odajeen took a minute to reply. "Perhaps. The feeling came around the same time that I felt her move last."

"I'm not sure I understand the relevance?"

"She bent forward over me... toward the table. Maybe that was when she took the amulet out? After that everything felt different, then this feeling began. It just felt uncomfortable at first."

Tillandra struggled to see how the two things were related. This was all new. Lani's skills were unique, they'd never seen anyone who could do what she could.

How on Dharatan can I understand this without help?

"Argggh."

Tillandra looked at Odajeen, her face was scrunched up and she had her head in her hands.

"What?"

"It's worse. The pain and the pressure. I can feel it, somewhere toward the back of my head, pushing at it, like it's..."

"Like what?"

"Like it's trying to get out. Do you think...?"

"Her? I don't know, Odajeen. I have no idea about any of this."

"Oh Thenis, what have I done!"

"Did she say anything to you?"

"When?"

"At all? Once she started?"

"We chatted briefly, when it wasn't working, but then she went silent after that movement and nothing. At first, I could still sense her but then that all changed."

"Was there anything you heard, or can remember about that?"

"No. It was only a feeling. I could sense her presence, and then it was gone. I could feel her body, but it was... lifeless is the wrong word, she doesn't feel dead, she just feels... gone."

Tillandra listened, watching as the woman rubbed at the back of her head.

"So, we have no idea if she could access your memories, or your journal, and we don't really know if what you can feel is related or not?"

She didn't expect an answer, the words were her way of talking through it. Odajeen said nothing.

"I think we need to move her to the college, somewhere where we can watch over her."

"I think I will retire here and get some rest. Hopefully this pain will go away."

The whole time they'd been talking Irdan had stood by the door not making a sound. Tillandra turned to him. "I will need your help, please?"

He nodded and walked toward Lani.

"Can you carry her on your own or do you need my help?"

"I should be fine." He bent down and wrapped his arms around Lani, slinging her up and over his shoulder.

Tillandra wanted to shout out *Careful*, but they knew nothing about what was right or wrong for the young woman. "Let's go."

"I'll come back and check on you after, Odajeen," Irdan said as he headed to the door.

They had only got a few paces from the room when Tillandra heard Odajeen scream. She turned and bolted back inside. The older woman was writhing on the floor in pain.

Irdan came back into the room and as he did so, Odajeen calmed. "What is it?" he asked.

"I don't know. Odajeen, are you okay?"

"Better now, but when you went it was as though the back of my head was being pulled from me."

"There's a connection between you then." Tillandra stood, trying to understand what was going on, but like everything else that was changing around her, she had too little information. "I want to try something, but it's going to hurt again. Only for a moment then I'll stop it. Okay?"

"Okay."

"Irdan, I want you to leave again..."

"I'm not hurting her!"

"Do as I say, or I'll get someone else to do it. It's only for a little moment, but I need to check if anything happens to Lani as well, when you leave."

His eyes bored in on hers.

"Okay?"

He stood still and silent for a moment. "Yes."

"Now."

They got outside and Odajeen's scream came again. This time Tillandra turned Lani's head to look at the young woman. *Oh no!*

"Back inside, now!"

"What happened?"

"Nothing good. Whatever color is left in her face was disappearing and she seemed to be dying before my eyes." She took Odajeen's hand. "For now, all we can do is keep the two of you together and I'll try to figure out if there's anything we can do. I think you should both stay here until I have had time to think this through."

"I'll stay with her."

"Okay. I'll be back as soon as I can. If anything changes... anything at all, send for me immediately."

He nodded.

Tillandra walked back to her office slowly. She wanted to have an answer, but her mind seemed to be empty of ideas. As if what the Lady of Stone had just told her wasn't enough to deal with.

What's her name? It's stupid not knowing what to call her.

She was a goddess, that much Tillandra knew for sure, but in all her dealings with her she'd never asked for her name.

It's like everything I do, I do badly. Even something as simple as that, I don't do.

She arrived in her room before even realizing she was there; her mind had been lost the whole walk back.

What a mess. What on Dharatan did they think they were doing?

The Lady of the Stone had asked her if she could kill Lani if she needed to, something Tillandra had no answer for. That choice might not need to be made anymore, if the girl didn't survive this then it would be a moot point.

Or... if we have to, to save Odajeen.

It dawned on Tillandra suddenly what the goddess had asked her. And in that moment, she understood why Odajeen had asked Lani to do what she had done.

If Tillandra had to kill Lani, she would be breaking the most important of their rules, of the magic that bound them all, and she too would have her memories wiped, her vision taken.

A chill ran down her back. Had Odajeen been faced with a similar choice, and she'd had the courage to do that?

Could I do that? To save us all?

She stood at the window in her office and looked out across the back gardens of the college, her eyes grazing over the colors of the flowers blooming in one of the boxes. One of the clusters caught her eye, the rich deep color.

Purple! That's it.

She hurried from the room in search of the young girl, and Gizen. The young girl was so new to them that Tillandra hadn't even thought about her being able to help.

While they had other healers in the city, none had the skill that this child had. Tillandra had been trying to shelter the youngster; everyone had wanted her to help them, so they'd needed to block access to her, and limited how much time she was allowed to use her skill.

In time the girl should be able to determine her own strength, but until she could, rules needed to be in place.

When she got to the student accommodation, she found Purple asleep in her room, with Gizen resting in a chair nearby.

"Tillandra?"

"Gizen, how is she?"

"She's fine, just taking a nap. I try to encourage them with her. So many people want to talk to her it can be exhausting."

"I understand that." Tillandra tried to smile but it was very forced. "I need her skills."

"Now?"

"Yes, I don't know if she can help but it's very urgent."

"Who?"

"It's two of them. Lani and Odajeen."

Gizen's face became concerned. "Let me wake her and get her something small to eat, can it wait that long?"

Tillandra nodded. She knew it likely wouldn't matter at all, but part of her wanted to say no and drag them both there immediately.

"Bring her to Odajeen's rooms when you're ready. You know where they are?"

"Yes."

16

LANI

hat did Odajeen do?

Lani struggled to think of her companion as Burgendetta. That someone lived two different lives was difficult to get your head around.

While she was anxious about where she was stuck, she also knew that the reason she was here was to answer the question about what had happened to Odajeen.

The fact that she had broken the killing rule the Jesters had to abide by wasn't in question. It was the details around it that the woman wanted to know. Lani couldn't waste this opportunity to learn what had really happened.

Accessing Burgendetta's memories worked exactly like it did with the other Jesters' masks. It was as if she had lived them, and could replay them at will.

What was different was that her own memories, the pictures she'd always been able to access, were gone. She had knowledge of recent things, and some concepts about her past, but it was sketchy and there were no images she could recall.

Inside Burgendetta's memories Lani became part of them, as though it was her that had lived them, mentally and physically.

Normally that meant she could see as them, but because Burgendetta was blind, Lani experienced things without sight.

Lani sought out the memory of Burgendetta, as Mother Folly, meeting with the man called Hembleth, and slid into it.

~

"Why is she so important?"

"She's very unexpected."

"That's not an answer."

"You were always very direct, Burgendetta."

"I need to know what I'm doing here."

"Her mother was a person of some importance in Enderk, in an unconventional way."

"Meaning?"

"For now, let's just say that it was important enough to the rulers there that she wasn't able to leave Enderk. She had knowledge that they didn't want known anywhere."

"And the girl?"

"We don't think they knew she existed. Given the way everyone else was murdered if they had known about her either she would have been killed or taken to Enderk. They did not seem to be aware to look for her."

"I still don't understand. If the mother was the one with the knowledge, then why did the girl matter? She is too young to have the knowledge..."

Burgendetta stopped and shook her head.

"... Unless she is the knowledge."

"I think you're focusing on the wrong things, Mother. You just need to keep her safe."

"You know I will."

"I have to go. Protect her, at all costs, and watch out for more of them."

~

Lani pulled out so she could think about what she'd just heard. They were speaking about her as a little girl, when she first arrived in Barnen.

The man said she was from Enderk. That went against everything she knew about herself; she'd always believed she was from Malamig.

While she did look mostly like other Mals, there were parts of her that didn't. But her mother was a Mal, she'd seen that when the block on her own mind had been removed.

Meaning my father is a Derk?

Lani wasn't sure how to take that information, or the way Burgendetta suggested that she was the 'knowledge'.

What does that even mean?

Her answers lay in the woman's memories so Lani went back to them.

Some time had passed and Burgendetta was lying in bed.

～

Hembleth hadn't answered much and only raised more questions. The man was so annoying, she could rarely get a straight answer from him.

As much as she tried, she couldn't grasp the relationship between the girl with the blue stone and Enderk, and why she was so important to Hembleth.

It was all Burgendetta could do to stop thinking about seeing the blue stone, the first color she could remember seeing and she wanted to see more of it.

She had to be close to the girl to see it, which didn't bother her as they'd be traveling together back to Anderwell.

Burgendetta thought that if they just left straight away it wouldn't matter about any Derks, they'd not find them on the road.

Something for tomorrow. She began to drift off to sleep.

～

As happened from time to time she experienced a vision as she fell asleep. Burgendetta could never control when they came but liked them, it was the only time she saw pictures of the world.

～

The Derk prisoner had been pretending he was more injured than he was. He did have bad wounds, but there was something compelling him which meant he was still a threat.

Burgendetta could sense he understood what everyone was saying around him. He heard the guards mention a girl, some young girl who had survived the attack.

The prisoner felt shame for being caught, for having been injured so much that he had been left behind by his comrades. Being left behind was the ultimate punishment for failure, to die over here.

Now that he knew there was another, he could remove some of his shame by finishing what they had started. Maybe no one would ever know, but he would.

Two nights later he drew in the guards to his cell, feigning more severe problems, and killed them both. She saw the surprise locked on their faces as he killed them easily, despite his lame arm.

Before he killed the last of them, he forced information about the girl from him. A knife cutting the eye was a simple method of causing pain that a man couldn't withstand.

It wasn't far to the inn where she was staying. The sign outside with the grain and sickle matched the one Burgendetta had been to earlier. Several more guards were on a sleepy patrol pretending to protect her room. He left both dead outside the room.

The young child didn't even know he had entered her room, and he cut her throat before she even stirred. The man didn't care now if he made it back or not, his work was complete, but he would try anyway.

Seeing the vision like that, as Burgendetta, broke Lani's concentration. She removed herself from the older woman's memories and found herself shaking.

It had only been a vision, and of course it wasn't real — if it had been, Lani would have died as a young girl. That was easy to think, but it took time to convince herself and settle down so she could go back into the memories.

~

Burgendetta had come awake from the vision as well. She was unsettled by it and forced her helper, a man named Dyaln to check on the girl. Even after he returned to tell her all was well, she couldn't share her unease.

The woman tossed and turned all night, not fully resting, knowing that the girl was in danger. One thing she'd learned many years ago was to trust her visions.

One way or another they told of something she needed to watch for, or to do.

She decided the best solution was to go and visit the prisoner herself, which required some help. Dyaln was sent off to seek a way to get to him.

Dyaln was able to find a guard on night duty at the cells, who was willing to let them in for a bribe.

"It's time, Mother."

"Okay, Dyaln, let's hope the guard lives up to his promise."

"You sure you want to do this?"

"I must."

They arrived at the back of the guards' building and were led to the cells. The guard locked them in with the Vrah prisoner.

"Now what?"

"I need to learn more about this man."

"He's lying on his cot; his hands are tied and on his lap."

"Is he awake?"

"His eyes are closed but I cannot tell."

"I need to lay my hand on his head."

Dyaln led her forward and she knelt beside the man.

"I have his hands."

"What do you want?"

"Just be still."

The man thrashed underneath her, but Dyaln had enough control of him, at least at that moment. Burgendetta laid her hands on his head.

~

Lani was surprised by what she saw in the memory. Burgendetta could see pictures from the man's mind, his thoughts, and memories, just like how Lani accessed the masks.

The irony wasn't lost on Lani that she was stuck inside the mind of the one person who could possibly help her. And this woman had that power stripped from her when she'd killed.

The prisoner was thinking about his ring, in his mind Burgendetta could see the orange stone in a black band and setting. He knows that others will be able to find it, to find him.

At some point they will come for the ring, they always do. He replayed the words he heard about the girl, from one of his guards. A cocky fool named Harsop. They thought he could not understand them when they chatted outside the cell, but he heard everything.

He was biding his time; she could sense it. Just like in the dream, he was planning how he would get free. The Derk knew where the girl was being housed.

A memory from the man showed him carving strange characters into the wall of the cell with a stone.

"Is there something on the wall, carved in over there?" Burgendetta pointed.

"Yes, but they look just like odd drawings, Mother."

"Thanks. You must remove them, no matter what happens to this man, understand?"

"Yes, but why?"

"Just do it, Dyaln."

The man thrashed beneath them.

If he didn't survive, when other Derks came, those letters would tell his comrades what they needed to know. That there was a girl who survived.

"It won't happen, Derk, do you understand? The girl will be fine. None of your kind will ever know."

Burgendetta could feel anger rising in his mind. All he could think of now was getting free of her hands and killing them both.

"She will die, as will you." The words came under his breath, slowly and angrily.

"What did he say, Mother?"

Burgendetta didn't answer her colleague, she was focused on the man under her hands. He was trying to move again but Dyaln's strength coupled with the injuries he had were enough to subdue him, for now.

"I will kill her, or others will kill her! Just like the rest." There was almost laughter coming through his gritted teeth. Burgendetta could sense the malice and complete determination in his mind. He would not rest until his job was done.

Burgendetta had never felt the way he was. She could feel his absolute compulsion and willingness to kill the little girl and anyone that got in his way.

It was almost as though she took on the dark stain from his mind and redirected it. Her hands slid down to his throat. She grasped there and squeezed as tight as she could, putting everything into it. The Derk began to thrash harder now, and behind her Dyaln called out.

"Mother, what are you doing?"

She didn't answer, all her effort was into trying to stop the Derk from being able to harm the girl.

She could feel the strength of the prisoner slipping away, his life being squeezed from him. Burgendetta knew she shouldn't, but she also recalled what Hembleth had said: 'Protect her, at all costs.'

Before she realized what had happened her hands were free of his throat. She had been pulled off by Dyaln and they stumbled backward several paces before he re-balanced them both.

"What are you doing, Mother?"

Burgendetta said nothing for a moment. She tried to control her own compulsion, the need to stop him from doing what he was planning.

"I don't know what came over me. It was something I could read in him... it..."

"It's okay. He's alright."

She could hear the man gasping on his cot.

"I should check on him."

"That's not a good idea."

"I'm fine, Dyaln, whatever that was it is gone now."

"Okay, if you're sure."

She stepped forward until she could feel the edge of the bed.

Shielding what she was doing, Burgendetta pulled a small vial from her pocket, removing the stopper cautiously, and as she fumbled with her other hand to sense the prisoner's body and head, wedged her thumb and finger into his mouth.

She quickly tipped the contents of the vial into his mouth and stood up.

He spluttered and spat some of it out.

Burgendetta could feel Dyaln grab her arms and spin her around.

"What did you do?"

"Get me out of here, Dyaln… now!"

That wasn't the moment that it all changed for Burgendetta, Lani knew that now. Despite the deaths she'd witnessed Lani still struggled with seeing someone killed.

Even when she had to save her own life she took no pleasure in the concept, and to see Odajeen try to kill the Derk upset her.

He wasn't going to last, Lani knew that. He'd ingested too much of the poison to survive. Which meant her own demise was imminent. Lani just needed to gather herself to watch it.

She needed to know, that was the whole point of why she was here, so she had to see it through.

They were back in Burgendetta's room.

"What did you do, Mother?"

"I had to, Dyaln, there was no choice. Listen carefully, I do not have long!"

"What do you mean?"

"He will die shortly, then they will take me. It's the price for such an act, and I did it willingly."

"I don't understand."

*"Don't waste time, you'll find out soon enough. He had left a message --
those carvings in the wall spoke about the girl, that she'd survived.*

You must tell the others that."

"What others?"

*"Whoever comes for my things, one of the Court. You must. More Derks
will come for him, he was sure they would seek him out. They can track this
somehow."*

Burgendetta held the black ring with the orange stone in it.

"What...?"

*"I took it from him. Somehow, they can follow them, he was going to hide
it in the bed, so even if he died, they'd find the message and know to hunt
her."*

"But—"

"I had to. It's that simple."

*There was a knock at the door of her room, where Dyaln had brought her
back to. She could hear him jump to his feet.*

"Who is it?"

"Ashantha."

*The sound of the door opening was clear in Burgendetta's memory,
followed by the words, "Mother, what have you done?"*

∾

Lani recognized his voice, the man who she'd found in the cavern. He
was there, which explained some of what he knew of her. She had to
watch more.

∾

"I did what had to be done, Ash."

"Why?"

*"Dyaln can fill you in on what I just told him. There is little time. I poisoned
him, and my time is almost up. I need to tell you a lot of things quickly."*

*Briefly she explained to him what Hembleth had told her about Lani, and
the need to protect her.*

"It must be you now, Ash. You must do this for me. For us."

"Why her?"

"I do not know, Ashantha, but you might want to pursue that more as well. There's things Hembleth would not tell me, he said he couldn't, but I find him tricky to believe at the best of times."

"This is all so crazy. There should have been another way."

"I knew at the time, Ash, that it was what I was there to do. For better or worse."

"Oh, Mother."

What happened next caught Lani by surprise. Without warning it was as though a door closed on Burgendetta's mind. What light made its way into her blind eyes disappeared, and her mind shut down.

At least that's how it felt to Lani. Clearly, she didn't die, but the memories stopped immediately at that point. That's where the wall appeared, solid and impassable.

She couldn't imagine how difficult it would have been for Ashantha and Dyaln to have Burgendetta there, clueless as to who she was. Her past erased.

She had the answers Odajeen sought now, the challenge was how to get back to her to tell her. One way or another she had to find her way out.

But how?

17

TILLANDRA

$\mathcal{W}$aiting for the two girls to arrive had felt like an eternity to Tillandra. Neither she nor Odajeen had said a word the entire time. Mostly she'd just stared out the small window and prayed for some miracle to help her.

She was feeling conflicted between her need to be decisive and make decisions for the benefit of everyone, versus the impact on one person. How she'd pushed Lani was one example.

When Gizen arrived with Purple in her chair with wheels, it was yet another example Tillandra had to deal with.

The young girl seemed so small and fragile, but her power in healing was beyond anyone they'd seen before.

"Hi, Purple."

"Hello."

"Did Gizen tell you what was happening?"

"Only that Lani was having some problems."

Tillandra smiled. That was one way of describing it.

"Are you okay about helping?"

"If I can."

"You're not feeling too tired?"

"No. I haven't had to heal anyone for a while. I'm being careful like you said."

"Good. The same rule applies here, too. If you feel like this becomes too much at any point you just stop. Alright?"

"Yes."

Tillandra pointed Gizen to the space behind the sofa where Lani and Odajeen were sitting.

"What's wrong with her?"

"You know how you have your skill to heal people?"

"Yep."

"Lani has her own skill. Hers is a little different, but she can see things in the past. She was using it on Odajeen, but something has gone wrong."

"What do you mean?"

"I mean that her mind is connected in there somehow and she won't come back. Or she can't come back. Does that make sense?"

"Sort of. Will it happen to me too?"

"What?"

"Getting stuck in there." Purple pointed to Odajeen's head.

"No, your skill is very different." Tillandra made it sound like she knew the truth, but in reality, she had no idea what the problem was, so she couldn't honestly know that something wasn't about to go wrong.

But then, like her discussion with the Lady of the Stone, she had to choose for the good of all, and not just for one. As far as they knew now, Lani was very important to everyone's future, perhaps more so than the young girls.

Look at me, willing to risk a child without any certainty.

Tillandra's heart rate sped up as she watched the young girl place her hand onto the top of Odajeen's. For a moment Tillandra held her breath but relaxed as she noticed that Purple's eyes were still focused in the room.

She wanted to ask the girl questions but thought better of it. For the time being she just had to wait as did the others in the room. Several frowns showed up on Purple's face, but she made no comment.

After many minutes the young girl removed her hand and took a deep breath.

"She has two minds."

"Who does, Purple?"

"Odajeen does, Mother. There are two different minds in her head, split by some wood."

"Wood?"

"Yes, it's like a round piece of wood."

"Like a mask?"

"Umm… yes, I think. I couldn't see… I didn't know how to explain… but like a mask."

"Did you find Lani?"

"Yes. She's behind the wood… the mask."

"Behind?"

"There's a front part, then the wood, and a back part. Way back there." Purple poked her finger at the back of Odajeen's head. "Lani's back there."

"Is she okay?"

Purple shrugged. "Don't know. I can just see her there."

"Is there anything you can do?"

She shook her head. "When I heal people, I see their wounds and they get a color which tells me what to heal. There's no color there. It's all just black."

"Black?"

"Dark. Like at night when there's no light."

"Okay. And you didn't see a way to free her?"

"I didn't look for that. Sorry."

"Don't be sorry, dear, I'm just asking."

"I was just looking to heal her."

Without being asked to the girl put her hand back on Odajeen's head. The minutes went by slowly while she waited.

"I feel like I should charge admission," Odajeen said quietly.

"I'm sorry, Odajeen." Tillandra said it but knew she didn't really mean it.

"Don't be, this is important to free Lani."

"Let's hope she can find a way." The words described the hopelessness Tillandra felt. Getting the girl to help was all the control she had over the situation.

The girl removed her hand and placed it in her lap. She seemed sad to look at. "I couldn't find anything to help."

"What did you see?"

"It's just like a wall of solid wood. I can't see how she could get through."

"It's okay, Purple. Thank you for looking. You've explained much more than we knew before."

"Sorry."

"There's nothing to be sorry about. I'm sorry that I made you do it." Tillandra turned to Gizen. "Thanks for bringing her, she's been very helpful."

After they had left, Tillandra returned to the window and stared out into the street.

"What next, Mother?"

She turned to look at Odajeen. "Maybe you can tell me?"

"Why?"

"I'm all out of ideas. With all of this. And I'm meant to be the one with all the answers."

Odajeen laughed. "I'm not sure I'm the right person to help. I didn't exactly make a good job of being you."

"I doubt you could have done much worse."

"Look at me, Tillandra. If they wiped my mind, then that means only one thing."

"That you killed someone. There had to be a reason you did it?"

"There's no record?"

"No, Odajeen. We know when but not why."

"Perhaps Lani can see, whatever is back there." Odajeen tapped her head.

"Unless we can get her out, we'll never know. Even then…"

"I am sorry, truly."

It was Tillandra's turn to shrug her shoulders. There'd been enough words spoken about it.

"Are you okay if she stays here with you?"

"Yes, it's the least I can do. What will you do now?"

"Right now, I have no idea. But there must be a solution, I just have to find it."

"Can I suggest something?"

"Why not? there can't be any harm in it."

"Go back to the source."

"What do you mean?"

"I don't remember who it is behind you, or what drives everything here, but the woman that spoke to me through Lani's brooch — who is she, can't she help?"

"A good point, Odajeen. I should have considered that... I'll think on it."

Tillandra didn't say what the problem was with that idea. She'd only just spoken with the goddess and been warned about draining the stones in the tower.

If only I'd known this before. But the stones, how much power do they have? Can I afford to leave here and go to Midderbuilt if they run out soon?

Another piece of information she hadn't been told. Useful information that would enable her to be better in her role. As she reached the top of the tower she still hadn't decided if she'd use them or not.

Being back there eased her anxiety at least. She took another look across the city. It was another of those choices -- take the short-term view or a long-term one.

In the end she chose to seek assistance; she had no other ideas on how to solve the problem. Tillandra placed her hand on the Mother Stone and let her mind drift into the feeling of the stone.

"Back so soon, Tillandra. You did hear my warning about draining the stones?"

"I did, but I need your help. It's important."

"What is it?"

Tillandra explained what was happening.

"This is not good, Tillandra."

"That I do know."

"You need to take me there."

"How do you mean?"

"Take the Mother Stone and connect me to Burgendetta."

∼

Tillandra was surprised by the request but relieved at the same time. If anyone was going to be able to solve it, then the Lady of the Stone was much more likely than herself.

The only time she ever had the Mother Stone so close to her was when she took it back to Midderbuilt, to the Citadel Stone, to recharge it.

"That was quick." Odajeen seemed surprised to see her.

"Your idea had merits, I'm going to try something. Sorry but I'll need to put my hands on your head."

"You might as well join the party."

She placed one hand on the stone in her pocket and her other onto Odajeen's head. As soon as she did, she could feel the power of the stone flowing along her and into the other woman's head.

∼

"What is your name?"

"That's a strange question to ask right now."

"It's been bothering me, that I don't know what to call you."

"You don't need to call me anything."

"You don't have one?"

"I have many."

"One that is more commonly used than any other?"

"Thenis."

"Oh."

"Disappointed?"

"No. I could have expected that."

"Perhaps." She said nothing for a short while. *"This isn't good."*

"Lani?"

"Yes. Like the young girl said, Lani is stuck on the other side of the mask."

"Could you reach her?"

"Speak to her?"

"Yes."

"No, it's not like she is in the Void. It is hard to explain, but that part of her is stuck in there."

"Is there a fix?"

"I can hear you both." The sound of Odajeen's voice in her mind surprised Tillandra.

"Another unexpected occurrence."

"What?"

"You being able to communicate like this, Bur... Odajeen."

"You're the god?"

"In a manner of speaking."

"In my head?"

"In a manner of speaking."

"That proves it, only a god could be so painfully capable of avoiding an answer."

"Thenis, is there a fix?" Tillandra wanted an answer.

"Only one way I can think of at this time, but you might not want to discuss it here."

"Because it affects me?"

"Yes, Odajeen, it does." The tone in Thenis's voice chilled Tillandra.

"Tell us!"

"Are you sure you want to know? Both of you?"

"Yes."

"Yes," Tillandra confirmed as well.

There was a gap before Thenis spoke again.

"The mask must be removed, in order to free her from behind it."

"How?"

"There is only one way the mask can be removed."

Tillandra could guess what that was, which was why Thenis didn't want to say it to them both.

"What is it?"
   "Only when you die, Odajeen, can the mask come free."
   "Oh."

18

TILLANDRA

*T*he map room under the college was often not the calmest of places, Tillandra knew that, but she'd hoped to feel more at ease than she did.

Down here the Court had their group discussions. Having just talked Odajeen out of wanting to end her own life to save Lani, Tillandra foolishly had hoped this might be easier.

She had explained it all to her colleagues, but in the end knew it was up to her to make the tough decisions. This was more to inform them rather than seek their approval. They needed to act now and stop discussing it.

"What are you proposing then?" Junther asked in his usual brusque way.

"It's time to get back out in the world. Many of you haven't been away from Anderwell in a very long time."

"There's a reason for that."

"Is there really, Junther?"

He stared back at her. "Who will oversee everything?"

"I will, and one other. As for the day-to-day teaching and management, there's more than enough people to get that done."

115

"You want us back in courts or houses?" Toolet's serious voice turned Tillandra's head.

"No, that's one thing I want us to do differently."

"Please explain?"

"There's simply not enough of us to go around. Where would be best to go? And once you're locked in with someone then what happens? It's not easy to move around or be flexible. Plus, if that goes wrong, like it did with Goran and King Nordahl, then that's a whole other level of problems."

"About him…" Junther started up.

"Later, Junther, please."

The look he gave her boosted her resolve. He might be annoyed but she was tired of this; tired of their debates, them always questioning everything, and tired of double-guessing herself. It was going to happen, she just needed to get it done.

"While the process of using couriers works, it's too slow across long distances. We need to get news from the entire continent quickly. The message from Ahn's court has taken the better part of two weeks to get here, and that's too long."

She kept going, talking over Lionel before he could say much. "Let me finish please! It's no one's fault, we're just too far removed. We have plenty of people to place in courts, with the Patroned and now all the hospitality teams coming along.

"What I see is that we should have members of this court, placed strategically in cities closest to the places of most interest. That way you can all better manage the local teams, and news can be spread back here as quickly as it needs to be."

"I see. Like trading hubs, but for information."

"Yes, Junther."

"Smart."

"What of our work here?" Bea joined in.

"You were already planning to be away, Beantic, before you ran into Goran. What would be different now?"

"True, true." Her neck twitch was fully activated today.

"It seems you've already made your mind up, Mother?"

"Yes, Lionel, I have. I still want everyone to understand the reasoning though. There's too much at stake for me to leave things as they are. I'm to blame for the time it takes to make decisions around here. It's taking too long, and we're being left behind."

The room fell silent. Tillandra was sure they could understand why. She also knew it was a major change for them.

"Beantic, I see no reason why you don't continue with what you had planned. Set up in Callet. Of all the places it's the most central. You'll need to make sure you can strengthen the networks to the north."

"Who else in the north?"

"Hallendell is already in Nkuku, which is close by, and Clannack in Laumua. That will have to do. Lionel -- you'll need to head to Okeans."

"What of Orwarn?"

"It makes sense to move him, but I don't want to wait for that to play out. You could be there in a week or so getting a read on what's happening. I'm thinking Orwarn will fill in where we need him, possibly Malamig or south, but I'd rather wait and see what we need before I move him."

"And me?" Toolet asked.

"You'll stay with me for now, mostly to bring Leo up to speed."

Everyone looked at the newest member of their court. He hadn't said a word since he'd arrived in the map room.

"Up to speed on what?" his voice seemed a little higher pitched than normal and he cleared his throat after he spoke.

"Being one of us, Leo. You've been here the least amount of time and have gone from being a new arrival to one of the Court. While the process says you were the chosen one, you still need to know what we do here, and be ready for an assignment."

"Assignment? Like school?"

The room broke out in light laughter.

"No. Like where I'm sending the others. You'll have to be put to work, your time staying in Anderwell won't be for long."

"Oh."

"Toolet, you need to fast-track him. You two have already formed a relationship, so you're to spend all your time with him -- go out and help him learn more in Lakeside and Jarv if you need to, show him everything he needs to know. He has no time to do the Circuit."

"Okay, Mother."

"Which leaves me."

Tillandra looked at Junther as he blew smoke rings above his head. "You're going home, Junther."

"I thought you might say that. Bundok?"

"I'm afraid so. With what King Ahn is up to, any foreigners will attract suspicion. Being a Skarian should at least cut you some freedoms others wouldn't get."

"When?"

"Yours is probably the most urgent... and the most dangerous."

The levity of the recent joke had all disappeared. Tillandra's last comment brought the seriousness of what she was asking back to the surface.

"As for Sinder, I'll work out what he needs to do. It will be easier now he doesn't need to get into the Court. He can just monitor from Vodotok and watch for anything Ahn tries through there."

"What of Hallendell? Are you going to pull her out?"

Tillandra had spent some time thinking about that over the last day. "No. She's in the most unique of positions. She's already in one court, and should she succeed in getting to the White City, who knows what we might learn?"

"Which leaves our old mate, Goran." Junther's sarcasm was obvious.

"I've thought a lot about that too. It's taking up too much of our time doing what we are doing. I think it's been helping but it's not a cure. He needs to heal completely or he's no use to us at all. If his alter wins, he'll be a prisoner forever, we can't afford him to be free."

"So, he'll stay where he is then?" Lionel asked.

"For now. Gizen came to me with one of her visions. I'm considering it."

"What was it?"

"She claims to have seen the young girl, Purple, healing Goran."

"What's the problem then?"

"Just that his skill is still there, albeit weak, and I'm not sure what his alter is capable of, that's all. She's only a young thing and I'm just concerned that he may try something."

"I might have an idea."

"Tell us, Junther."

"I could touch him, that would give her time to try her healing on him. I can control the level, so it just disables him but only as long as I touch him, rather than completely paralyzing him. It's possible that will be enough to keep the other one at bay, allowing her to try."

"Interesting idea." Tillandra was about to ask the room what they thought when she caught herself. *Stop doubting yourself or delaying things -- make a decision for Thenis's sake.* "We should try it. First I need to ask the girl, I need to watch how much she does."

Here she was again about to use the young girl for their own needs.

"If you want me in Bundok quickly then it needs to be done tomorrow at the latest. I'll need the day to organize things."

"I'll see to it. As to everything else you just need to get onto it. We can all communicate when we need to. But that's the other reason for Toolet and Leo to be here with me initially. So that it's not all coming through me - I'm not sure how much I can do if I was receiving connections all the time."

"There's one other reason for you all to be dispersed, which I haven't mentioned yet."

All their eyes turned to her. She explained what she'd learned about the amulets.

"I don't know what is going to happen, but if we get notice that another one has surfaced, then whoever is closest will need to hunt it down."

"But how? We can't all take the box with us." Junther sounded agitated.

"Ashantha didn't need the box. The box is the place to bring them back to, but he used his glove as the pouch. It was enough, especially as we know more about them now than what he did. You all have a glove like that, so you'd do the same."

"You've really thought this through, haven't you?"

"Yes, Beantic, I have. It's time we got ahead of them."
"Them?"
"The Derks."

19

KARPENMOR

*D*espite pondering who might be behind the delays to the remaining two families, Karpenmor was none the wiser. For that to have any value he needed to understand what not being here would mean.

There would be loss of face if they weren't here for the enthronement ceremony, but at this stage it looked like they would still make it.

It was as though he was missing something important but couldn't find out what it was. A little like the ceremony itself, he knew little about it.

Up until recently he hadn't paid much attention to how Uksod ran things. That had changed once he'd broken free of the amber brandy that had dulled him.

He was the heir to the throne now that his birthday had passed, and he wanted to do it well. There were those about the palace that hadn't fully adjusted to him taking charge, but they were becoming fewer by the week.

Uksod never had a problem — people followed his orders immediately. Karpenmor knew that was because people feared the Regent and what he might do if they didn't follow his requests.

No such fear existed around Karpenmor's requests, which was how he wanted it, just not the lack of obedience.

Surely, I can have authority without fear?

Somehow, he needed to learn how to have people willing to do his instructions without having to resort to the same methods Uksod used.

He approached the Vrah compound, his intention being to spend some more time in the library. It was there he had discovered unique historical records and he was looking for something that covered the period when his father, Schevenal, was enthroned.

It might well be an unnaturally long time ago, but it still had to have happened. When he took over from his own father, there would have been a ceremony.

Karpenmor's hope was that he might gather some insights into how it was run, who was present, and what rules surrounded it.

Does it even matter? I will be the High Prince; can't I create whatever rules I want?

Setting such a first might not be the right way to start his rule, or not. Handling everything in his own distinct way might be exactly the right thing needed in Enderk.

He had questions about the Vrah and One's loyalty. While they were his protectors and served him directly, and not the priest or his religion, Uksod's influence couldn't be ignored.

The priest's life had been much longer than normal men, which meant One had served him the entire time. Irrespective of Karpenmor's position, bonds would have been formed that might be slow to break.

Can I trust One when I take over, or is he Uksod's puppet?

He doubted One was anyone's puppet, but he appeared to be extremely loyal to Uksod, which was understandable. Or perhaps he was just loyal to the head of the realm.

Since Uksod had been incapacitated, Karpenmor and One had a few awkward interactions as they dealt with the new relationship.

If it didn't change, Karpenmor wanted to discover more about the rules of replacing leadership of the Vrah. He expected their library would hold that information at least.

Behind the palace proper Karpenmor stopped and looked up at the massive mountains that protected the rear of the city. The sheer rock face rose further than his eyes could detect and was the best defense anyone could ever wish for.

Inside the compound everyone gave him their acknowledgement, a small dip of the head, but no one spoke. It was the way of the Vrah; they would answer when questioned but unnecessary speech was avoided.

At the northern end of the compound Karpenmor could make out what appeared to be a messenger arriving. They dismounted and hurried into the building.

There was always some form of activity happening within the boundaries of this complex.

Inside, on his way to the library, he saw the rider hand over a package to One. The leader of the Vrah dismissed the man and walked toward Karpenmor.

"Highness." He dipped his head.

"A gift?"

"Not so much, but important. Perhaps you would care to see what it is, Highness?"

That piqued Karpenmor's interest. "Certainly."

"It would be best in my office."

The leader of the Vrah held his hand out to gesture Karpenmor down the hallway, which Karpenmor followed.

"What brings you to us, Highness?"

"I was about to visit the library, One. Nothing particularly exciting."

The two men walked without further words until they were behind the closed door of One's office. He gestured to Karpenmor to sit on the soft chairs to the side of the room, near a small fire.

One opened the pouch and tipped the contents onto the small round table that sat between them. Seven rings rolled out, all identical, the same rings every Vrah member wore.

"These are the rings returned from Dharatan, from the failed mission over there."

"Rings of the dead." He said it out loud not as a question, just a fact.

"Yes. They have been couriered from the southern city where the new team is camped."

"Is that near Anderwell?"

"Yes."

"A long journey."

One shrugged.

Karpenmor bent forward and picked one of the rings up. As he did so his head swam, it took all his effort to retain his poise and not show anything to One.

Something about the ring felt strange in his hand, his palm and fingers were tingling. There was a similarity to how his father's pendant had felt, although that had a blueish stone in it, not the tiny amount of amber that each of these rings held.

"I've never seen one up close before, One. They are simple but there's an elegance to them. There's a number on the underside."

"Each has a unique number, Highness. It is the number allocated to a recruit when he becomes a Vrah. That stays with them until they die or become one of the ten."

"The ten?"

Karpenmor thought he saw a small eye-roll from the older man. He didn't have to explain such things to Uksod.

"My senior lieutenants, Highness. Their numbers are assigned to them by me. If a Vrah is elevated into the ten, they give up their number and take up the ring of the position they fill."

"I see. Outside of the ten does the number mean anything?"

One shook his head. "No, it is only the number they draw from the pool of rings when they pass initiation. Whatever that number, it is theirs for life."

Karpenmor looked at the ring in his hand and read the number carved on the underside. "Ninety-three."

"Ah. I did not expect he would fail."

"What do you mean?"

"He was the leader I picked for the team that was sent over there to recover the amulet. He is... was... quite the soldier. My expectation was he would make quick work of the task."

"What happened?"

"We lost them all, so the only report is that which Uksod was able to discover."

"Uksod? How would he know?"

One looked at him. Karpenmor could see the hesitation to answer, it was an interesting test.

"He has an ability to speak to any Vrah wearing a ring."

"Oh, does he now?"

"I thought you would know, Highness."

"There are a number of things I have to learn, One. But I will get there. What did he report?"

"The person they hunted was a young woman. Ninety-three had captured her but then something happened. He did not know what. Then they were all lost."

"Lost? You mean killed."

"Yes."

"Not just a young woman then, she clearly has her own soldiers who are not to be trifled with."

"All things considered, yes."

"Things?"

"There are seven rings here, Highness. To have killed this many of our highly trained assassins is most unusual."

"What do we know of this young woman?"

"Little, Highness. Each time we've gotten close to her she has eluded us. That she carries the amulet, we are certain of now. Who or what protects her, I do not yet know."

"You said what protects her. What do you mean?"

"There are things outside of my knowledge, Highness, but to lose so many of my men, could mean…"

"You can say it."

"Magic, or those who wield it."

Karpenmor looked at the man. He was very serious. "That's a strong claim."

"It would be better discussed with Uksod, Highness. That is his area of expertise."

So it seems.

"Yes, as soon as he recovers, I will make sure to have him bring me up to speed. What of the hunt for the girl?"

"Those who recovered these rings believe she is holed up in the city of Anderwell."

"And they haven't sought her out?"

"Without Uksod it's hard to communicate effectively over such a distance. I had hoped for more information to come back with these rings, but it appears there is none."

"We cannot just wait for Uksod can we?"

"No, Highness, I will be sending word back with the messenger as soon as he has recovered."

"Thank you, One. I've taken up enough of your time."

Leaving the man's office, Karpenmor headed toward the library. He had more questions now than before, including why he could sense something in the ring. More than ever, he wanted Uksod to recover. The man would be able to answer what One could not.

20

LEO

Nothing much had changed for Leo since he'd become a member of the Court, except now he was expected to spend time in serious meetings. It all felt a little strange to him, more like someone was playing a prank on him than it being real.

He'd learned how much it took to run things behind the scenes, or a little of it at least. It had never occurred to him who did the things that kept everyone looked after, but now he was intimately involved in it all.

There was little time for him to hang out with his friends, and they'd all become a little stand-offish since he'd been elevated. Which meant when he wasn't in a meeting or being taught something he had time to kill, which he did by wandering the city.

Since he'd put the mask on at the Audition, Leo had noticed the oddest thing he could now do. At first, he'd thought he was losing his mind, but he'd worked out how to use it and now he practiced whenever he was alone.

He was able to detect who had magic and who didn't, as well as what their skill was. If he looked at someone through the corner of his eye, just a little out of focus, he could see sparks of color popping from them.

Like the woman he had seen on the street earlier that morning. She had blue and yellow flecks coming from her, and when he concentrated on the color a voice in his head told him what it was: Acrobatics.

That had made sense, the woman he had seen was a performer, preparing to do a show out on the street. Many of the students had colors around them, but not all.

Leo wasn't sure that this new capability of his was particularly useful, but it did make for much more interesting walks around the city and college.

He knew he should discuss it further with Toolet or Tillandra but there always seemed to be something else more important than his colors.

They were definitely more interested in his other ability. The stir from when he'd turned into a rat hadn't died down, even though he was less than impressed by it.

I can turn into a rat! What a great power that is.

Maybe if he could shape-shift into something like a bear or bird… but so far, he couldn't even properly reproduce being a rat.

It sure wasn't going to impress any girls, that was for sure, most of them couldn't stand rodents and screamed even just seeing a mouse on the other side of a room. He could cross a narrow rope easier than anyone else, woop-woop. That didn't make him feel very special at all.

"There you are!"

Leo looked over his shoulder back into Toolet's office from the balcony where he'd been staring across the back of the college. "Given I'm meant to be with you I assumed coming here would be best."

"And I went looking for you, while you were here the whole time."

"If only we could communicate to each other."

"Ha, Ha. If only. That might need to be the very first thing I teach you, because it sounds like it's going to be very important."

"I didn't want to ask in the meeting, but how will everyone be able to communicate quickly from those places?"

"Come and sit down, we've got so much to cover, it will be exhausting."

"You don't have any classes?"

Toolet gave off her nervous laugh, like she did randomly throughout the day. Leo didn't pay it much attention anymore.

"They've all been canceled; other teachers will take over until I've got you up to speed."

Toolet poured them both a goblet of her usual white wine, placing hers on the high table beside her padded chair before jumping into it. "Where to begin?"

The older woman closed her eyes and began gently massaging her temples while Leo just sat there watching her.

"The masks we wear are more than just a way to brand us as one of the Court. No one else can see them or knows we're wearing them. As you can tell, we can't distinguish them either. They're carved from a special wood in a forest in Daskare. The wood carries its own magic and is part of a communication network."

"Network?"

She nodded. "We didn't know as much up until recently but when Mother went to get your mask, she learned more about them. Not only can we communicate to each other but there's a tree network where those who have the right skill can communicate."

"A tree network?"

"That's what I said, didn't I?"

"Yeah but that's a little hard to believe."

"So, a piece of wood, melding into your face is acceptable, but the tree that it comes from can't do anything other than make masks?"

"I see what you mean."

"You need to suspend your skepticism if we're to get you up to speed quickly, Leo. What served you as a student, allowed you to protect yourself from relationships, will only slow us down."

"What do you mean?" He felt embarrassed by what she said, but he knew she spoke the truth. When he passed the Audition, it was after he had to face his truth, that he pushed everyone away through sarcasm and distance.

"I don't need to explain it to you do I -- just get over it, okay?"

Leo nodded.

"Let's ignore the trees for now, so far I've not used one. I'm going to teach you how to use your mask so you can speak to the others, and they you."

She went on to explain about the life force requirement and spent a lot of time talking about the cost, and how much toll it took on the users. Leo listened and tried his best to be serious but even though he knew she wasn't pranking him, it all felt a little fanciful.

He was a doer, someone who needed to see it in action before he'd be convinced. And talking was just like class. The bit that stopped him in his seat was when Toolet started telling him they used rats.

"Rats?"

"Typically, yes."

"Ewww."

"Coming from you that's funny."

"What do you mean?"

"You know exactly what I mean. You turned into a rat during your training."

"Doesn't make it any better. I didn't choose a rat, it just happened."

"That's another thing we have to work on."

"What?"

"Your ability to shape-shift. You need to be able to use it at will, when required, and to choose what you turn into."

"How would I even..."

"I listened to what you talked about previously and you've turned into other things, you just hadn't realized it."

He wasn't sure what she meant.

"When I queried you about your past, you eventually talked about that time you had been captured hiding between the tents listening in to people. You talked about how you almost slid into the tent and could hear and see things more easily."

"And?"

"I'd bet good coin, Leo, that you became a snake or similar when that happened."

"A SNAKE?"

"Yes, or maybe a lizard."

"Lizard? You think this makes it better?"

"It's unlikely it was a worm as you appeared to be able to see and hear very well."

"A worm? So you really are just making fun of me. If that was true, why didn't someone see that? I got caught as me, not some creature."

"You've no control over it, Leo, like I said, and we need to change that. We don't want you turning into a rat then one of us grabbing you to use."

"Why, what happens to the rats?"

"I told you how we use the life force of the animal. With rats, they are small and using them this way kills them."

"That's horrible!"

"They're rats, Leo. There's more of them than we can ever kill off. No one misses them."

"But..."

"What, you're the king of the rats now are you, Dent?"

"Don't you start." The nickname his friends had chosen had stuck and he wasn't losing that.

Toolet was chuckling at him and had a big grin on her face. "It is what it is, Leo. We use the rats. You can use other animals, but do you really feel like you want to do that to a dog or something else?"

He shook his head. He didn't want to do it to anything.

"For the first time, I'll be the one who initiates the call. It's not the most pleasant of things."

"What do I do?"

"I want you to go to your little office and sit at the desk." She then explained to him what he would need to do, and how he would know.

Leo waited in his small office thinking this was all part of a joke. The whole first year trainee prank thing. Except just like she told him, he could hear a knocking sound.

He looked left and right but saw nothing, there was no one else around, and the sound, despite it seeming to be in both ears, was in truth coming from somewhere in the center of his forehead, or thereabouts.

She'd told him he needed to close his eyes and focus on the center of his head, so he did. Nothing seemed to happen, not at first, but he kept at it, his heartbeat picking up the more the knocking continued.

He saw or felt a darkness that emanated out from him, then he slipped into it. He thought he could hear someone speaking, but it was very faint. Leo tried to push into it by concentrating harder but that didn't work.

Whatever it was he fell out of it, and was sitting back in the chair with small sweat beads on his face.

Toolet appeared a minute or so later.

"You're trying too hard."

"What does that mean?"

"Have you ever meditated before?"

"Not that I'm aware of, no."

"Right. Well, you don't get to calmness by forcing calmness. You have to let it come to you, not the other way around. Tell me what you experienced."

Leo did and felt a little daft trying to explain it.

"You did the first part right. When the knock came, you focused here." Toolet tapped the center of her forehead. "That's good, but it sounds like once you started to move into the Void…."

"Void?"

"Yes, that's what we call it. That blackness, it's where all of the communication happens. When that happens, you just need to wait for it. Stay focused on the same spot in your head, and breathe, don't force it. I always think it feels like I slip there, it pulls me into it, rather than me pushing my way in."

"That makes sense. The more I tried, the further it seemed to be from me."

"Shall we try that again?"

"I guess."

21

UKSOD

*I*f Uksod didn't know better, he'd think someone was sitting on his head it felt so heavy. He wanted to lift it off his pillow, but he couldn't muster the will.

I'm so exhausted, did I not sleep at all last night?

His entire body felt empty as though he was little more than a sack of skin and bones.

What is going on?

He tried to remember what he'd been doing yesterday but his mind was foggy and struggled to grasp hold of anything.

Ever since Yantarnaya had bonded him to the circlet on his forehead he had never been plagued with ill health, not the mortal kind at least.

I've drained myself again! What was I doing?

That was the only thing that could harm him now -- when he overused the use of his power, the payback was this exhaustion. He'd done something bad a number of years back and been unconscious for a week.

How long this time? Did it feel as bad as this?

Everything seemed worse right now, but then it always did. The events of the present always seemed much more pronounced than distant memories.

Uksod took several deep breaths and gathered his wits about him. He could hear the crackling of a fire and the faint humming that rose from the Debrua Stone deep under the mountain.

Incense was burning, so he was in his own rooms, even if the blend being used wasn't what he'd use. *If you want something done right, best you do it yourself.*

With a concentrated effort he forced his eyes open. It surprised him how much strength that took him for something so simple. Even the dim light in his chambers caused him to grimace, and he caught movement to his right.

"Eminence! You're awake." Trorn appeared beside his bed.

Yes, fool, stating the obvious.

With another focused effort he pushed himself up.

"Let me help." Trorn moved forward and helped prop pillows behind him.

If there was one thing Uksod hated it was feeling like an invalid, or worse, being treated like one. He knew he should be grateful for Trorn, the man was just helping, but still it grated on his frail nerves.

At least now he could see about the room. As low as the light was it still created a dull ache behind his eyes. Not that he would close his eyelids, Uksod wasn't sure he'd open them again.

None of that really mattered, what he needed was a drink. His tongue was rough, and his lips felt cracked and sore.

"I imagine you'll want this more than anything else."

Trorn held a mug and brought it over to him. Uksod wanted to hold it himself but his desperation for it and the difficulty he had moving his arm made him just accept the help.

The taste of the ale was the sweetest thing Uksod could remember. Even better was the feeling of it sliding down his aching throat.

Whatever dryness that had baked in there, the ale cut through it and softened the edges. It was as though the ale was filling his body up with air, it felt that good.

So weak, what on Enderk was I doing?

It had been many years since the last time he pushed himself this much, and he should have remembered why -- this was not a smart move, but there must have been a reason.

What was going on? Why did I need to do this?

"We were so worried, Uksod, this is the worst I've ever seen you."

Uksod wanted to reply, but he couldn't seem to speak despite focusing his will.

"What is it, Uksod? Are you okay?"

He was able to nod at least.

"You can't talk?"

Uksod nodded again.

"That's okay, there's nothing you need to say, not now at least."

Yes, there is. How long was I out? What happened?

"When you were found, Karpenmor was very worried. I assured him that you would be fine, just to give it a couple of days."

A couple of days, that was all. Thank Yantarnaya.

"But weeks, never before have you been out for so long. I thought you would never recover."

Weeks? How many weeks, man -- tell me!

"But there's color back in your face, you're on the mend I can see."

How long?

Trorn turned away from him and headed to the side table, filling the mug again.

That better be for me. Hurry, man, I'm dying here.

Uksod's number two came back and slowly tipped some of the ale into his mouth, holding a cloth under Uksod's chin with his other hand.

I'm not a child!

As the liquid ran down his throat, he was able to move his tongue and lick his cracked lips.

"More?"

Yes, fool. More! What do you think I'm licking my lips for? If I could speak I would.

Despite his frustration Uksod managed another nod. He could handle the begging for now. The sooner he drank and ate the quicker he would get his strength back.

"Karpenmor will be pleased to hear that you're awake, he has been here almost every day for hours watching over you."

The boy, here? I would not have expected that from him.

Uksod focused back on the ale dripping into his mouth. Everything else could wait. Hopefully the sooner he restored his strength the quicker his memory would return.

Uksod's head swam a little and he closed his eyes. The ale was good, but he needed to let everything adjust now that he was awake.

But I need to be on my feet. There's much to do... I just can't remember what.

"I see you're still tired, I'll leave you be."

He started licking his lips and opened his mouth, albeit slowly, while looking at Trorn.

"More ale? I think you've had enough for just now. It will only make it more difficult when... when you need to get rid of it."

Trorn had looked away from Uksod when he'd said it.

You wouldn't speak to me that way if I was up.

"Someone will be through to help clean up in a little while."

He understood. If he had been out for many weeks, then they had been cleaning him and dealing with all his body issues. It was more than that, this was a look of pity, as if he was an invalid. The priest's superior now confined to his bed unable to even feed himself.

Not for long, Trorn. I don't need your pity or anyone else's. You should know better.

"I'll be back in a little while with others, and we'll get you out of that bed and into a chair."

He didn't wait for Uksod's approval, as he would normally, he just turned and left.

That angered Uksod, which he enjoyed. It was another thing that made him feel more normal. The man was just trying to help, he was his right hand.

No doubt you've had to deal with things you're not ready for. That's why you're so keen for me to be better.

He tried to move his body but struggled. For now, he'd just have to accept the position he was in. Food would have been good, anything to eat. Now that he was awake his stomach had stirred as well, and he felt as though he could eat a deer all on his own.

In order to distract himself from that thought Uksod probed the stone in the circlet on his head. He felt nothing from it. That didn't surprise him, his strength was so depleted, but he wanted to know for sure.

What has been going on while I've been out? The boy's been visiting has he? That is surprising, I'd have not thought he'd have cared.

Uksod knew that Karpenmor had hardly visited his own father when he'd been confined to the amber room, which made it even more interesting.

Perhaps the lad realizes how much he needs me? That would be a nice correction. He was being petulant, I remember that much at least.

For him to have drained himself this much, Uksod knew he would have used two bodies at least. Which meant a very long conversation or multiple.

Who on Dharatan would I have needed to do that with?

Uksod closed his eyes and tried to focus on what had been happening. Some memories began to bubble up as his body woke more.

He and Karpenmor had returned from Ponte, that was some time before... then the boy was doing something.

What?

There'd been questions about the enthronement, and the bridges, but nothing else.

I'm sure of it. Who was I speaking to?

An image of a priest in different robes came to Uksod's mind. A tall man, someone Uksod knew.

What's his name... I know him. Fuling, that's it.

Something to do with this priest letting him down. It had to be about the amulet, surely. The amulet that the girl had.

Girl... that's right. A girl has the amulet.

More snippets came back to him. Fuling had failed to capture her, she was gone now. Out of reach... or something. He had spoken to this priest, and then someone else. One of the Vrah.

But who, what did they tell me? Why was I so desperate to push so hard? I can't remember. I need to remember.

22

TILLANDRA

Knowing she could speak to Thenis through the stones was a double-edged sword for Tillandra. The goddess only answered what she wanted to, or what she could, and there was no guarantee that Tillandra would get what she needed.

Then there was the effect on the Mother Stone and its companions in the tower. Weakening that shield was not something she wished to hurry along.

Somewhere nearby the Derks were likely waiting to find a way to Lani and her amulet. At the moment the stones shielded them from finding her exact location.

Tillandra knew that it was only a question of time before someone came inside looking for the girl, despite them having every guard on alert.

Carnus, the Ngaherian, had brought them news about what he'd seen. He was definite he'd spotted someone leaving the city via the rope, but they'd never returned.

His view was that they'd spotted him on their tail, so they knew not to return the way they had. Whatever it was this mysterious person was up to, Tillandra had to believe it was related.

She'd insisted that everything about the way the city was secured should be changed. Now every parapet was heavily guarded day and night.

You'd need to be invisible to get over the walls. The gates of the city were partly closed now, and inspections increased, slowing everything down.

Anyone remotely looking like a Derk was denied access, and Carnus had been stalking walls and gates like a one-man army. They'd placed guards as discreetly as they could all around Odajeen's place. There wasn't much more they could do.

I could do with a dream.

Some guidance to add surety to the decisions she was making. While on the outside she'd acted with determination telling her colleagues what everyone was to do, inside she questioned everything and lacked any form of certainty.

Bracing herself, she entered the cells below the college and saw that everyone had already arrived. Today they'd try and resolve the Goran situation once and for all.

Either he'd be healed, or he'd spend the rest of his time down here, their prisoner. He had taken up too much time and energy already.

"What are you all up to?" the angry voice of Zoran called from the bars of his cell.

Tillandra turned to the guard and quietly said, "Lock the doors and wait outside and don't come in no matter what, understood?"

"Yes, Mother."

Turning back to the group, she looked at Junther. "We'll let Beantic overwhelm him first, then you're up."

"Do you think all of you can force me out of him? Is that what this is? And why did you bring the kids along, Mother? That's not very sporting of you."

"Go on, Beantic, I don't want to listen to him any longer."

"Already started, Mother, it will just take some time, he's fresh this morning."

"I can tell, you jittery one. Go on, shake your head, you don't bother me."

Tillandra watched Beantic and could sense her power building.

Even though she directed it toward Goran in the cell, it pulsed out to the sides as well, brushing past her.

Once Beantic had a strong control over him she nodded to the others. Lionel opened the cell door letting Junther move in. He dragged a chair in and sat at the foot of the bed, reaching out with his only arm, placing the hand on Goran's ankle.

"You can start. He can't move, not even his mouth. Best she gets on with it while I can control his breathing."

Tillandra picked up Purple, chair and all, and carried her into the now cramped cell. She placed the chair up against the bed and stood directly behind it protectively.

Gizen stood outside the cell. "You can do it, Purple. Just like we discussed."

"Okay." The young girl's voice was very quiet.

Tillandra watched as Purple leaned forward and place her hands on Goran's head. One was on his forehead and the other near his ear. She began to hum, a small beat with her eyes closed.

Several times Goran's body shuddered, unable to fully move, but it looked as though he was wrestling with what Purple was doing. The little girl continued to hum a simple tune over and over while her hands stayed motionless on Goran's head.

It went on for at least an hour, before Gizen spoke. "That has to be enough, Purple, surely you can't do much more?"

"All… most." The girl's voice was croaky and weak-sounding, not timid like before. "There." Purple pulled her hands away and slumped back in her seat. Tillandra looked down and could see how pale the girl was.

"Quickly, Lionel, get her some air and something to drink. Gizen, go with her and make sure she's okay."

Once Purple was gone, Tillandra left the cell and watched as Junther let go, stood up and hurried outside. She shut the cell door quickly and locked it.

"We've done all we can now." She said it as much to herself as anyone else.

"What now, Mother?"

"You lot should get on with what you need to. I think I'm going to wait here for a bit, to see if there's any change."

She sat in the central area watching the bed where Goran lay, contemplating what came next. While he was still alive, they couldn't replace him in the Court, but if he didn't make it, then they would have to run another Audition.

There were still the two remaining Prospects from the last one, Sabant and Aakesh. It was the first time Tillandra had reflected on them since Leo's ascension.

The girl, Sabant, had struggled since he had been the one chosen. They'd all been a little surprised it wasn't her; she'd appeared the one most ready, but then that wasn't how it worked.

Whatever it was within her she needed to accept and face, she mustn't have been able to, whereas Leo had. *Perhaps I need to spend time with her.* Yet, it wasn't as important as Lani and Goran at this point in time.

Thenis had stated that the only way she knew to get Lani free was for the mask to come off, which meant Odajeen dying.

Earlier the goddess had impressed on Tillandra that she might have to face such decisions, the death of one for the benefit of the many, but Tillandra couldn't imagine making such a call.

There must be another way, surely? Lani got in there, why can't she get herself out?

Having Lani's skills were useful, and supposedly the prophecy spoke about her, and how she was needed to help them prevail. At least that's the interpretation that they'd settled on with what they knew.

But if she was stuck, or lost, in Odajeen's mind, would it matter? That amulet was going nowhere, it was where they could manage it.

I could just put it in the box and let it be. But if she dies from it, then that means I killed her.

Tillandra wasn't ready to do such a thing. She still couldn't grasp what sort of force must have made Burgendetta do it.

Movement on Goran's cot broke Tillandra's train of thought.

"Goran, you're awake."

Tillandra could see his eyes move toward her, and then lock on her, staring as she moved closer to the door of his cell.

"Can you speak?"

He didn't say a word, he just stared at her. Seeing his frail physical state and the gauntness of his face, on top of how scruffy he was, brought out her worst fears.

Maybe this is all there is now.

"He's gone."

The sound of Goran's croaky voice took her by surprise.

"It is you."

"I need a drink."

"Of course." Tillandra went to the outer room, returning with the jug and a mug. After filling it, she pushed the mug through the access slot.

Goran stood slowly and shuffled across to the small ledge and began to drink. After the first few sips he began gulping it down, liquid running down his thick beard as it overflowed from his lips.

When he had emptied the mug, he pushed it back through. Tillandra filled it and pushed it back, and he drained it again quickly. When she gave him the third, he took it and went back to the bed and sat again.

"That's better. I felt like my throat was buried in the desert."

"What do you mean that he's gone?"

"Zoran, he's locked away."

"How?"

"That girl, it's what she did. She found a place to put him, in here." He raised his grubby right hand and touched his temple.

"She put him somewhere -- I'm not sure I understand."

An awkward silence fell between them. Tillandra wanted to go and fetch her colleagues, but she also needed to speak to her friend while he was still himself.

"I've never talked about him before, maybe I should have."

"Zoran?"

"Yes. He never used to be there, or not like he was after the Audition. That's when he came out properly."

"Why did you not say?"

"It was all too new, and I was ashamed. I thought something was wrong with me."

"Something was wrong with you."

He looked to the floor.

"It's not your fault, Goran, we all have things wrong with us, that's what makes us who we are. But by hiding it you couldn't get help from us."

"It wasn't like you wanted to help. I've been an outer for a long time."

Tillandra looked at him, the sadness that had enveloped him wasn't just now, it was the thing she'd mistaken for shadows. He was completely shrouded in it, like a gray cloak.

"That's not entirely true, Goran. You behaved extremely out of character and caused a lot of harm with what you did in King Nordahl's court."

"What he did."

"Sorry?"

"That wasn't me, it was Zoran."

Tillandra should have had that realization before. Now that she knew there was a second person within the one man, it explained everything, or most things, especially Goran's stark behavioral changes at times.

The Court had never been able to make sense of how he'd done what he did, but the answer was simple now. He hadn't, it was Zoran.

"You prove my point."

"What?"

"How on Dharatan would we have known that, Goran? You never told us, did you?"

He shook his head; his shoulders were still slumped and his energy was very low.

"There was little choice in what we did. We couldn't make sense of any of it, and you refused to take any responsibility for it. Putting you back on the Circuit as penance was the softest of the suggestions that came up at the time."

"Like I said."

"What?"

"On the outer."

"Oh, give up the pity party." Tillandra wanted to help Goran, but she was getting tired of this response. "You never told anyone about what was going on and yet we're supposed to feel sorry for you and always be on your side."

Goran said nothing.

I'm not copping this poor me routine. This could just be him trying to manipulate me and I'm done with all of that.

Tillandra turned and left the room, locking the gate behind her before handing the keys to the guard outside.

"He's all yours."

She felt like an angry child stomping up the stairs and almost burst into laughter as she broke free on the upper level, taking in the cooler night air.

The college was peaceful with everyone in their homes or asleep and she relaxed, taking her time before heading to her office. There was no way she could sleep now, not after all the events of the day.

Tomorrow some of her colleagues would leave Anderwell, and then it really would be left to her to make the decisions. At least this one was dealt with.

Either Goran was going to heal properly, or he wouldn't. As much as it pained her heart to have to be so cut and dry with one of her colleagues, she knew they'd spent too much time dealing with him.

ARBERY

rbery was stunned, this wasn't exactly what she had in mind when Kalling had proposed the offer to her.

"You're pranking me, aren't you?"

The wiry courier smirked at her. "You don't like it?"

"I'm not sure there's anything to like or dislike, this is a shell, not an inn."

"Where's your vision, Arbery?"

"Vision, I'd need a wagon full of magic to make this anything."

She had been very excited when he'd told her his plan the week before, and it had taken all her willpower to not mention it to Dedrick. Despite her husband needing something to lift his spirits, she was glad she'd not said a word.

To show him this would have broken what little hope he had left. The building that Kalling had brought her to was the remnants of an inn that had been all but destroyed by fire two years before.

Now the charred beams, broken walls and dirt was all that remained of what back then had been known as the Horse and Cart. Arbery just shook her head. He couldn't be serious about this.

"Here's the thing, Arbery, we can't afford for you to just suddenly be the new proprietors of an inn that's all made. There'd be a lot of questions, the type that would attract attention, and we don't need that."

That made sense to her.

"I know it doesn't look like much…"

"Much? It doesn't look like anything at all."

He rolled his eyes at her. Despite her response he seemed to have a cheeky smirk permanently on his face. "… but this is perfect for you."

"How?"

"With the grain issue that everyone is facing, it makes a lot of sense you'd be looking to do something else. Of course, you don't have lots of capital behind you to just change things, but if a distant relative happened to help fund the purchase of this derelict building and some helpers arrived to work on rebuilding it…"

"… then it wouldn't seem particularly abnormal."

"Now I see why Goran liked you. You can see the vision."

"That makes sense. Who would be the helpers?"

"There's a troupe heading this way who, let's say, can do more than just entertain. They have a mix of skills including building and the like. More than anything it's just more hands with the same interests."

"Won't that look strange to others?"

"No, they'll still do entertaining in the evening, but during the day they'll trade out their labor for somewhere to sleep. And you have two rooms available back at the bakery. It probably wouldn't hurt to have some extra people staying there when things get worse."

"You're not wrong."

"And we'll be able to fund a bit more, discreetly, so you can offer some of the affected people with no work a little part-time labor to help."

Arbery could see it all now, everything except what would happen to the bakery.

"What about the bakery?"

"That's the shame in all of this, but long-term it won't survive."

"No? Dedrick will be devastated."

"Initially you'll keep up what you do, he'll bake, and you can oversee the building. But between you and me, and no one else, even him, the emmer supplies are running low. Things are going to get a lot worse. He'll have nothing to bake except what we can get to you."

The thought of them losing the bakehouse bothered her even through the excitement of having an inn.

"I guess once he sees the inn taking shape, he'll be fine."

"It's the best I can do. Eventually you'll just have to let the bakery go, or sell it to someone else. It could be converted, but it won't matter. When you rebuild the kitchens, make them bigger and put in one of the ovens he needs. Long-term he can still bake some things, just not like this."

With the vision Kalling had painted in her mind, Arbery cautiously walked around the shell of the inn. She could start to fill in where things would have been. The kitchen toward the back lay where the courtyard would have been, or half of it. There was enough room to extend it if need be.

It was a huge piece of land compared to what they had now and, given the rest of the town was built out, a lot more than she could have expected. This wasn't quite the opportunity she had hoped for, but her spirits picked up as she began to see what it could be.

They'd be on the inside of this group, and part of something bigger than just themselves.

"We could use it like a bakehouse still for those that need one. It would be a way to keep our connection."

"Perhaps, but you are going to need to have some separation. In the end the running of it will be up to you, within the parameters of what we expect."

"Of course. And what will that be?"

"Why don't you convince your husband of the task first? When you're both on board then we'll need to begin several things, one of which will be your additional training."

"When do you need to know by?"

"Yesterday, Arbery. There's a lot happening you don't yet know about, and we need to have things underway. I'm about a month behind the schedule I was given, and I need to catch up."

"Catch up a month?" She shook her head.

"One more thing. You've maintained the secrecy of our family since we brought you on board, but this goes to another level. Once you're a Keeper in the network, there's no turning back."

"Okay."

"It's a lifelong commitment, Arbery. For both of you! There is no out."

Arbery wasn't sure she liked the way his tone had changed, albeit only slightly, in that last warning, but then she'd always known they were locked into something that they probably couldn't leave.

"I'll talk to him tonight."

"As soon as you can agree, and I'm confident you will, then I can set things in motion. But I need to be away tomorrow heading south again to find the things you'll need."

"Like I said, tonight. Will you stay with us, at the bakery?"

"No. I have a favorite place I like -- nothing against your hospitality -- but I'll be there. You'll see me first thing."

"Alright." Arbery watched as he left the gutted building. "Oh Thenis, what are you asking of us?"

She spent more time walking all corners of the yard and looking at all aspects of the site. The more she did, the more excited she became. *They really are giving me an inn.*

When she barred the door after their last customer Arbery looked back at Dedrick, who was wiping his forehead with his apron. A crust of white flour was left behind, making her smile.

"What?"

"You and flour. If it's not on your legs and hands, it's over your face."

"Not for long."

"What do you mean?"

"I didn't want to say anything, didn't want to worry you, but I don't think we have more than a couple of weeks of emmer left. I still can't find anymore."

Arbery figured now was as good a time as any to give him the news. "I might have a solution."

"Have you a secret farm tucked away I don't know about?"

She looked at him. Despite the worry that he must have been carrying and not sharing he was remarkably upbeat. "No, fool. But I might have secured a small extra supply to keep us going short-term while…" She paused, nervous about saying it out loud.

"While?"

"You know I was out for a bit today?"

"Yes. You never did say where."

"We had a visitor."

"Who?"

"One of them." Arbery pointed to the small wooden carved jester's head behind the counter, that was the only symbol for those coming by to show they were part of the network.

"Oh, and?"

"They want to give us an inn."

"An inn? Really? So why are you hiding it from me, isn't that good news?"

"It's complicated, but I was worried about you, about the bakery. If we do this, then we won't be able to keep this up."

"Keep this up?" He looked about the tiny shopfront. "What is it we're keeping? This tiny place, struggling to make anything for anyone, wondering if we're going to get attacked for a small sack of emmer?"

"You know what I mean. This is your life, you're a baker."

"I'm a baker, wife, because I don't know what else to do. I'm here because it's how we feed ourselves and put a roof over our head. But it's not my life. You're my life. Anything else is just what we do to survive. If you wanted to move to Nedor I'd walk away from here tomorrow."

Arbery was shocked. As much as she knew this man, he still surprised her, and her love for him shone through the flour and worry she'd had all day.

"No need to move town, love. But the inn isn't quite ready for us."

"So, this is the bit where you let me know the catch?"

"Sort of."

Arbery went through the story with Dedrick, staying up half the night discussing it with excitement. All the concern she'd had about convincing him was unfounded. They were going to have an inn, just liked she'd hoped for.

KARPENMOR

hat else don't I know?

That question had plagued Karpenmor through the night. The more he had become involved in the day-to-day running of the palace, the city and beyond, the greater his thinking on it.

He had slept, but it had not been an easy rest. Whenever he stirred his mind had begun to ponder more things. Before the sun had risen, he'd given in to his latest waking and come outside.

Standing out on his balcony he was forced to constantly brush his face clear from his thick red hair, blown by the wind whipping over the balustrade.

The waking city below seemed so unfamiliar to him despite having lived here all of his life. He had been down in the city so rarely that it was something that he knew about but not of it in any real detail.

At this time of day, a blanket of quietness lay across everything. None of his guards or servants knew he was awake, leaving him completely in peace.

Few sounds echoed up from below and he could imagine he was anything, anyone. Mostly he imagined what being the High Prince would mean long-term.

With Uksod out of action, Karpenmor had stuck his nose into

everything. For the first time he could remember, he wanted to know how things ran around here.

Much to the dislike of his chancellor and other administrators he'd asked many questions, reserving his judgment for now. He wanted to understand how everything worked.

He hadn't done as much of that with One as he possibly should have, up until yesterday at least.

Maybe that's what disturbed my sleep last night?

There was more going on than what he had discovered so far. At times it seemed overwhelming; it would be easy to defer to everyone else and go back to drinking the amber brandy.

Karpenmor shook his head and stretched out his shoulders. *I haven't thought about that stuff in a long time. Why did Uksod keep me on that?*

Another question he could ask the priest when he woke. *If he wakes.* Karpenmor wanted the man to wake, he wanted him to be available to question and to learn from.

Focusing back on the city below he watched as progressively throughout the city fires and lanterns were lit, twinkling like stars.

Most of them came from TimberTown, the poorest section of the city. Many of those down there would be heading off to fulfil their roles serving those in the wealthier areas of the city.

So many people down there, living out their lives unconcerned by the things bothering Karpenmor. And had no concept of what filled their thoughts, what concerns they had.

For the first time in a long while Karpenmor wanted to get out into the city. To walk about and learn more about all of that as well.

Why not? I'm in charge now.

Uksod was always against the idea, without ever providing a satisfactory answer, but the old man had little say now. Karpenmor turned and walked back through his room and opened his outer door.

The two guards outside didn't flinch.

"I am going for a walk — out in the city."

Karpenmor set off heading toward the great stairs that led down to the lower levels. One of the guards followed silently behind him; no doubt others would join in as they got to the gates.

There was nothing he could do about the guards that would accompany him, but Karpenmor hoped the early morning dark would give him some degree of anonymity. He wanted to see the city as it was, not as others tried to make it look for him.

Inside the large entrance doors to the palace two Vrah appeared startled by his approach. It took both of them to move one of the large stone entrances, his arrival surprising everyone.

Other guards outside quickly joined in and both doors were open in time for him to walk through them. Karpenmor nodded his appreciation but didn't stop nor speak, and continued down the long stairway that ended at the circular road.

It was here carriages and people arrived before coming inside the palace, separated from the front of the grounds by a large body of water.

Checking over his shoulder he noticed that his escort had grown, with three of the guards from the doors locked in step with his main guard. Facing back to the front he let a small smile form.

He knew it was a silly thing but keeping them on their toes and alert by being spontaneous made him feel good. If he had to be followed everywhere then making them react was a tiny way he could exert his own control.

I still don't feel like I'm in charge, do I? I shouldn't care one iota what they think, and yet I do.

As they circled to their right Karpenmor could see several Vrah coming from the opposite direction toward the gates. The nearer the two groups got to each other he was able to see that One was accompanying one of his men who led a horse.

The horseman had mounted and departed through the gates before Karpenmor reached them. One appeared to be waiting for his arrival. As they closed on each other he nodded at the guards, who fell back from their proximity to Karpenmor.

"Highness."

"Good morning, One, I am surprised to see you out here so early."

"As I am you, Highness."

The other Vrah had stepped back leaving the two men space to talk without being overheard.

"Such times are the only peace I get from the constant interruptions and business of the palace."

The leader of the Vrah looked at him. While his mouth never moved, Karpenmor felt as though he could see the tiniest indication of a smile at the edges of the man's eyes.

"The same reason I am out here, Highness."

"A messenger?"

"Yes, Highness. He heads back to Ponte, best to leave at first light and make good use of the coming daylight."

"Another message to Ponte? Did mine not go already, One?"

The Vrah leader was a little slower in his response. "It did, Highness, this was a different message."

It was another case of Karpenmor sticking his nose into the business around him, but he couldn't help himself. With the bridges closing in on being completed he was very curious about everything happening there.

"Something important, One?"

Again, the response was slow enough to be well considered.

"Just another request from Ngahere, Highness. It got the standard response."

"What type of request?"

No gap this time. "To send a delegation here."

"I don't believe I've ever seen a foreign delegation here before, One."

"We always refuse them, Highness."

"They get rejected automatically?"

This time One's face struggled to hold its impassiveness.

"That has always been my instruction, Highness. I was told that I didn't need to bother Uksod with them when they came, simply to wait an appropriate amount of time then send an identical rejection."

"I see."

Karpenmor could see the man was conflicted, he'd only been following his orders. There were so many touches of Uksod on everything it irked him.

"And what is that message?"

One's discomfort had disappeared now.

"When you return that which is ours, we will consider entering discussions."

"What exactly does that mean, One?"

The man was slow to respond. "That I do not know, Highness. I was simply told to use only those words."

Karpenmor didn't believe that at all. The connection between One and Uksod was still strong. *For now, at least.*

It was a reminder of the things Uksod had knowledge about, which Karpenmor did not. He needed to fix that; he couldn't have these gaps of information.

"Next time you receive such a request, please confer with me on it. I think we'll want to consider how they are handled moving forward."

"Of course, Highness."

"The bridges will be close to completion soon; we will need the Ngaherians to comply if we're to finish the last one on their side. Perhaps it's time we received one of their delegations."

One nodded but said nothing.

"You said they come once a year?"

"Usually, Highness, but recently that has changed."

"How many?"

"This is the third."

"They've sent three this year?"

"Correct."

"Are they all the same?"

"Usually, yes."

Having to pull these answers from One was wearing very thin with Karpenmor.

"For Tarna's sake, One, tell me!"

To his credit, or training, One didn't bat an eyelid to the rebuke. "This one was different; they were more persistent and direct."

"How so?"

One was quiet for a moment. "Perhaps you should read it for yourself?"

"I think that would be a good idea."

"It's in my office if you'd like to accompany me there."

Karpenmor nodded and they turned and headed east toward the Vrah compound.

If nothing else, One, you've managed to keep me inside the walls.

When they arrived in One's office, the leader of the Vrah was quick to take a partially rolled scroll from his desk and hand it to Karpenmor. At times like these he was thankful for all the training Uksod had put him through.

His ability to read meant he had no need to rely on others, or to have them sanitize what they read.

"There is nothing here to explain what it is they wish to discuss."

"Nothing, Highness, but the wording is different... more desperate."

"They do repeat themselves... of the urgency. I would have wanted to know what this is about before I rejected it outright."

The room fell quiet.

"If Uksod was well I would ask him why he doesn't accept any delegation from the Ngaherians."

"I believe it's not just them, Highness."

"Sorry?"

"My instructions have always been to reject any delegation requests. That no foreign emissaries and their parties should come to En Carta or be allowed on Enderk soil."

"How on Enderk will we improve our relationship with these barbarians if we don't hear what they have to say?"

"It is not my place to debate reasons, Highness, I have simply been following the orders I have been given."

Karpenmor knew it was going to take people time to adjust to his rule. This was just another example of why he hoped the Tenebrosity would be full this time around, and he could be enthroned. The reach of Uksod's tendrils were everywhere, even in such simple instructions, the ramifications could be far-reaching.

"It's too late to stop your messenger?"

"He will be on the Great Plains by now, Highness."

"Perhaps I'll need to send another message."

One said nothing.

"Let me think on it — I'll come back to you later today."

"Highness."

Karpenmor turned and set off back to his rooms. He wanted to think about the reasons behind the Ngaherian requests before he replied.

Why are they so persistent suddenly?

~

As he approached his chambers, he saw Trorn.

"Looking for me?"

"Ah, yes, Highness."

Uksod's second in command was nothing like the head priest. He almost seemed to stammer around Karpenmor, uncertain of how to behave.

"What is it?"

"I have news, Highness."

"Tell me!"

"Uksod is awake, Highness. He is better."

"How is he?"

"Weak, but able to speak."

"I should visit him then." Karpenmor went to change direction, his guard almost walking into the back of him.

"Ah… could I suggest waiting a little, Highness? He's resting again, just the waking and speaking seemed to exhaust him."

Karpenmor's motivation to see Uksod was for information, and he'd likely bombard him with questions. It wouldn't be ideal for the older man. Reluctantly he agreed.

"I will leave it a few hours then, but it's important I get to speak to him next. Please keep others from him."

"Of course, Highness."

When Trorn had left Karpenmor entered his quarters and sat on a sofa, rubbing his hands. Finally, some good news.

25

TILLANDRA

Sometime during the night Tillandra slipped into one of her visions.

~

She was looking down on something that was hard to grasp. There were wispy images of people, sounds of them talking, all coming and going.

These images and sounds floated, crisscrossing their way through a ball of darkness. As Tillandra tried to understand it her focus was pulled toward a particular image.

The face even though it was faint and transparent was still familiar. It was Lani and there was a connection coming from her, reaching outward.

Someone appeared to grasp that connection, a figure that Tillandra did not recognize. A woman, whose face bore some resemblance to Thenis, but it wasn't her.

While she couldn't hear what was being said, Tillandra had an ill feeling from the woman. Something about her set all her instincts on alert. She wanted to tell Lani to get away, but Tillandra wasn't there, her voice went nowhere.

The woman looked briefly in Tillandra's direction, a smirk on her face, as though she had heard. She called to the girl, using her name.

Lani responded to the voice as though she knew it. She moved a little toward her, almost as though cocking her ear to listen.

The woman beckoned to her with her hand, and her fingers seemed to grow out like massive ropes in Lani's direction, looking to wrap around her and drag her in.

One of the nails grew like a massive talon. Tillandra screamed to the girl but it didn't matter what she did, the woman's powers were so strong she was unable to influence how Lani thought. The girl began to step toward her.

NO!

The woman turned toward Tillandra, this time looking directly at her. Her eyes blazed orange and she swept her left hand as if to knock Tillandra away.

Tillandra recoiled from whatever the woman had done, flailing backward in the vision, trying to stop herself spinning.

She woke thrashing her arms to stop herself falling, her body covered in sweat with Milfred stood over her.

"M-m-mother, are you okay?"

"What... what's the matter?"

"You were screaming in your sleep. You woke m-m-me."

Her mind cleared and she propped herself up. "I'm sorry, Milfred. Just a bad dream. What time is it?"

"Just before dawn."

"I'm sorry, you can go back to bed, I'll be fine."

"I wouldn't sleep anymore now, I'll make us a drink."

"Sorry, Milfred."

Tillandra waited until he had left her room before swinging her legs over the edge of the bed and sitting up properly.

What on Dharatan was that about? That wasn't good at all, how does she know about Lani? What do they know about Lani?

There was the other side of that question which caused some concern to Tillandra. Did Lani know the other woman? If so, how? What was their relationship?

Normally she'd just ask Lani, but that wasn't possible to do.

That space seemed familiar. Like... like the Void.

"That's it!" Tillandra surprised herself speaking out loud.

It did feel a lot like the Void. What was the other woman doing there? Could they also access that space? It made sense that anyone could, but that meant there was danger there as well.

Was she speaking to Lani now, while she's in Odajeen's mind, or before that? Or later? Is it showing me that Lani will get free, but she's friendly with this other woman?

So many unknowns, Tillandra hated how obscure her dreams were. Gizen's visions all seemed direct and clear, proper foretellings, unlike the abstract visions Tillandra saw.

Another idea came to her.

Can we speak to her in the Void?

Tillandra wanted to kick herself for not considering that. If she was visible in the dream within the Void, then maybe she could get to speak to her.

Then she could warn Lani about the other woman, they could work on a solution together. *Either that or we need to call to her, like the woman did. Odajeen could try calling her out.*

What had seemed hopeless last night suddenly felt possible. Not just one thing to try but two.

She dressed quickly and hurried down the stairs, eager to try what she'd just learned despite her tiredness and the earliness of the day.

Milfred turned as she hurried through.

"Sorry, Milfred, no time for that now."

Before he could reply she'd already hurried out to the street and toward the gardens behind the college.

I hope the little tree will work, I'm not keen to use a rat this time.

She sat beside the tree that Peka was tending, restoring it to what it should be, and laid her hands on it. This still felt awkward to her, more than it should, given what they did with rats.

Once she'd slipped into the Void, Tillandra cautiously looked around, now worrying about how safe and private it was in here. She couldn't sense the other woman there, nor any hint of danger.

Within a few minutes she had found her calm inside the Void and focused on Odajeen's face, seeking it out, like she would any of her other colleagues.

In here she struggled to hold onto the thought of Odajeen's face.

She tried to grab an image from her mind and bring it into the Void but it kept slipping away.

After minutes of trying, Tillandra swapped to seek out Burgendetta. This time she was able to feel something, an object at least. The mask was there still part of the network.

She tried to connect to it, sending the knock, but it didn't feel the same. While she could sense its existence, she couldn't connect with it.

Even trying to see through the mask didn't work either. That made sense — if she couldn't connect to it for communicating then it was unlikely she could do anything else.

So how could that woman speak to her?

Tillandra pulled out of the Void and let go of the tree. She knew that there was no certainty it had happened, or was happening now, where Lani was, but it frustrated her anyway.

Her excitement felt as though it had been sucked from her, and the ball of worry that sat in the pit of her stomach had replaced it. She stood and slowly walked back toward the front of the college, as the sun rose behind her.

How long was I trying that?

It had been only just light when she had sat down but now the morning was in full swing.

I will still get Odajeen to try calling out to her, what harm can it do?

As she walked around to the front of the college she found a small group gathered outside.

"Mother, there you are. I didn't want to go without seeing you first." Bea hurried her way.

"It's that time?"

"Yes, Mother. If I don't go now, then when?"

"True, there's always going to be enough reasons to stay. I wish there was another way, I'll miss you."

"We can talk whenever you want. Sort that stuff out with the trees, then it won't taste like dung using those beasts and we can communicate more easily."

"Yes." Tillandra didn't need to share what she'd just been doing; it was time for Bea to be gone.

"Keep us all in the loop, Tillandra. We're one connection away."

"I will. You're right though, the sooner everyone is away the quicker we'll all adjust."

"And don't forget about Kooka!"

"What do you mean?"

"He's got to be replaced, Mother. He's struggling with it but the sooner that's done, the easier it will be on him. And the cart has to go back out."

"But who?"

"No idea, but that's why you get all the riches." Bea laughed at her own joke.

"Thanks for nothing."

They hugged before Bea went and clambered up on her horse. There was nothing else to say and the first of their group to depart turned her horse and led her small group away.

I hope I made the right decision.

26

UKSOD

$\mathcal{S}$taring around his chambers, Uksod was becoming agitated. He usually never spent more than his sleeping hours here and the sight of it was tedious to him.

He wanted to be up on his feet, not lying in bed, hardly able to shift his own body weight. At least now his memory was returning quickly.

That was always the biggest worry when he drained himself so much, whether it would harm him in other ways. Once again, he was fine albeit feeling hopeless stuck in his bed.

With his memory back he knew that Schevenal's amulet was south on Dharatan, in the city of Anderwell. At least that is what the remaining Vrah had told him back then. What had happened in the last few weeks was anyone's guess.

Maybe One would have more to update him with if the assassins had thought to send word. Despite the length of his unconsciousness the distance was vast, so at least one message might have arrived.

That depended on whether they had achieved any success. No one ever rushed to send bad word, that was always much slower to arrive.

It would be much more convenient for me to reach out to them directly, there's no avoiding me then.

Uksod knew that wasn't going to happen anytime soon. Little of his strength had returned, and from his previous experiences, he knew that it would take him several weeks to fully recover.

Walking was still a struggle even with a helper. On his own he was unable to do more than stand while holding onto something. At this rate Karpenmor would have complete control of everything without Uksod even able to raise his voice.

As if summoned by his thoughts, the door opened, and the young prince walked in.

"Good morning, Uksod. How do you feel?"

"Better every day, Karpenmor." It wasn't a complete lie.

"That is good to hear. I visited you several times since your recovery, but you've been asleep every time."

"The fastest way to healing, at least that's what the physick says."

"Of course. I can leave you to rest if you're still too tired?"

Uksod steeled himself and pushed his body more upright while forcing his face to show nothing. It took most of the strength he had but it wasn't like he needed it for anything else.

"Can I get you anything?"

Uksod shook his head.

Karpenmor sat in the chair close to the head of the bed, forcing Uksod to twist his head around.

"I will be fine within a day or two."

Karpenmor let out a small awkward laugh. "You think? There's no rush, Uksod, everything is under control."

So I hear, you seem to be taking to this like a fly to horse manure.

"I may look old and sick, Highness, but this is not the first time I've experienced this, and it will pass quickly. I shall be back to my normal duties in no time."

Karpenmor studied him, looking deep into his eyes. "I was quite worried, Uksod. The thought of losing you was not something I wanted to contemplate."

Oh really?

"I am not going anywhere, Karpenmor, but it is nice of you to say so."

"You're my only remaining family, Uksod, despite us not being blood. It was you who raised me, whether or not you liked that task. Father... he wasn't much."

Uksod let the silence linger, trying to work out what the lad was up to. He didn't trust this sudden expression of emotion.

"Perhaps it's coming to a time when you should step back and ensure you don't wear yourself out?"

If Uksod could have, he would have slapped the boy on the cheek. "Now you're being dramatic, Karpenmor. I shall be fine; this is the result of something more significant than age. When I'm better I will explain it, it's probably time you know. Nevertheless, she would not allow it."

"Who?"

"Yantarnaya. I am her servant as much as I am yours. My role is at her will, and I serve her until she has no more need of me."

And that better not be anytime soon either.

The look the boy gave Uksod seemed almost cold, not the boy who was being tender moments before.

"Well either way, once I've taken the helm officially it will diminish your burden, Uksod. Being both High Priest and Regent has been a large task you've borne for a long time. That will soon be at an end."

And there it is. He really has changed just in these last few weeks. There's a desire or resolve that I haven't seen used in this way before.

"Assuming, of course, that this eclipse is in fact the Tenebrosity."

"I've continued preparations, in case it is."

"So I've heard."

Karpenmor raised his eyebrows.

"You've been making Trorn prepare for the ceremony."

"Without knowing when or if you would recover, it seemed the smart thing to do, Uksod. We don't want to miss the timing."

"Thankfully that won't be necessary, now that I am better."

Karpenmor didn't reply.

"I would be..." he chose his words carefully, "most upset to not be able to handle your ceremony, Karpenmor. You, yourself, just said how I am the only family you have, and that's the same in reverse. For me, seeing you through to High Prince will be a monumental occasion. How could I not want to be the one who oversees it?"

Karpenmor looked at him. This time it was warmer, although Uksod was unsure he could really read the lad anymore.

"Sorry, Uksod, I didn't think about the way you might feel about it."

"I… I can oversee the preparations from here. Trorn can continue, but I can make sure he's not missing anything."

"If you're sure you can manage it?"

It was Uksod's turn to send a cold look to the lad. His continued playing on his weakness irritated Uksod.

"Is it true that families Six and Seven are not in the city?"

"Yes. There's something happening there I cannot understand."

"Tell me, perhaps I can assist."

Karpenmor explained about the delay, and what he'd learned from the family priests.

He would have Trorn send the two men to him. Whatever was going on did not sound normal at all, and for once, he wasn't the cause of it. So, who was?

"That sounds most unusual. And you haven't discovered the cause?"

"No. I even sought some assistance from Lady Natillian, but to no avail so far."

"Lady Natillian?"

"Yes, I've been trying to get to know the leaders of the Imperial Families."

"A wise move, Highness, but remember I warned you to watch her. She comes across as a proper and self-effacing woman, but underneath she is very different."

"Oh, come on, Uksod, she was very pleasant, and her granddaughter was most charming."

"Granddaughter?"

"Yes, Bhoomi. She is quite the picture." Karpenmor's whole demeanor changed when he mentioned the girl.

What has she done to the boy? He's smitten with her granddaughter. She would have loved my absence, the perfect opportunity to present her offering.

"I see. We'll need to get to the bottom of the family delays, that's most improper."

"Agreed. I wanted to punish them for being late to the capital, until

I heard about the problems they've encountered. One and I will find out who is behind it."

One can fill me in on the rest.

A yawn escaped involuntarily from Uksod's mouth.

"You're not well, Uksod, I've worn you out. We can discuss it in a few days, once you're stronger."

The words were annoying enough but the way he stood and patted Uksod's blanketed legs made the old priest feel embarrassed.

He's treating me like an ancient, or worse, an invalid.

"There are other things I want to ask you about something I came across, which was most interesting. Perhaps when I come back next, you'll feel up to it. Rest now, I'll send the physick to check on you."

Karpenmor left, closing the door behind him.

Uksod wanted to rush after him and punch the boy in the face, or smash something at least, but all he could muster the strength for was to slide back down in his bed and fall asleep.

27

UKSOD

*I*f nothing else, lying around for so long allowed Uksod some time to reflect on the changes happening around him. While he'd previously resisted his loss of power as Regent, there was little he could do about it now.

He'd received an update about the impending eclipse and his priests were certain this was the one. Which meant that part of his role was almost complete.

The lad still had much to learn, and Uksod would need to guide him for as long as the boy would let him. They needed stability here in Enderk not changes and chaos.

That was why Uksod had planned who his bride should be, not that the boy knew anything about that. Within Family Six he'd had his eyes on the daughter of the family head, Twarden.

She was low down the pecking order there, with her father having nine children. As the youngest she wasn't expected to rule within her own family.

The connections would be important in maintaining the balance within the family dynamics. Lady Natillian and the Family Five had grown in their power over the last decade and were becoming too dominant.

Her influence on some of the smaller families meant her sway within the imperial dynamics was growing. Uksod didn't find it a coincidence that Family Six had been delayed and Natillian had been putting her granddaughter under Karpenmor's nose.

She could well be behind the delays, keeping Twarden well away from the boy. A subtle move perhaps, enough to build a connection that might be difficult to break.

More reasons I need to be back to full strength and diverting his attention. He doesn't need to be falling love-struck with so many things to get done.

We don't want him making any decisions of significance until he's bonded. Then we'll be able to control what he is doing.

Karpenmor might think he was his own man right now but that would change once he was bonded to the amulet. That was the power of the stones cut directly from the Debrua, like the one in the circlet on Uksod's head.

With those bonded, Yantarnaya could directly influence the wearer and control them through her power. Uksod knew the price of what he'd agreed to when he'd accepted the bond.

Karpenmor wouldn't get the same choice. Once the girl was removed from the amulet it would bond to him whether he wished it or not, like it had to the King on Dharatan.

I need to get to the Debrua, that's the quickest way to recover.

Uksod pushed the blankets and sheets from his legs, before swinging them over the side, and sitting himself there, feet on the ground. He waited a minute or two, letting his breath and heart settle, before pushing with his arms to a standing position.

He wobbled weakly as he stood. Walking was possible but only by propping himself against the wall. Getting down to the stone would be almost impossible, he needed help.

One slow shuffle at a time he moved around the wall until he got to his main entrance. He had to rest for several minutes, sucking in breaths, until he felt strong enough to open the wooden door.

As he'd hoped there was a solitary Vrah posted outside. The guard looked surprised to see him, or perhaps the state of him.

"I need a body, but a man, someone capable of helping me. Do you understand?"

"Yes, Eminence."

"And tell no one else, just get them to me, quickly!"

Uksod gritted his teeth until the guard had hurried away, taking all his strength to pretend he was well. By the time the guard returned he'd only just made it back to sit on his bed.

The servant brought into his room looked afraid.

Rightly so.

"Thank you, you may go." Uksod dismissed the guard who closed the door behind him.

"I need help to go somewhere. You'll have to help carry me there."

The man said nothing but nodded. Uksod was happy that he knew his place in the way of things and didn't have to try to force him.

He pushed himself up again and wobbled, the man cautiously stepped forward and awkwardly wrapped the priest's arm behind his neck and shoulders.

Side by side they walked forward. Uksod hated that he needed to use such a lowly person to help him move, but he wouldn't have anyone else see him this way.

It was bad enough that priests had watched over him and bathed him while he'd been unconscious.

Walking was slow going and the man had to twist them both sideways to get through the door into Uksod's office. Finally they made it to his temple room.

This was the part that Uksod knew was the turning point for the servant. What he was about to see meant he would not be returning to his normal life.

He unlocked the hidden door and told the man to walk them through. Once it was shut behind them, he stared at the endless stairs leading downward. There was no way he could do this without the man's help.

Despite the obnoxious smell, Uksod was grateful to be here. He could sense the vibration from the stone coursing up through the floor of the caves and into his legs.

Every step was slow, sapping all his energy while he concentrated on making sure his feet were steady and on a step.

When they finally reached the bottom and turned from the sheltered stairwell into the open chamber, the orange glow that lit everything blinded him momentarily.

The servant stared in awe at what he'd been exposed to.

"Over there!"

Uksod used his free arm to point at the massive tear drop-shaped amber stone. The vibration of it was immense down here, especially because of how weak he was, and already Uksod felt a little better.

When he reached the stone, he placed his hands upon it. They tingled so much it almost felt like they were burning, but he couldn't let go, the power that flowed into him was intoxicating.

~

"There you are!"

"My goddess."

Uksod knew she would want the details of what had happened, despite her likely having some sense of it already.

"Why you don't just use the stone to do your work, Uksod, I don't understand. I assume you persist with using bodies to do what you do because you like it. It's such a weak process which is why it drains you so."

Uksod knew she was right, but he had his reasons.

"All this because you won't come down here. Your cup is already full, Uksod. Go on, reach out to someone with a ring."

Despite her assurances he was still hesitant after how much he'd depleted his physical strength.

"I'll protect you, my weary priest."

Uksod couldn't see her face with her so deep inside the stone, but he could detect a smirk around her words. He had become used to the ever-present teasing from her, after so long acting as her servant.

The easiest person to test this on was close by and while they rarely communicated this way, he wouldn't need to say much.

"Uksod?"

"Yes, One, it is I."

"It is most unusual for you to reach me like this."

"Needs must."

"You are well now?"

"Yes… and no. I will explain tomorrow. I am sorry for bothering you but I needed to test my strength."

"Understood."

"And, One."

"Yes?"

"No one needs to know I spoke with you."

"Of course."

Uksod let go of the connection.

"See, old man, I told you that you were recovered."

This was the main reason Uksod didn't use the stone to communicate like this. Yantarnaya was privy to everything said, and who he was speaking with. That was an intrusion he didn't want on a regular basis.

"Is that One still useful?"

"Very, Goddess. I can trust him implicitly."

"You will have need of men like him where you have to go."

"Go, mistress?"

"You haven't forgotten already have you, Uksod? You're not meant to be languishing here. I need you over there, finding the rest of the amulets, and spreading my influence."

Uksod hadn't forgotten, he just wasn't in any hurry to leave the comforts of life here in the capital. His recent trip with Karpenmor to Ponte had reminded him of how little he enjoyed traveling.

At least in Enderk he was treated royally wherever he went, but over there where he'd be traveling in secret, it would be rough and unfriendly.

"The boy still evades me, Uksod. Perhaps we need another way while I wait for you to get his amulet back."

"Such as?"

"I am looking to you for ideas, that's why you're here. When he took the drink you used to give him it made it a lot easier."

"He refuses that now, somehow he worked that out."

"There was something else too, Uksod, I'm sure of it, something he uses to shield himself. That's why we need him bonded sooner rather than later."

"I'm trying, mistress."

"Yes, you are, Uksod."

Uksod felt a brush across the stone in the circlet on his head, followed by a tiny sharp prick. He pulled away from the stone and looked back at the servant staring at him and the stone.

Enjoy it while it lasts, it's going to be the last important thing you see.

2 8

UKSOD

If he had thought he was going to bounce back to his normal physicality, Uksod was wrong. He'd only made it less than a third of the way back up the stairs when he began to struggle.

His thighs felt empty, and his knees ached, but worst of all he was struggling to breathe. He needed to stop every ten or so steps to rest a little, before pushing on.

Thankful again for the servant who had helped him down, he once again had to lean on him to continue. The man sweated even more than Uksod and it spread onto his robes, making his skin itch.

He had never been one for close contact and had to focus on what he was doing to avoid retching from the smell and feel of it. Without the man he was not going to make it back up.

While the energy that the stone had replenished gave him a certain type of power, it didn't provide as much assistance in matters of the flesh.

His body's atrophy from the multiple weeks laid out in a bed surprised Uksod. It was another reminder of how old his physical body was.

The other part of him that was used when he accessed the magic was fully restored but his physical strength was going to take a little more time. Now he could get up on his feet it would return quickly.

Being unable to move and take care of himself was one of the things he detested above everything else. While he was in the body of an older man, he had stopped aging hundreds of years back.

He had maintained a physical capability that pleased him and allowed him to do what he did. Without that he sensed what it would be like to lose the power she gave him, and he didn't like it at all.

It was the reminder of what she had given him and what would be the cost if he lost her favor. Perhaps he would die quickly — that would be better than living out his last years as an invalid.

A memory of watching Schevenal in the Amber Room, incapable of looking after himself, flicked across his mind causing his skin to shiver.

Not me!

They reached his chambers after what seemed like a lifetime. His robes were drenched and all Uksod wanted to do was to wash himself and change, but there was something else to take care of first.

He rested on the edge of his bed for ten minutes, catching his breath, before he felt ready to stand again. The servant waited off to the side, saying nothing.

It was as though the man was in a dream. His eyes looked slightly glazed over as he reflected on what he had seen down below.

You should feel lucky to have seen what no one else but me has seen.

Uksod walked to his side table and filled a mug with ale, downing it quickly. He was sure the man behind him would love one, but that wasn't how things worked, nor would he need it.

He considered using the man to communicate with Fuling again. Uksod was very keen to learn where the man was and what he was up to now.

But just thinking about it caused his body to tremor. He didn't fully trust himself or even what Yantarnaya had told him. She'd said he was fully recovered in that side of himself, but he wanted to feel completely normal before he tried.

He put his mug down and slowly opened the middle drawer that his body shielded from the man behind him. Inside was a blade, mostly ceremonial, but it should be sharp enough. He ran his thumb gently along the edge to check.

It had better do.

There was a small doubt in his mind that his body would let him do what he was planning. He contemplated getting the guard to do it but dropped that thought.

If he couldn't use the other method, then he'd do it this way. Some people might be bothered by getting their hands dirty, Uksod wasn't. He enjoyed the feeling of watching the light leave someone's eyes.

Tucking the blade behind his back he walked slowly toward the man. He was near enough to the door that he was away from Uksod's bed and other furniture.

If the man had any concerns, he didn't show them, he simply stood where he was waiting to be told what to do next. Uksod didn't rush, and stopped in front of him, reaching out to him with his right hand, placing it on the man's shoulder as if in a friendly gesture.

Uksod whipped his left hand around from behind him and slammed it into the man's middle, near the top of his stomach. As the man reacted, trying to pull away, Uksod wrapped his right hand around the man's neck and tried to hold onto him.

The servant was younger and stronger, and pushed back, hitting the wall behind, only helping Uksod. He pulled the blade out and rammed it back in again, repeating several more times, blood streaming across his hand.

What fight had been in the servant fell away as he dropped to his knees. Uksod removed the blade and when the man slumped forward, wiped it across the back of the man's tunic.

That will have to do.

"Guard!"

He stepped over and opened the door, beckoning the Vrah in.

The guard showed no surprise at what he saw. He ran his eyes over the priest, checking he was okay.

"I'm done with him."

Uksod stepped back and turned, walking to the side table. He placed the blade back into the middle drawer and slowly pushed it closed.

He grabbed a cloth and tried to wipe the blood from his hands. "I'll need some water to clean these, and have someone clean up after you when he's gone." He tossed the soaked cloth over by the dead man and walked to his office.

The Vrah would sort it all out, as they always did. When they were controlled by Karpenmor, and not him directly, it was all going to be a little different.

He didn't need the lad knowing about everything he did down here, which reminded him he needed to finalize another of his plans.

The Vrah were here to protect the High Prince and his family, they weren't specifically there for the priest. While the two roles were intertwined there was no conflict.

But if Uksod needed something doing which went against their directions... *I can't have that.*

He needed his own men at arms. Those dedicated to just the priests, and by default, Yantarnaya, who would support his needs. Perhaps some of the Vrah might wish to join? That would be tricky to oversee.

Perhaps there was a way to have Karpenmor agree to the idea, and formalize it, without him having to do it himself? It would make it much easier.

And... if he could have One head it up, then that would suit him even better. Uksod needed to work out whether the Vrah leader was amenable to such an idea, or not.

While they had worked well together for his term in office, he was Vrah, and their loyalty was to the throne. Uksod needed to test this out discreetly.

If he was going to have to leave En Carta, then he would need his own people. He needed some time to get this sorted. At least Yantarnaya didn't expect him to leave until Karpenmor was enthroned.

That will buy me some time. It wouldn't hurt if everyone thinks I am still recovering, while I plan everything.

Leaving his home of so many years wouldn't be easy to do, and he cared little to be on the road, but they did need to retrieve the amulets.

Yantarnaya was right, it was up to him to take care of it. Not only to get the one back from this girl Lani, but also the others. If two had surfaced, more would as well, and he needed to lead that charge.

First he needed to get Karpenmor enthroned and focused on building the armies. If they were to take control of Dharatan and destroy the Citadel Stone they were going to need more than just the jewels.

Uksod couldn't do it all, he just had to accept it. Too much was changing quickly for his liking but he couldn't undo it. Everything they wanted was closer than ever.

As the night wore on he lay back on his bed, a real exhaustion creeping over him.

All in good time, I just need to be careful, until I am back to full strength.

29

TILLANDRA

The college was beginning to feel empty to Tillandra, which was a ludicrous thought given how many people it held. But with the other members of the Court departing, her close contacts were shrinking.

With Junther also gone, the weight of it all sat firmly on her shoulders now, and not for the first time she wondered if she was up to it.

Perhaps she should have discussed what had happened to Lani with him and Bea before they went. Except that would have delayed them even further, and she needed them on the road.

Maybe one of them might have had a better idea on what to do. Better than Thenis? I doubt it.

Candles lit her office as she sat behind her desk doing nothing but second-guessing herself. As usual. The large building was quiet of people noise, but the creaking and groans the building made never ceased.

Tillandra listened to them like the words of an old friend. Across the room lay the piles of journals that she and Lani had been working through.

The process of the girl putting on the masks of past Jesters still fascinated Tillandra. Due to the effect of people having their minds wiped by trying to wear one, they'd never considered them anything but relics of their old friends.

From time to time she had wondered why they came away from the dead person's face and were stored in the map room. In the materials she had access to, there was no mention of why.

Now that Tillandra had seen what Lani could do, it made more sense that the masks were not lost. *Who else might be able to do the same? How could we find out without harming anyone who didn't have the power?*

Lani's transformation when she wore them was unnerving. The first time she'd put Ashantha's on, when they'd first met, Tillandra had been startled.

The girl's face, shoulders and arms changed into Ash. Her friend, whom she knew was dead, sat before her, and when the girl spoke it was with his voice.

Wearing the masks allowed her to read his journal, breaking the magic that hid its words from anyone but the owner. It had always seemed such a stupid use of magic, that there was no way to learn about the things their colleagues had stored in their journals.

She could understand it while you were alive, it granted you privacy on things you wanted to record. But after they were dead it was just another frustration in not being able to learn more about those who had come before.

Until now.

Who is Lani really? Thenis has said the prophecy relates to her, that she's important, but why? She has unique abilities... is it because she's linked to the amulet?

Tillandra didn't like that thought. It would mean that the amulets were more intertwined with their lives than she knew. If the people linked to amulets could access the masks... was it the jewels that gave that power?

Does that mean that Lani is one of them? Is that what the dream was showing me... or is she between both worlds?

She struggled to accept that the girl was working against them. She'd been able to access the tower, which was guarded by the Mother Stone.

It didn't make sense that the stones that were there to protect

Anderwell would let the enemy inside, to their most important place. And the girl had been helping to uncover information for them.

Or is she trying to learn something for the other side? Is she a plant here to find the other amulets?

Tillandra couldn't believe that Thenis wouldn't know that and wouldn't have warned them more than she had already. That ultimately made her dream make more sense.

Lani was at risk of being influenced by the woman Tillandra had dreamed about. There was still a possibility she could be drawn to her, to them, and that was the choice Tillandra had to be prepared to act on.

Can I harm her to save us all?

That Lani had become trapped was a help, she was stuck in there, and her body was useless to her at this point. Unless she was hunting for knowledge inside Odajeen that she needed.

Could she harm Odajeen from inside?

Tillandra didn't know, nor would the older woman. They were all guessing at this point. Lani was doing something no one else had done before.

She decided to check on Odajeen, perhaps the woman had felt something. They'd all been so busy focusing on how to reach Lani, they hadn't thought about the other option.

Could Odajeen push Lani out of where she was? If she could still feel a presence, was there some way she could help get her out?

Irdan let her into the room, her protector still showing his displeasure at what had happened to his charge. Tillandra ignored him and approached Odajeen, sat beside Lani on her sofa.

"Any change?"

"Nothing, Tillandra. How about you?"

"Still nothing tangible that might help. Can you still feel her?"

"I'm not sure if it's her, but I still have the ache in the back of my head. Like something is pressing there."

"Have you tried to do anything with that?"

"What do you mean?"

Tillandra laughed, although there was little humor in it. "Like force it to move or push at it… something like that?"

"Yes, I've even rubbed at the spot."

"And nothing changed?"

"No. It just feels as though what's inside is too big for my head."

Tillandra stood without speaking, looking at the two women. Thenis had said the only option she knew of at the moment was if the mask came off, but Lani had got past it to get in there. Tillandra still believed there had to be a way to get out other than that and there was no guarantee that Lani wouldn't die with Odajeen.

"I'm all out of ideas at the moment."

"I've had one."

"Go on."

"You probably won't like it."

"Just tell me, Odajeen, I'm stuck."

"What about using the amulet?"

She was right, Tillandra didn't like it. "We're not taking that thing out, it's dangerous."

"It was out when you found me, wasn't it?"

"Yes, so?"

"What if it was that which Lani used to get in? Or it was the thing that helped her get in… we know nothing about it do we?"

Tillandra could see the logic behind what Odajeen was saying.

"It was out, but we have no idea if that mattered or not. It was dangerous to everyone here just having it out on the table."

"No one touched it."

"It's not just that. You know we think they can track it."

"The Derks?"

"Yes, that's how they kept up with you."

"But even here?"

"I don't know. The magic that shields Anderwell is meant to protect us from the outside, but she brought that in here. I don't know if it will stop them sensing it."

"It was just a thought. Maybe that is what she needs to get herself out, or maybe it's that which will jolt her free."

Tillandra spent a moment pondering the idea. The more she did, the more she had to agree that it had merit. The question was whether she was willing to chance the Derks locating it, coming to Anderwell or not.

Was this the question she had been posed by Thenis? Could she just leave Lani inside, safely locked away, or would she expose them all to those hunting her by getting the amulet out?

"Have you thought about how?"

"It's in a pouch, isn't it?"

"Yes."

"And you were able to use the pouch to put it away when you came earlier?"

"Yes."

"Then just like that. I open the pouch and squeeze it out. Then you can do what you did to put it back, or I can."

"You can't see, Odajeen. If you touch it…"

"Then I die, I know. Then the mask falls away and she is free."

"Possibly."

"What do you mean?"

"We don't know for sure she'll be free, that was just the only idea Thenis had at the time."

"I'm willing to take that chance. I've lived a long life, Tillandra. The girl is needed, much more than I am."

Tillandra looked at the older woman, fully understanding what she was saying. "I don't think we need to go to that extreme."

"I'm not saying I want that to happen, it's just in case something goes wrong. Is there anyone else you'd sacrifice other than me?"

"I don't want to sacrifice you or anyone else."

"We're hypothesizing about something that won't happen anyway. I'll be very careful with it, the pouch protects us, we know that. It's no different to how you've done it before."

Tillandra sat in silence.

"It's an idea, Tillandra, You make the decision, but you asked for ideas so there's mine."

30

GORAN

*E*very part of him itched. Goran had been dirty before, many times in fact, but never this dirty. The beard he wore was long and unkempt, even his matted hair felt unclean.

Maybe this was a good sign, the fact he recognized how dirty he was could be a good thing. Or not. Maybe it was another indication that his mind was broken, and being itchy was another sign of his body being out of sync with his head.

He wanted a bath, a proper one, and a shave. He wanted daylight, and to look at the sky, and ale. He really wanted ale. Not the lightweight stuff that they gave him here, which was little more than flavored water.

Real ale, in a noisy tavern full of people. And lasses. A grin formed on his face.

Now that is an idea I haven't had for a while.

The cell Goran had been confined in was big enough to walk about but there was no outside light. What light there was came from lanterns on walls in the open area outside the semicircle of cells.

His guard, Hulfer, sat across in the far room, bored with his duty. As much as the guards were meant to stay away from him, they were people too.

Down here in the stuffy dungeons, it wasn't too hard to get them into a conversation, and Hulfer had been easier than his replacements.

Goran was still too weak to use his skill as much as he'd like. His ability to influence people around him was a perfect accompaniment to being an entertainer, or when he'd been Nedor's Jester.

Trickling out tendrils across a crowd to build their enthrallment, get others to cheer and call out, all built the mood that made him one of the most sought after on Dharatan.

At least until the incident with Nedor's daughter, which hadn't been him, but Zoran. Not that it mattered to anyone anymore.

One on one he was able to influence a person much more directly, which he used when seeking information or for fun when gambling. It was weaker at the moment, so he had to be careful using it.

Zoran had tried to use it all the time while Beantic and the others had been working on him, which left his reserves of that strength weaker than they should be.

Goran needed his body to be strong and his overall health to help build it back up, and that meant better food, ale, and fresh air. None of which he was getting down here.

"What news from above, Hulfer?"

The guard looked up at him, Goran startling him out of his doze. The older guard stood, shaking off his sleepiness and walked into the room closer to Goran's cell.

"Awake now are ya?"

"Not that it makes much difference." Goran pushed a thin weak tendril out at the man, enough to keep him engaged.

"Much the same, Goran. Hot and dry."

"You're not really a great storyteller, are you?"

"Were I one, ya think I'd be stuck down here smelling you?"

Goran laughed. It was another reason he picked Hulfer to work on, at least he had a sliver or two of humor in him. When they'd spoken it had helped Goran feel more normal.

What am I thinking? I am normal. It's Tillandra and the others that are making me seem different.

He knew deep down they weren't going to let him out. Tillandra's face had shown pity not friendship on her last visit, then she'd stormed out angry with him.

And Junther, well that old windbag had never been on his side, Goran knew he'd always vote against him. The faint memory of how he'd used his paralyzing skill on Goran made him itch again — it was a terrible feeling.

They'll either keep me here or find a way to lock me away with the Broken.

None of his colleagues had been to see him in days, which wasn't a great sign either. Goran had pretty much figured out that whatever they were planning for him wasn't going to be to just let him go back to normal.

Which is why he needed to do what he had planned.

"Can I get a refill?" He held his wooden mug through the access slot in his door toward Hulfer.

"I'll get the jug."

Goran's skill meant he could influence the emotions of people around him. He used it in thin threads, plucking people's feelings like a bard might play their lute.

That was where Zoran misunderstood it. He would use thick bands or waves of it, overwhelming one person but not controllably. Goran had been mixing several threads ever since Hulfer had started his shift.

One of which was safety, and comfort, while also keeping him sleepy. That meant the man hadn't yet placed the keys back on their hook by the main outside door.

"You're a good man, Hulfer."

"Golden tongue they should call ya. Only saying that cos I have what you want."

Yes, you do.

As the guard approached, he had to use multiple sensations to make the old man value the jug he carried as though it was a priceless glass vase.

The man's knuckles were almost white with how tight he was grasping the handle.

Just a few more minutes.

"Put ya mug on the ledge, be easier to pour."

Goran did as the guard asked and leaned against the cell door.

Hulfer put one hand out to hold the mug, the other holding his jug, all his focus on what he was doing.

Just as he was almost done, Goran reached through and grabbed the man's wrist, yanking it toward him, the mug flying inward and all the water spilling out.

"What ya doing?" Hulfer blurted out as his head bumped into the cell door.

The guard was too fixated on the thought in his head to hold onto the jug which left him unable to fight back. Goran spun him around and then hooked his arm around the man's throat.

He'd done this plenty of times before and squeezed until he could feel the man's breathing slowing.

If he went too far, it was all over for both the guard and Goran. He might be an outcast from his peers, but he was still bound by the magic that made him who he was.

Killing the guard was definitely not on his agenda for today. When his hand relaxed its grip, the jug dropping free and shattering on the floor, Goran knew it was enough.

Carefully Goran slid him down the bars to the floor before removing the keys and freeing himself. He dragged Hulfer into the cell, gagged him with his own belt and locked him away.

"Sorry, Hulfer, you were just the easiest target."

Standing on the outside of the cell felt fantastic. Even if he still had a lot of work to do to get free, it was something. What he had to make sure was that he didn't get caught again.

He had at best another hour or two before another guard would check in on things. In that time he needed to be free of the college and out of the city.

That wouldn't leave him much time to gather things he might need, if anything it would leave him with few options but to head to Lakeside.

With time against him, Goran headed to the outer door. He locked it from the outside before climbing the staircase toward the outside world.

The door at the top was locked which didn't surprise him but would make it harder to sneak through any other guards out there. No one would be expecting Hulfer to come out, so he'd need to act quickly.

Goran primed his skill ready to use it to help buy him some time if needed, and gently opened the door. The room was empty, so he released his skill, closing the door and locking it.

This was too easy for him, that was how little a threat he was considered.

I can use that to my advantage.

He approached a window of the entrance room he was in and looked out. The sky showed it was pre-dawn, the first pinches of light just beginning to show.

That explains the lack of people. Get moving, Goran, we don't have long.

His rooms would be the first place they'd look. If he thought he had enough time, he'd have gone there and tried to leave a clue about where he wasn't going to head, but time was the thing he didn't have.

There was a place that no one would look, he was pretty sure of that. As long as it was still empty. Goran doubted anyone else had even thought about it, he hoped at least.

What he didn't need was to go there and find it occupied by someone else. But he had little choice. He wanted, hoped at least, to find a change of clothes and a few other necessities before he left Anderwell for good.

31

KARPENMOR

*V*isiting Uksod in his quarters like this still felt unusual. Up until this incident, Karpenmor had never ever been in the priest's private rooms.

He felt awkward being here, coming to visit the man who for so many years had been his de facto parent and supervisor, while he lay sick in his bed.

Uksod's face had always appeared to be this old, ever since Karpenmor could remember. There had been no detectable changed in his appearance, or none that the inattentive young prince had noted.

Karpenmor could see a frailty that hadn't been there before. His physical presence was not the same, which was not something he could say about Uksod's eyes.

Unless he was mistaken something had changed with the priest, his eyes had a sparkle much more familiar to Karpenmor.

How far can I push today, I wonder?

"Uksod, how are you feeling today?"

"A little more normal, Highness. There's improvement but... I don't want to overdo it."

"Of course. Do you feel up to discussing a few things?

Uksod nodded.

189

"How many of the ceremonies leading up to the eclipse are necessary?"

"Sorry?"

"I've been digging into the planning of the event, and while I know you'll oversee everything, it's like I'm a party trick."

A smile crept over the priest's face, not something Karpenmor was used to seeing.

"I think you are exaggerating, Karpenmor. But it is going to be the biggest event the realm has seen in hundreds of years."

"But so many?"

"If, as it has been predicted, this eclipse is the Tenebrosity, then you will be crowned High Prince, something no one alive has ever witnessed, Highness."

"Except you."

"Sorry?"

"You said no one alive."

"Yes, well…"

It was a fact they both knew that others did not, but Uksod's life-span was such that he had seen Karpenmor's father throned.

"It was not the same for your father, Highness. His enthronement came only two decades after the High Prince before him."

"So many things you know that I do not."

"What is bothering you?"

"Do I really have to sit through a parade of potential brides?"

Another grin came across Uksod's face.

"What's so funny?"

"I was expecting something serious, and you raise this."

"It appears it is serious to everyone else."

"Indeed, it most definitely is. It will happen every year until you choose a bride."

"What?"

"There is a process, a way of things, Karpenmor. Once you come of age to become High Price, it is expected that you will marry."

"Perhaps I will… at some time… but not now… I'm not interested."

"You showed some interest in Natillian's granddaughter."

"Not to marry… I was just… she's a very charming girl."

"You might want to be careful about where you show your attention. Some might take it as misleading."

"What do you mean?"

"Just be careful that you don't send any wrong signals that might be misconstrued."

Karpenmor didn't think he was sending any signals, nor was he interested in taking a wife in the foreseeable future.

"When will this parade happen?"

"It's not a parade, Highness."

"It feels that way. Like they're going to present their offerings for me to pick. It seems like a cattle market just for brides."

"I think you're thinking about this all the wrong way, Karpenmor. It is known as the Dance of the Brides, where each family presents one woman from their family, hoping she would be selected for you to court."

"I don't wish to court anyone."

Uksod said nothing.

"A dance?"

Uksod lifted his eyebrows in acknowledgement.

"Which means I'm expected to dance with them all?"

"Of course, Karpenmor. Should you choose not to, that woman is excluded from future years' dances. And so it goes until there is one left or you pick your bride."

"You're kidding me?"

"I am not."

Karpenmor rolled his eyes. "Given how important this is, shouldn't I know when it's going to happen?"

"Seven nights before the fourth eclipse of the year, Highness."

"So, I have some time."

"A little."

A thought crossed Karpenmor's mind, distracting him from the conversation.

"What is it?"

"You said every family will present someone?"

"Yes."

"Then the two families that have been delayed would not likely be in the capital."

"Delayed? Who has been delayed?"

Karpenmor could see the levity the priest had shown earlier was gone. A serious look had crossed Uksod's face.

"Six and Seven, both are well overdue from arriving in the city. If they don't make it in time, then they are excluded?"

Uksod nodded. "That would be correct."

He felt a little foolish, like he should understand more about what was going on, why Uksod was suddenly showing concern about the topic.

It was a simple dance, what did it matter anyway? He wasn't about to marry one of these girls, even Bhoomi, as lovely as she was. If some didn't make it, so be it.

"Was that all, Highness?"

Karpenmor was a little surprised by how quickly Uksod wanted to end their conversation. There was more he wanted to discuss.

"No. I wanted to ask you about some things One couldn't answer for me."

Uksod appeared to sit a little more upright at that. "Such as?"

"When you were out, he had some rings arrive back from Dharatan."

"Dead Vrah?"

"Yes."

"Ah. How many?"

"Seven."

"So, it was all of them." It felt like Uksod didn't mean to say that out loud.

"What do you mean, Uksod?"

"What did you want to ask me about them?"

Karpenmor stared at the priest, who had deflected his question. "One said that you can communicate with them?"

"With the rings?"

"With the Vrah when they are wearing them… is that true?"

"Yes."

"That's how you got so sick isn't it? Communicating with them."

There was silence while Uksod stared at him, a strange look that was neither friendly nor threatening.

"It would appear, young man, that you've learned a few things while I have been absent."

"Then it's true?"

"Yes."

"I didn't know that."

"You've never asked before." The priest stared back at him. "I imagine, Highness, that there's a million things I haven't told you, which you've neither asked nor shown any inclination to know. Until now."

Karpenmor felt thrown off by the man's confidence and how he kept changing the questions he answered.

"What about the girl?"

This time it was Uksod who paused and seemed a little thrown off. "What girl?"

"The girl, who has the amulet. The one who killed all seven of our men."

"Ah, her."

"Does she have a name?"

"I believe her name is Lani."

"And who is she?"

Another pause.

"Someone who has your amulet, and who would appear to be very capable at avoiding our men."

"Killing, you mean."

Uksod didn't reply.

"Who is she working with? She must have a large army, or many soldiers protecting her."

"We do not know at this point."

"What's the mission all about?"

"Getting your amulet back, Karpenmor, surely that's obvious."

"It isn't going very well, Uksod."

"No, Highness, it is not."

"How will we fix that? Once I'm enthroned, I can go and hunt it myself."

"It's not going to be that simple, Highness."

"Why not?"

"Presently large groups of Derks are not allowed on Dharatan, and you're not going to be going over there without protection. I didn't spend all this time just for you to rush off and get yourself killed."

"I'm not going to get myself killed."

"And yet some of our best assassins' rings have just returned because of that very reason."

Karpenmor knew the priest was right, but he was frustrated.

"Much better than a silly dance." Uksod's face tightened even more if that was possible. "What's going to happen next?"

"When I am well enough, I will have to speak to them."

"Can't they just enter the city where she is hiding out and capture it?"

"Not if those that are protecting her are there also. I need to find out more about what our team has discovered before we rush into anything."

"How long?"

"How long for what?"

"Until you're well enough, Uksod?"

"That is hard to tell, Karpenmor, but likely it will be several weeks."

"That long? What can I do?"

"Nothing, Highness. You just need to let me recover. I will discuss it with One, once I am well enough and find the best approach."

"And me."

Uksod nodded. "And you, Highness, of course."

"Does the amulet have magic?"

"That's an odd question."

"Is it like that?" Karpenmor pointed at the amber stone on Uksod's forehead, set in the circlet he always wore.

"Somewhat. And yes, there's magic within it."

"Her having it, isn't just about Yantarnaya wanting it back, it's powerful?"

"Yes."

"Is the girl important to it?"

Uksod delayed his response again, which Karpenmor noted. "No, she's just the thief who took it."

Karpenmor crossed the room. He was unable to sit down, with so many things flitting around in his head.

"How long does a leader of the Vrah normally hold their position?"

The question appeared to catch the priest by surprise. "—They usually serve until they die, or... Why the question, Karpenmor?"

"I just wondered about One. He's not the youngest of men, and — well, I'm not sure he's going to be right to serve me."

"You don't trust One? What has come over you, Highness? That man has led the Vrah since you were a baby and protected you continuously."

"At your direction, Uksod."

"Only because I was Regent."

"I hope that's true, but sometimes it can be difficult for people to let go of their old ways and habits."

Neither said a word for more than a minute before Karpenmor broke the silence. "I've taken up too much of your rest, I'll leave you to recover."

He turned without waiting for a replay and left hurriedly. Everything was changing, himself included, and Karpenmor felt decidedly uncomfortable in not knowing who to trust or what he should be doing.

32

UKSOD

I can't keep this up.

Uksod waited for ten minutes until he was sure the boy wasn't coming back before he pushed off the heavy blankets covering him and sat on the edge of the bed.

Ever since he'd visited Yantarnaya in her chamber his energy had been almost at full strength. The Debrua Stone had replaced any weakness in his ability to use his magic and his body was already beginning to rebound.

Keeping up the illusion that he was unwell wouldn't last forever. Especially if he had to keep watching Karpenmor looking at him as though he was an invalid.

His path ahead was pretty clear -- he needed to get Karpenmor's amulet back and seek the others. If he was going to have to head to Dharatan sooner than he had thought, he needed to accelerate his other plans.

Fuling had done a half-decent job of building a religious compound in one of the eastern realms, but it wasn't enough. Uksod needed more bases to station his priests and hide his men.

Men that he could rely on to protect him as their highest priority. There would come a time when the things he was trying to achieve for

196

Yantarnaya might not align fully with Karpenmor's, and he couldn't leave his own protection to chance.

While he hoped they'd remain on a similar path, he wasn't going to be around to steer how the lad made decisions, and watching how quickly he was taking control he might struggle anyway.

At least until he was under Yantarnaya's control. And that required him to get the amulet back. It would be much simpler when he was bonded to the amber and she could control him directly.

Uksod was ready to get back to running things here in the temple, even if from his quarters. He opened the door, grabbing the attention of his guard.

"I wish to speak with One, as soon as possible, in my office." Uksod didn't wait for a response, closing the door and barring it. He was getting sick of people just wandering in unannounced.

He dressed into fresh robes and footwear before heading through to his office and sorting the fire. The room was cold; he'd never let any of the servants in there.

Once he had a small blaze underway, he set the right amount of incense in his fire cages, a unique device he'd had made that sat in the upper corner of his fireplaces, so that it smoldered slowly.

Uksod settled at his desk and let his mind wander over the things he needed to deal with. The first one was the likelihood that one of the families had deliberately interfered in the travel of Six and Seven.

It was only a minor thing, and up until the conversation with Karpenmor, he'd wondered what the reason would be. Their delay could easily be explained away to weather or any other number of reasons so they wouldn't lose standing in his eyes.

But missing the courting dance, that is a different matter.

It might not seem like a great deal when casually looked at, but Uksod knew better. He should have woken to the possibility much sooner, but his thoughts were still a little sluggish from his illness.

He had been discretely grooming the daughter of the head of Family Six as someone to catch Karpenmor's eye. Too many things were happening at once, and he'd forgotten all about it.

If it was another of the families involved, then who was it?

Lady Natillian seemed as likely as any other, particularly now that he knew about her candidate. He had missed the girl when he'd been reviewing each family's possible entries to the dance.

Natillian, ever the cunning one, had kept the girl well out of sight. *I never even thought about a granddaughter, she's so deceptively young-looking. I should know better.*

Worse than that, the girl had already caught Karpenmor's eye. He didn't trust Natillian's family at all, and them being second strongest of all the families was enough of a reason to avoid Families One and Two being joined by such a pairing.

Much better a weaker family like Six, that would raise their standing and bring some more balance to the dynamics of the Imperial Families.

Uksod hadn't been able to influence that much in recent times, there'd been no events that could alter the balance while he had to keep Schevenal under wraps.

Karpenmor's coming of age was going to make this much more interesting. It was poor timing that Uksod would need to be away from the capital; he needed to find a way to keep Natillian away as well.

She's far too clever an opponent to leave unattended. I'd better get a look at this granddaughter as well, perhaps I can change how she appears to the boy.

Uksod also wanted to speak to the Vrah near Anderwell, but he was a little anxious about using a body again so soon. He could of course use the Debrua Stone, but then Yantarnaya would be listening in to the whole exchange, not something he wanted.

Uksod didn't understand the difference, but she didn't have that access when he used a body.

Maybe it wasn't that she didn't have access? Perhaps she just wasn't that interested in his day-to-day actions? As much as Karpenmor thought Uksod knew everything, there was a lot about their goddess that was a mystery to him.

He heard a knock at his office door.

"Yes?"

"It is I, Eminence."

"Come."

The leader of the Vrah was a welcome sight for Uksod. He hoped the man wasn't about to bring him more problems.

"You seem much better, Eminence."

"I am, One, but the heir can do without knowing that for the time being."

This was the first of his subtle tests. He needed to be sure about where One's mind was at.

He could see the Vrah leader had a small smirk on his face.

"You find this amusing, One?"

"No, Eminence, just that you're clearly back to your old self, scheming already."

"Not so much scheming as preparing. It seems our young heir has certainly taken many steps forward in his leadership, quicker than I would have imagined. Which means I need to be a little cautious, that's all."

"Cautious of him?"

"Perhaps a wrong choice of words. It is just to my advantage if he and some others think I am incapacitated, at least for a little longer. Are the guards to be trusted?"

"Most likely. But things have changed. If they were to be asked by his Highness directly, I would think they would tell him the truth."

"Then we need to make sure that doesn't happen." Uksod rubbed his bald scalp, kneading his tight skin. "Swap them out in a few hours, and make sure that you do that every four or so hours. I'm in no danger. And you, One, you won't tell his Highness?"

"I see no threat to him that would warrant me to say anything. Were I asked I would tell him the truth."

Uksod wasn't surprised at the answer, One had always been loyal in his role.

"That's appreciated, One, but such a stance will create conflict in the future. I am not sure such a position will be tenable when he has ascended to the throne."

One's face became deadly serious.

"I was not meaning any disloyalty, Eminence.

"Nor did I think you were, One."

Uksod rubbed his thumb over his first finger as he watched the man.

"It has not escaped my attention that it will be difficult to transition. I have been doing this for a long time, for you, Eminence."

"For us all."

"Of course, but it has been your rule I have been under. I am not sure it might not be better that another takes the reins for the new Prince."

Uksod was happy to hear it but needed to tread cautiously.

"That is understandable. I wouldn't have thought you were ready to hang up your weapons so readily, you aren't that old, One."

"It might be easier than its alternative."

"What if there were another option?"

One behaved cautiously this time, taking his time before replying. "Such as, Eminence?"

"With Karpenmor running things in Enderk, I will be able to get to our goddess's work. She has wishes for me, over the seas."

"On Dharatan?" There was almost a tinge of excitement in the man's tone.

"Yes. I will need to have my own small company of men at arms, there to serve and protect myself and my priests."

"Not under the Prince's command?"

"Not directly, One. We would all be Derks, which means in a way yes, but he would be advised to leave us alone, by Yantarnaya."

"I see."

"It would mean travel, and you would be hands-on."

"Are we not getting too long in the tooth for road trips, Eminence?"

"It would appear not, One."

They both sat quietly for several minutes.

"The idea appeals, Eminence, but how will the Prince take such a request?"

"Leave that with me, I think he'll be okay if I present it at the right time."

One nodded.

"For the time being it's business as usual, and right now, I need a body."

Uksod's tone was direct and commanding.

"You are capable of this?"

Uksod looked sternly at the man. "Yes. I don't need to be questioned."

He could see One suitably rebuked by the man's slight change in posture.

"The usual place?"

"Yes."

"When?"

"As soon as you can, I have a lot to catch up on and I don't know when the lad will be back to visit me."

He watched the Vrah leader let himself out through his office door then went and placed the bar back across it. He needed to be away for a while, and he didn't need anyone coming in.

33

UKSOD

*H*aving someone like One to do as he needed was important to Uksod. The Vrah leader had always served him well while he had been Regent.

He'd never had any reason to question the man's loyalty and was grateful for that. Besides, Uksod doubted he'd have the patience to train someone new.

Once he had left En Carta there'd be no time for hand-holding nor delays. The man would fit in nicely to what Uksod needed.

That left Trorn, who was a different proposition altogether. His second in charge had been protected from their real mission for too long.

With Uksod incapacitated as he had been, the flaw in that had been exposed. Instead of Trorn knowing everything and being able to improvise, he'd been too easily controlled by Karpenmor.

Uksod needed to bring Trorn into his plans more, and to give him more things to control, despite the thought causing Uksod to cringe.

I still prefer to do it myself. Others never seem to do it the right way.

Part of his reluctance was ego and the rest fear. Uksod liked being the center of everything, he loved the power it gave him over everyone else.

But he was still at the whims of *Yantarnaya's* power and while she'd given him centuries of attention, he never lost the awareness that she could replace him with another if she chose.

Lately she'd become more agitated and even threatening, which made him very nervous. She had never guaranteed his life, just that he would live a very long life and rule.

How long and under what conditions she'd never been clear on. So he pleased her as best he could, working toward what she wanted -- getting free of the Debrua Stone.

To do that required all the amulets. For all this time she'd always been certain they were hidden not destroyed, and their surfacing now validated that.

Thus, her patience was running thin. After so long waiting, to have two already surfaced pushed all the wrong buttons on her.

She wanted them all and now.

Karpenmor's sister was proving more than difficult, she was near impossible to pin down. Uksod had no desire to honor Yantarnaya's wish to meet the girl, all he was interested in was getting the amulet back.

To do so she had to die. Neither his goddess, nor Karpenmor, need be any the wiser. Bringing her back here would lead to problems that no one needed. Especially not he.

The new amulet that had returned had been gifted to King Unx, back in the time of the Great Fair, and had now returned to his descendant.

Should the others follow the same path then he would need to be on Dharatan ready to intercept them. Once they bonded to their new owner things became much harder, especially with them weak after so long away from the Debrua Stone.

Getting Unx's grandson, King Ahn, to come to Enderk would be problematic; trying to get several of them would make everything too complex.

Uksod's best option was to be ahead of everyone.

Right now, he needed to appease Yantarnaya by getting back the one amulet he could potentially control. That would buy him some time, and make things easier all round.

While he was still very anxious about using a body, he had no choice. He didn't want Yantarnaya listening in so he'd just have to suck it up and do it.

Inside his shrine he barred the door back to his office. While he didn't expect anyone was going to get through his outer doors, no one would break the sanctity of this room. Once inside, he opened the door to the lower chamber and passed through.

One level down the stairs he stopped and turned to a door set into the wall. It had been some time since he'd used it, but it was another way he could move around the chambers that others did not know about.

The key for it hung around his neck on a leather thong. This key opened several locks around the underground temple complex, and it was the only copy.

He hadn't used it on this door in quite some time and the lock resisted the key.

Patience is the key to everything. Timing of everything is what matters most, something the lad and Yantarnaya don't understand.

After working it for a period of time, left and right in tiny twists, the lock finally began to move. He repeated the process until everything operated more like it should.

This needs more maintenance; I will have to do that myself.

There wasn't much Uksod cared to do himself, after so many years of having others at his beck and call, but such areas were off limits to everyone else.

Next, he had to work the door, and its hinges groaned with being forced to work. Once he'd opened it enough, he slid through into the dark space inside.

Before closing the door, he used the dim amber light from outside to help guide his hands up the right-hand edge of the back wall. Careful not to snag his palm on possible splinters, he found the latch he was looking for.

The wooden wall popped open an inch, and he leaned against it. It too was difficult to move, and it took all his remaining strength to budge it further open.

This should be swinging open easily. And I'm half-exhausted already which will not do, I need to recover my strength better than this.

He was dripping in sweat by the time he was able to get through into the space behind it. Once his path ahead was open, Uksod pulled the door to the stairs at his back closed and locked it, before hanging the key back around his neck. Then he moved into a study room deep in the temple.

The wall he had entered was lined with bookshelves, the middle one open. It was much easier to close and the small click that followed told Uksod it was locked. Nothing told anyone else that it was movable and the latch on this side was not easy to locate.

From this room it was a short distance down to the chamber that Uksod was heading to. The man that had been left for him was gagged and bound to the benchtop, ready for what he was about to do.

Just another person with no purpose. There were so many of them that bred in the city without any role other than to serve. Whether it was to farm or mine, clean or cook, they were replaceable. They had little insight or intelligence and were driven by their base instincts, breeding like vermin.

At least you get to go out serving the greater good.

Uksod almost smiled as he stood looking down at the man. Fear flooded the man's eyes. He tried to speak through the gag, but it was all just garbled.

"There, there. Don't be afraid, this won't hurt a bit."

This time Uksod did smile, as if it might calm the man. It did the opposite, with him thrashing in his bindings briefly. As soon as Uksod laid his hands on him the energy he drew stopped the man's fight.

He wanted to be in and out, he'd strangle the body if he didn't drain him completely, but Uksod didn't want to overuse the power no matter what Yantarnaya had said.

～

"Eminence?"

Fuling's voice in his head caught him slightly off guard. "Who else talks to you this way?"

"No one, I was just surprised. It has been some time."

"There has been little need, that's changed. What news from your side?"

Fuling filled Uksod in on the resistance coming from across the border, and that their plans for a military strike quickly toward Watersend would not happen.

"That plan is of less importance at the moment, Fuling."

"Oh?"

"We need him to come to Enderk, the amulet he is bonded to needs to come home."

"Bonded?"

"That's what it did to King Ahn, it connected to him permanently. Do not ever try to touch it now that it has, it will kill anyone that tries to do so."

There was a short gap. "Good to know."

"It will be affecting his behavior, his thinking."

"This might explain the changes in him."

"Tell me."

"He's much more vigorous than he was before and behaving somewhat unusual. Almost from a different era. I know that makes little sense."

Uksod thought on that briefly. "Perhaps that's to be expected."

"Eminence?"

"The amulet has its own power, which is very old and tainted by who it was bonded to before. He needs to come back here. If we can have him back here with it, then I can do something to adjust that."

"While I have encouraged the plan to source wheat from Enderk, he's resisting any suggestion he should come himself."

"Tell him you've received word they will not deal with anyone but himself. He'll meet the new High Prince and negotiate directly."

"That might work."

"Do you have any wheat left?"

"No."

"Nor will you. Before long your neighbors will fight each other for some, if things continue. We will be the only source, and whoever gets the best deal done, will become very rich amongst the realms."

"This he'll understand."

"How are the boats progressing? I have been out of contact with the port."

"We are still learning. Getting there safely without being seen from shore is costly. At best we get two of three across the seas."

"What's the worst?"

"Some have never made it back. We lost five in one trip."

"I might have another solution for this too if you cannot fix that problem, but you must get him here!"

"I will try."

"Do more than that, Fuling. Tell him the Ngaherians are keeping it all for themselves, anything that will stir up his emotions."

"I will do all I can, but since he's had the amulet, he seems able to resist my use of the ring."

~

That done, Uksod needed to make one more connection. It had been months since he'd last spoken to his plant in the city of Anderwell.

When the man was within the city, he was unreachable, some magic blocked any attempt. Which meant they'd agreed the man would leave the city every full moon and wait for several hours so if needed Uksod would contact him.

Now he needed the man's help. It was a relief to connect with him quickly — Uksod knew he didn't have long left in the body he was using.

~

"Good, you're there."

"Yes, I was expecting you last month, but you didn't come."

"I was tied up. I do not have long, be quick."

"I found the team close by and told them where the girl is within the city."

"Have they tried to get her?"

"No." The man paused before he continued. "The city has been locked down and is under heavy guard. It is almost impossible for them to get inside now."

"Impossible?"

"Anyone that even looks half like a Derk is being denied, and the ways I could use before have been blocked."

"You can't get into the city?"

"I can, but I cannot bring them in those ways."

Uksod was frustrated.

"You will have to get it."

"What?"

"The amulet."

"I thought you wanted the girl as well?"

"Not under these circumstances. It's too difficult. Kill her and get the amulet. Give it to the team, they can get it to me."

His contact said nothing.

"Is there a problem?"

"It will be difficult."

"Isn't everything?"

"Most likely I will blow my cover here."

"The amulet, that's all that matters. You will be well-rewarded when you do this, you can live anywhere. Get it done, and soon."

Uksod felt the connection cut out abruptly. The man under his hands was dead. He lifted his hands and shook them as if removing the dirt of the body from them.

The effect on Uksod's energy was strong as well. He'd overdone it, but at least he could just top up at the stone. Both conversations were necessary even if neither filled him with the greatest confidence.

He needed some wins. Surely one of the two could get what he asked done, if not both?

34

TILLANDRA

*T*illandra knew she needed to make decisions and not spend so much time deliberating over everything. Logically it made sense but the idea of exposing the amulet was not such an easy one.

No one could detect it here within the city, not while the stones in the college tower had power. That was how Tillandra understood it.

Yet the jewel within the amulet wasn't powerless and Lani had explained how she could sense it reaching out for something whenever it was out of the pouch.

And then there was the basic danger, the simple fact that only Lani could touch it. While Odajeen had offered herself to do it, that wasn't practical.

The delicacy with which it would need to be extracted from the pouch required sight, not just courage. It was a risk, a significant risk, and if anything went wrong, Tillandra would be lost.

I cannot ask anyone else to do it, if anyone is to do it, it has to be me.

Wandering around the city hadn't helped her make the decision so she returned to her home. Milfred was nowhere to be seen, which she was glad for.

For no reason other than as a distraction from her current thinking she sought out the book in her office. Without Lani able to read the journals it was the only remaining source of historical information.

Moving the books that hid it on her shelf, she pulled the silk cloth-wrapped book out and put it down on her desk. She sat and opened the book using the small paper bookmark she'd left last time as a guide.

The page appeared differently to her, parts of it now didn't look anywhere near as damaged as they had, and words previously illegible were easily readable.

It meant the Occultation had receded more, making the knowledge easier to access. As she'd been told, it also meant that the other amulets would come too, if only she knew where.

As she read, more names became evident to her — not just Schevenal and Truegen but others; King Unx was listed there.

The great-grandfather of Ahn was there, and now his amulet has returned.

Tillandra looked for other names and compiled a list of the rulers of the day. It would give them somewhere to start looking for history about them. Whether or not knowing more about each ruler would help locate where their amulets might turn up, she wasn't sure, but any information was better than none.

Whoever had written this book seemed to have been compiling the written word of several different scribes because the style changed on pages. Some of the accounts covered the same topics, those that spoke of the amulets all described them as beautiful jewels, almost lustfully.

Only one account contained in the book wasn't fawning over the gifted jewels. Tillandra went back to its beginning and carefully picked through it.

She's made her way here, aboard an unlikely vessel. I can sense her presence -- it's all around, and yet I don't think even she knows what she is doing. Even she is a carrier for the vermin that rides on her back across the waters.

Tendrils reach out from those gifts, like the arms of the cursed beast in the ocean. So many arms each wriggling and moving their way in many directions, snaring those who come close. You can feel it in the air, like a smoke.

The taste of it is there if not the sight, for me at least. It is as though I can sense it on my tongue or in my nose, yes, it is faint, so subtle and light that I could almost ignore it if it wasn't for the acuteness of my senses.

It takes all my resistance to block its effects. I have had to meditate twice today already, seeking assistance from Seth. I am not sure if she listens to me or not, but I meditate and pray for her guidance.

Others around me have been enraptured by the reach of that evil goddess. I dislike calling her such, but I cannot find any other word to describe her. She has powers, this I can feel, and she is known as the one who disappeared, but she is here.

Somehow, she is here, like a wind whose source is distant, but felt wherever it blows. It must be those amulets that has brought her, that is the only thing that makes sense. Rare is it that I wish for sight, but this is one of those times.

To see what it is that everyone has spoken of, described in such amorous terms, would help me better understand what it is that is happening. What it is I can feel around me. Maybe it is my inability to see it that is protecting me?

~

There were still parts of pages that were either damaged or hidden from Tillandra by the power of the Occultation, leaving gaps she couldn't read. But a picture was forming in her mind about what might have been happening back in the times of the Great Fair.

~

No one notices the blind man, which makes little sense. It is as though they think having no sight makes you stupid or crazy. Without sight I listen more, smell more, pay attention to space and the feel of many things.

I am able often to get closer to conversations than another might, as though my lack of vision is a sign of my compliance for confidentiality. Foolish as it is, it serves me well. These nights I hear conversations amongst courts of envy and greed.

Those who not many days before were ready to meet with their colleagues from the other realms are plotting the worst of things. It is her; I know it is her, that's the way she would work. These amulets are the very cause of this pain, and they work against those who wear them.

Her name I will never say out loud, silly of me I know, but I am no more or less than any person, my irrationality is what makes me a person. I write it here so that others may know it is Yantarnaya I speak of.

Few have heard her name here on Dharatan, but I listen. Even to the gods I listen and if you listen hard enough and long enough you will hear things not even meant to be heard.

Sometimes I find myself in a place that is sightless. I can tell that, even without eyes. A place of nothing, and yet there I hear many things. If I meditate for days on end, until my body is almost lifeless without food or water, as I have done several times, I find my way there.

That is where I first met my Seth, who instructed me on my path. It is also there I heard the other one's name. The goddess that went away, that they had lost. But she isn't lost, and while I pray to Seth to tell her that she is here, and she is found, I do not know if my goddess hears me. She is here, it is her that comes on these tendrils.

It is like a wave of them, breaking across these fields. I can do nothing to stop them. But there is ill here, and it is breeding quicker than rats or even pesky flies. Even now I feel it on my skin, creeping up my nose, wanting into my head.

I must meditate, I feel myself giving in. I am beginning to want to see the amulets. Despite the impossibility of that, the thought is there, that is how I know it is not natural. I must meditate.

The description that the person gave of the place where they found themselves when meditating sounded very much like the Void. That would make sense, although this person didn't sound as though they used magic to get there.

Was it a man or a woman? Tillandra couldn't tell from the writings. The subsequent accounts she read were from others who had noticed the increased tension within the fair. She kept going, hoping for more from the blind writer.

~

How odd, how could they have written that? That makes little sense. They must have been using an aide to do it, hopefully they didn't change the wording to suit themselves.

~

There were still many pages that she could not read, but Tillandra knew they weren't really blank. The mottled inky tone of the page was simply the obfuscated writing she was blocked from. *For now.*

The next set of pages were of accounts leading up to the first of the fights.

It was recorded by people very confused as to what was happening. As noted by them, the original reason for the Great Council meetings was to avoid such occurrences across Dharatan, but to start a fight there was without precedent.

Soldiers from the Kysten guard and those from the northern parties clashed over small things. Bit by bit everything began to unravel. Other guards turned up in efforts to stop the initial fighting, but it escalated. The event descended into a battleground, the attendants that accompanied the rulers running in desperation for their lives as everyone became an enemy.

Then even they began to turn on those from other realms. Slowly the writing was from a fewer number of scribes, as though others were drawn into the fray or killed. Tillandra couldn't really say, at this point she was so embedded in the story she was filling in the gaps on her own.

Perhaps those are actual visions, not my imagination.

As she thought the idea, chills ran along her arms, a signal she was more correct than wrong. Then she came across some more from the scribe she had been looking for.

~

There is nothing I can do, I have hurried away out of fear for my own self, into a rock cluster that I feel will protect me. Here with my aide, we hide hoping to be ignored by everyone overcome with this madness.

No one is safe, now even the rulers are directing the fight. At first it was just small groups that started, but as though gripped by paranoia, or simply base fear, rulers pulled their troops around them and created shields, before pushing one way or the other to overcome an enemy.

It is as though they are all enemies, it is madness. It is her. She is responsible for this, the gifts that Schevenal brought, they are all her doing. I doubt even she could foresee what would happen.

What good a jewel to control if there is no control? What else could they be? I have thought long and hard on it, meditated for hours, and all I can sense is the amulets were sent to control people. To turn them to her.

What is that sound? I can hear winds, I think it is winds, coming from my left. The west, is it the west? My aide will not leave the shelter either, nor could I make him. It is hard to know which way is which tonight, but I hear sounds of a storm.

Maybe Seth has heard me, bringing one of her storms to calm this madness.

~

Tillandra was fascinated by the words this person had put down on paper. Tingfurlew had told her about the storm that changed Sahro and surrounding realms, but this person was writing from within it.

~

It feels like a day has passed, I feel as though I am shouting, but I cannot easily hear. We were almost buried alive in our rock cluster. I am thankful I brought an aide with me to help, I would not have been able to get out on my own.

We sit on the side of a new dune, looking across a vast desert. That is what I am told, nothing that was here before still exists. Only sand.

For a whole day, or so it seemed to us, winds tore around us, screeching like they were in pain, then the screams of people weaved amongst the noise. I cried, the sounds were horrific, and the level of the noise was vast.

My hearing is dulled and still rings from it. The air is now clear, and I can smell everything. There is no death here, or no smell of it. There is no smell of her here anymore either. What happened to those amulets, I know not. But I cannot feel them anymore. All gone.

Perhaps sand is a burial ground to mute their calling. How deep must it be to cover the tendrils up? Are there people, I ask my aide?

He answers there are, many wandering aimlessly on the desert below, some calling out, others injured or silent in the aftermath of what occurred. If this was my god, I am now scared of her power. Never had I realized she would deliver such wrath on us.

The scope of this is unfathomable. I must meditate. I must meditate and pray. I do not want to anger my god.

~

Tillandra closed the book, letting the story behind the words sink in. She couldn't imagine what it would have been like to survive such a thing.

The writing, if it was true, and she couldn't see why it wouldn't be, answered more questions. The amulets had been sent by Yantarnaya and they were for nothing good.

If she'd been reluctant before about exposing Lani to the amulet, now she was frightened by the idea. Whatever good that might come from it, the risk was high.

This isn't going to get any easier.

35

LEO

*I*f this wasn't the creepiest thing he'd ever done, Leo didn't know what was. The rat had gone still in the sack under his hand, but Leo's heart rate was still up.

"Focus, Leo, before you use it all up."

Her words didn't help the squeamish feeling he had but he persisted anyway with what Toolet was telling him.

Breathe, Leo. Go into the Void.

Over the last few weeks, he had been getting well practiced at the meditation that Toolet had been teaching him and settling himself into a peaceful state.

He wished someone would have taught him this years ago, it would have helped with his turns. Those moments when he couldn't do anything but run away and keep running until he'd burned his anger or embarrassment away.

What was that?

The problem Leo had was holding onto the thing she called the Void. It appeared like a blackness in front of his face and head, which had taken some getting used to.

He accepted that but whenever he tried to move into it, like Toolet had told him, he struggled to stay with the concept. This time that was different.

He visualized a small version of himself stepping into it. As he took his first steps his whole self felt the difference and he scared himself back out of it.

It took him another minute to reclaim the calmness he needed and to bring the black space back.

This time he moved further in, the area he had moved to was wavering and shrinking, then he popped out again.

Breathe. Focus.

The next time he was able to stay in there much longer. Long enough that he could try the next step. Leo brought an image of Beantic's face into his mind.

Like Toolet had said, that image appeared across from him inside the Void. It shimmered and almost disappeared, but he was able to bring it back, taking all of his concentration.

Once it was stable, he pushed out at it through the darkness with an intention to knock on it. When Toolet had explained it to him it sounded stupid but being here now he understood somehow what she meant.

"Hello?" The voice was faint and cautious.

"It worked!"

"Who is that?"

"Ah... it's me, Leo."

"Oh... that explains why it's so unfamiliar... and weak."

He felt embarrassed when she said that and immediately the blurry distant image he'd begun to see of her faded more.

"Hold... to it... Leo..."

He calmed himself and shook off his feelings. Her face began to solidify more, and her voice became a little stronger.

"That's it. Is this your first time?"

"Yes."

"You're doing better than I did."

"Really?"

"Hang on to it, Leo… you can't let your emotions run free in here. Maintain your focus."

He did, but it was becoming harder to control. His breathing wasn't helping, and he could feel the shape of the space he was in waver.

"I think your rat is about done. Good work, Leo."

And then she was gone. Leo opened his eyes and wiped away the sweat that had formed on his brow with his sleeve.

"You reached her I see."

"How…?"

"… you were speaking out loud."

"Oh."

"There's nothing unusual about that, Leo. We all do it, but you don't need to. When you've practiced more, you'll be able to distinguish that voice and your voice."

The feeling came suddenly, and Leo had to turn to avoid it hitting Toolet. The contents of his stomach erupted from his mouth, uncontrollably, all over the floor.

"There we go… right on time," Toolet said.

Leo couldn't reply. He suddenly felt dreadful. His stomach convulsed several more times, and his brow was covered in a cool sweat. He collapsed where he was.

Another voice entered the room, but he couldn't work out who it came from, and his eyes needed to remain closed if he had any chance stopping the vomiting. "Is he alright?"

"Yes, well no, but he will be. He's just conducted his first calling."

"That explains it then. I'll get someone to help with this mess."

"Thanks, Mother."

Hours later Leo was able to sit normally in a chair and sipped slowly at a light ale that Toolet had brought to her chambers.

"That was horrible."

"It's only simple ale."

"I meant the calling -- more specifically what happened after."

"That seems to be the problem of using rats."

"What do you mean?"

"Up until recently it was just something we accepted. You do get used to it, it's rare to get sick like that when you've done it many times, but it's never pleasant. Cost of the job, basically."

"Not worth it, I'd say."

"It's worth it, mark my word. When you do have need to communicate with someone, it's better than any other thing you could do. Think about it. Beantic is somewhere on her way to Callet. She'd be well over halfway there now, and yet you were able to speak to her clear as day."

"Not so clear."

"It will be when you get the hang of it, and get used to the…"

"… Not sure I want to get used to that. What did you mean about 'up until recently'?"

"Ah yes, as I was saying, Tillandra discovered that there's other methods we can use that have no sickness with them at all. Which explains why using a living being feels the way it does."

"I don't understand."

"You get sick, as best we can tell, because you use the life force of the rat. And that seems to carry with it parts of itself which seem to upset our bodies."

"Like it's illness?"

"We aren't sure, Leo. It could be that, or it could be simply because you're trying to ingest a dirty animal."

"Ingest?" His voice went squeaky.

"Not by mouth, but that's the best way to explain it. You're taking in whatever makes up the life of the rat."

"What about a chicken?"

"What do you mean?"

"Well, we eat chickens, maybe if I used a chicken, it wouldn't make me sick?"

"I'm not sure it's connected to the same concept as eating, Leo. I've told you the best we know or have discussed."

"What was the way that didn't make you feel sick?"

"I haven't tried that, only Tillandra has."

"And?"

"It was using a tree."

His face must have looked disbelieving to her.

"I'm serious, Leo."

"What tree?"

"One in the forests in Daskare, to the east, where Peka is from. And another elsewhere."

"Why there?"

"That's where she was taught it by the woman who made the mask you're wearing."

"Umm…"

"The Carver is a unique person that uses very unique trees to create the masks we wear, the one you put on in the Audition. Those trees are part of the magic that allows us to communicate."

"Now that makes some sense. Because we wear the mask that allows us to connect with the tree."

"So it seems. That's partly what Peka is doing here, tending to the tree out in the back garden."

"I've seen him out there. That wispy-looking tree is magical?"

"It's young and hasn't been cared for. He is caring for it and strengthening it. We could use that, instead of the rats. At least when we are in Anderwell."

"That's pretty cool. Maybe I can use that instead?"

Toolet shook her head and laughed. "No, Leo. You need to be able to do this whenever not just around a tree like that."

"Oh."

The sound of knocking caught him by surprise, and he looked around the room, trying to work out where it was coming from.

"What, Leo?"

"That knocking, where's it coming from?"

"There's no knocking here, Leo, that will be someone trying to speak to you. I'd suspect it's Beantic returning the connection to you, to save you having to use another rat."

"Oh."

"Don't worry, it has none of the sick side effects. Just don't stay long there, you're tired from your efforts and this will tire you more."

"I'm fine."

"Sure you are."

"What do I do?"

"Go back into the Void and focus on the knocking, the rest will be the same."

The taste of sick lingered a little in his mouth, not quite enough to stop him from trying but close to it. He closed his eyes anyway and focused on calming himself.

All his practice paid off as he was able to drop to the ideal state quickly. Not using the rat seemed even easier and the darkness appeared before him.

He could see a shape in it, off in the distance, and as he moved within, he could see the face of Beantic again.

～

"Hello, Leo."

"Hello, Beantic."

"You know you can call me Bea, as well."

"Okay."

"How do you feel?"

"Better now, not so good earlier, though."

He could sense her laughing. Not at him but at the event.

"Yes, it's not the most pleasant of things even when you've been doing it a long time, but the first few times are disgusting."

"One way of putting it. Where are you?"

"Diwedd, do you know it?"

"I have heard of it."

"Pass on that location to Mother, I will be on my way to Callet tomorrow. I should be there within the week."

"Okay."

"There's more."

"Okay."

"She needs to know that the issue with wheat is dire."

"Wheat? The shortage?"

"It is much worse than that, Leo. Crossing through Rohumaa into Lletem there are now much bigger patrols of soldiers, and travelers being questioned. There is none anywhere and a tension is building that looks very troublesome. Here in Diwedd there's talk about Ngaherians holding out on everyone. Tell her I will find out more about it."

"Okay. Aren't we meant to do something about it?"

Beantic laughed again. "We are, we will if we can, Leo. That's for Mother to decided, but we can't magic up wheat."

Her face began to shimmer and began to head backward.

"Hold your focus, Leo."

"I'm trying."

"It's probably too much for your first time, pass the message on, I'll send more."

∼

With a jolt Leo found himself out of the Void. There was no extended goodbye or ceremony, one minute she was right there in front of him, and then she wasn't. He opened his eyes to see Toolet staring at him.

∼

"And?"

"You were right, it was Beantic."

"What did she want?"

Leo filled her in on what the other Jester had told him.

"Best we go share that with Mother."

She turned and headed off at full pace, forcing him to jump up and hurry after her.

36

KARPENMOR

He was nervous which wasn't anything new, but it bothered Karpenmor that he was having trouble controlling his response. At this moment he felt like he might throw up, and it was all over nothing.

Almost nothing. He had requested a meeting with Lady Natillian to see if she'd learned anything about the delays as he'd asked last time.

But that wasn't the reason for his nervousness, or not most of it. It was his hope that she would bring Bhoomi. He knew it was silly, he didn't even know the girl, but that was the cause of this feeling.

He'd changed his clothing twice already and had been pacing his balcony for the last hour trying to find peace, but it was reluctant to come.

What is wrong with me?

Of all the things that he needed to be thinking of, Lady Natillian's granddaughter was the least of them.

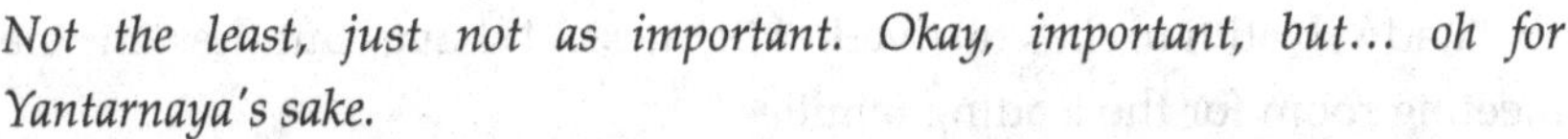

Not the least, just not as important. Okay, important, but... oh for Yantarnaya's sake.

Something twinged in the back of his head as he said the goddess's name but then it disappeared. He would have thought more on it, but the sickness in his stomach brought his attention back to his present state.

It wasn't that he didn't want to see Bhoomi, he did, but he had thought he would have heard back from Lady Natillian regarding families Six and Seven.

He couldn't ignore the fact that she was the leader of her house, and an opponent all things considered. It was possible she might already know and be choosing to hold it back from him, although he couldn't understand why.

Should he push her in this meeting? Exert his authority over her and demand what she knew? He couldn't even prove she did know anything. And then what? How would she respond to him moving forward?

I don't have to be the same as Uksod, I can have decent relationships with the families, if I choose.

Karpenmor's thoughts were interrupted by a knock at the door to his chamber.

"Enter."

It was Aika who came through the door, her face always downward and her shoulders slightly hunched. Her family's poverty and the harsh way they'd raised her contributed to her manner.

Karpenmor didn't approve of the way she carried herself, even less today with the anxiety he was feeling.

"Stop it, Aika!"

She froze in her spot. "What, Highness?"

"Stand up straight!"

Karpenmor regretted snapping at her, she didn't even look at him. Awkwardly she straightened her shoulders, her head still downward-facing.

"Better. As my aide, Aika, you can't slouch around the place."

"Sorry, Highness."

"You wanted me for something?"

"Lady Natillian has arrived, Highness. I have put her in the meeting room for the leading families."

Karpenmor didn't reply, which appeared to make the girl anxious.

"That was correct, wasn't it?"

"Yes, Aika. I was just thinking how quickly you pick up on instructions. I haven't ever had to tell you something twice."

She didn't say a word, and her eyes refused to look directly at him.

"Yet, I sense a question in your statement. Is there any reason why I wouldn't want to meet her there?"

She said nothing.

"Aika?"

"It is wrong of me to listen to you when you're speaking to yourself."

"Speaking to myself? What on Enderk do you mean?"

"You have been annoyed recently, Highness. You have several times cursed this woman and others out loud, when I have been near."

"Have I now? And what have I been saying?" Inside, Karpenmor found this exchange humorous, but it was a useful exercise in the boundaries that his new assistant had.

"It is not for me to repeat such words, Highness."

"Aika, I command you!" The words grated on his own nerves, let alone how she would take them, but he needed to see if she would do as she was told. "Look at me, Aika." While he said it with a soft tone, it was still a command.

She reluctantly shifted her head and looked at his chin.

"Up here, Aika." Karpenmor pointed to his eyes.

She looked directly at his eyes, and he saw her light brown eyes for the first time. There was a yellow hint reflecting off them, her eyelids wide open, almost in fear.

"You called her a witch, Highness. Why hasn't that witch come back to me when I asked her... things to that effect."

Karpenmor could see her face was blushing and he almost laughed but pulled it at the last moment.

"It's okay, Aika. I know I said those things, and I asked you to repeat them."

She looked away from him again and he didn't say anything of it. He needed to build trust between them if he she was to fulfil this role the way he wanted.

"Do not be afraid to tell the truth to me, Aika, I need that from those who work for me. Understood?"

"Yes, Highness."

"Then I totally understand why you might have been concerned. But she is one of the leading families and though I am annoyed at her it would be rude not to see her in that chamber. Is she alone?"

"Yes, Highness."

Karpenmor's face must have shown his disappointment.

"Is there a problem, Highness?"

It intrigued him that despite not looking directly at him she could still see his expression. "No, Aika, just wondering. Let's go."

"I will come with you?"

"Only to the outside, in case I need you for anything."

She seemed to relax a little at those words. He wondered how she could get through the day like this, with so much anxiety from everything he said.

She'd better get used to it.

Now that he knew Bhoomi wasn't going to be there, it meant he wouldn't be distracted and most of his own anxiety dissipated. When he entered through the door opened by his guard, Lady Natillian stood from the chair she had been sat in.

"Your Highness." Her knees dipped slightly, and she bowed her head.

Karpenmor heard the soft click of the door behind him. "Lady Natillian, alone this time." He regretted the words the moment they left his mouth.

He almost sensed a touch of delight in her face at his words. "Your invitation was for myself. I didn't presume to bring anyone else with me."

"Of course," Karpenmor quickly replied, "I am pleased you have come." He moved to a chair opposite where she stood and sat, beckoning her to follow.

"You requested this meeting, did you not?" Her face carried a slight crease of concern.

"I did." Her face relaxed. "Although only because I hadn't heard from you since our last meeting. I had expected a response."

That caused a tightening round her eyes, which she tried to conceal. "My apologies, Highness. I have nothing to report about your request, I did not want to waste your time with empty words."

Her age was difficult to tell. While small creases did line her eyes and mouth, they were small details not large marks. Everything about her was always manicured or sculpted. Her hair was crafted into a double bun on her head, without a single loose hair.

"You have had no information regarding what might be behind the cause of their delay?"

She paused and while her eyes never left his, Karpenmor sensed there was a hint of resistance there.

"I do not, Highness, or none more than I expect you know already?"

"And what is that?"

"Only that a bridge appears to have collapsed and that the families have had several misfortunes on the trip, losing horses and the like."

Karpenmor nodded. "This I have heard."

"Then I have nothing else to add, Highness. That is all I know."

Without the distraction he'd had last time he had met with Lady Natillian, Karpenmor was able to concentrate more on how she responded.

He was not so sure what she told him was the truth. Something about her manner gave him cause to mistrust her. If she knew more about it, she wasn't about to give it up easily.

"I hope your Highness understands if I had more information, I would share it with you. My family and I are here to cooperate and support you."

He looked at the older woman. This was a game to her; he could see that. She was well practiced at overseeing her family and no doubt had little chance to play such games with Uksod.

Karpenmor didn't think the old priest would spend much time focusing on what she or the others wanted. His only goal was to keep them away from the palace and what had been happening to his father.

"Of course." He could have lied as well, but he didn't. "It is a major inconvenience to all our planning. The coming events include all family heads."

"I understand, Highness. What will you be doing about it?"

He paused and looked at her. It seemed to be an innocuous enough question.

"In the most part nothing. There are those events which must happen at a certain date or time, and they'll have to continue. Where needed the family priests or other members will fill in."

"I see."

"However, we most likely will need to rearrange several of the more important events, or so I am advised."

"Can I ask which?"

"The Dance of the Brides might have to be shifted. It would appear this is of great importance to all families."

This time she did let a small grin form on her face. "You don't see it that way, Highness?"

"Best I do not comment, Lady Natillian. I'd be glad if it was already over."

"That will upset everyone's planning."

"I imagine it will, it has within the palace, but it would be best to let everyone be part of it."

"And if they don't arrive on time?"

"Unless the street has informed you otherwise, Lady Natillian, I believe they will be here."

She paused for half a minute before replying.

"Such words of the street are generally ill-informed, Highness, but there is nothing I am aware of to say other than what you believe."

"Thank you for your frankness. While I had hoped to learn more, it's time I focused on getting ready for what's coming."

"Could I bother you with one more matter, Highness?"

"Yes?"

"It occurs to me that with these rearrangements an opportunity might have presented itself. I wouldn't want to presume anything, but our family, I, would be honored if you would join us at our city compound for a dinner. I realize you have many things to attend to, but it would be a great honor and it would be a way to learn more of our new High Prince."

Karpenmor was intrigued by how quickly she'd put this idea

together. Was it really a chance idea or was it already planned that she was going to ask? He sensed she wasn't finished so let her continue.

"Of course, I understand that your time is very busy. With much of my family here, including my children, and grandchildren..." She paused a touch at that, just enough that Karpenmor sensed it was deliberate. "I doubt they will all be here at the one time again."

That would mean Bhoomi would be there too, he would get to see her again. It shouldn't matter but it did.

"Your whole family indeed. It was your granddaughter that I met last time you were here was it not? Bhoomi?"

She smiled at him. "Yes, Highness."

"How many children and grandchildren do you have, Lady Natillian."

"A lot, Highness. It would be quite the party."

It would be a lot more fun than being stuck in this palace.

"Send the invitation to my staff, I am sure I can fit that in."

"Thank you, Highness."

He stood and left the room, his mind totally back on Bhoomi, so much so that he didn't even notice Aika slip in behind him as he headed back to his chambers.

37

GORAN

For the first time in a while, Goran was pleased that things in Anderwell were slow to change. No one had thought to tell the landlady of Ashantha's rooms he wasn't coming back.

She'd kept the dead man's room spotlessly clean. Someone would need to tell her otherwise, but it wasn't going to be Goran.

This was the last place anyone would think to look for him which made it the perfect spot to plan his next steps. He was glad for the clear head.

While the room was clean it was also barren of anything useful to him. It felt more like a rented room in an inn than anyone's home.

There were no paintings on any wall, only a single set of spare clothes and next to no personal belongings. Ashantha had never spent a lot of time in Anderwell, he was one of the Court always out on the road.

Goran thought about how Ash's room at Henri's in Callet had more personality than this. Not that either man was still alive. The deep sadness about Henri's death bubbled up inside Goran.

He'd not thought about his friend in a long while, but it hurt almost as much. There were no tears, but he could feel the ache in his heart.

Henri had always been a good friend to him. He still couldn't believe that the man was dead. As had been Ashantha. Two good men dead all because of the foolish expedition to Enderk.

As he sat in the room memories flooded back about how heated those discussions had been amongst the Court. Whether or not Ash should go across the seas.

In the end it had come down to a vote and it had been Tillandra that had determined the final decision. She was their Mother, she had that right, but it had caused a rift for a while.

He knew that she carried the guilt of that decision, and a couple of the Court were never shy of reminding her she'd made that call. Goran couldn't hold it against her, not for that at least, but he missed the man, nonetheless.

In hindsight it was the correct decision, the amulet had come from his expedition, and this Lani woman. The jewel wasn't right, there was something about it, he just wished he'd been more awake to learn more about it.

As for the young woman, he guessed she was still somewhere here in Anderwell. Maybe she too was locked up in a different place.

It doesn't matter. I'm not part of that anymore, they made that clear.

He stretched out on the bed, hoping to get some rest, then to work on what he would do. The room was safe enough, it was on the third and top level of a building.

The ground floor was a candlemaker's shop, and the proprietor of that lived on the middle floor. He'd made his way in from the rooftop staying quiet and would leave the same way. No one needed to know he'd been here.

Ironically, he'd wanted to be back in Anderwell for years, back with his family. Now he was planning on where to go to be far away from the same people.

There's nothing left here for me now.

He didn't consider the others as family, not the same as he had before. If he were caught again by them Goran didn't doubt he'd end up back in that cell, or another.

And what for? What have I done to deserve that?

He'd broken no rules, done nothing to harm anyone, he'd simply been affected by his alter. And yet they'd locked him up and drugged him.

So where to then?

He was alone now. There wasn't any support network, or inns he could just stay in as part of his work. Of course, he could still entertain and his skill was still his to use.

Gambling and entertaining would need to be his trade until he found another option. It would require a little finesse to make his way without leaving stories about him as he went.

There would be none of his best performances to be had anymore, he'd just need to do enough to earn a bed and money for the next leg of his trip.

Perhaps I could find a patron and just serve them hiding in plain sight.

It wasn't as though he could completely hide though. His ring would track where he was, they'd be able to see his general location on the map in the mask room. If they wanted to hunt him, it wouldn't be so hard.

What he didn't know was how much they'd hunt him. He sat up now that he'd realized they would know he was still in Anderwell. He couldn't stay here any more than he could just disappear.

Maybe Tillandra might try to contact him through the mask, but in that he had a choice. There was no way to force him to answer and speak to them.

The ring was a harder thing to avoid. Goran didn't know any way to get it off, not without chopping off the finger.

I wonder if the magic would let that happen?

Maybe there was a way he could seek his own answer to that. But not here and not now. He had only one immediate thing to do, and that was to get out of Anderwell.

If he wanted to be free he had to leave, get on the road. While the Circuit wasn't open to him, he did have an extensive network of contacts all over the northern part of Dharatan, many of whom were only known to himself.

There were plenty of places he could stay and get help, he just had to make that decision and act on it. Which was part of the problem.

Knowing what he needed to do, the truth of his situation now was forcing him to make a final decision. Leave and be gone forever. There was no coming back from it.

Deep down it hurt. He didn't want to be away or an exile, he wanted things to go back to how they had been.

Stop moping, what's done is done.

Until they had word out about him, he shouldn't have any real troubles just walking through the gates. Even then he could influence that a little, he'd just need to change his appearance.

Goran tugged at the locks on his head and ran his hand through his scruffy beard. Both needed to go, his hair particularly was distinct enough here in Anderwell, it would be a beacon right to him.

There wasn't anything in the room to help with that. He'd need to divert to somewhere that might have a suitable blade. That meant holding off for a little while longer.

His best bet was a smithy he knew that liked his drink and was a creature of habit. The man would be finished before the last of the sun dropped below the walls and off to get his first ale.

Goran wanted to be off now, but he had to bide his time until sundown came. He looked out the window and could tell it was an hour give or take.

Not too long.

He changed into the only set of clothes he could find in Ash's room. Normally they would have been too small for him, but his captivity and illness had left him a shadow of his former self.

They weren't a perfect fit but they were clean. Goran bundled the others up; he would dispose of them elsewhere so as to leave no trace here.

You're not one of them, not anymore. You're not wanted, despite still having the mask and ring, they'll lock you away if you stay. They made the choice, not you; you can't trust any of them anymore.

Goran had to check himself to make sure it wasn't Zoran speaking. It wasn't, it was his own thoughts, and they rang true. It was nice to have his own thoughts to himself.

Whatever it was that the young girl had done to him, he liked it. Having Zoran locked away right now was one less problem for him to deal with.

No one else was putting ideas into his head, it was his choice about what to do and how to do it. He rubbed his face vigorously and shook his head just to make sure it really was only him in his mind.

The truth hadn't changed. He was an outsider on the run, unlikely to ever return. He couldn't believe it had come to this.

The door to the room pushed open suddenly and Tillandra strode in, a serious look on her face.

"Clever choice, Goran. I wasn't sure where you'd go."

KARPENMOR

*B*rooding on things wasn't new to Karpenmor but today he felt stuck in his thoughts. He wasn't feeling as in control of things as he would have led others to believe.

It wasn't any one big thing, just a number of little things all stitched together.

Like his meeting with Lady Natillian. First, he tried to be clever and use her to learn more about what was behind the delays to the other families but had learned nothing at all.

Then he wanted to put her in her place for not getting back to him, but instead he'd felt silly for even thinking he could, and again ended up empty-handed.

Worse than that, he'd played the benevolent leader and agreed to her request without any deep thought. Now he would have to attend a social gathering of her family all because of his desire to see Bhoomi again.

And he did want to see her again. The more Karpenmor tried to not think about her the more she popped into his mind at the oddest of times.

He could see images of her face in his mind without even trying.

And he liked it. More than that, it was stirring feelings in him he wasn't familiar with.

When he'd turned sixteen Uksod had started sending him women to pleasure him, which he'd accepted at first. He'd thought that was something he was meant to do.

But like everything Uksod planned for him, it wasn't what Karpenmor wanted, and he put an end to it. The idea of just using them like that felt wrong.

Nothing had ever been said about it, and it never happened again. Of course, Karpenmor could demand whatever he wanted now, but he didn't.

Even just thinking about that linked the idea of it with Bhoomi and made him uncomfortable. She was attractive to him, but he couldn't think like that.

Karpenmor knew she was being put in front of him by Natillian deliberately, and for this very reason. He had to put her out of his mind and focus on other things.

He cursed himself again for agreeing to go to their event. Having agreed to theirs, now he'd also receive invitations from the other families.

His choice would be to attend them all or offend some or all the families, raising the status of Lady Natillian if he did so.

His face flushed as he thought about how silly he'd been, and he felt agitated by his folly.

Not so clever, Karpenmor!

Wanting to be in control was completely different to having control. It was almost as if he was forcing himself into a position to have to be more like Uksod.

He could simply offend everyone and do whatever he wanted, but that went against his desire to be a better ruler than Uksod.

Karpenmor laughed. Not so long ago the idea of being in charge of Enderk was the furthest thing from his mind. Back then he'd happily left Uksod alone to do what it was he did with no concern about the decisions he made.

Now Karpenmor was basing who he wanted to be on doing the

opposite to how Uksod ran things. He wasn't even sure if he could do what was going to be required.

It was too late to go back now. He would be crowned soon enough and the time of Uksod ruling was over.

Should I keep him as my chancellor, to help run things, at least until I have a better grip on everything?

There were already chancellors who looked after everything from running the palace to finance and supplies. It would be better if they reported to him directly, leaving Uksod more as a mentor, not a decision maker.

A knock came at the door to his room. He still felt agitated and annoyed by the thoughts in his head, and didn't want to deal with anyone.

"Go away! I am not to be disturbed."

Whoever it was didn't repeat the intrusion, which he was grateful for. Even being curt like that cut him a little. He disliked being rude to others, but the sense of authority made him feel better also.

I need some time to myself, it's almost impossible to get these days.

He needed to be anywhere but here, somewhere where no one wanted him to decide on anything, and somewhere he could turn his mind away from everything and everyone.

The last time Karpenmor had been able to be completely free of anyone else's demands had been when he was much younger. It seemed a lifetime ago, but for many years Uksod hadn't bothered too much with him and let him do whatever he wished.

With no friends in the palace, as if there would be, he had been left to roam within its walls. There was always a Vrah guard somewhere close by, which defeated that purpose as well.

Karpenmor had begun to make a game out of finding ways to lose them. Being much smaller he was able to find places he could get into that a grown person could not.

That had been when he found the many hidden passages and tunnels within the palace complex. No doubt the Vrah hated him for what he had done, but he would disappear for hours, hiding from them and everyone else.

Will they leave me alone in here or should I go somewhere else? Where can I be completely alone?

The palace had plenty of rooms and chambers, many of them often empty for long periods. That hadn't always been the case, Karpenmor had read about grand parties and social events in the palace -- before his father had gone to Dharatan.

Before the madness took him, it seemed as though he liked to ensure the palace was alive -- regularly entertaining and filling the place with people and sounds. How stark in contrast it now was.

Much of the palace was devoid of life, with rooms unused despite always being maintained, and much of it felt cold and unlived in. Those were the rooms that young Karpenmor loved to hide in.

No one came looking for him there and he always found all sorts of things to play with: weapons, books, and maps. None of them he understood but they made it fun for him back then.

He knew the perfect place. Karpenmor walked toward his bed, looking up at the ledge running along the entire wall. The last time he'd used this he was only ten or so and had to climb up on furniture to access it.

Now tall enough, he ran his hand along the ledge until he felt the small lever hidden there. Pulling at the lever caused the panel where he stood to pop open from the wall, less than an inch.

Back when he had first found it as a ten-year-old, it was as if a fantastic new world opened to him. As a young boy he hadn't realized the whole purpose of it, but as he grew, he could see the eye slots behind the wall, carefully hidden in the decor, and the narrow but usable space that led away down to the lower reaches of the palace.

He hadn't liked the idea that people could spy on him, but then he discovered no one seemed to use it. Dust built up and was never disturbed, except by himself, and cobwebs lined the corners and turns.

As he stepped into the darkness he sneezed, causing even more dust to blow up into his face. He'd not been here in over a decade, and it appeared no one else had either.

He pulled the panel closed, which left him in almost complete darkness. His ability to just about see in the dark was still there.

Karpenmor hadn't ever really understood it but it was never

completely dark to him in spaces like this — certainly after the first time he had been somewhere new.

It was as though his mind stored a map of it and he could follow it. His memories of the place showed him a view of it that let him walk safely despite the lack of any light source.

He descended through the narrow passages until he was in the lower levels. It was like he had only done it just the week before, every step he took leading him exactly to where he wanted to go.

The lever he reached out for was exactly where his memories showed it to be, even if they had been from a ten-year-old. He pushed on it and the secret door in front of him opened.

It was stiff from lack of use and scraped heavily on the floor as he pushed it open. Karpenmor wasn't worried someone would see the marks, the chamber he had arrived in had never appeared used or cleaned in all the previous times he had come there.

He went to a shelf on the side wall and ran his hands over it until he found the flint and steel before lighting a lantern he'd left in here. The large room he was in was left exactly as he remembered it.

39

TILLANDRA

She had expected Goran to be surprised, but the look on his face caused Tillandra to be concerned. He'd turned with a start at her voice, but now he was evaluating the situation in exactly the way she would if she was cornered.

There was both fear and a threat in how he was scanning her and the room, which she hadn't expected.

"How did you?"

"What? Find you? We all have some tricks up our sleeve, Goran."

"I'm not going back in a cell, and if you even think that's appropriate then you're not the person I thought you were."

"It was for your own good."

"You locked me up as a prisoner, which confirms what's been bothering me for a while."

"It wasn't you."

"Whose body was it then?"

He was right, and it was what had bothered her the most when they had first locked him up. But Zoran wasn't the person they wanted running around in Anderwell, or anywhere else — not now that they knew him.

"Yours."

"Exactly, but you chose to treat me like a prisoner."

"Your alter isn't exactly the nicest of people."

"Did he, or I, harm anyone?"

"Only you."

"You locked me up, and left me there, as though I'd committed a crime. Tell me what crime did I commit, Tillandra?"

The way he used her name, stung. It wasn't a kindly tone, but a cold and distant one.

"You were unwell."

"Like I thought. What was the long plan? Leave me in there until I rotted? Or did you have some other scheme in mind?"

"I just wanted you to be safe, to be you." Even she heard the lack of conviction in her voice. He was right, she'd known it all along, but she had continued with it anyway.

"So what now?"

She looked at his eyes. There was still no warmth in them. Tillandra had no idea what she'd expected to happen when she found him, she'd just wanted to make sure he didn't leave Anderwell.

Finding him had been the easy part, although it wasn't something she wanted him to learn about. She could see as if from his mask which meant she could do better than just see what city he was in.

She could tell where he was at any time and he would be none the wiser.

No one needed to know that. His trust in her would be completely gone if it wasn't already. Nor did she know what he would do with the knowledge.

Despite him appearing to be himself, Tillandra couldn't be sure what that really meant anymore, or how long it might last. Purple didn't understand what she did enough to read anything from him, all she could do was treat him for his injury.

"How do you feel?"

"Physically, or about what you did?"

"Physically."

"Fine, there's nothing wrong with me that a decent bed, some ale and a few good meals wouldn't fix."

"And a bath." Tillandra regretted it the moment it came out of her mouth. Her attempted humor fell flat and she stood awkwardly just inside the door to Ashantha's old rooms.

"There's no light-hearted way around what you have done, Tillandra. I can't stay around this place anymore."

"You can't want to be back out on the Circuit; you didn't like it before."

"I don't mean the Circuit, I mean with all of this, with you… and the others."

It was as though the breath rushed out of her. Tillandra had never considered that those in the family might choose to go their own way. It wasn't what they were here for, they were elevated to do a job. No one — that she knew of — had ever stepped away from their role.

"Leave?"

"I'm not one of you, this has been made abundantly clear to me now."

"That's not true, Goran."

"Isn't it? It was bad enough leaving me on the Circuit, but this… this is a whole other level."

"You were unwell."

"So you keep saying. When other people get unwell do you keep them underground in the cells?"

Tillandra didn't reply. They were circling back over the same ground. He was right despite her believing the circumstances were not normal.

Everything was different, every day. She had done what she thought was right at the time even though now it sounded terrible coming from him.

"Nothing to say. That says enough in itself."

"I'm sorry."

"For what? Not answering, keeping me prisoner, isolating me? What exactly?" The tone of his voice had become even sharper than before, and it was enough to break her out of the sense of sadness she felt toward him.

"Oh, come on, Goran. What exactly are you upset about? You were a mess, you know it, I know it, and before you cut your fingers to shreds playing your pity harp let's remind ourselves that no one but you knew anything about your alter up until now."

Now that she was started, she began to feel anger welling up inside.

"I've been your advocate the entire time from when you went rogue. It's easy to play your poor me routine now, but when the events happened in Nedor, how were we meant to know? You never said a word. Not a day since have you ever explained why that happened, or what was behind your… more interesting moments… so that we could understand.

"And regarding the cell, and keeping you locked up, if you think that was easy, then your head is stuck so far up your own behind you can't see daylight. I sat down there every day, watching over you, praying you'd come back to us.

"Everyone did, whether they wanted to or not didn't matter, I made sure everyone took their turn. And guess what, none of them complained, none of them judged you. Everyone was worried for you. It nearly tore Junther up when I asked him to use his touch on you."

"You did what?"

"That was how we got you back. Don't you remember?"

Goran shook his head.

"He held your arm to sedate you so that young Purple could heal you. She was in pain the whole time, but she never let up, and she doesn't even know you. These aren't people who disregarded you, Goran. We just had no clue what to do… and…"

"And?"

She looked at him. Maybe a touch of the harshness was gone from his eyes, maybe not. Perhaps she was getting through to him now.

"And Zoran is not the nicest of people to get along with."

"Hah. That's an understatement."

There was hope where this conversation was going. He was slowly engaging with her, not just attacking her, albeit very slowly.

"So where to from here?"

"Come back to the college, Goran. We need to sit down and work through all of this. It's a lot to get over."

"And if you don't like the answers or how it's going, what happens then? Some guards turn up and you put me back, or does Junther lay his hands on me again?"

"It's not like that at all. You're free now."

"Only because I took my own actions."

"How did you get out?"

Goran stared at her. He shook his head, and then something changed. She couldn't tell what it was, but he seemed colder again, like she'd lost.

Suddenly she felt a little woozy, like she needed to sit down. Goran helped her. She could kind of sense that. Everything felt different, and she was struggling to remember what it was she was doing here in Ashantha's old rooms.

That's right, she'd come to check on them, to see what to do about them. She sat on the bed he'd used and looked around the rooms as though she was forgetting something.

Had someone else been here with her? She felt like someone had, but it couldn't have been Ashantha, he was dead. It was all a little strange. She was feeling very confused, as though she didn't know what she was meant to be doing.

This room, she'd come here for a reason.

What was it?

She wanted to get up and then head back to her office, there was something very important she was meant to be doing, but her head felt a little heavy, she really did want to have a rest.

A small rest won't hurt, this bed will do.

Tillandra lay down on Ash's cot and before she knew it, she was asleep. It was only when she woke that her memory was clear again.

"The little gimp, how dare he."

It had been a long time since she'd worked with Goran on his skill, but she knew the feel of it when she was free of it. He'd convinced her to have a sleep and forget him.

That it had come to this nearly brought tears to her eyes. She'd always liked Goran, and he was right in many ways, they had treated him poorly, but it was for his own good.

Now he was totally distant from them and free. Should she just let him go -- to leave their Court? There was no precedent for that, none at all. At least now she was not going to feel bad about using his mask to track him.

40

ODAJEEN

*B*eing stuck in her room with the lifeless body of Lani was starting to get on Odajeen's nerves. At first her sense of guilt had been enough to fuel her patience, but that had dwindled now.

She did still feel guilty, but it wasn't enough to help her sit still for days on end doing nothing. To leave the room she'd have to take Lani with her, and that wasn't practical.

It had been several days since she'd suggested to Tillandra about using the amulet, and there'd been no response.

The fix was simple in her mind. *I said I'd risk myself to try the amulet, what's the harm in it?* Anything to try and help free Lani.

It was selfish, Odajeen knew, she wanted her life back, or at least part of it. She did feel very bad for Lani, given it was her own suggestion that had led to this, but she wanted to be free too.

Despite pondering other solutions, it seemed obvious to Odajeen that the amulet was involved in it. It had been out when Lani had become stuck, so to her mind that meant she'd used it, somehow.

Why not try the same thing in reverse?

Yes, there were risks, she knew that. Apart from Lani, anyone that touched the amulet died, but Odajeen had already accepted that risk.

No one else need be in here, or risk themselves, she could just try it herself. If she died, then hopefully Lani would get free, which was a win in one way.

Her life had been good, or good enough, and Odajeen knew she didn't have that many years left anyway. She wouldn't touch the thing deliberately, she wasn't that ready to give up, but if it happened, it happened.

What had the voice said? You will need to make a great sacrifice? It was something like that.

If saving Lani involved her sacrificing herself, then so be it. Odajeen had lived two lives, the second of which had been very fulfilling.

She had no idea if her first life had been a good one. It had ended from an event which wasn't good, but deep down she had a conviction that there was a valid reason.

That didn't really matter anymore. Her hope that Lani could access her memories and give her the details had been foolish and she'd put the girl in danger.

All the risks she'd taken to get Lani to Anderwell would be in vain if she couldn't help resolve this. As much as Tillandra had been kind to her, the current Mother Folly was prone to procrastinating over decisions.

She'd learned that much in the little time she'd spent here. Perhaps this was better than how Burgendetta had been? She'd never know now, but something needed to be done.

I could do it without anyone knowing. What can go wrong? If it kills me then the mask will fall off, that's what they said -- then she will be free.

Odajeen didn't want to consider that it wouldn't help. She needed to cling onto some hope.

The amulet was in its pouch on the table, exactly where it had been since Tillandra had got it back inside. All she had to do was tip it out so that it was available to Lani.

Someone else could put it back later, or Lani could if she came free.

Enough already.

She'd spent days debating it back and forth. Her decision was made.

Just get on with it, old woman.

Slowly she moved forward until she was perched on the front of the sofa. She paused again each step, testing her resolve. After taking several deep breaths she reached out until she could feel the edge of the pouch.

Turning it so it was far enough from the edge that nothing would fall off but still within her reach, Odajeen readied herself.

Pinching the other end of the small bag, Odajeen gently pushed against the hard lump inside. Little by little it moved away from her fingers until she heard the clink of it falling onto the table.

Odajeen kept hold of the pouch. It was the only thing she could use to pick it back up again if she needed to, not that she wanted to try that. All she could do now was hope that whatever magic was within that amulet could reach Lani.

Good luck, girl.

Unsure what to expect, The minutes passed with more excruciating slowness than ever.

There was a risk that the amulet would attract the Vrah, but Tillandra had told her the stones blocked them being able to detect it.

Or at least that's what she'd been told. She didn't care, what was more important was that Lani got free. Odajeen had to trust that all the extra guards she'd been told about could protect them anyway.

Then she began to sense something else in the room. It was a strange feeling, something she wasn't familiar with, and she didn't like it either.

It wasn't hard for her to understand what it was, especially after how Lani had described the amulet to them. It was doing something to her mind, she was just thankful that she couldn't see it.

From how Lani had explained what had happened to people she'd met, they all became enamored with the amulet and wanted to possess it, with invariably fatal results.

Just help her get out of there and stay out of my head.

Odajeen jumped slightly at the click of the door. She instinctively closed her fist around the pouch as though it would hide what she'd done.

Expecting it to be Tillandra, she waited for the berating, but no one spoke. Odajeen could sense someone come into the room, and the door closed quietly again.

"Hello?"

Whoever had just come in said nothing. Odajeen knew that wasn't a good sign, especially with the amulet out on the table.

She very slowly leaned her body forward a little at a time, trying to not show what she was doing.

"Who is it?"

Again, no reply. She didn't expect one now, but it was a way to cause a distraction from what she was thinking to do. Hopefully they wouldn't expect it from her.

Her fingers relaxed in her left hand, and she let the pouch unravel a little as she did it. If they were beholden to the spell it cast, then putting it away would be her best option.

Tillandra had made it sound like if you got the pouch close enough it almost pulled the amulet inside. Odajeen hoped that was true, and that she didn't touch it by accident.

As quickly as she could she shot her arm forward toward where she thought the stone was.

Odajeen could sense the man dash toward the table, and suddenly she could feel the grip of his hand around her wrist. "No you don't!"

Her fist closed tightly around the pouch again before he could grab it, and she felt his other hand start to prise at her fingers.

He was much stronger than her, and she had clung on to it as much as she could, trying to wriggle free of his other hand.

"HELP! Irdan!"

The man let go of her wrist and punched her in the side of her face. It was all she could do to not let go of the pouch. Her eyes teared up as the side of her face began to burn.

No one came to her help which wasn't a great surprise. If he was able to come through the main door, then there was probably no one close by.

Odajeen didn't know how long she could hold on. As soon as he had the pouch, he could take it and go. Out of all the things she was willing to accept, including her own death, someone else getting the amulet wasn't one of them.

That's it. My sacrifice.

It didn't matter if she died, she'd already accepted that. But he wasn't going to get it.

"You can't have it."

Her fist was hovering somewhere over the amulet on the table. She didn't know where but she needed to find it. With what strength she had left, she pushed downward with her fist.

The man was more worried about prising her fingers free than bothering with the movement of her arm.

She kept pushing toward the table. The ball of her palm reached the table, his hand was still wrapped around hers, keeping the rest of her hand off it.

He pulled her hand up slightly, his other pushing at her face, trying to cover her mouth. Odajeen reached forward to where she expected the amulet to be.

One of her fingers came free and then another. His strength was winning and now he had a grip on the fabric of the pouch as well. She didn't have long to hold out. But it meant his hand was outside hers which was what she wanted.

Why can't someone come when you need them?

With one last effort she pushed her arm a little more forward before she conceded. Everything changed in an instant. His grip loosened immediately, and she felt his body drop with a crash onto the table.

Her lungs were screaming for air, and she sucked in what she could. The crash of the table was the only sound apart from her in the room.

I've killed him.

Odajeen knew what she'd been doing. It was a last-ditch effort but the only way she thought to prevent him from getting the amulet.

All that noise must have been enough to get someone's attention. The door flew open on cue, right when she no longer needed their help.

41

LANI

*L*ani tried to imagine what was happening outside.

What do I look like? Is anyone doing anything to help?

She couldn't rely on anyone out there helping. None of them had put her in here, and in the end they might not know how to help.

Nothing had changed since she'd been in Barnen, no one else had her back, it was up to herself to look out for her own interests. She needed to solve her own problems.

Maybe Tillandra might prefer this, with Lani locked away she couldn't cause her harm, or threaten anyone with the amulet.

It's always about the amulet.

That stone was involved in her being in here, somehow she needed to connect to it to get out. But so far she'd had no luck finding it, or even a hint of it.

Which made sense. With her lost to them, she was certain they would put it back in the pouch. All she could hope was that at some point they might get it out, and that Lani would notice.

Now she knew what had happened to Burgendetta, Lani was ready to get free. While there'd be more things to learn, she had enough.

Out of nowhere she felt the air around her change. It was a strange feeling, not like a breeze or even a smell, but there was something different.

If she didn't know better, she would have thought someone else was in the space with her. Instinctively she turned her head in all directions as if to look before remembering she had no sight. Then her right forearm began to tingle like it did when the amulet was close to her and out of the pouch.

Is it out of the pouch?

The idea excited her, it meant that the outside did have an influence on her.

Connecting to the amulet was easier than she'd expected. All she had to do was turn her thoughts to the sensation on her arm and it was like the tendrils that connected to it were grasping her mind.

Slowly she followed the lines back toward the amulet. Lani could sense the outside, in the strangest of ways. But the barrier blocked her path. Even like this it was there, holding her back from slipping out.

Lani wanted to cry out in frustration. She felt like if only she could see then there'd be a clue as to how to get around it, but without the experience of Odajeen her senses weren't sharp enough to feel out what she needed to know.

She tried to reach Odajeen or anyone that might be near the amulet, like she had been able to way back when she'd been held prisoner in the cart. There were presences out there, wisps of them that she could sense, but nothing tangible to grab hold of.

It felt exactly as if she was in a cage and even though she could push her arms through the gaps in the bars, everything was just out of her reach. Occasionally something would brush over her, but she was too slow to grab it.

This is interesting.

"*Who is that?*"

Lani gasped in surprise. The voice wasn't familiar to her and there was something about her tone that concerned Lani. She was speaking into her mind, like the Lady in the Stone did.

Who I am doesn't matter so much, not now at least.

"Why not?"

You seem to have yourself in quite a predicament.

"How can you speak to me when no one else can?"

Through the amulet.

"Where are you? Can you help me?"

I'm not where you are if that's what you're asking. As for helping you, that I do not think I can do, not yet at least.

"Great. What do you want then?"

Don't you have quite the attitude?

The woman stopped speaking and Lani wondered if she'd gone completely. She wanted to ask but she also knew that sometimes waiting can be better than speaking. In the end the voice returned.

I would help you, but the stone is too weak. It needs to come home.

"The stone?"

In my amulet, the one which you have taken.

"I didn't take it; it was given to me. I didn't want it."

Yet you still have it.

"It bonded with me; I cannot let go of it."

I know. That was most unexpected.

"So everyone keeps saying."

Everyone?

"The other lady… the Jesters."

Jesters? I do not understand that. Who is the other lady?

Lani suddenly realized she'd said more than she should. The tone that had bothered her in the woman's voice was even more pronounced. She didn't know why it bothered her, but she needed to be a little more cautious.

Tell me, Lani, who are these people?

"How do you know my name?"

I know many things, Lani. I know where you come from.

"Where?"

I asked you first. Perhaps we can share our knowledge, that's what friends do isn't it?

"We're not friends."

But we could be, couldn't we? Friends can help each other. Wouldn't you like to know more about yourself? About how to disconnect from that amulet.

"Yes. You could just tell me."

But then what do I get for sharing that knowledge?

"Friends don't barter their sharing; they just help each other."

Again, the silence.

One thing at a time, Lani. You seem to be locked away somewhere strange, but I cannot work out what it is that's holding you there. I could help you if I knew what it was.

"I'm in someone's mind."

More silence.

How on my soul can you do that?

"I just can."

Then why are you stuck?

"This was different. I tried a different way and there's a barrier stopping me getting out."

Lani was being very cautious about explaining the exact facts behind her predicament. This woman was clearly someone like the Lady of the Stone — she had to be or how else could she be speaking to her? Yet where that other Lady brought with her a sense of peace and helpfulness, this one made Lani's skin crawl.

Or the sensation of her skin at least.

"If you can speak to me through the amulet, why haven't you done so before?"

You don't normally connect to it. The few times you have in the past I was not ready for it, I missed you.

"Missed me?"

I am not just sitting around waiting for you to randomly connect to the amulet. By the time I turned my mind to the amulet you had stopped using it.

"I do not like it at all."

You'd like to be free of it?

"Yes."

That can be arranged.

"How?"

You need to bring it to me, then I can help you remove it.

"Why can't you do it from here?"

It is not such a simple thing, child. And it is weak, I am hardly able to speak with you as it is. No, you need to bring it to me, then you can be free of it.

"Where is there?"

What?

"Where are you? You said I need to bring it to you, where is that?"

A long way from where you are. You need to come to Enderk, to En Carta."

"That's a long way from here. Couldn't you just meet me closer?"

Ha, if only I could. No no, you need to come here. It will be worth your while.

"How?"

"There's someone here you will want to meet."

"Who?"

Your brother.

Lani was stunned. She'd not forgotten the memory of Burgendetta talking about another child, but this confirmed it.

"Brother? I don't have a brother."

Ah, but you do, Lani. And he would be very excited to meet you.

"Who is he?"

Not now.

Lani wanted to know more.

"Who is he? Why doesn't he come and get me?"

I've told you already you need to come back here if you want to be free of the amulet.

"I've not been to Enderk, how would I get across the water?"

That I can help with. We have some people not far from you who can bring you back. You've met some of them before.

"You want me to go to those men who wanted to kill me?"

They don't want to kill you, Lani, sometimes they just get a little over-enthusiastic about their work.

"I don't trust them… Last time it was like they would just kill me."

You can trust me, Lani. They won't harm you; I very much want to meet you.

"I'll think about it."

Lani needed to stop speaking to this woman and try to get herself out. She'd confirmed the amulet had to be out of the pouch and this was valuable time Lani needed to try to free herself.

There was a warning in the back of her mind not to trust this woman, not to believe everything she said. It was so hard to know what to do stuck inside here.

Come to me, Lani. I can help.

Lani didn't reply and focused back on the sensation of where the tendrils were coming from. She sought a better connection, a way to feel the power of it like she had previously.

Suddenly everything changed. The barrier slammed back into Lani, and she was alone behind the mask. Sweat dripped down her face as though she'd been physically exerting herself and the silence was absolute.

What happened? Did they put it away again?

"Agh! How can I get out if you take it away!" she screamed into the empty space she was in.

Her emotions were a mess.

I have a brother! Is it true?

All at once her life was flipped on its head again. Why had her mother not told her about her brother? Or the Lady of the Stone?

42

TILLANDRA

Sitting on the edge of the bed, Tillandra wasn't sure what to do next. Her natural reaction was to hunt down Goran and bring him back, to try and talk sense into him. That was good in theory, but he had already manipulated her once, and he wasn't keen to listen to her, so her options weren't great.

If Junther hadn't left she could get him involved, but Goran wouldn't easily let him anywhere near him. Beantic was the person she needed but it was too late now, she was already on the road.

Why do I want to bring him back?

The change in him was very clear, he wasn't going to just change his mind from a conversation. Tillandra cradled her head with her hands and scrunched her eyes. She'd messed up again and this was the result.

She wanted to cry, to return to her place and lock herself in her room. Goran had been someone she trusted; she'd backed him all along and it hurt her that he'd not trusted her.

Just another mess I need to clean up. It'll just have to wait until we've solved the problem with the girl.

At the thought of Lani, Tillandra stood and decided it was time to check in on the two women. The closer she got to Odajeen's house, the faster she wanted to go, without understanding why.

Something felt wrong, but there was nothing to tell her what it was, or even why she felt that way. Humaas never needed to run but Tillandra came as close to it as she ever could.

Her natural strides at full pace were closer to a horse running than other races walk. It only took her a few minutes to traverse the city and arrive at Odajeen's building and she didn't even knock before bursting into the room.

What confronted Tillandra stopped her in her tracks.

The scene in the room was very different. Odajeen was sat on the edge of the sofa, beside Lani, with something gray in her hand.

A man's body lay across what had been the table and he wasn't moving. He looked familiar.

"What happened?"

"He tried to take the amulet."

Tillandra turned back outside and yelled. "Guards! Guards! Where are you?"

She turned back once she saw men popping out of buildings nearby. By the time she had reached the body, she already knew who it was, and a shiver ran down her back.

As she knelt down, Tillandra closed her eyes before flipping him over. She wasn't sure what she was surprised at more, the amulet she could see underneath him out of its pouch, or the face of Milfred lying there dead.

"What on Dharatan?"

"Mother?" Odajeen wasn't sure what the other woman had seen. "Who is it?"

"Milfred, Odajeen. What happened here?" She almost screamed at the blind woman.

"I told you; he came for the amulet."

"Why would he? I don't understand."

Men had begun entering the room. Irdan pushed his way through them. "Odajeen, are you alright?"

"I am now."

Tillandra turned to them all. "Back up and get out. We'll deal with the body later. Now!"

Irdan was reluctant to leave she could see, but when he saw the amulet beside the man's body, he too left, closing the door.

"Give me that pouch!"

As she looked at the amulet she noticed that the amber stone was glowing. Not just reflecting light but there was something deep inside it almost like the flame of a candle.

It hadn't done that before. Just another thing she had no knowledge about. Cautiously she opened the pouch and held the opening out as she moved it near to the amulet.

The pouch seemed to suck the amulet inside and closed itself around it. All the orange light that had been emanating from the amulet disappeared as she tied it off.

Tillandra stood up, her eyes still not believing what she could see and her heart breaking at the sight of her friend lying at her feet.

"Speak, Odajeen, and don't leave anything out!"

When the woman was done, Tillandra was no happier and none the wiser about why Milfred lay dead at her feet.

The facts seemed to speak for themselves. It wasn't as if Odajeen could go and get him and bring him here. He hadn't been around any discussions about the amulet — how did he even know about it?

She knelt and searched his body. He looked just like the man that had cared for her these last years, yet it didn't explain why he was there. Or why he was trying to take it.

Inside the front pocket of his tunic, she felt a small hard object. As Tillandra took it out she gasped.

"What?"

"It's one of their rings."

"Whose?"

"It looks like what I've been told the Vrah rings look like."

"Amber?"

"Yes, a small stone. There's something engraved underneath but not that I can read."

"What does it mean?"

"It means that things are not well here at all."

"Is it connected to the amulet glowing?"

"I have no idea, but I am going to ask the one person who might know."

"Who?"

"It doesn't matter. Can I trust you to not do anything like this again?"

"Yes."

Tillandra wanted to laugh. Her own voice had sounded like a teacher scolding a student and Odajeen's like the child in trouble. Except there was nothing funny about it at all.

"I'm going to put it back inside her tunic, and it should stay there unless I say otherwise."

"Of course." Her tone was more normal now.

Maybe if Tillandra hadn't deliberated on her decision so much none of this would have happened. None of that mattered anymore.

If Odajeen's idea had merit, nothing had changed with Lani. Perhaps it needed more time to work? Tillandra didn't know, and right now she wasn't willing to try it again.

"I'll leave more guards. If he was one of them then more might be coming." She looked at the older woman and realized that she was suffering for her decisions.

"You couldn't do anything else, Odajeen. He would have killed you once you'd heard his voice."

"It doesn't make it any easier. I feel useless sitting here."

"Right now, you stopped the amulet being taken, and that's a good thing. If she was alone, it would be long gone."

She left and headed back to the college, then climbed the many stairs up to the tower. Immediately she felt lighter and the weight of what was happening seemed a little smaller.

The power of the stones washed over her, and she took a few moments to let the feeling sink in before she laid her hand on the Mother Stone and sought out Thenis.

I am here.

"I need your help."

Doesn't everyone?

"The issue with Lani just took a side turn."

In what way?

Tillandra explained what had happened to the Lady in the Stone.

None of that is good. Not only the spy but the glowing amulet. Let me check with someone.

That the goddess was as concerned as she was didn't make Tillandra feel any better.

We think we know what the glowing is.

Tillandra hated how these conversations went. It was as if she had to drag the answers out.

"Are you going to tell me?"

Yes. The only reason we can think is that there was another connected to it.

"Another?"

Yes.

"Who?"

Yantarnaya.

"What?"

Like I am, talking to you here, through the cuts from the Citadel Stone, she could do the same through the amber. If you could see how the stones you hold look now, they too glow.

"That isn't good."

No, it is not. What is her status, she is hard to see.

"Nothing has changed. Odajeen's idea didn't appear to change anything. We've found no way to help her, which is why I am here."

There was a long silence, that worried Tillandra even more.

You must bring her to the stone.

"Midderbuilt?"

Yes.

"There's so much to do here I can't see how I can leave."

Why does it have to be you, Tillandra? She needs more than one person to protect her, especially after the attack you've just mentioned.

"Isn't it too risky?"

You've just told me they nearly got to it there. Either they would have taken her back to Enderk or killed her.

"Understood."

And soon, Tillandra -- do not delay. This is very serious, Lani must be protected from her, from them, at all costs.

Tillandra had nothing else to say and within a few moments she felt the presence of the goddess leave. As she broke her connection to the stones her calm dissipated along with it.

That's going to be quite a challenge.

She left the tower and distractedly headed out of the college down the main front stairs into the forecourt, almost walking into Carnus who had blocked her way.

"Where is Lani?"

His stern voice brought her back to the present. "What do you mean?"

"What have you done with her?"

"We've done nothing with her, Carnus. What on Thenis's name do you mean?"

"I don't believe in that name... Lani hasn't been around in many days. I have looked for her and she hasn't even been back in her own room."

"Oh."

"Tell me, where is she?"

"I think you better come with me."

HALLENDELL

Things had been relatively quiet for some time now and Hallendell had fallen back into a comfortable routine. After the attacks on the group known as the Watchers there had been no sighting of them.

The Master General in Nkuku had been floating around almost gloating since his quashing of the dissenters. She didn't doubt that he'd sent word back to his ruler in the capital Kamasa, that they had put an end to the group.

Except Hallendell knew better. Their leader, Watcher, was alive and in hiding, and he'd return. The opportunity to harm his organization hadn't come from anything the military had done; it was purely on the back of the Vrah attack.

Her time here was becoming a little meaningless. The goal wasn't for her to be here, but to make it to the White City, Kamasa, so she could get close to the Supreme Commander.

While she had visited it several times — an event considered very rare, that an outsider would be allowed in — she still struggled to see how she could leverage her position here to get her moved there.

The Jesters had never been even close to getting inside, and she'd achieved much more than anyone else ever had. And while helping the Watchers had been something, it didn't get her there.

Being tucked away in the Citadel wasn't all bad. She had little to do with what the rest of her colleagues had to deal with around Dharatan. This posting had been a relief to her once she'd settled in.

It was a harsh way to live but she was protected and, for all intents and purposes, ignored. That meant no eyes staring after her, no need to wear a costume all the time.

Hallendell was certain Tillandra understood that's why she never asked to leave. While it was a nice thought to think about returning to Anderwell and seeing all her colleagues, there were things she'd prefer to keep.

One of the freedoms she had in her role here was being allowed to walk the entire compound, like she was this morning. It was a routine that she kept up every day she could. Part of it was to check the marker in case Voince had left a message.

There had been none for more than a month, which was unusual, but then with Watcher out of the city there were few needing her help.

I need to remember to send them something when I can.

As she rounded a corner toward the side of the kitchens a small man, almost entirely covered in flour, stepped out the side door and sneezed. Hallendell rarely laughed, she'd never found life particularly amusing, but she couldn't hold back a chuckle that burst out of her at the sight.

"Funny, am I?"

The little man's long red hair stood out despite the clouds of white dust that had blown into the air. Every time Hallendell tried to look into his eyes to gauge him, she found herself unable. It was if her eyes kept slipping off his.

"It... it was just..."

"It's okay, I know how funny I look."

Hallendell felt embarrassed by her behavior. She shouldn't be judging anyone for how they look.

"You really are that uptight, aren't you?"

"Excuse me?"

"Relax, Hallendell, why don't you walk with me for a moment."

Now she was particularly perplexed. He used her name as if he'd known it forever and yet she couldn't ever recall meeting him before. It was entirely possible that he'd heard of her in the kitchens, but right now everything felt strange, putting her on full alert.

Who is this man? He's not Morskan either. Although there are other servants who aren't, it's still rare.

She cautiously walked behind the man as he left the doorway of the kitchen and headed toward one of the inner courtyards.

"Things are about to change around here."

Hallendell didn't reply, she wanted to keep the little man talking.

"Another amulet is about to surface, and it's going to be near to you."

"How do you know about the amulets?"

The man stopped and turned his head to look at her. His eyes bored in on her, yet she couldn't hold their gaze. "I know of many things, Hallendell, including who you are."

A chill ran up the middle of her back and the hairs on her arms prickled. "What do you mean?"

"Not here." He turned away and continued walking.

Hallendell was a little scared about what was happening, and while she didn't have a blade tucked away under her robe, she knew how to use her body well enough to defend herself.

Once they were completely alone on the far side of the courtyard, the man pushed himself up onto a bench and invited Hallendell to sit as well.

"I'll be fine standing. Who are you?"

"I have many names, but if you wish to have one, you can call me Hem."

"Hem? What sort of name is that?"

"What is any name? What is Hallendell? You people get so hung up on such things when they mean so little."

She didn't know how to reply to him. Everything about him upset her sense of calm: his look, the way he spoke, and the deep-set confidence that emanated from him. He was not threatened by her, or even being in the Citadel in any way.

"I know of the amulets, and of your group. You need to be more focused on getting the amulet before these people do."

"These people?"

"The Morskans. Don't waste important time playing dumb."

"Who are you?"

"I'm on your side, that's all you need to know. The rest you'll just have to trust me with."

"I'm not inclined to trust anyone."

He laughed at her, a good-natured laugh, and Hallendell looked around to see if anyone else had heard and was looking their way.

"Be at ease, we are perfectly safe here. For now."

"How do you know? These people are very suspicious."

"Yes, they are, but right now they cannot see us, nor hear us, I made sure of that."

"How?"

"That would be telling. I do not have long and wasting time explaining everything will just delay what else I need to do. We know another amulet is coming."

"Coming?"

"Returning from where we locked them away."

"Locked them away?"

He rolled his eyes. "We hid them all, in what we thought was a clever way, except it's breaking down. The amulets are getting free, and the one coming will head toward the White City."

"How do you know where it will go?"

"Because of whose amulet it was. It belonged to the previous Supreme Commander, and so it will seek out the current one."

"Let's say I get to it, what then?"

"You need to get it to Midderbuilt. That would seem to be the best place."

"Why?"

"Anderwell is becoming too dangerous for them, it will have to go to the very place we don't want it. Don't ask, I don't have enough time to tell you."

Hallendell didn't believe she could find anyone more frustrating to deal with than Morskan leaders, but Hem was running a very close second.

"You need to know about how dangerous they are."

She looked at him but didn't say a word.

"If it reaches the Supreme Commander and bonds with him, then touching it will kill you instantly. Not only that but you'll have to kill him to get it more than fifty feet away from him."

"Nothing challenging then?"

It was his turn to say nothing.

"And before that?"

"You can touch it but be warned it will impact you, even you Jesters will struggle to control it."

"So, I'd be damned either way."

"You'll need to improvise. At Midderbuilt it can be controlled."

"Right. If I can get it and take it there, to a city I am not allowed to enter, I'll be safe and my job done."

"That's about it."

"So where is it?"

"It hasn't surfaced yet, but it will within days. Word will reach here when it does, once you know you need to get there first."

"So just up and leave on a rumor?"

"It won't be a rumor. When it arrives, it will make an impact. You'll have to follow its trail and cut it off before it gets to Kumasa."

"Easier said than done."

"The last one came out of the desert. If this one follows suit, then that's where it will come from."

"That's nowhere near here. If it crosses from the desert to Kamasa it will go direct."

"Then you need to get there, however you can."

"Impossible."

"Nothing is impossible, Hallendell. You just need to find a way. Listen... People will speak of the jewel, it will not be able to be hidden, that's not in its nature."

"I don't take my orders from you, or anyone else."

"I will let Tillandra know and tell her what I have told you. She'll confirm what I've said."

"Don't worry, I'll speak to her as soon as I can."

"Good."

"Hem, that's your name?"

"Yes. Why?"

"Just that when I am talking to her, the description crazy little old man won't be very helpful."

"Just do it, Hallendell."

"I heard you."

"There's another thing you should know."

"What's that?" Hallendell could hear the skepticism in her voice.

"Be very careful handling the amulet. It can kill."

"Great."

"If it's bonded to its owner then no one else can touch it, to do so you die instantly."

"How will I know if it's bonded?"

"They won't let go of it easily, and it would need to be a ruler, or descendant of one."

"And if it isn't bonded?"

"You can touch it, but its effect is strong."

"What effect?"

A noise from the other side of the courtyard caught her attention, and Hallendell turned to look. There was no one there but it sounded as though the door to the kitchen had banged closed.

She looked back toward Hem, but he was nowhere to be seen. All that remained was a white outline of his butt on the bench and a small pile of flour under where his feet had hung.

I must be going mad. What a story this is.

44

KARPENMOR

The mustiness of the room was a little overpowering and Karpenmor had to take shallow breaths to let his senses adjust. He tried to remember how long ago it was since he'd last come here but could not.

That it was full of furniture and books meant at some point in time it had been used. Karpenmor had been coming here since he was young and seen no one else which meant such a time was long ago.

He had wanted privacy and that's what the room offered although it was a lot dustier than he remembered. There were several large sofas that he could relax into, perhaps even take a nap.

When he'd been smaller many of the other rooms down here were either locked or too heavy for him to open. Karpenmor decided he might investigate the level a little more before returning to relax here.

The main door to the room was as heavy as it looked, and the handle took all his strength to twist.

Definitely not been used in forever.

As he pulled the door inward the hinges groaned, but he was grateful that the door cleared the floor and didn't scrape like the other had.

Karpenmor only opened it enough to poke his head out, silencing the hinges, the noise seeming to echo in the empty hallway. Surprisingly there was a touch of light off in the distance such that he could see the length of the hallway to his right.

He didn't expect to see anyone but knew it was best to be wary just in case. Karpenmor didn't want anyone else knowing he was using this place; it might be the only safe place he had after his enthronement.

Just as he pulled his head back into his room ready to close the door, he heard a distant sound of footsteps.

Who else is down here?

His lantern would be an easy giveaway if someone else came to this hall. He killed the flame and placed it to the side before sliding out of the gap in the door. Closing it wasn't an option, the sound would only alert whoever was down here they weren't alone.

The footsteps had come from his right and that was the way he moved, using every trick he knew to keep his steps silent. If nothing else, years in the palace trying to evade and avoid the Vrah had taught him some skills.

The corridor turned sharp to the left just ahead, and he slowed before dropping silently to his knee. Anyone keeping an eye out would be looking at head height, so being much lower would help him avoid being seen.

Taking a long breath, he edged his head slowly around the corner. Down the hallway a sole torch sat on the wall throwing light in both directions.

Karpenmor could see no one, but there was a door opposite the torch.

Is someone in there?

To find out he'd have to approach the door but there were no other places to hide. If someone came out then he would be seen, there was no way to avoid it.

Instead, he chose to wait for a while to see what happened. A person or people were using this level for something, and he wanted to know more, but discreetly, at least for now.

Noise of the door being opened ceased all thoughts and Karpenmor stared, waiting to see who would emerge. A man stepped out of the room not bothering to close it.

The man turned in Karpenmor's direction, startling the heir, before he looked back the other way and headed off in that direction, taking the torch with him.

Uksod! What are you doing down here? And walking?

Karpenmor pushed himself to his feet and followed quietly down the hallway. At the doorway Uksod had just exited Karpenmor stopped and looked inside.

A man lay on a stone table, his hands and legs tied to keep him from moving. He didn't appear to be breathing.

What on Enderk? Who is he and what was Uksod doing with him?

Karpenmor left the room and headed in the direction Uksod had gone. He heard the distant sound of a door closing and hurried toward it.

Around the next bend he was less cautious than earlier, hoping the door meant Uksod had gone into a room.

Slivers of light shone out from under a door on his right. He tried to see through the keyhole but it was half clogged with dirt and what he could see showed nothing.

The light went out suddenly within and there was the sound of another door being dragged closed.

Was it a trap? Was Uksod inside waiting to see who had followed him? Surely he hadn't heard me, why would he expect anyone else to be here?

It didn't matter to Karpenmor anyway, he was the heir, he could go anywhere he liked. He'd be more interested in grilling the priest about how he was suddenly so miraculously up and about and yet hadn't informed Karpenmor.

He wrenched the door handle and pushed the door into the room. It was dark and hard to see anything except he could tell there was no one in there.

After fumbling around for a bit, he found the lantern and lit it again. Uksod wasn't coming back so he wasn't worried about being discovered now.

Ahead of him the wall was covered with a massive bookshelf. There wasn't another door anywhere to be seen on the two other walls, which meant he'd gone out through one in the bookshelf.

Karpenmor couldn't find it or how to open it. After probing and prodding for a period he killed the lantern, closed the door and retraced his steps.

He went back to the room with the prisoner. Inside were two large stone tables, running away from the door, with a gap between them that a person could walk down.

The man didn't appear to have moved and Karpenmor shook him. He could feel he was dead and pulled away, bumping into the table behind him.

Who is he, and why is he in here, dead?

The light from the torch outside didn't show any injuries, and there was no blood nor any giveaway smell. Before he could inspect further the sound of men's voices drifted down the hall toward him.

Quickly looking around the space he found a nook on the back wall he could squeeze into. He watched two men enter the room, both Vrah.

"He didn't even close the door this time."

"Who would care? No one else knows of his work down here."

"At least it's only one this time."

"And he isn't here. Finding him collapsed last time was most unusual."

"And concerning, the way One reacted meant something."

"Perhaps. They have a long history, sometimes I think One is as old as the Regent."

"Enough, let's dispose of this, and get back to our posts."

After untying the man they dragged him out of the room, slamming the door behind them, leaving Karpenmor in the dark.

He wriggled out of the space he'd squeezed into, scraping his elbow as he did so. Karpenmor rubbed the small wound and thought about what he'd just discovered.

The men had suggested Uksod killed the man and did it regularly. Was this related to how he had gotten so ill? He didn't seem to be bothered at all about taking the man's life.

The thought angered Karpenmor. Just more things the old man did which he wouldn't allow to continue.

Killing people, whoever they were, to further his own means wasn't acceptable. There was no solving it now, but he was adamant the old man couldn't continue to kill his people like this.

There would be a reckoning, no doubt an unpleasant one, but it could wait until after the ceremony was done.

After waiting for what he hoped was long enough, he left the room, closing it more quietly than those before him.

Quickly he made his way back to his own hiding room, and closed it tight, leaning against the door. He'd learned something today; he just wasn't sure exactly what it was.

He relit the lantern in here and looked around, the idea of peace and quiet a distant memory.

45

KARPENMOR

Karpenmor dropped into the sofa nearest him and tried to make sense of what he had just learned. Uksod was well enough to get around and was faking his illness.

That was one thing and concerning in its own right. But not only that, he had killed someone in an unusual manner and doing so was what previously had led to his illness.

What magic are you using, Uksod? And to what end?

The only way he was going to get answers would be to confront the old man, but for now he wasn't ready to do that. Knowing what he did gave him an advantage, something he could use should he need to.

He stood up brushing off the dust from the old sofa and stretched his back out. While he had been down here for some time he wasn't yet ready to head back, his head wasn't calm at all.

For the first time since he'd come in he stood, and took in his surroundings. Not completely unlike the room Uksod had gone into, this one had at one time been someone's study.

There were shelves of books lining most of the walls, a desk and chair on one side, and many half-burnt candles on the desk, shelves, and ledges.

Intrigued by the idea that someone worked down here doing an unknown task, Karpenmor decided to investigate more.

Dust covered everything, not just speckles but layers of it. He had to brush it off the spines of the books which caused him to cough.

None of the ones he had pulled had any titles, they simply had a number carved into the spines. He traced his finger along the highest row he could reach until he got to the left-hand end. The first book there was labelled eighty-four.

He pulled books from different spots randomly and took them over to the desk as well as his lantern and began to flick through them.

To have such a series of records here, they must be about something that was important.

For all his time in the different libraries both in the palace and the Vrah compound, none had books labeled this way. If nothing else, they had taken his mind off of Uksod.

The books he had chosen were ledgers of some kind, summarized periodically with notes about the trade being recorded and events surrounding it.

～

… Extreme winter weather caused significant delays in the deliveries reaching Ponte. The milder conditions allowed them to reach Comerc over the land bridge without further delays…

～

Comerc? How come I have never heard of that place?

Any tiredness or wooziness disappeared from Karpenmor as his inquisitiveness grew. He read through every book he'd pulled from the shelves, finding most of them referred to this place.

Karpenmor couldn't recall any map or book he'd studied before mentioning it, which was even more curious. Before he put the first batch back on the shelves, he scratched their numbers into the desk using a letter knife.

Every ledger he flicked through recorded all the goods sent to this place and in return all the coin and jewels that returned. It didn't take him long to realize that Comerc was a place of trade.

Maybe it's a trader's market and not a city or town?

The fact the land bridge had been destroyed made any such trade difficult if not impossible. *Which might explain why this sort of ledger no longer exists.*

Karpenmor stood, needing to stretch himself. He'd been hunched over the ledgers for quite some time. He had no desire to leave; what he wanted was to find out more about Comerc.

All the books he could see in this room were all labeled the same way, which wouldn't give him the answers he wanted. He pulled at drawers and shuffled through random papers without succcess.

Tucked in the corner of the room in the dark he saw a stack of scrolls, wedged upright into a box-like stand. The tallest of them was dry and he opened it very slowly onto the desk.

The paper was close to cracking and once opened he weighted the corners, so it didn't curl back up too quickly.

Whoever had created the map had painstakingly outlined every part of Enderk, places Karpenmor hadn't ever been. The level of detail contained within was amazing to him; he hadn't seen anything similar in any of the libraries above.

As his eyes moved left across the map past En Carta he saw that the map didn't end at the coastline. The land bridge was drawn in detail west of Ponte and joined with what he knew as Dharatan.

There his question was answered. Labeled on the nub of land poking out toward Enderk was the location Comerc. Roads ran to it and out from it including across what looked to be a border.

That was our land!

He stared at it for minutes, taking in the revelation that Enderk had owned land on what they now called Dharatan, and not just an outpost, this looked to be a city with lands around it.

We controlled the land bridge.

Suddenly things fell into place for Karpenmor. He had heard people discuss that Enderk had lost so much after his father's disastrous expedition to Dharatan, but there was never any detail.

Perhaps that detail had been suppressed or lost over so many years.

Or perhaps it had been hidden as Karpenmor had never read about it or seen any other maps showing it. *Uksod's work no doubt.*

The pain of losing your own city and people, cut off and isolated after the land bridge collapsed, would have been immense.

What happened to the city… to our people?

The peace he had sought was lost now. Karpenmor wanted answers, he wanted to know more. The person who would know was Uksod and, ill or not, he'd need to answer.

46

KARPENMOR

As he made his way back up to his room through the hidden passage Karpenmor pondered what it was that bothered him the most.

That Uksod was playing him for a fool, pretending to be sick when he wasn't, or that there was more to it than that. That perhaps the priest wasn't working for him but against him.

Why else is he hiding what he's doing?

His natural instinct was to rush in and confront him about it, but he was beginning to learn he needed to think first and act slower.

He laughed. *When did I suddenly become so thoughtful?*

Without even trying he'd already begun to change. Once he was High Prince his whole life would be about determining how to handle matters -- day after day.

There was some benefit in knowing that Uksod was well — Karpenmor would be able to better gauge his loyalty and support, by proposing things to the old man that would force him to show his hand.

What was more intriguing though, was the information he'd learned from the map. It wasn't dated, but it didn't take too much to work out that it was prior to the collapse of the land bridge. It raised so many questions.

How long after the collapse of the bridge had the city remained populated by Derks? Had the Ngaherians captured it and renamed it their own? Were there Derks still over there?

It was just another matter to discuss with the old man. Why hadn't they kept it? Only Uksod would know; he would be the only person that knew anything dating back that far.

We have a lot to talk about, old man.

Karpenmor was thankful that he'd gone off on his exploration today. While he didn't get the rest and peace he'd sought, he felt invigorated by what he now knew.

As he stepped back into his room, Karpenmor could see it was already dark outside. He'd been gone much of the day; no doubt people would be searching for him.

He picked up a goblet of wine and drained it quickly, his mouth parched. He lifted the bar on his door and opened it.

The guard outside turned to look his way.

"Send for some food, I would have my dinner served up here please."

Just a nod, before he turned and headed off. Karpenmor recognized the man's face, he was one of the guards that had cleaned up after Uksod.

And here he is guarding me. Who can I trust?

He remembered the image of the dead man on the stone table, causing bile to rise in his throat. He refilled his wine cup and washed it away.

Uksod seemed to have no reservations about harming others, it was a major difference between him and Karpenmor.

That needs to change. His ways aren't my ways. And it's my direction they must follow!

Karpenmor knew the transition was causing issues within the palace and he wanted Uksod's knowledge, but he didn't want the priest running things, not even small things.

That might hurt the man's pride, but there was no way around it.

The more he saw how Uksod did things, the quicker Karpenmor wanted the change.

I'm sure he isn't working against me.

He could have let one of the other families in, but he hadn't. For hundreds of years, he'd kept Karpenmor's father alive in the Amber Room, and ruled with a firm hand, keeping everyone else at bay.

What does he get from all this?

Having Vrah guards doing Uksod's dirty work came from one place, One. The priest and the leader of the Vrah had worked together for a long time.

Karpenmor couldn't be entirely sure about One's loyalty either. As the leader of the Vrah he'd been directly connected to Uksod for his entire career. Changing his allegiance could also prove to be difficult.

How could I replace him? I certainly couldn't outfight him.

As far as he knew it was an earned position, one which was only granted when the previous leader died. *Is that what must happen? I will not do that.*

Perhaps he needed to find a way to test One's loyalty as well. How, he wasn't sure. A knock at his door brought a servant with his meal, something he no longer wanted.

All this reflection in his head wasn't helping, causing his stomach to churn. He left the food on the table where it had been served and headed toward the Vrah compound. He wanted to search the library for information on Comerc.

On the way he decided to see what One knew about it. Word of his arrival traveled fast, and One came to meet him before he'd reached the leader's office.

"Highness."

"One, sorry to bother you so late."

"It is not so late, Highness. What can I help you with."

Karpenmor didn't want to be standing in the hallway, it seemed an odd way for him to be greeted.

Was the man hiding something in his office? Or was he trying to control the meeting?

"Your office perhaps?"

There was a slight pause before One nodded and turned, beckoning Karpenmor to lead. "After you."

Karpenmor felt something wasn't quite right but couldn't pick up on what it was. The office smelled stuffy and there was a hint of incense in there, not that he'd ever seen One burning any.

The room was empty, and One seemed a little more comfortable when he returned to his side of his desk. Uksod had been here recently, the incense confirmed that.

He doubted few other priests spent enough time in this office to leave that aroma. Karpenmor wondered what it was the two of them were up to.

"How can I help, Highness?"

"I have some questions for you."

"Would you like to sit?"

Karpenmor did, even though the offer didn't seem genuine from One.

"Have you spoken to Uksod about the team near Anderwell?"

There was a pause before One answered. He appeared to be considering his words carefully. "I have not yet, Highness."

"And no more word from your team near there?"

"No, Highness. The target still appears to be inside."

"The young woman, or the amulet?"

His directness was catching One a little off guard. "The amulet, Highness. Although my latest directive was to try to bring the young woman back as well."

"From?"

"Sorry, Highness, what do you mean?"

"Where did you get this latest command from?"

"Uksod, Highness, it was he who was giving us our instructions about this matter."

"But he has been unwell for many weeks, so your instructions must have been that way for all this time?"

One's eyes narrowed very slightly, but enough for Karpenmor to see that wasn't correct. Things were happening around him that he wasn't aware of. The reminder he'd given himself before coming tonight was valid, he had to be vigilant of everyone.

"Yes, Highness. Just before he was unwell, he had advised me that were it possible, she should be brought back as well."

"And you've sent that message to your squad? How long does that take usually?"

"Many weeks' hard riding once they land, Highness. It all depends on how long the boat trip takes."

"I see."

Karpenmor wasn't convinced. "Tell me, One. Why is it your assassins are failing at this task so badly? It's been many weeks that they have known this woman is in Anderwell, if she's even still there, and yet they're unable to get her and bring her back to us."

There was no hiding the glare this time. Karpenmor knew he was challenging the Vrah leader, but that was his job. When he was enthroned all of this was his to command, and it was as good a time as any to test him.

"A very good question, Highness. And one I do not have an answer for. I have sent more squads to assist, and one of them will return immediately with more information."

"That seems a very slow process."

"It is, but I do not have a better way to get information."

"Of course. I couldn't find out much about the city last time I looked at our research. Perhaps we need to find out more about it?"

"I hope after this mission is over that we will have exactly that, Highness."

Karpenmor stood abruptly. "Thanks for your time."

"Highness," One replied as he too stood.

Karpenmor saw himself out and slowly retraced his path back to the main palace. He had no patience to search through books tonight, his mind was again circling over all the things happening — not the least of which was knowing that Uksod had been in One's office not very long before him.

47

HALLENDELL

$\mathcal{H}$allendell came wide awake, unsure what it was that had woken her. From how dark her room was she could tell it was still deep in the night.

She braced herself ready to spring up and tried to detect if there was anyone else in her room. Nothing moved and she couldn't hear anything unusual.

Very cautiously she moved herself until her feet were on the floor and sat there trying to work out what the danger was. Her instincts rarely let her down.

Without making a sound she crept to the door, placed her ear up against it and listened for any noise from outside. The door was still barred which would block anyone forcing themselves in.

Was that it, had the door rattled with someone trying to get in?

She couldn't hear anything outside. It didn't mean that wasn't what had happened. They could have left once they detected the door wouldn't open.

Next, she checked her window. It was still open, but exactly as she had left it. It would take someone as agile as her to get in that way, and she was pretty certain she'd have known if someone was coming in that way.

A blood-curdling scream broke the stillness and Hallendell knew exactly what it meant.

There was no way she'd get back to sleep now and if the soldiers were torturing someone at this hour it was important. She was curious to know more.

Without lighting her lantern, she fumbled around until she found her black robe and slipped out of her room.

While it wasn't the first time that someone had been tortured within the Citadel, it was unusual for it to be done in the middle of the night.

Not that it would bother the Master General here in Nkuku — he derived great pleasure from it, especially if it was related to catching Watcher.

Usually, the sounds were muted by the activities of the day. Hallendell reached the rampart level and crossed over, heading in the direction of the prisoner cells.

She paused and considered seeking out a rat. She did need to talk to Tillandra about what the man Hem had told her, as she had struggled with how much to believe.

With the soldiers busy below it would be a good time to do that... except she wanted to learn why they were doing it now. Something told her it was important.

She moved cautiously, using the shadows to hide herself from other eyes and headed toward the screaming.

More screams followed the first, with no pattern to them. The closer she got to the location of the cells she could hear someone talking with force and the sound of crying.

It only confirmed to Hallendell that someone was being tortured and increased her desire to know who.

The cells were a roofed rectangular building with a wide corridor down the middle. All ten cells faced the corridor with both ends open making it easier for soldiers to monitor without having to be inside.

Deftly she lowered herself down from the walkway onto the roof of the cell block. Crouching, Hallendell stepped silently along the ridge line.

Each of her footsteps were deliberately slow, allowing her to manage her weight and any chance of sound. A third of the way along she lay down, beside a vent in the tiled roof, and placed her ear to the small gap.

"He's gibbering."

"Do not kill him without him giving up what he was doing."

"Thieving, no doubt."

Hallendell didn't recognize the voices, but she knew they'd be soldiers. She wished she could see who it was they were hurting.

"We've seen none of these Watchers in ages." The name was said with clear scorn. "If he's in the city, then he's up to no good."

There was a brief silence, then the clang of metal and a hiss, seconds later there was another scream. It sounded as though it was right below her.

"What are you doing? Tell us, you cannot survive this."

A grunt followed and sobbing. Then another scream as what Hallendell guessed was a hot metal prod was branded onto the prisoner.

"Woman."

"What? Hold up, don't do that yet. What did you say?"

The man who was being tortured sounded horribly unwell. "Woman."

"What woman? What do you mean?"

"Tell the woman. Watcher needs her."

Hallendell felt a chill run down her back. This was way too close to home for her. The man sounded delirious now, he must think he was keeping his message safe, not handing it to his enemies.

"Quiet, you lot."

"What woman?"

"The one that spies."

She heard the sound of slapping against skin, more grunts and a whimper or two.

"Funny skin, tall. She watches for us. In the palace. Get it to her. Watcher... needs her."

"What did he say?"

"You heard him as good as I did."

"You... give him water, keep him alive. And you, watch him and don't let him die. I need to get the Master General, he'll want to hear this direct."

Hallendell heard footsteps coming underneath her. Then the man stopped, and she heard him again. "And you two, perhaps it might be wise that we guard the tower that the witch lives in."

It was all she needed to get her moving again. Hallendell had no idea who it was that was below, but it wasn't hard to guess that one of Watcher's men must have been captured.

Her problem now was staying safe. Even if she could talk herself out of this, which she doubted, she wouldn't be allowed out of the Citadel anytime soon.

Blast you! She stared down at the roof. There was no time to linger, she moved as quickly as she could over the roof back to the walkway, clambering up and then sprinting back toward her room.

While the guards wouldn't be in a rush, expecting her to be asleep, they wouldn't dally either. Being up higher than them and fast on her feet, she easily beat the guards to her tower.

She barred the door and dragged her robe over, blockading it as best she could. Quickly she made up a pack of things she couldn't leave behind. Her costumes were among those things.

As an afterthought she dragged her bed over to the door as well. It wouldn't delay them forever, but with that wedged between the post in the middle of her room and the door it would buy her extra time.

They'd come, she knew that. There was no love for her here amongst the soldiers, and there'd already been suspicion of her before. That the Master General enjoyed her skills wouldn't be enough now.

His action would be swift. Hallendell clambered out the window of her room and made her way down, leaving the way she did so often. This time she took her kabel rope with her as she didn't expect to be coming back anytime soon.

With her cover blown the need for subtlety and discretion was gone, so she set off quickly toward the one person she could trust. Ducking patrols roaming the city was easy, but Hallendell's heart still pounded.

If she was caught now there'd be the same treatment for her that she'd heard in the cells. Her colleagues would not be happy with her, but she had no choice.

As she rounded the corner, she could see the Good Companion Inn was sitting quietly without any soldiers nearby. Hallendell rushed toward it and leapt higher than most could to grab at the tall fence surrounding the courtyard.

With her athletic abilities, her feet ran up it as her hands pulled her upward, and she flipped up and over, landing heavily on the ground below.

What she hadn't counted on was the large dog walking toward her, snarling. Then it began to bark a warning to all. It was preparing to attack and Hallendell had nothing at hand to fend it off with.

The animal wasn't quite half as tall as her, but it was thick across the chest and legs, and its jaw was massive, the drool visible even in the poor evening light.

It barked several more times before the door at the back of the inn flew open, banging against the wall as it did so. Two people came out, both brandishing blades, although that wasn't where Hallendell's eyes were focused.

"Looks like your thieving is about to stop once and for all." A man's voice.

"Get Voince, urgently."

"I'm here." Hallendell recognized the voice. "Is that you Hal?"

"It is. Think you can call off the beast?"

The man whistled and the dog seemed to ease a little. "Monster, back!"

Another whistle. The dog looked almost disappointed but walked backward several steps before turning and heading to the man. Hallendell relaxed and looked at Voince.

"This can't be good?"

"It isn't and I don't have much time."

"Quick, come then!"

48

HALLENDELL

$\mathcal{V}$oince had her helpers moving within minutes of Hallendell finishing explaining what had just happened. Some were wrapping food and grabbing skins.

"Load one of the horses we have for couriers, she'll be needing a fast one."

The youngster scurried away out of the kitchen toward the courtyard out back.

"Poor Lospa."

"Who?"

"The one they caught; I know him."

"Sorry."

"You'd probably recognize him if you saw him. He was a bit slow on things but loyal to Watcher. He's been running messages for months now."

"They're close to coming back then?" Hallendell realized she wasn't on top of what was happening.

"Yes, it seems they've got everything in place. Means the Master General must have word somewhere. I'll need to let him know, they have a leak, or they've worked out where they're coming from."

"I wish I could help."

"You're burned now, there's nothing we can do but get you out of here."

"Do you know the little old man I spoke of?"

"I don't, sorry."

"I should speak to Mother; I need to get answers."

"Not tonight you're not."

A young man in his late teens walked into the kitchen with a serious look on his face but waited for Voince.

"What is it, Joime?"

"Bad news."

"Spit it out."

"City gates are all locked, and there seems to be increased patrols in the street."

"They know you've gone. Sheeves!"

"What next then?"

The Keeper turned to the young man. "Go tell them to unload the horse, we'll need to get under the walls first. Send me Bernica."

"Yes, Voince."

Within a few minutes a young girl aged about twelve arrived. "What you need?"

"I need you to get to Draflo, outside."

"Okay."

"Tell him we'll want a horse, ready to run, within an hour. We'll be loading it. Got that?"

"Horse, one hour, a runner which we'll load."

"Good, now go and don't get caught!"

The youngster didn't wait, she turned and started off in a run out the back.

"She'll be alright?"

"They'll never see her, she moves so fast. And being so small she can duck through the shadows without being seen. Even if they do, she plays the homeless orphan so well they have no idea she's a runner for me."

"Is she?"

"What?"

"An orphan?"

"Lord no, she's one of mine."

Hallendell's face screwed up in confusion.

"She's my youngest. Before your time here."

"I never knew."

"No need to tell and the less who know, the safer she is."

Hallendell just nodded. "So what am I going to do?"

"We're going to smuggle you out through one of the tunnels. Once you're under the walls you'll have a horse and some supplies, but you'll be on your own."

Voince exited the kitchen leaving Hallendell alone for the first time since she'd arrived.

This is madness. How on Dharatan did this happen? I was so careful; it wasn't even my fault.

As much as she wanted to be annoyed at the lad that had been captured, she couldn't. It wasn't his fault, most would have given up their secrets under such treatment.

Her life was changed now, and for better or worse, what she had to focus on was getting away safely. While she waited, she rifled through her bag and grabbed some of her items to change her appearance.

Hallendell even caught Voince a little by surprise when she returned.

"Smart move, it took me a good moment to work out what was going on. In this dark, you'll not be recognized by anyone except up close. Shame about your height."

"I'll accommodate for it."

"It's time to go, the longer we wait the harder it will be."

"I'm ready."

"You're going to need to lug a bag, I'll take the other. I don't want more than the two of us out there together."

"I'm fine. Let's go."

A swivel panel in the back courtyard wall let the two women out into the alley that ran down the southern side of the inn. It was dark and empty, and they hurried along it slowing at every intersection to check they were free to cross.

Hallendell could tell they were heading to the southwestern side of the city. Getting through the inner walls was easy enough, there were friendly buildings that had passages to the outer city.

That was where things got more difficult. Voince raised her hand behind to stop Hallendell.

"Wait."

Hallendell watched her squat down in the shadow and followed suit. A minute or so later a group of four soldiers passed by, far enough across the roadway that the women remained hidden.

Voince waddled forward and poked her head around the corner, in both directions before standing. "Quick."

She darted across the road into the alley directly across from them with Hallendell right behind her, only slowing to navigate the barrels and detritus littering it. "That's not usual."

"I didn't think so."

"There'll be more, they're expecting you to run."

"Maybe I should hole up and wait."

"That just makes it dangerous for us all. If someone gives you up, we're all done."

"True"

Hallendell knew the Master General would hunt her until his dying breath. As much as he'd appreciated her skills as his jester, she knew he was ruthless and wouldn't spare any resources to make her pay.

Several blocks from the outer city wall Voince slowed and turned into a very narrow lane if it was even that. They both had to travel along it sideways to get to the doorway she wanted.

Voince knocked four times then waited. After half a minute she repeated the four knocks. A short while later there were two knocks on the other side. Voice replied with three knocks.

Hallendell could hear the sound of sliding bolts, then the door began to open. A pair of eyes and a long beaky nose peered around the edge of it.

"It's you." The man quickly opened the door.

"No time to explain, I need the tunnel."

"Not tonight."

"What do you mean?"

"There's soldiers outside the wall, waiting for anyone coming out."

"What?"

"Get in here, can't have you being seen."

They stepped into the dimly lit room and the man closed the door, before sliding one of the many bolts on it closed.

"This isn't good news. It means they're aware of our moves."

"Just lucky I reckon. This aint no city of fools despite what we might think. They're just covering any places that someone might want to use to get out."

"Maybe." Hallendell could see Voince thinking through what was going on.

"What about your girl?"

Voince turned to look at her sharply. "What do you mean?"

"Wasn't she going out the tunnel."

Voince laughed. "Not that one, she uses one that others can't -- or not easily."

The Keeper then scratched her chin before turning to the man.

"You know the long rabbit hole?"

"Yes."

"Get there and when Bernica comes back, tell her to go back. She's to let Draflo know the rider is coming through there."

The skinny man raised his eyebrows at Voince. "You sure?"

"It's our only way, now go."

He looked at the door, "You bolt all of them for me?"

"Done, now go!"

Hallendell started sliding the other five bolts closed on the door they'd come through. "Why was he worried?"

"You won't like it, but it's the only option you have."

"Just tell me."

It's a tunnel, of sorts. Narrow and you'll have to slide along on your front. What are you like in small spaces?"

"I'll cope."

"Bernica will come back and help you drag your bags; you'll have to push one in front and drag one behind you. It'll be slow going but it's all I can do."

"Maybe I just leave one behind."

"Your stuff?"

Hallendell shook her head.

"And you'll need some supplies, we'll have to halve what I was going to give you but you need some else you'll not get far."

Hallendell knew she'd said yes to this, but her stomach was flipping. Of all the things she hated, small, confined spaces was something she could only tolerate for very short periods of time.

My only other choice is to wait, but she knew they wouldn't rest until they found her. Just like they had with Watcher.

"Let's go."

~

The entrance was in a basement of a building across the road from the outer wall. Voince wasn't joking when she had said it was narrow. No wonder her daughter was the one that went through it.

"This looks fun."

Voince didn't reply but picked up the lightest of the two bags and pushed it into the hole.

"Berncia was told to come back for you when she's delivered her message. She'll make much better time than you, you just need to push on as far as you can on your own."

"Okay."

"Safe travels, Hall."

They hugged. "Thanks for your help, I'll see you when I see you."

"I hope none too soon, now be gone with you!"

~

The air in the hole tasted of damp soil, and Hallendell's shoulders ached from constantly rubbing against the sides of the tunnel.

It was dark, her bags blocking any light that might have helped. The process of pushing one bag forward, dragging herself after it while pulling the other one behind her with her right foot, looped through its handle, was slow.

Her face was sweaty, and she'd made the mistake of wiping it several times. Now it was covered it with dust and grime. Twice already she'd had to pause and talk herself calm about the narrow space.

Hallendell knew it was just in her mind, but it was a compelling fear that had to be managed. At the moment it was held at bay, but she had no idea how much further she had to go.

The young girl hadn't returned yet, which created more anxiety. *What if she had been caught? Or wasn't coming?* Everything had changed in a heartbeat, but she could trust Voice, that she knew.

She stopped again and closed her eyes, taking slower breaths and letting her calm return. It took longer than it should but once it was done, Hallendell pushed the bag forward and slid after it. Her knees were beginning to complain as well, no doubt the skin on them was close to breaking.

Suddenly the bag in front was tugged at and instinctively she pulled back on it.

"It's me, I'll take it now."

"Oh, thank Thenis."

"You've done well, we're about halfway."

It should have made Hallendell happy, but the thought that she still had so long to go made her want to cry. She let go of the bag and watched it move away from her and began to try and follow. The youngster seemed to be much quicker at this than her, and before she knew it there was only darkness ahead of her and the distant sound of the sliding bag.

49

TILLANDRA

*T*illandra still hadn't had time to process everything that had been going on. The thought that Milfred had been working against her had never crossed her mind.

They were meant to be safe in Anderwell, this was their place where others left them alone. But if Milfred was working for the Derks it meant nothing was safe.

Who else is there?

She didn't have time to think about it right now, but it only high-lighted the importance of getting Lani away from there. Thenis's words were doubly as important now.

While she hurried with Carnus to Odajeen's, she diverted to gather others. All of them seemed equally perplexed about what they were doing but she only told them to follow and more would be explained when they were there.

At Odajeen's door she stopped and turned, blocking their way. "What you'll see in here will surprise you." She looked directly at Carnus. "Not everything will appear as it seems, but there's been a very recent turn of events that is very concerning. No one is to touch anything or anyone, understood?"

Carnus didn't nod like everyone else, but it didn't matter. The pause before going in was as much for her as any of them. Tillandra needed to brace herself for what she had to face again.

"Follow me."

One by one Toolet then Kooka, Leo and Carnus came into the room. Irdan had been nearby, but she waved him away, there was no need to explain all of this to him.

There was a collective gasp when everyone saw the body on the floor.

"Who is it?" Odajeen had turned toward them.

"It's me, Odajeen," Tillandra answered, "and I've brought some of the others."

Carnus moved toward Lani and stared at her. He was less worried about Milfred's dead body on the floor than the others.

"What's wrong with her? She's not moving."

"She's alive, Carnus. Let me explain."

If a look could harm, then his was stabbing her.

"Why don't you all find a spot to sit or stand and I'll tell you what I can."

Carnus was the only true outsider and there was no way Tillandra could explain the situation without at least giving away some detail she'd have preferred to have kept quiet. Kooka knew how things operated but some of what she told would have been new to him as well.

"She's in her head?" Carnus looked at her like she was as mad as one of their broken.

"Lani's mind is, yes, as ridiculous as that sounds."

"What is the fix, Mother?" Toolet asked.

"Then…" She pulled the word at the last second. "I have discussed this with the Lady of the Stone…"

"Who?" Carnus interrupted.

"… I cannot discuss everything with you, Carnus. At least not now. Please just listen."

She let her words hang there for a moment before continuing.

"The amulet is involved in all of this, and him." Tillandra pointed to Milfred.

"What happened?"

"He wasn't who we thought he was, Toolet. He had this." She held out the amber ring.

"No way."

"Yes, and he came in here to take the amulet. Odajeen tried to keep it from him and in a struggle, he touched it. Leaving him like this."

"Dead." Leo was staring at the man on the floor, his eyes wide open.

"Yes, Leo. I can't explain it all but contact with the amulet has been made again, and now him. It's not safe for Lani to stay here. Which is why you're all here."

She looked at each of them slowly.

"Lani needs to be taken to Midderbuilt, to the Citadel Stone."

Toolet gasped. "How?"

"Not easily. The trip through the desert isn't easy at the best of times, it will be much slower with a wagon. Lani must be kept hidden, at all times. Kooka, that's why you're here."

"You need a driver?"

"We do. While your time with the Fool's Cart is up, I'll have you help this one last time."

"Of course, Mother."

"You can't go without Odajeen, she's connected to Lani until this is fixed. Irdan and Vefed will follow wherever Odajeen goes, but Carnus, I would ask you to go and be Lani's guardian."

"I would go anyway, that is my task."

"Good, because there will be danger in this."

"Do you want me to go, Mother?"

"No, Toolet, you're needed here."

"Does that mean you're going, which is why I am here, so I know where you'll be?"

"Slow down, Toolet. I am staying here, I cannot be away, nor can you. But... we do need one of us on this journey."

Tillandra turned to look at Leo.

"Him?"

"It has to be. You've taught him how to use it haven't you?"

"Only just, he's very green."

"He'll have to make it work, he's the only one that we can spare."

"I'm here you know; you can speak to me."

Tillandra wanted to laugh, it was very much Leo to speak out where others might be intimidated.

"You will have to step up, Leo, and handle some things that you aren't experienced in."

"I'm not sure what that means, but if that's what you need."

"It is."

"I'm concerned, Mother. Maybe it would be better if it was me."

"It can't be, Toolet, but I understand what you're saying. You have two days to have him ready, that is all the time there is."

"What about Milfred?"

"What do you mean, Kooka?"

"If he's one of them, then they know where we are. Are there more of them?"

"Yes. But we don't know where, or how many. That he tried to get to it in the city means they must be close by. He would have had to give it to someone."

"Is he the intruder?"

"Maybe, Carnus. We'll not know now."

"Can they take it from her?"

"Sorry?"

"The amulet?" Toolet asked.

"I doubt it. Either they must take her, or they will have to kill her. That's the folly of what he was trying to do. Unless he was going to do just that and Odajeen saved her."

The room went silent.

"The amulet must never leave the pouch again while you're on the road. Is that understood?"

Everyone nodded.

"And if anyone touches it, you'll drop dead just like him."

"Great."

"It's no joke, Leo. Look at him!"

For once the young man said nothing.

"We'll plan to get you away without attracting any attention, but you will need to be very cautious. Once you're on Death Road there will be no other help for you."

"Death Road?"

"That's the name of the only trail west to Watersend, Leo."

"Brilliant, this is really going to be a carnival isn't it?"

Tillandra ignored him. "There are some other details for some of you, including how to get Lani into Midderbuilt and some messages to deliver along the way, but I'll discuss that with those who it affects. Any questions?"

All stayed still or, like Toolet, shook their heads.

"Good, then you need to prepare. I've done this trip multiple times, it's hot, dry, and hard. Hopefully Seth will hold off any storms while you're out there, you need no extra hardships."

One by one they emptied from the room, leaving just Tillandra, Odajeen and Lani.

"All of this because of me."

"Are you going to stop with this attitude of pity, Odajeen? You were once a Mother, you made hard decisions and led others like me. Be that person, the others will need someone to guide them."

"I..." she stopped.

"Better. There's no going back, and it may have been that the only way to free Lani from the amulet was to do this anyway. All that's changed is that it's happening now and differently to how it was imagined."

Tillandra left her and walked slowly back home. Not being the one heading to Midderbuilt felt strange, as would her having to entrust her city pass to Kooka.

There were many things the group would have to face, with no certainty Lani would be freed by Thenis, but there was no other choice.

As she reached her door a wave of dizziness came over her and she had to brace herself against the door frame. Her mind began to drift off as if she was going to faint but instead she slipped into another waking dream.

Once it had passed, Tillandra opened the door and stepped into her kitchen, expecting to be greeting by Milfred. A wave of grief washed over her as she thought about him.

I can't believe it.

Tears formed in her eyes, and she couldn't stop them. She sat at the kitchen table for ten minutes until the tears and sobs had passed.

Only then did she replay the vision she'd just had. She rarely received her dreams that way, normally they came while she slept.

Unlike the normal dreams this one was very clear about its message.

The only reason for sending Purple that Tillandra could see was for healing. She only hoped it was to fix Lani and nothing more serious.

50

KOOKA

It felt good to know that he wasn't about to be stuck in Anderwell. Kooka had known that the Fool's Cart needed to change hands, and he'd agreed to it, but didn't like it.

Sure, he was tired of it in some ways, but he still couldn't let go of the feeling that had haunted him ever since his first run. *Who have I missed or left behind?*

Every child, or person, he'd rescued and brought to Anderwell was thriving. They didn't all take to it easily at first but over time the consistency of their life won out.

No one attacked them or belittled them. There were no nights sleeping rough in the heart of winter wondering if they'd wake in the morning, nor weeks without anything to eat.

Most never told anyone their stories, it was too harsh, and Kooka was the only one that knew their truth, or the parts he had observed. None had lived an easy life before Anderwell.

Despite his desire to save more of them, his body wasn't what it used to be. Things ached every day and it was harder and harder to climb in and out of the wagon.

It meant that this trip Tillandra had put him on was a good compromise. He wouldn't have to care for the people coming with him, not like on the Fool's Cart at least, but he got to be on the road again.

After the length of time he'd done that for, it was the part he knew he'd miss the most. Being settled in Anderwell as he had been since arriving was very comfortable, but the itch to travel was an ever-present companion.

The wagon was laden with the supplies he had best determined they'd need, especially items to help repair the wagon if needed. Tillandra had warned him about how hard it would be — not that he needed reminding.

Mostly he avoided running the Fool's Cart down Death Road, but he had needed to do it once. It was a difficult trip and several of the kids he had brought suffered ill health from it.

Normally there was a ceremony when he left with an empty cart, those of the Court who were in Anderwell would see him off, and many others besides.

This trip was very different, if anything it was being done in complete secrecy. The wagon was a covered one, which would be needed to keep Lani and Odajeen protected from the weather, but also, as Tillandra had highlighted, from prying eyes.

She'd spent some time with him sharing information on who it was that was chasing after the girl, or more particularly, the amulet. Kooka didn't like that they were transporting something so dangerous, but it wasn't his decision to make.

The brute, Carnus, stood across the narrow road from Odajeen's straight as a column, looking away. *He might be uptight, but I'll be glad for him if we get into any trouble.*

The door opened and Irdan and Vefed carried Lani as well as guiding Odajeen out to the back of the wagon. Cautiously they moved the two women into the back and up toward the front where a bed of sorts had been made.

Kooka then started loading the supplies in behind them. It was the first time Carnus moved, and he helped all three of them to load the many baskets and wrapped packages.

Once they'd made a wall at the back, Kooka clambered up into the wagon. "Pass me all the water pouches."

He lined them between the bed and the supplies so that they were all wedged upright. There seemed a lot of them, but their group wasn't small and who knows when they'd find replacements?

When he climbed back down to the street, he brushed off his tunic and hands and looked to see Tillandra and others coming toward them. He could see she had brought Purple with them, in her special chair with wheels.

Saying goodbye to her was going to be hard. Ever since they'd arrived, he'd become closer and closer to her, especially since Gizen had started caring for Peka.

"Mother."

"Kooka, are you almost ready?"

"All except the people."

Leo stood beside her, with a pack slung over his shoulder. Kooka reached out his hand for it and slung it up with the others in the back of the wagon.

"This one too."

Kooka raised his eyes as Tillandra handed him another.

"I thought you were staying?"

"I am, it's for Purple."

"What? No!"

"Yes, Kooka, she needs to go with you."

"Why?"

"I can't say for sure, and I've discussed it with her. I had a vision, and she has to go. It's important, we just don't know why."

Kooka looked at her. "You're okay with this?"

The little one nodded at him, a sadness hung across her face.

"Well, then I'm glad to have you. I wasn't looking forward to saying goodbye, I'd miss you too much."

As if a match had been struck, Purple's face lit up, her eyes opened, and her mouth turned upwards. Kooka was touched that the sadness she was showing before was because he was leaving.

"We'll not be able to fit that in, sorry." He pointed at her chair.

"Doesn't matter." Purple spoke for the first time.

"I'll put you with the women inside, okay?"

Purple nodded, and as Kooka was about to grab her, Carnus

stepped in and hoisted her up as easy as anything. He turned and walked her over to the back of the wagon, placing her on the supplies.

The young girl dragged herself by her arms across to where Odajeen was. Kooka could hear them talking quietly and left them to it before turning back to Tillandra.

"Any more surprises?"

"No, but you'll need this." She handed him a small package. "It's the token to get Lani into Midderbuilt. Only one person can use it so I am unsure how you'll make this work, but perhaps you can go in and get Tingfurlew to help walk her in."

"I guess we'll just have to deal with that once we get there."

The sound of horses approaching made Kooka turn to look back down the street. It was Irdan and his brother leading their own rides and a spare for Leo. Carnus had refused one when they'd met to plan everything, and no one was inclined to argue with him.

Toolet walked to Kooka and reached out to hug him. He bent down and let her. "Be safe."

"I will, Toolet."

"And don't let Dent get into trouble."

At that Leo turned and scowled at her. She gave him a smirk.

"Dent?"

"He can tell you if he wishes."

Kooka stood up. "Let's be on our way before the lanes get too busy."

No one said anything else, and he walked to the front of the wagon, patting the nearest horse on the rump before climbing up to the seat. *This wood doesn't know my butt, I guess it will have time enough to learn.*

The wagon began to move, and they headed away from the two women left behind. Steering the wagon didn't require much attention and Kooka made sure to take in all the buildings and parts of Anderwell he wouldn't see for a long time.

It had been his routine every time he left the city. He savored the view of everything, trying to lock them in his mind as a memory to remember why he was away and what he was bringing the kids he found back to.

Except this time there were no kids to find.

I hope we'll be coming back.

It was the strangest thought he'd ever had, and Kooka didn't know why. A chill ran down his back as he pondered it. He wasn't sure he wanted to know why he was bothered. He'd signed on for the journey, he'd just have to handle what came along when it did.

You're getting too superstitious old man.

51

TILLANDRA

It began, like they all did, as a minor tickle at the bottom of her chest. Tillandra knew what it meant, but there seemed little she could do to stop them turning into a full-blown coughing fit.

Her stomach ached, as did her back and shoulders. Everything connected to her chest had been used too much over the last week as she'd progressively got sicker.

Overnight she'd flipped between coughing or the shivers, neither of which were pleasant. Her head felt foggy from the lack of sleep and food. She could stomach liquid but not food, anything she'd eaten had ultimately come back up from the violence of her coughs.

At this very moment she was sweating and pushed the blanket to the side.

In the fireplace a small smoldering fire kept any moisture from the room. That was the best advice the college physicks could offer.

Darn that Purple went with Kooka, she could be useful right now.

Tillandra would love to know how the group was traveling but had no strength to attempt anything like that. It was the most dangerous time to use the magic, when your body was exhausted.

Only Toolet was left to look after her now that everyone else was on the road. She'd not expected to lose her aide when she'd decided to send everyone away.

Toolet was more than capable of managing things in Anderwell, so Tillandra would just have to lie here until she got better.

If I get better.

Feeling sorry for herself wasn't unusual, especially as tired as she was. She turned to her other side slowly, grimacing as her muscles ached at the effort. At least on this side she could watch the daylight arriving through the windowpane.

Her eyes began to flutter, and she felt as though she was about to pass out, but it wasn't that, it was another dream coming. Tillandra didn't know why they were coming so quickly one after another, but over this past week she was dreaming every other day.

Everything about the city gleamed, sunlight bouncing off the sparkling white stone. In the vision the street was nothing but white.

In the distance a tower reached high above everything else, and it was toward there that the dream moved. She observed people as they progressed down the streets in an unusually ordered pattern.

Everyone was on foot, there were no wagons or carts to be seen, and they all walked no more than two abreast on the right side of the direction they headed.

No one rushed past others, all seemed to be moving at the same pace, which was quite unusual. Typically, such city streets were bustling with chaotic sounds and movement.

Heads all dipped as they passed the person through whose eyes the vision was being generated. Whether this was from respect or fear wasn't detectable.

The road ahead was unnaturally straight, every stone appearing to be lined up perfectly with the next. If you were to stand at the corner of a building and run your eye down the road, nothing would jut out from the line of sight.

Guards stood either side of a timber gate near the bottom of the tower. In such a solid place, all stone and precision, the presence of a wooden item was out of place.

The gate was swung open by the guard on the right who nodded and dipped their head as she passed through. A brief pause looking upward as if to acknowledge the stairs about to be climbed.

Step after step the vision moved up inside the tower for what seemed an hour. Every hundred or so steps was a landing with a closed door.

On occasion the eyes would pause at an outside window and look out away from the city across an endless forest that encased the rear of the city.

At one landing, high within the tower, the vision stopped and moved toward a guarded door. The man that waited there nodded and reached into his tunic to pull a cord, holding a key, over his head.

He turned to the door and unlocked it, swinging it open. As soon as the walker had passed through, the door closed leaving the dimly lit room quiet.

Several thin gaps between stones allowed for tiny slivers of light into what was clearly a cell. Little fresh air squeezed into the space and the smell that filled the room turned the nose of the visitor.

In the center of the room hung a woman, her arms extended above her head, bound together, and suspended from a hoop high above. She dangled her feet which were splayed on the floor, not supporting her weight.

She wore only short pants and much of her torso was covered in tiny cuts long since dried and crusted. Her lips were cracked and split, and her eyes looked dark, whether from the dim light or the torture she'd clearly been through.

"We'll try this again, shall we?" The man's voice cut through the silence of the vision.

A single eye opened but only partly. The man turned and went to a side table and ladled some water from a bucket, tipping it toward the woman's mouth.

She poked her tongue out slightly and lapped what she could of the small amount he tipped across her. Much ran down her chin and across her chest ending by her feet.

"Tell me what I want to know, and you can have as much as you want."

The woman closed her eye, her only level of defiance. She flicked her head slightly at an attempt to move strands of her ghost-white hair that was half-stuck to the side of her face.

The man put the ladle back in the bucket and moved to another table, picking up a small whip. As he unraveled it very slowly, caressing the leather strands, twisted together to give it strength, he seemed pleased with himself.

He then proceeded to light candles around the room until he could see the woman fully. The strangeness of her skin didn't bother him at all. With all the work he'd done to it, the odd blotches of pink and white that made her look like a patchwork was masked by all the welts.

"Where is it?"

No reply.

"I know you have the jewel, now tell me what you did with it?"

The crack of the whip as it flicked onto the woman's back cut through the silence of the room. She shuddered only slightly at the fresh wound, but her head never moved.

Tillandra fell out of the dream in tears.

"It can't be!"

She was shivering but couldn't tell if it was from the fever or what she'd just seen.

Oh, my Thenis, what has happened to you, Hallendell?

It took all her concentration to force herself upright, suffering a coughing attack as she did so, before she could take her next step. Using the wall, Tillandra pushed herself upright and shuffled around, one hand and one step at a time.

She grabbed a robe and, with more effort than it should require, put it on herself, before continuing to the door. Tillandra had no idea how she'd get down the stairs, but she was going to have to try.

There was no one there to help her, not like there used to be.

At the bottom of the stairs, she only just made the bench by the table, collapsing onto it to rest. Her mind was already far away, replaying the vision she'd just had of Hallendell suspended in the tower.

The White City. What on Dharatan has happened?

As if by a miracle the cook that Toolet had arranged for her opened the kitchen door, her face aghast at what she saw.

"You shouldn't be up."

"Get Toolet." Her voice was rough and faint. "Quickly!"

It seemed an age before Toolet arrived to find Tillandra still propped on the kitchen table.

"What is it, Mother?"

As she retold the vision she'd just had, tears ran down Tillandra's face.

"We don't know that it's real, do we?"

"It was one of my real visions, Toolet, not just a bad dream."

"How do you know?"

"I just do."

"I will try and reach her, there must be a way to validate this. Didn't you speak to her not so long ago?"

"I did."

"And she was still in Nkuku, correct?"

"Yes."

"Then I'll see what I can do."

"Thank you. We have to save her!"

"Let's find out whether she's in danger first, this might just be from your illness and nothing more."

Tillandra looked at the little woman, wishing that she was right, but the feeling running through her body didn't agree at all.

CLANNACK

On the sticky days like today there were two things that helped Clannack survive Laumua: the ocean breeze and white wine. Today he was extremely grateful that he had both together.

Predicting when the breeze would come was a game played throughout the city, but there were none that could get it right all the time. Even the elders couldn't truly tell you when. They all had their methods, from the way the gulls flew, or the time of the low tide; some would even use parts of their anatomy.

"I can feel it in my blood."

Clannack paid no heed to any of them anymore. His first year stationed here he'd sought out someone that could give him the knowledge, but it was a fool's errand. There was no pattern that he could determine and most of the year it was too hot to waste the energy thinking of it.

And, man, did it get hot here, despite the coastal aspect. The air became so heavy and moist it felt like a hot blanket, not something you could enjoy. While Clannack preferred the blancs grown in Northern Thabeng, on days as hot as this one, if it was white and wet, he'd drink it.

"Fishes!"

That was another thing he still didn't understand about the Ngaherians, their toast. No one would ever explain why they toasted the fish, but it was what everyone did, and so he followed along.

When in Ngahere, be like the Ngaherians!

The sun was long since past its high point and while there were still several hours left in the day, the heat hadn't abated. So, like most days, Clannack sat outside on the balcony of his ample room, his wide feet perched on the low outer wall, lying back in his chair which was tilted precariously on its rear legs.

A bead of sweat formed on his right temple, and he waited until it had formed enough weight to begin its descent. It seemed a silly concept, but the wetness brought a tiny cooling as the breeze flowed up and over him from the shorefront below.

Waves lapped gently on the stony beach below, the sound of boots crunching across them as workers hurried to finish their day's work. He'd become used to the less than pleasant odors that would waft up at times, it was the price of being close to the ocean in a fishing city.

Laumua was the capital of Ngahere and had the largest port which meant a large fishing trade. Everything about the city was focused on the ocean. The Queen's compound here backed onto the water which contained the wing that Clannack lived in.

His role as secondary councillor to the Queen was relatively new, certainly in Ngaherian terms. There were plenty who had little time for an outsider in their Queen's company, but she had become accustomed to him.

Being male was another reason that brought much consternation amongst the traditionalists, as it wasn't considered right that a man should have the ear of their leader.

None of that mattered, not while he had her ear, or part of it anyway. Clannack still didn't feel secure in his position even after nearly two years. Maybe it was the Queen's manner that made him feel that way, he wasn't sure.

I mustn't have much more wine; I need to get ready for the journey north to Kuwaha.

Clannack wished that they might travel by boats direct from here in

Laumua, but Queen Vika would have none of it. In her mind boats were for fishermen and nothing else.

He loved the idea of sailing out of sight from land to see what lay across the vast eastern ocean, past Enderk and further south. Many didn't share his interest or enthusiasm for it.

Few of his colleagues in Anderwell shared it either, not that it mattered. For now, he had to stay in Ngahere, but when an option presented itself to go further afield he wanted it known he had first pick.

The Queen preferred land under her feet and being able to seek counsel with the trees, that's what she'd told him when he asked her about traveling by boat. One didn't argue with her for long, and his influence was too small.

She'd completely change her mind if it was a river. The Queen liked to travel by the canoes that were unique to their people, but no major rivers existed on the direct route to Kuwaha.

He'd been unable to learn why they were going north, which was just another frustration. Traveling by foot would be slow and hot, not knowing why just made it annoying.

Be damned with it.

He righted his chair, grabbed the jug of wine and topped up his goblet. There was no chill left in it, but it was wet and tangy. Soon enough evening would set in and any breeze that remained would peter out leaving the buzz of insects and sweat.

I should be telling Mother where I'm going, but that seems all too hard right now, when I have little else to tell her about. Best I wait until there's real news.

The Court had been unsure about what value having someone in Laumua would provide, but when notice went out that the Queen was seeking a foreign councillor, it was too good an opportunity to miss.

So far things had been dull, up until the events in the Tombs. That had set tongues wagging harder than a cow's tail. Banishing the man known as Carnus had been something to tell, not that it had made any sense to him or the Court at the time.

What made it even more intriguing for Clannack was the news that Carnus was now in Anderwell. It had taken several connections to learn the whole story, which was a limitation of the way they could speak.

There was only so much you could do with even multiple rats before both parties tired from it, or worse, felt sick. Long tales weren't suited to it, it was best for short messages and instructions.

Clannack had nearly let it slip to the Queen that he knew where Carnus was one day when he'd let his guard down. Of course, it was the wine's fault. Only a servant slipping and throwing a platter across the room had distracted everyone enough, that the matter had been overlooked.

It wasn't something they cared to hear about nor how he'd have known that information. He'd learned that banishment was rare but complete. There was never discussion of that person again and they were never allowed back into Ngahere.

The rules that these people lived by revolved around a strange sense of honor. What was given was also taken away, as the warrior's mother found out. She went from a place of respect in their society to an outcast, forced from her home to fend for herself again.

The poor woman had a story that many couldn't match. Her daughter had shamed them and been banished, causing the father to take his own life as payment to restore their honor. It left the mother and son as neutrals in their society which he'd changed when he'd entered the Tombs.

That was all over now.

What is he up to, following that young woman? And how can I even attempt to find out anything about him here if I can't talk about him?

Tillandra had set Clannack an impossible task, trying to learn more about why he might be chasing Lani. Clannack had formed some unique friendships in the city, but none he felt he could trust with this level of inquiry.

Should word get back to the palace, and the Queen, then he did not know what the outcome might be, nor did he want to find out. He'd just have to keep frequenting the places where stories got told out of the mainstream and see what bubbled up.

Another thing he was trying to learn more about, was people talking about a large number of Derks coming across the water. Mostly it was all rumor, with no hard evidence, but one fisherman had reported that he had been late coming back one day and had spotted an odd craft further out to sea.

It wasn't a Ngaherian vessel, and it didn't match any others he'd seen before, but his view of it was distant and he'd had to race back into shore in the fading light, so he had little to tell.

Clannack had hunted for more information but so far no one else had anything more to add. He hadn't reported that back yet either because it was just as likely to be a fake story as it was true.

There was no harm in listening, that was the job they had. He just wished there was more of it. A story like that could keep him busy for weeks or longer. That beat the monotony of daily attendance on the Queen, listening to her people's requests.

Maybe I'll hear something more interesting in Kuwaha. It will be good to be somewhere different.

GORAN

So bloody hot, every single minute. What fool am I to come this way.
Goran lay on his cot staring at the light coming through the roof of cloth. The oasis he was camped at had little on offer as far as comforts, and he was sick of sitting in sand.

His leg ached a little, something he'd had to accept because he had no zongle weed to dull it. He still didn't know why he'd chosen to come this way; it would have been simpler to head back north, but Death Road had lured him, and he'd followed.

There was nothing of interest to see and he'd chosen to walk it — alone. That meant living inside his own head the entire time, something which he'd typically avoid.

Zoran hadn't surfaced at all, at least not yet. Whatever the young girl had done to him had at least helped temporarily which he was pleased for. For the first time in a long while he felt more like himself, even if he was in pain.

Nor had anyone from Anderwell followed him, at least not yet. He listened, expecting riders to come for him, wondering how that would end. Each day his strength was returning, he wouldn't be such an easy mark anymore.

At first, he'd planned to cut off his locks and shave his head, to change his appearance. But then Goran realized that all she had to do was look at the table in the map room and she'd know where he was no matter how he looked.

Maybe I still will once I get to a city, then they'd never locate me. People get lazy with what they observe about someone else.

So far there'd been little traffic coming from Anderwell, most of it was heading east toward his home base.

Old home base. It's not my home anymore.

Without anything strong to drink or weed to smoke Goran couldn't drown in his victim thoughts, they just didn't stick the same. As much as he tried to dwell on them his mind was clearer, the heat and exercise simply purged them from his head.

He knew he'd made this decision; he'd created his reality and now he wanted to accept it and move on. He needed to make his own way, with and without his skills.

Perhaps there might be a reconciliation in the future, perhaps not, but that wasn't his goal. Goran wanted to find out who he was, the real him out here in the world, unprotected by the Circuit and his insulated network.

It was more than a week's walk to Fort Layder and there was no rush for Goran to get there. He'd enjoyed the few days in Hesb but the temptation to slip back into his normal ways was high and it was still too close to Anderwell.

What he didn't want was to wake up in a cell hungover with one of his old colleagues staring at him, ready to take him back. He wasn't a fool, he knew eventually he'd slip up, drink too much, win too much from the wrong patron in some inn and get into a fight.

Perhaps he'd win the fight, perhaps not, but there'd be a time he'd get locked up for it and Goran wanted that to be a long way from anyone he knew.

"Master G, you stay another night?"

"So it seems, Jaskle."

"Little traffic today."

"Just me for company, isn't much of a party."

The man who manned this oasis laughed a croaky but happy

laugh, not a pinch of malice in it at all. "You think I live here because I want company?"

Goran smiled back at him. "I guess not, Jaskle."

"It all good, Master G. If people come, all good, but just as happy to be alone here. Just me and the sand."

"There's no one else?"

"Once, Master G, but he was killed. Now just Jaskle. Better that way."

"Oh, I'm sorry."

The tender of the oasis waved a hand at Goran and shrugged. He looked to the west. "Spoke too early, Master G."

"What?"

Jaskle pointed one of his long skinny arms. "Wagon coming."

"How can you tell?"

"Sand dust, too much for horse. Just know."

Goran was amazed at what the tender could supposedly see. All he noticed was the desert and swirls of sand everywhere when puffs of wind blew up.

"They'd want to be quick, that sun doesn't have much more left in it today."

Jaskle nodded and set about lighting the torches and lanterns that surrounded the oasis. All up the covered space could hold thirty or more people and numerous animals. Jaskle lit all of them no matter how many people were there.

Easier for the late ones to see it if it's lit, Master G, he'd said last night when asked.

Goran stood and stretched out the aches in his back and legs, helping light what was left as he waited to see who might arrive. Just as the last of the sunlight dropped over the dunes to their west a wagon rode in slowly with a short man sat up on the bench guiding his single horse.

He had a mop of dark hair, not dissimilar in depth to Goran's, tied back behind his head, and a huge beard that almost reached to the bottom of his short legs.

What struck Goran most was the massive grin he had on his face, as though he'd just struck gold.

"Welcome, traveler," Jaskle called out.

"Greetings. So glad I made it, didn't want to have to spend another night out in the sands."

"Don't I know you?"

"I've been here several times before, Jaskle, yes indeed."

"Can't recall your name, Master, forgive me."

After steering his wagon to the side and tying the horse up he clambered down and walked to them.

"Don't worry none about that, Jaskle. It's Rainbow that people call me."

Goran could see why. The beard that had looked white in the distance was a range of bright colors, strangely blended through the hairs. It made him smile.

"And who might you be, stranger?"

"This is Master G."

Goran walked closer and held out his hand. The strange little man grasped it firmly with one of his own and puffs of dust erupted from the joining.

"Sorry about that, darn chalk is everywhere on me."

"Chalk?" Goran noticed that the man still held onto his hand. There was something about him that made him feel completely at ease, even if a small corner of his mind noticed the grip.

"Yes, sorry. I'm a chalker. That's what's in my wagon, I've been selling my wares over in Watersend and places."

Finally, he let go of Goran's hand and he could see pink and blue dust all over his palm. It made him smile.

"See, the smallest of things can bring happiness, Goran."

That broke the spell on Goran's mind. He hadn't mentioned his name at all. He looked at the little man suspiciously, but the strange man winked, laughed and headed back to tend to his horse and wagon.

"Water and grain for the horse please, Jaskle."

"Of course, Master Rainbow. Coming right up."

Goran went back and sat on the edge of his bunk, his nerves very much on edge. The ease he'd felt earlier was gone, and he was watching the stranger very carefully.

The odd man was of dwarven stature which gave Goran some advantages, but he'd felt the man's strength in his grip.

Is that why he hung on so long? Letting me know he could crush it if he wanted?

There wasn't any avoiding him tonight, that was for sure, and Goran didn't think he'd sleep at all. Tomorrow he'd definitely be leaving, without question.

Jaskle prepared food and a hot drink for them around the fire, and then left the two of them to eat. It was the oddest thing, but the tender never ate with his guests, in fact Goran hadn't seen him eat at all.

Explains how thin he is.

"Don't be so worried, Goran, knowing your name doesn't lead to me meaning you harm."

"You've got me at a disadvantage if you know me. I don't know you."

"Oh, you do, you just don't recall is all."

"I think I would remember you."

The old man laughed an infectious happy laugh that seemed to fill the entire oasis and seep out into the desert. "You of all people have spent much time in my company, Goran, but I'll discuss that another time."

"What do you want?"

"Want? What makes you think I want anything? Just an old chalker heading east."

Goran studied him but all he got back from the man was happiness and fun. He let his mind slip back a little and began to push out his skill but suddenly felt a slap across his face bringing him back to the present.

"Don't be doing silly things like that."

Goran rubbed at his chin. The man hadn't moved and was still sat across the table from him.

"What?"

"Let's cut the silly talk, Goran. I know who you are, what you are, what you can do. You're a bit clumsy at it, but that's what happens when we let people have toys they aren't trained for."

Goran shook his head; he was quickly getting lost and more frightened than he'd been in a long time.

"You've got work to do, Gambler."

"What do you mean?"

"There's no option to run away and waste your position."

"I'm not running away."

"True, hobbling then, but still my point remains. You can sulk at
Tillandra all you want, not me though."

Goran stared at him. "I'm done with them, with all of it."

"You're not."

Goran shook his head.

"Let me be very clear, Gambler..."

"My name's Goran."

"... Gambler, you're needed. What's happening is much bigger than
your petty grievance with how you were treated when you were being
an arse."

"Petty grievance? What would you know?"

The old man's face lost all the smiles it seemed to hold and his eyes
bored into Goran's. "Enough. Your other half is contained -- for now --
and that's all that matters. You've got work to do, there's no debating
it."

"What?"

"See, that's not so hard, is it?" It was as though the sun came back;
Rainbow's face lit up with a wide smile. It was almost as if he had
multiple mouths there was so much smile on his face.

"What do you think I'm going to do?"

"I know that when you leave here, you're heading northwest."

Goran was a little confused. "The road goes west."

Rainbow nodded; little clouds of chalk leapt off his beard. "You'll
not be following the road."

This time it was Goran who laughed.

"You need to catch up to the knights."

"Knights?"

"This will go slow, Gambler, if I must repeat everything. Listen up
good now. There's a party of Skarians that have cut across the land,
heading north."

"What are they doing?"

"Now that's a good question. They're hunting amulets." That word gave Goran pause. "With them is the man who found the last one."

"The one Lani has?"

"No, not that one, there's another."

"I didn't know that."

"Because you've been so busy being someone else, and running away, your friends are trying to solve this on their own."

"Where is it?"

"King Ahn has it."

"Is that a bad thing?"

"Perhaps, perhaps not. Only time will tell."

"What am I to do against knights?"

"Stop them getting another amulet."

"Another? There's more?"

"Many, but they're not all coming at once."

Goran shook his head. "Where are they coming from?"

"Can't tell you, sorry. But we don't want these knights to find another."

"And you think I can stop them… how many are there?"

"Just a handful, easy for you."

"I can't survive out there, it's desolate. I don't have a horse or anything."

"One will come."

Goran shook his head.

"Tomorrow don't be worried. You can go tomorrow, all will be fine."

"Why can't you do it?"

"Me?" Rainbow laughed again. "I have some other things to do, Gambler. But don't worry, I'll be watching you."

At that Rainbow stood and wandered to his wagon, clambered up in the back and lay down. It must have taken him all of a minute to fall asleep. Goran listened to the raucous snoring and dropped his head into his hands.

What in Okicheck's name is this all about?
Exactly.

Goran couldn't be sure, but that other voice in his head sounded very much like Rainbow. He sat and stared at the wagon where the dwarf was sleeping, wondering what was about to happen.

GORAN

*A*cross the oasis the snoring emanating from the wagon Goran was looking at continued. The old man asleep in it had shattered any sense of calm that Goran had been feeling.

He didn't understand how the man knew so much about his identity and even his injury. As far as Goran could recall he'd never met the man before, despite the man saying they'd crossed paths many times.

I'd remember him, that's for sure.

A listless wind occasionally drifted through the covered area and reached Goran, bringing with it more of the evening chill. With the sun long gone the desert temperature had dropped dramatically.

This oasis was partly protected and insulated by a sand wall, more like a dune, at its southern side. It only buffered the weather a little, and Goran was wrapped in borrowed blankets from Jaskle.

His brain was getting foggy from tiredness, but he was reluctant to let it win. He had lain down earlier trying to sleep but his eyes refused to stay closed. This little man worried him much more than any of his colleagues in Anderwell.

Why would I follow this man's direction anyway? I'm not part of that anymore.

It was a natural reaction -- Goran had never liked being told what to do, even if it was sensible. When he was told to go north his first reaction would be to go south.

But for some reason he kept thinking about the possibility of Skarian knights being out there in the desert. Even standing alone from the Court, he didn't like that idea.

And if it was about them hunting another amulet, then it wasn't a good thing. He'd missed so much being locked away in Anderwell, including the news Rainbow shared about King Ahn having already found one.

The one Lani had was one too many, and yet this chalker claimed there were many more. Even without knowing everything about the amulets his instincts told him they were a bad thing.

Why were the knights hunting for another one? What did Ahn want with more? Are there even any knights out there?

If there was ever a time he would have liked to have a smoke it was now. He could do with something to just block it all out and let him sleep. *The man will be gone tomorrow, and I can keep on my way. This will all pass over.*

Eventually the weariness took control and Goran did fall asleep to the sound of snoring.

The sound of raised voices snapped him instantly awake.

"I cannot spare a horse, stop asking. I have told you already, they are not for sale." A dark-skinned man stood towering over Rainbow by the water pond.

"The gray one will do just fine. I have the money here for it."

"Are you deaf, old man, is that the problem?"

Goran could see Jaskle tucked behind Rainbow's wagon, watching the conversation. Rainbow wasn't fazed by the loud voice of the tall man, and he started pulling a pouch from inside his tunic.

Standing beside the animal pen were two other men, dressed similarly to the man Rainbow was negotiating with. Both were armed and paying close attention to what was happening.

If for no other reason than to balance the odds, Goran stood and dropped his blankets. Shaking his head, he stretched out and stood part way between both groups.

"You're awake, Master G, so good to see. I was just getting you your horse." It was Rainbow using the name that Jaskle called him. Goran didn't understand why but nodded without saying anything.

"Stupid old fool..." The man stopped what he was saying when he saw the gold coins that Rainbow had tipped from his pouch onto his palm. He slowly looked over to his companions and Goran noticed him raise an eyebrow in an apparent signal. "Perhaps there is a price, but not for the gray, maybe the brown closest to us."

Rainbow still had his ridiculous grin on his face. "Show me."

The horseman smirked, and turned toward the horses, leading the way. Goran readied himself -- it was clear that the trio were going to try something now that they'd seen the money Rainbow carried.

He didn't move but calmed his mind and sought out the Void. Right on the edge of it he reached for his skill and grabbed three threads and pushed them out toward the men.

It was as if they hit a wall halfway across the space.

No need, this is all going to plan. It was Rainbow's voice in his head.

Goran was partly embarrassed that his skill had been batted away so easily but also uncertain about Rainbow's confidence. This looked as though the situation was going to turn violent very quickly.

True to his word the horseman went into the pen and turned the brown horse around so Rainbow could inspect it. Goran noticed him slowly freeing his arms from his split robe, the hilt of a sword appearing on his hip.

"This horse is too young, and isn't well muscled, she will not do."

"Don't worry, fool, you won't be taking any of our horses. But I'll take that pouch off your hands." The horseman had slid the sword out now. It was a short, curved sword that he handled as though he knew how to use it.

"This pouch?" Rainbow remained very calm.

Goran looked back and forth keeping his eye on the other two men, who didn't appear too concerned by what was happening. They clearly believed their companion could easily handle the little old man.

"Pass it here!"

Rainbow tossed it the few feet that stood between them. It landed in the spare left hand of the horseman and immediately a puff of colored cloud popped out of it surrounding the man's head.

He waved his sword arm up dangerously near his own head, grasping the pouch so he didn't drop it. The more he squeezed it the more the seemingly endless supply of what Goran knew had to be chalk streamed out of it.

If not for the threat the man offered, and his companions, Goran would have laughed at the sight. He was now completely covered in chalk dust of many colors, but his face was being crushed by what seemed like a solid helmet of it.

The sword fell first then the man dropped to his knees, coughing and spluttering. As quickly as it had arrived the chalk fell to the ground and the man stared at Rainbow before his eyes rolled back up in his head and he collapsed face-first into the sand at their feet.

His two companions had drawn their weapons and cautiously walked toward the gate to the pen.

"You want some sunshine as well?" The pouch had appeared back in Rainbow's hand and as he smiled at them all the chalk began to flow up from the ground and into the small felt bag.

Both of them stopped and looked at each other. Neither appeared to have much idea what was going on, but any confidence they'd originally had was severely dented by what they'd seen.

Evidently not enough to completely deter them, and they pushed the gate open and held out their blades toward Rainbow. In an instant what looked like a multi-colored rope rushed out of Rainbow's hand and wrapped around the men's ankles.

They fell, dropping their swords as Rainbow pulled back on the rope. Then it continued to swirl around the men, turning them back and forth as it weaved a cocoon over them.

When it was finished Rainbow turned to Goran. "Slow learners, Gambler. It appears they aren't the brightest little rays of sunshine at all."

It wasn't the magic that startled Goran, he'd seen plenty of it, but the skill of how he wielded it that impressed him.

"I guess we can choose whichever one is best now."

"What makes you think I want a stolen horse?"

"Not stolen, Gambler... I'll pay them for it. Just because I bested them doesn't mean I'd thieve from them."

"I don't need a horse; I'm not going out into the desert hunting your mythical knights."

At his words Rainbow's face went stern and dark. "Keep your words to yourself, fool! We are in mixed company."

Goran could feel his face reddening and wanted to turn and hurry away.

"The gray is the best horse for you. Get it and what you need from their supplies. You'll need a week's worth at least."

Despite wanting to say no, Goran found himself following every word Rainbow said. By the time he was done his horse was fully laden, he'd said goodbye to Jaskle, and both he and Rainbow were heading west on Death Road.

He's using my own skill on me.

I am.

Get out of my head.

"If you weren't so stubborn, Gambler, I wouldn't have had to."

"Goran."

"No, my name is Rainbow."

Goran shook his head.

"This is where you go north."

"What?"

Rainbow pointed his arm. "That way. You are days behind them, but if you start off that way you'll catch up."

"You're very confident about what I'll do."

"I know your capabilities, Goran. You're one of mine."

"Your what?"

"Look for a vulture. That's your guide."

"A vulture?"

"That's what I said."

"It will guide me?"

"That's what I said."

Goran shook his head; the whole idea was ridiculous. *This is how they get rid of me, send me into the desert to die on my own, no one having to lay a hand on me.*

"Stop your poor me routines, Gambler. No one wants you dead, except for yourself. Follow the bird, you'll be fine. Start trusting in yourself and stop blaming others. That's my advice."

With those final words it was as if Rainbow had whacked his horse on the rump. The gray reared slightly and bolted away from the wagon straight into the desert. It was all Goran could do to stay upright and on the horse.

By the time the horse had slowed, breathing heavily, its skin sweating, they were both a long way from Death Road. Looking back over his shoulder Goran could see nothing at all but sand.

He continued to let the horse plod its way forward in the direction it had been going, the sand looking the same on all sides. After another hour Goran spotted a single bird circling ahead of them a little to their right.

A vulture you said. Let's hope that's what it is.

He pulled on his rein a touch and turned the horse toward where the bird was. *Let's see what happens next.*

Part of him was excited by what had happened. He felt like he was back at work, doing what he should be doing.

55

UKSOD

*H*e'd only just got himself back into his bed when the outer door swung open and Karpenmor walked in.

"Highness."

"Uksod, I wanted to check on you. How are you feeling?"

There was something brash about the young man that cautioned Uksod. Something was different and the heir had an almost challenging look in his eye.

"A little better, Highness. It comes in bursts then slides away again."

"Soon you'll be back on your feet then?"

Uksod could sense the words as almost a challenge. It wasn't so much a question as a statement.

"Too soon to tell, Karpenmor. I can't rush it along." He forced a cough out of his chest. "You seem agitated, Highness."

"Do I?"

There was something bothering the lad, Uksod knew this behavior. When he was younger it was easy to quash, either through direct use of power or brandy, neither of which would work anymore. He needed to be subtler than that.

"Could you get me a drink?"

Karpenmor stared at him for a moment, before moving over to the side cabinet and grabbing a jug. When he got to the bedside table, he filled the goblet and handed it to Uksod.

"Thank you."

The heir put the jug down on the table and sat in the chair next to it. He sat there brooding for minutes and Uksod left him to it, sipping on the ale while he waited. It would come out given time, he just needed to let him stew.

"Why have I never heard of Comerc before?"

Uksod nearly spat out his mouthful before forcing it down and turning his head. "Where did you hear that name?"

Is this what this is about? That's an easy thing to handle.

"I saw it, on an old map."

"What sort of map?"

I thought I'd got rid of all of them, or at least they're hidden amongst my secret things.

Uksod became a little concerned that the boy had found his private chambers.

"A map, Uksod, one with lines and names. Don't change the topic. I asked you a question."

"Which was?"

"Why haven't I heard of it before?"

"Because it's never spoken about. Ever."

"But…"

"What? You're the heir, so you should know everything?" Uksod knew it was a dangerous ploy to challenge him when he was this uptight, but he needed to push the attitude back to where it was controlled.

"That's a little juvenile don't you think? I mean you've been actually paying attention for a few months and somehow, I'm meant to have told you about the entire history of Enderk in that time."

Thankfully for Uksod, Karpenmor's face softened, and his eyes dropped.

"You're right, I'm sorry. And you've been unwell."

There was still something about the word unwell which he said with a twist in his tone.

"And it's not a topic that is spoken about."

"Why not? It's huge."

"Because I made it that way."

Karpenmor looked at him but didn't say a word.

"The story of it is best kept hidden, Karpenmor, for now at least. It was hundreds of years ago and there is no one alive who knows of it or could remember what happened."

"Except you."

"Except me. And I feel it every day."

"Your age or the loss?"

"The loss. Don't be trite, Karpenmor. It was YOUR father that lost it, not me."

"What happened?"

"You know of the land bridge, and the great storm that destroyed it. It cut us off from Comerc. We couldn't get back to Dharatan for almost a decade."

"How come?"

"The barbarians lined the cliffs and beaches with guards, but also, we didn't have much skill in boating back then. There had been no reason when we could travel to Dharatan on horse or foot. Any attempt to land men was met with force and death. So we stopped trying."

"Our people… what happened to them?"

"I've never been able to hear the truth of that. By the time we were able to get people onto the mainland there were no Derks to be seen. If any did survive, they would be long dead by now."

"They killed them?"

"Perhaps they died naturally but I doubt it."

"Outrageous!"

Uksod held his tongue. It was good the boy was focused on this, especially given his desire to complete the new bridges. Maybe it would keep his mind off other things.

"Had I known of this before I would have pushed harder for us to get there."

"The bridges are being built, Highness."

"We can reclaim it then."

"It will not be so easy, Karpenmor. After so long the Ngaherians think of it as their own."

"It's ours!"

"It was, yes, but they've claimed it through force and even the name is changed."

"Is that why you reject their requests?"

"Sorry?"

"The Ngaherian delegations. One advised that you instructed him to always reject them out of hand."

"Ah, that. Yes, and did he tell you of the message?"

"He did."

"Then you know why I have never entertained them, here or even at the border. Not that it has ever worked but the message has been sent every year since they first began requesting a meeting."

"How long has that been?"

"Twenty years maybe. Ever since the new queen took over."

"Doesn't it make you wonder why?"

"Of course it does, Karpenmor, but what is the point of a meeting when there's nothing I could do about getting back what I wanted?"

Karpenmor sat quietly for a minute before speaking again. "They've just recently sent their third request this year."

Uksod smiled. It was most likely that his wheat plan was finally starting to come to fruition.

"You like that?"

Is now the right time to tell him about the plan?

"It means they are getting more desperate, Highness. That is a good thing."

The lad shook his head, and Uksod could see his confusion written on his face.

"Before you... your father passed, I put a plan into place on Dharatan to change our leverage with them."

"What did you do?"

"We attacked the wheat stores in several realms, and their seed stock. The idea being that it would slowly destroy their capability to produce enough wheat to feed themselves and they would need to look for help."

"Us?"

"Yes."

"I sense a but."

Uksod smiled again, this time because it was good that Karpenmor was finally thinking for himself, not just a child. "The plan was a little too effective."

"What do you mean?"

"What One and I put in motion we expected to be a three-to-five-year plan. Something to subtly erode their stocks and capabilities."

"Why so long?"

"At that point we were increasing our shipping capacity, but it was slow. Without that we wouldn't have the capability to get the replacement wheat across to Dharatan."

"But now we have the bridge."

"We will, much sooner than I had planned, which is a bonus."

"What went wrong with the plan?"

"Nothing went wrong, per se, it was just a lot more effective than we imagined."

"How so?"

"Almost the entire stores in Ngahere, Malamig and Lletem have been depleted. Even their latest crops are failing."

"Can't they get it from other realms? Why would they come to us?"

"Before we knew how effective it would be we set plans in motion in the few other realms that produce enough wheat to be helpful. We didn't want them ramping up their crops in subsequent years."

"And it wiped them out as well?"

Uksod nodded. He explained how they had delivered the infected rats into the stores and soaked the seed stock with a solution that weakened them.

"I would like to have known this earlier, Uksod."

"I understand, Highness, but like I said, when exactly would I have informed you of it?"

"Do we have enough to supply them all?"

Uksod noted how well the boy was changing topics when he didn't want to answer a question. "Almost. Enough to save them from themselves."

"What does that mean?"

"Unlike our society, Karpenmor, their people believe they have a say in how their countries are run. When they run out of wheat it will cause unrest within their cities and towns, people will fight each other and then they'll turn on their leaders. That's when a supply will help the rulers keep control, ease the concerns."

"We'll be their savior?"

"Exactly, and we wouldn't want them to know how much supply we do have. The less they think we have, the higher the price they'll be willing to pay to beat out their neighbors."

This time it was Karpenmor who smiled.

"You like that idea, Highness?"

"It's given me an idea."

"What, pray tell?"

The smile remained. "Now that would be telling, Uksod. All in good time. Best I let you rest, I wouldn't want to slow your recovery."

Uksod again heard the way he stretched out the word recovery.

Cheeky little snot, but you're up to more than that aren't you? I need to keep a closer eye on you. Especially where did you find that map?

56

JUNTHER

*I*t was true, Junther knew he was grouchy, but that didn't mean there weren't things that made him happy. Mostly people just annoyed him more often than they didn't.

Living in Anderwell he'd been able to live a routine that was neither exciting nor horrible. Routines made him happier, inside at least; he wasn't going to waste energy expressing his feelings externally.

Whatever people thought of him didn't really matter. As far as he was concerned, that was their problem. Life hadn't been easy for Junther when he'd been younger, and it had taken him a long while before he'd moved to Anderwell.

Having only one arm made him easily spotted by normies who disliked those that were different. He had suffered more than enough beatings before he'd even become a man.

When he'd been less than twenty years of age, he'd met the then Driver, Ruport, but the whole idea of being stuck with a bunch of crips didn't appeal at all.

Life had become too harsh in Daskare where he'd grown up, so he'd traveled. First west thinking that their similar kin might be more kind, which wasn't true.

It didn't actually matter where he went, the only place that didn't judge you for your physicality was Anderwell. Eventually it all became too much, and he'd arrived at the gates on his own feet.

Much later he'd befriended Ruport before he'd given up driving. It bothered Junther thinking about his long-since passed friend. He looked to the sky and said a silent prayer.

He didn't know why people looked up, rather than down which was where the bodies got buried, they just did. As his eyes dropped back down to street level, he followed the head of his horse as it walked slowly along the cobbled streets of Bundok.

When they'd ridden through the gates an odd feeling had swept over Junther, part sadness, part pleasure. It was the first time in almost thirty years that he'd been back to where he'd grown up.

So much of it looked exactly the same, just the people looked different. Faces which he should have recognized in familiar stores, he didn't, the people he'd known there long gone.

No doubt some he looked at might have been their offspring, which meant they might have been some of those that tormented him.

Let them try now.

A twisted grin formed on his face. The idea made him feel better despite knowing he couldn't afford to display his skill publicly if he was to keep a low profile. His role here was to learn what was happening and feed information back to his colleagues.

The sight of The Wise Owl was very welcome after the weeks it had taken him to get here. At his age such travel came with more aches than anything else.

He'd happily take staying put over constantly having to be on his horse. Off down the roadway Junther spotted a crowd gathered, enough that they'd blocked it completely.

Despite not having worked out on the Circuit for many years, he knew that any such gathering was filled with knowledge and continued on his way toward it.

What's a few more minutes?

Closer to the crowd, Junther could see a procession of knights, soon followed by other people also riding. It didn't take much to recognize the man, King Ahn, by the crown he wore.

More knights came behind him. Junther dismounted and tied his horse to a post, before getting amongst the people watching.

"What's all this then?"

The woman he had spoken to turned her head in his direction before answering. "The King's heading away, it's been on all the criers' lips. You deaf, old man?"

Junther wanted to cuss the rude woman who wasn't much younger than him but said nothing. He didn't need to create attention with a tirade of snarky comments directed her way.

Back at the inn he secured his horse and, not seeing anyone to attend to the animal, grabbed a bucket of water and placed it where she could reach it.

I'll get someone to tend to her in a bit.

Grabbing his satchel and slinging it across the shoulder of his missing arm, he headed toward the back of the inn. A tall man, about half Junther's age, stood leaning up against the wall beside the door, puffing on a pipe with a long stem.

"Welcome, stranger."

"Greetings, I'm looking for the Keeper."

"Found'm."

Junther held out his only hand and lifted the ring so that the man could see it.

"It's a long time since I've seen one of them down here. I'm Akvitte."

"Junther. Nice to meet you, Akvitte. Sorry none of us have been around."

"Plenty of those on the Circuit to keep me busy, always something to be done around here."

"I'm hoping that includes serving good ale?"

"Indeed it does. I'm done here anyway. Let me fix you one, and I'll get the lad to tend your beast. Staying long?"

"That was the plan."

Akvitte turned inside the open door and led the way. He didn't waste any time before getting a jug placed in front of Junther. "Looks like you've been on the road a few days."

"Straight from the college."

"Best you wet your whistle then. Can I fix you some food before we settle you in?"

"Bread and cheese would do."

"Only bread you'd be getting is rock bread, no wheat to be had down here."

"That bad?"

"Worse. We've been out for about a month, and no sign of any, not in the short term at least."

"Whatever you can give me is fine by me, sorry I didn't know."

Akvitte shrugged.

"Before you go, what's going on with the King? I noticed a procession heading east past the end of the road."

"Chasing the wheat, they say."

"What's that?"

"He's off to try and get us some wheat supplies."

"Where from?"

"They've not really said, but it can't be Kysten, they ain't got any either if you listen to what everyone through here says."

It's worse than we knew. Too much news from the north and not enough from down here. Thank Thenis I'm here.

"He was heading east though."

"Thabeng then, but you'd have rocks in ya head if ya thought they'd have wheat. See what I did there?"

Not that funny.

"Yes, and you're right. The rock breakers aren't the most likely source of wheat. Strange."

"Can't help ya with any more than that, boss. Maybe one of the others will have more to tell."

"How many do you have residing here right now?"

"Six there was this morning, but that might change now the King's moved on."

"Why's that?"

"He's a bit of a killjoy. With him gone we're likely to have less rules about the city. Might see some more flow through."

"I guess I'll get to know them well enough by the time I'm through."

"Let me get you that food."

By the time Junther had eaten his fill the ale had his head a little fuzzy. A little was deliberate because he knew in all likelihood his travels hadn't ended.

He was down here to watch over what was happening with the King, who'd inconveniently just left the city. That meant either he would have to wait here until he got back, or he'd have to head off in the same direction.

No rush, a group of that size won't be traveling fast. I can at least get one good night's sleep.

After washing and handing over all his spare clothes to Akvitte to have cleaned, Junther had spent the rest of the day waiting in the main room for the Circuit members to finish their work and come back to the inn.

That turned out to be a waste. As far as learning where the King was heading, none knew any more than he did. What was interesting though was the confirmation about some of the news they'd already received.

"Ya'd swear he be his younger kin."

The Morskan called Hian who sat across from Junther had an interesting way of talking.

"Why's that?"

"I only seen him twice or three, but tha people also say it. His face, smooth, not a crease. And upright, stood tall like he lost half his age."

"Interesting. And this all happened after the men gifted him?"

"Ya right. That was when, says all that was there. Some fancy amulet. Magic, that's what it be."

"What's that?"

"Everyone be talking it. He got magic, he got. That's what changed the King."

"A bit of gossip, I'd say, Hian. I wouldn't put too much stock in that."

It had been a fun evening catching up with faces he knew from the college and to see who they had become since. To them he was one of the many teachers they'd had, none had ever seen him on the road.

All the talk had taken its toll after the travel, and he headed up to his room. He knew tomorrow he'd have to leave, but at least for tonight he was going to sleep well.

57

CLANNACK

Clannack was thankful for his size, it was the one thing that he had in common with the Ngaherians. His height at least. The rest of his body was fairly large too, but not in a normal way.

His disproportionate feet, hands and head bothered other people. Clannack had accepted how he was built at a young age, and to this day still couldn't understand what caused others so much discomfort that they detested him like they did.

His parents had done all they could to protect him when he was young, but it didn't matter. Until he'd grown large, others picked on him relentlessly. At least his parents hadn't shunned him like many normies did when they bore broken children.

Once his parents died there was nothing to keep him there. His near neighbors did all they could to make his life uncomfortable, trying to take the small house away from him.

Never to his face of course, always behind the scenes. In the end he had set off to travel, looking for a place that didn't discriminate so badly.

He ended up in Anderwell just before his eighteenth year and it was as if he'd shed half his body weight. Clannack hadn't realized how much of his feelings he'd carried around with him, hidden under his smile and politeness.

Being able to just walk around without anyone even noticing him initially made him feel invisible, then he realized that was normal for most people. He had loved his time there and hadn't ever had to fight.

Not that he didn't mind having to punch the daylights out of someone if they deserved it, as rare as it was that he ever let it get to that. But when it did, Clannack had to admit he did enjoy it.

Everyone treated him as useless until they discovered how much strength there was in his odd-sized body. The thought brought a smile to his face, something the walk of the last week had not done.

Ngaherians were stubborn people, and the Queen the head of it. If there was a reason to be stubborn, she'd find it and lock in on it like a mosquito on warm blood.

So walk they had done. Clannack was just another large body in a column of them. Some were warriors, the others human pack horses. If you asked one of the carriers, they'd tell you Ngaherians had no need for horses.

It didn't make sense to Clannack, but then much of their culture didn't. Nearly two years in, he still found them a frustrating nation of people. At first, he'd thought it was purely those around the Queen.

There was always a different attitude in royal courts and the important key members of the society that surrounded it. But it wasn't that; in Ngahere, Clannack had found everyone thought this way.

He carried his own belongings in a sack slung across his shoulder, one of his large mitts holding the top of it resting against his upper chest. With his other he flicked his thick black hair off his forehead and away from his eyes.

The white streak of hair that ran from above his right eye to the back left of his head was as noticeable to him today as it had always been. It was that which first caught others' attention, then they would see him, and notice how large his head was even for his size.

Within Ngahere it was his whiteness that stood out more than his size. They were used to large people -- they were the largest people on Dharatan. At times some of them actually scared Clannack, and he wasn't easily intimidated.

Ngaherians had a chocolate color to their skin that wasn't dark in and of itself but against his skin, the contrast was stark. He was as white as you could get. Despite years being outside, his skin had never changed color.

He'd seen others, who had lighter skin tones, go red or brown from a lot of exposure, but not him. He was as close to an Enderk skin as anyone else, despite his being from Lletem.

They were only a few hours from Irava, having recently passed through Kekahi. For Queen Vika it was an opportunity to visit each of the towns and cities on the route. Clannack had expected they'd follow the coast for speed, but he was mistaken.

The inland roads they had followed were surrounded by trees except when they were near to towns, and the view never changed, just the person in front or endless trees to the side.

No doubt they would be held up in Irava, dealing with local matters of law, and some formalities to do with the Queen visiting. It was difficult for Clannack to enjoy such visits as he had no network here to speak of.

Building contacts took time and he was rarely allowed away from the capital. When he was it was always with the Queen. Since leaving Laumua he hadn't spent much time in her company, except in the evenings when he was expected to stay close enough that he could be summoned quickly.

For what I can't imagine. All they do is camp, drink and talk of the woods.

He wasn't sure what it was that annoyed him about the Ngaherians. Maybe he was a chauvinist, and being directed entirely by female leaders was what bothered him. Except it never bothered him about Mother Folly, or his elders in the Court.

Clannack didn't know, he'd pondered it for the last year, trying to work out why he found this assignment such a chore. In truth he did little. He got to spend almost every afternoon and evening on his balcony looking at the sea, and he was never in danger, at least not any mortal kind.

His life was pretty easy, except... something about them just bugged him. He lifted his eyes from the man in front of him and saw his favorite first councillor, Nikora, walking his way.

You can think with sarcasm, can't you? She's about as favorite as mosquitos are to me.

"Clannack!"

Where most people called you like they were asking a question, to see if you were there or would respond, Nikora barked like a cranky dog.

"Nikora?"

She turned when she reached him so that she was now walking alongside; the march didn't stop for anyone, except the Queen.

"Her Highness wishes you to attend to her this evening."

"About?"

"You need to know nothing more than your attention is required. When camp is set and you've..." she looked him over with disdain "... cleaned yourself appropriately, make your way to her chambers."

"Of course, Nikora." He looked directly into her eyes and let a playful smile form on his face.

She frowned and strode off without a word.

It's that attitude that drives me crazy here. They are all full of it to varying degrees, it's as if because of their size, and lack of fear of most people, they are better than everyone.

That's why Nikora dislikes me, because I'm neither bothered by them nor scared, and I let her know. I wonder what's in store for me tonight? Maybe the Queen has had enough of Nini for one night.

Clannack wanted to call Nikora by his pet name just once to see her reaction. It would be the greatest insult to her, she who projected her strength and smarts.

For him, an outsider, to call her a pet name might just cause her head to fall off her shoulders. Clannack burst out laughing, which was one thing he did that they never did. He laughed a lot, and often.

His big hearty laugh disturbed the men walking around him, enough that the one in front turned and stared at him while he marched.

Clannack stared back, poking his head forward in mockery of the man's seriousness.

"Something the matter, good mate?"

The warrior grunted and turned forward again. Clannack considered singing. That would set a saw amongst the ancient trees, and cause chaos. It was okay to have entertainers in the court, inside at the appropriate time, but otherwise no.

They are so bloody serious, these people. So uptight, it's like they haven't figured out how to enjoy anything.

There it was, the thing that Clannack had known but couldn't put his finger on. The thing that made his assignment so hard: there was no enjoyment in their culture. Not in the way that he was used to.

He didn't mean like Callet, that place took it to the extreme; no, just simple enjoyment. Now that he thought about it, even in the city the children didn't rush about screaming and laughing.

Everyone and everything were so focused on their honor, their law, their rules, that they were constantly uptight. He wasn't sure if it helped now that he'd put it into words, but at least he knew. This had to be the least fun place on Dharatan.

58

KARPENMOR

He had woken annoyed, and it wasn't shifting. Karpenmor was finding it harder than ever to sleep since he'd taken on the responsibilities of ruling.

Now with what he'd learned recently it was becoming even more difficult to the point that he was only managing four or so hours each night.

A lack of answers to what he should do was bothering him. How much should he trust Uksod? Then there was One, and where the Vrah leader's loyalties really lay.

He still hadn't come up with an ideal way to replace the man from his position, and for now had switched from researching that to learning as much as he could about Comerc.

Even he was unclear why that bothered him so much -- all he knew was that it did. It had triggered him in a way he'd not expected.

He wanted to undo the past, to claim back that which they'd lost. In part it was because of the role his father had played in losing the city, which he understood, but another part of him was outraged.

When he'd learned of the stolen amulet a similar feeling had come over him. Was it patriotism?

The idea that the barbarians had inflicted these things on him — on his people — seemed to fire up his hatred.

And there he was, lying in bed, his head hot with anger fueled further by the knowledge that he couldn't get back to sleep.

Karpenmor threw on a robe and walked out to his favorite place, his balcony. Early light crept through the Ashar Pass, long before it would clear the mountain tops.

He could see a small group of Vrah dragging someone through the gates from the city toward their compound. *What are you up to I wonder?*

Of course, there were a myriad of things that happened day-to-day that he wasn't aware of. That was one of his conflicts, wanting to know it all but then not. He had to let people do their work.

He could ask One what they were doing, but it would come across as strange that he was questioning what was most likely normal activity.

Would Uksod question him about it?

Karpenmor added that to the list of things he had no answer for. He turned his thoughts back to the land bridge and Comerc.

I wonder how much further the engineers have progressed? It is getting so much closer; I should be there.

By now One's messenger would be getting close to arriving with the latest rejection message for the Ngaherians. Karpenmor should have sent someone immediately to cut them off and stop it.

If he'd acted quickly, he could have halted that message getting any further than Ponte. Sending another one now would not make a lot of sense.

Messages weren't going to be enough for what needed to happen next. Soon enough the Ngaherians would know what was coming -- they'd see the bridge being built once it started on the last Step.

The current relationship between Enderk and Ngahere wasn't going to suffice for what he needed to do. Things were different now, because of the bridges and him becoming High Prince.

While there would be a lot of history to try and push aside, he knew he had leverage now. Uksod's plan to destroy the wheat was an easier selling point than some of the other things they had done without for all this time.

Historically they had taken tin and other mined products from Enderk, but he didn't know if they'd still need it. And of course, there was a lot of amber to share.

Dharatan had blocked the import and ownership of amber for longer than he'd been alive. He didn't know why, but perhaps that mattered as well. No doubt there was an underground market for it, but if they could trade it openly it would be a boon for Enderk.

The key to this was to place the Ngaherians as the key to trade on Dharatan. Let them profit from being the portal that all goods came through.

Someone needed to ensure they finished the bridges and finally connected to Dharatan. His desire to see the connection between the two continents re-established had turned from a wish into something much more important.

The reconnection had to happen, by force, if need be, so he could reclaim that which was taken from them.

I need to be the one negotiating this.

He walked back through his room and opened his outer door, turning to one of the guards. "Bring Aika to me, please?"

The guard nodded and hurried away. Karpenmor left the door open and went and sat on his favored sofa, watching the door for her arrival. If she'd been asleep, she made quick work of appearing wide awake and ready for her work.

"Highness, how may I serve?"

"I wish to see the High Chancellor here in my chambers."

"Now?"

Karpenmor wasn't sure if that was confirmation or a serious question.

"Yes." He kept his voice calm, but his response was still definitive.

"I will wake him, Highness."

"And have them bring me breakfast would you please? I'm starving."

"Of course, Highness." She turned and disappeared from his sight. The sound of her running echoed back down the hall.

"You can close the doors now."

One of the guards outside reached through and pulled the door closed. Karpenmor waited on his sofa. The chancellor was not as quick at responding to his request as Aika had been, and carried a scowl when he was introduced by the same guard.

"Chancellor, so good of you to come." Karpenmor knew he'd inconvenienced the man, but he wasn't in the mood to care. He wanted action taken and he wanted it done now.

"What is so important that it couldn't wait?"

"Highness." Karpenmor stared at the man, who had served Uksod for nearly fifty years.

"My apologies, Highness." His old face wasn't anywhere as practiced as Uksod's in hiding his emotions and Karpenmor could see him react to the rebuke.

"And do you usually question why you are summoned?"

"Apologies again, Highness. It seems I am ill-prepared this morning to serve you properly."

"Perhaps you might be past your prime, Chancellor?"

If the air had been thick between them before it was solid now as Karpenmor rose from his sofa.

Perhaps if he'd had more sleep he might have acted differently, or maybe it was his frustration at the way people were just not heeding his commands as he wanted them to. Either way his frustration came out.

"I don't care for your manner at all, you're done here. I am removing your title, your time in the palace is over!"

The elderly chancellor's face was the color of a beet and his eyes enraged, but he said nothing.

"What are you waiting for? Go! Guard!"

Immediately one of the Vrah rushed through the door.

"Take this man away, he is no longer in my employ. Take him to the gates and throw him out and bring me his second."

Karpenmor knew that his mood had been sour since he'd woken but he wasn't going to cop such attitude from one of his primary aides anymore.

Just after the room cleared, Aika hurried in with a platter of break-fast and placed it on the table before where he stood.

"Thank you, Aika."

"Anything else, Highness?"

"No, not for now." Looking at her eyes he could see the anxiety in them. She was still on edge whenever she was around him, or perhaps it was his mood making her cautious. "I appreciate you bringing this so promptly."

She simply nodded and left, closing the door behind her. He began picking through the fruits while he waited to see who would arrive next. It wasn't long before the second chancellor, Nagel appeared, reluctantly entering the room before the guards closed it quickly behind him.

"Good morning, Highness."

Karpenmor looked up at the man, who wasn't that much different in either age or appearance from the first. "It would appear you have a new job, Nagel."

"I do, Highness? What is that?"

"High Chancellor."

"But... but Voldif?"

"Voldif has been retired. I need people ready to do their best work for me, Nagel. Is that you?"

"Ah... yes... of course... but..." The man looked at Karpenmor before continuing. "Yes, Highness, and thank you."

"You're welcome, Nagel. I have your first job already."

"Of course, Highness. May I enquire as to its nature?"

"I wish you to precede a delegation to Ngahere."

"Precede, Highness?"

"Yes, Nagel. I realize typically you might conduct discussions in matters like this, however in this circumstance it will be me."

"You're going to Ngahere?"

"Close enough, Nagel. The bridges are almost complete so I will go to Step Six."

"Ah, yes. If I may say so, Highness, the news of the bridges has created much excitement."

Karpenmor studied the man, happy that if nothing else he was willing to be open with his leader.

"It is a key moment. Which is why I need to be the one to negotiate with them. There is a lot at stake to negotiate, not only finishing the bridge but the future trade between our nations."

Karpenmor finished explaining what he needed from the chancellor and then sent him to prepare.

"Leave tomorrow, Nagel. No later. And another thing, keep this to yourself. And I mean entirely to yourself, even your traveling companions need only know you're going to Ponte. Understood?"

"Yes, Highness."

For the first time in days Karpenmor could feel his spirits rising. Now he had to pull it off and get back before the eclipse. He just needed a few things to go his way.

TILLANDRA

*I*t was as if a heavy curtain had been drawn back from over the top of her. Tillandra woke feeling normal, or as close to normal as she had in weeks. Cautiously she sat up then swung her legs over the side of the bed and stood.

Everything felt right: her legs had plenty of strength in them, her head was clear, the only thing was the tickle in her throat. That was still there, which meant she'd cough soon enough.

I'll see how that plays out, hopefully it won't wipe me out again.

This last week had been a washout. She knew she'd dealt with some things but mostly she'd been here in her room with people visiting her. Now she could get back on top of her work.

Not until I've washed though.

When she reached the ground floor, she stood in the cold kitchen looking around, feeling very alone. Normally Milfred would have a fire going and even be making her a chai.

She still couldn't reconcile what had happened, what he'd been, and it was even harder because he'd been so close to her for these last few years.

How could I not have known?

It took her longer than it should to take care of setting a fire and getting water warming for her bath. Tillandra knew she was going to have to do all of this for herself now.

She couldn't imagine allowing anyone else into her house and her life like Milfred had been, not for a very long time. Everything she did in her own home brought back memories of the man, making it almost impossible to free her mind.

The image of Hallendell being tortured had been burned into the back of her mind and was the unlikely savior from her own thoughts.

Focusing on that allowed her to push everything else away, even if temporarily. Tillandra was happy to be receiving regular visions again, that pleased her, but in this instance the image was frightening.

Striding across the courtyard to the college she lapped up the sun on her arms and the freshness of the air compared to her room. A cough formed and stopped her in her tracks for a minute before she could continue on.

There it is. It's not going to derail my day, not today.

Toolet was coming out of the main college entrance just as she arrived.

"Mother! Are you feeling better?"

"Much, Toolet!"

"I was on my way over to your place."

"Saved you a trip then didn't I? My office?" She pointed her arm back inside. Toolet nodded before turning and heading that way.

"It's a relief to see you back up and about."

"I doubt it's as good as it feels to me. What do you know?"

"I've been in the map room just now."

"And?"

"Hallendell isn't in Nkuku, she's moving westward."

"Toward the White City?" Tillandra could feel her chest tighten.

"That's unclear. If so, it's not the most direct route."

"I'll need to reach out to her."

"Are you well enough? I can do it."

"I'll use the tree, it's fine. Anything else?"

"Ah… I checked again on Goran, he's out west as well."

"What do you mean?"

"Death Road. He's been heading toward Watersend, up until recently."

"What is he doing?"

"Hard to tell. He's headed northward into the desert."

"The desert? That's kind of a relief, I thought you were going to say he was heading toward the others."

"No, they're still slowly crawling west, but he's a long way from them. I've no idea why."

"Maybe he'll answer me if I try." Tillandra knew she could look through his mask if needed.

"I worry about him, Mother."

"As long as he stays away from Lani, that's the most important thing. We need to decide about him, I know, we will."

"There's so many things to take care of."

Tillandra stopped walking. "Is there anything else?"

"Not really, just matters about the college, but nothing you need to be worried about."

Toolet had paused a little while she was answering. It was only subtle, but Tillandra noticed.

"What is it?"

Toolet raised her eyebrows.

"There was a pause, something's bothering you that you're not telling me."

"Clever. It's Sabant, our Prospect."

"What about her?"

"She's not been seen, in about a week."

"That doesn't seem much to be worried about. And she did need to get over not being selected in the Audition."

"Her room looks as though no one has used it for as long, and no one can say when they last saw her."

"Doesn't seem much, why does it bother you?"

"I'm not sure, Tillandra, but I'm worried about how she took things. She wasn't the same after Leo was chosen. I'm concerned about what she's thinking. We can't just have her disappear on us."

"Understood. Hopefully she's just taken some time away, there's no way for me to track her, she doesn't have a mask or ring."

"I just hope she's not done anything silly."

"We have enough to worry about. I'm glad you mentioned it, but we'll just have to hope she shows up in a little bit. She'll need food and a bed, Anderwell has a lot to offer."

"Hopefully."

Tillandra didn't go into the college but watched Toolet make hard work of the many stairs before turning and heading to the garden where Peka had been tending to the tree.

What she saw shocked her as she rounded the corner into the garden. The wispy-looking tree was as tall as the wall and its trunk was now wider than the average person.

That is unbelievable. What a difference Peka has made.

She lowered herself down beside the trunk of the tree and looked up at all the new young branches filled with leaves. The sight lifted her spirits.

Even the touch of the tree was different. Last time she had been very cautious laying her hands on it, not wanting to damage the sapling. This time the pulse of the tree was strong, and her hands vibrated as she laid them on it.

Slipping into the Void was easy, and she could sense energy flowing back from it into her, strengthening her. It was a boost to her recovery.

Her first effort was directed toward Goran. She still had affections for her colleague and couldn't just write him off. *What are you up to, Goran?*

Looking through his mask she could see he really was deep in the desert. He seemed focused on a distant bird directly ahead of him.

She watched briefly before seeing that there was little she could tell from seeing where he was. Trying to speak to him was a waste of time. Twice she knocked hoping he'd answer, but he didn't.

A little annoyed, she switched focus and sought out Hallendell. Again, she used the mask to check on what the woman could see first.

It was a relief to see her out in countryside, apparently riding a horse, and not in a cell being whipped. Tillandra sent out the knock and waited.

Knowing that Hallendell was riding, Tillandra waited patiently and tried again a few minutes later. It was a relief to hear her speak.

"Mother?"

"In All Jest, Hall."

"It's good to hear your voice. Sorry for the delay, I was riding."

"Riding?" Tillandra forced herself to sound surprised.

"Yes, things have changed."

Tillandra was relieved that the woman was out of Nkuku, but not so happy that she was still hanging around Morska.

"I don't like that you're still there, Hal, but you can't ignore Hem's wish."

"He is real then?"

"Yes."

"I hoped he was just a dream."

"You need to be careful."

"I'm well aware, Mother, but if there is another amulet then I need to get to it."

Tillandra wanted to tell her about her dream, but it served no purpose, like Toolet said. Maybe it wasn't a vision, a foretelling, but just an illness-induced dream.

"Then what?"

"He said take it to Midderbuilt, that it wasn't safe in Anderwell."

"I'm still not sure why there is better than here but do as he says. When I know more, I'll let you know. I am glad you're away from there, I've never been that happy about your assignment."

"No point dwelling on it now, it's over and I can't go back there."

Tillandra walked slowly back to the college. She felt a little better knowing their colleague was safe. If anything it was a double win. Hallendell was away from her likely torturers, and she was in pursuit of another amulet.

60

GORAN

There were plenty of things Goran knew that the average person did not. One of those was the presence of magic, or skills, which is how the Court referred to it.

In all his time, though, he'd not ever seen such magic as was behind the vulture he followed. Every day when he woke, he found a bird ahead of him in the distance.

Throughout the day he headed in their general direction, always a long way behind but not too far that he lost sight of them.

At the end of the day, they circled over the spot where he'd find shelter, food, and water. Nothing elaborate but enough to sustain him in his pursuit of the supposed Skarian knights.

For more days than he could recall all Goran had to look at was sand, dunes and dunes of sand as far as he could see. Up and down he rode, letting the horse do all the work while he held on and watched the bird ahead.

Maybe there aren't any knights out here. This man, Rainbow, might have been sent to lead me to my death.

His mind had been wandering most of the day and there was little he could do to stop it. He was hot, so hot, but despite it he wore a heavy coat to protect him from the sun.

On his lips cracks had formed on top of other cracks and he wouldn't waste what little saliva he had to lick them. While each night there was always more water, the worrier in him conserved everything, unsure when his luck would run out.

What had Rainbow called me? Gambler. How did he know? He's right, even this journey is a gamble. Is it a trick to kill me or is it real? And yet I rolled the dice on it.

In a way Goran didn't mind if it was his last trick. The pain of what he'd faced recently had sucked much of his inner strength from him.

Others would tell him that he played his pity game, the poor me story, far too easily, but he was pretty much done. The fight to be himself didn't seem worth it anymore.

Rocking gently as his horse plodded through the day made it easy to sink into the depths of those feelings and an acceptance that if it was his end, it was okay.

Isolation and too much time to think were always his downfall. Usually that's when Zoran came free as well, but the benefit there was Goran then didn't have to think at all.

Now all he had was himself. And the sun and sand.

Somewhere in the back of his mind a warning bell rang out, but he pushed it away. Pictures of his friend Henri drifted into his mind, and he lost himself in those images.

Suddenly his face was rocked backward with massive force and his left shoulder pinched and screamed out at him. Air burst out of his nose and mouth and as he sought to suck more in, his mouth filled with sand.

Goran opened his eyes as he raised his head, looking for danger. Spitting sand out of his mouth he saw he'd fallen from his horse and was lying on the ground.

There was little sunlight left in the sky and he pushed himself up, desperately fumbling for his water sack before trying to clear his mouth.

His heart was racing as he tried to work out where he was and what was going on. His horse was only a few feet from him, thankfully, but he couldn't see the vulture in the sky anywhere.

Crap.

Now fully awake he frantically looked in all directions but it was nowhere to be seen. Goran had no idea what to do — without the rest stop he would be lucky to survive another day.

He clambered back into his saddle hoping the extra height would show him the way forward. His chest tightened as he began to think about his options.

All he could see was sand, everything looked the same, only shades of color from the sand made any contrast and even that was rapidly disappearing with the setting sun.

To the north a flash caught his eye. It passed quickly but he was sure he'd seen it, then it happened again. It was in the opposite direction to the setting sun.

It's like the way sun bounces off metal. Could it be?

With little time left before he ran out of light, Goran had to make a choice. The wakeup call of what had just happened made him choose the less risky option.

He slid out of his saddle and walked toward the rough location of the light he'd seen. Goran didn't see it again and tried to stay in a straight line toward where it had come from.

Maybe it was my imagination.

As he crested the next dune, he readied himself for the unexpected, knowing he'd be more visible than at any other time.

Thankfully he saw nothing, but then he wasn't sure he was heading in the right direction anymore. His doubts crept back in.

Maybe they've gone down below the crest. It was as positive a thought as he could muster for now.

If there was someone close by they'd be looking to settle in for the night as well, set up camp or the like. He needed to be more careful now.

Goran quickly started to look for somewhere to tie up his horse. Off to his right a shape caught his attention. He reached for his blade as he tried to work out what it was.

The shape moved upward, spreading its wings before heading back the way he'd come, not getting more than a few feet above the sand.

It's keeping out of sight as well.

He'd been right to be more cautious — if he trusted the bird then it was staying low so as not to bring attention to him. Goran walked to the darkness where the bird had been perched.

There was a protrusion of rocks poking awkwardly from the sand. He was just able to get the horse under, and tied it up, facing outward.

A pool of water bubbled up inside a formation of the rock, with a thin trickle of it running down the edge, across a white crystalized line that reached the sand on the ground.

Moss-like plants made a small mat around the base of the rocks ending at the sand. The water was enough to sustain them even with little light.

Goran pulled his larger coat off his shoulders and threw it to the side of the cavern-like space, before he pulled the hood of his tunic up over his matted hair and took a shorter blade from his saddle.

He patted the horse gently. *Don't worry, old mate, I'll take all this off when I get back.*

Goran climbed up the longer side of the dune toward where he'd seen the reflection. Crouched low and with the last of the sun to his back, he slid down the next dune and crawled up the other side.

It took two more before he found the beginnings of a camp.

A handful of knights were pulling together a series of tents on long poles. They had with them a train of horses carrying their supplies.

Even in the diminishing light he could tell the symbol of the ice bear on the knights' armor. These were the people Rainbow had sent him after. There were four others who weren't clad in armor.

One wore the characteristic long robes of a priest, while the other three were dressed like anyone else. The man closest to Goran seemed twice the age of the other two, but that was about all he could tell from this distance.

Goran crept backward until he was on the downside of the dune and turned, seeking what remained of his previous tracks to find his way back.

Next time I need to leave some markers or I'll end up lost.

Back at the rocks he set to completing his routines, freeing the horse of its burden and saddle before feeding it.

Just as there had been each night, a sack was sitting there, unaffected by animals or weather, almost as though someone was ahead of him leaving it for his benefit.

One day I'll want an answer to this.

He drank and ate the crusty bread like cakes and gnawed at the hard cheese. There were some dried meats in the bag as well and Goran ate half of them, before wrapping everything back in the sack and adding it to the saddle bag.

They are here, just like he said.

Goran was comforted by the fact that Rainbow had told him the truth. He wasn't going mad, there were knights out here as he'd been told.

I need to tell my colleagues.

Goran stumbled across the thought. *I have no colleagues anymore. It's just me.*

Rainbow had told him to pull his head in and that he couldn't run away. Had he told Tillandra what he'd asked Goran to do? Would he smooth things over with them all?

He felt conflicted despite the bravado he'd displayed to her; Goran did want to belong with the other Jesters. That's why it hurt so much to have them reject him.

This was what he wanted -- to do the work they did to protect their world. It was why he'd felt so much better once he'd settled into the task.

Would Tillandra forgive him for what he'd done? Had she told the others? The others wouldn't forgive him, that's for sure.

But... they should know about this. Do they know something we don't about where the amulet will show up? I need to know more.

Outside the rocky outcrop moonlight lit the night. *It's enough for what I want.*

Goran grabbed the two ropes hanging from his saddle, and left his hideaway.

He climbed back up the side of the dune where some of his footsteps from earlier were just visible. At the top he placed the end of one of the ropes down and slowly let it unfurl behind him as he clambered downward.

On the far side of the next dune, he did the same thing. His hope was it would be enough to help find his way back, otherwise he'd have to survive the night outside.

Ahead, light from what he assumed had to be campfires made it easy to know where his prey was. Goran climbed almost to the top then lay down on his front and slid forward.

Sand worked inside his tunic, scratching at his skin, as he looked down at the men preparing their meal. He froze at the sound of metal rubbing together, closer to him than the men down in the camp.

Very, very slowly, he slid backward and waited on the downward side of the bank.

All Goran could hope for was that whoever the soldier was they weren't going to see the grooves he would have left in the sand. If they were up at the same height as he had been then he was in big trouble.

61

LEO

If this is what being a Jester is all about, I'm doomed.

Leo was walking alongside the wagon on the opposite side to Carnus. Several times he'd walked alongside the massive man, trying to start up a conversation.

That had gone down as well as a rat in a bakery. Even simply remembering the look Carnus had given him, made him want to crouch and hide.

Kooka was one who would talk. He had no shortage of things to tell you about, which Leo enjoyed most evenings, but while they were traveling, Purple occupied the seat beside him.

For whatever reason, Kooka spoke very quietly around her and only to her, which meant Leo was left striding along, or riding on his horse, each of which ran out of favor quickly.

No one needed Leo's opinion on anything, not that there was much that required a lot of decision making. There was only one road to follow across the desert, from waystation to oasis, and repeat.

He was trying to at least learn a little more about where they were heading, but there wasn't much to be learned from this motley group. None had ever been to Midderbuilt; the closest Kooka had ever been was Watersend.

Kooka had stopped the wagon and waved him alongside. He motioned Carnus to come around the same side.

"What's up?"

"It might be nothing, but we've got company behind us."

Carnus immediately turned that way and stared. "How can you tell?"

"There are sand swirls happening back there with some regularity. Normally that means riders."

"That would be normal, right?"

"Could be, Leo, but who can tell? Out here you can get sand pirates that live within the desert and come out to raid those traveling along Death Road."

"Great."

"Nothing to be done about it but keep your eyes open. We passed a waystation just before, it's the last one before tonight's stop. I might pick up the pace, we'll be better off there than out here on the road, no matter who it is."

Carnus said nothing but moved to the back of the wagon and stayed behind once Kooka started it moving again.

The sight of the camp was a welcome relief to Leo. While they'd not seen anything else, other than sand swirls, being in the semi-shade and protection of the oasis felt better.

Kooka took charge and backed their wagon into as safe a spot as he could, after some stern discussions with the tender of the camp.

"The girl in there's unwell, and I'm not leaving her out, no matter what you say."

The tender only gave way when Carnus walked in and stared at him.

"Over there, out of the way, but it means you only get two beds tonight."

"I won't need a bed," was all Carnus had to say, before he went back to the slight rise at the entrance of the camp.

Leo used the barrel of wash water to wipe all the sand and grime off his face and arms before getting stuck into the food that was available for them.

When he was done he took a large plate and skin up into the wagon. Odajeen sat up when he came in.

"Thank you, Leo. Will you stay with me for a bit?"

"Sure. Any change?"

"No. But then I don't expect any." She didn't say anything else and chewed slowly on the dried meat, looking out at the waterhole that the camp was based around.

Leo stared at Lani. The young woman looked dead; it was the only way he could explain it. If it wasn't for her chest rising and falling ever so slightly as she breathed, you wouldn't know she wasn't.

He knew that Odajeen soaked a cloth and squeezed drinks into the girl's mouth, but she hadn't eaten since this had first happened, and you could see her body wasting away.

"What's happening out there?"

"What do you mean?"

"It feels tense, Leo. I didn't catch what was said when we stopped earlier."

"Kooka noticed someone behind us today. But we've not seen anyone, and now the sun's going down, not sure we will."

"Is he worried?"

"A little, but I don't know why."

"People travel this road, just like we are. I'm sure it's nothing."

Leo was about to agree when the sound of people screaming came rushing into the wagon. He knew it wasn't the screams of pain, but of an attack and he slid across the wagon to get out.

As he dropped to the ground, Leo rushed to his horse and pulled his sword free. He couldn't see Carnus but the sound of steel ringing from just outside let him know where the trouble was coming from.

Kooka carried Purple and pushed her into the back of the wagon. "Stay here!" He turned and headed up the slope toward the sounds.

Leo took off behind him.

"Leo, stay with them! Someone needs to protect the girls."

He stopped, unsure what to do. Slowly he turned and headed back to the wagon, relieved that he hadn't had to face whoever was outside. He just hoped Carnus was as good as he looked mean.

His body riddled with fear, Leo looked from side to side unsure what he'd do if someone broke through. He was the last stand to protect the three women inside the wagon.

For much of his life Leo had been the subject of cruelty. He'd been beaten regularly, tied up, tossed around and much more. Rarely if ever, though, had he been worried about his life.

There was the time that he'd been caught with a merchant's daughter, not doing anything, they were simply talking and holding hands. That hadn't stopped the merchant getting his guards to take Leo out into the surrounding forest with instructions to 'finish him off'.

By what seemed chance at the time he'd managed to escape; when the men had been focused elsewhere, he'd slipped out of their ropes.

Since he'd learned about his skill, Leo had wondered if it hadn't been him that had slipped out of the bounds.

The ropes had been tight on his wrists and legs, and he was tied to the tree while the guards went and readied their bows. What he now recalled of the escape was the ropes literally falling off him and he moved quickly away.

Was I a rat then too?

At this moment, he was as worried as he had been back then. Was this the end, could he protect Lani and the amulet? Leo was fighting his natural instinct to just run, that's what had kept him safe up until now.

But he couldn't, he had a job to do. He gripped his sword tightly and focused on that to keep him grounded, watching for any signs of attackers.

The tender also had a sword ready and paced about the camp area, waiting for whoever was outside to come in. "Bloody pirates. Attacking an oasis... never heard of."

Leo ignored him and listened to the sounds of fighting outside. He hoped there weren't too many more than Kooka and Carnus; if they were harmed then it would end badly for everyone.

Feeling helpless wasn't something Leo liked, but he'd been told that Lani and the amulet had to be protected at all costs.

Leo didn't like the finality of a statement like that, but it was enough to silence his desire to run and hide.

The sound of feet landing in the sand to his right caught his attention. A man dressed completely in black stood in front of the tender with a curved blade in his hand, about half the length of the tender's sword.

The tender wasn't a small man, but he didn't appear confident at all.

"Leave here! There's nothing for you here, the rule of the Oasis protects everyone."

The man in black paid no attention to his words and moved forward quickly, his blade sweeping in circles in front of him. The tender stepped backward brandishing his sword out straight, and Leo could tell this wasn't going to be a fair fight at all.

The tender struggled to block the sweeping attacks, poking his sword forward and missing completely. The attacker used his blade to push the sword outward before stepping inside the arm and slicing across the tender's midriff.

Everything seemed to down slow for Leo. His eyes filled with tears and if he hadn't been frozen to the spot his feet would have looked to run.

The tender's eyes popped wide open, and he looked downward toward his badly cut stomach just as the man in black brought his blade back, turning his wrist completely over, and slicing the man's throat.

Blood shot out and the tender crumpled instantly into the sand. He was dead and it had only taken the attacker less than a minute.

Leo saw the man in black turn toward him and knew he was done for. He was no better using a sword than the tender and he could feel his stomach clenching as he thought about his own guts spilling out.

Leo focused on the man's eyes, which were dark and emotionless. He didn't even show satisfaction at what he'd just done.

As the man moved slowly toward Leo, the hopelessness that he felt started changing.

It began to merge with an anger, which grew quickly. Leo had never been able to control his emotions and for once he was happy for it, at least he'd die fighting, not peeing his pants.

Suddenly he felt his sword drop from his hand and he was confused. A sense of shame came through.

How could I be so scared that I drop my only weapon?

But it was only a fleeting thought. There was something else there, the anger was still growing, and it was fiercer than he'd ever felt before.

He opened his mouth to yell at the man but what came out was a growl, a deep strong growl, and he saw confusion in the man's face.

Something had given the man reason to back off, and Leo didn't know what. The attacker was backing away and trying to circle back toward the way he'd come.

Leo moved forward, his anger overriding all sense of safety now. He could smell the man's fear, that's what he sensed, and it felt strange. Strange but good. Leo had never felt dominant over someone before.

It attracted him, drew him to the man in black more. Leo wanted to taste the man's fear.

What am I thinking?

Everything he wanted to do was overridden by this sensation. Around him he was aware of sounds and smells he hadn't noticed before. The blood pooling below the body of the tender smelt sweet to him, he wanted to lick it.

Sweet Thenis, no!

He jumped forward. It was the most amazing thing he'd ever done — one moment he was still growling that deep guttural sound, staring down the murderer. Next, he bounded forward then leapt at the man in black, batting his arm and blade away before pushing him down.

Then he opened his mouth and bit in… and tasted the man's fear. And his blood.

Oh Thenis, what have I done?

~

"Leo! Leo!"

It was Kooka's voice that he could hear, waking him. What had happened?

Slowly Leo came back to consciousness and instinctively patted himself down to see what was hurt.

"You're fine, Leo. How do you feel?"

His hand reached his upper chest, and it was all wet and sticky. He smelled his hand and looked down. It was covered in fresh blood.

"What's this?"

He saw Kooka look at Carnus, who simply shrugged, and then he looked back at Leo. "You killed him."

"Who?"

"The Derk."

Leo was confused, he didn't understand what Kooka meant. He began to sit up, and Kooka grabbed his arm, pulling him up off the ground. That was when he saw the man who'd killed the tender.

Leo turned and threw up, all sorts of things coming out of his stomach, which he didn't want to look at. The man in black's tunic was shredded and his throat was wide open, as though bitten through by a...

Wolf!

"Did I...?"

"Yes."

He collapsed to the ground, the memories he'd had of his last memory coming back to him.

"Sorry, lad, there's no easy way to say it, but yes you did."

"Did you see?"

"Only the end. We yelled at you to stop."

"Did I?"

"Yes. Then you changed back."

It was then that Leo finally realized he was sat there stark naked. He frantically grabbed at his clothes lying beside him and roughly pulled on his tights. He left them and went to the water barrel and dunked his head, scrubbing off all the blood.

He couldn't seem to wash it all off, and it was Carnus that came and stopped him. The man's powerful hands locked on each of his wrists. "Stop!"

Leo looked at him, feeling the shame at what he'd done, what he'd become.

"There's nothing there. It's all in your head."

"What?"

"The blood. It's your mind wants to wash away the thoughts. Nothing but time can do that."

Leo's shoulders slumped.

"It's not a bad thing, Leo."

"I ate that man!" Leo's disgust at himself was easy to hear in his words.

"Would you rather he killed the women? And you, like he did the tender?"

"No."

"Then you did what you did, to save them. What good if they had died, and our mission failed?"

He knew it was the truth but the whole concept made him want to be sick again. He shook free of Carnus and left the campsite, throwing up until all he had left was sore muscles.

When he returned to the camp, Carnus and Kooka had cleared away the bodies.

"How many were there?"

"Seven, it would seem."

"And?"

"All dead. We will inspect them in the morning light. How are you?"

"How do you think?"

"It will pass, just give it time."

"I doubt it."

Leo went to his bunk and lay down. There was no way he was going to sleep but he didn't want to speak to anyone.

6 2

TILLANDRA

$\mathcal{I}$n spite of the many issues Tillandra was facing she felt remarkably upbeat. Her overall wellbeing had continued to improve, and her cough had mostly subsided.

She could feel the smile on her face as she walked the college checking on everything. It wasn't something she did regularly but today it felt like the right thing to do.

She paused at most of the classrooms and observed the students and teachers at their work.

She still marveled at how someone had the foresight to create Anderwell the way they had, and how it had developed into the bustling environment it now was.

Within its walls many people, even those who had no magic ability, but who had suffered for their physical or mental problems, now lived in safety and with purpose. Despite her feelings about the faults she believed she had, being the head of this place did make her feel good.

"There you are!"

Tillandra turned at Toolet's voice. "You need me?"

"I think so."

"What's wrong?"

"Leo contacted me, but he couldn't hold his connection properly, I think something has happened… he sounded shaky."

"Didn't you say he was struggling with it?"

"Maybe, but this seemed different."

"Why didn't you call him?"

"I thought it quicker to come to you, you're the only one that's used the tree."

Tillandra shook her head. "We need to change that; anyone can use it. Let's go, I'll try to reach him."

She didn't wait once they reached the tree in the college garden, dropping down to the ground and putting her hands on its trunk.

"Hello?"

Leo's voice was very shaky, it wasn't the connection that was the problem. "Leo, it's Tillandra, are you okay?"

"There's been an incident." His voice faded out almost to nothing as he said it.

"Stay with me, Leo. You need to focus."

"I'm trying."

Then he was gone. Tillandra's sense of calm had evaporated in an instant. Something was very wrong, and her mind jumped to all sorts of conclusions.

Is Lani alright? What about the others? Is Leo hurt, is that why he can't hold onto it?

She reached out for Leo again and waited, praying he would answer.

"Hi."

"Leo! Are you okay? What's going on?"

"Yes. I guess."

"You scared me, your voice is so weak, you couldn't even hold your connection."

"I couldn't use the creature. My heart wasn't in it."

Tillandra didn't understand what he meant; it didn't matter at this second.

"What's happened, Leo?"

He said nothing for longer than Tillandra expected. "Leo?"

"I'm here. We were attacked."

"By whom?"

"Derks."

Tillandra gasped. "Is everyone alright?" She knew something had to be very wrong based on how Leo was responding, but she had to know. She wanted it straight.

"Yes."

"Everyone?"

"Yes. No one is injured, nothing major at least."

"What do you mean?"

"Carnus, he has a couple of scratches, I guess. But that's all."

He described the attack to her and that Carnus and Kooka had killed all the Derks, bar one.

"One got away?"

"No."

"Then what, Leo? Do you have a prisoner? That's good, maybe we can learn something from them."

"No."

"What then, Leo?" Her voice sounded agitated, even in the Void.

"I killed them."

"Oh." It then dawned on Tillandra that young Leo was struggling with killing someone.

"Is that your first time, Leo?"

"Yes."

"That explains why you're sounding out of sorts. It is not something pleasant to have to do."

"No…"

"It's not a nice thing, Leo, none of us like it, but what would have happened if you hadn't?"

"They'd have killed Lani and the others."

"You saved your wards, there's nothing more you can do, Leo."

"It's not just that."

"What do you mean?"

"I turned."

Should I ask, or just wait? When he said nothing else, she spoke. "What do you mean, Leo?"

"Into… a wolf."

The others in the Court had speculated about what Leo might be able to do once he'd been elevated as one of them. All their skills had expanded or changed after they put on their mask.

Leo changing into other forms was to be expected, she only wished she understood more about it to guide him. As far as she knew, there hadn't been any others in their past that had carried this skill. She'd have to ask Thenis about it.

"Tell me everything, Leo. It's alright."

Except it wasn't. By the time he'd finished, Tillandra could hear the pain coursing through him. Every part of him was conflicted. She could hear the logic, which he understood, about the need to defend himself. It wasn't that which was the problem. It was the way he'd killed the man, the ferociousness, and the lack of consciousness.

They hung there in the Void without words for minutes. She struggled to find words to comfort him. It was always difficult to console someone after the first time they killed but this was on a different level. *He wasn't ready for this trip, it's my fault.*

"You should come back, Leo."

"What?" He sounded angry.

"This is too big an event to not have support around you. I think it would be wise that you return to the city, and we can learn more about this."

"I don't want to learn about it! I want to forget it!" She could hear the strength was back in his voice, which if nothing else was a positive. "Besides, if I wasn't here, then she might have been taken, or worse."

"Who?"

"Lani. If I wasn't the one protecting them, then no one would have been."

"What about Irdan and his brother?"

"They've been gone for days."

"Where did they go?"

"They are riding ahead and checking on each destination. We're expecting them back today."

"Perhaps they should stay close in future?"

"Yes."

Tillandra sensed the opportunity she needed to anchor Leo's fluctuating emotions. "You did a good thing, Leo. You're right, without you, Lani could have been taken or killed. The whole mission would have failed, and bad things would eventuate."

He didn't say a word.

"Thank Thenis for you and the others. How is Kooka?"

"He's fine, a few scratches, he said it was Carnus that did most of the damage."

"Odajeen? Purple?"

"Scared but safe. She knows what happened to me, she hears things. Everyone is looking at me differently."

"That's bound to happen, Leo. I don't think any of them knew your skill anyway, which is a mistake, I should have explained it to them."

"But a wolf?"

"I can't imagine a rat would be much use in that situation."

He laughed back at her.

"What next then?"

"Keep going but keep the brothers close. Don't wait about, get moving and stay moving. We're going to need to start dealing with all these Derks, but I doubt you'll have any trouble from them immediately. They have large distances to reach you."

"Okay."

"Get Lani to Midderbuilt, Leo, and soon."

"Yes, Mother."

"And go easy on yourself, Leo. I'm here if you need me, but you need to control yourself better. Your last connection was too weak, you weren't deep enough."

"This way is much easier."

"It is, but you can't rely on us being able to reach back to you. You need to manage it at your end."

"Okay. There's something else."

Tillandra didn't like the tone in his voice. She couldn't imagine what it was because he'd accounted for everyone.

"What? Just give it to me."

"We discovered their temporary camp. Where they'd set up waiting to attack us."

"And?"

"There was someone else there."

"Just tell me, Leo!"

"We found Sabant."

"WHAT?"

"Sabant. She was in the camp, tied up as a prisoner."

What in Thenis's name?

"She says they tortured her. She has been beaten and cut. She could hardly talk; they hadn't fed her in days."

"Did she say why they took her?"

"No, we've only just found her."

"Question her when she's better, Leo, we need to know what they know."

"Okay. She's very scared and shaken."

"Wouldn't you be? Look how you're feeling."

"True."

"She'll need you, Leo."

"She hates me!"

"You're the closest person she knows, you need to be her friend. Things like this can change people. You need to be gentle with her, let her tell you what happened when she's ready."

"Okay."

"We'll talk again once she's better and you've had a chance to watch her."

Tillandra sat out in the garden for a while after she broke off the conversation. All of this was a troubling turn of events. The bliss she'd been feeling half an hour before had crumbled now.

At least we know where that girl is.

ARBERY

Drizzling rain hung across the town and the wind that blew had an icy chill to it. Arbery's fingers were close to numb and in this very moment all she wanted was to be back in the bakehouse.

Her inn had a roof, thank Thenis, and all the side walls were also complete, even if some windows weren't. She was standing under the half-repaired roof of the outside open stable. When it was completed, it would house a dozen or more horses and equipment.

Right now, it kept her dry while she took a break, sipping on a mug of hot milk and spice. It wasn't a drink she'd ever tried before the helpers had arrived. Once the quiet man had made her the first one, she'd fallen in love with it.

He was mute and communicated only by hand, which she was slowly getting the hang of. The others had said his name was Viraji which Arbery now used.

She sipped some more and looked at her new home. Or it would be if they could get the inside finished. They were digging out what would have been a cellar in the building before it had been destroyed by fire.

When Kalling had offered her an inn and a permanent spot within the Circuit, it had been all her dreams come true. Then he'd shown what it looked like, and her heart had sunk.

Since then, it had just been hard work. She and Dedrick worked split shifts at the bakehouse, until it closed around middle day. He'd be there early like now, and she'd go back soon to finish off and clean up.

Dedrick wasn't himself, that was for sure. There was so little to bake with and he was making small flat breads and little rolls that weren't much better than rocks.

He wouldn't stop, not until there was no form of grain at all, but his heart wasn't in it. The only reason he kept going was for the people who needed something to eat.

Especially the very poor who ate meats rarely; without the breads they had little at all. He hated what he offered but he wouldn't give up, not now at least.

Once the outside was done, then he'd begin to build the extension to the kitchen which would house a baking oven. They'd cleared a spot for him to start. He wouldn't let anyone else work on it, and she respected that.

Gidie walked out the back door with a spring in his step. The podgy man, who she now knew was around her age, looked not much more than Tiber had. His extra body size shook under his tunic as he walked, adding extra dimensions to his appearance.

Of the four men that had shown up to help, just like Kalling had said they would, he was the closest thing they had to a leader. Gidie was the singer in their troupe and Arbery watched him perform several nights a week.

These men had been incredible, working all day, before heading out to earn their money playing for the townsfolk. Everyone in Little Big Rock had fallen in love with them, even more so because they'd hung around much longer than other troupes usually did.

Because of that they didn't make a lot, day to day. They couldn't and wouldn't tap out the people who were all beginning to struggle, but they made a show of it.

Several of the Rock's nobles had tried to hire them for private shows, which they'd so far refused. Gidie said they often did this, to increase what they would get. He'd told her they'd do a few performances just before they left and make enough to cover their time here.

She wasn't sure how they did it, but they brought food and drink almost every day, which had removed that burden from her. Arbery wanted to pay them, they were building the inn with them, but Gidie had said that it was all part of the deal.

It was a Circuit inn after all.

"Miss Arbery, you need to come."

"What is it, Gidie?"

Arbery's face dropped. The last thing she needed was another problem. There'd been more than enough delays due to structural issues or rock they could hardly get through in the ground.

"We found something."

He turned with a flourish and headed back into the inn. Arbery followed wondering what it would be this time.

"Down there." Gidie pointed at the ladder into the basement.

"We really need stairs here."

He chuckled. "We will, Arbery, all in good time."

She clambered onto the wooden ladder and carefully made her way down into the cellar. Her mood lifted a lot when she saw how much space had been cleared.

Lanterns that hung on all the cleared walls showed a space half the size of the building above, with only an eighth still full of sloped dirt and bricks.

The three others were stood to the side wiping sweat from their brows with their sleeves, which left dirty streaks across their faces and foreheads.

Everyone was gathered around a shallow hole in the ground looking at what they'd discovered. A shovel looked to have marked the top of a small black box.

"What is it?"

Gidie was behind her, and she startled slightly at his voice. "A box, but we've not opened it."

"Why not?"

"Not our place, Miss Arbery. Best left to the Keeper."

A tiny smiled formed on her mouth. She loved the times he used that term. Soon enough it would be what she was called by everyone. Arbery couldn't wait for that to happen.

She knelt at the hole and brushed the rest of the dirt off the top of the box. It looked as though it would have been shiny if it was cleaned, and the scratch on it was minor.

Arbery picked it up and instinctively shook it. Something rattled around inside. She shook her head, knowing she should be a bit more careful until she knew what was inside.

"I think I'll take this upstairs, and we can open it in the light."

Everyone was interested to see what it contained and gathered around her in the kitchen area which was the only place with a bench.

Arbery placed it down and just stared at it. The latch was fiddly, clogged with dirt. When she was finally able to flick it open, she paused again, a little nervous about what they might find.

With a sigh she opened the lid. The inside of the box was covered in felt and there was a single ring inside. She'd never seen anything like it before. It had a strange-looking band, and the stone was orange.

It twinkled in the light, almost as if it contained a light of its own, but something very weak. Arbery picked it up and held it up to the light.

"There's like a light inside."

The others had all crowded in. Gidie spoke. "That's amber."

"I thought amber was banned?"

"Pretty much is, Miss Arbery."

"Might explain why someone buried this here. They didn't want it found." She could see there was something carved on the underside. Holding it above her head so the light got into the underside she tried to read what it was.

"I can't make out what that means, it's not our words."

Gidie looked. "Derk."

"What?"

"I don't know what it means either, but I know Derk lettering when I see it."

Arbery put it in the box, then banged the lid closed and latched it. "In that case then, we've never seen it. Not to any local, right?"

"Yes."

"You'll tell your lot then?"

"OUR lot, Arbery."

"Of course, our lot."

"I'll get word back, but we're not carrying that with us. You need to keep it safe, until I find out what Mother wants doing with it."

Arbery didn't like the idea of that. When she'd held it an odd feeling had run through her, one that made her feel queasy in her stomach. As soon as she'd put it in the box that had disappeared.

On top of all that, she knew full well that no one was allowed to have amber, so she should hand it in. But she wasn't part of Little Big Rock anymore, she was joined with the travelers. It was their rules she followed now.

A shiver ran up her back when she picked the box back up reluctantly. *Best I take it and hide it back at the bakery for now then.* None of the others said a word, they all went back to their work.

Arbery decided her hot drink didn't matter anymore. She found her coat and wrapped the box in it before setting off to tell Dedrick what was going on. No doubt he'd know the best place to hide it.

6 4

UKSOD

There was failing and then there was complete failure. Uksod hated both, but he was now the one who had not only failed to achieve what he needed to, but in essence had failed completely.

He stared at the two bodies laid out on the stone tables in his chamber deep under the palace. One had died from his use, the other he had stabbed out of pure frustration.

Now backed up to the wall he pushed his body as though he was trying to go through the rock. It was the only thing keeping him upright. He got nothing back from the men on Dharatan.

No sign of life at all. It had been stupid of him to kill the second body instead of taking a break and trying again.

What does it matter? There's more where they came from.

Why weren't they close to Anderwell? *It's like they are in the middle of nowhere. Why out in the desert, and who, or what killed them all?*

He knew he should have paid more attention to their exact location; he would need to give it to those who would need to recover their rings. *I can locate them next time.*

One wouldn't rest until it was done, that Uksod knew. They'd been successful retrieving all the rings from the most recent dead Vrah,

383

which was a win, but still there remained one that had never come home.

Barbarians had never killed Vrah, the assassins had always been too good, too fast, and always operated in the darkness, up until the attack on Karpenmor's mother.

In theory that had been successful, at least at the time. They'd killed the woman before she had let anyone alive know about her secret.

Uksod didn't doubt that if someone else knew the truth, it would not have stayed hidden all this time. It was too powerful; it would be too catastrophic to the empire should it come out that Karpenmor was not a full Derk.

Two failures had come from that event, one they'd only discovered more recently, which was the survival of the girl, Lani, Karpenmor's sister. Her existence was much more problematic than the words of the mother.

The other failure had been the loss of thirty-seven's ring. While Vrah only retrieved bodies of fallen comrades if they could, they were all trained to bring back the rings.

His had never been found. Uksod had never been able to locate it, which bothered him more than its actual loss. To the Vrah, not having the ring was a wound to their code.

Why were you all the way out there?

These rings in the desert needed to be retrieved. He could only surmise they were following the girl if they'd left the proximity of Anderwell.

She had become expert at avoiding Vrah attempts to kill or capture her.

I might as well do that now. I shouldn't have been so hasty to kill the second body.

He went to the door and opened it.

"I need another one!"

The guard looked at him, stepped to the door and saw the two bodies, before nodding then turning and hurrying away. Uksod knew they would never question it, and when the guard returned, he brought more Vrah.

Uksod waited in the far corner of the room until it was cleaned up and his new participant was strapped to the nearest table. He did a basic check of his energy and felt okay. He knew this second effort would tire him, but this was too important to put off.

If he had to, he could go to the Debrua Stone and fix that soon enough. Not that it would hurt his image with Karpenmor if he appeared to be unwell again.

Unless the boy had already figured it all out.

Enough worrying about that petulant boy, I need to find these rings.

As soon as he took control of the body on the table Uksod pushed his mind out toward where he'd located the rings. It came easily to him, and he spent the next few minutes zooming in and out of the location so that he could identify it more easily.

It proved to be a futile effort, but Uksod tried to detect the men who'd worn the rings. There was nothing to find.

He zoomed out, hunting for the amulet, that it might lead him to Anderwell where they knew it had been. There was nothing there.

As Uksod began to draw his mind back toward Enderk a tiny flicker of light caught his attention. Way off to the north it was a very weak speckle that he only just noted.

As quickly as he turned his mind to it the light disappeared.

Was it just my imagination?

It happened again. A weak light, very weak, but he rushed toward it. The light was struggling to stay in existence, but he felt it with his mind.

It's thirty-seven's ring! Where?

Uksod could tell the amber stone had little power left in it. It was free from whatever must have hidden it until now but was very weak. He rapidly sought out symbols that would give him the location.

Then it was gone, as suddenly as it had appeared. *Perhaps that was the last vestige of power it had. All gone now.*

Not that it mattered too much. He had located it, the rest wasn't up to him. One and his men could hunt it now, and bring it home, Uksod could tell them where to go.

This time when he pulled back out of the Void, he wasn't angry. It hadn't taken all of his energy to do what he'd done; he was tired but not too much. Nothing a good rest wouldn't fix.

His legs were a little wobbly at first but his motivation to tell One what he'd found out, the good and the bad, was enough to drive him forward.

Rest was for later. What was needed now was to discover who could get the rings back to En Carta, and who could hunt down the missing ring.

One's office was empty when he arrived from the passage he'd used. He doubted the leader would appreciate that he'd come without warning, not that Uksod really cared.

It wasn't the office that Uksod wanted anyway, and he headed to the library. The Dharatan map that hung on the east wall was what he wanted, and he took a moment to focus in on his memory of where the light had been.

Uksod poked his finger to the town that matched the location he'd seen in his mind.

"There you are!"

Uksod startled slightly at the voice behind him.

"One, you were next on my list. You won't believe what I've just located here in Little Big Rock." *What a stupid name for a town.*

CLANNACK

*U*nlike other rulers and lords Queen Vika cared little for lavish accommodation when traveling. Clannack entered her modest tent structure which had little adornment or items of comfort.

"Clannack, thank you for coming."

"Your Highness." He gave his customary head bow.

The Queen looked at the guards on the inside of the door. "You can both wait outside.

"Do you know where we are heading, Clannack?"

"Only in generalities, Highness, but not for the purpose."

"That's what I like about you, always straight to the point."

It was rare praise from the Queen, but he knew she'd flip on an eye blink, so he provided no response and just waited.

"We are heading to Kuwaha. Have you been there before?"

"No, Highness."

She nodded her head but didn't reply immediately.

"It is a very different city to any of ours."

Clannack was a little confused by that statement and it must have shown.

"I forget that you do not know all the history of our people, Clannack. Kuwaha was not always a Ngaherian city, once it belonged to the Derks."

"That I did not know."

"Enderk extended onto Dhratan, its border in land that is now all Ngaherian. Kuwaha was the only city on this side of the land bridge, and no one was ever allowed across there from here."

Queen Vika sat very still. The chair on which she sat was little more than makeshift, certainly not a throne.

"The city was wrapped in the walls that still stand today; they extend all the way to the cliffs. Only traders were allowed within the city, never any soldiers. It was known as a holy city."

That did get Clannack's attention. "Holy?"

"Yes, it is littered with what back then were temples."

"Not now, Majesty?"

"No!"

Her tone changed in an instant. Clannack knew he needed to stop replying and let her finish.

"It was run by priests and was a harsh place. Punishment for breaking any of their rules was extreme. In many cases flailed bodies were hung from the outer wall to be eaten by birds and other creatures."

Clannack didn't want to break her story so stayed quiet.

"Up until the destruction of the land bridge, the city was an enigma. Traders came and went to strict locations inside, did their business and left. There were no inns to stay in, no sound of enjoyment, and by all reports passed down to me, those that did enter never saw many other people at all."

Wind flapped the sides of the tent, breaking Vika's train of thought momentarily.

"Once the bridge was destroyed by the great storm, all of that changed. Soldiers from the south that chased the escaping Derks from the Great Fair through Ngahere, were blocked at the city walls. They attacked and eventually broke into the city. The results were bloody on both sides, but the Derks won, isolating themselves even more. Now they were alone and without supplies on Dharatan."

She took a long drink from a goblet she had been holding.

"The residents of Kuwaha blockaded the city and refused to deal with any barbarians as they called us. That their city had been invaded was a final straw."

She stopped as if contemplating the story.

"The folly of it all. They had few supplies and no relief from Enderk. They literally starved to death. When my kin finally entered the city, the scenes were horrific. Bodies piled up inside the temples, in what appeared to be sacrifices. I'm told that the priests hung onto power using extraordinary means, including eating their own people."

Clannack's stomach turned at the thought and he paced across the tent.

"Now you might understand our position on religion?"

The policy the Ngaherians had around religion now had some context.

"While it is now a city of our own, it is not a popular place, nor one I would choose to visit regularly."

"And so why now, Majesty?"

"We need the Derks' help."

"We do?"

"The wheat problem is a lot more dire than we've let on. There is nothing left in reserve, and our current crops are failing at an alarming rate."

"Failing?"

"Yes! Not only is it suspicious that the stocks of so many were destroyed but this year's crop has been weak, if not completely useless. We have spoken to the trees to seek their wisdom but there are no answers. Something or someone has brought this upon us."

Someone most likely.

"That's why we're going to Kuwaha. I need to get a delegation across to Enderk and to have them hear my request."

"Has anyone ever been there?"

"Occasionally, but none bar one has ever been reported to have returned. Reports that one made his way back last year popped up to the north, but no one has been able to prove it."

Ashantha must have been seen.

"It might explain the presence of additional Derks in black that have been seen arriving."

"So they get killed over there?"

"Or worse. I do not know."

"Why do you wish to deal with them?"

"We need wheat, this cannot go on like it is. Already our neighbors pressure me, believing we have more to sell to them. Even amongst our people you can sense the tension growing. We'll survive but the longer this goes on, the more problems it will cause. The last thing I need is soldiers on our borders sent to harvest our own produce."

"Surely that won't happen?"

"Who can tell, Clannack? These are the oddest of times. Word has it that the Skarians are mobilized on the borders of Sahro."

That caught Clannack by surprise, and his face twisted at what he'd just learned.

"I need your assistance. Every year we send a request for a delegation to meet with the Derks, to go to En Carta."

"Their capital?"

"Yes. Every year they are rejected."

"How do you deliver it?"

"There is a small station on the cliffs. When we finally returned to basic relations with them some hundred years ago, the steps of Kuwaha were built down to the ocean, and a small compound was allowed for their officials."

"In Kuwaha?"

"On the outskirts of it at the edge of the cliffs. It is a small, fenced compound that can only house a dozen or so people. Most of them are guards, but when they wish to trade with us, that is where it's done, outside that compound."

"That's where the Derks have to come through?"

"Yes. We restrict the numbers, one in for one out. But it's a facade."

"Sorry?"

"There's more Derks traveling around than we allow through the gates. They must land by boat elsewhere, it's hard to know how many there really are."

"Why isn't it Ngaherians guarding the steps?"

"They wouldn't do any business with us if we didn't agree to this setup."

Clannack was surprised that these stubborn Ngaherians had given in to such pressure.

"There are things we trade that my predecessors desired. Now that door is open, it has become very difficult to close it again."

I wonder what that is. Maybe she'll tell me.

"I've sent three requests this year."

He looked up in surprise. "Three, that's a little…"

"Desperate? Yes, it is. But I am sure they have plenty of wheat, and I want to get them talking."

"Has it worked?"

"No. I just received word the latest request has been rejected. Which is why you're here."

"I don't understand."

"I want you to go over there."

"What?"

"We need an emissary to go, someone official to force their hands, and you're known to be close to me. They would take you seriously."

Clannack wasn't stupid, he suspected he was being chosen because he was the most dispensable.

"You want me to go there, to the place that no one has returned from?"

"I want you to try."

"What do you want me to try?"

"I doubt very much that you'll be allowed past the guard station at the cliffs, but I want the representation made. I am hoping that you not being Ngaherian will make a difference. Every time they reject us, we receive the same message. *When you return that which is ours, then we will negotiate.*"

"Kuwaha?"

"It's the only answer that makes sense. Whoever reads our messages knows their history. I don't think a Ngaherian can get through to them, hence why I think you're the person to do it."

Clannack could see the sense in it, but her willingness to throw him to the wolves was concerning.

"And if they let me through?"

"I doubt that will happen."

"But if it does?"

"Then I would be trusting our fate to yours."

Or more particularly, you'd be leaving my fate in their hands.

"It is a lot, Majesty."

"I cannot force you, Clannack, but I believe you want what is best for all of us."

Her use of the collective 'we' was the first time she'd ever included him in such a statement. He was very aware he was being played by her right now, and she probably knew he understood that as well.

His options were very limited, and she knew it. Perhaps not for the same reasons as he knew but she was leveraging the person whom she believed him to be, very cleverly.

If he refused, he had no doubt that he would quickly be on the outer and, with some subtlety, removed from court. After all his work to get close to her, that wasn't ideal.

He took to pacing again to allow him time to think. His nerves were on edge, and he needed to think through any choices he had, or how he could flip this.

Sounds came to him from outside, little things but enough for him quickly to establish that there were more than just two guards outside. The entire tent was surrounded by warriors.

Nikora had stood off to the back without speaking the whole time, but she carried a pleased look on her face. She enjoyed watching him being put in this position.

Clannack was pretty sure if he didn't agree to this, he'd be set upon the moment he left the tent, if not before.

"I would be proud to serve you in this way, Highness. While I am unsure how I will be more successful than any other, I will give my utmost to seeking a solution to the current problem."

I hope that sounded official and convincing enough.

"Good. I am so pleased. We will be camping outside the city, at our next stop. Like I said, I have little desire to be in that city, so you will go on with a guard from there."

A guard of course. To make sure I follow through and don't just run off.

Clannack dipped his head in acknowledgment.

"Thank you, Clannack, I am very pleased that you will be doing this. You can leave me now."

The nice queen had disappeared, and she was back to her matter-of-fact tone. He shouldn't have been surprised.

He turned and left the Queen's tent heading quickly for his own space.

There were big risks with what he was being asked to do, especially meeting with Derks, but there could also be significant wins if he could learn more about them.

After passing his tent, Clannack stepped out of the main camp as though going to relieve himself in the dark surrounding forest. Slowly, and as quietly as he could, he pushed deeper into the dense bushland.

He sat himself down with his back to a tree and let himself drop almost into the Void. This was where he had the most access to his magic.

He sent out several strands, one straight ahead, the other to his right, and let them weave through the air. Like a fishing line he could sense the energy of creatures brushing against the strands if they were close.

A few insects flitting around brushed over them, then he was able to sense something more like he was hoping for. He'd never told the others that he didn't always use rats, not that anyone ever discussed it with him.

He needed to use what he could find close at hand. The snake that was loitering a distance away was too dangerous; even though he could control its thoughts most of the time, snakes had a dominant instinct to bite, and he'd suffered a few previously when trying this.

Clannack felt the fox as it sniffed its way through the bush nearby. Its ears and nose perked at his first touch in warning, but then Clannack had control and brought the creature toward him.

It was only a young fox and not as suspicious as it should have been. Clannack hated that what he would do would rob it of any chance to grow older, but he needed help and as fate would have it this was his closest and best option.

With his extremely long arms he was able to get his hand onto its back before it turned to snap and he sent it to the ground, semi-conscious. The strands retracted immediately and Clannack focused now on the energy of the animal.

Slowly he drew from it and pushed deeper into the Void, sending out his request as he did so.

66

GORAN

It was the silence that had Goran most concerned. If the soldier, or soldiers he'd heard were still moving then he would know where they were. But there was nothing.

Either they were at their destination and had no need to move further, or they'd discovered the marks Goran had left behind and were considering what to do about it.

Skarian knights wore full armor most of the time, which made no sense to Goran, but then neither did being a full-time soldier.

Even more ridiculous was wearing the armor out here in the middle of the desert. For Goran it helped when they moved, they made sound, except for now.

What have you got yourself into this time, Goran?

He still found it unusual when talking to himself that Zoran didn't show up. Not that he wanted his alter back, but after so many years of it, the absence was as uncomfortable as the lack of noise around him.

Some noise drifted over the dunes from the camp, but it wasn't from there that he'd heard the sounds of the knights.

His choices were limited: he could either lie here and wait through the night and return when the sun began to rise, or head back now.

There was so little light that he doubted he'd be seen unless someone was perched directly above him. And his hunger determined his final course of action.

Goran's food and drink was back with his horse at the rocky outcrop, and as slowly as he could he began to slide himself down the side of the dune.

No one called out, nor did he hear any armor movement, so at the bottom he stood and aimed as best he could across the valley he was in.

To his relief, once he began to climb up the far side, he found the rope he'd left behind. The idea had been a good one, and he coiled it as he trudged heavily up the sand.

As he reached the crest Goran looked back, grateful to see no one on the opposite side staring back at him. At least he was undiscovered, and as fast as he could he clambered through the sand and down the other side.

The half-moon made it light enough that he wasn't in complete blackness, and he located the second rope easily enough. With both looped over his arm he was able to get back to his horse easily.

Relieved and tired, Goran sat and ate just a little of his remaining food. He still didn't trust the birds he followed and that more supplies would exist for him in the future.

As much as he wanted to believe in it, in what had already happened, he couldn't. He still struggled to believe he was even out here. Rainbow had told him he would, and he had followed.

He used my own skill on me.

At first, he thought he was being led out here to die, but the knights were here, like Rainbow had said they would be. Which was a different sort of problem.

Now he needed to figure out how to deal with them.

Have they found the amulet already? Or are they still looking for one?

That he had no answer for. He would need to follow them and learn what he could while he figured out some way to overcome them, if it came to that.

Will the vulture still come now that I know where the knights are? It would be easier to follow from a distance that way.

Goran wished he knew more about the amulets. Whatever the

Court had learned about them while he'd been locked away hadn't been shared with him.

Nor had Rainbow been informative either. All he knew was they were powerful and not to be left to chance who had them. It was enough. Somewhere deep inside he knew it was a truth even if he didn't have anything else to support it.

He tossed and turned a lot through the night. Every night was the same since he'd entered the desert, something about it deeply unsettled him.

There was such a lack of other sounds in the desert and yet it wasn't quiet. When he lay still at night he could sense a humming noise, or more correctly a beating sound of some sort.

Like a pulse beating, deep in the ground, almost not there, and yet it was. As though the very ground was the surface of something that was alive, and you could hear its heart beating way below.

If he had any weed or drink he'd have used that to block it out, shut down his mind so he could get some quality sleep. But he didn't, and it had been a long time since he had. Even the thought of it wasn't as pleasant as it used to be.

Day came quicker than he thought it should, and he stretched himself out before saddling the horse and packing what few things he had ready to set out.

Turning his ear to the direction of the camp he heard nothing. No doubt the soldiers would already be up and about, packing down their camp if they weren't already underway.

He assumed they'd travel like him, avoiding the hottest parts of the day, which meant early mornings and late afternoons.

It didn't take long to prepare himself and he pulled the horse free of the outcrop and walked toward the far side, still unsure the best way to manage following his prey.

He had no plan on how to overcome them if and when they got an amulet. At this point he just wanted to stay close enough to have whatever inspiration he needed, and act on it.

As much as he was feeling isolated out here, the voice wasn't something he wanted to hear.

"You're a long way from anywhere, traveler." It came from behind him, above where he'd rested the night out.

Goran turned, the sight not something he was happy about. Three knights stood on the crest of the dune, two with bows, nocked and pointing directly at him.

I didn't know knights used bows.

It was a silly thought, but nonetheless it was true. They'd been smarter than him and waited him out. What he didn't understand was how they'd got there without making a sound.

Unless they were here before I got here last night?

"As are you. Why the weapons?"

"We're a little concerned as to why you've been following us?"

"Following you? I think you're mistaken."

The tone changed as the man in the middle, who'd been speaking, moved downhill toward him, his right hand resting on the hilt of his sword.

"Don't take me for a fool, traveler. We've known about you for two days."

Fool. Thinking you were smarter than them.

"How exactly could one man like me be a threat to soldiers like yourself? Where exactly are you from, by the way? You don't look to be local?"

"None of that matters to you. Now, we can do this easily, or we can put a couple of arrows in you, that choice is up to you."

"Do what exactly?"

"Head over to our camp."

Goran shrugged. Now was not the time to act out any solutions. As it was, this might work in his favor. Now at least he didn't need to worry about how to follow them.

"Would you like me to lead the way?"

He saw the soldier smile through his open helmet, turned and led his horse in the direction of where the camp had been last night.

67

CLANNACK

They had not been wrong when they'd said the city looked like nothing else he'd see on Dharatan. As Clannack approached on foot, he tried to take in what he could see over the wall.

Even the wall was completely different. The edges were hard, with none of the attempted softer corners. The caps and roofs of the turrets and columns were all angular, like triangles.

Inside, the pyramid-like tops of buildings were everywhere. And it was all dark stone, none of the white marble or sandstone that existed in many cities around Dharatan.

Nor could he see much wood, it was all stone. He didn't even know what the stone was, and as they walked along the road leading to a gate, he ran his hands along the wall.

It feels smooth but looks rough. How peculiar.

This close Clannack could see portions of the wall which had clearly been repaired by Ngaherians or others from Dharatan. The stone didn't match any more than the finish.

Based on the history he now knew, it had to be sections of wall that were destroyed when the city was first overrun.

Once inside the gates the first thing Clannack noticed was how quiet it was. While Ngaherians weren't people that abounded with frivolity and fun, their other cities and towns were still filled with people noise.

Inside Kuwaha everything was muted and slow. No one rushed anywhere and people walked in straight lines following each other. Several times his party was frowned at until they got into a line and held the group pace.

As frustrating as it was it allowed Clannack time to observe the city. Vika hadn't lied when she'd told him about the influence of religion on the place.

Despite them no longer serving the purpose for which they had been designed, the number of buildings that would have been temples was ridiculous. On every corner there was one, which meant in some places your vision of the city was framed entirely by temples.

Each looked identical to the others, not similar, but identical. Even now, with signs mounted across their facades to name the business inside, the likeness of them amazed Clannack.

Carvings in other buildings were all of the same person, a woman, portrayed as tall and lean, not Ngaherian at all. Her nose was sharp and while not long, it dominated her face, below strong brows.

Clannack couldn't help but observe how the harshness of how she was portrayed reflected the other architecture throughout the place. When they reached the mayor's building in the middle of the city, he was both relieved and overwhelmed.

This building sat alone, taking up the size of a large square. It was surrounded by the equivalent of three road widths on what appeared to be all four sides, although the back he couldn't see.

While the space accentuated the building's size, it wasn't needed, with both the height and the size in general being larger than anything else nearby.

Despite being middle day and a clear sky above, the amount of light at ground level was minimal, as though night was about to consume everything.

As he looked about his surroundings all he could put it down to was the stone. If he had to guess at it, he would have suggested that the stone absorbed all the light.

That's just silly, but what else could cause it? It isn't as though we're in the shadow of anything.

Unlike many other realms, Ngaherians didn't have a lot of pomp or ceremony within their internal forms of government, and Vika hadn't sent a herald forward to announce Clannack's coming.

Instead, he had to join the queue inside the building to see the mayor and deliver a letter which introduced himself and his guard. After an hour of waiting, he'd had enough and called a solider over.

"What?" The woman's attitude was so typical of those with power in this country and how they dealt with foreigners.

Clannack handed the letter to the woman and stared hard into her eyes. "This is from Queen Vika, for your mayor. I'm not going to wait around here for hours so deliver it to her for me."

The woman looked back at him with equal intensity. "Stay here."

Clannack laughed. *Where else would I go?* The woman didn't look back at his sound and walked toward another guard, passing on the letter, and hopefully his message.

This was repeated several times until it arrived at the mayor's table. She looked annoyed at being interrupted, or as Clannack thought, perhaps she was always that way, given how everyone around here seemed to behave.

Is it this city that does it? There's nothing nice about it at all, I can feel it in my bones.

Gestures were made, passed down the line of guards to the woman that Clannack had started with. She came closer to him. "Come. Just you." She looked at his escort, all of whom showed no response.

Clannack followed her and they approached the table, the mayor looking at him with a level of disdain. "This is him? A foreigner?"

The guard nodded.

"You carry a message from our Queen, why is that?"

"Why is what?" Clannack's mood was matching everyone else's, and he knew in this moment, if only now, he had the protection of the Queen's guards and her rule. He wasn't putting up with her attitude.

"Excuse me? You'll address me in the right manner or spend your next hours locked away."

Clannack shrugged and extended his massive body to symbolize how little he cared about their physical size. "Feel free and watch what happens when my guard report back to the Queen on how you've treated her councillor. Speak to me as you would her, or we'll wait to see how she takes your delay on the mission I am on."

It was as though all the air in the room was sucked out as a maelstrom arrived. He knew what those in earshot would be thinking, 'How dare this foreigner speak such to the mayor.'

Her face went pale. Clannack didn't know if it was in rage at what he'd said or that she'd recognized exactly what was happening here, and the error in judgment she'd made.

"You are he?"

Clannack nodded. "Clannack, Second Councillor to Queen Vika. If you had read the note, this wouldn't be needed."

At first her eyes never left his, then she looked down and opened the letter. Clannack could see she read it twice before she looked up at the guard alongside him. "We'll retire to the rooms behind here, bring him behind me."

With that the air returned and a few quiet mutterings could be heard. He walked alongside the guard assigned to him, not caring what everyone thought.

Now that he'd seen this city, Clannack wasn't particularly sure he'd ever want to come back here, once he returned from this mission.

If I return.

The mayor sent everyone else away once they were in the room and looked at him for at least a minute before speaking.

"You did not have to challenge me so."

Clannack shrugged more casually this time. "Perhaps it's the feel of this place, but I had no desire to be spoken down to either."

She nodded. "Understood. And even more so with this mission you have been given."

Clannack realized that to them he was a dead man. These were the guardians of the gate who knew no one returned. It was getting to him, that he had no choice, more so since they'd come into the city.

Maybe everyone that's gone has simply gone without hope. This place would have sucked out any hope you had. I need to get going before it affects me the same.

"There's something else the Queen doesn't know yet."

"Which is?"

"I think it best I show you. We've only noticed it this last week, and a message was dispatched to Laumua yesterday."

Clannack held off telling the woman that the Queen wasn't there, he wanted to know what was bothering the woman.

"Come with me."

He followed and they were accompanied by guards as they went out the back of the room, and through the building until they were outside.

His escort, who was still inside, would have conniptions if they knew he'd given them the slip this way. Clannack could see the city opening up a little bit as they walked along the main roads away from the mayor's building.

Nothing prepared him for the wall-less cliffs that appeared as they turned a corner on his left. The road ended up ahead, and he could see the expanse of ocean that bordered the back of Kuwaha, as well as the comical-looking symbolic gate of the Derks.

This clearly wasn't what he was being shown, as different to the rest of the city as it was. He could see the land away from the cliffs which would be the closest Step to land. The others further off were harder to make out in the distance.

They turned again and climbed stairs up into a tower on the back of one of the last buildings facing the cliffs. When they reached the top, only the mayor and Clannack went in.

"This is one of our watch towers. For decades we've monitored them, always trying to keep an eye on the Derks and the ocean. They line this side of the city."

"Okay."

She beckoned him to the Long Eye that stood on a leg, allowing it to be at head height without needing to handle it. He'd seen smaller Long Eyes before, boat captains used them, but they were easily managed and some even fit into the inside pocket of a coat.

This one was longer than his arm, and as round as his leg. He put his eye to it and was amazed at how clear the image was. It was pointed across the Step closest to them to the island behind.

What he saw caught him by surprise. Not just the bridge that the Derks were building but the number of buildings that now existed there and the supplies surrounding the people working.

The bridge was almost halfway toward Dharatan, and a smaller number of people were on this side of that gap, building back toward it. He stood up.

"That changes everything."

"I thought you might say that."

TILLANDRA

In the not-too-distant past Tillandra's dreams were a rare event. Not so rare as to be unhelpful but nothing like they were now.

She didn't know if it was the receding Occultation that was the cause or not. What she did know was that they were coming every few days now.

Many were still a collection of strange symbolism, but others were much more realistic. Determining which were messages and which were only dreams had originally caused her problems.

Thenis had given her some insight into telling the difference except now she was having to deal with many that were things to act on.

I have more than enough to do already.

When she woke, she used a new routine, sitting in bed and recording in her journal what she could remember as the morning light crept through her window.

Many of them made little immediate sense to her but having them written down let her spend more time with them as she sought out what they might be telling her.

Her most recent dream was filled with orange. The only relatable way to describe it was that she was a bird, circling Dharatan so high up that all she could see was color patterns.

Orange was highlighted everywhere in lines and dots across Dharatan. *Is that the Derks?* If it was then it was even more concerning than she'd ever imagined.

Moving lines of orange were running from Enderk across the Steps toward Dharatan. They appeared stymied by a barrier on the very edge of Dharatan, a wall holding them back.

The amount of light kept building and Tillandra could see that it would overrun the barrier if it was left to keep building. *The orange wave?* The prophecy from Nkuku hadn't been ignored, but it had made little sense up until Lani had arrived.

Now that the color orange was confirmed as being symbolic of the Derks, or more correctly their amber, the threat had become more real. As she sat in her bed, Tillandra didn't need anyone to tell her the meaning of this dream.

The Derks would soon move to cross into Dharatan one way or another, and when they came it would be in a wave. The rulers of her realms were not ready.

Why hadn't we been given more knowledge sooner?

The prophecy in Nkuku was about that city being the defenders against the orange wave. If that was true it would mean the Ngaherians were defeated.

How in Thenis's name would that happen? Tillandra knew how much of a warrior society they were. Their physicality was incredible as she'd witnessed with Carnus.

If his whole nation would be pushed aside either something powerful came to bear on them or the numbers arriving would be massive.

Is that why the bridges are being built? Or do they have many more boats than we know about? Where would they land?

Tillandra closed her journal and dressed into day clothes before hurrying to the college. Most of her colleagues might be away but the one that remained was as good a sounding board as any of them.

∼

"That's frightening, Mother." Toolet looked as though she'd been awake for hours.

"An understatement."

"Then we need to warn Queen Vika. They should prepare surely, being on land they'd have much higher odds against boats if they are aware of it?"

Tillandra thought about what she said. They did need to 'influence' what happened, but this would be a much more direct form of information. Would they have to show their hand?

"But how, Toolet? We don't want to let them know how we know, and I'd prefer not to expose Clannack in that way."

"True..." The small woman dropped down out of her desk chair and paced the room. "He has that difficult woman's ear, which is useful. Losing that now would be disastrous. We need more inside information, not less."

"Everyone needs to be told, but our reach isn't that long."

"Perhaps it is."

"What do you mean, Toolet?"

"It's something that Clannack came up with in Ngahere, but the concept could be used anywhere."

"Go on."

"Our Circuit is the perfect place. Rulers make two types of decisions, one from ideas of their own making -- often the most foolish ones -- and others that come from the pressure in their realms."

Toolet stopped her pacing and went to the table where she had refreshments. She poured two goblets of ale, held one up to Tillandra until she took it, then quickly swallowed the entire contents of her own one.

"We can use the Circuit to spread a tale. If suddenly a watered-down version of the prophecy starts to be told in every inn and market square it will grow in populism."

Tillandra laughed. "You're right."

"We'll be stoking anti-Derk sentiment, but given how prolific you think they've spread around the land that's not a bad thing. All we'll be doing is bringing recent events to light."

"So, we mix in elements of the attacks, which will give it credibility, but then add stories of how the Derks are coming... I like it. How did this come from Clannack?"

"It didn't specifically, but he'd been working on a small group of people in Laumua, that would spread a story when fed it and then he monitored how long it took to reach the wider community."

"And?"

"It worked much quicker than he'd imagined. He only used it in very basic circumstances but was very surprised how willing the general population was to believe and spread his tales."

Tillandra stared at Toolet as she processed what her colleague had just told her. It was simply an extension of what they already did but in reverse.

Instead of gathering information, and then feeding it back to the decision makers, this attacked ideas at the simplest of levels.

"I like it, and we're perfectly placed to make it happen. Make it happen, Toolet, and fast. Just go lightly initially. If Clannack was surprised in his experiments, we wouldn't want to overdo it."

"Sure. I'll get word out. I'll start with Bea. Given what's happening with Hallendell, she's the best suited to act on it."

"Tell her that if any of those who have completed their loops are around, they should go back out straight away, and not return. This is too important to wait for the next troupes to arrive in the north."

"Okay. Then I'll speak to Clannack."

"No, leave him to me, I want to learn what he's up to."

"What do you mean?"

"He's not in Laumua, he's north, close to Kuwaha."

"Okay, I best get started then."

Tillandra turned and left, heading for the back garden. She wanted to speak to Clannack now, if she could. Her pulse was beating quickly, and everything had a sense of urgency about it.

I hope my dream was correct, otherwise we're about to start something that will be very hard to put back in the box.

"Mother?"

"In All Jest, Clannack."

"In All Jest, to you as well. Your timing is impeccable."

"What do you mean?"

Tillandra sat dumbfounded as Clannack explained what he'd just seen. At one point she almost let go of the tree, their connection wavering.

"Are you okay?"

"Yes, sorry, I just lost my concentration. You're sure?"

"Couldn't be surer, Mother. They have bridges all the way across to Step Five, and they're approaching Step Six."

"How on Dharatan?"

"However they are doing it, they have a mass of supplies building on the island I could see."

"None of this is good, but it reinforces what Toolet and I have just decided."

She told Clannack of the plan.

"Wow, I didn't think we'd jump to such a large experiment, so quickly."

"We don't have any choice, Clannack. I cannot see any faster way to build suspicion and fear than to stir it up in the populations."

"I agree."

"You need to do your own version with the Queen."

"What did you have in mind?"

"The barriers on the Ngahere side must go up, she needs to prepare for an attack."

"Impossible."

"Why?"

"Like I said, she was about to send me over there, even if it meant me not coming back. They have no wheat and she's worried about what will happen without it. She wants to trade with them."

Tillandra thought about what he'd just said. It all made a bit more sense now. The wheat problem had to have originated from over there, this was their way across. Leveraging it to finish the bridge would get them access.

"We need to stop it, Clannack, or at least restrict what they have access to."

"If I get her offside then I might get pulled from the mission to meet with the Derks. Surely that's got to be of greater value."

Tillandra felt squeezed. Her dream made it feel like it all had to be solved now but Clannack was right. It wasn't just about the bridges — getting information from the Derks was why she'd sent Ashantha away in the first place.

If all of that hadn't happened, they'd be much further behind than they were now. What else could Clannack learn?

"I don't like it, not after what happened last time."

"I know what you're saying, Mother, and I feel like the reason she wants to send me is, she feels I'm expendable. But this is the best option we have to find out what they are up to."

"I know."

"Right now, Queen Vika can say no to letting them build from this side, there's nothing they can do about that. At least not for now."

"Meaning?"

Clannack told her about the history of Kuwaha.

"Perhaps they intend to take it back anyway, there's possibly an alternative plan."

"We need to monitor the coastline, there's been rumors about boats crossing the water for some time."

"I can't help with that, all of her focus right now is on the wheat."

"Keep me informed, Clannack, and stay safe!"

"I'll do my best, Mother."

When they were finished, Tillandra decided she needed to stretch her legs and climbed up onto the walls, walking around the ramparts, looking out across the land surrounding Anderwell. What had earlier felt like urgency now felt more like dread; the future the prophecy had hinted at seemed much closer now.

69

HALLENDELL

*H*allendell was surprised at the way she felt. For the first time ever having little order felt good, not having to be on constant alert in the Citadel was freeing.

She was in Lahti, and she did normally prefer order and a schedule, without it her anxieties grew.

Staying in Nkuku has been her way of hiding from the world. Blaming others for how they treated her and why she'd stayed there was a convenient scapegoat.

It was true that people stared, and she'd been mistreated for much of her younger life because of the strangeness of how she looked, but it was the lack of order that bothered her the most.

While the order of her previous role helped, she could never rest lightly within the Citadel. She had always felt one moment from discovery and, as it had turned out, it was a valid concern.

Hallendell finished her daily stretching routine. Being able to do the things she could required a certain degree of unnatural flexibility, and that needed some maintenance.

After leaving Hurok she'd crossed the river, and border, into Lletem, staying briefly in Ffiniol. From there she'd ridden to Urrun as quickly as she could.

The small city at the foot of the mountains felt safe, and she rested two days before heading along a rough track following the river. She forded the river at a sheltered spot before reaching her current destination.

Hallendell's hope that she'd be unknown arriving in Lahti played out, and she found herself a small inn to stay on the southern side monstered by the mountains that the city sat beside.

The river continued on past the city, narrow and sluggish, constantly in shadow from the size of the spires rising above it. This part of the city was dark and damp, but it suited Hallendell.

What she hoped to locate were those in the underbelly of the city, those who knew things others did not. While they wouldn't trust a stranger, they'd be happy to profit for sharing what they knew — at the right price.

Hallendell sought out the urchins that called this part of the city home. She walked slowly through the lanes and narrow roads where the buildings were smaller, in worse repair, and in many cases empty.

They were never truly empty; there would always be those that would take ownership for themselves as long as they could. People who didn't want to be found, or for anyone to know which building was theirs.

Hallendell spotted a young boy perched on a step, carving something with a little knife. She shuffled slowly, making herself less threatening to him, not that he seemed particularly bothered by an adult.

He stopped what he was doing and looked up at her. The left side of his face was wrinkled, the skin ridged and folded over on itself, parts smooth, others as though it had been pulled and stuck together.

Only fire did that to a person. His left eye didn't exist, everything there was sealed off. Hallendell hated to think what he'd gone through to get that.

"What you making there?"

He turned his right ear closer to her. "Say 'gain?"

"What... you making... there?" She tried to slow it down as much as possible to help him.

"Don't need to talk like dumb, just can't hear unless it's facing ya."

"Sorry."

"A bird. Little tit." He held it up.

Hallendell was amazed at the likeness of the wooden bird he was carving, the front half at least. He'd begun at the face and was working his way back.

"Wow."

"What?"

"That's amazing."

He shrugged.

"Do you carve a lot?"

He nodded and focused back on what he was doing.

Hallendell sat on the same step and let him carry on. She didn't need conversation to fill the quietness. There was a beauty in having company that needed no conversation.

She watched how meticulous he was with his cuts, but more than amazed that he was able to recreate it without a drawing to model, or a live bird to copy.

For no reason he stopped and turned to look at her. "Where you from?"

When he finished asking, he turned his head back around facing forward, which meant his ear was closest to her.

"Long way away. South." It wasn't a complete lie, that's where she was from.

"Why here?"

"Passing through. You?"

"Born here."

"Parents?"

He shook his head and touched the left side.

For a second she was confused, thinking they'd caused his injury.

"It took them too."

"Too?"

"And my brother."

"I'm sorry."

He shrugged again. "Long time now. Can't live backward."

His simple approach caused a little smile to form on her face. Children seemed so resilient at times. "Where you stay?"

"Thieves. I cook and clean. Not a good thief, too easy to remember me."

She nodded; it made sense. Hallendell was happy that at least he had a place to stay safe.

"Can you help me?"

"What?"

"While I've been traveling, I heard a story about a thing. But I don't know if it's true, or even where it might be."

"What thing?"

"A jewel. Some say it's got magic in it, some say it's bad, but sounded more like just a Teller story to me."

The boy was quiet for longer than before.

"Such thing here."

"Here?"

"In the city."

"Really?" She didn't want to be too enthusiastic, while the boy was being open, he had no reason to trust her.

"Why you hide your skin?"

His question caught her by surprise.

"What?"

"Under that paint. Why do you hide it?"

"How do you know?"

"Just can."

Now Hallendell was truly curious, this lad had something more than just a simple patience.

"Too many people stare, call me names, I got tired of it." He didn't need to know the rest.

He shrugged. "I get that."

"Yes, I can see you would."

"Should I wear paint?"

"Do you want to cover up?"

"Sometimes… I'd just like to be normal."

"You are, not your fault that you got burnt."

"Was."

"What do you mean?"

"I started it, was playing with the fire, and…" His mind wandered off.

"How old were you?"

"Four maybe."

"Then not your fault. Wearing paint doesn't hide the truth… what's your name?"

"Twodet."

"Well, Twodet, you don't need worry. Let me tell you something though."

Hallendell told him about Anderwell and the Fool's Cart. He was both surprised and amazed about it.

"I go there."

"Wait until the cart comes, Twodet. It's safer that way. I'll let it know you're here. They'll come for you."

"It's safe for me?"

"Safer than anywhere you've ever been."

He seemed pleased about that.

"It's in the council building."

"What is?"

"Your jewel. It came last week."

"It's real?"

"Seems so." He shrugged again.

"What have you heard?"

"Gossip. Street says it shines orange."

"Really?"

He shrugged again.

"You going to take it?"

"What makes you say that?"

"All the thieves talk about is how to steal it. They say worth more than a life's coin."

"That much eh? Any of them tried?"

"Three not come back yet."

"Yet?

"Been gone many days, no one seen them."

It was useful knowledge. If practiced thieves hadn't returned then it was well guarded. Not that she didn't expect that. She doubted they'd taken it and run, not three of them. But then they weren't her, either.

She'd be able to get to it, one way or another.

Hallendell sat and watched him as he carried on carving. After an hour, she stood.

"Don't forget to watch out for the cart, Twodet."

He nodded and looked back at his bird. Hallendell walked away wishing she could take him with her straight away. It always hurt knowing there were so many of them out there.

70

CLANNACK

No one spoke. Clannack stood still, as still as he could, not wanting to break the silence in the tower. His eyes had a sudden desire to twitch and an itch on his nose appeared from nowhere.

For once he controlled his need to shuffle and twist whenever in a tense situation. His arrival back at Queen Vika's camp had begun a conversation he hadn't enjoyed.

She didn't believe him, and he'd had to challenge her to witness it for herself. After that she'd not said a single word to him, it was as though she had already cut him from her court.

It wasn't what Clannack had hoped for, if anything it was more extreme than he'd seen from her in some time. On the trip to Kuwaha, he'd tried to understand what was triggering such a response but came up dry.

Either she had wanted to see him gone, and sending him to Enderk was the easiest way for her to accomplish this, or... *Maybe she did think I could help solve this for her?*

Without her willing to talk to him he had no way of finding out and so he stood still, waiting for the air to break.

Vika stood up straight after looking through the Long Eye for what seemed the twentieth time. "This is not good."

She walked to the stairs and descended from the tower, accompanied by her immediate guards, the mayor, Nikora and last Clannack. He had followed without direction but if his time was done, he wanted to hear everything he could.

At the distance he kept he couldn't hear what the mayor and Queen were discussing, but once back inside the council building, they all moved into a small meeting room.

The Queen held the guards back to wait outside, and Clannack paused ready for the doors to be closed on him.

"Come on, Clannack, what are you waiting for?"

He didn't reply but entered the room and she closed the door.

"It would seem that you were quite correct in your assessment, Clannack."

His instinct was to play the fool and say something snippy, but he bit down on his teeth holding his jaw closed. He was on a tightrope standing over a drop to a deep cavern out of sight below.

Queen Vika turned to the mayor. "Gimau, how is it that I have heard nothing of this bridge building?"

The mayor didn't appear ready for her queen's arrival, mentally or in any other way, and her nervousness was apparent to the three others in the room. "It only appeared to us several days ago, Majesty."

"What do you mean, Gimau?"

"The Long Eye only reaches a set distance. What you're seeing now, wasn't visible four days ago."

"Four, you just said, several. Don't play words with me, Gimau!"

"Four days ago we couldn't make out that a bridge was there. We could make out people but nothing to capture our attention. There are always people on the nearest island, and we don't spend much time looking further than that. Then two days ago on this Step we noticed many more people, and then materials arriving. It was at that stage we started to change our focus, and slowly the outline of the far bridge came into view."

Clannack could tell that the mayor needed a drink. Her voice was cracking and she sounded breathless, but there was no way he was moving to help her or anyone else right now.

"Out on the edge it's fuzzy, as you would have seen. But we can see it has changed even in two days."

"Why haven't I been told?"

"I sent a runner yesterday just before your man here arrived."

"No one reached us."

"To Laumua, Majesty. I am so sorry that we didn't know of your location, but I sent someone to the capital with word."

The Queen didn't respond, Clannack knew she couldn't rebuke the mayor any more for that, her approach had been deliberately kept quiet.

"We should sit. Can we have something to drink, Gimau? We will be here for some time."

The mayor went to a side door to the room and spoke quietly to an aide outside.

Clannack was internally happy at the meekness the mayor was exhibiting, compared to how haughty she'd been when he arrived. Even more so that he'd been included in this.

"Nikora, Clannack, sit. This is not what I expected."

"Will this not provide us the trade route we desire, Majesty?"

"It would, Nikora, but at what cost? We have no walls, no barrier here at all. How many of their men would enter with a bridge?"

"Of course."

"We do not appear to have much time. Would you not agree, Clannack?"

Her look had softened toward him, more like the way she had been prior to her decision to send him to Enderk. That made it easier for him to speak more freely.

"If they are this close, then I tend to agree, although with only two days of information it is hard to gauge. I didn't see that many supplies on the near side when I looked."

"Agreed. It would be a slow process to get them up to the top, especially the large beams. That will slow them a little."

"Once it's finished, they'll be able to rapidly build the final leg."

"Only from that side."

Clannack didn't respond.

"Your advice, Nikora?"

"I sense your reaction here would be to block access to the cliffs?"

"It's one of them."

"You know my process."

Vika waved a hand at her.

She turned to Clannack. "What are the positives in a bridge existing?"

"A connection? Trade?"

"Yes, and I would think leverage."

"Which would be what, Nikora?"

"You want grain, amongst other things, and they could supply it if what we know is correct. That means you are in a unique position, not just for us, but for all of Dharatan. They would know this too. Allowing them to finish it would mean they owe you a favor." Clannack noticed Nikora was puffed up with her own importance.

"If they'd honor it."

"Of course. What of the negatives?"

"Their soldiers!" The Queen quickly added.

"Easier access to Dharatan, and specifically Ngahere, is a problem."

"Be more specific, Clannack?"

"Queen, it's not just their armies having access, if that wasn't bad enough, but we already know there's spies and others that are arriving without our knowledge. Then there's the amber."

None replied immediately to that.

"It's outlawed by agreement of all the realms. I have never learned why, but it is a rule we've enforced. I do not know what would happen if more came."

"The same could be said for the numbers allowed on Dharatan. While we can claim innocence for any arriving by sea, we cannot for those by land. We are meant to be the gatekeepers."

"Yes, all that." Vika's annoyance was obvious, even to her. "None of this is new, but how the other realms might respond is something I don't know."

"Trade, Majesty?"

"It's an obvious route for them to take."

"Sorry, I don't understand." Clannack had to ask.

"The other realms could simply block trade with us. No wood, or other items sold to their markets would hurt us... a lot!"

"I see. But they will want the grain."

"Perhaps. If they think we're taking advantage, then perhaps they might hold off on that. We'd be the filling in the pie being cooked slowly to our demise."

Clannack knew she was playing the antagonist on all topics; it was her way of deciding on matters. He needed to make sure they controlled what was going on.

"I doubt that other realms could hold out as long as you could, Majesty."

"What do you mean?"

"Everyone is struggling with the wheat shortage are they not?"

"They are."

"Then word being spread to their people that they are choosing not to trade wouldn't go well..."

She interrupted him. "You are the clever one, aren't you?"

"Whatever the end result will be, Majesty, we need to be in control of it."

"You're right, Nikora. And Clannack, it would look like you won't have to travel far to complete what I wanted from you. I still think you will be an important key to this puzzle."

"As you wish, Majesty."

She stood and circled around the outside of the room. The major had said nothing the entire time, and Vika stopped across from her.

"Gimau, how many troops do you have here?"

"In the city? One thousand, perhaps a few more."

"And?"

"Sorry, Majesty?"

"I sense there's something else."

"There's another thousand in exercises."

"Get them all back. We'll want half of them to rotate through building duties."

"Building?" All three spoke as one.

"It's time we had a wall on the ocean side of the city. The little gate they have right now will not suffice. From today no Derks enter Ngahere without my personal approval. Clear?"

"Yes, Majesty." The mayor looked worried.

Clannack understood why — Vika wasn't leaving Kuwaha anytime soon, she'd just signaled her intention to oversee this entire thing.

"There's more. Every Derk in the city is to be moved into controlled living. I want them housed in that section of the city closest to the gate. None is allowed to roam without guards. Two per Derk. And only within shortened day hours."

"That will cause a number of problems, Majesty."

"Solve them, Gimau. I'm not debating this. Nikora, word along the coast. I want patrols, everywhere. Any Derks landing are to be arrested on sight. If they resist, use force. They can be held by us or die here, that's their choice. Until I have what I want, then we need to ramp up our leverage."

"Yes, Majesty."

"Right, then we'll move into our quarters and set up office, for now the capital will exist here in Kuwaha."

The room quickly emptied except for Clannack. He sat there thinking through everything that had just happened. It wasn't the way he'd have liked it to go but he held only a little sway.

At this point the Queen was hedging her bets; building some sort of wall to signal her intention to block the bridge but wanting to negotiate on trade.

It meant she was looking for leverage points to negotiate with, and that meant compromise. How much she would be willing to give up was what concerned him.

TILLANDRA

There seemed little reason to go home for anything but sleep these days. Previously the companionship of Milfred had helped make sure each day ended in comfort while he catered for her.

Now she chose to stay in the college, her office feeling more comfortable than her empty kitchen.

Clannack had spoken with her again; in fact, she'd had so many discussions that Tillandra was feeling exhausted. She knew she needed to watch herself.

Toolet could take over speaking to people while she let her strength rebuild.

The response from Queen Vika wasn't all Tillandra hoped it could be. Building a barrier was one thing, but if Clannack's summation was correct, it wasn't going to stop the bridge being built.

Tillandra didn't know how long it would take for word to spread about Derks, but it would be hard pressed to overcome a desire for wheat.

Some positive news was the rounding up of Derks within Kuwaha and along the coast. If nothing else, it would make Ngahere a no-go zone for Derks coming over by boat.

It would take a lot of people to watch the entire coast, so it was only a temporary fix. With such a massive coastline the boats could go either north or south landing in Rohumaa and Kysten or even Malamig.

Small boats meant only a few at a time, but even those had been enough to cause problems. If the rumors of larger boats were true, then they could ship an army without anyone knowing until it was too late.

I need to get those realms thinking the same way.

Every additional piece of information made her feel worse, the dread that surrounded her was growing in strength. The prophecy about the orange wave coming and her most recent dream all appeared to be real.

Linking back up to them by bridge wasn't something Tillandra could see anything good coming from. Perhaps Vika might block them altogether, but Tillandra doubted it.

The Derks had been clever, thinking longer term and working on the wheat. Now they had the leverage they wanted to get this finished.

She wished she had time to go north and see the bridges for herself. While she didn't want them to be there, to see the engineering would be something of great interest.

No matter what she thought about it, the Derks were coming. She needed a plan, a way to respond, and she needed to come up with it quickly.

The Court's influence in the north was limited, if it wasn't for Clannack they'd have no one close by anymore. Hallendell was out of Morska, and Nedor was closed off ever since Goran's efforts there.

The sooner Bea could start to mobilize people north of her the better they'd be, for information if nothing else. They needed to be watching.

She needed to help find Watcher. If what Hallendell had told her was true he was still alive, and they would need him in place before long.

As strange as the tale of the Watchers had seemed decades before, it now made much more sense. If she could get someone close to him it would help, while Clannack handled things much closer to the Derks.

~

A knock at her door broke her train of thought. "Come."

The door opened and Gizen stood there with her sensing stick.

"Hi, Gizen."

"Tillandra, can I talk with you?"

"Of course, come on in."

The younger woman entered and deliberately closed the door, then using her stick walked to the chairs on the other side of Tillandra's desk.

"Sit there, please."

She used her hand to feel her way around it then dropped into the seat, moving her stick to the side of her leg.

"How can I help you?"

"You can't, but I have something to tell you."

"Oh?" Tillandra was slowly getting used to the woman's manner. She never said more words than necessary, and apart from the time she spent with Peka, showed little joy either.

"I had a vision."

Tillandra leaned forward, resting her arms on the desk, and focused totally on Gizen. If the woman had one of her visions, then it meant something important. She never had idle dreams, and unlike Tillandra's, they were easy to understand.

"There's a man in the desert, a prisoner. You need to know this, but I don't know why, all I know is where he is, and the people that have him."

"Can you see what he looks like?" It was the strangest thing that the woman could see images in her dreams despite her lack of sight.

"Yes."

Tillandra waited, knowing that Gizen would say more when she chose to.

"He had long hair, but it's matted, all clumped together. When he walks it rocks about the back of his head. He rocks because of the way he walks."

"What do you mean?"

"Like one leg is shorter than the other, makes him limp or rock along, but maybe that's walking on the sand. He wears a ring."

"Like I do?"

"Yes."

Tillandra was beginning to worry now about where this was going. "You said he was a prisoner?"

"Yes."

"Who are these other men, do you know?"

"They wear armor, which doesn't seem smart in the sun."

"Is there an insignia on their armor?"

"Yes… a bear, do you know it?"

Tillandra nodded, she knew exactly who they were. "And where in the desert?"

"Northwest from here. A long way."

"How can you tell?"

"It's like I am a bird."

"I'm confused, Gizen, what do you mean?"

"When I get the vision, it starts as though I am a bird, up very high, I can see all of the land around me. Then it swoops down, and I can see the people."

"You've had it more than once?"

Gizen nodded her head but was quiet.

"Why have you only told me this now?"

"I didn't understand it before, but when it came again I could. And it told me to tell you."

"It?"

"The vision. I get a feeling of words, a direction, it is hard to explain. I just know what is needed."

Tillandra sat quietly while she thought about why Gizen was getting this dream. There was nothing the girl could do but to tell them, unlike her other visions which had brought her to them.

"He's one of us, Gizen."

The words stuck a little in Tillandra's throat, but she knew they were right. Goran was one of theirs and would be until the day he died.

"Oh."

"How many are there?"

"Six, and three others, who seem to be the ones giving directions."

"Not in armor?"

"No, the main one, he's… much older and scruffier."

"Thank you, Gizen. If it comes again, please bring me updates, even if they don't seem to be much at all. Okay?"

"Of course." Gizen stood without any other words and left Tillandra's office.

Why in Seth's Sands are you out there, Goran? Did you stumble across them?

There was only one way to know for sure, but she didn't know if he would speak to her. First, she visited the map room. While she trusted Gizen, Tillandra needed to be certain about the facts.

Sure enough, the blue light which was Goran hovered above the map in the direction the woman had said. Tillandra looked at where everyone else was.

As it stood, he was as close to them in Anderwell as anyone else.

Next, she went to the garden. She felt drained of energy, which wasn't a great way to use their skills, but time wasn't on her side.

The tree didn't seem to weaken her anywhere near the same and had none of the side effects of using a rat, it was the best option she had.

Slipping into the Void she used the method she'd learned that allowed her to see outward from the wearer of a mask. It was intrusive on the wearer, but this was important.

Goran sat on a horse, riding in the hot sun. Even she could feel the heat just from what she could see. Ahead of him rode soldiers, not fully armored but still wearing enough of their heavy uniform that Tillandra thought they must be dying.

At the front of their straggly line rode a man who wore a ragged coat and wide-brimmed hat. Goran looked down, and she could see his hands tied to the horn on his saddle, confirming that he was a prisoner.

It was hard enough to watch as they rode slowly, she couldn't have imagined what it would be like to be there. The horses plodded methodically through the sand, nothing like the camels she preferred to use.

What are you doing out there, Goran? And what did you do to get caught by these soldiers?

As the sun settled, they stopped, and the knights began to unpack several of the horses that had trailed behind them. Within a short time, they had set up a proper camp, with high tents for shade, both for the men and their animals.

Tillandra had procrastinated enough. Despite it being unlikely he'd respond to her, she had to at least try to speak to Goran.

She sent out the sensation of knocking, and waited, trying not to get her expectations up. He would know exactly what was happening, the question was whether he would answer.

"I wondered when you would reach out."

"In All Jest, Goran."

"If you say so."

"Where are you?"

"You know, Tillandra, don't pretend otherwise."

"You're still angry with me then?"

"Not so much, just pragmatic, and I'm sorry for what I did in Anderwell."

"Putting me to sleep, that was cute."

"I needed space, and it was the first thing that came to mind."

"Why are you in the middle of the desert, Goran?"

"It's a long story."

"I've got as long as you need."

By the time he'd recounted the visit he'd had on Death Road and what happened next, Tillandra wasn't happy that he'd been sent by one of the gods without any support.

"Cursed Rainbow."

"Who is he?"

"One of the gods, Goran, you couldn't tell?"

"I suspected, but he is quite disarming. Why would a god come to see me?"

"To get you to do the work they want done. They told me we'd get help when amulets showed up. I was stupid to assume they'd come to me and not the nearest source."

"What do you mean?"

"He's come to you because you were closest to the knights. And Hallendell to another amulet."

"She saw him as well?"

"Another. They're very active at the moment."

"Rainbow was quite animated about stopping the amulets. She's left Nkuku?"

"She had no choice, one of the Watchers was interrogated and gave her up. She was exposed."

"That's not good."

"No, thankfully she got out of the city, but she's on the run from them. How many soldiers are there?"

"Too many."

"What do you mean?"

"Too many for me to handle on my own. I can maybe use my skill on them for a minor delay, or one or two for something more significant, but getting away from here isn't an easy thing to do. They'll be able to follow me no problem."

"You're right in the middle of nowhere, you need help."

"So I'm screwed."

"I'll figure something out."

"I won't hold my breath."

"Don't be like that. Just stay close to them, and even more so if they get the amulet. We'll get you help, just buy me some time."

His tone softened. "Okay. I'm sorry, Tillandra."

"For what?"

"For everything."

"You can make it up to me next time we see each other."

~

She stood up from the ground and shook her head. *Go on, give me something else to deal with.*

72

KARPENMOR

It was a surprise to Karpenmor how sour a mood he was in. He knew he wanted to get to Ponte soon and arrange a meeting with the Ngaherians, but he didn't think this was the cause of how he felt.

Waiting for his carriage to take him less than a mile wasn't helping. Nor was wearing formal attire doing anything.

His collar felt too tight, and he constantly felt like he needed to swallow. The silver tunic seemed to be sliding all over his skin such that it felt uncomfortable.

Aika had said it was the finest silk, something produced only in Enderk, which was extremely popular amongst the Imperial Families. He couldn't remember wearing it before and wasn't a fan.

Yes, it was very smooth compared to the rest of his tunics but that didn't stop it bothering him. Aika had said he would get used to it. Karpenmor wasn't sure he wanted to.

Oh Yantarnaya, why am I being so petulant?

Karpenmor half expected a reply, although that hadn't happened in recent times, thankfully. It was something he wanted to understand better. While he didn't like her in his head he felt as though he should have some form of communication.

I am the High Prince!

No doubt he'd been muttering and shaking his head a lot in the last half an hour, his mind not letting up as he waited. Finally, the carriage pulled around to where he was waiting at the bottom of the entrance steps to the palace.

All his servants and advisors seemed on edge, and while he knew it was because of how he was behaving, part of him was happy with it. His petulant side just wanted everything his own way.

Because I'm the High Prince! And yet, I'm not. And isn't that exactly how Uksod treats everyone?

Aika seemed glad to have him climb into the carriage. "Try to enjoy the event, Highness."

He nodded, afraid of what sarcasm might roll off his tongue if he spoke. She looked on the verge of tears and he didn't want that. He'd already upset her when he came to wait for the carriage despite her advising him it wasn't ready.

Now he had to live with how everyone reacted to him. If he couldn't shake the feeling, then tonight would be a disaster. With his cabin curtained off, and finally alone, he closed his eyes and tried to calm himself by controlling his breathing.

The carriage began to move and the rocking of it and his breathing seemed to help. He shifted his focus to what he was about to attend but it didn't help his uneasiness.

Why on Enderk did I accept this invitation? I'm in no mood for petty small talk.

But that wasn't true, not entirely. Karpenmor knew that the information he was receiving in the palace wasn't entirely accurate.

He had caught out the two closest people to him in a lie, or at least in not telling him the truth.

Which called into question what else he was hearing... or not. If he couldn't rely on the leader of the Vrah to give him information, then perhaps he needed to go.

And as for the Regent, there were many things he wasn't sharing with Karpenmor. He had taken many steps to rule outright within his palace, but it wasn't complete.

He would never be able to trust everyone one hundred percent,

Karpenmor knew that. He had a pragmatic approach to it, but while an individual here or there was one thing, his security force and the religious leader of their country was another.

The carriage pulled to a stop, and he opened his eyes. Karpenmor took a deep breath and relaxed a little. It would have to do.

The door to his left opened, and one of his Vrah guards beckoned him out. He did his best to do it gracefully although he wasn't sure he pulled it off.

Brushing his coat and tunic flat he approached the steps as Lady Natillian walked down them, her green dress clinging to every part of her body. Despite her being much older than him, Karpenmor noted how well she wore it.

At that moment he was glad he wore the silk tunic, showing he was at least connected to the fashions. Her dress looked to be of the same fabric.

"Your Highness, you honor us with your presence." She bowed slightly as was their custom.

"Lady Natillian, it is you who honor me, inviting me into your family circle."

Being the first family to entertain me will definitely have the other families envious. I am sure their invitations are already on their way to the palace.

He held his arm out, as Aika had instructed him, letting Lady Natillian loop hers through it, and they proceeded up the stairs. The main building in her compound was a beautiful construction with several columns highlighting the curved, tall, bronze doors through which they walked.

How many people does it take to keep them from tarnishing I wonder?

It took some concentration to not shake his head at his own thoughts, and he brought his attention back to his companion.

"How many hands will I need to shake tonight, my Lady?"

Her head turned a little toward him, a small grin forming on her mouth. Surprisingly she wore few of the marks of age that other older ladies in the court had. "A few dozen or so, Highness. I did limit those in my family clamoring to be here."

No doubt to leverage them when needed.

The doors to her ballroom opened as they approached, and he

could see she was reasonably true to her word. If there were twenty couples in the room, that would be the most of it. There were almost as many servants as attendees.

Several horns played an entrance as they stepped in, and he wanted to cringe. He maintained his composure, focusing on the people he could see.

As he scanned the room, he kept a small smile held firm on his face, and wondered where the person he sought was. Then he saw her and he almost stumbled, quickly gathering his step so only Lady Natillian would have noticed.

She turned her head and quietly spoke. "Are you okay, Highness?"

"Yes, thank you. A little misstep."

He tried to casually return his look back to where Bhoomi stood. Her hair was tied up in a bun, and her face makeup highlighted her sharp nose, lean cheeks, and chin.

She also wore a silk dress, hers turquoise, dipping low in the front, but long to her feet. Karpenmor brought his eyes back to where he was being led and restored his calm.

Wow. I hope I get to speak to her tonight.

Slowly they walked around the massive room, with his hostess deliberately showing him off. Of all the power plays another family could make, to have the heir on her arm was a statement.

The room was split in two, the southern half filled with tables. Everyone was mingling at the other end, with drinks being served by the army of servants.

Karpenmor accepted and sipped, very slowly, a soft red wine. People had begun to chatter again, and the noise was completed by the sounds of a harpist on the stage nearby.

Lady Natillian left him with some of her family, but hovered close by. Karpenmor wondered if anything would be asked tonight, or if this was the preparation for a later time. He was very aware of how far out of his depth he was, at least at this time.

That was why he'd agreed to her invitation. In order to rule the way he wished, he would need to know more about the Imperial Families and how they operated.

There was no politicking in Uksod's methods, his rule had been absolute and through force. Karpenmor had no such desire.

It wasn't that he didn't expect to have to exert his power to rule, he would do what was needed, that he knew. Whether it was from his own loneliness, locked away in the palace, or from his desire to be more inclusive, he intended to entertain the Imperial Families. At least until he understood them better.

As if reading his mind, Lady Natillian returned to his side as his current companion nodded and excused themselves.

She slowly turned her head to his. "Forgive me, Highness, if you already know this, but are you aware of the incident involving families Six and Seven?"

Immediately she had his full attention, and he twisted his head to look her directly in the eye. "Humor me, I cannot always be sure I hear everything."

"Two bridges falling despite normal weather and no obvious reason, certainly caught my attention."

He nodded, wanting to see where she was going with this.

"If one was a suspicious person, perhaps they'd wonder if it wasn't deliberate."

"But for what purpose, Highness, and who?"

It took every scrap of concentration to keep his face straight, his eyes unwavering and to pause at her words.

She said bridges. Even I did not know there was more than one. What is she trying to tell me? Unless... He couldn't afford to let his thoughts wander or he'd show his emotions to her. *Was it her?*

"It seems you have learned more of the delays than at our last meeting."

Whether it was his fixed stare at her that caused the tiniest of flinches in her appearance he didn't know, but something had caught her out, or in what she'd expected.

"Only in the last day, Highness. I did think you would know."

Really? Did I catch you out?

"It is something I am still learning more about, but I will get to the bottom of it. I wouldn't want to comment more without having all the information available to me."

"Of course, Highness, and sorry for bringing it up."

About that he knew she was lying, she brought it up deliberately. There was no mistaking she had a reason to raise the matter, he just wasn't sure what it was.

"Let me finish introducing you to my family members."

"Of course." He wanted nothing of the kind but followed her toward the guests.

It took all his will to not yawn and to feign interest in everyone he was introduced to. Thankfully Lady Natillian controlled it so that he was only with each small group for a matter of minutes.

Until he reached the group containing Bhoomi. She was accompanied by another of her sisters, and two brothers. Karpenmor forgot their names the moment they were said, his eyes focused on Bhoomi's, his heart beating very quickly.

"Forgive me, Highness, I need to check with my Chief Steward about the next event."

Karpenmor nodded and watched Lady Natillian head to the side. Bhoomi's siblings quietly sidled away one after the other with polite excuses, leaving him alone with Bhoomi, and yet surrounded by everyone in the room.

"Are you enjoying your evening, Highness?"

"It's very pleasant, Bhoomi."

"You remembered my name?" She blushed.

"How could I not?"

This time her face reddened, and he wasn't sure if he had done something wrong or not. Then a gong sounded making them all turn to the stage.

73

KARPENMOR

*I*f anything, Karpenmor was grateful for the distraction. The sound that silenced the room and made everyone turn was the introduction of their hostess for the formal part of the evening.

Out of the corner of his eye he tried to watch Bhoomi. *Why was she embarrassed, I just said the truth of it. I couldn't forget her if I tried.*

Her face appeared calm again at least, whatever he had done she seemed to have recovered from. Lady Natillian was welcoming her family and guests; he was mentioned first.

Then everyone was requested to make their way to the tables to eat, and Karpenmor felt very self-conscious as people parted in front of him.

"They are waiting for you, Highness," Bhoomi whispered.

He looked at her. She had leaned a little closer, and he could feel the touch of her breath on his cheek. He looked into her deep green eyes and lost himself for the briefest of moments.

"For what?"

"To go to your seat."

"Of course."

Karpenmor became very conscious of the room around him, and

everyone now looking his way. He felt the blood rushing to his face and wanted to kick himself.

He nodded once at Bhoomi, and turned, walking toward the table below the stage. Once he arrived, servants held his seat, and served him a drink the second his bottom touched the chair.

Everything to be a performance.

At that point it was like all the air returned to the room and guests began to fill their seats, in some form of pre-organized order. Karpenmor knew he should be paying attention to who sat first, so that he learned something about this family and those it placed in high regard, but his mind was elsewhere.

He couldn't stop trying to catch a glimpse of Bhoomi, who had only just began walking toward her own seat. For someone so young the position she held appeared relatively high in the pecking order.

While he was waiting it gave him a few moments to contemplate the news that Lady Natillian had delivered. That she had mentioned two bridges could have been an accidental error or deliberate.

Why does she want me to think she knows more about this than others do?

And why hadn't he been informed of this by others, particularly One or the family priests? As High Prince, or soon to be, he should have known about this.

That's the problem though isn't it? I'm not crowned yet, and some seem to think that allows them some latitude. Or is it more than that?

Whoever is behind this delay it's related to the families; it has to be. A power play of some sort.

Lady Natillian approached her seat, the last person to sit. Karpenmor felt confused about protocol for such a situation. It was typically required etiquette that men stood for ranking women in their society. But did that apply to him?

The other men on the head table were looking toward him as though their actions depended on him, and he had no idea what was meant to happen. He couldn't afford to offend Lady Natillian, so he stood as she approached.

Once again it was as though everyone breathed with relief. He didn't move to hold her chair, a servant was already there, and he was their ruler, but it had crossed his mind.

Where have I seen such things?

Karpenmor tried to recall at what time he would have observed such behavior in others, and he couldn't remember. There was much Uksod and his tutors had tried to drum into his reluctant young head, that there was a good possibility it had been told to him at some point.

As food began to be served, he let his gaze drift back to where Bhoomi sat to his right. She was focused on her plate and listening to an elderly man sitting on her right.

Karpenmor loved to look at her like this, he didn't feel so awkward at a distance. He wasn't sure if it was the way the light around her table fell on her or just the way she was, but to him she was the most beautiful thing he'd ever seen.

A group of musicians had begun to play, and the room felt more relaxed, and he let his eyes drift across the room, watching the rest of the family.

As expected, it was an exquisite meal, better than any he'd eaten in quite some time. No doubt his staff could prepare similar, but he never asked for anything other than simple foods.

Karpenmor typically avoided rich foods. One thing he had learned while growing up was that those who retained a degree of self-control around food and drink appeared to be the healthiest.

It also explained his lean frame, which was not just because of his youth.

"Is the food not to your liking, Highness?"

He turned his head to Lady Natillian, noticing a touch of concern on her face.

"It is all most lovely, don't worry, my Lady. To be honest I've been a little captivated watching everyone, and the goings-on. I can't recall the last time I attended such an event outside of the palace."

Karpenmor realized it wasn't just her watching him and quickly chose an item to taste. He felt like an animal in a cage that everyone was watching, waiting to see what he'd do.

The conversation with the hostess covered no new ground, only gossip about those in her family that she felt inclined to talk about. None of it interested him and he struggled to refrain from both yawning and looking toward Bhoomi.

Is it a coincidence she is on my right, as is her grandmother, affording me an easy view without offending my hostess?

He was sure that Lady Natillian was very aware of her impact on him, but despite that he still struggled to not do it. Like when you bit the inside of your mouth and couldn't leave it alone with your tongue.

Thankfully he had not been expected to dance when the meal was finished, instead he sat with his hostess asking banal questions about different family members.

When it came time for him to depart, Bhoomi was far removed from him in the great hall, and he could see no way to speak with her again without bringing it to everyone's attention.

He thanked Lady Natillian for the evening and was never more grateful than when the door to his carriage closed behind him and it began to move.

Back at the palace he found his aide already returned and waiting for him. "So, what did you learn, Aika?"

"Mostly gossip, as is the way in the servants' quarters of such houses."

"Nothing of use then?"

"I didn't say that, just that mostly it was idle gossip. But what was curious was the lack of talk about one topic."

"Which was?"

"The delays to the other families. I specifically probed the topic, and it was as though I was speaking to myself."

"How is that curious?"

"Normally such a thing would be one of the main topics amongst the servants. With one or more houses not following protocol, the bridges and other interference with them, there would be no end of speculation, gossip and professed facts."

"Interesting."

"It was…" She stopped again.

"Speak, Aika." He wanted to shake his head at her but let it pass.

"It was as though they knew a lot about such a thing, but to say so would be detrimental to their house."

Karpenmor nodded as he had his own suspicions about it.

"But to what end?"

"Perhaps that's where the thing they would talk about fits in." She had become particularly nervous now.

"Whatever it is, unless you're behind saying it, I will not bite the hand that delivers the message."

"Well... it's..."

"Spit it out, please. I'm tired from all those pomps needing me to be polite, just tell me."

Her face reddened, not unlike how Bhoomi's had, and he was worried he'd again said something out of place. *Why am I worried about how my aide feels?*

"Everyone was interested in whether or not you'd taken a liking to Lady Natillian's granddaughter."

"Which one?"

"You know which one, the one that came to the palace with her."

"Ah, Bhoomi."

"Yes." Aika's face seemed to be even redder if that was possible, and Karpenmor was clueless as to why.

"Why are they concerned about that?"

"It would appear that your hostess tonight has been working this for some time."

"Working what?"

"Making her ready to be someone you would be attracted to, that she could be a worthy... woman for you."

Karpenmor felt his own face flush this time, which was silly, he'd known what Natillian was up to. It was the idea that the whole topic was discussed so publicly that embarrassed him.

He turned from Aika and let his thoughts settle. "You did well, Aika, you're a natural at this."

It was easy praise for something that really wasn't anything spectacular, but he needed this young woman to retain her honesty. A little praise was an easy way to reward her.

He dismissed her for the evening and removed the formal clothing, glad to be unrestricted and able to breathe easier. Was getting Bhoomi in front of him worth interfering with the other families?

Karpenmor was already part of the royal family, he didn't need to aspire to anything else, but he needed to better understand the political advantage Natillian was after.

There was only one person who could tell him the truth, Uksod. He already had a less than favorable view of the leader of Family Five, no doubt he'd deliver a biased interpretation of these events.

74

TILLANDRA

*H*er options were slim. Sending soldiers into the desert to rescue Goran was mad enough; not having an exact location to tell them was insane.

That meant either herself or Toolet would have to accompany them, there was little other option. She needed to find her friend and debate who.

Tillandra was happy to go, in a way it would be easier. Spending some time out of Anderwell would suit her, relieving her of this constant barrage of problems to handle.

Except she knew they wouldn't go away, and it would be more difficult for her to handle them out of the city.

Fussleguts. It means it must be her then.

Thenis had told her that their highest priority was getting the amulets and while Goran wasn't near one, that had to be the reason the knights were out there.

Somehow, they had a sense of where they would come, or maybe the scruffy man who seemed to be leading them, was someone special — the man who'd found Ahn's amulet.

How would he know? Is he another god working against them?

Tillandra suddenly was even more worried for Goran. Surely if this was a god then Thenis would have warned them of him? It didn't matter who he was, she still needed to send aid for Goran.

How many men? They'll need a lot of supplies. Or can we send a fast-raiding party and a second one to bring supplies?

Absent-mindedly she arrived at the foot of the stairs to the college. Tillandra looked up at it and reveled in the majesty of it. *Who would have thought that taking in the broken would lead to this?*

She found Toolet in the little woman's office.

"That man sure has a penchant for getting himself in trouble."

"That he does, Toolet."

"What to do then?"

"We need to send help."

"Who?"

"That's why I'm here."

"Me?"

Tillandra shrugged. "I can't see who else, Toolet, can you?"

"Gimbden?"

"I feel like he needs to stay focused where he is. The army across the border hasn't moved, and we need one of us watching that."

Toolet sat quietly up on her padded chair for a minute.

"I guess it's me then."

"It has to be one of us, Toolet. How else can we point them in the right direction?"

"Good point."

"And I can't divert Leo after what's just happened. Someone needs to be around Lani not just for now but when they get to Midderbuilt. She needs all the protection we can give her."

"When do I leave then?"

Tillandra wanted to say today and was about to answer when she noticed her colleague's eyes glaze over. She suddenly appeared to be elsewhere.

I wonder who she's speaking to.

∾

It was several minutes before she became present again.

"Sorry about that, it was Bea."

"Everything alright up there?"

"Yes, but she had news. A Vrah ring has been discovered in Little Big Rock."

"The name is familiar, but I can't place it."

"It's in Malamig, we're setting up a new inn there. A woman named Arbery."

Tillandra recognized the name and had to think why it was in her mind. Then it clicked.

"She was the one that helped Lani at the beginning of her journey and then sent a message to us about her."

"Correct."

"How in Thenis's name did she find a Vrah ring?"

"Apparently it was buried underground up there. They found it when excavating. It was in a box, a black box. That sounds exactly like the one Tingfurlew gave you for the amulet."

"Now that's interesting. There's only one reason to use a box like that, to block it."

"But why bury it?"

"Maybe it wasn't intentionally buried, Toolet. The site was a derelict building, wasn't it?"

"Yes."

"So perhaps it was just stored there and then it got buried... I don't know. But someone didn't want it found, didn't want the Derks to find it."

"She wants to know what to do with it."

Tillandra laughed.

"What's so funny?"

"I'm getting more questions than answers at the moment. We don't need it, there's nothing I can do with it. Tell Bea that it should be kept locked away or bury it again for now."

"Okay."

"And make sure they know to keep the box closed. Else they'll end up with visitors they don't care for."

"When do I leave?"

"As soon as the men are ready. Probably in the morning."

"I've got a bit to get done then."

"It can all wait."

"Well, I have a few hours up my sleeve, I can at least finish what I was working on."

Tillandra turned to leave. "I'll let you know once I've spoken to the captain."

By the time she'd finished discussing what was needed, she was feeling hungry and wiped out. The day had passed quickly, and she'd skipped eating completely.

There was one place she knew she could rely on for food and headed to the dining room in the college where all the students ate.

As she entered the main college a guard rushed her way. "Mother, come quickly."

"What is it?"

"Toolet, she's had a fall."

Tillandra didn't waste time grilling him, she just hurried along behind him. He led her to the main library on the first floor.

As they rushed in the main librarian was standing bent over on the left-hand wall. Tillandra wanted to push past the guard knowing she could move quicker than him.

"What is it?"

"Mother, she fell."

Toolet was lying on the wooden floor, not moving. Her tiny body looked lifeless.

"And? Is she alive?"

"Yes, I think her arm is broken."

"You think?" Tillandra regretted the sarcasm, but the way her arm was pointing didn't leave anything to the imagination. "Where's the phsyick?"

"On their way."

Tillandra kneeled and checked Toolet's breathing and felt for her heartbeat. The librarian was right, she was alive. Her face was pale, and she was unconscious, but it was something.

It took more than an hour to wait until the physick had come and had her moved. Tillandra couldn't watch as they set her arm back in place.

The pain woke her friend briefly, before she passed out again, and in the end, she left them to their work, on the proviso that as soon as Toolet woke they had to come for her.

She's not going anywhere.

By the time that was over the dining hall was empty, and she had to scrounge a simple meal up from the leftovers in the kitchen.

She ate it without tasting it and needing some fresh air, took a goblet of wine and went to the front steps of the college.

Now that night had fallen it was much quieter and didn't look so odd for her to be perched there. Once her wine was finished, she felt calmed enough to head back to see how Toolet fared.

The sound of a sliding stick caught her attention and she saw Gizen and Peka coming her way. A smile formed on her face when she saw the little boy who seemed to be growing quickly here.

Not as much as the tree he tended but the food and surroundings were working wonders on him, and his life wasn't in danger.

"Tillandra?"

"Yes, Gizen, what is it?" She braced herself for more bad news.

"I had another vision."

"Of Goran in the desert?"

"Yes."

"Tell me."

"It was different to the ones before. I think they are live."

"Live?"

"I mean current. Some dreams come in advance to tell me I should go, others are immediate, like seeing you in that basement."

"I see."

"It's showing me him as he is today and it told me to go."

"Go where?"

"To him. I can lead you to him."

"Really?"

"That's the feeling. I should take you."

"It won't be me that goes, but you can lead the soldiers."

"Okay. What about Peka?" The boy had wrapped his arms around Tillandra's long legs and would not let go. She was absentmindedly patting his back.

"He can stay with me."

"When will I go?"

"In the morning. It's urgent."

"I better tell him I will be going away."

"It won't be long; you'll be back just as quick." Tillandra hoped it would be true, she wasn't as convinced as she tried to sound.

"We'll see."

Something about the way the younger woman had replied sent a chill down Tillandra's back. It wasn't a vision of her own, but it worried her.

The ease with which she'd just told the woman to head off on this mad chase through the desert disappeared and in its place a dread began to grow.

75

HALLENDELL

*L*ahti wasn't a place Hallendell wanted to stay. While it wasn't Nkuku, it was still Morskan, and the military ran everything here.

There was a lot more freedom than she'd ever seen under Master General Izpen, but then he was a particularly nasty man. The general in this city was a little different.

He'd learned the hard way with the amulet. On its initial discovery he'd treated it like a city monument, allowing the public to enter the council building and observe it from a distance.

Proud to show off his opulent new gem until the first attempts on it had happened. Hallendell had heard all about it in the inns and washhouses all over the city.

It was the only thing people could talk about. The amulet had the entire city in its grip, the center of every conversation and what anyone thought about.

Not that you could get to see it anymore, not since the attempts to steal it had begun. That made sense to Hallendell, that the local thieves would sense the opportunity of a lifetime.

Except the stories she heard weren't just about practiced thieves, but anyone that spent too much time around it. More than a dozen locals had just turned without warning when inside the building, crossed the line and made a run for the amulet.

All of them had been cut down. Several guards charged with clearing up the bodies had gone mad and tried to reach it as well.

Now, as she'd heard, bowmen lined the upper level far enough away from it to be what they considered safe, all armed and ready to shoot the next person that tried.

And none of the public were allowed in, it had been closed off. Some told Hallendell that even the General no longer went inside, but she couldn't confirm it, nor did it matter.

Word had been sent to Nkuku and the Master General that it had been found but was too dangerous to bring to them, that it would be better if they came for it.

And so they waited.

Amongst those who dwelt in the underside of the city there were many plans to try and get in, but for all their scheming, none could come up with a plan that would stick.

Hallendell couldn't see how she could do it on her own, so she'd been working on a plan to get some help, enough to cause the distraction she would need.

She didn't have long to pull it off; soon soldiers would arrive from Nkuku, and most likely Izpen himself. Hallendell needed to be long gone by then.

There were two doors into the council building, one at either end. These were heavily guarded, but the rest of the long building had none.

Not that it needed any, there were no windows on the first two floors. That helped her in lots of ways — climbing wasn't an obstacle and few people at street level would notice someone gaining access that high up.

The night previous she'd conducted a dummy run, dressed in her all-black outfit, nearly invisible in the dark of night. She'd reached the third-level windows without issue and then scaled to the roof.

Almost all of it was glass, a dome that would have allowed the light in during the day, and moonlight at night. Lanterns below lined the lower level, and Hallendell could mark out in her mind the layout of the building.

On the ground level a sole pedestal stood with what looked to be a glass box on top of it. From what she could see, that held the amulet.

On the third level a walkway encircled the open hall below, with offices opening off of it. It would be those that had the windows she'd passed on the way up.

At night the guard numbers were much lower than in the daytime but still there were too many for her to slip past. She couldn't see them from the roof, but there had to be soldiers at ground level as well.

There was only one way she was going to pull this off, and it was going to be very hit and miss. It had two components that were both unpredictable.

Even if she knew all the people she would need personally, it would still be near impossible. *What had Hem said? Nothing's impossible, you just need to find a way.*

Something else bothered her as well. Ever since she'd been up on the roof looking down at the stone, she'd felt its touch. It was subtle but it was there.

She could remember how it felt while she was up at the edge of the glass, looking down. It was as though it called out to her, wanting her to help it get free.

The more she focused on it the stronger it grew. She felt it like fingers trying to grab hold of her mind, to grasp it and twist her toward it.

If it hadn't been for her training and her ability to concentrate her will, she doubted she could have held out, but she pushed back at it.

She shook herself, trying to forget the way it had felt.

If that's what it does to me, no wonder it pulls at those who might be weaker in their resolve.

It also meant she knew taking the amulet was going to be the least of her problems.

Today she had set her plan in motion. Now she had to hope it worked. Time was against her, and the longer she remained here, the more she'd be remembered.

She had one chance to get in, get out and run like the wind toward Midderbuilt.

With the city so transfixed on the amulet and why it was being held there, she'd been able to plant seeds in the minds of a few less than savory characters that there was more at stake.

That the building was filled with other amber gems and coin and that the other members of their guilds who'd tried to get in, were still alive, being held inside.

She bought drinks and fed the stories, strategizing with those that would listen about the best way to break in, fueling them with a plan to smoke the guards out.

People had listened and bought into the idea. But whether they'd act on it was one of the factors she couldn't count on. Nor if they did manage to break in, what would happen with fire and smoke.

It was the best she could come up with at such short notice and all she could do now was hope. She had her tools of trade with her, and waited off to the side of the square that fronted the council building.

Through the early evening, groups of men had been gathering, hushed at first, but their bravado growing as their numbers swelled.

The guards out the front were watching them carefully and in response drew more of the men from inside the building to back them up.

Part of the plan has worked at least.

Hallendell had hoped they'd be more worried about an attack outside than anything inside, at least short-term, but again it was only an educated guess.

More and more men entered the square, some carrying weapons along with more yelling and posturing. She could see some wagons being rolled in behind the men, and could only hope it would be wood to start a fire.

She couldn't linger there any longer and hurried along the road parallel to her target. At the identical spot to the night before, she burst from the shadows and sprinted to the side of the building.

Had anyone been watching they would have been amazed at how the black shape leapt and seemed to bounce upward with the speed of an animal.

Her grip pulled on small ledges helping propel her upward, until she found the ledge of an upper window. With a small pause, Hallendell pulled her body up above her hands and was squatting on the ledge.

She looked down in both directions, but no one had seen her, or if they had they were paying her no attention. The sounds from the front kept growing, which gave her a little more freedom to be aggressive opening the window.

There were no locks, no one would have deemed them necessary up here, but the window felt as though it had never been opened. It took a lot of yanking upward, almost causing her to lose balance at one point before she was able to break the seal on it.

With that done it opened more readily, to two-thirds of its height. It was enough and she swung her feet through, followed by her head, until she was standing in a dark office behind a desk.

Hallendell paused to see if she'd been detected but all she could hear was the clamor at the front of the building. Slowly she began to open the office door out to the walkway.

She didn't need it open much to see that there were still bowmen on both sides of her and more further away. The only positive was she could begin to smell smoke from inside the building.

Hurry up, I don't have all night.

KARPENMOR

hy hadn't Uksod told me about this?

The news he had learned at the dinner party wasn't trivial. If it hadn't been for the distraction within the room, he might have given away his lack of knowledge.

The Dance of the Brides that he'd thought of as an inconvenience was something much more significant. This year's dance, being the first since he'd come of age, was when the nominees were presented.

While the dance would be held every year at the same time, only those who danced this year could attend in future years, until he selected his bride from one of them.

This is ridiculous. I should be able to choose who I want.

And suddenly it all became a little clearer. The reasons that someone might try to delay other families made more sense. At least on the side of the families, from his point of view it was all a sham.

Were families Six and Seven not able to present their aspirant at the dance, then they would be excluded from contention.

They would have no opportunity to link their family to the royal family, a once in an era chance to lift their family's position in Enderk society.

It seemed even more likely to him that Lady Natillian could be directly involved despite her surprise and pleasantness on the surface. Her family had the most to lose if another below her became cojoined with his.

Family Five was the second most powerful family in Enderk, and no doubt she had no desire to see that change. Linking her own family would create a gap between the others that would be cavernous.

But should that not happen, then who would be her biggest threat? From what he understood, Family Seven was not so far behind hers to be a concern for Lady Natillian.

That she'd blocked both families made it much less obvious who the target was. It might appear more of a simple series of bad luck events, although he didn't believe that at all anymore.

She'd done everything perfectly to get Bhoomi seen by him and for the two of them to become a little more familiar. And it had worked, that was true.

Was Lady Natillian worried about the competition? Perhaps there was someone equally as lovely that she feared would steal Bhoomi's chance?

Karpenmor doubted there could be anyone more lovely than her, but it was a possibility, or more likely it was about reducing the numbers. A one in four chance was much better than one in six.

She would have no idea who he might fancy, but reducing the odds would be a smart play. And of all the families she was best placed to pull this off.

Her lands were closer to the capital than Six and Seven's. She'd quickly taken up residence in the capital in preparation it would seem for this event.

That other families quickly followed limited what she could do but not so much those who had to pass over parts of her land. If anyone was behind it, she was a prime contender.

What of the Vrah riders that had left days before, heading toward the east? Had One sent men toward the delayed families? If he had, why? *Why didn't he do it in discussion with me?*

Sleep had avoided him, and he wandered the halls of the palace, occasionally seeing servants hurrying from place to place as though expecting him to ask for something.

As it was, he just wanted peace and quiet, he wanted to be able to get his head clear about what was going on around him. How much of this did Uksod know? He would know all the rules behind the dance and yet he'd said nothing of it.

He was very concerned about the delays. Why was that? Was he involved in sending out the riders? Between him and One they think they can still run things behind my back!

Now he felt angry again. His face felt flushed, and he wanted to yell in frustration. He needed everyone to follow his commands, Uksod wasn't in charge anymore.

Footsteps running toward him caught his attention and he turned, bracing himself in case of danger. He didn't need to as his Vrah guards were just a few paces behind him.

They were like his shadow, he was aware they were there, but he forgot about them, accepting them as part of himself. A messenger had halted by the guards, slightly out of breath.

"Let him through."

"I have word from Ponte, Highness."

"And?"

The messenger seemed flustered, and quickly pulled the tube from his satchel. "Sorry, Highness."

"Thank you, get some rest and refreshment." He waved the man away.

More good news about the bridges, I hope.

Karpenmor opened the tube and pulled out the message, reading it as he continued on his way to his chambers. Halfway there he stumbled on the steps and almost fell.

Fool.

He waited until he was back in his room and alone before he finished reading.

The Mayor of Ponte's message was concerning but not unexpected. The good news was that construction had reached the final Step.

They were building back from Step Six, meaning there was only one more bridge to be built. The other news was the response on the Dharatan side.

The Ngaherians had expelled the small guard station on what he now thought as the Cumerc side of the water and sent them back to Step Six. They'd been told that any other Derks were being rounded up and held in the city.

Not just that but the barbarians had begun to build a wall blocking access to that side.

So, they aren't as happy as I am about the bridge?

Karpenmor chuckled. It was a little more aggressive than he'd expected, but he hadn't believed they'd just let him finish it without some form of response.

Everything would need to come at a price and Uksod had done one great thing in creating the wheat shortage. There was leverage and he had more if he needed it.

This was expected as long as they didn't become too hostile. The longer he left it, the worse things would become. A meeting was required; he needed to respond to their delegation request.

It was time the Ngaherians were received as they had requested. He would welcome them to Enderk, just not here in the capital.

Karpenmor threw down the letter on his desk and rubbed his head. He was running out of time to get all this done quickly. The enthronement was not so far away, but he knew there was no one else he could trust with this.

Uksod was still pretending to be unwell, and he was uncertain about what the priest might do, which left no one else of seniority that was in his pocket.

That he needed to change, and his first choice was easy. But to solve this situation he couldn't send them on their own. And as he hadn't yet been crowned, he would need to make sure his side of the delegation was represented suitably.

It was clear now what he had to do.

He opened his door and looked at his guards. "Bring me Aika, quickly."

She appeared quicker than he imagined she would, looking tired.

His assistant must have been awake the whole night as well. *She is diligent, I'll give her that.*

"I need you to arrange some things."

"Of course, Highness, what do you need?"

"Find Trorn and send him here, then you will need to go and prepare yourself."

"What do you mean, Highness."

"We're going on a trip." He filled her in on the details and what they would need. "It's to appear as though we're going on a ride out to the temple at the crossroads, nothing more."

"I understand."

"You need to make sure we have additional supplies in your party, and we'll meet you there. But that's only between you and me, are we clear?"

"We are, Highness."

"Excellent. And there's one more thing."

"Highness?"

"You'll be known as Chief Steward from now on."

Her face flushed and her eyes were startled. "I…"

"You don't need to say a word, Aika. It's done. Now go."

His face was covered in a grin wider than he could remember. Karpenmor was pushing his horse as hard as he could while still holding on, much to the dismay of the two guards accompanying him.

Ahead he could see his target and he didn't want any delays in getting there. As they approached the Lone Temple at the Prince's Junction, he slowed his horse.

Here, out on the plains north of En Carta, the temple looked sizeable, and yet he could only see it from his balcony in the palace because he knew it was there.

The plains spanned such a massive distance, things looked tiny when viewed with normal eyesight. The covered waiting area at the front of the temple offered shade and a resting point for the animals.

Karpenmor slid off his mount and handed it to a young man waiting for them inside the compound. His guards quickly followed suit and fell in lockstep beside him as he headed toward the main complex.

A flustered priest hurried out through the wooden doors which were so tall and wide they didn't look as if they had ever been closed. No one man could move them.

Karpenmor had remembered this temple from his riding lessons. At those times it had been a shelter from some rough weather, but he'd never stopped here in his later years.

On his trip to Ponte with the caravan they had passed by with hardly a glance, his mind elsewhere, and Uksod much more in control. *Not so much anymore, old man.*

"Your Highness, we are not ready to receive your royalness, my apologies."

"Your name?"

"Jaycee, Highness."

"Jaycee, there is no need for bowing and fawning, I am merely passing through. Your temple looks perfectly resplendent to me, and it is I who should be apologizing for disrupting your work."

"It is no trouble, Highness. What can I do for you?"

"Can you tell me where my Chief Steward is?"

"Chief Steward, Highness?"

"Well to be correct, Stewardess. She was sent here ahead of me with guards."

"You mean, Miss Aika?"

"Chief Aika, yes."

The priest dipped his head. He clearly hadn't known his previous guest's position in the palace. *That will change.*

"Bring them to meet me in the gardens."

"Of course, Highness."

The others arrived quickly, Aika, eight Vrah and Trorn.

"Highness," Trorn was the first to speak.

"Trorn, so good to see you, and Chief Aika."

"Chief?" It was Trorn that spoke in surprise, although Karpenmor could see the query written on her face as well.

"Yes, you traveled with my Chief Stewardess, Aika, did you not?"

"I didn't know, Highness. And my apologies if I didn't use your correct title, Chief Aika."

"That's okay, Trorn, it's a new position for her and she's quite humble about letting others know. It doesn't surprise me in the least that she's not said a word."

Karpenmor turned to the temple's priest, Jaycee. "Thank you, for aiding my party, that will be all for now."

"Of course, Highness." The priest turned and went back toward the temple doors.

Once he knew they were alone, Karpenmor addressed the party. "You are all here under some pretence, not the real reason I gathered you."

No one said a word. He turned to the Vrah. "Who is the leader of your group? The most senior?"

A man, shorter than most, but enough age to show he had earned his role, nodded. "That would be me, Highness."

"And your number?"

"Sixty-one, Highness."

"Sixty-one, your mission is now different than explained to you. You are to include the two men who came with me and prepare yourself for a long ride."

He looked at Trorn. "You will be accompanying us, Trorn, as will you, Aika."

"Where are we going, Highness, if I may ask?"

"We are on a fast ride to Ponte."

"Ponte?" The priest didn't contain his surprise. "All of us, Highness? It's so close to the eclipse…"

Karpenmor raised his hand and interrupted him. "I'm aware, Trorn, but there's little choice. Hence why it will be a fast ride, no caravan like my last visit. Each of you will get to learn the reason for the trip when we arrive, for now all you need to know is it is important. Freshen your horses, and Aika, arrange the distribution of the supplies."

"Highness."

Everyone began to disperse and headed to where the stables were housed. Trorn remained and stepped a little closer.

"Can I ask why you need me on this trip, Highness?"

"You can ask, Trorn, but for now I will not answer. But don't worry, there's nothing bad about to happen. It will be fun."

Karpenmor doubted the priest would enjoy it one bit, in fact he'd not known the man to ever leave En Carta. He was needed, if not for the negotiations, but as a symbol of the past.

What little he could find about Cumerc told him it had been a particularly religious city. A waypoint for Derks on Dharatan, and as such he wanted a priest with him when discussing its return.

And he would be discussing its return, soon enough.

On top of that, he knew Ngaherians banned priests and religion of all sorts in their realm, so all the better for him to bring one with him.

He needed to leverage what he could. One way or another he needed the bridge completed. As it was, Trorn would hold more standing than Aika. She wasn't ready for something like this yet.

Everyone is surprised, just as I wanted them to be. It's time people realized Uksod and One don't run things around here, I do.

77

LEO

*L*eo hadn't found the desire to speak much over the last few weeks. Since the attack the entire group had been eerily silent, even in the cities they passed through.

He stared out at the never-ending sand surrounding them and wondered when the trip would end.

Carnus mostly hung back from the group watching their tail, while Irdan and Vefed stayed close by. They were unhappy to find there'd been an attack while they were away and wouldn't let Odajeen out of their sight.

As they crested a large dune Leo stared into the distance, a glimmer of hope rising out of the horizon.

"Is that Watersend?"

Kooka looked perkier than he had for days. "It is, Leo. We'll get a good bed and feed there."

"We have an inn there?"

"We do, a good one and all, the Clown Prince."

"How safe will it be?"

"As safe as anywhere. We need to stock up, and I don't know about you, but my behind could do with something else to sit on, and I'd love an ale."

They still had hours to go but the sight of the distant city lifted Leo's spirits. They needed lifting or if nothing else he needed something new to think about.

Ever since the attack he couldn't stop thinking about what had happened. At times he wanted to experiment with it, to figure out how in Seth's name he could control it, but mostly he just wanted to forget it ever happened.

No one gave them a second look as their cart rolled slowly along the cobbled streets of Watersend. Despite the odd shape of the city from outside, inside was much like any other.

Kids loitered in lanes and doorways, some playing and others spotting new targets for their masters. *You'd be wise to stay well away from us, kids.*

Leo knew what street thieves looked like, he'd been amongst them half his life. He knew when they thought they had a mark. Thankfully for them they saw the guards and turned their attention elsewhere.

"This is it," Kooka said as he pulled the cart into a courtyard behind a building three stories high, toward the north wall.

As they'd pulled in a youngster had dropped down from a barrel they were perched on and ran inside.

"Here I was about to give a bollocking to whoever parked their wagon in the middle of my yard, and then I see it's you, you old fool."

"That's like a donkey calling a horse slow." Kooka clambered down and the two men embraced, both laughing loudly.

"Been far too long since you brought your type of smell here, Kooka. I see you're still collecting little ones." He tilted his head in Leo's way.

"'Fraid not, old purveyor of tasteless ale."

Leo climbed down awkwardly and walked over to the Keeper. He held up his ring as he did so, still something he was taking time getting used to.

"Oh! Well excuse me, you're a new one."

"Leo." He held out his hand, and the Keeper shook it warmly.

"Wessen, Leo. Welcome to the Clown Prince. What you up to if you've stolen the Driver to come out here?"

"I'm retired from that, Wessen."

"Really?" Then a big grin formed on his face. "You really are too old then." Wessen slapped his right arm on his leg and bent forward, laughing at his own joke.

"Enough of your silliness. We need to unload our cargo and find somewhere around here that serves food and drink of a reasonable quality. Know anywhere close?"

Wessen poked Kooka gently in the middle and turned to the wagon. "You've cargo? Must be valuable if you want to unload it."

Kooka leaned closer and spoke quietly. "Just some people we'd prefer to not make a song and dance about. If you could get us some rooms, we'll help the ladies up there."

That caused Wessen's eyebrows to rise. "You'll want them fed up in their room?"

"Yes, but one of those two will take it up and sort them."

"Sure. What about him?" he said, nodding toward the Ngaherian. "He looks like he was born angry."

Kooka laughed. "If it wasn't for him, I'd be rotting in the sand somewhere out on Death Road. He won't say much but he can eat a horse and look for seconds."

"Right you are. What about the little one?"

"She'll stay with them overnight, but she can eat in the main room with us."

It took them a while to get everything done, and Leo took a bath before he joined Kooka, Purple and the brothers down in the main room. Carnus had told them he would eat upstairs and watch the women; he'd not let Lani out of his sight since the attack.

"Feel better, boy?"

"I do, Kooka, you should give it a try."

The older man smiled. "I'll do that when my stomach is full enough to put me to sleep."

"So how much further to…"

"Don't say it, son, even though anyone can see where we go when we leave, best to not broadcast it. More than a week. You'll want to drink and eat what you can, everything on that trip will taste like sand again."

A man entered the inn through the front door and seemed to

bounce his way toward their table. Leo found his bright and vibrant energy surprising after the drabness of the recent weeks.

"Kooka!"

"Who told you?"

"Wessen, he sent a runner."

The two shook hands, and Leo noticed what appeared to be a ring on the man's left hand.

"You'll be wanting to meet young Leo."

He reached out his hand and lifted Leo's left before he knew what had happened. The mask on his ring went blue as the man put his alongside.

"Gimbden, Leo. A pleasure to meet you."

"Hello."

"Hello?" He laughed. "I heard you're full of words, and all I get is a hello."

"Give him time, Gimbden, before long you'll wish you never asked."

"This is all a bit new for me."

"I'd say it would be. Now what's going on and who's this lot?"

Leo twisted his head to the table next to theirs where Irdan, Vefed and Sabant sat. None of them spoke.

"They're with us, it's a long story."

"I'd better take this chair then. And who is this lovely young lass?"

"Purple." It was the first thing she'd said all day.

"What a lovely name that is. It's my favorite color as well."

"Really?"

He winked at her, and Leo warmed to his colleague and his light-hearted manner.

The men leaned their heads in toward the center of the table while Leo and Kooka took turns to explain what they could that Gimbden didn't already know.

"And you're all going to Midderbuilt?"

"That's the plan."

"What about the broken one?"

"Who?" Kooka looked surprised.

"The young woman sitting over there with those two."

"Why?"

"I can sense she's not well." He tapped his head. "She's shook up in there, she needs some help."

"And you think you're the man for the job?"

"Not so much, but there's others here who might help. Besides, where you're going you don't need any more liabilities. I mean you've got Leo after all." The grin on his face was enough for Leo to know it was all said in jest.

"Easy, you."

"But seriously, from what you've told me about her, and what happened at the Audition, she needs some time to heal. Maybe I can coax her back, or if nothing else find out what happened with the Vrah that took her."

"We'll think about it." Kooka had looked back at Sabant a couple of times before he answered.

"When are you heading off?"

"Tomorrow, we need to get there before something goes wrong."

"Something else you mean, besides being attacked, a woman stuck in someone else's head and all that?"

"Yes, all that."

78

UKSOD

The news had shocked Uksod.

"What do you mean, he's left the palace and not come back?"

One held his gaze, unfazed by the loudness of Uksod's voice.

"He left this morning with four guards for a ride."

"A ride?"

"Yes, Eminence, they were going to the Lone Temple."

"Did he say why?"

"No."

"Fool boy. When were you going to tell me?"

"I am telling you now, Eminence."

"Don't be cute, One."

"We don't tell you every time he goes for a walk or a ride, you've never asked for such a thing."

Uksod knew it was true.

"How long has it been?"

"They went early this morning, when they weren't back by mid-afternoon, I sent other riders."

"And?"

"I'm still waiting on their return."

"Get me their numbers, perhaps I can locate them myself."

"Sorry?"

"The numbers of the guards, their rings!"

One faltered briefly in his gaze, recognizing he hadn't been quick enough to understand. "There's more."

"Great. What is it?"

"It would appear that he had planned a longer exercise than just the temple. A second party left before him, his aide and Trorn amongst them."

"Trorn? Where did they go?"

"I do not know but they headed north also, with supplies on some extra horses and two more guards."

"What does the Prince think he's up to?"

"I could not say, Eminence."

Uksod shook his head and stared at the Vrah leader. "It was a rhetorical question."

This time One said nothing.

He had played out his illness for a few extra days, but it had gone on too long now, Uksod realized. Being unseen in the palace also meant he wasn't getting all the news he would normally.

If I wasn't already about to get back to business, this is forcing my hand.

While he'd been a little weak from the incident he'd wanted to remain away from general view. The last thing he needed was everyone to think him frail and weak.

His health was fine, and he needed to be above ground, paying more attention to what Karpenmor was up to. It was great that the lad was stepping into his role, but after so much planning Uksod didn't want him to mess things up.

He needs some guidance.

"Where do you suppose he's gone, One?"

"If he's not still at the temple, then there's only two options."

"I'm not a fool, One."

"To go east would mean he was looking for the other families. West and I'd suggest he'd be heading for Ponte."

"Why so?"

"The heir received a communication from Ponte several days ago. I was unable to receive it before him."

"You don't know what it said?"

"No, Eminence."

"Not very helpful. What's happening out there that we don't know?"

"The bridges are almost completed, that I do know, but I am unaware of anything else, anything urgent."

"Find out more, One. I tend to agree with you that would be his more likely destination. You'd better send more men after him, we can't have him suddenly come to harm when he's almost at the finish line."

"Finish line?"

"The enthronement, One. After so long, preparing everything, I'll be very unhappy if something were to throw this off track. You seem to be a step behind today, is there something wrong?"

"No, Eminence."

"Tell these later guards that the heir must be back in the capital in time for the dance, I will not have that messed up."

"They would force him, Eminence?"

"That would prove difficult, I'd suggest 'strongly encourage' might come across better. I'll prepare a note for Trorn. While I could pass a message through one of your men, he might not believe it."

One nodded.

"We'll have to assume he's heading for Ponte, but that can be confirmed with those you sent earlier when they cross paths."

"Of course."

"What of the other task I set you?"

"I sent the men, as you ordered, Eminence. They were under very strict instructions."

"When would we expect them to arrive with their packages?"

"If they had no delays, within a few more days."

"We don't need any more delays, One."

"I cannot predict how the family leaders will react to your message."

"They had better react the way they were told, and send their candidates back with your men. I didn't spend all this effort with Seven to have it fall apart now."

One stood wordlessly.

"There has to be a leak, One."

"What do you mean?"

"That we have been grooming the girl from Seven, someone found out. And I'd suggest Natillian is behind these delays. She knows the rules, and has the most to lose."

"We could take some action?"

"It would be too obvious. No, not while she's here and her grand-daughter is here. But we could make it much more difficult for them to meet with the lad."

One nodded.

"At least he's made that easier for the moment, taking off like this. Have Natillian's compound monitored, using some of your more specialized team. I want to know if it's her and anything else she might have up her sleeve."

"Eminence."

"And find out how she knew."

"It could be anyone, Eminence, there are so many servants and workers within the Seven family it would have only taken one to see a message, or one of our riders."

Uksod knew the man was right, it would be a wasted effort trying to find such a person. And it mattered not now, he needed the girl in the capital in time for the dance.

It didn't matter whether Karpenmor fell for her immediately, just that she was one of the contenders. For now.

"That will be all, for now, but let me know when your riders get back."

You might not want to attend the dance, lad, but you will, and even more importantly over time you'll need to choose the right person.

Lady Natillian's granddaughter was an oversight from Uksod's research. He'd not heard about her being the choice until far too late.

He'd been too confident in what he'd been planning that he'd forgotten how much of a player Natillian was. He wouldn't put it past her to delay the other families, in fact he wouldn't put it past her to take even more direct action.

Which I will have to take myself if your granddaughter gets too close to the boy. It would be such a shame for her to be harmed.

A smile formed and he felt even better than he had when he had risen this morning. Being back to his old self felt good. It was time for him to visit Yantarnaya, which might as well double as a chance to check on the guards with Karpenmor.

He'd hardly reached the bottom step when she began.

Uksod, you remembered who I am, I am touched.

"How could I forget, mistress?"

Indeed. What news do you have for me?

"Most things progress as they should. The bridges are near completion, we're preparing for the eclipse and coronation of the boy."

And yet you seem less than enthused.

"There's some wrinkles, as there always is, nothing I can't handle."

Is he ready?

"Perhaps more than I expected."

What does that mean, Uksod?

"He appears to have a mind of his own."

Uksod felt like she was laughing at him, or at least smirking, there was a definite sense of smugness to her.

"He's becoming quite the independent man, doing whatever he pleases."

What's he done now?

"Run off on an errand, or the like."

You need him leashed so we can direct him better. All the more reason I cannot wait till this enthronement is done and you can head off.

"Off? Where to?"

You know exactly what you're to do, Uksod. You need to be the one to build our allies on Dharatan. More importantly to fetch the amulets.

"We have the Vrah."

Which hasn't worked out so well. They need someone to oversee them over there and I'm tired of waiting.

Karpenmor's amulet is a long way from here. It will take time.

Excuses. There's more already, Uksod, and the rest will come. You need to get them, all of them.

"More of them already?"

Yes. They are weak, which is why we need them back here. We need them all, Uksod, even one less and I cannot get free.

"Understood, mistress. It will take time."

It's taken many lifetimes already, Uksod, this is nothing in comparison. What about the location of the Citadel?

"Nothing concrete yet. People are hunting, but until we have all of them, we have time."

So best you get moving, old man. No time for you to be lingering in this city. Get me my amulets, so I can charge them again, then you'll set out for the Citadel Stone. And finally, I can be free.

Uksod knew that was the deal, it had always been the plan, but leaving the comforts of Enderk wasn't something he was looking forward to.

It's time to place the beacons as well, Uksod.

"Where?"

On the Stepping Isles, and back in Cumerc. Placing them there will help me reach further into Dharatan. Get it done.

～

Uksod had plenty of time to ponder her commands as he climbed back to his office. He'd known this time was coming. Up until the boy's coming of age Uksod needed to be around, he was the Regent.

That need was over, and shortly he'd be free to set off on his own. He'd be without the reach he had over here, in some cases, like traveling through Ngahere, he'd have to travel incognito.

While there was at least one base for him in Rohumaa, they needed more places to stage what was coming. He needed to find people willing to feed them information and to house beacons of amber.

It was still illegal within Dharatan, but he knew coin could buy a lot of favors. And once the beacons were in place Yantarnaya could ensure the hosts wouldn't veer from their support.

While trapped inside the Debrua Stone all she could do was reach out and touch her people using amber. Cities and towns throughout Enderk were filled with it, not just in temples but many buildings.

All primary temples had a larger round stone, smooth and polished, located within the central spire which acted like a relay.

This helped her influence people without them needing to wear stones, like Uksod did. These weren't cut from the Debrua, like his gem, but they still helped, albeit in a more subtle manner.

Uksod needed the right-sized stones to make this happen, big enough to reach a distance, but small enough to be carried and hidden.

Across the city, in the market district, he found the carver he was looking for. This one was a skilled enough craftsman for this task, not at the level of the Lapidarist that had carved the amulets, but he would do.

"Highness, many years since you need Gehnant."

"Not Highness. Eminence, Gehnant."

"Sorry, sorry."

"I have a big job for you, worth many coins."

"Gehnant, very old, Eminence, not many stones left in me."

"Only you, Gehnant. Only you, can do this job for me. I need the round balls, like you've made before."

"Such hard work."

"Valuable work, Gehnant. Many balls, much coin."

Uksod shook several pouches and placed them in front of him. "There's much more of this to come as well. You need to get started straight away."

The old man shrugged and slid the pouches toward him. "Of course."

Outside his small workshop and house, Uksod turned to one of his guards.

"Stay here, he's never to be left alone. No one steals from him or knows what he's doing. Understood?"

The Vrah nodded and Uksod began his walk back to the palace. By the time the enthronement was over he'd have some of the amber stones at least.

79

KARPENMOR

*R*iding into Ponte was both a relief and exhilarating. Karpenmor was tired from the hard ride, and camping rough, and his grand plan to get here quickly had been hard on them all.

But all his tiredness disappeared as they approached the city. He could see the first bridge in the distance, arching from the Ponte gate. He couldn't wait to travel across them and see the other side.

There had been no warning for the governor of the city that they were arriving this time, and they reached his residence without any welcome party.

The guards at the city gates had dispatched their own messenger, and a harried governor arrived at the property shortly after them.

"Highness, you honor us with your visit. My apologies, I did not know you were arriving; we could have been better prepared."

"There was no time, our trip was very rushed. All will be fine. We need baths and food."

"Is this all of you, Highness?" he asked curiously.

"It is, Governor, and we will not be resting long here. Tomorrow I would like to be crossing the bridge to see the results you have written to me about."

"Of course, Highness. It is most magnificent."

The pair walked up the stairs to the residence, as servants bowed at Karpenmor's arrival. "I have another request for you."

"How can I help, Highness?" The Governor seemed to have regained his composure.

"I need a cloth maker, the very best."

"You wish us to make you some clothes?"

"Not for me, for my Chief Steward. She has nothing that suits her new position." Karpenmor stopped and beckoned Aika to catch up to them. "This is my Chief Steward, Aika, she will be organizing my things, but she also needs to be dressed appropriately."

"Understood, Highness."

"Know that she is very humble, Governor, and she will reject the offer, but you will ignore her only in this matter, and I expect she will have a full wardrobe ready for her. When we leave, the extras will be shipped back to the capital."

"As you wish, Highness. Let me go and get this matter begun for you."

Karpenmor watched the red in Aika's face slowly dim and slip away, nowhere as quickly as the Governor had left.

"You do not need to dress me, Highness."

"I disagree, Aika. You are now my Chief Steward, and you should be dressed appropriately."

"Do I not look correct to you?"

"It is not me for whom you dress, Aika. I know who you are and what you will do for me. But it is those who you will need to deal with that need to see you for the role you have."

"You honor me, Highness. I am very worried I will not be able to do this job you ask of me."

Karpenmor snorted. "Enough of that. You are more than capable, Aika. Your job isn't just to arrange my days, but to watch out for those around me."

"Watch out? What do you mean, Highness."

They had reached his rooms. "Come in, Aika."

When the door was closed, he turned to her and spoke quietly. "There are those who would like to have their own needs met more than mine, or who might want to see me fail. You must watch for them, and everyone else who has their own reasons for what they do. I need someone close by my side who only wants my interests to be protected. Who can tell me the honest truth even when I may not want to see it."

"I see, Highness."

"You might think you are not that person, but you will learn."

She bowed her head quickly.

"Tell me, Aika, is there someone that you have seen who isn't looking after my interests?"

She stared at him blankly, not expecting the question. Karpenmor waited patiently for her. He had to admit he liked watching the pressure he was applying to her.

It took her a couple of minutes before she responded. "Lady Natillian, this woman I would not trust."

"A good catch, and why would you not?"

"I sense she's up to much more than there appears on the surface."

"In what way?"

She was still uncomfortable to be speaking so directly with him. "She appears too smug with how well her introduction of her granddaughter has been going."

Karpenmor wondered if there wasn't a touch of jealousy about Bhoomi in her comments. He didn't understand why though, Aika was pretty enough in her own right.

"Perhaps she's just confident?"

"I just think there's a lot more happening that we don't know about. Could she be behind the bridge collapse and delays?"

"That's something I have been considering. What do you think about it?" Now that he had her talking, he felt pleased in his decision. He needed a confidant to discuss these matters with, and not Uksod.

"To what end? That they miss the dance? Is it that important?"

"It could be, Aika. Only those who attend the dance can attend the future ones. Then within the dance there are more rules, with the intention of eliminating candidates until there is only one left."

"Such a callous way to determine who you would marry, Highness."

He smiled. With that he was agreed.

"I think it's all about the power that comes from being linked to the royal family. At this time, she's the second most powerful family. If another gained more influence..."

"It seems a lot of work to eliminate the competition."

"I agree with that. Let's worry about it another time. For now, refresh yourself, you're about to be manhandled by tailors. Get whatever you want, there's no limit to this, including formal clothes. You will be in my company for many things, and the title of Steward is temporary, it will do for now. We ride tomorrow early, have everyone ready."

"Of course, Highness."

Karpenmor waved her away. As much as it pleased him to have her here to be on his side, he wanted his own bath and a rest from watching eyes.

Fog draped over the city, and Karpenmor could feel the early morning chill under his coat. They rode slowly toward the gate leading to the Stepping Isles.

He stopped as they approached it and beckoned the Governor to him. The man had looked very unsettled when he'd told him last night of when they'd be leaving this morning.

"Governor, does this gate have a name?"

"None, Highness. It has sat here as a beacon to the past and future, but we've not known what to call it and the Regent gave no advice."

"Then it can be known henceforth as Schevenal's Gate. My father was alive when this was built, and I would like all to remember him as they ride through it."

If the Governor had been surprised, he showed nothing of it. "A fine name, Highness. I will have it done."

"Let us proceed then."

The fog was so heavy that the detail of the arch only came into view as they rode single file through the gateway itself. Four Vrah ahead of him, the rest behind Aika and the Governor.

A light wind brushed over them and he wobbled a touch in his saddle. *I wonder what it is like up here when a real wind is blowing?*

By the time they had reached the second Isle, the sun was above them and the fog had all but lifted. The first of the guards rode ahead and stopped others from traveling the bridge while Karpenmor's party was on it.

They made good progress and by late afternoon, Karpenmor pulled up his horse and looked ahead. He could see the last Step ahead in the distance and with it the land of Dharatan.

The idea of these bridges had been exciting enough but to see the progress they'd made in such a short time was astounding. Across Step Six he could see the distant blur of the barbarian land, and what used to be called Cumerc.

That city will be ours again soon. You might not be ready for it, but we are.

"Let's ride, I want to be there before dark."

Karpenmor kicked his horse forward and had he been able to see the Vrah behind him, he would have seen the leader roll his eyes and set off after him.

HALLENDELL

Timing was everything, but it could also be her enemy. Hallendell had until daylight to get to the amulet or she needed to be long gone.

The entire building would be searched for damage once it was over and she had no intention of becoming a Morskan prisoner. There was no way that could end well for her.

She was able to detect the smell of smoke squeezing under the door and chanced opening it again. She could make out more smoke beginning to build up.

The bowman in her line of sight had pulled his tunic up to cover his nose and mouth. If nothing else, keeping him distracted would serve her purpose as much as him leaving his station.

There still wasn't enough to obscure her yet, so she closed the door and waited. Once she began to hear the guards outside coughing, she pulled up the cloth tied around her neck to cover her mouth and nose and opened the door.

On her right she could no longer see the bowman. Either he'd left, or he was blocked by the smoke. Either worked for her. The nearest guard on her left was visible and focused entirely on the ground floor below.

Hallendell knew she'd be unlikely to get a better chance to do what she needed to do. She took a quick shallow breath to calm her racing heart, but not deep enough to suck in lots of smoke.

Her speed on her feet didn't allow the man any time to react even if they registered her attack. Using a silken belt, Hallendell looped it over his head and around his neck.

He dropped his bow and grabbed at the belt. Hallendell held on as he bucked against her, pushing him into the railing so they didn't fall backward.

She was very practiced at the balance of holding on long enough to make someone unconscious but not to kill them. It was a fine line, and one she couldn't afford to cross.

When his knees buckled, she eased the pressure and dropped him quietly to the floor. There was no time to move him and Hallendell prayed she'd applied enough pressure that he'd be unconscious until after she was done.

Using the belt, she tied his hands behind his back and stuffed a cloth in his mouth to gag him. The negative of all this smoke was that it limited her visibility as well.

All she could do was to rely on her memory from earlier, and trust that. Hallendell climbed up the wooden pillar beside the guard's body and with hands and feet pressed into both sides of the roof beam above it she moved, feet-first, toward the center of the hall below.

The smoke was perfect for what she was doing while it lasted. If the attack outside stopped and the doors were opened to allow fresh air in, she'd have no cover at all.

She'd be visible to everyone, and an easy target for all the bowmen.

Concentrate!

Hallendell's feet reached the intersection of all the ceiling beams, that arched in from every pillar of the room. When she scouted it out, it had looked very strong — how strong it really was, she was about to find out.

The entire plan hinged on her being able to lower herself down on her cable, so she was directly above the case holding the amulet. If this wooden frame couldn't hold her weight she was screwed, there was no other way down.

Using her feet, Hallendell pushed the wooden structure while hanging on with her hands. Her eyes were watering from the smoke. It was very thick here, and she was struggling with the exertion and not being able to take deep breaths.

The wooden frame didn't move so she pushed harder. Still, it remained firm. Next, she moved her body halfway into the frame, still hanging with her hands to the beam she had used to get here.

Slowly she moved her body weight onto the frame ready to hold on tighter if needed. The frame didn't appear to move or buckle at all.

A good sign. Now I just have to try the whole thing, there's no way I can tie the rope and hang on at the same time.

With little time to contemplate things, Hallendell moved the rest of her weight, so it was fully in the circular frame she was now inside. Nothing moved at all. Quickly she pulled her kabel vine rope from a pouch tied to her tunic and looped it through the roof beam, still preferring that to the frame for her support.

When it was locked off correctly, she let the cable fall, sliding it through her hands so she could control the fall. Once it ran out, she slipped on the gloves she wore when using the rope and lowered herself out of the frame.

She could sense the stone below not as strong as it had been before, but it was there. She had to focus away from it, or her mind would get lost there.

Without the smoke Hallendell would have been perfect target practice for the bowmen, but now she was a ghost inside a cloud of smoke. Flashes of orange speckled the smoke below. Initially she thought it was the amber stone, before she saw they came from the front of the building.

The entrance is fully on fire.

Her time was running out. If the outside of the building was beginning to burn then inside would be alight in no time. She had to get the amulet and get back up and out before then.

Sweat ran down her back in a steady stream as well as soaking the band tied around her forehead, which she wore for this exact reason. She needed her sight, even if it was smoke-filled.

When her feet touched the floor, she looped the cable around her waist. She couldn't afford to lose sight of it, and the smoke down here was the thickest.

It had been another gamble she'd had to take, which was how much visibility there'd be down here. Thankfully it blocked any sight of her.

If her calculations were correct, she would find the case immediately to her left. Hallendell reached out very slowly and felt something hard there.

There was also a strong sense of something else probing at her as well. Hallendell knew what it was and shuddered at what it was trying to do. Again, she locked her mind off to it as best she could.

Turning left she stood before the case and, placing both hands around it, lifted the glass, hoping there was no lock holding it in place. There wasn't.

She lifted it and tilted it slightly as she carried most of the weight on her left arm so her right could reach under. This was the moment when she'd find out how powerful the amulet really was.

Her hand wrapped around the amulet; she could just see it when a small movement caught her attention.

A clear glass pebble had been placed on top of the case and was rolling down the top of the case. She pulled the amulet out, and dropped the case back in place, but too heavily as her left had reached out for the pebble.

Too late, it hit the floor and shattered. The sound barely registered compared to the sound of the box. Immediately she dropped the amulet down inside the front of her tucked-in tunic and began to pull herself upward.

A whoosh passed her shoulder almost hitting her. Another grazed her shin, causing her to grimace. *That hurt.*

More whooshes came but were all lower, she'd already pulled herself upward at least twice her height. There were probably more arrows flying below but she could no longer hear them now over the sound of the fighting and the crackling wood burning.

It took every bit of her strength and practice to get herself up the rope, her hands straining inside the gloves, the rope almost cutting through them.

Hallendell wanted to take in deep breaths but couldn't. Her eyes wept and whatever it was coming from the amulet was pushing against her mind.

The physical exertion and effort seemed to help her focus and shut it out. She knew that wouldn't last but for now it was enough.

Once she'd reached the top, she hurriedly transferred herself back onto the crossbeam and began the painful slide across it. This time she worried less about being visible or making any sound, confident that the guards would be focused down below.

Her timing couldn't have been better, for as soon as she'd retraced her path back across the beam, she found the bowman awake and trying to wriggle himself free.

Hallendell was grateful he was more worried about his being caught out than alerting a colleague.

A kick to the side of his head slumped him back down on the ground again, and she removed his bindings before dragging him back to his post.

She used the gag to cover the small graze on her leg that the arrow had caused and retraced her steps through the office and down the wall. More soldiers were beginning to arrive at the square to her left and she knew the attack would be over soon enough.

While Hallendell felt bad for those she'd used to help her steal the gem, she knew it was important. And feeling it constantly working on her mind, she understood why they needed to get it far away from everyone.

She hurried off away from the building, disappearing into the shadows. By the morning, the city would be full of soldiers hunting the thief. This was one gem they would not stop looking for, especially General Izpen.

81

CLANNACK

During his time in Laumua, Clannack had come to see the Ngaherian warriors as fit and strong, but lazy in many other respects. The average soldier flaunted their physicality but were little more than meat lumps with brains.

Watching them in action now forced her to change that view of them. Once they were issued a command their whole nature changed, and they sprang forth with action and didn't stop.

What had once been an open skyline was now filled with the makings of a wooden wall. The Ngaherians had removed the old gate and started building the footings and posts as close to the edge as they dared.

Second teams came through and began to build frames for simple ramparts once the initial wall sections were braced. That was only the beginning of things.

Queen Vika had sourced stone from other cities and outlying settlements needed to build the real wall. As it slowly began to arrive in the city piles were created twenty feet back from the wooden wall. Soon builders would begin on footings for the real wall.

Clannack had many days left alone to his own devices as the Queen spent more time with her generals than her councillors. It was to be expected; they were behind the logistics and manpower needed.

He nosied around gathering information where he could, but unable to get direct access to Vika at this time. Clannack spent many hours using the Long Eye to watch what the Derks were doing across the gap between them. Their half of the bridge proceeded quickly, and it wouldn't be long before there was little else they could do.

They too had begun the construction of a large gate on their side of the final bridge and walls to either side of it. Clannack could make out the formation of towers either side.

He doubted this was an immediate reaction to what the Ngaherians were doing; they seemed to be a long way ahead in their planning of this situation, Clannack assumed they'd always designed such defenses.

The tension was building throughout the city as though a war was coming. Clannack wondered if it would get to that. At this point Vika held most of the cards. Without her consent and help, the bridge on this side would never get completed.

Any Derks that had been in Kuwaha were being held in what must have been historic dungeons from when the city belonged to the foreigners.

Clannack hadn't been in there but heard they were a dingy and horrid place. Word had been sent to start rounding up Derks across the rest of Ngahere, of which there should be few, but that rule had become more and more relaxed over recent times. He wondered how many they would find.

Both sides were bracing for potential conflict which meant Clannack's role of negotiator was not going to be easy. What he needed was time with the Queen to understand what he could bargain with.

Will the bridge be enough? Will she even allow it?

While her approach was hostile it was required. If she'd done nothing when the negotiations began, she'd appear weak and begging for what she could get.

This way the Derks would need to resolve her concerns and console them to allow the bridge to be finished, something he wished he could stop.

The Court might not want it to be completed, but there appeared little they could do about it. At best he might be able to delay it, but the Derks would push on.

Will they launch an attack to take back the city if they have to?

Vika was using him, and he believed it was mostly because he was not one of them. He was disposable as the first negotiator. Should that not work out then there were other options, including Nikora.

Clannack needed to make sure he remained in the middle of things, so he could keep the Court abreast of everything. And besides, he had no desire to die at this time either.

Whatever was coming to Dharatan was going to be centered around this city, the bridges and the Ngaherians. Clannack needed to remain right where he was and to be highly valuable to Vika.

Two of Queen Vika's personal guards approached where he stood watching the construction.

"Come, the Queen wishes to see you."

Clannack disliked their directness, the guards thinking they too could command him. It didn't matter he was a councillor to the Queen, they still spoke to him as a foreigner.

He followed them anyway.

When they entered the council chambers, he saw Nikora was talking to the Queen, and a side table had several respected generals leaning over it.

The Queen finished the discussion she was having then sent the generals away.

"Clannack, I have missed your council."

"I have always been available, Majesty, but you did not call for it."

"There's a lot going on, Clannack, more than I needed to bother you with."

He stood and watched her, wondering why she'd chosen now to speak with him.

"But now that the walls are in progress, and we have troops arriving, I feel we can address the real issue."

"The bridge?"

"And the Derks. What they want, really, and what to do about it."

Clannack waited again. He didn't want to assume anything with her, she'd ask him for his opinion when she wanted it.

"I wasn't lying when I told you I wanted you to be our chief negotiator. Nikora rightly argued against it, that it needed to be her, but there's too much Ngaherian blood involved. We will struggle to distance ourselves from the past. As will the Derks. Which is why using you, an outsider, is an advantage, or at least I believe it will be."

It made sense, he'd played this around in his head ever since she'd told him about the history of the city.

She beckoned him up to the dais and then behind her chair. There was a table with a map laid out. It showed the coast of Dharatan, and the islands that spanned the sea over to Enderk.

"To have reached this far they have had to build from both sides, there's no other way I know of."

"Agreed."

"Which means they must build from this side. They need us, they know that, we know that, so then it's a question of what is the cost."

"You intend to let them finish it?"

"I will if the price is right."

"And what is that price?"

"I do like your directness, Clannack."

"Well, for me to negotiate I need to know what I can negotiate with."

"I've thought long and hard about it, Nikora and I have been over it as much as we can, but I'd also like your input on what we've decided."

"I'll do my best."

"The first point is whether we even allow the bridge."

"Are you prepared to block it?"

"Yes, and you need to make sure they understand that."

He nodded.

"They have invested a lot of effort to get to this point, I believe they will be very motivated to complete it. That they say one thing in their messages, but still having built the bridges makes me think they are willing to bend."

"Or they are willing to use force."

She looked at him seriously for a moment. "We considered this. It would be hard for them, certainly, and even harder now we are ready for them. But we can't ignore that option."

Nikora spoke for the first time. "We've sent for more soldiers to prepare forces along the closest coast areas, the most likely landing places for such an attack."

"This is information you do not need to tell them, Clannack," the Queen carried on. "If they are scouting this option they will learn on their own."

"Sure."

"It's my view they want this land bridge restored. There would be a lot of advantage to them to be able to trade like they used to, and in much larger quantities than we allow now. Without inside knowledge of their realm we don't know how much they might be struggling, what they might need from us. Learn what you can, it might be the key."

Clannack nodded.

"Ultimately, I want exclusive trading rights from them to Dharatan. I want to make Kuwaha the trading city it once was, but under our control."

There it was, her ultimate price, the thing that she wanted out of it.

"And what will you give up for that?"

"Only access to Ngahere. It should be enough."

"You know what they will ask for?"

"The city returned, it's what they always ask for."

"And that is a definitive no."

"Absolutely!" Her face darkened at his question.

"What wriggle room in this is there, if any?"

"I will not give up the city, Clannack, not now, not ever. They will have to pry it from us with blood."

Clannack didn't like those words being spoken. He knew sometimes such ultimatums became true sooner than the speaker wished.

"When will this begin, Majesty?"

"Soon, Clannack. We will send word and wait for them to set the time. I doubt they will come here, you will have to go to their island."

Clannack nodded, having expected nothing less.

"What do you think, Clannack?"

"I think I am going to be the wheat in the grinder between you and their emissary."

82

KARPENMOR

There was little natural cover on Step Six. The bushes that survived were low and wide, clawing their roots into the dry rocky soil to ensure they survived.

Karpenmor could see that the way the buildings were being constructed was different to the mainland. The roofs were flatter, and shaped to help the wind swoop over them and not get caught beneath.

The men trying to secure the beams on them had to be secured by ropes as they battled the force of air trying to take the wood away.

"I was not expecting you, Highness," the most senior Ponte councillor shouted across the howling sound. "There is nowhere that's safe enough for you built here yet. Perhaps back on Step Five?"

Karpenmor nodded. He would have to return across the bridge tonight, it had taken much longer than he'd realized to get here.

The early bridges were now fully finished but the last two were still incomplete. The sides and barriers were still being built which left Karpenmor feeling more exposed than he'd have liked.

Not that he showed any concern, praising those working on them as he passed. The winds grabbed your attention as though they might pick you up and take you over the sides. The sight downward was not for the faint of heart.

"I want to look across before we go back."

He handed the reins of his horse to the councillor and walked the remaining distance to the western side of the island. Within seconds he was encircled by Vrah.

There it is.

Karpenmor couldn't believe he was looking upon Dharatan from land. It looked much as Enderk did, the buildings while some distance away had a very familiar feel to them.

Cumerc.

"It is something else is it not, Highness."

Karpenmor could see that that the councillor was referring to the bridge now beginning to extend from this island toward the mainland.

"It is, your work here is most pleasing. To see so many of them complete..."

He was proud of the work that had been achieved. Since his last trip out to Ponte the progress was astounding, almost as if the workers too could feel the significance.

"How long until you extend as far as you can?"

"Several more weeks, Highness."

"You need the other side to begin." The councillor was smart enough to know it wasn't a question. Already on this side rock was being placed on foundations to create the gateway and walls that would mark the gateway to Enderk.

For now, at least.

"How much time until this wall and gate will be finished?"

"Four or more weeks until it's high enough to attach gates, but we will need to give it time to strengthen and settle, especially in these winds."

"Keep up the good work, tell the workers how pleased we are about what they are achieving."

"Highness." The councillor took his cue and nodded before stepping away.

Aika approached his side.

"What do you think of this, Aika?"

"It is impressive, Highness, and frightening all the same."

"Frightening?"

"That we are this close to reconnecting with them, it is an unexpected event."

Karpenmor hadn't thought about how it would appear to those who didn't know it was occurring. He'd just been focused on getting it finished, on getting back what was theirs.

It would explain what he could see across on the opposite cliffs. That the barbarians feared the reconnection shouldn't surprise him.

And so you should be scared, once we can get our men there, then Cumerc will be returned to us by force if need be.

"Have they agreed to the bridge, Highness?"

He chuckled and turned to look at her. "No, Aika, they have not, which is why we are here. I wish to oversee the discussions, to help them see the light."

"What if they say no?"

"That is not an option. One way or another they need to agree."

"By force?"

"Not yet, and hopefully that won't be needed. We have some things that I think they will want."

Karpenmor turned and faced the rest of the small group that had accompanied him. "Trorn?"

"Highness?"

"How's your fear of heights?"

"It does not worry me, Highness."

"Good. If they do not send someone here, then I will need you to go with Aika to their side."

"Of course, Highness. When should I prepare for?"

"Let's give them a day."

Trorn stepped back and Karpenmor turned to head back to his horse.

"Councillor, do you have somewhere we can stay on Step Five?"

"I have already sent someone back to prepare it for you, Highness."

"Thank you. We'll head there now."

Karpenmor didn't doubt that he was taking the councillor's own accommodation from him. *He can do without it for a day or two, perhaps he'll have more buildings ready quicker.*

He turned away from the bridge under construction and spoke to the leader of the team surrounding him. "We'll walk, have someone bring the horses."

With that he set off, truthfully glad to be off the horse and stretching his aching muscles.

It was dark when they finally arrived in the simple building constructed for the councillor. The roof was effectively a dome, and it was only high enough for you to stand in the center third of it.

This will do.

Karpenmor sat and thought about what had been achieved in such a short time. When he'd first gone to Ponte they had only just begun, but now they were almost done.

The timing couldn't be better. He knew he had to be back in the capital soon, but if they negotiated this correctly then by the time the enthronement was done, he could come back and oversee the opening of the bridges.

His father might be remembered for them coming down but all of that would disappear once it was known that the son had restored them.

Even better would be the recapture and populating of Cumerc. That might take a little longer, but he was in no doubt that this was going to happen. Yes, he wanted to find the amulet, his amulet, and he would. But that was going to be harder than this would be.

All that mattered was the connection was finished, and the entire span of bridges completed. On each of the islands, buildings had to be constructed to hold all the supplies they would need.

Right now, everything was exposed to the weather which made the place extremely inhospitable. Once the basics were in place then the barracks would need to be built to house the army that would be spread over the entire span.

Not that the foreigners need to know that.

There was a knock at his door. "Come."

Aika entered, battling the wind to close the door. She looked around at the minimal quarters and seemed disappointed.

"What is it, Aika?"

"Your room is very small, Highness."

"It will suffice. Where do they have you staying?"

"They do not at this point. Tents are being erected. Although they look as though they will blow away if the wind gets any stronger."

"That will not do. You cannot stay out there with the soldiers and workmen."

She shrugged. "Is there anything else you need from me before I settle for the night, Highness."

"No, Aika, there is not. But this won't do, not for my Chief Steward."

"You keep using that term, Highness. I am not sure what it means for me."

"It means you're to be my right hand. I need someone I can trust by my side, and someone who has my best interests at the front of their minds and decisions."

She dipped her head. "I am not sure I am the best person."

"Of course you are. Enough, my decision is made."

"Highness." Aika dipped her head again and turned to go back outside. "There is one other thing, Highness."

"What is it?"

"Do I have to cross the water?"

"Only a little, Aika, why?"

"I cannot swim, Highness. The water frightens me."

"Perhaps it will not be needed. If they send their people to us, then you will not have to leave. But I will need you there if they do not, I cannot trust the priest alone."

She said nothing, but he could see she was more than a little frightened by the ocean below. "But the bridges, they don't bother you?"

"Not if I don't look down, they do not. It is not the height that upsets me but the thought of falling into the water."

"Tomorrow we will know what is necessary. Perhaps it won't be needed."

Aika left the hut, and Karpenmor had needed to fight off a thought to tell her to stay. He was bothered by her having to sleep outside, for no real reason, but the temptation had been high.

There was little room in here, they would have been very close, and it had stirred some thoughts in him which he pushed away, letting her go.

Not her. Not now.

83

JUNTHER

I'm too old for this.

Junther hadn't slept well in weeks. Despite staying in inns most of the way he still felt sore and grumpy. He missed having his bed, and his pillow, not some lumpy construction that most of these places offered.

Following the King's trail hadn't been difficult, a mass of soldiers and advisors traveling as they were left behind obvious signs.

Currently he was in a small coastal town a little way from where the Skarians were camped. Junther had been surprised they remained on the coast and had not headed inland.

The only information he had at this point was the route they were on; he had nothing else to share with his colleagues. Once the travelers had left the south, they'd gone almost incognito, or as much as a patrol of knights could.

There was no ceremony or pomp around the King, and you'd be forgiven for thinking he wasn't with them. They clearly wished to avoid recognition and any attention that would attract.

Most of the larger cities were skirted using their coast-hugging boats which they resorted to regularly. Even that was strange — why not use them the whole way?

Perhaps the King isn't the biggest fan of being on the water?

Junther needed to travel much quicker when they went on the ocean, making sure they never got too far out of sight.

Or there's the option that he's no longer with them? Did I miss him leaving the group?

Junther's doubts had grown the further north they'd traveled, so he decided he needed to revalidate that the King was there. It would mean getting much closer to them than he'd been so far.

As long as he didn't stumble onto any sentries, he should be fine. Last night he'd purchased a small Long Eye, that he hoped would save him needing to ride too close to them.

Before he'd finished up at his inn the previous night, he'd heard some of the locals talking about where the group was camped close to the Ngahere border.

It was early and he stretched again, trying to force his aches to depart, before he went to his horse at the back of the inn. A light fog lay across the roofs of the nearby buildings and the chill caused him to shiver.

As there was no hurry at this time of the day, Junther walked the horse for a bit, letting his hips warm up. No one was up to much so early in the day, and he didn't think the Skarians would be either.

If the directions he'd heard were correct there wasn't much cover before he'd be in wide open land. The small hills he'd traveled over this last half mile were the last of them.

Junther pulled up and followed a well-worn trail away from the road. At a copse he tied his horse up and took off on foot, climbing to the top of the first hill. Lying on his front, he crawled to the peak and pulled his Long Eye out.

There was no movement on the next hill, nor any guards that he could see. That surprised Junther.

Maybe being on the road so long has made them drop their guard. Or something else is up.

He got to his feet and walked causally down the far side of the hill as though he was out for a stroll. It was an unlikely story if he was caught, but there was little he could do about it now.

On the top of the next hill, he saw why there were no guards here. The camp was almost completely packed up, ready to set off.

Bugger. They'll be miles away from me by the time I've recovered my things.

Foolishly he'd not brought his belongings with him. The long and uneventful trip had lulled him into accepting that the soldiers would maintain their habits, except today they hadn't.

Using the Long Eye, he swooped across the camp. The last tent standing appeared bigger than the typical ones he'd seen previously. An older man stepped out of it, one of the few people not wearing armor.

He had a white goatee beard and his head was bald on top with a small band of white hair that wrapped the sides.

That's the King for sure. At least this wasn't a complete failure.

Junther slithered backward and once he was clear of the peak turned and hustled down the hill, nearly tripping twice, only righting himself at the last moment.

Once he was back on his horse, he kicked it into a gallop back to the town. He gathered up everything he had and got back on the road with enough supplies for a couple of days.

While they had a head start on him, they wouldn't be traveling at any great speed, or at least that's what he hoped, if past behavior could be trusted.

He stopped at the Skarian camp site that he'd seen them vacating but found nothing of interest.

Didn't expect to, but better to check than not.

Once during the day he'd gotten a little too close to the knights, spotting them ahead in the distance, so Junther had slowed his pace, and taken more breaks.

While he wanted to stay in touch, he didn't want to be seen by them. They were sticking to the coast which meant he'd bet money they were heading toward the Stepping Isles.

Junther wanted to catch up to them then, but he didn't want to be recognized from earlier. That would make them suspicious of him, and he might need to get a lot closer there.

The sun was dropping over the plains when he reached a small coastal village. There was no sign of the camp, and when he left the village there were no signs of the trail heading north either.

He back-tracked and rode in a circle around the village, unable to find where they'd disappeared to.

He looked at the last spot where their horses had all gathered, just to the side of the village square. It was right beside the jetty filled with small fishing boats tied up.

How?

He found the inn next, and went in, setting up at the bar in the main room.

"What'll you have, traveler?"

"One of your better ales would be fine, Keeper."

The man limped toward a large barrel on the side of the bar and scooped the mug he held into it, bringing it back to Junther.

"There you go."

"Thanks. I've earned it today."

He took a sip.

"Always quiet in here?"

"Aye. Not a big place, we are, although I thought we were in for a change of fortune I did."

"Oh?"

"Big group come through here hours back, and pulled up, I was licking my chops. I doubted I'd even have enough mutton for them, was about to send the boy to get some more for me."

"What happened?"

"They gathered at the jetty, and before we knew it, a bunch of wide boats turned up and they all got on, horses and all. Took 'em no time at all, I'll tell you."

"That is interesting. Strange thing to see no doubt."

"Ruined my day it did. I'd got my hopes up and all."

"I bet. Strange such a big party up here. Not seen them before?"

"Not that many, no."

"What do you mean?"

"There's been them armored knights coming around for some time. They never stay here mind, but they ride up the coast and go again."

"Some time you say?"

"Yeah, last year, maybe a bit longer, I'd say. Strange lot they are. Some said they're southerners, but I can't see why they'd be all the way up here. Nothing of interest up this way."

"I wonder where they were heading?" Junther didn't even realize he'd said it out loud until the Keeper answered.

"They went north they did."

He nodded and took a big drink of his ale.

Now what am I going to do?

UKSOD

In a way, not having the boy around made things easier. While he was still the Regent in theory the palace had settled into the heir ruling while Uksod had been unwell.

There was little point in changing that now, with only a matter of weeks until it should all be official, but Uksod was enjoying being the decision maker, even if only for a little while longer.

Preparing for the enthronement without having to run things past Karpenmor just made it easier and Uksod was grateful for it.

What did bother him was the lack of messages back from Ponte. The Vrah messenger that had been dispatched should have either returned themselves or sent a rider by now.

It was a long haul, but the messengers were trained to ride without sleep, and to deliver their message.

Unless of course the boy didn't let them return. For someone who had no interest in anything for so long, he's definitely slipping into the role easily.

Uksod felt a touch of pride in how Karpenmor was responding, even if it also annoyed him.

A servant finished laying out a small meal on his table in the main hall, where he was going to meet his first appointment for the day, Lady Natillian.

She'd requested a meeting with Karpenmor and Uksod was interested in getting more insight into what she was up to. Deliberately he didn't meet her in the designated rooms, and as she approached he saw the surprise in her eyes, despite her trying to maintain a neutral expression.

Just need to keep you on your toes.

"Lady Natillian, so good to see you. I hope you don't mind us meeting here, I've not eaten yet and I have such a busy schedule I thought sharing breakfast today might solve two things at once."

"Eminence, of course. Will the Prince not be joining us today?"

"My apologies, my Lady, but he's not available for the next few days. I hope I can fill in for him suitably." Without giving her time to respond he continued, "And who is this lovely creature accompanying you?"

Uksod knew too well who it was, he'd had the Vrah investigating the granddaughter since he'd learned about her.

"This is Bhoomi, my granddaughter. She came to town to witness the enthronement and learn more about the capital."

"Join us, Bhoomi." He didn't stand for either of them but beckoned to the chairs across the table from him with his hand. The two ladies sat, and Uksod could see Natillian assessing what was happening. She clearly had expected to see Karpenmor.

"Can I ask the reason for the meeting, Lady Natillian?"

His directness would help to keep her on the back foot, even if only a little, which he needed with her. He'd always considered her the most capable opponent.

She usually played her hand very close to her chest, and rarely came to the capital, but the length of her stay and the direct approaches to Karpenmor meant a lot.

"A courtesy visit to see the heir, and to confirm that the dance will still be going ahead."

"How nice of you." He paused and maintained eye contact, while placing a piece of fruit in his mouth. "And why would it not?"

Her eyes remained on his the entire time. "Just that we seem to have some families not in the capital. I was just curious, we're all of course very excited for the event."

Uksod admired how well she remained calm and was able to sound so confident in her delivery. He still believed she was behind the delays.

"Minor details, Lady Natillian. It would be most unfortuitous to break the tradition, such a bad omen to do so… no, the dance will proceed as planned."

She let a small smile form on her face.

Deliberate or real, I wonder?

"That is good to hear, it does take such a time to get ready for an event of the type. What if the other families miss it?"

"I wouldn't worry about that, Lady Natillian, either they are here, or they are not, the rules do not change."

Uksod saw no point in informing her that they would be here, he could almost guarantee. He needed no more interference from her or anyone else.

"And would I be correct in guessing that you'll be the candidate for your family, Bhoomi?" He turned his full gaze on the young woman, causing her to flinch ever so slightly.

She flushed a little at the intensity of his question and stare, but before she could answer, Lady Natillian did.

"Yes, she is, Eminence. We're so very proud of her."

"How wonderful, such an important event. How are you feeling about it, Bhoomi?"

Lady Natillian didn't interrupt this time.

"It is quite imposing, if that is the right word. Forgive me, I am a little nervous."

"That is okay, young lady, and understandable." Uksod wondered if her appearance wasn't a little contrived for his benefit.

"And I believe you've already met the heir several times, is that correct?"

"Yes, Eminence, I have."

"And what did you think of our soon to be High Prince?" Uksod wanted to smirk, there was no room for the young woman to sidestep this question.

"He is a very kind and interesting person. I have been honored to have spent some time with him."

Nicely answered, young lady. It appears you have been learning a lot from your grandmother.

"Yes, he is. Perhaps it won't make you nervous for the dance. It must help to have met him already, I'm sure. I doubt any other candidates will get such an opportunity now with his days so busy."

She smiled delicately and didn't answer, another sign that she knew how to handle herself in important company. Uksod's words were for Lady Natillian more than the young woman. He wanted her to be very aware that he knew what she was up to.

You'll not be saddling this mare to our heir, at least not while I'm still around. A very clever play, she is quite the delightful one.

"Please enjoy the meal. I must apologize but I have another meeting, and with so much to plan, I cannot spare a minute anywhere."

Both women stood and he gave a simple head bow before he turned and left the hall, a grin on his face. The slight to the second most powerful family in the realm was something he wouldn't have done when he was sole Regent.

She is going to be quite an appealing match for young Karpenmor. I need to find a way to make sure he prefers my choice.

It seemed a simple thing who might marry the High Prince, but it had become more and more evident to Uksod over the last decade or so that such things never were.

After the events of Schevenal's disastrous trip to Dharatan, which saw the deaths of all the family heads, the rule of Family One had not been challenged.

Uksod knew that in some circles it was seen as a deliberate act by Karpenmor's father to secure his long-term family dominance, but there was no way to prove such a thing, nor anyone strong enough or willing enough to challenge the rule of Enderk.

Yantarnaya had made it very clear to Uksod that she needed Schevenal's family to be in control, that the amulet was bonded only to them and without the Lapidarist it couldn't be changed.

If there was no heir to control the amulet, then she could never destroy the power holding her within the stone. Anytime she mentioned it she sent bolts of pain through his amulet as a reminder of how much pain he would suffer if that ever came to pass.

His role was simple. Find a way for Schevenal to bear an heir and make sure there was always a descendant of his alive for when the amulet was rediscovered.

He'd set about building his power as Regent and squashing the dissent he was aware of, but it rarely showed its head. For hundreds of years the families fought internally while factions within tried to build their own power.

That suited Uksod -- the longer they did that, the less they were focused on En Carta, Schevenal and why he was hardly seen, and Karpenmor.

Over time the fighting settled, and each family began to focus outward. At first, he didn't pay much attention to it, but then conflict between the Imperial Families began to reappear.

Historically it was something that had always been part of their culture. Battles over rights of access, trade, resources, and land.

Periodically the ruler of the time would intervene if the troubles appeared to be growing too big. What had been concerning Uksod wasn't this, it was that the disputes had all but disappeared, and those that appeared all ended mostly in favor of one family -- Lady Natillian's.

She'd become increasingly powerful and adept at handling the other families closest to her. Natillian's building of borders across her land was another deft move to exercise her control of the south.

While there was no outright coalition formed, there had been little examples of the impact that might have on the realm — attempts at controlling internal trade around goods that had never been restricted, delays of passage of goods through their territory and the like.

None of it was particularly significant separately but when combined, the power she'd built was becoming concerning to Uksod. What wasn't needed was her granddaughter inside the imperial palace with the ear of the High Prince.

No, that wouldn't work at all.

The plan Uksod had was much better. He'd nurtured the daughter of Pratala, head of Family Six, indirectly of course, to be the candidate for the dance.

At that time, Karpenmor had been easily influenced by Uksod's words, and it looked as though it would be easy to pull off the relationship that made the most sense to him.

Back then the bridges did not exist either and the boats being built down in Haakan were very important to his future plans.

Family Six's expertise in boat building was such that finally they were beginning to get vessels that could not only carry significant numbers of people and supplies, but were better able to navigate the turbulent seas between Enderk and Dharatan.

It was the only viable method to get an army over there at that time, so he'd been careful to ensure Family Six was always well looked after.

Linking the two families through marriage would be mutually beneficial. That connection would see Six grow in stature and influence even more.

Perhaps now with the bridges Natillian saw her chance to knock them out of importance. With the boats not needed and keeping the daughter out of the dance they'd be of no matter.

The more he thought about the reasons for why it had to be Natillian, the greater he believed it.

No. Bhoomi, as lovely as she might appear to be, will not do. Perhaps she needs to be removed from the equation.

Few people were bothering him day to day, even less with Trorn absent, which pleased him as he had something else he needed to do.

He approached the guard by his office. "I need a body."

"Now, Eminence?"

"Yes. I'll head down shortly."

It was one of the things about the Vrah he loved, the absolute commitment to following commands from those above. It would become much harder once Karpenmor was High Prince, which is why he needed to get his own soldiers.

He didn't want to have to beg Karpenmor for what he needed, and his priests were not the right people to fulfil these commands.

This time it was a woman strapped to the table, a gag held tightly in her mouth.

Uksod closed the door and looked her over. He could imagine she was a worthy bed companion, not that it mattered to him. His pleasure came from what he was about to do, not the other.

⁓

He sought out the barbarian priest and was pleasantly surprised with what he discovered. The man was somewhere around the Ngahere coast.

"Uksod, I am glad you have reached me."

"And why is that, Fuling?"

"I am with the King, and we are nearing the place you call Kuwaha."

Cumerc, but then you wouldn't know would you?

"That is good news. You managed to convince him?"

"I am not sure it's all my doing, but he accepted that we should approach the Derks ourselves. He believes the Ngaherians are holding out on everyone."

"Tension, I like it. You will face resistance there, Fuling."

"As expected, but we come prepared."

"The bridges linking the islands are nearly completed. Only the last remains. Should there be issues with the Ngaherians, you only need to cross to Step Six, and I'll see that you're allowed all the way to En Carta."

"Understood."

"There might be one complication."

"Which is?"

Uksod explained about Karpenmor being the heir and his presence in Ponte. He wished he knew what the boy was up to and where he was exactly, just another reason he needed the boy leashed.

"You are not in control?"

Uksod didn't like the tone of the question.

"More than enough for what you need to do. Our objective is

different to the Prince's. You need to get the King here to En Carta, then much more will be revealed."

"Can I wear my cloth in your country?"

"You can, but I wouldn't wear it anywhere within sight of Ngahere, or you'll never be allowed back there."

Uksod couldn't help but smile as he left the dead woman behind. Things weren't all bad, progress was being made, even his mistress would be happy.

LEO

After the respite in Watersend, Leo could almost handle the sand again. Almost. It had only taken the first day before he could feel it once more inside his clothing, rubbing against skin.

The others didn't seem bothered by it, but it bugged Leo constantly. He rubbed at the collar of his tunic where he could feel grit against his neck.

He looked up and had to blink his eyes, unsure about what he was looking at.

"It's something else isn't it, lad?" Kooka asked.

"Is it moving?"

"Yes, it is, that's what I've been told."

Off in the distance a huge peak stood tall over the desert. Unlike any other mountain he'd ever seen this one was spinning, or a spire of sand was moving, fast enough you could see it.

"It's incredible."

"No one knows how or why, just that it does that and always has done."

"It's sand, isn't it?"

"Yes. Mount Qum, or the Spire of Sand as everyone refers to it."

"That's where we're going?"

"To the city underneath it, yes. Midderbuilt."

For the rest of the day all Leo could do was stare at the spire as they rode closer. Occasionally a small caravan would pass them, mostly guards and several merchants, heading back to Watersend.

Kooka and Gimbden had explained about the gems that came from the mountain, and the master craftsmen that inhabited Midderbuilt fashioning them for merchants.

The gem trade was centered in Watersend, because no one was allowed into Midderbuilt. Even at their destination, the Traveler's Rest, no one was allowed to trade in the jewels, to keep the nefarious away from the city.

Leo wasn't sure exactly how they were going to manage to get Lani into the city as there was an issue with them having only one pass -- Tillandra's.

This was something he was going to have to resolve with their contact inside, a man called Tingfurlew. They couldn't separate Lani and Odajeen, both needed to get into the city.

He struggled to sleep through the night. The concept of the spinning mountain fascinated him, and even though he couldn't see it in the dark of night, he couldn't stop thinking about it.

When daylight arrived, he was out watching it again, sitting near Irdan who had stayed on guard all night. Kooka came from his rest soon after.

"Not long now, Leo. We should be there today."

"Okay, then the fun begins."

"Fun?"

"I have no idea how we're going to manage getting them in."

"All will sort itself out. Our first job was to get them here. And shortly we'll have achieved that."

"I guess."

Leo didn't like that all of this was falling on his shoulders. The older man was a better candidate for making decisions. His brooding was interrupted by a knocking in his head.

Here we go.

$\sim$

"In All Jest, Leo."

"In All Jest. Mother?"

"Yes, Leo. Can't you recognize my voice?"

"I guess. It's all so new."

"Never mind. Where are you?"

"Kooka says we'll arrive at Traveler's Rest today."

"You're close, good."

"I've no idea how I'll get them in, unless they relax the guard."

"That they will never do, Leo. One pass, one person."

"What if I have to separate Lani and Odajeen?"

"That would have to be a last resort, Leo. A very last resort. I may have an answer, it's very odd, but I need to tell you anyway."

"What?"

"Last night I had a dream, which was quite strange, but your location would explain it. I saw a stream coming from the mountains."

"A stream of water?"

"Yes."

"Out here?" Leo laughed.

"That's what makes it strange, now listen."

"Sorry."

"It's before the city, and it means something. I've never seen such a stream out there. In the dream I saw someone moving back up the stream, and into what looked like an opening. I don't know if it is for you or not, Leo, but I wouldn't have seen it for no reason. Or I doubt it. The dreams always mean something."

"I've seen no stream so far."

"In all the times I've been to Midderbuilt, neither have I, Leo, but I needed to tell you. Pay attention for signals that might relate to such a thing."

"I will."

"How is everyone?"

"Tired and quiet. We've all said all we can."

"The women?"

"Odajeen is more patient than me. Both her and Lani are alive and stuck in the back of the wagon."

"I hope this works."

"Me too."

~

She was gone as quickly as she'd come, and while it was nice to hear someone else's voice, Leo wasn't any more at ease after it.

A stream out here? Sounds like a silly dream, nothing more.

He didn't discuss the conversation with anyone else, he didn't want to sound stupider than he often felt. For now he'd just keep it to himself.

They set off north, the wagon groaning as it struggled over the sand road as it had done ever since leaving Anderwell. The noise was almost pleasant to Leo, his mind following the creaking as the wheels rolled, drifting into a half sleep.

As they neared their destination, Leo noticed the road was packed a lot firmer and had rock crushed into it, so that it didn't shift with the sands.

A huge stone cliff face climbed up to their left, and he could see a path cut into it. Past that, a huge outcrop hung over the camp beneath.

"Traveler's Rest," Kooka said.

"What a strange-looking place. I guess Tillandra was wrong."

"What do you mean?"

Leo explained her message and dream to him.

"You fool, Leo, you should have told us this when it happened."

"What difference would it have made? There was no stream of water out there, I would have seen it."

Kooka shook his head and raised his hand to stop their group.

"I saw something back a few hours."

"What?"

"It was an odd rut or path cutting down through the hillside. Now that you've told me what you have, I'd say it was an old stream, cut into the side of the hill."

"I didn't see any water."

"Nor I, but the dream might not be exactly about the present. It could be symbolic. We'll have to go back."

"You sure?"

"One thing I am sure of is that you were given a message, and we should follow it."

Leo felt stupid, both because they'd have to head back the way they came, but also because he should be smarter than this. He was a member of the Court; he was meant to be a leader.

~

"That!"

Leo looked where Kooka was pointing. The last two hours had been painful, having to backtrack away from the rest stop. Looking at what Kooka had seen, Leo was disappointed. It was a stretch that this was what Tillandra had dreamed.

"It could be anything."

"It stood out to me, boy, for no reason. As if I was meant to see it. I might not be special like you lot are, but I know what's normal and what isn't."

"Okay."

He wasn't convinced but they were here now.

"I'll go take a look. Why don't you set up here until I check it out?"

"Okay."

Leo tied his horse off to the wagon, took a water skin and began to climb up the hillside, glad to be back on his feet. The rut that he followed was strange, and he could see Kooka was right, only water could have created it.

As he followed it up, he poked at the ground, but it was rock hard and not a drop of moisture to be found. If there'd ever been any water it was long gone.

A strange dream.

He followed the rut around rocky outcrops and out of sight of the people below until it came to an end at a rock wall. Leo looked back and couldn't believe how high he seemed to be.

The distance seemed a lot further than he'd walked, and the sun hadn't moved that much.

More magic?

Kneeling, Leo inspected the end of the rut and could see there was a gap under the rocks that came from inside the mountain. It was only big enough to fit his hand in if he wriggled and squeezed it through.

There wasn't any water inside either, but he could feel cool air blowing over his fingers. Carefully he pulled his hand back out. He got to his feet and tried to find other holes or access points around the rocks.

There was nothing else, just the single point that water must have flowed from in the past.

How on Dharatan are we meant to get inside? Surely the point of showing this was to help us.

GIZEN

I dislike horses.

Gizen said as little to herself as she did others. She'd never worked out why people had to say so much, most of it was just twiffle, in her mind.

It was why she preferred to be alone. Anderwell was the first time in many years she'd been surrounded by so many people.

This trip was much more her style. Despite being with a squad of thirty soldiers, they hardly spoke.

Gizen presumed it was early morning, by the way the group rose and packed up camp before they set off.

First the captain would ask her if she'd had another dream. If she had, she'd point in the direction it showed, if not they carried on the same way as the day before.

Then they rode, and rode, and rode. And rode. It was so hot, and dry, and without sight, Gizen was very aware of the grains of sand that found their way into everything.

At times she tried to count the grains she could sense, her mind giving up eventually as the number was too great. They sheltered during the hottest part of the days, using canvas and poles as makeshift covers.

While it kept the sun off them, the heat never dissipated, not until the sun dropped each evening. She could now tell the end of the day by the way the temperature changed, and welcomed the cool shift that hit them as soon as it was gone.

Some nights they continued to ride; the captain explained to her one of the times it was because of the moon in the sky. When it was bright enough to let them see their way he kept going.

Gizen hoped the soldiers were feeling better than her. They would need to be when the time came to rescue Goran. Herself, she was exhausted, physically, and mentally.

Her mind kept drifting off for the sensation of water. All she could think of was to be able to drop into a bath. That was one part of Anderwell she'd fallen in love with.

Without warning a dream took her over. Gizen knew the feeling well, and before it fully took hold, wrapped her scarf around the horn on her saddle and her wrist, to save from falling.

~

She was the bird high in the sky, circling now as it dropped in height, closer to the desert below. She could see two groups of people, one camped and one riding.

~

As quickly as it had come, it went. She shook her head and called out for the captain.

"I am here."

She pulled up on her reins and stopped the horse.

"All stop!" His voice roared in the quiet, but she could hear the squad stopping.

"They are camped over there, more permanently. There are trees and water." Gizen pointed her arm in the direction she'd sensed in the dream.

"Out here? A miracle."

"There are guards, circling the top of the dunes, while the camp is in the valley beneath."

"How many guards?"

"Four I think, spaced out, they walk around looking outward."

"Any idea of how far?"

"Not far, we should be careful now. I cannot tell the distance, but I am sure it is close."

"Then we need to be more wary of our approach. Let's set up camp, it's late enough anyway."

Gizen listened as he got down off his horse and instructed his men about what he'd learned. Occasionally she heard parts of the conversations.

"Siffen, you'll need to do your thing. Unseen of course."

"Of course, Captain. Any idea how far?"

"No, but her words likely mean close. The rest of you, set up this site as well as sentries, for all we know they could already know about us. We're not in battle mode."

It took an hour, give or take, before the activity settled. Gizen was led to a sheltered spot dug into the sand. She took the time to nap, as she doubted they would need her.

She was awoken by someone rocking her shoulder.

"Miss Gizen?"

"Yes." Her head felt groggy. It was the captain.

"Are you okay?"

"Yes, I was just sleeping. What is happening?"

"We've located them, you were right."

"Where?"

"Half a mile away. If you'd not stopped us, we'd have been spotted for sure."

It's not me, it's the dreams.

"What now?"

"We wait. Our scout will maintain his watch over them and if they move, we'll follow."

"If they don't?"

"Then we'll do what we came here to do."

Gizen wasn't entirely sure what those instructions were. She'd been told they'd be rescuing Goran, which was reasonable enough, but she knew Tillandra had left out other things about why he was out here.

It doesn't matter. My task is done.

She went back to sleep. It seemed the easiest thing to do, and she was of no use to anyone else.

When she woke this time, the temperature was cooler, as was typical when the sun was down. It felt as though she had slept through the night, but she couldn't tell.

Normally she'd hear the sounds of the soldiers, even if they were sat down they were never completely still. Unusually there wasn't anyone she could sense close by.

There's no one here.

"Hello?"

No one replied. *Flackengruff.*

Gizen stood up and using her stick, prodded round the covered space she was in. The tent roof was still there, as were its poles and baggage. But no one else.

The light touch of the sun on her face told her she'd left the cover of the shade. It had to be the early morning rising sun.

They're attacking with the sun behind them.

Gizen wasn't even sure why she knew that, it was almost as though the idea wasn't even hers but was put into her head. Whatever they were doing was happening now.

She had a basic sense of the direction of the enemy camp based on where she'd been sheltered and did her best to head in that direction.

Walking was hard for her in the sand, she'd only done a small amount of it on this trip and struggled to navigate the soft surface and the slopes.

Taking it slowly she found a strange rhythm climbing an upward slope. As she crested the top, she could sense a breeze that hadn't been there just before.

No sounds of fighting came to her, so she proceeded on, falling face first on the downward slope. As she tumbled the stick fell from her hand and she rolled several times before stopping.

Gizen sat up spitting out sand from her mouth and brushing it from her face and eyes. It took her many minutes to crawl back and locate her stick, then she cautiously made her way down the slope.

She wished she'd drunk something before she set off from the camp, now she wasn't sure how she'd find her way back there. Her mouth was dry, her lips coated with sand and the sun was heating up quickly.

There was no consistency to the rise of the next upward slope, and as she reached the top she cautiously moved forward, probing to detect when it went downward. Off to her right she could hear sounds of people and turned in that direction.

You're a fool, Gizen, what can you do?

Now the sounds of swords clashing and men screaming replaced the constant sound of air over sand. Rarely did she ever think about sight, but now she truly wished for it.

It had been too long since she'd ever been around such fighting, and she had no way of telling who was friend or foe. She froze, unsure what she should do, listening to the sounds in what seemed like the next valley.

She listened and turned her head sideways trying to decide where she should head next.

Suddenly everything near to her changed and she could feel the presence of someone, or something. It was very different to how she usually detected people.

Gizen felt frightened without even knowing why. She turned to her left in the direction of the sensation. The feeling changed — what had seemed like one thing seemed to separate.

One sensation crumbled away until she couldn't feel it at all, but the other remained, stronger than it was before. It began to form into a shape in her mind, becoming clearer and stronger as the seconds passed.

The color of orange appeared in the darkness of her mind, and the shape or outline became very clear.

It's shaped like an… amulet.

HALLENDELL

The cave Hallendell was hiding in smelled dank and she needed food. The minimal supplies she'd escaped Lahti with were almost gone.

For two days she'd hidden here watching for pursuers but so far hadn't seen anyone. She knew that southwest was the only direction she should go, but something held her back.

Normally she'd describe it as her intuition, but the feeling wasn't exactly that. Hallendell couldn't tell if her gut was just confused or because she was feeling a little unwell.

She checked the cut on her leg, for the fiftieth time, and it still looked normal. *The wound's fine.* Her mind seemed clouded as well, a fogginess that she only associated with overusing her magic.

On her first day traveling south she'd been focused and knew what she was trying to do. She needed to head toward Hillview and get supplies to cross the desert toward Darkside.

But now there was confusion where that clarity had been. She was having trouble remembering why she needed to go to Midderbuilt. There had been a conversation, with someone. *Who?* They'd mentioned a person in Midderbuilt, she was sure they had, but now that name was lost to her.

Who in Thenis's name is it?

Her eyes flicked open again, and she saw that it was dark outside.

What happened, how could I have slept so long sitting up? What on Dharatan is going on?

Hallendell could tell something was wrong, and a thought briefly poked through the fogginess of her mind. She grabbed hold of it and forced it out from where it was hiding.

The amulet, that's what it is.

She stayed as focused as she could manage and pressed her mind outward and saw the fingers of orange. The same as she'd sensed in the council building back in Lahti.

Each thin finger was wrapped around her imaginary body almost entirely. It had encased her and was squeezing. Each tendril traced back to a central ball of them and another thick band led off into the distance.

Hallendell didn't know where that was heading but she pulled her mind away from the fingers and looked around the cave, sweat dripping from her brow.

It will take complete concentration to stay on top of it if I can. How did the girl manage to carry hers all the way... That's right, she had something that shielded her.

The word Midderbuilt popped back into her thoughts. Something about that place resonated with the shield.

I need to head there!

Without waiting, Hallendell gathered her meager belongings and left the cave walking out into the early evening air. Cautiously she worked her way down the hillside and found her horse, still tied where she'd left it.

Even that isn't clear thinking. If anyone had found it, they'd know someone was around here.

Right now, she felt clearer of thought than at any time in the last day and a half. She knew it wouldn't get any easier and took the horse by its reins and began to walk.

All night she headed in a southerly direction, switching back and forth through the hillside until the sun began to rise.

For now, that will have to do.

Hallendell found a spot well hidden within the bush on the flattest land in all directions and made a resting spot. She watered her horse with the skins she'd been able to fill at a stream that they'd stumbled across.

She needed food but it wasn't the first time in her life she'd been without any for days. She knew she could survive.

There must be a village around here somewhere. I'll have to risk seeing people if I am going to make it to Midderbuilt. I'd best grab some sleep.

When she woke, the sun had passed well over the top of them. Hallendell felt very confused, she wasn't sure exactly why she was lying on the ground, in the bush.

I'm meant to be heading to Kumasa, am I heading that way? Why can't I remember?

Something floated across her mind, the name of a place, but she couldn't grab hold of it. Her vision seemed cloudy, and she struggled to hold onto any thoughts.

Kumasa. White City. Got to go.

As if driven by a force inside her, she stood, brushed herself off and grabbed her horse. Using the sun above, she plotted a course north.

Hallendell found a trail that had been used many times before and mounted up before choosing the northern direction. It wasn't directly that way, but it would suit well enough.

Just before sundown she found her way to a tiny village of a dozen buildings and farms. As she approached, a man carrying a shovel stopped what he was doing in the soil and looked at her.

"Ho, stranger!"

"Hello."

"Where you heading?"

She wasn't sure why, but she didn't want to tell the man the full truth.

"North, I think I got myself a bit lost."

"If you're out here, I'd say you have."

"Where are we?"

"Well south of Lahti, this place doesn't even have a name." He laughed. "You're a day's ride from anywhere large."

"Oh."

"You'd be best stopping here the night. We'll be able to put you up and feed you."

"That would be very helpful."

"You in some trouble?"

"No." Her defenses jumped up immediately. "Why do you ask?"

"No reason, just not often a woman comes through her on her own. You look scared of something or someone."

"Sorry, I've been wandering the last couple of days and I'm almost out of food and not slept well."

He leaned his shovel up against the fence beside him. "Come on then, I was about done, let me take you to someone who can help out."

One part of Hallendell was telling her she should be more cautious, she should just keep going, while the other side was thankful and glad to stop.

She chose staying here and was glad for it. The simple but hot meal and bed in a stable was more than she could have hoped for. In the morning she had a meal of bread and fried egg, drizzled with honey the farmers said they collected close by.

They loaded her up with extras, enough to get her to the next town, and she set off on her way. Once back on the road she struggled to stay focused and just followed the horse, her mind almost completely fogged over.

A big gust of wind almost blew her off the horse, she was that unstable. It was only an instinctive reaction to grip on that saved her, before she pulled her horse to a stop.

Hallendell got down and tried to work out where she was. She couldn't properly remember the last period of time. There was a loose memory of a village and sleeping somewhere, but she didn't know where she was.

North, go north. Why? I thought I needed to be going south.

Her head ached every time she tried to think through where she was meant to be doing.

What am I doing out here?

She led her horse off the road and into a copse of trees. It was going to be dark soon and she needed to settle in for the night. The sky was cloudy and that meant there'd be little moonlight, she couldn't afford to keep going.

Her eyes opened and Hallendell was clueless as to what was going on. Her head felt a little clearer as though she'd been sick. She looked down at her leg, and the graze from the arrow was a little red around the edges but otherwise seemed to be healing.

She had no idea why she had been feeling off, and took a moment to gather herself, breathing strongly in and out, slowly, and as deeply as she could.

Once she felt more centered than she had for a while, she grabbed the horse and mounted, looking at the road, and deciding that she'd be able to make a good distance south following it.

About halfway through the day, she approached a small village of what looked to be about a dozen buildings and plots. Something about it felt familiar, although she couldn't remember being this far south in Lletem ever before.

Usually, such places housed people who were friendly but kept to themselves and she rarely spent much time bothering the people. She slowed her steed and let it walk through the village.

On the outside of the village on the south side, she saw a man with a bullock and a plough working the soil. He looked her way and waved.

She waved back and he stopped the animal and hurried in her direction. Hallendell pulled up and waited for him, thinking it was the courteous thing to do.

"What happened?"

"Sorry, what do you mean?"

"Why are you back, I thought you were going north?"

"When was I here before?"

He looked at her with a cautious gaze.

"Are you sure you're feeling okay? We were a bit worried about you."

"I feel better than I have in days, thanks, but I don't recall ever being here."

"That's very odd, miss, you were here but a day ago."

HALLENDELL

The farmer looked up at her with concern, and slowly grabbed the reins of the horse.

"Why don't you stay with us again today?"

Hallendell went on alert. She wasn't quite sure if it was because of the assertiveness of his actions or because she wasn't sure he wasn't right.

"It's fine, thanks."

He looked at her for a long time before releasing the reins.

"You sure?"

"I am thanks. I think I might have been suffering from an illness, but I'm feeling perfectly fine. Sorry that I don't remember."

"That's all good, I just don't want you in harm's way."

She smiled.

"I think I'll keep going while there's good light."

Hallendell nudged her horse forward and let it walk until she was well out of the village. Several times she looked back over her shoulder and saw the farmer stood where she'd left him, watching her go.

Once she was out of his sight Hallendell kicked the horse into a trot and stared ahead at the road she was on. As she rode, she processed what had happened as best she could.

Her mind did feel reasonably clear, and she felt like herself. She knew she was part of the Court, and several times looked at her ring. It crossed her mind she might want to contact Tillandra and let her know what was going on.

Except as soon as that thought took hold her focus drifted a little as though there was something wrong with the idea. She couldn't hold the thought long enough to action it.

With a shake of her head, she'd be fine again but after several occurrences of this she put it to rest. The section of road she was on looked completely new to her, and an hour before sundown she came to a crossroads.

The right arm of it looked to cut due south into the hills, while the road ahead bent more eastward. She was trying to decide the best course of action between the two, but her eyes keep darting to her left.

On that side, the road went more north than anything, which meant it would at some point join back up to the one she'd come from. While she appeared to come from the west, her memory was good enough to know that not long after the village it turned more northerly.

I don't want to go north!

Except she did, or part of her did.

Bloody amulet, stop it.

Hallendell tried to focus her will as though she was reaching out using her skill to one of her colleagues. When she did, the drag to her left weakened… a little.

As soon as her resolve eased, the desire came back. She could sense exactly what was happening and needed to find a way to stop it. But she didn't know what.

Her eyes began to feel heavy, and she let them close for a moment while she tried to think the problem through. When she opened them again it was dark.

She was still sat on her horse just to the side of the road, where it was chewing at some grasses. No one else was around but still she felt threatened.

Everything about what she could see was filtered as though something thin was covering her eyes. Hallendell brushed at her face but there was nothing there.

Deep inside the Jester knew she was being affected by the amulet but at this moment she couldn't do anything to stop it. All she could understand was the desire it had to go north.

The feeling overrode everything else, even the danger of riding at night, or the need to eat. Hallendell gathered the reins and moved the horse forward, taking the left road and moving slowly that way.

It could have been two days or three, she no longer knew how many, before she came to a wide river. There was no bridge, and the water was deep and moving fast. Hallendell knew there was no crossing there.

She went to the right, following the narrow trail along the river until she came to a bridge that spanned a narrow stretch of the waterway.

Once over she kicked her horse along, pushing the pace as though the need to get to her destination was urgent. Somewhere inside, it was as though a woman's voice was calling out to her to stop, but it was muted, and she plugged on.

Several days later Hallendell came to a town that appeared to have grown out of the deep forest behind it. She got down from her horse and walked toward the closest inn.

It was quite some time since she'd washed or eaten a full meal, let alone had an ale. A man took her horse from her and scowled when he looked at the condition of the animal.

She cared nothing for his opinion, and stumbled her way into the inn, getting an equally unfriendly look from the woman behind the bar.

"I need a room."

"You'll be taking a bath before you use any bed of mine."

"Yes. I've been on the road a long while."

"Hmmpf. Sit there while I get water drawn and heated." The woman pointed to a stool at the bar and slid a mug of something toward her.

Hallendell did as she was told and took a sip from the mug. The fresh ale was like a magic potion for her, the taste almost the best thing she'd ever had.

After the first three sips she ended up drinking the rest in one go. A burp burst out from her mouth by accident, not that she cared. Had she been watching the room, she'd have seen several men there who looked up and frowned.

One of them got up quietly and slipped out of the inn, unnoticed by her.

Sometime later the woman returned and led her to the washroom. Hallendell dumped her bag on the floor and stripped her filthy clothes off.

The woman went to take them away, but Hallendell gripped her arm, looking deep into the woman's eyes.

"I need to sort them first."

The woman's eyes were part angry and part scared as she looked back. "Sorry, miss. I'll leave you be."

The water was warm, not hot, but good enough for Hallendell and by the time she'd scrubbed the dirt off and cleaned her hair it had taken on a chill.

A large cloth had been left for her to dry and she found the cleanest items in her bag to put on. They still needed cleaning, but they were better than what she'd last been wearing.

She took the amulet, wrapped in a green cloth, from inside the tunic lying on the floor and placed it into her bag which she slung over her shoulder.

Outside the washroom she found the woman waiting and handed her the bundle of clothes.

"Finally. I thought you'd drowned yourself."

Hallendell had nothing to say and after an awkward silence the woman showed her down the hall to a room.

"Yours." She opened the door and let Hallendell walk in.

"Thank you."

The woman walked off taking the dirty clothes and Hallendell shut the door before lying down on the bed and immediately falling asleep.

The sound of a man's voice cut through the fog in her mind. She could hear the tone of it but not the words. Was someone trying to reach her?

Who can reach me? What does that mean?

She knew there was something she could do, that others could not, but the idea escaped her.

What is that voice? Whose voice?

Slowly she opened her eyes to see her room filled with men. Despite the groggy feeling in her head, she went to move and found herself bound to the bed.

"Hello, Hallendell."

The voice was very familiar. It took a lot of focus to get her sight clearer. When it was clear enough, she saw the face who'd just greeted her.

Izpen.

Where did she know that name from? His face looked very angry.

"I've been hunting for you for some time, but even better not only do I have you, but also the thing the Master General will reward me greatly for."

In his hand he held the amulet. The daylight coming in through the open window made the orange gem in it shine brightly.

Oh no!

CLANNACK

*H*alfway down the steps, which was a very generous term, Clannack had a moment. He grabbed the rope tethered to the cliff face and stopped, closing his eyes.

Everything was moving and the tight rope helped to ground him against the wind and swaying of the wooden steps. Looking down didn't help but there was no other way to walk safely.

He began again, a gap now between him and the two male Ngaherian warriors in front of him. That didn't bother Clannack, what did was the thought he'd have to climb back up again.

Let's hope I don't have to do this multiple times.

When they finally reached the bottom his group stood on a rock ledge, which made do as a jetty, waiting for the boat to cross from the island the Derks called Step Six.

Wind swept through the gap between the mainland and the island, whipping the sea into a frenzy of changing directions while it gathered strength from being squeezed between the land.

Across the water he thought he could see more steps that appeared to be cut into the island rocks, which made Clannack feel a little better.

Watching the boat coming their way didn't inspire him with any confidence. Multiple times it looked like it was heading into rocks that jutted from the water to the north of where he stood.

Each time the men rowing corrected its course and brought the boat back in the right direction. Their ability still didn't make him feel any better about what was about to happen.

When it finally sidled up to the jetty everyone was given directions to get on board quickly before the oarsmen pulled away again. The boat was two identical halves, and the rowers simply changed the way they faced and rowed back toward the island.

Clannack didn't mind being on the water, but this was as rough as he'd ever experienced, and it turned his stomach a little. Not enough to make him sick, but several of the warriors looked greener than their normal color.

Once free of the mainland things became easier and the final stretch was driven more by the current than the oars, with the boat landing on a small beach at Step Six.

Two other boats were beached there and tied up to a massive brass hook embedded in the rock face. It was why they controlled everything between the two countries, as the Ngaherians had never had any need to build such bases to cross the span.

For the Derks it was the only way to do any trade at all, but seeing this properly Clannack could see why any previous threat of the Derks invading had never been real: it was simply too hard to move anything in large quantities to the mainland.

It made sense why the Derks were landing in other locations down the coastline, this spot was far too treacherous.

Their party was led by six Derk guards up the steps cut into the side of the cliff. Each step had been carved very precisely, in a way that master craftsmen would do it. They followed the natural shape of the cliff, but their height and width were identical, making them much easier to walk on.

Every half dozen steps a pole had been fixed to the outside of the step face, and through it two ropes were tightly strung providing a handrail, and protection. The rope looked very weather-worn.

These have been here a long time.

By the time they reached the top Clannack was exhausted. He

wasn't unfit by any stretch of imagination, but the climb took a big toll on him.

Compared to the Derk guards his party looked wiped out. One thing was for sure, the Ngaherians weren't about to launch any attack using this path either.

A surly man met them at the top dressed in a black robe, which ended where it brushed over the straps of his sandals. A symbol was stitched into the front of it in a light-colored thread, contrasting with the main garment.

Clannack knew he was a priest and subtly checked the guards that had accompanied him. As expected, each had a sour look on their face, only weakened by their exhaustion.

The priest bowed slightly dipping his head. Clannack copied him.

"Welcome to Step Six." His accent had a nasal tone to it, subtle but obvious compared to the Ngaherians.

"Thank you."

Clannack brushed his hair off his face again, the wind was making a hard time of it for him.

"Perhaps we should retire inside, out of the weather?"

"That would be good, although I doubt my companions will accompany us." Clannack raised his eyebrows to the priest.

"Understood. They can shelter over there if they so desire." He pointed to a set of canvas shelters that were being buffeted by the wind from the north but were open to the south.

Clannack turned to the closest guard who nodded, and he watched them walk that way. *I guess everyone will have to trust what I say was discussed then.*

A smile formed on his face as he followed the priest into a tent big enough for six or seven people to stand comfortably. Inside a younger man was sat on a large chair with two armed guards on each side.

The priest stopped Clannack and spoke quietly to him. "Sorry we were not introduced. I am Trorn, senior priest to our goddess, Yantarnaya."

"I am Clannack, Councillor to Queen Vika of Ngahere."

The priest stepped forward toward the young man.

"Your Highness, may I introduce Clannack, Queen Vika's emissary and councillor."

He turned back to Clannack and continued. "Respected Emissary of Ngahere, I am honored to introduce the heir to the throne of Enderk, his Highness Karpenmor Redne."

Clannack hoped that his surprise didn't show on his face. The Prince of Enderk was out here on this wretched island! Of all the things he'd expected this wasn't one of them. While he tried to rearrange his thoughts Clannack dipped his head in respect.

The young man stood and walked toward him, causing the nearest guards to spring to alert, an air of tension suddenly forming in the small space.

Karpenmor raised his hand and directed them back to their position. Clannack watched the two men in black reluctantly do so, but could sense the others in the room edge a little closer toward him.

Even more surprisingly the young man extended his hand toward Clannack. "Very pleased to make your acquaintance, Clann... Clannack, is that correct?"

Clannack shook the young man's hand which despite his average build was remarkably strong. He was almost as tall as Clannack, which was something else he hadn't expected.

"Correct, your Highness. It is my upmost pleasure to meet you. I have to admit I was not expecting someone of such position to be here."

"It came about by chance; I was visiting the Steps to see progress on this most exciting project. One might think the stars aligned as this would seem most fortuitous."

"Indeed."

"Join me. I am sorry our hospitality is quite meager, but our supplies are still catching up with our progress."

Clannack made a note of the comment. It was only a small thing, but he had to remember everything he could about this meeting, and not just for the Queen.

"Some liquid refreshment would be all I could ask for. The journey, or climb, is quite challenging."

"It certainly looks that way."

The Prince said nothing else while his servants quickly appeared and placed drinks in front of them on the table, first offering the Prince his before handing an ornate wooden goblet to Clannack.

Karpenmor raised his goblet, looking at Clannack. "To our future relationship."

"To our future relationship."

Both men drank from their goblets. Clannack noted that it was an exquisite white wine, a varietal he did not know, slightly tart at first, mellowing to finish with a hint of spice.

"You like?"

"It's most unique, and yes I do."

"These grapes come from the south of our country, Clannack. It might appear they are another thing we have that could be of interest to your people."

Clannack noted that the Prince wasn't going to waste time with too many pleasantries. The meeting proper had begun, which suited him fine. He didn't wish to spend a night here, and the idea of climbing back up the cliff in the dark held no appeal.

KARPENMOR

It was taking all Karpenmor's effort to not stare at the strange features the man across from him had. The only other barbarians he'd seen were the warriors that accompanied this emissary Clannack.

Karpenmor didn't think he was of the same race, but the meeting made him realize how little he really knew about Dharatan. Reading things in a book was one thing, experiencing it firsthand was something else.

What was it my tutor used to tell me? 'You cannot learn to swim by reading a book, you must get in the water.'

Clannack was as tall as the Ngaherians and himself, and almost as thickset as the guards he brought with him. His head and hands were quite different, they were much bigger than the rest of his body.

Focus.

"It would appear we have a number of things to discuss, Prince Karpenmor." The man's voice was smooth and quite gentle compared to the way his body looked.

"Indeed, the most important of them regarding the bridge."

"Yes, quite a feat. Queen Vika was notably surprised, as we all were, when we noticed what you were up to."

"It is an important piece of history."

"How so?"

"Are you aware of the land bridge that used to span these islands, Clannack?"

The head nodded, distracting Karpenmor. "Yes, I am."

"The events of that were disastrous, particularly for the loss of connection between our continents. Restoring it to how it once was, or at least a semblance of how it once was, is a moment in history."

The emissary didn't respond immediately. "Assuming that it can be finished."

"And why would it not, Emissary Clannack?"

Again, the man paused, obviously to Karpenmor choosing his words carefully. "At this point in time, Queen Vika, hasn't approved any such construction on the Kuwaha side."

"Cumerc."

"Sorry?"

"Cumerc, that's the name of the city you're referring to."

"No, it is known as Kuwaha and is a Ngaherian city."

This time it was Karpnemor who held his tongue. He'd expected resistance but wasn't prepared for how it would annoy him. The man must know it was an Enderk city.

Is this the first bargaining chip?

"That you may view it as, Emissary, however prior to the land bridge collapsing the city belonged to us and was known as Cumerc. It was the central trading station between the two continents."

"My knowledge of history would agree that all that time ago it was an Enderk city, but like many places, time changes names, people and boundaries."

This man is quite prepared to challenge me.

"That may well be the case, Clannack, but it does not sit well with us, that one of our cities was taken from us."

Clannack looked at him, neither friendly nor hostile and paused for a short while. "I can appreciate that it may not."

The city is definitely a trigger point, as it is for me. Not that it is unexpected. What else matters to this man, or his Queen?

"Word has it, Emissary, that there has been a major problem with the wheat on your fair continent." Karpenmor emphasized the word fair as much as he could, dragging out the sentence.

"Yes, there has been. Supplies are limited." Clannack didn't want to outline exactly how dire it was, but he expected the Prince already knew, especially if, as the Court assessed, Enderk was behind it.

"Then there's ample opportunity for us to help. We have had several bumper crops over the last few years and our stores are bursting with spare grain."

"We had received word from your advisors that this might be the case."

"I would offer to hurry it to your markets, but there is a major impediment."

"The bridge."

"Of course, Clannack. You've taken the trip over water to get here, do you believe we could get a decent supply to you using that method?"

Clannack shook his head. "I do not. But I am not sure the promise of some wheat will be an enticement to the Queen to just open this pathway. There are other factors to be considered."

"Such as?" Karpenmor knew full well what the emissary meant.

"Such as the law of the land. All of the realms of Dharatan have a long-standing rule regarding trade and access for Derks."

"You'd let your people starve based on some historic bad blood? Surely, we can all agree that the past has moved on. Was it not you who just said that this city you call… Kuwaha, I think you said, is part of the changes of time?"

His opponent let a small smile form on his face, and paused for a few moments.

One to me.

"Agreed, Prince Karpenmor. Noting of course that Queen Vika is only one of the rulers on Dharatan, she cannot decide on a change for all the others."

"This seems quite strange to me."

"How so?"

"None of the other realms border with Enderk. It is only your-selves who connect to us if this bridge were to be completed. Why should the decisions of others impact what you do with your land?"

"A reasonable point. Were we to find a way to any form of agreement regarding all of the matters in front of us, an enforced exclusivity would go a long way to helping with any decision making."

Karpenmor chuckled, in a friendly way. "I expected that might be part of your approach. It is worth considering, given the connection would be directly between the two realms."

There was a sense of urgency to the emissary, he didn't have any desire to be anything other than direct. This also suited Karpenmor. In reality he wanted to be on his way back and would have been if it hadn't been for the arrival of this man.

He was going to leave Trorn here to negotiate and force them to deal with a priest, just a leverage point to twist the Ngaherians' nerves.

Ah that's it. He cannot be Ngaherian, or he would object to Trorn's presence. I wonder where he is from, and why does he represent the realm if he is not one of them? Very intriguing.

"You appear to be already building a wall to block the bridge, that is concerning."

"Until any agreement is made, there is no bridge. The Queen felt it wise to fortify the cliffs in case there was any hostile intent."

"It would appear that the hostile intent is all on your side, Emissary. After all it is us bearing the cost and expertise to build these bridges."

"Yet you also have what appears to be the beginning of a wall on your side also."

"True." *One to him.* "Simply a way of setting the border."

"Which is all ours is doing."

"To be frank, I had expected you would be here to ask how you could help, but that doesn't seem to be the case."

"One could say on our side of the divide that an approach prior to now to discuss such construction might have been seen as a less forceful way of conducting things."

Karpenmor studied the man. Things were going more or less as he expected, but his opponent wasn't giving anything away. He wanted to slow things down a bit, perhaps that might help.

"I think there are many things to think on, Emissary Clannack. I believe we should rest, and I can discuss with my advisors, and think on the matter. You and your men should stay, it's not a good time to try to get back, and the winds seem to be growing. We'll accommodate you for the night and meet again in the morning."

It was a command, not a request, and Karpenmor watched to see what the reaction would be. The huge face didn't give too much away, just a little scowl crept in, before being calmed away.

He'd been right, the man wanted to get back today. Karpenmor didn't know if it mattered but at this point in time he felt as though he had the upper hand.

"Trorn, can you coordinate someone to set up shelter for them all, and have them fed? Then we shall discuss these matters ready for the morning."

"Yes, your Highness."

Clannack stood as Karpenmor did and dipped his head before heading out of the tent. A smile crept onto Karpenmor's face. While there wasn't a lot of headway, he was enjoying this... a lot.

LEO

He looked around the rock face, on both sides. Leo couldn't get any higher up the mountainside than where he was now.

If this is meant to be the way in, then it should be right here.

Looking down from where he stood, Leo was confused. He'd only walked and climbed a reasonably short distance, or that's what he'd believed.

That's not what he saw now. The wagon seemed about half-sized, and Kooka very small sat upon it. He shook his head, it made no sense, but then nothing about his current life did.

With no way in he began his descent, part sliding, climbing and finally walking along the last of the dry stream bed until he was back beside the wagon.

Once again it only took him a few minutes, but the distance was much further than he could say he'd covered.

"What did you find?" Kooka seemed impatient.

"Nothing promising."

"How did you get up so high so quickly? Is that your thing?"

"What do you mean?"

Kooka shrugged. "I've been around the Court for a long time, Leo, I know that they all have certain capabilities. Things that the rest of us don't have."

"No, I just walked and climbed, and suddenly I was much further up than I should have been."

"Magic."

"Yes." Suddenly Leo realized he hadn't been thinking clearly. "That's it, Kooka."

"What is?"

"What you said. No, I didn't use my skill to get up there, but that's how I get in."

"You gotta slow down and fill me in, I have no idea what you're saying."

Leo did and gave Kooka an explanation of what he could do, but also of what he found up there.

"You're going to shrink and go into the mountain?"

"I don't see any other option. It makes sense, that's why it's like that. If it was someone else, I'd say the way in would suit their skill."

"If you say so. But whatever you need to do, you need to do it soon."

"Why?"

"I don't want to be camped out here overnight, there's a storm brewing over the desert." Kooka looked east and Leo saw what was bothering him.

"I'm going now."

The climb was just as quick as the first time and Leo got to the spot where the stream begun. *That's the easy part.*

Toolet and he had tried ways to practice him consciously moving into the form of an animal, but with mixed success. Several times he'd become a rat, despite his displeasure at it, but both times it was almost by accident.

Another time he'd become a rabbit but couldn't stay there. That one made him feel quite unwell because he was much more aware of the process, as it happened too slowly, or that was how Toolet explained it.

Because he could sense what was happening his mind and body

got in the way. It was the best guess they'd had about why he'd been flickering between himself and the rabbit.

When he'd become the wolf, it had been outside of his control and he'd lost any sense of what was happening, no way to mimic it. Not that he wanted to repeat that.

I'll just try a rat, that will be simplest.

Leo sat and folded his legs, resting a hand on each knee, bringing his breath under control. As he calmed himself and slowed his thinking the sound of thunder rumbled off in the distance.

It doesn't matter. Let it be.

Nothing happened. He opened his eyes and was still sat there looking out across the desert. The black clouds had moved closer, and the thunder was louder.

A crack of lighting off in the distance made everything feel more ominous. The desert seemed to be moving in all directions, as though the storm had whipped up the sands.

Leo closed his eyes again and tried to change himself. He pictured a rat and told himself to become one. More thunder rumbled and his anxiety began to build.

I need to solve this, quickly.

Nothing changed. He opened his eyes and looked down the hill. He could see Kooka staring up the hill, and Leo wasn't even sure if the man could see him up there.

The light of the day was disappearing fast as the black clouds scuttled across the whole of the eastern sky, bringing an early night. Leo heard someone climbing up and looked to see Irdan's head coming up through the rough path below him.

"Leo," the man shouted up at him, "we have to go. Kooka has warned this storm is too dangerous."

A heavy drop of rain hit Leo on the nose. *One more time, you can't just give up.*

More drops fell, some of them landing on him, others punching up dust from the dry stream bed, or sliding off the rocks. Leo closed his eyes again.

He didn't think of being a rat, he just pushed into a rat. *That's the difference. I didn't try to shape it, I just moved there.*

Everything smelled different, and he kept moving his head looking left and right. The view was very different, and even though in the deep part of his mind he hated this, it was the first time he was alone doing it by choice.

The hole under the rocks looked large to him at this size and Leo wasted no time before walking into it, and climbing up into the dark tunnel.

He could see more than adequately despite there being no light source. The space opened into a narrow tunnel which headed directly into the mountain.

Letting go of the image of the rat, he felt himself come back. Leo was standing inside the tunnel now, finding it much darker than it had been moments before.

He put his hands out and touched both side walls. Turning to his left he used both hands to scour the dark wall. There had been something he'd seen when looking up that he didn't recognize.

His left hand came to it, and he could feel it was a lever of some sort. It pushed inward and as it did so the rock face began to move. He pushed it more and the rocks opened enough for him to slide out.

Irdan had reached his spot now.

"Bring them up, Irdan."

"Who?"

"Odajeen and Lani."

"Kooka says we must go and now, or this storm will be too much."

"You must bring them up, I can get them in here."

Leo followed him down and told Kooka what he'd found.

"There's no time, Leo."

"There has to be, Kooka. This is what we're meant to find."

The older man shook his head. "Quickly, let's get them up there."

Irdan and Vefed dragged the two women out of the back of the wagon.

"Great, you bring us out now it's storming."

"We're here, Odajeen, but we have to carry you, for now at least."

"Okay."

Leo looked at both women, and thought they were both looking very weak. Lani's skin was almost see-through, she was so thin, and Odajeen looked much older than he remembered.

The crack of thunder overhead made him jump.

"Quickly, everyone," Kooka shouted as a gust of wind made all the canvas on the wagon flap violently.

The journey up the hill should have been near impossible with the two guards carrying the two women, but somehow a few minutes later they stood outside the entrance.

Leo went inside. "Push them in and I'll guide them." He could see no other option. Lani came first, and he grabbed hold of her, and stepped back slowly.

As she came, Irdan pushed Odajeen inward but then stopped.

"What's wrong?"

"I can't pass through."

"What do you mean?"

"See." Irdan pushed his hands toward Leo, but they stopped in mid-air as if there was a barrier there.

"Great."

Irdan turned away and Leo could hear him talking. Then Kooka's face showed through the gap to outside. He tried the same thing but couldn't push through.

"We can't stay here. You will have to do this alone, Leo. We'll get to Traveler's Rest and wait for you there."

"Okay."

Leo shook his head; he had no idea how he'd manage to get these women to wherever they were meant to go. Kooka left and he was stuck there holding Lani upright when another crack of thunder echoed outside.

"Odajeen?"

"Yes."

"Can you walk?"

"Of course, I'm blind that's all."

"You're going to need to come this way. I'll step backward and lift Lani. You need to follow."

"Okay."

It took longer than it should, but they reached a spot in the tunnel where there was enough space for them all to stand together.

"Hold her up, I'll be back soon."

Leo ducked back down the tunnel to the opening. As unthinking as he'd been recently, he knew he had to protect this entrance. It wasn't for others to know about. He pulled the lever and the rock face closed, plunging him into complete darkness.

92

LANI

$\mathcal{I}$t felt as though someone had lit a lantern, such was the change to how the space felt. Up until this point Lani's mind had felt like it was partly shut down. Her resolve had been dwindling.

She'd wondered how she could ever get free. Then the light turned on. Except it wasn't light, but that's as well as she could explain it.

Then someone spoke to her.

"Hello, Lani."

"Who are you?"

"You know who I am."

"Do I?"

"We've spoken before."

"From the stone?"

"Yes."

"Where am I?"

"In Burgendetta's mind."

"That I know. I meant..."

"You're almost at the place where I live, under the mountain."

"Midderbuilt?"

"That's the city people live in, yes."

"What am I doing here?"

"We need to solve this problem you've created, young woman. Some friends of yours have brought you to me."

"Who?"

"That matters not, I want you to relax and let me use you to try and figure this out. It might feel a little odd."

"Odder than being trapped inside someone else's mind?"

The lady murmured. "Perhaps not so strange."

Lani didn't notice a lot, in fact her mind felt clearer than it had in some time, almost as though it had been dipped in a cold bucket of water.

Who would be with me? Odajeen? If so, then her men as well.

I wonder who else? Is Tillandra one of them? She will be so mad with me for doing this.

When the voice returned, there was still no emotion in it, no way for Lani to determine how the woman felt about what she'd learned.

"Your helpers are bringing you to the stone. When you're there I will try and see what I can do."

"Is there anything I can do?"

"No, not at this time."

And then she was gone again. While previously Lani had been anxious about getting free, now she felt a sense of hope which brought with it impatience. She wanted to be free.

She walked back and forth inside Odajeen's mind trying to burn off the uneasiness she felt, the desire to be free. As she did so she also recognized that her ability to access Burgendetta's memories was about to end.

When I get out of here, there's no way I'm coming back.

She slipped back into the old Jester's memories.

Lani found herself back at the table in the room under Anderwell. Not her, but Burgendetta, standing in the dark room looking at the table.

Every time Lani had come back to this memory she wished she could see what the others could. They had described blue lights that hovered above the surface pinpointing the position of the rest of the Court.

Burgendetta could not see them nor the map of Dharatan carved into the massive wooden tree trunk that filled nearly half of the room.

She knew that many seats were placed around the table, but she was the only person in the room.

On the wall to her left Burgendetta knew there were masks, the faces of passed Jesters, but she could not see any of them. She thought of one, but Lani had never been able to get the name from the woman's memories.

Lani rolled backward in time, letting the memories scroll past in her mind until she felt something that caused her to stop. Burgendetta was somewhere deep inside the ground, that's how it felt, or what she knew in her mind.

In front of her there was something that pushed light into the eyes of the blind woman. And there was a humming. The same stone Lani was near now.

Burgendetta held the Mother Stone in her hand and could feel the massive stone before her drawing the little one to it.

When Burgendetta reached the stone, the Mother Stone fitted perfectly into a hole made just for it. A sense of relief flooded through the woman's body, and she turned and walked away from it.

Lani felt Burgendetta sit down and relax.

"Burgendetta, welcome back."

"Thank you, Thenis. The stone was getting very weak, I could tell."

"You mustn't leave it so long. The very most is twelve moons, or you'll drain all the protection of the city."

"Understood. This is all so new, were there but a guide..."

"It is new to us as well, many of these things were not quite accidental, but we had to create without a lot of planning."

"What of my question?"

"I cannot find anything to aid you, I am sorry."

Lani felt the body she was in shrug.

"I see trouble ahead for you, daughter."

"More than what you have laid on me already?" Burgendetta's words were not filled with pain, almost humor.

"I'm afraid so."

"What is it?"

"That I couldn't tell you if I wanted. The future is locked out of your comprehension at this time. You will probably never remember these words, but I am sorry."

"Ominous, but that is okay. I have endured plenty in my time, what will be one more thing."

The goddess said nothing back to Burgendetta and Mother Folly settled into her rest on the cushions.

At least I'll feel good after this recharge.

Lani moved further back, excited by what she'd learned about the Lady in the Stone. It was hard to know what was important in the life of the woman. Several times Lani stopped to watch memories, only to find them everyday moments of no consequence.

She watched the Audition that made Burgendetta one of the Court, which had been ten years, or thereabouts, before she'd become Mother.

So much magic, so much mystery.

The images raced past. Lani had decided she wanted to go back to the very beginning, to some point where the young Burgendetta had been born blind or become blind.

The streets were dark and threatening. Burgendetta scurried along the shadows, avoiding the men in black. Not the soldiers, they afforded her no attention.

Lani was startled, she'd reached a memory where Burgendetta could see.

The priests were the ones who had taken her mother, she'd never come back from that. Now Burgendetta hunted for scraps like the other young in this city.

Clouds hung over the city, and drizzle had been falling all day, making the paths muddy and any pavers slippery. She paused at a corner and checked around it carefully before racing across and down the next road.

The smell caught her attention. Food cooking, somewhere close by, rich meaty food. Her stomach grumbled and ached at the recognition. The last thing she'd eaten had been part of a rat, roasted over a fire of wood scraps.

She'd had to share it with Gyen. The girl was younger than Burgendetta, and just as desperate. Burgendetta knew she should only care for herself, but her heart didn't work that way.

Cautiously she homed in on where the aroma was coming from. Strangely it seemed to be emanating from the back of a warehouse that was usually empty.

It wasn't going to be anyone rich, that much she knew; they never came into this part of the city. She scurried into a narrow alley alongside the building and found some loose boards part way along.

Inside there was a small gathering of the soldiers around a fire. None of them spoke. That much she knew about these Vrah, they rarely said anything.

She felt safe enough hiding from them. Typically, they'd ignore the street kids and go about their business. Suddenly a tall man walked into the room, wearing the clothes of a priest and all the soldiers stood at once.

"What is this? Clean it up, I could smell you up the road, everyone will know you are here. Fools."

The fire was extinguished and the pot that had been on it taken to the side of the room and pushed away.

"Is this everyone?"

"Yes, Uksod, it is."

"Have you brought me those who I need?"

"Not yet. We waited until you would be here."

"What? Now I must wait? What was the point of me arranging this? What's your number?"

"Seventeen, Eminence."

"I am not his Eminence, or not yet at least. Do not mistake my orders for things you should think on ever again. When I give you a command, follow it without question."

"Yes, sire."

"Get me someone, and fast, and bring reserves."

Burgendetta slid quietly along the wall, seeking the pot the men had discarded. It would still have food in it she knew, and her stomach was driving her decisions.

She reached it and nearly scalded her hand touching the side of it. A small gasp escaped her mouth as she pulled her hand back. Worried she might have alerted the guards, she froze and held in the pain in her hand.

When no one came she tried again, this time not caring about her hand. It was already slightly burned so she used it as a spoon.

Burgendetta put it inside and while the food was hot it wasn't unmanageable. She scooped the thick stew up and pushed it into her mouth.

Her eyes closed as she savored it, letting it slide down her throat. Without thinking she sucked her fingers before stopping. The sound of footsteps headed her way, and she opened her eyes.

A strong hand grabbed her and pulled her out of the shadows.

"Who is this?"

"Never seen her before, sire."

Burgendetta wanted to cry. Of all the people she wanted to avoid, this priest was one she'd heard about. He might have even been the one that took her mother.

"Can you use her?"

The priest looked at her. "No, she's too weak and small. Get rid of her."

"She's harmless, shall I just let her go?"

"Harmless? These leeches bleed the city of its purity. Perhaps I can practice with her."

"What do you mean, sire?"

"Put her on the table and strap her down."

"I thought..."

"Just do it."

Burgendetta looked up at the man. He was much younger than she'd thought, everything except his eyes. And the thing on his head seemed to be burned into his skin.

It should have looked pretty, she thought, with that orange jewel set in the center, and all the small gems down the sides of the gold, but something about it was repulsive to her.

Maybe it was all the pink skin around it, where it seemed burned to his head. Parts of it were wrinkled but freshly so. It made her want to be sick just looking at it.

"What are you looking at?" The priest looked down at her.

She couldn't speak even if he needed her to.

"You don't like what she's done to me? Pity you. Close your eyes, this won't hurt a bit." He chuckled; it was a sound that made her skin go cold.

"I said close your eyes, child!"

Burgendetta couldn't. Something was stopping her from being able to close her eyes. She wanted to, she wanted desperately to get away from here.

"CLOSE THEM!"

The priest was angry, shouting at her, but still, she couldn't. She didn't understand why he was so mad, but she couldn't stop looking at the horrible way his head looked, and it must have been showing on her face.

He placed his right hand on her chest, and something changed in her. What little strength she had fell away from her and she felt almost sleepy, but still her eyes wouldn't close.

"You think it's revolting to look at?" It was as though he was inside her mind. "Well, I'll fix that."

His left hand reached to his neck and pulled a pin from the cloth there, a long thin metal pin with a shiny gem on the handle. Burgendetta felt as though she should be worried, as though she should care, but everything was dull now.

The priest brought the pin toward her, and with a smirk on his face he brought it down.

NO!

Burgendetta wanted to squirm, to scream, but there was nothing but what she could do in her head. Then he pushed it into her eye, and she screamed.

The burning pain pierced through everything else, and she felt sick. Before she could gain control of herself, he pushed it into her other eye and the pain was too much.

As she slipped into unconsciousness all she heard was the priest. "Perhaps that will teach you a lesson, live with that. Take her away."

Burgendetta succumbed to the darkness.

~

Lani pulled out of the memories, her face full of tears. She couldn't believe what she'd just seen. Odajeen hadn't been born without sight, they'd taken it from her.

93

GORAN

The fight was hanging in the balance. Goran was wriggling around on the ground of his tent, one eye out the opening, while he tried to free his bindings.

He could tell the men were from Anderwell, Tillandra had sent help for him. *That wasn't what I expected.*

Goran knew she could watch where he was on the map, but that was a pretty general position. Somehow, with a bit of luck, they'd found the Sahrian knights out here in the middle of nowhere.

It meant that there was another one of his colleagues with them. Someone would have had to be in contact with Tillandra. *Or is it her?*

That would make some sense, she had always been the one more on his side than against.

It doesn't matter right now, I need to get free, to help.

He rolled half out of the tent and sat up watching everything happening around him. One of the soldiers on his side came close by.

"Help me!"

The man looked and hurried his way, watching for an attack.

"On your front," he barked.

Goran was nervous but did so anyway and could feel a blade

between his hands. Suddenly they were free, and he turned and stood. Now he needed a weapon.

"Are you Goran?"

"Yes."

"Then stick with me, you're who we're here to free."

"I need a weapon."

"Let's get you away from here first."

The man turned south and started moving through the sand, Goran following. They clambered up the side of the dune to the top, and found a body.

"Oh Thenis, not Phetir." The soldier shook his head but didn't spend any more effort over what he couldn't change. "Take his sword."

Goran picked it up from the sand, noting it too had blood on the blade. At least the man had hurt someone else.

"Damn, what is she doing?"

Goran looked to where the solider was facing. A woman was stepping slowly across the sand toward something he couldn't focus easily on. It looked like a person but was draped in a heavy robe.

As she got closer the other figure seemed to be diminishing. It was more like an apparition than someone real. Goran had heard about such things in the desert, images that were imaginary.

But the soldier can also see it.

Automatically they both started toward her.

The apparition disappeared completely, or more accurately crumbled, the robe the only thing Goran could still see across the width of the dune.

"Who is that?"

"Her name is Gizen. She's blind though, I don't understand why she's out here."

Gizen? That name doesn't sound familiar.

"Where's she from?"

"Anderwell, like us. Enough questions, we need to get to her."

The woman didn't look blind to Gizen, she was walking directly to the robe. When she reached the spot in the sand she bent down and picked an object up.

Goran felt a twinge inside as though something had shifted. It was an odd sensation and passed instantly but it warned him an event was happening that shouldn't.

He spun around, looking for danger close by. Usually such sensations kept him safe from covert attacks, but not now. All the fighting was in the valley or across the dune to his right.

That was when he saw one of the knights climbing up the side of the dune closest to Gizen. He wanted to call out but it would make no difference. If she was blind, she couldn't defend herself against a physical attack.

The woman turned his way, as if sensing him, and he saw the sunshine glinting off something in her hands. The light that came from her hands was a deep orange, not that of the sun or the sand and a shiver ran down his back.

It's an amulet.

She started walking back across the dune, in the direction Goran and his companion were heading, but they were still too far from her.

Will it affect her like Lani? She's not dead from it, that's something.

The knight was getting closer to her, Goran couldn't help himself.

"Gizen, quicker, there's someone coming."

A sound broke his focus. It had come from behind and he knew what it was. *Armor.*

Goran spun and pulled his sword up. Another knight was trying to creep up on them. "No, you won't!" Goran kept walking backward, keeping him somewhat in touch with the soldier from Anderwell.

He looked across his shoulder and could see the knight closest to Gizen getting far too close. "You must go help her. Don't let the knight get that thing she holds!"

The soldier looked back at Goran, then nodded and headed off.

I hope my arm is ready for this.

After so much time in captivity and so little training the one thing Goran wasn't practiced in was fighting. *But there's only one of them.*

As the man got closer, Goran pushed out his skill at him, immediately getting a reaction. The knight stopped briefly, his eyes letting Goran know it had worked.

The knight pushed on while Goran pushed thoughts back at the man. He would be difficult to master, being a trained soldier. His orders and reactions would be instinctive, which meant they often overrode thoughts.

Suddenly the man was upon Goran, making it almost impossible to do both things. Their swords came together, the shudder reverberating down his arm.

He pushed the thought that he was a friend, a simple thought, but easy to use. It was just enough, Goran could feel it, the responding attack paused just a little.

I've got to use that.

Changing position was much harder in the sand, more so for the knight wearing half of his armor. Goran stepped back, trying to keep the man coming forward.

Usually that wasn't ideal but if he could tire the knight, as well as use his skill it gave him a chance. He had to spin quickly, the knight was better than he and an unexpected strike came under his guard.

The tip of the blade just brushed against his tunic. *Too close.* Goran pushed the thought out again as he jabbed his blade forward in an effort to keep the man away.

Another couple of steps backward, poking his sword forward, parrying an attack, more steps. Then he focused his will and pushed a strong thought at the man. *You're wrong.*

The knight's thoughts were interrupted just long enough for Goran who'd changed his direction in anticipation. He stepped forward as the knight's sword arm had dipped enough to create an opening and drove forward.

Goran turned side on to avoid the man's blade and pushed his own into the throat of the man, just above his chest armor. It was a feeling he'd never liked, the way a blade punctured the skin before sinking deep in.

A spurt of blood hit Goran in the face and he pulled away, bringing his sword out despite the drag on it. The knight fell back, his hands grabbing at his neck.

Goran didn't need to worry about him anymore and turned to look toward the woman as he brushed his eyes clear with the sleeve of his tunic.

The soldier and knight were fighting, and Goran headed toward them as fast as he could. The young woman had stopped walking, turning her head in different directions, unsure where to go with the sound of the men so close to her.

"This way!"

She didn't appear to hear him. Goran knew he had to get to her, to the amulet. All his past came back to him in a flood.

He knew he was still one of the Court, when all he could think about was getting the amulet and taking it somewhere safe. All his angst and grievances washed away.

Thirty steps was about all there was between them. Goran could see that the soldier from Anderwell was being beaten. He couldn't will anything to help him, the distance was too great, his energy was weak and trying to run was taking all he had left.

Everything seemed to happen slowly as the soldier was cut down by the knight. The Skarian didn't pause even for a breath, pushing forward toward Gizen.

Goran couldn't get to her, he needed to do something. He had to stop to focus his will and he pushed out a simple thought. *Stop!* It had no effect. He grabbed everything he could and pushed again.

Was that an effect? Did he slow?

It wasn't enough and Goran tried to rush to her, twenty steps left. The knight was closer, only five or so. Gizen heard the knight and turned to him, holding out the amulet toward him.

That stopped the knight in his tracks, his eyes staring at the light coming from the jewel, gaining Goran valuable time. Fifteen steps… twelve… ten. The knight moved forward again, looking at the amulet in her hands.

Goran was only five from her, his sword out in front ready to knock her down if he had to. The knight was quicker than him and reached her first. The Skarian stepped forward and drove his blade into Gizen's middle.

"No!"

Her hands flew open, and the amulet spilled out. As it did so the knight let go of his sword and reached out to catch it. Just as Goran reached them.

His first swing cut one of the knight's hands off, his second half severed the other. The amulet fell out and the man looked up as though seeing Goran for the first time, horror across his face as the pain kicked in.

Goran's next attack was straight through the neck, like he had done to the previous combatant. It had always been his favored way of ending a fight, no one ever attacked again after it.

The knight went down, and Goran dropped to his knees beside Gizen, the sword still in her as she lay in the sand, tears running down her face.

"Gizen?"

"Yes…" Her voice was surprisingly strong.

"I need to pull this out. Then I'm going to bind the wound, we'll get you some help."

"Where? Out here, there's no one."

"I'll figure it out."

"That's another amulet, isn't it?"

Goran remembered the jewel and spun on his knees. It lay in the sand, light shining on the stone, and instead of happiness, his heart felt crushed.

There was nothing good about it, somehow all he could see was the danger in it. Unlike how it seemed to enrapture others, he wanted to bury it where no one would ever find it.

You will not, Fool.

He knew the sound of that voice. Goran didn't need to look anywhere to know where it came from. It was inside his own head.

Oh no!

94

TILLANDRA

Tillandra sat before the tree wanting to admire it and just enjoy the beauty of it, but she had a sense of dread. No dream had come but something had happened, she could sense it.

At least using the power behind the tree meant she could more easily use her skills, without the cost. Her first connection was to the desert.

"How badly is she hurt, Goran?"

"It's not good."

Tillandra wished Purple was with her and not the others. She had sent Gizen into harm's way and the woman had been hurt, probably fatally.

A coldness in Tillandra's heart surprised her. Yes, she did care that she'd sent the woman into a dangerous situation, but not the way she might have at other times.

I had little choice.

That was the price of the win that had come out of it. Goran now had an amulet, which had been kept out of the hands of the Skarians.

We got an amulet, that counts.

"Are there any prisoners?"

"None. The soldiers wouldn't give in, but one of the others he ran off into the desert. Should we hunt him down?"

"Leave him be. What of the amulet?"

"What do you mean?"

"How do you feel?"

"Horrified by it…"

He said nothing else, and Tillandra could sense there was more that he wasn't saying.

"What is it, Goran?"

"I think it doesn't affect me the same."

"What do you mean?"

"Everyone else is drawn to it, our soldiers, even Gizen seems drawn to it, as were the knights that attacked her, but for me it repulses me. I have to stay a distance from everyone in our party."

"That's the first positive thing you've told me."

"Sort of."

"What is it?"

"I think it brought him back."

"Him?"

"You know. I don't even want to say his name."

Tillandra realized who he meant, Zoran. "Are you sure?"

"Not about the cause, but he spoke to me. That's the first time since when the young girl did her healing. I think it's him that's affected by this, which is why I'm not."

"You can manage him, Goran. You did for a long time."

"I'm not so sure. But something about the amulet seems to have pulled him free."

"Keep it safe, Goran. If anyone can, you can. It makes sense even."

"What do you mean?"

"You've had to fight an opposing side of yourself for a long time, you've developed tricks and skills to manage that… no one else has such experience with that effect. It might just protect you from the amulet."

He didn't reply. Tillandra knew he was still there, but he wasn't speaking, so she just waited, letting him think through whatever he could.

"Are we closer to Midderbuilt than you? Should I go there?"

It was a good question. She wasn't sure that anywhere was safe for the amulets, not while they weren't locked away in something like the box Lani carried.

But with Lani already at Midderbuilt, sending an unprotected amulet there was fraught with danger. It was the last place they wanted the Derks to think of as significant.

Goran needed a decision, and they were a touch closer to Anderwell.

"Come home, Goran." It felt good to say that to him. "Run fast and bring her home, maybe we can save her."

I need to send more help to them. Maybe a physick can help keep her alive long enough to get her here.

~

Tillandra tried to reach Hallendell but there was no reply. As much as that was usual for her fellow Jester, she wasn't stuck in Nkuku any longer.

The dream she had worried Tillandra, so she switched to seeking out the woman's mask and trying to see through her eyes. What she saw next broke her heart.

Hallendell was being led by a group of Morskan soldiers, her hands tied in front of her and a long rope leading her. For now, at least, she wasn't being tortured.

What are we going to do for her?

The Morskan capital, Kamasa, also known as the White City, was a fortress and allowed few inside that didn't live there. If they were taking her there, as her dream had suggested, she was in a lot of danger.

I must do something.

Her options were limited. Because of the distance, there was no one particularly close, but also everyone was doing something she needed them to do. *Not everyone.*

Tillandra shook her head and changed her thoughts to Junther. She focused on her friend and his ridiculously long white hair. Normally it would cause her to smile but not today.

～

"In All Jest, Mother."

"Junther, In All Jest to you too." Their relationship was usually one of casual banter, she tried to force herself into the mood.

"How are you getting by, old man? I've been worried your body might just stop on you out on the road like this."

"Ha, your jokes are as good as your cooking, Tillandra. Weak or overdone. Our investment in Milfred is the best thing we ever did, or you might not have survived."

That ended any chance of frivolity she had. He didn't know about what had happened, and now she had to retell the story, she could sense fresh tears running down her physical face.

"I'm sorry, Mother, I truly am."

"Enough, tell me what you know."

"I know I don't want to be in Kuwaha. This is the most horrible place I've ever been."

"You're inside then?"

"Yes, but only just. And it's particularly difficult to stay unnoticed now."

"Have you seen Clannack?"

"Is he here?"

"Yes, I thought you knew."

"I've spoken to no one else, there's been no time, not after the King and his troops boated away from me."

"What do you mean?"

He explained that they'd taken ocean transport, and he'd had to ride very hard to catch up.

"There's a lot going on up here, you can feel the tension in the air."

Tillandra passed on Clannack's information to him.

"I won't be able to get close enough to King Ahn now. I'm not sure what use I can be."

"We want to know where he goes next, and if they return home, I need to know where they go, and when they might be back."

"What about the troops on our border?"

"I think with him away they are at a standstill, there seems no current intent to invade. Gimbden has many eyes on them, and our own forces are prepared -- as best they can be."

"So, you think it hinges on whatever the King is doing up here?"

"I can't answer that with any real insight, Junther. Perhaps they underestimated our preparedness or response and are rethinking whatever they were up to. Alternatively, they might have been preparing for the amulets."

She told him about the amulet that Gizen and Goran had.

"Is it coming back to Anderwell?"

"At the moment. I'm not sure that's ideal but I need to ask now we have one."

"Can we trust him?"

"I want to think so."

Junther was silent, and Tillandra knew there was no point in continuing the discussion, he'd be anti-Goran as long as he lived.

"I might need you to head west."

"Nedor?"

"No, the White City."

"What?"

She told him about Hallendell.

"I'm not sure how I'll get in without being caught myself but give me the signal and I'll be gone that second."

"Just let me think on it a little. She's not there yet."

"She's a lot closer than I am. What about Bea?"

"I'm reviewing all options; I just need to find the solution that fits best. I can't afford to lose two people."

"She's not lost yet, Mother."

"I know… I know, but you didn't see the dream."

"And from what you told me she was alive in that too. You'll figure it out."

"Don't get recognized by Ahn's men, Junther. You are going to be needed back in Sahro."

"Of that I'm very aware, Tillandra, and I've been chasing them this whole journey. This is the first time I've ever been in the same place as them."

~

Tillandra stood up, her mind less at ease, not just with what was happening, but knowing she was now making decisions that were potentially sacrificing one in favor of a bigger goal.

She wasn't sure how she felt about that, or how easily she'd made that call. But it was done now, she couldn't undo it even if she wanted to.

95

LANI

*L*ani didn't want to go back and see any more of Odajeen's life. Reliving what the woman had gone through as a young child had been very difficult to stomach.

The way the Enderk priest Uksod, a name she would never forget, took her sight was horrific. She hated the man for what he had done so callously.

Previously she'd not grouped the assassins chasing her as representative of the entire race but after seeing this she wasn't so sure.

Lani had wanted to believe that their goddess, that's how Lani saw her, was being honest with her, but seeing what her people did made that difficult to swallow.

Even the city that she'd seen Odajeen living in as a young girl had repulsed Lani. The memories she'd experienced with eyesight did little to comfort Lani.

The place appeared harsh and had a horrible feeling to it. Any curiosity she had to go to Enderk to learn of her past was quickly diminishing.

The more she thought about Odajeen, the more she had to admire the woman. Burgendetta had been brutally blinded and left to fend for herself, which she'd done. Then over time she'd become a Jester, rising to be Mother before giving it all up.

To save me.

After losing her memory and surviving for many years, without even knowing why, the woman had helped Lani, and now Lani had put her at risk.

Is she at risk, or is it just me?

Despite everything she was thinking and feeling Lani felt better than she had in a long time. Much better. Her mind was clearer, and she felt generally stronger but she couldn't explain it.

There was a vibration that had come with the sense of light when she'd arrived at Midderbuilt, and Lani assumed it was connected.

It must be the effect of the stone.

~

"You're here now."

"Is that why I feel this way?"

"It is the Citadel Stone. That's part of its effect when you are so close. It raises your vibration to match its own."

"Who brought me here?"

"That's of no consequence. We need to concentrate on how to get you free. I need you to tell me everything about where you are, what you can see."

"I can't see anything. I'm seeing life as Burgendetta did and she was blind."

"Interesting. You need to go back to the beginning and explain everything since you got in there. Even before if you can, I am not sure which part of it will help."

~

It felt like hours passed with Lani explaining what she had discovered, the things she had done, and the impressions she had from where she was trapped.

Thenis asked many questions, some which Lani didn't understand the purpose of, but she did her best to answer. When it was done, the goddess spoke again.

"I need both of you to rest now."

"What do you mean, both of us?"

"Odajeen is there with you."

"I see. Is she okay?"

"She lives and can behave normally, but she is weak as are you. She can't leave your company, or she becomes very sick. Odajeen has suffered much doing this."

Lani felt sorry for the impact this was causing, but not guilty. It had been Odajeen that had asked her to do this.

"How long has it been?"

"Many, many weeks."

"Really? It feels only like days here."

"Much has been happening while you've been lost in there. But none of that matters. Rest and let the stone recharge her and your health. I need you both strong."

Lani knew she had fallen asleep. Not because she was lying down, she still couldn't do that, but by the way she felt. It was as if someone had wrapped their arms around her to allow her to relax while she stood.

And she had slept. The deepest and most refreshing sleep she could ever remember.

"Good, you are awake."

"How long?"

"A day, that is all."

"I have never felt so refreshed."

"So Tillandra says. It is but a shame that more cannot experience the power of the stone, but… it must be hidden."

Lani knew enough to understand why. Especially with the amulet.

"Where is the amulet?"

"Now, it is in the box, with the man who brought you here."

"Box, what box?"

"You do not remember?"

"There's memories I cannot access, in here I only know what happened from the time I arrived, or Burgendetta's memories."

Thenis explained the principle of the box, and how it helped her, as well as affected her.

"If it's in the box how come it didn't harm me?"

"I suspect it did, but because your body is not awake outside of here, no one would know. That was why I needed you to rest, to boost you back to full strength."

Lani was grateful for it even more.

"We do not want the amulet exposed near here, it is a beacon of sorts to those who wish to find the Citadel Stone."

"I see."

"Let us begin. I am going to give you some things to try, and I will see if I can assist you or at least learn more about what is happening."

"Okay."

"First and the simplest, I want you to focus on Odajeen. Bring her into your mind, as you remember her from the last time you saw her."

Lani started focusing, trying to bring the woman's image into her mind, but nothing came. She stumbled inside her own mind. It was the thing she'd always been able to do, to recall things, and even knowing she was not herself, still it frustrated her.

"It's okay, Lani. I just wanted to test it. As you told me, in there you're not you, not properly."

The goddess said nothing for what seemed a long time.

"Now I want you to focus on the room you were in, the last memories of the time before you transitioned. Can you do that?"

"I'll try."

Images did come to Lani, but they weren't strong ones, and she needed to really concentrate to see them in that space between her eyes.

"That's good. They aren't strong enough yet to help."

"Yet?"

"I'm still guessing, but we need your conscious to be more connected outside of the mind if we have any chance of drawing you out."

"Alright."

"Can you feel the mask, or what you think is the mask?"

Lani reached out and moved a little until she felt the barrier of the space she was in. Running her hands over it she nodded.

"Yes. I think that's what I can feel."

"Try to push yourself out through it. Maybe imagine it like it's a breath and you're being blown out."

Lani shook her head. Initially, she found herself trying to blow, not where she was.

She imagined a cloud of air behind her, and then turned it into a wind, pushing at her back. As good as her imagination was, she couldn't actually feel it, and she didn't move anywhere.

"Your mind isn't willing to accept that."

Lani felt disheartened, she'd thought the goddess would be able to just do something magical and extract her. These exercises felt stupid and weren't working.

Over the next period Lani tried multiple ways to get past the mask, or the barrier that existed. Nothing worked and Lani didn't feel anything that came close to the way she'd felt when she'd been pulled in here.

Everything felt different, and while she didn't know why, she knew they were approaching it wrong. She'd been connected to Odajeen's mind and…

"Wait, there was something else."

"What is it, Lani?"

"When I got stuck in here it was because I was connected to the amulet."

"You didn't mention that earlier. It's important."

"I didn't remember it. When we were trying things to access her memories nothing was working, and I took the amulet out and used it."

"What do you mean used it?"

Lani explained about how she could access the power within the amulet, and it gave her an ability to do things.

"This is even more concerning."

"If we take the amulet out of the box, I can access it, maybe that's all I need to get out."

"I told you why we don't want to do that, Lani."

"Do you want me to stay here?"

"No. I need to discuss this with my siblings."

"Okay, but nothing else has worked. I have no more ideas. Can she still find it even here? Can't you block it, somehow?"

"We do, Lani, but as the Occultation breaks down, we don't know if the amulet might pierce the shield. It's not something we want to test. I will be back."

Thenis was gone for what seemed hours, but Lani knew it was probably only minutes.

"We've agreed to test it, we think the shield of the Citadel will hide it like it does for the others."

"The others?"

"Not something you need to know about at this time. We've asked Leo to do as discussed. They will take it out, but they need to be very cautious as you know."

∼

Lani could feel the change. Suddenly there was a connection that didn't come from within Odajeen's head. It had a weight to it and it dragged at her like it was trying to pull her.

As she let her mind drift toward that sensation Lani felt a different power also pulling at her. It was as though the two were fighting against each other.

One felt loving and she got the sense of the bright light she'd felt when she arrived in Midderbuilt.

That's part of the problem. I need to go to the other one.

Lani focused away from the Citadel and let what she thought had to be the amulet take over her mind. It felt very different and despite its size pulled firmly at her.

Following that path was difficult, as though walking into a gale. Each step required her to push with all of her will just to get closer, fighting toward it.

Lani couldn't move. She was held stuck in place, the power of the pull from behind her was growing the closer she forged toward the amulet.

All of Lani's will was being tested. She pushed harder again, but the Citadel was doing everything it could to stop her getting to it. *It's making it worse being here.*

Despite everything she tried, the strength of the stone she was being charged by wouldn't let her reach the amulet. Gritting her teeth and putting all her effort into dragging her mind to the sense of the amulet, Lani pushed.

The sudden sound of a snapping noise echoed through the space she was stuck in. She recoiled backward tumbling over herself, then it all went black as she passed out.

CLANNACK

Clannack was glad that he was summoned early for their negotiations. The Prince took no time in beginning. "Cumerc must be returned to us."

"I beg your pardon?"

"The city, you call it Kuwaha, but its name is Cumerc, it was ours before you captured it after the fall of the bridge."

Clannack had been ready for this point to come up.

"Its name is Kuwaha, and I discussed this with you yesterday. At the time of the bridge collapse we were in a battle with your people who had attacked many on our lands."

"Our people were under attack, chased from the Great Fair fighting for their lives."

"If this is the case, why did they not seek protection in this city of yours, if it was that important?"

"I cannot say, I was not there, but thankfully they sought the safety of our homeland. Had they not they would have been trapped when the land bridge collapsed and perished at the hands of your people like those left behind."

"Not my people, Prince Karpenmor. It is true that the city was captured, but as happens in the times of history, cities change hands, borders move, and realms that once were are no longer. This discussion cannot be about undoing the past. It must be about the future."

Karpenmor stood up. "If you're not willing to compromise then there's little left to be said."

Clannack did not stand, but his eyes never left Karpenmor's as the Prince stepped away and left the tent. He hadn't expected such an aggressive step at this stage.

Maybe this is his way to gain concessions? If he feels we have all the leverage, does he need to use the city as his starting point?

Clannack waited a little longer then sent for word on when the Prince would return.

When the priest returned the news wasn't what Clannack had hoped for. "Prince Karpenmor has advised that at this point he sees no reason to continue, that your stance is clear."

Clannack knew this was part of the game, or at least that's how he interpreted it. Now it was his play.

"Then advise the Prince that our negotiations are over. He will have no bridge to Dharatan."

"You would leave?" The priest seemed surprised.

"It is good to see priests here act as errand boys. We have no use for them in Ngahere, even for that role. And yes, I do not intend to sit here while your master plays games."

The priest reacted as expected, a look of scorn appearing on his face.

Clannack turned to his guards. "We leave, gather your things."

"He will not be pleased."

"Nor my Queen on how I have been treated. Advise your master that any attempt to stop us leaving will be considered a hostile act."

Clannack knew the Ngaherians needed little preparation to depart, and he turned on the priest and began walking toward the steps down the cliff.

No one blocked their path, and at the bottom a boat was ready for them. The journey across to the mainland was as rough and unpleasant as the one that had brought them.

At the top Clannack headed directly to the Council building. Upon entering the meeting hall, he was met with a sight that did surprise him. A party of armored knights stood behind a guest stood in front of the Queen who sat on the makeshift throne.

She looked up as he walked into the room. "Clannack, welcome back. Your timing is perfect. Come forward."

Several of the knights had turned to see who it was she welcomed. More than double the number of Ngaherian warriors lined the main room, while others stood back in the side sections.

He approached the dais on which she sat and dipped his head. "Your Highness."

Standing to Clannack's left was a man with a small crown on his head. Not a tall man, nor was he broad, but he still commanded the space in which he stood.

If it's knights, you must be Ahn.

"King Ahn of Daskare, may I introduce my most esteemed councillor, Clannack. Clannack, we have a most important and interesting guest."

Clannack dipped his head to the King, less than toward the Queen, but respectful enough. "Your Highness, you're a long way from home."

The King studied him and nodded. A certain arrogance in it. Clannack had heard about him, so his manner wasn't surprising.

"This is true, but then such times demand journeys like this. May I introduce to you my Great Chancellor, Fuling."

The man beside the king bowed, more graciously than Clannack had, but said nothing. The man didn't look at all like an administrator, if anything Clannack would guess he was a priest in disguise.

Queen Vika spoke. "What brings you so far north, King Ahn?"

"Much, your Majesty. I have been on a mission to secure our wheat supplies."

"You have been affected as well?"

"We have, as have all the realms, it would seem, from our travels. No one seems immune from the plague, has it also affected Ngahere?"

The Queen took a moment before answering him. "There are those seeking to suggest that we are holding out on others, King Ahn, they are greatly mistaken."

"What of your neighbors?"

She raised her eyebrows at him.

"The Derks. I have been led to believe they have wheat to offer."

"Have you? And where did you hear such a tale?"

It was the King who paused this time.

"There are many talking about this, and yet there's none to be seen. It makes us wonder why."

"What are you suggesting?"

The air in the room was becoming tenser.

"Nothing at all, but you asked why I was here, this is the reason."

"May I ask what brought you here, and not to our capital?"

Clannack had wondered about that as well. Why had they come here and not to Laumua?

"We had planned to cross the sea and make contact with the Derks. That was until we discovered how treacherous the waters were. Then I saw the bridges. I came to see how they were progressing and was equally surprised to find you here."

The Queen rose, signaling the end of the meeting. "You and your men are welcome to stay as our guests. Why don't you all refresh and we'll meet again this evening to discuss these matters further."

Clannack watched as the guests left the hall, his mind wondering what the truth was behind their visit. Queen Vika turned to Clannack.

"An interesting turn of events. Now why don't you tell me what happened, Clannack?"

There wasn't that much to tell, she too was surprised that the Prince was the one he'd met with.

"A strange set of occurrences. The Prince and now the King. All turning up at the same time."

"Is it possible they were planning to meet?"

"I do not know, Clannack, but I don't trust coincidences. Your rejection of the negotiations was the right move no matter what. Without our cooperation there's no finishing the bridge, and without anyone to discuss it with he's stuck."

"He was definitely trying to… put us in our place, your Highness."

"Then he learned an important lesson. You did well, Clannack."

"I was unsure how they might respond. There is a sizeable force over there already, I'm not sure we'd have had an easy time of it should things have become physical."

"What next?"

"I think, Majesty, that we wait until we hear from the Derks. Without us there is no completing their bridge."

"I was meaning with the King."

"We need to know what he's up to. What's concerning is that he was intending to sail directly there. We would lose any exclusivity with the Derks were that to happen."

"For now, he's said he cannot. It might be a stunt to get the best leverage with us he can. The best option is the bridge."

"You still believe in making a deal?"

"Our grain is about to run out as well, Clannack. Without it we'll face our own problems. Our people need a lot of food."

He knew that Tillandra wouldn't be happy that the bridge might get completed but Vika was ready to deal, and he was sure the Prince of Enderk would also.

It was all going to come down to the price.

"Why the wall then?"

"I'm not a fool, Clannack, and this will be the most important connection point between the two realms. While I have no idea about the truth of the distant history, I still don't trust them. I want to be able to control who passes through and protect our side."

"I saw plenty of soldiers on their side. They might be amassing an army on our doorstep."

"They'll need more than a bridge to defeat us, Clannack. It would take some miracle or magic to get past the defenses we'll put up."

A shiver ran down Clannack's back. *She might not know what she just said.*

"So, I am to go back and negotiate for the return of the city?"

"No! That is not what I said. That decision is a long way off. Your job is to find a way, if there is one, to let them finish the bridge without that happening."

"Okay." Clannack didn't hold out much hope that would work out, but he would try. At least he would know about the circumstances of any agreement to share with his colleagues.

"I'll be going back?"

"We'll wait for them to send word first. And when you do go, you'll state I have to approve any final deals, that way you have a final out."

"Noted."

The Queen had been remarkably calm and logical about what she planned; it was a side to her he wasn't used to seeing. Too many things were converging all at once and Clannack pondered again about the coincidences. He didn't like them either.

97

LANI

The pain in the side of her head woke Lani. She couldn't recall anything as painful as this, but then she had so few memories of her own she had nothing much to compare it to.

Am I free?

She opened her eyes, but nothing was different, she was unable to see anything, her sight still absent.

Am I still in Odajeen's head?

"Yes, Lani, you are."

Lani grunted.

"Tell me what happened."

Lani told her everything that had happened. Little by little the pain in her head was easing and with it came the clarity she'd sensed just before she'd passed out.

"I can't do it in here."

Thenis didn't respond.

"Coming here was the right thing to do, I needed to be replenished, to have the strength to do it, but the stone in here won't let go because of the amulet. It's holding me back from being able to get back to myself."

"Are you sure, Lani?"

"I felt it, before the end happened, the resistance was the Citadel Stone. I have to get away from it to be able to get free, I think I can do it now."

"That would mean exposing the amulet outside the protection the Citadel offers."

"I'm open to other ideas but I don't have any. I sensed what was holding me back and it's the stone in here. I am certain if it wasn't for that I could have pulled myself out."

"You must get free, Lani. You mean too much. No one else has the ability to do what you've done."

"What does that even mean? Apart from the fact the amulet connected to me, there's nothing special about me. Who do I mean so much to? I was of no interest to anyone until the amulet came along. I didn't want any of this!"

"This is no time for you to be that person, Lani."

"What person?"

"The victim. You've lost most of that attitude recently, but you were full of it in the beginning..."

"I am a... I understand what you mean. I can't do anything in here, I have to get out. It's the only way to do it."

It occurred to Lani that she didn't need Thenis's permission, she could just get outside and do it anyway.

"Be patient, I need to discuss this with my siblings. What's your plan?"

"Initially just to be outside, away from the Citadel Stone. Somewhere I can try again, but not so far away in case I need to come back... to get my strength back."

"Wait for me."

It wasn't as though she had any choice. Without any way to speak to the others who were there with her she couldn't physically make Odajeen's body do anything.

One thing she hadn't considered was what affect her being in here was having on the older woman's body. Now that she'd learned of the life Odajeen had lived, Lani wanted to ensure she did no more harm to her.

Lani wasn't even sure if she could tell the woman the truth when she got out of here. *There we go.*

She now felt more positive about getting out than she had at any time since it had first happened. It wasn't *if* she got it out, it was *when* she did.

Odajeen would want to know about what Lani had learned, and everything she had discovered was all unpleasant. Maybe if she had more time to look she'd find all the good in her life, but Lani's priority was getting free.

~

"We agreed you will have to try. What comes of it we'll deal with when it happens. The primary goal is you get free."

"Okay."

"Your friends are moving you out from under the mountain."

"Thank you."

"I've done little to help you, Lani. What I will say is you need to focus forward, let go of the past, it's behind you now, it has no purpose in your life."

"Easy to say. How will I know when they do it?"

"I spoke to Leo. He will wait until they get you to the campsite and will set the amulet free again. I hope you'll be able to tell."

"I hope so too."

~

And again, she waited. Time passed, filled with her anticipation and frustration. Of all the things she hated, being at the mercy of others was the worst.

When I get out, I will never do this again.

Would she even remember what had happened, or would it be like this in reverse? That hadn't even occurred to her until now.

The irony wasn't lost that she might do all of this and then have nothing to tell Odajeen anyway.

"Are you still there?"

"Not for long."

Lani quickly shared what she had learned with Thenis on the promise that she could share them back to her or one of the Jesters if Lani couldn't remember.

It was an odd request, but the goddess didn't seem concerned at all.

The vibration had gone now, and Lani had to guess she was outside the mountain. What came next seemed like her last hope. If it didn't work, would she be stuck in here forever?

Would she be stuck until Odajeen died or would there be no way out? What of her own body, would it eventually waste away? Or would she go crazy lost inside a dead person's mind?

The whole idea was too bizarre to think about, she just had to get out. One way or another. *This has to work!*

98

LEO

The tunnel ended and Leo fumbled around for the lever he'd used before. His left hand bumped into it, and he breathed more easily as it opened.

Being under the mountain had been something else. He wasn't sure what happened, but he'd never felt more alive and ready to act.

Except he'd been stuck inside looking at the massive white stone for what felt like two days.

Both women now looked much better, still worryingly thin, but fuller. *That makes no sense.* But it did.

There was something about them that mirrored how he felt. That was the best way he could explain it, he felt full, not just energetically but in ways he had no words for.

Sunlight burned his eyes, and he shielded his forehead while he peered out. Irden and Vefed were on their feet, surprised to see him.

"Help me with them."

Leo shuffled out sideways lumbering with Lani on his shoulder, Odajeen following behind. He was glad to hand the two women over to Odajeen's guards. He wasn't a big person and the effort of dragging Lani hadn't been easy.

Looking back at the opening to the mountain he wondered what other strange and magical things he would experience. The stone was one thing, but the lady that spoke to him was something he would never forget.

Her voice was like a warm fire just for one, as though its heat wrapped around just you to keep out the cold. When she spoke to him his heart filled and he just felt better than he'd ever felt.

She told him what they needed to do. Leo didn't understand any of this, and he still didn't care that much about the why. He was happy to do it, about being one of the Court.

His life was no longer just about him being driven by some personal cause, or motivation, he was now part of something else. He didn't need a reason to do it if it was needed.

Just do it.

And he would.

"Get them back to the wagon."

Kooka came to meet them. His face had dropped when he saw Lani still being carried.

"It didn't work then?"

"I was told that it almost worked, and that Lani cannot do it in there."

"That's disappointing."

"She needs to be close to do it, but not that close. I don't understand it, but that's what I was told."

"Anything else?"

"No, just that she'll want to be close by and that maybe we'll need to take them back in again if she runs out of strength."

"What does that mean?"

"I don't know, Kooka. I don't know."

The old driver shrugged his shoulders and looked to Odajeen's guards.

"They're settled, Kooka. What now?"

"I think we go back to Traveler's Rest, Irdan."

"You sure? Won't we attract attention coming and going like this?"

Kooka tilted his head toward Leo, "This one says Lani needs to stay close to the mountain for now."

"Okay."

Kooka looked out across the desert. "At least the weather's better."

All Leo saw was sand, and he was already sweating from the heat. If the camp was undercover, then he was all for it. No one spoke as they began moving their way north.

Leo could feel the disappointment within their small group. Maybe it was only him that had noticed the difference in the two women, but that was the thing he clung to, that gave him hope.

Otherwise, he had no idea what they might do. At some point the group would look to him for advice, and he was so new to this he wouldn't know what to do.

After a couple of hours, he tied his horse to the back of the wagon and climbed in.

"Leo?"

"Hi, Odajeen."

"Is something wrong?"

"No, why?"

"You don't normally come in here when we're moving. You don't normally come to me at all."

"It's strange."

"What is?"

"All of this. One minute I was me, then next thing I know I'm in Anderwell and suddenly I'm meant to be someone important."

"Why do you think you're important?"

"The role I now have."

"That doesn't make you important, Leo. Not in the way you're saying it."

"What does that mean?"

"You're important to your people, the Jesters and those they help, but you, yourself are not important. Do not forget that, or your pride will ruin you."

"I think I understand. What I mean is that now I have to make decisions… that affect other people. Like you."

"What decisions, Leo?"

"If Lani can't do what she is trying to do, get free — from in there — then what? I'll have to decide what we do next."

"Perhaps."

"Who else?"

"Anyone can suggest an idea, Leo, and yes, maybe you will have to be the one. But then why worry?"

"Because... it's important."

"You're very concerned with important."

"That's not what I meant."

"Is there anything you can do about it in this moment?"

"No."

"Then there's no need to lose any time worrying about it. When a decision is required, someone will make it or help you make it. Let it be."

Leo thought about what she'd said. She was right, and it only made him feel more unsuited to being one of the Court. But then she'd been a Mother Folly some time ago, so maybe that's why she was so smart.

"How are you?"

"Okay."

"I mean after being in there, I didn't ask you if anything happened to you. You look better but...?"

"I feel better, Leo. There was a thing in there, something, it was so familiar and yet it wasn't, I cannot really explain but my body does feel stronger."

"You look fuller."

She laughed.

"What's so funny?"

"That's an interesting way of describing it, Leo, but I can't think of a better way of saying it. I do feel fuller, thank you."

"Why you thanking me?"

"For asking, Leo. And for taking me there."

"It was what was needed."

"Exactly."

"What?"

"You decided based on what needed to be done, did you not?"

"I did."

"And so, you shall again."

"You're very wise." He felt a little silly saying such a thing, feeling like he was a child again.

She laughed, "I'm just old, Leo, which means I've got more experiences. I'm not sure that makes me wise, just experienced."

Leo didn't know the difference, but anyway despite her laughing at him he wasn't bothered by it. Normally he'd have gotten angry at someone laughing but she was different. Calmer and settling.

The wagon rocked to a stop, and he climbed out the back to see what was going on. Before him stood what had to be Traveler's Rest. The whole sight was quite something.

A rock ledge hung out over the top of it from high above. The camp had been made under the ledge, with tents, and nothing permanent, as though no one was allowed to live here, only pass through.

Kooka was talking to the guards who controlled access through the simple outer fence, which wouldn't hold anyone back and was purely symbolic.

The little he heard of this place, no one would breach the rules, otherwise they'd be banned from the camp and from ever carting goods for Midderbuilt traders.

Leo carried the pass that Tillandra had given him which would allow Lani into the city, although that wasn't needed anymore.

A narrow path wound its way up the cliff face toward the city, steep and only wide enough for people to pass each other. A gantry above him controlled the only trade passage, a lift, that allowed delivery up and down to the camp.

Heavily armed guards were everywhere but many of the people in the camp were hidden from view either within or obscured by the rows of tents.

Leo walked with the wagon as Kooka started it up and they followed a pathway just wide enough to get through the row of tents. There were people of many races here and most had serious looks on their faces.

No one was welcoming, and he was glad when they stopped at the spot allocated to them. Kooka backed their wagon into a spot between two tents.

"Let's get the women out and into the tents without anyone seeing them. Let everyone think we're protecting rich cargo, rather than people."

No one had anything else to say and they waited until night fell before moving Lani and Odajeen into the tent tucked further away from anyone else.

Leo knew what he'd been told to do, he just wasn't sure when. That wasn't something the Lady in the Stone had told him.

99

GORAN

The desert favored no one. Every day without fail it was hot, dry, and relentless. The cold of the nights affected Goran the worst though.

He'd taken control of the party, or what was left of it, and pushed the survivors continuously back toward Anderwell. They didn't respect the sun during the day and rode from first light until everyone was done late in the afternoon.

Dragging a wagon was slow going but it carried Gizen and three other injured men. The girl wasn't doing well and rarely spoke.

Goran wasn't a healer and knew her best chance was getting her to the physicks back in the city, if they could ever get there in time. He held little hope for the soldiers, several of whom were in a very bad way.

None of the Skarian knights had survived and Goran had made sure to loot their camp for any supplies he could, and then they'd left immediately.

Time was his biggest enemy now, followed by getting lost. One of the soldiers swore he knew the right path back, which was fine, Goran had no clue and there was no vulture to follow this time.

He rode a good distance back behind the wagon and far from

anyone in their group, so that he could keep the effect of the amulet away from them.

One of the front riders had turned and trotted back toward him.

"Riders coming quickly, Goran!"

"Where?"

The soldier turned and pointed out toward the left a little. Goran could see the swirling sands that gave them away and nodded.

"Be as ready as you can."

Goran loosened his coat and made sure he could access his sword quickly but kept moving forward. He knew that they were not in good shape. If they met another group of knights, things wouldn't end well.

It seemed an age before the riders came into view and it was a relief when they did. A flag flew from the leading rider showing they were from Anderwell.

Alongside him a tall woman strode, keeping pace with his horse easily. *Tillandra.*

Goran had stopped along with the rest of his group, and he slid down off his horse, glad to be standing for a change. He was anxious to see her for the first time since he'd tricked her but equally surprised to see her out here.

His mouth felt sour, and his stomach tightened, his anxiety surprising even him. Tillandra had slowed to a normal pace and walked toward him.

"In All Jest." That she used their Court greeting pleased him.

"In All Jest, Mother."

She kept walking, putting him further on edge, but she just wrapped him up in her long arms and cuddled the air out of him. Of all the things she could have done, this was unexpected but very welcome.

"It's good to see you, Goran, and that you are well."

He pushed himself free. "And you, Tillandra."

They stood awkwardly for a moment.

"I didn't expect you."

"After what you told me I figured it would be a long crawl back. There's a physick with us, maybe it's enough to get her home."

Goran shrugged. He didn't hold out much hope for any of the injured. "How far are we?"

"Three days' ride at least with your wagon. Unless there's a way to get her back quicker."

"She can't ride, she's not well at all."

The physick had already leapt into action and had clambered up into the wagon. He poked his head out as the two approached.

"Can we get these others out? It's putrid in here and I need room."

Tillandra turned to the soldiers that had ridden with her. "Let's get a camp set up so we can move the others out to be seen to."

It didn't take long before the wagon had become the center of a shelter protecting everyone, and the three injured soldiers were moved onto the ground.

After a long hour the physick climbed out of the wagon and approached Tillandra. "She's very weak. Looking at her I'd say she's lost too much blood, but it's hard to know. The heat and dirt aren't helping."

"Until we can get her back to the city there's not much we can do about that."

"I'll check the others now."

He walked to where the injured soldiers lay.

"I warned you she wasn't well," Goran said.

"I know, but it might be enough. We'll leave first thing and just keep pushing."

Goran had little to say. His exhaustion had hit him hard now that there was someone else to take over, and he could see the same thing on the faces of the surviving soldiers.

"Come on, let's check on her." Tillandra gently grabbed his upper arm and directed him toward the wagon.

Once they were inside, he stopped her before they crawled over to Gizen.

He took the wrapped amulet out from his tunic and held it out to her.

"You need to take this, please."

Tillandra pulled out a gray glove and slipped the package Goran had into it, closing it up tightly, before slipping it into a pocket in her tunic.

"Thank Thenis."

"What?"

"It's gone from my head. Whatever that glove did I can no longer feel it."

"Good."

"It was strong, Tillandra, everyone could sense it. I had to ride several lengths back from them all otherwise they'd start to feel it.

"What could you feel?"

"Like it wanted me to go east, always toward the east. Kysten, I think."

"That's one of them gone for now, I can put it away somewhere it won't affect anyone."

Gizen's croaky voice caught their attention. "Mother."

"Yes, dear, I'm here." She shuffled over and Goran followed her.

"Peka?"

"He's fine, Gizen, he's in Anderwell with Toolet."

Goran could see the girl almost smile then she passed out. The two Jesters sat there quietly watching her breathe, making sure she was still alive.

Suddenly saliva bubbled out of the young woman's mouth then she began to speak, but even Goran could tell it sounded different to her normal speech.

"Men of cloth…"

"What's that, Gizen?" Tillandra asked.

"… carry the poison…"

Goran could see she wasn't conscious, or not normally. She lay there and he reached over and wiped away the drool around her mouth.

"… a city reborn… harbors more…"

He could see Tillandra knew they were hearing something unusual and said nothing.

"… watch for them… they bring the dark…"

More minutes passed and she continued to drool but her eyes never opened.

"… the wood will fail but the wall must hold…"

Goran had pulled his journal out and was writing it all down."

"… faith must be broken, the source cut off… the children of the light can break the source…"

Then she slumped again, and they watched while the sky turned dark. Outside the soldiers had set torches to provide some light. Goran and Tillandra stayed with the girl.

Out of nowhere she coughed and called out, her voice back to its normal self. "Tillandra?"

"Yes, Gizen, I'm here."

"I knew."

"Knew what?"

"This would happen, I saw it."

Goran saw Tillandra's eyes widen. "What do you mean?"

"The amulet, this…" She patted her wound gently. "The dream, it showed me this."

"You never told me… I would never have sent you."

"I always do what it shows me. It's the way of it…"

Goran couldn't believe that this young woman had willingly come out into the desert knowing what was ahead of her. A tear formed in his eye.

"It's okay, girl, we have a physick here, we'll get you back to the city where you can recover."

"I won't."

"Won't what?"

"Make it."

"You don't know that."

"I do."

The wagon seemed way too small to Goran now, and they sat silently contemplating what this woman was telling them. He could see Tillandra's sadness written on her face.

The girl bucked slightly, grimacing at a wave of pain that had coursed through her.

Tillandra simply held her hand and stared at the girl. Goran didn't know what to do, he could see the girl's life slipping away.

She coughed periodically over the next half an hour. Each one hurt

Gizen but she never said another word. Tillandra let out a little gasp at the same time as he sensed it.

"She's gone." Tillandra's eyes were filled with tears, and she choked on her words.

Goran nodded. There was nothing to say.

After they buried her in the sand, Goran and Tillandra sat off to the side of the fire burning in the middle of the camp.

"What was that?"

Tillandra looked at him with raised eyebrows.

"The words, you heard them."

"You wrote them all down?"

He nodded.

"I know what it sounded like, but…"

"Why her?"

"Yes. But then why not her? She saw so many things. I should never have let her come out here…" Tillandra dropped her head into her hands.

Goran didn't understand all of what Gizen had said but enough of it sounded like the main prophecy to at least give them reason to pay attention to it.

Who are the children of the light? What did that mean?

"I'll write you a copy, then you can think on it."

They didn't speak again until morning. The loss of the girl had hit Tillandra harder than it did Goran, and he knew not to push her.

"If I had brought Purple, she could have saved her."

"You don't know that Gizen said she knew this was going to happen. The young girl would be safer back in Anderwell than out here, you don't know what you might have ridden into."

Tillandra laughed. "If only. Purple is with Lani and the others."

"Oh."

"It's too much. First Hall, now Gizen."

"What's happened to Hall?"

Tillandra caught him up on what had happened to their colleague.

"That's it."

"What?"

"What I'm going to do."

She stared at him, confused.

"I'll go and get Hallendell."

"You can't."

"I have to. Being out here on this mission reminded me what I'm here for. I'm no good stuck in a city doing one thing, I need to do it."

"I've already sent Junther."

This time it was Goran that laughed. "That old fool, it'll take more than him to do it. He'll need help."

"I can't lose any more, Goran."

"I'm not going to get lost, Tillandra, and if we don't help her, we'll all lose her."

Back and forth they argued for nearly an hour, but her heart wasn't fully in the fight. He hadn't planned on staying in Anderwell anyway and if Gizen hadn't been hurt he wouldn't have been going back there with her.

Being out on the road was the best use of him. It felt strange to say goodbye to her again so soon but there was little choice.

Tillandra gave him two of the soldiers who were willing to lend a hand, and then they helped the others pack up and head back to Anderwell.

Goran gave one last wave before Tillandra turned and followed them. Now he had something important to do, and they needed to get moving.

He turned his horse and headed north, toward the Lletem border. It would be the fastest way, if not the most direct.

100

UKSOD

As much as things seemed to be going well and visiting Yantarnaya could have been rewarding, Uksod still preferred to use a body.

Once he'd become accustomed to the after-effects, the feelings it stirred within him had become extremely enticing. He reached out, hoping the priest would be wearing his ring.

"Fuling, you're close."

Uksod waited, hoping the man would be able to answer quickly.

"Uksod."

"You're in Cumerc?"

"A place called Kuwaha."

"That's the same place. It was originally called Cumerc, when it was ours."

There was a short gap in reply. "Now it makes sense what was discussed."

"Tell me everything that has happened."

By the time he'd explained what was going on at this point, Uksod had to admire what Karpenmor had done. That he was on the islands negotiating was more than Uksod had expected.

"Can you bypass all of that and just get to the island known as Step Six? If you do, I can have you brought directly to the capital."

"We were trying to do that until we discovered the Queen was here, so we're hiding our intent at the moment."

"Perhaps you need to just do it anyway."

"The Queen has guards blocking access to the only steps down."

"I see. Force?"

"Not such a great idea. There is a large contingent of warriors here and a limited number of us. We were only allowed a small number in the city."

"I see."

"There's a lot more of their soldiers camped outside the city as well. It would appear they have taken the bridges as a threat."

"Interesting. I am glad the bridge is not finished then, or they could try to come across it."

"They seem to be here more for building the wall."

"What wall?"

"You've been here?"

"Of course."

"They've begun closing in the cliffs including where the steps come."

"That isn't ideal."

"I noticed one thing."

"Which is?"

"Where the bridge would be built, they have not yet built anything."

"A sign that they expect to accede to the Prince then?"

"That was my view on it."

"You need to get the King here."

"He wishes to come, there seems to be an urgency in him since arriving here."

"It's the draw."

"What?"

"The amulet he carries is being drawn toward its source. It would be influencing him."

"I will push for a resolution to this matter, but both sides want the city, neither seems willing to bend. Can you advise anything?"

"Only that the city is of no importance currently. We'll get it back soon enough. We want you and the King here; this cannot be blocked."

"I will do what I can."

"It is important, too important to be held up for long."

"Understood, but the King has his own mind at times."

"I'll work on that too. Anything else?"

"They really don't like our kind here, do they?"

"No, they do not. I must go but will reach out again soon."

He left the dead body and decided he should go see his mistress anyway, she'd be pleased with how things were progressing.

"I can sense the amulet, Uksod, it is close."

"Yes, it is, mistress."

"How long until it gets here?"

"Soon, there are a few minor delays. The Queen of Ngahere was in the city on the other side, making it more difficult for him to get across."

"How is it being solved?"

"We're working on it. I have been in touch with the priest, the boy isn't helping either."

"I thought you were getting him back?"

"Working on it, but he can't be dragged back like an infant, he's the heir, and he's negotiating with this Queen."

"Hasn't he become quite a handful?"

"Yes, he has."

"The amulet must come back to me. I will want to speak to it."

Uksod knew it needed to be recharged but he didn't understand what she meant about talking to it.

"Down here or in the Amber Room?"

"The Amber Room will do. No need to bring others down here, that's your privilege is it not?"

He could tell she was toying with him again and chose to ignore it. She'd changed since the stones were free, now she teased him sarcastically rather than berating him so much.

"I did wonder if I'd need to take it from him and bring the stone down here."

"You cannot touch them, Uksod, same as anyone else. Once bonded they will kill the person who touches it."

"What of Karpenmor?"

"What of him?"

"Will he be killed if he touches the amulet this girl carries?"

"Yes."

"Then she needs to be killed, there's no way around it. It would be much easier to get it back if we simply did that now."

"No! I've told you I am intrigued by her, I want to have her here before me, to probe her mind and learn about her before we do that. And besides..." She didn't finish her sentence.

"Besides, what?"

"She's a descendant is she not?"

"Yes."

"Then she could birth another. All we need is another boy."

"That would be extremely hard to explain to the families. let's hope there's no need for it. It will create turmoil we do not need."

"Perhaps we need better control of these people, Uksod."

"We've discussed this many times, Highness. Surely, we want everyone putting their focus on what we want to do in Dharatan? Rather than fighting each other?"

Yantarnaya did not answer, leaving Uksod unsure if the conversation was over or not.

"What would you have me do, Highness?"

"Keep doing what we planned, to get the amber across the islands. We should have done more of that before now."

"I have large stones being cut, and we will ship them out. And then they can keep making more to store on the last island ready to place in Cumerc."

"You think they will give that back to us?"

"We will take it back, one way or another. We need such a base, a fortified position on Dharatan to attack from."

"In these matters you've always been of one mind with me. Will the boy be able to lead the army you will need?"

"That will need to be seen. To be fair, while I was unwell, he did take control of some things, has shown some capability."

"Good. I sense our time is coming."

"There is something else, Highness."

"What?"

"I will need more rings."

"Does the Vrah not have enough?"

"It isn't for them, but for others, like how Fuling has one."

"Why?"

"I will need to have more than one man available to speak to, already I am unable to speak directly with Trorn..."

"Who is Trorn?"

"My number two here in En Carta."

"Why can you not speak to him?"

"Karpenmor took him with him on his escapade. It would be advantageous were I able to speak to him now and know what is happening there."

Uksod was met with silence.

"What would be better is that the Lapidarist were still here."

"He has been gone a long time Highness, you..."

"I know what I did to him, Uksod. He could not be allowed to leave."

"He was the best."

"We need another, you must find me another."

"His brother has gone into hiding. I doubt he would do the work anyway."

"Because he worked for them?"

"Yes, and you killed his brother."

"You people get so sentimental about such things. There must be others,

Uksod, you need to find me another. If you want your rings, then do what I asked you before and find someone capable."

"Yes, mistress."

Uksod held his thoughts to himself until he was a long way up the stairs. He knew he'd dropped off the search for another lapidarist who could handle the Debrua Stone, because all his focus had gone into the pursuit of the amulet.

He would speak to One. There had to be more with the Vein, he just hadn't found out how to locate them. Getting more rings would be important for him, using amber wasn't enough, it needed to be from the Debrua.

Once out of the caverns he headed straight for the Vrah compound.

"Eminence."

"Any more word of the Prince?"

"Only what you already know. I have instructions for messengers to be sent daily in both directions so that when anything changes, we'll be the first to know."

"The guest I have been expecting is in Cumerc."

"A guest?"

"A king from the south of Dharatan, and his priest."

"A priest in Cumerc? The barbarians there will kill him, if they find out."

"He travels incognito, One. Fear not, he is a smart man. They will be coming here; he will have soldiers with him."

"Okay."

"The King must get here as quickly as possible. I hope Karpenmor doesn't delay that."

Uksod explained to him about his other problem, and the need to hunt down any lapidarists that had extraordinary talent.

"Most end up in a city far to the west."

"Do you know its name?"

"I will find it; I have read of it before. It is on the far side of the desert. It is likely that we might find one there."

"We would be noticed over there. It is so remote and it's too difficult to access. We can be smarter than that, the ones we seek can come from anywhere. They would get noticed in their towns when they are young, before they get trained and taken to that city."

"You wish for a child?"

"Perhaps that is best. Then we can train them as we need."

"Would any exist here, in Enderk?"

Uksod thought about what the Vrah leader said.

"There is no reason that they might not, we have not been looking. Send out people to every family, town, and village, urgently, One. Find me a child who can work with gems and stone unlike others."

He left One and headed back to his room. *Why hadn't I thought of that earlier?*

KARPENMOR

He was feeling a little foolish and very much out of control of the situation. The emissary had left the island without a word which meant the power was back in the barbarian's hands, and Karpenmor had caused it.

He could have been more conciliatory and taken a smarter approach to dragging out what he was trying to achieve.

Had he also overplayed their desire to get Cumerc back? What he wanted was the bridge completed, everything else was irrelevant at this point.

With the bridge restored they'd easily retake the city; it would just be a matter of time. Now he had pushed himself into a corner that he needed to get out of.

To make matters worse he was running out of time. He only had a small window of time that he could be away from the capital, and he needed this resolved.

What better present to grant himself for his confirmation as High Prince than the completion of the land bridge?

He would need to send a placatory message with the aim of continuing the discussions or face the reality he would need to leave and schedule this for another time.

He had been tempted to send his own emissary but that would have meant Aika, as Trorn could not set foot in the city -- not until it was restored to Derk control.

Aika wasn't ready for that type of meeting, not yet at least, and he couldn't afford any further bungles. In the end he'd sent a message advising he was returning to En Carta.

It was the only way he could push things forward and not appear too desperate. They would see through it, and possibly might call his bluff, but he had few options remaining.

In his favor was all the items they could trade. Wheat was central to it, as was their silk, amber, spices, and tin. There were many things Enderk was rich in that were valuable to the foreigners, he just needed to find a way to get what he needed.

If he had to, he'd highlight their superior knowledge in sailing craft, something they would have to utilize if he couldn't pull off this deal.

The boat builders in Six's territory experimented with vessels much larger than any that the barbarians had seen. They sought a way to cross the wider seas with sizeable forces and without the losses.

Before the bridges had seemed likely it was the only way they had to get enough soldiers to Dharatan. If he couldn't reconcile with this Ngaherian Queen, then they'd need to do it that way.

It would start with retaking Cumerc, then he wouldn't need anyone's permission to complete his bridge. All they would need to do was hold the cliffs long enough to build the last half.

Aika stepped into his tent.

"What is it?"

"A delegation is returning, Highness."

"How long?"

"They are on the water."

"Thank you, Aika. Get the meeting tent ready."

"Already done, Highness, I did that as soon as we saw them heading down the cliffs."

"What would I do without you, Aika?"

She blushed at his words. There was still that about her which he didn't understand.

He went outside and was met with the blustering wind that never seemed to stop on this island. Four wagons of wheat were parked close by.

"Aika, have one of the sacks brought into the meeting tent, as well as the small pouch of amber jewels on my side table. Place them in front of my seat."

"Yes, Highness."

He went back into his personal tent until he was advised that the delegation was in position within the meeting place. He slowly made his way there flanked by Vrah.

He sat in his makeshift throne, facing the party, looking at Clannack, the emissary.

"I must apologize, Emissary Clannack, it appears you were insulted by my earlier absence, which was not intended. I did truly wish to reconsider your words."

The man looked at him, perhaps surprised by the tone he was taking but showing little on his strange face.

"I thank you for your words, Prince Karpenmor, perhaps we can start things again. We received your message that you are returning to your capital, we did not want to waste this opportunity."

We both need this to happen, don't we? So give me an indication of how.

Both stared at each other, the feeling in the tent frosty and not just from the cool temperature outside.

Karpenmor turned to Aika and nodded. She walked forward and pulled out a knife, putting the chancellor immediately on edge.

Aika sliced the small sack that lay at one end of the table, before putting the blade back in its sheath.

The wheat within spilled out, across the table and onto the ground by Clannack's feet.

"Would your people not wish to have such wheat, Emissary? We have so much I fear we might have to burn much of this year's crop before it goes moldy."

"You know we would, it all comes back to the price, Highness. My Queen understands that there's a lot of history regarding the city I have come from. You must be aware that the sudden appearance of your bridge is more than enough to cause concerns from our side."

Karpenmor knew the man was correct, he would behave no differently. What he couldn't work out was what he would do in their shoes.

"I see. You still don't trust us."

"Do you us?"

"I would agree that there's a lot that needs to be rebuilt, and not just the bridge."

It seemed to Karpenmor as though the emissary had relaxed a little in how he sat. Maybe they were getting somewhere.

"Perhaps Highness, we might find a way to take smaller steps. Do we not both want the same thing?"

"Which is?"

"The bridge makes sense, to reconnect our peoples as they were so long ago. You speak of trade but that won't just be in one direction. There will be many things from Dharatan of benefit to your people."

And we'll get them in time.

"Our alternative is simply to bypass Ngahere altogether."

"And how do you propose to do that?"

"We have the boats that could fulfil such a goal, Emissary, we could deliver many goods south or north as need be."

The Queen's man sat still and said nothing.

"Our people are very skilled on the water. We already have large boats in numbers that it would be very easy to deliver loads to the south coast directly, without Ngaherian interference."

"At what risk?"

"It's true that the seas are difficult, and not everything would reach its port, but we build better vessels every day. Wheat, gems, spices, tin, and much more could be delivered."

"But it would be safer and guaranteed to travel by road."

"Perhaps. Only if such a road exists and we can use it. With no bridge it's a pointless exercise."

"Surely, Prince Karpenmor, you didn't build all these bridges for no reason? If the boats were all you needed, you'd be doing it."

The man was good, Karpenmor had to admit. He was trying not to give up an inch. He leaned forward and opened the pouch in front of him, spilling the polished amber across the table.

The emissary looked at them for a good while before looking up. "Such beautiful gems, but banned from Dharatan."

"Why is that, Clannack? Why do you deny your people such wonderful gems?"

His opponent looked at him and back at the stones on the table.

"I do not know the reason, but it is a long-standing custom, which all of the realms agree to."

"What would it take to convince them it's a silly tradition?"

"That is not something I can answer, Highness. Perhaps a topic for another day."

"What is it, Clannack? What does your Queen wish me to concede to get my bridge built?"

"The city is off the table, as we've already mentioned. However, she is willing to allow more Derks within its boundaries. To create a true trading center."

Karpenmor liked that they were finally getting down to the details, without rubbing it in his face about control of Cumerc.

"For the bridge?"

"And exclusive rights to control the trade through Enderk."

"Within the city, perhaps, not all trade to and from Enderk. You overreach yourself, Emissary."

After a brief pause the man opposite him replied, "Understood, and of course I mean trade that crosses through the gate."

"I think it best put that you can tax or levy whatever crosses through, but it would seem a step too far that you control what can and can't come through."

"If it is going to enter Ngahere then it's nothing more than already exists on any other access point."

"It's not enough."

"I don't understand."

"You want us to build this bridge, which you profit from. You get your wheat and we make you look good to all the realms across the land, and yet we get nothing in return."

"Is the reconnection not enough?"

"No. Not from where I am coming from."

"You know the position in regard to the city, I am struggling to see what else I can offer."

Karpenmor wanted more than he had but did not know what that would look like. The bridge mattered most but to back down this much he needed more.

Trorn signaled him. "Give me a moment, Emissary, to convene with my advisor."

They stepped to the back of the tent.

"What is it?"

"Perhaps, Highness, you could bargain for the temple."

"Temple? What temple?"

"Facing where our bridge points is the primary temple built in the city. Access to it would be of significant value to us."

Karpenmor cared little about a temple, but it was potentially just the right thing. To have the Queen concede such a thing would look as though he hadn't caved completely.

"A worthy idea."

They returned to where the man from Ngahere sat.

"There is one thing."

"Name it."

"The main temple in the city. Return it to us and I would consider that compensation." *For now.*

He could see the surprise on the other man's face. "I cannot see Queen Vika agreeing to this."

"I am being most diplomatic, Emissary, I have accepted your conditions, perhaps your ruler needs to do the same."

"I will have to discuss this with her."

"I expect no less. However, my time is short, as advised I have to leave for the capital. You have until tomorrow."

Karpenmor stood. As far as he was concerned this negotiation was finished. Once the emissary had left the tent, he allowed himself to relax.

I hope they don't try to delay me; I have no time to lose.

102

CLANNACK

He had expected this conversation to go as it had done; Vika was unhappy with the news Clannack had delivered.

"You expect me to honor that?"

"I expect nothing, Majesty, I am simply telling you what was said."

"Too much."

"What is, Majesty?"

"There's too much happening all at once. Look at these." She handed him some letters.

Clannack read them and looked at her and Nikora. "Are these for real?"

"I received them earlier, they are very real." The first councillor's face looked as serious as he'd ever seen it.

"Both Malamig and Morska are threatening action if we don't deliver wheat. Do you believe they will?"

"The situation is growing worse by the day, Clannack, I'd be a fool not to take them seriously." The Queen had stood and paced the room. "One border to protect is enough, to have to protect three would stretch us."

"I can't believe things have come to this." He shook his head. He needed to relay this to Anderwell and quickly, but he hadn't had one spare minute in days.

"The timing worries me. It's almost as though the Derks knew of this or have promoted the idea somehow."

Clannack knew what the solution was, even though Tillandra would hate it. "The bridge solves everything, Majesty. Wheat for all, including us."

"I know, Clannack!" Her tone was not friendly. "But this is too much to ask. He would know this."

"How long can you afford to hold out?"

She stared at him for a while. "It's the only reason I keep you around, Councillor, because you aren't afraid to ask me such questions."

"He seems very serious about returning to the capital. If he leaves now, how long might it take to resume talks? Did you not tell me your previous advances have all been rejected?"

"They have, but he needs us to finish his bridge."

"He did threaten to bypass us altogether."

"So you said. Can we believe they really have such boats?"

"Up until recently I'd not have believed much about them, but these bridges are something to be admired. If they can build these, why not bigger and better ships than we've seen?"

She stood still, looking directly at him, considering what he'd just said.

One of the stewards entered the room.

"I wondered how long it would be until the King wanted to learn of your negotiations." She turned to the steward. "Bring him in."

Clannack knew what the Queen was like when she was in this mood, it was not an ideal time to have King Ahn around. She returned to her makeshift throne.

"Queen Vika, thank you for seeing me."

"You are our guest, King Ahn. How can I help you?"

"As you might expect, I am keen to hear how the negotiations are proceeding."

"Slowly."

Her abruptness was noted by the other ruler and his posture stiffened.

The Queen had Clannack fill the King in on the Prince's latest offer.

"I fail to understand what is so bad about this offer?"

The atmosphere in the chamber was becoming tense and Clannack waited for the Queen's next response.

"Then you know little of our ways."

"A temple. That's it, you give them back a temple to use and benefit from it immensely."

"It is not possible."

"Would you reject the opportunity completely?"

"At that price, yes I would."

"Stubborn, that's what you're being. Wasn't this city once theirs?"

"Before it was lost to them. And now it belongs to us."

"What harm would it cause you to give them what he asks for?"

"Why give them anything? They need this bridge; it wasn't us that built it."

"But you will profit from it, controlling all trade with them."

"What is it you really want, King?"

"What do you mean?"

"You turn up here never before seen so far north, at a time this bridge is ready to be built, willing to settle with this..." she chose her word carefully, "enemy of ours that we've tolerated for so long. Why here, now? What is in it for you?"

Clannack could see the King was wrestling with himself, wanting to rebuff Vika's attack, but being mindful of his position.

"I do not appreciate your tone."

"Is it not a fair question under the circumstances?"

"I am here, Queen Vika, because the word amongst the realms is that you have wheat and are holding out on us. I was quite prepared to sail there and secure our own supplies. I see that you do not have any for yourself, but you have the solution. If not, then boats will have to do. But I cannot go back to my people empty-handed. The winters in Daskare are extremely cold, and we need food to survive."

She sat in her makeshift throne, looking at the King and his chancellor, without saying a word for several minutes. She stood and came down off the dais to stand in front of the King.

"You are right to do so, as are we. Everyone is suffering from the blight that has attacked our wheat. Our trust of these foreign neighbors of ours is very low, we are suspicious about everything they do."

"I can see that clearly. But perhaps the distrust is about a time long passed and you're missing what might be a new beginning."

"Maybe you're right, maybe you're not. What I don't like is being pushed into making a decision under someone else's timeline. I'll have your meals prepared in your accommodation this evening if you'd excuse me. Tonight, I fear I will be poor company as I review this matter."

It wasn't an offer, and the King didn't contest it. He was a guest here and the Queen had made her intentions clear.

Clannack knew he was in for a long night; she'd want to thrash out an alternative from him and Nikora. The idea of allowing a temple to operate in her lands was nearly as bad as handing back the city.

He sighed and followed her from the hall.

103

KARPENMOR

Karpenmor was all but done waiting for a response from the Ngaherians. Time was up and he needed to be leaving to get back to En Carta. He wasn't going to miss the likelihood of his enthronement, bridge or no bridge.

The negotiation had a deadline too and he had already told Aika to prepare for their departure. While he might have not made a perfect job of it so far he had to stay true to his word.

He'd said he would be leaving and that they had today to answer, he needed to stick to that.

How would Uksod handle the Queen? He'd simply show force and bribery.

That's what I've been doing one way or another. Twisting their needs to my own. He stood near the edge of Step Six looking back toward Ponte, unsighted off in the distance.

So many people in motion now, so much activity. It was something that excited him, and he was proud of what his people had achieved.

What will they come back with? Or will they delay it?

Karpenmor wished he knew the full extent of the impact of the wheat shortage. He should have grilled One about it before he'd left the capital.

Depending on how bad that was would determine whether they changed their position or not. He had already given ground about Cumerc but he wasn't going to give up everything, that would cause him to look weak.

If it didn't happen today, it could take months. And he didn't have months to wait. His plans were coming together, and putting these things to bed would let him move his focus to bigger issues.

Or I'll make good on my threat to supply others. All this work on our boats might now have to pay off.

Aika hurried to him. "There's a party on the other side, Highness."

He followed her across the island and looked down to where he could see a group at the bottom of the steps on the Dharatan side.

"I should go back inside then."

"I will get you when they have arrived."

He nodded and walked away, his guards always a few steps behind.

It took an hour before the delegation arrived in the meeting room. Karpenmor walked in and was surprised to see a tall, muscular woman in the middle of the group. *The Queen has come.*

Twice the number of Ngaherian soldiers lined the rear of the tent they had gathered in. An equal number of Vrah circled behind Karpenmor, while many more surrounded the outside of the tent.

If the meeting took a bad turn there would be a lot of bloodshed.

The emissary spoke. "Prince Karpenmor, may I introduce Queen Vika, of Ngahere."

Karpenmor dipped his head to the imposing woman. While he matched her height or close to it, she was twice his physical size, and he did not wish to get into combat with her.

"Welcome to Step Six, Queen Vika."

"It is a pleasure, Prince Karpenmor."

"I was not expecting you; you must forgive the humble accommodation we have here. Our facilities on these islands are very basic... at this time."

"I apologize for not giving you notice but I felt it prudent and hopefully more efficient for me to attend, so that we might resolve the differences."

"I hope that we may."

Then the emissary introduced the other guests. "Additionally we are accompanied by King Ahn, of Daskare, and his Great Chancellor, Fuling."

Karpenmor struggled to hide his surprise. "It is my pleasure to meet you as well, King Ahn."

"And you, Prince Karpenmor."

He struggled to remember the location of the realm this man was from, but what he did know is it wasn't close. "You are a long way from your homelands."

"We are, perhaps fortuitously."

What captured his attention even more was the jewel he wore on his chest, which hadn't been visible until he'd removed his coat.

It's an amulet.

It had to be, Karpenmor could tell, even though he didn't know why. He struggled to keep his eyes off it.

"I invited the King here as an observer, so that the other realms might know the truth of our agreements. If we may begin?" Queen Vika words broke his fixation on the jewel.

The discussions continued for nearly four hours. Much of it was tedious and official, trying to set the stage for an agreement. All the previous ground had to be covered now that it was her speaking and not her emissary.

Both stated their positions about the city, Cumerc, before they finally got to the offer of the temple.

Karpenmor could sense the tension that had formed around it. "The bridge is not enough."

"Allowing you to practice religion within our lands goes against everything we are."

"Allowing such a beacon of our culture, our religion, to lie wasted in the city our traders would pass through is not acceptable either. This was our city, Queen Vika, and it still holds much historic value to us."

She didn't reply but her body showed how steadfast she was holding on this issue.

"You want to benefit from our people but do not accept that religion holds a primary role in our society. We're back in the same place, the bridge is not nearly enough to balance what you will gain from it."

He turned to Aika. "Ready yourself, we will not be here much longer."

The air in the room had become frosty, the agreement all but abandoned.

"What about the other options to ship wheat south, Prince Karpenmor?" King Ahn spoke up, attracting a fierce stare from the Queen.

Karpenmor's mood improved, but he managed to keep his appearance unchanged. "This will have to be the way, King Ahn. We can discuss this between ourselves, as it will not need Ngahere."

"The bridge will be the most practical way, Prince Karpenmor, you've already built much of it."

"That can wait, Queen Vika. It will happen over time, one way or another."

"A threat?"

"No, just a reality. How long can you live without wheat, I wonder? Will you need to buy from the King to satisfy your people's appetites? That seems unnecessary and expensive."

Karpenmor wished he could smile, but knew he was already pushing the woman firmly. He needed to complete the deal, not push her so far away it became impossible.

"You are pushing a hard line, Prince Karpenmor."

"I don't see how, Queen Vika. If anything, I have been more than accommodating."

"How so?"

"My people will wonder why we cannot reclaim our city, and yet I conceded on that point, for the sake of the future. I have taken a long-term view, that forging a new relationship will benefit us all. And yet you offer me nothing. The bridge offers you as much as it offers us, if not more. Sure, we profit from the trade, but that's only coin. In return we're asking you to give us back a single building, to allow our people a bastion of their religion where they will trade."

The emissary Clannack leaned toward the Queen and spoke quietly into her ear. Her eyes turned to him and stared for half a minute before she looked back.

"My advisor has presented a possible solution."

"I would be keen to hear it.

She sat upright and appeared to swallow as though the taste of what she was about to suggest soured in her mouth.

"Were we to wall off the section between where the bridge would land and this temple you are speaking of, to create a neutral ground, the place of trade, then perhaps..."

She let the matter hang between them, not wanting to finish the idea.

"Think of it as a safe trading space, Prince Karpenmor." Clannack finished it for her. "The land would belong to both parties but would be overseen by Ngaherians. The markets for trade could be built there as well. This temple would be walled off from the rest of the city, allowing it to be restored."

"An interesting solution, Queen Vika." She still seemed to be struggling with the idea.

"Any priests that stay within the temple will never be allowed to enter the city."

The Queen looked at him. Now she was finalizing the terms, rather than arguing against it.

It was only words, but he agreed. She added more detail, but Karpenmor cared little. Once they had a foothold on Dharatan they could take back the rest of the city.

The bridge would enter the city directly in line with the temple and would be walled off as well, the gates from it being either side of the temple and surrounded by guard houses.

Everything coming through that wasn't for Ngaherians would be taxed by her, something he thought was very smart, and she'd have the final say on what and who could or couldn't pass.

"And the restrictions on our people must stop."

"What do you mean?"

"If you want our traders to sell their goods, they need to be able to travel the lands."

"I can grant them access to my own land, but I cannot guarantee that of the other realms."

"I would be happy to have them in Daskare," King Ahn spoke up. "We will have to encourage our peers to do the same."

"Make sure you encourage them firmly."

"And what of our trade?"

"What do you mean, King Ahn?"

"With the bridge completed it will allow traffic in both directions. And there is much that we could trade with you. I for one would be very keen to visit your capital and learn more about your people, Prince Karpenmor."

Karpenmor looked at the older ruler. There was something about his request that felt welcoming, as though he should just take him back with him. A feeling that wasn't of his own making.

The amulet he wore caught Karpenmor's attention again. This man wore one openly, but not the Queen. Karpenmor wondered whether he should just take this amulet as his own.

It would be much easier. Except, somehow, he knew it wasn't the one he was chasing. He couldn't explain why, but the sensations he had when looking at it, almost repulsed him.

He could admire its beauty but he didn't covet that one. *It's her.* The gleam in the stone, the sensations he could feel, weren't normal. *It's Yantarnaya at work.* He slowly slipped his hand into his tunic pocket, rubbing his thumb over the pendant he had carried with him.

"I am sure you will find it most interesting, King Ahn. En Carta is a beautiful city and her people are most wonderful." A smile crept over the King's face. "But not until the bridge is complete, then we can discuss other options."

The smile disappeared and the conversation ended. He stood, signaling their agreement was finalized. He held up a goblet and toasted the deal.

"To a new beginning."

"To a new beginning." The words echoed around the tent, some sounding happier than others.

Karpenmor watched them go down the stairs before turning to Aika.

"We go now."

"It's already well past middle day, Highness."
"We go now, Aika. Every mile we cover is one closer to home."
"Yes, Highness."

104

LANI

*S*he was literally in the dark. Lani had little idea about how she'd be able to do what she had told Thenis. It had been an idea, something that had come to her.

And now she needed to pray that it was real, that it would work. She was done with being lost inside Burgendetta's mind. Lani wanted out.

Without the vibration she'd felt under the mountain she had no idea when the amulet would be taken out of the box it was in. She hoped she'd sense it, otherwise all of this would be in vain.

Twice now she'd been able to connect to it, but last time she was held back from using it to try and get free. She'd convinced herself and Thenis that it was the Citadel Stone which blocked her.

Lani didn't really know for sure, and the longer she was away from the power of the Citadel the more she began to doubt her gut instinct.

Maybe it was just her wanting it to be true, so she'd allowed her mind to trick her into the idea. How exactly would she get free?

She was so close and yet further away than ever, waiting on others to do things for her, that might possibly help. Possibly being the key word. Lani hated relying on others, she always had.

When it came, the change was so obvious that Lani wondered why she'd even been concerned. The amulet was out of the box she could tell.

The pull of it began as a tiny tug at her mind, the smallest of spots. Where she would normally be hesitant, she leapt toward it, opening her mind.

It came faster than she expected, grabbing at her. She felt her thoughts as they raced along the tendrils of the amulet, connecting to the power behind it.

Something was very different out here, without the shield of the Citadel. It was stronger than she'd ever felt it from the beginning.

Lani felt like she had been stretched out of any natural shape. Most of her body was still anchored back in Odajeen's mind, but part of her was out, the connection between them very tenuous.

She no longer felt so confident, any sense of bravado was replaced with fear. The link between her thoughts and the rest of her felt weak, she had to push against the amulet.

It didn't want to let her go and she could feel the tendrils wrapping around her like fingers wrapping her mind, holding it back.

The connection wavered for her, she couldn't keep going or it might snap. Lani wanted to cry, to curl up on herself and sob her way out of it.

Thenis's words came back to her, to give up being the victim, that she needed to solve this. It was enough to stiffen her resolve.

If I can't get away I need to bring me with it. That's it!

The whole idea was as simple as it was ridiculous. Rather than trying to get back to her body, she needed to bring her body here.

After all I want out, not back in.

It was a choice, another choice Lani needed to make. She had to choose to get out, and not run from the fear of what she needed to do.

It wasn't just for her either, it was to free Odajeen, this woman who'd given her so much without even knowing her. Lani needed to get out.

Come to me.

As much as she tried to will it, nothing worked. Commanding her body was useless. Out here she seemed to have access to her real memories, parts of them.

It was hard to stomach, her mind was in two places, she was losing control over how it worked. Some memories surfaced, about how she used the amulet before.

To control the bowman and the men on a boat somewhere. She'd tapped into the amulet and let it run with her thoughts, to feed off them and power them.

She sought the stone out; it was near her somewhere close to her actual body. Lani let her thoughts go and a source of power flooded through her mind.

Like lava it crept slowly down the pathway back to her body. Painfully slow. Lani wanted to scream, to make it hurry before it was too late.

As if responding to her it sped up and she could sense the rest of herself behind the barrier. *Pull me free.*

There was the tiniest of movements, a shift, then it settled.

Pull me.

The power within it flooded through her and now it felt as though the far-away part of her was moving, but weakly. Something heavy held on and pulled back against her.

Lani had to reach out with imaginary hands trying to claw at herself, to fetch herself from what held it back. Again, she let the power flood through her.

Everything about her body felt wrong, the vision she'd had of herself inside Odajeen's mind was broken now. She was twisted and elongated.

Her mind knew this was all wrong, that she was in danger, but it was too late now. She'd used the stone's power and she couldn't let it go.

The feeling of it was too enticing and she wanted to be free, she really did want to be free. And the stone wanted her free as well.

Connected for this long, this deeply, she felt linked to it in a way she'd never been before. It knew her, somehow, it was linked to her, she belonged with it, to it.

A chill ran through her, as she recognized the truth of that last thought. She wanted to pull away from it, to get free from it, not just Odajeen.

The power of it was too strong for her, and she felt parts of her almost splitting as the amulet now tried to suck her from her prison.

Whatever it was that held her back, the mask, or something else, it held on with almost as much strength. Lani felt as though her imaginary body was about to snap, her legs ripped free.

She felt ill and her thoughts were so confused, she wasn't sure if she was heading to safety or not. It had become too hard to breathe and everything felt compressed.

A pain ripped through her and she screamed out which was the worst thing she could have done. There was no air to breathe back in, nothing to suck into her chest.

Her neck felt as if a rope was tightening around it, squeezing her throat. Lani couldn't hold on. The amulet had taken her, it was killing her, she was sure of it.

She'd made a mistake, this wasn't the way to do it, she'd been lured here, it wanted to kill her. As her mind began to shut down the only thing she couldn't understand was why?

It had wanted her free, why would it do this?

Off in the distance where her feet might have been Lani sensed a strange sensation of weight. It was rushing at her out of her control.

She wanted to get away from it, but she couldn't do anything, she couldn't even scream so tight was the crushing of her neck. Then the weight slammed into her, pounding up from her feet, driving a force upward through her body, forcing her mouth open, letting her suck in several breaths.

All Lani felt was pain. It started where the weight had hit her and spread upward. She couldn't take it anymore. Everything went black.

105

LANI

She could hear the sound of voices, distant voices, unclear and muted as if Lani was under water. She gasped for breath without thinking.

Thankfully there was no water and air flowed into her chest. It hurt to breathe but paradoxically it also felt good. There was something different about how it felt before.

Smells.

She could smell things, people, smelly, smelly people. And that came with a recognition that where she'd been in Odajeen's head there had been no smells.

And there was pain. All of her hurt, from her toes up through her legs, into her chest and especially her head. The sides of her head still felt like they were being crushed.

Almost like how her old headaches had felt. *My old headaches… that's a memory.*

Lani tried to access her memories and this time they were hers. She could see what had happened leading up to being trapped, she could see Anderwell and Tillandra.

What about the other memories?

With a gasp of breath, she sought out the things she'd learned as

Burgendetta. Those were there too, just like they were with the other masks she'd used before.

Thank Thenis.

For a passing second Lani expected to hear the goddesses voice in her head, but it never came.

I was right, I am free.

Lani tried to turn over but every part of her was so sore it hurt too much, and she gave up. She felt so heavy, as if her body was being pressed down by something.

Even her eyelids were heavy, like they were attached to a weight, she could hardly open them. It was dark here too, but a different sort of darkness.

The blindness has gone. Please!

She tried to open her eyes again but the pain in her forehead stopped her. She locked them closed again, praying for the pain to ease.

And she passed out.

When she came to there was a different pain, coming from her eyes. *There's light!*

Around the outer edge of her eyelids she could see light and it hurt. The pain in her head had eased considerably and this pain was only in her eyes.

There were more noises, and they were clearer this time. The sounds of people, talking, moving, banging things. And there were smells of food, and more people.

Everything was muted as though her hands were cupped over her ears but not as much as the last time.

"I think she's awake."

That sound was much closer, and sounded familiar. Lani tried to remember who it was, but the name wouldn't come to her.

It will.

She was confident now, Lani was positive she was free of Odajeen's mind, but the experience must have hurt her body and she needed to recover.

"Lani. Lani, can you hear me?"

She gathered strength in her throat and went to speak but nothing came out. The pain she'd experienced from the squeezing as she pushed to get free from Odajeen's mind came back to her and she could feel how tight her throat still was.

"Get her something to drink, quickly!"

Yes, please.

Her head and arms were still too heavy, she didn't have the will to lift them. Instead, Lani focused on her eyelids.

I want to show them I can see.

Now that the voice had mentioned a drink her mouth felt drier than the desert. She couldn't remember ever feeling this thirsty and all she could think about was water or ale.

Anything, bring me anything. Quickly!

With the thought her body instinctively tried to swallow but all she felt was scratching, the way swallowing fragments of glass would feel.

Then suddenly her head lifted on its own, she could feel a strong hand under it, and the sensation of liquid on her lips, spilling down her chin.

She wanted to weep at the feeling, but her eyes were just as dry.

The flavor of the ale that was being dripped into her mouth tasted better than anything she could imagine.

"Just a little at a time. Don't overdo it or she'll be sick." It was the deep voice of a man, again familiar, but she was unable to put a name to it.

Lani licked her lips and took in more of the ale. Her throat eased enough that she was able to swallow without so much pain. Her stomach began to stir as well, liking the liquid but stimulated now and grumbling for food. As it did, she could feel how hungry she was, how little energy her body had.

Her nose was flooded with smells, even the ale had a smell she wouldn't normally recognize, but mostly of the people around her.

I'm free, I'm free. I am, aren't I?

All Lani wanted was to be able to see to confirm it, but her eyes wouldn't open.

"Don't forget to wipe her eyes, with a wet cloth. They're probably crusted closed." That was a woman's voice, and she knew it; it was Odajeen.

"Oda..." The sound was weak and crackly coming from her mouth.

"Yes, Lani. Don't bother speaking yet, just let your body settle. You're back, girl. Thank Seth!"

Tears finally came to her eyes, running down her cheeks.

All the sensations were coming fast, almost too quickly for her to grasp. Something damp crossed over her face, rubbing at her eyes.

Once it had been removed, she tried her eyelids again.

"Arggh!"

She'd opened them too quickly and the pain of the light hitting them had been sharp. Tears came again this time as it brought the memory of what had happened to Burgendetta back to the front of her mind.

It would have been so many times worse than that.

"Easy, girl, don't rush things, there's no hurry." The male voice again.

But there is, I need to see, you don't understand.

Next time she moved them very slowly, the tiniest sliver of an opening, and let the light in, adjusting to it. When she felt safe, she moved them some more, letting in more light and she waited.

At first the image was blurry with her eyelids still only partly open and the tears flooding them. It took almost all her strength to lift her left arm and brush her tunic across her eyes. It worked; she could see.

She was in a tent and there were people crowded in there, kneeling beside her and standing over her.

Lani looked up at a brute of a man standing above her. *Carnus.* She smiled at him; he didn't return the favor.

"You're back, girl?"

"I am."

Lani could see the smile on Odajeen's face beside her. Someone was behind her, and she turned to see Kooka bent over, holding her upright.

"Hey there, girl. You gave us a right fright you did."

The warmth in his smile lifted Lani's spirits even further. All these people had come with her, to look after her and help her. More tears flooded her eyes.

"Maybe you can deal with that." A boy about her age pointed to the ground in front of her.

Lani looked and saw the amulet on the ground. "Oh! Where's the pouch?"

Someone placed it in her hand and without thinking she snatched the jewel up, letting the pouch draw it inside. She closed it and let it fall into her lap.

"What happened?"

The group laughed spontaneously, even Carnus had a small grin on his face.

"We thought you could tell us." Odajeen sounded very curious, and Lani knew she was going to have to have a long talk with the woman, at some point.

"We should get you to eat and drink and recover before we discuss things," Odajeen said. "Leo, tell the others, but she'll want to wash. This is very good news, girl."

Leo, that's it. He's one of the Court.

Lani wanted everything and all now. More ale, food and yes, a wash. Suddenly with the idea put in her mind from the older woman she could sense how grubby her skin felt.

"Where are we?"

"Traveler's Rest, under Midderbuilt," Leo replied.

It was the camp that Thenis had mentioned. They were a very long way from Anderwell, and the amulet had been out. She was free but at what cost?

Had she just put these people in danger?

"You are weak, Lani." It was Kooka that was speaking now. He turned and looked up at the brute still stood staring at her. "She's not going to be able to walk easily, Carnus, you'll need to help her."

Carnus nodded and reached for her.

106

UKSOD

That Karpenmor was on his way back to En Carta should have made Uksod feel better, but there was a bitter taste to it all. His sourness was due to the finality of what would happen when the boy was crowned.

It was ridiculous and he knew it. He'd had more than enough time to prepare for it, it was always the goal, and yet after centuries of control, which he enjoyed, the concept irked him.

While the Prince had been out negotiating with the barbarians, Uksod had noticed the changes that had already crept into the palace.

Servants didn't respond to him the way they once had. They did what they had to, but there were quite a few newer ones that he could tell were more used to the Prince's approach.

With time I could change that. You just think you're safe, that's why.

He eyed one of the servants walking by and sized them up. *It wouldn't take much for word to spread about how you lost your life.* He snapped his fingers. *Just like that, gone in an instant.*

Maybe a few of them should turn up on his table underground, he could prolong the task, let them feel every part of their life slipping away… their eyes seeing him last.

Uksod turned his thoughts back to the Prince. He should already know the specifics of what the boy had negotiated and yet no word had been received.

And he thought the boy had limited the Vrah's tasks. No doubt the lad smirked as he kept hold of all the messengers turning up and not letting them return.

One could only do so much, especially at a distance, but he would discuss it with him anyway.

The lad had been a surprise package. When he'd weaned himself off the amber brandy, which had allowed them to influence him, Uksod had worried where it would lead. The boy had been more than malleable before then, not so anymore.

But the result was better than he'd expected. While he wasn't doing what Uksod directed, in the end what mattered more was getting the bridges completed. If he'd been able to negotiate that, Uksod would care little for his method.

He had to admit there'd been more progress of late than in a very long time. And now that he could see the lad was capable to rule the capital, it would free Uksod up to take care of the bigger issues.

Of spreading their word. *Of my real rule.*

"Uksod!"

Her voice felt sharp as it intruded on his privacy.

"I am here, mistress… as you know."

"Snippy again, old man. Is this the new you? I am not sure I care for it that much."

He felt a twinge of pain in his forehead as she reminded him of what she could do.

"How can I serve, mistress?"

"That's more like it."

The pain stopped. Uksod waited. She hadn't turned up for no reason, and he would have to wait until she told him. Patience wasn't a strong suit of hers.

"The girl has used the amulet again."

"Where?"

"In that infernal desert. What is it with the amulets and the desert?"

"I do not know, mistress. It is something I need to investigate more."

"You'll be able to soon."

He let that pass. "What is she doing with it?"

"Connecting to it, did I not just say that? The amulet is stronger than before."

"How can that be?"

"I do not know, Uksod, but if it was here, like I have been asking for, then perhaps I would be able to answer you."

"Sorry."

"She has a way to mask what she's doing with it, Uksod. I don't like that, but then I want to know how, why. That's why I want her here, so I can find out what how she does what she does."

"Can you tell me more about her location?"

"The desert, Uksod, lots of sand. What more is there to say?"

As irked as he felt, pushing her in this mood would only lead to pain for him. Uksod bit his tongue. "She's in the middle of the desert?"

"No. There are mountains there, she's with other people, many other people. Big mountains... one of them is moving... that strange place."

"I know of the place you speak of."

"Good. Does that mean you have someone there who could get to her?"

"In this case, yes. He's been there a very long time, just in case."

"You please me, old man. Sometimes you are useful, your ability to plan ahead impresses even me."

Uksod wasn't foolish enough to take her praise to heart, she'd stab him with it just as quickly.

"I want that girl and stone brought back. Then we'll have two."

"Yes, mistress. What of the other one?"

"It's lost to me again. Maybe it's run out of any power it had left."

"The others lasted longer. I think perhaps it might be shielded from us."

"By whom? My siblings?"

Uksod was intrigued by her words. She rarely mentioned the other gods. The one time he'd raised them he regretted it immediately.

"Remember the box I told you that Schevenal had? It was that which hid the amulet from you. This girl must have something like that because she hides it as well."

"It is not surprising they would be interfering."

"Where was it the last time you could sense it?"

"The desert as well. But it was going directly toward that city, Anderwell."

"Interesting. They must have a shield, or shields. They keep popping up in this story."

"At least I can feel the one close by, getting closer. When will he be here, Uksod? It's teasing me to have it so close."

"Soon enough. I expect he will attend the coronation, now that Karpenmor is on his way back."

"If he really has got them to agree to complete the bridge then your tasks will be much easier. Get him ready to lead, and you'll be able to go. Perhaps this King coming will be a good chance for you."

"What are you thinking?"

"You could return with the King toward his homeland, as though an emissary from us. Blending in with their people will be much easier will it not?"

"Perhaps. It is very close to Anderwell, I think it's time I investigated that place."

"You might have to be the one to find this girl, Uksod, no one else seems to be able to. There's one thing I know you can do."

"What's that?"

"Whatever it takes, Uksod. You've always done anything to get the result I need."

"And what if there's no option but to kill her and take the amulet?"

"Then you would do that in the blink of an eye, and the amulet will be mine. I am interested in her, Uksod, but much more concerned with the amulet being back here. Either on her or her brother."

"When will we tell him about her?"

"We won't unless it becomes necessary. Imagine telling him then you have to kill her, like you killed his mother. Think clearly, old man."

"Of course." Uksod always felt sillier than normal when he was around Yantarnaya. Sometimes he wondered if it was the stone working on him, a way to make her feel better about herself, being trapped in there.

"You have much work to do. I want all eight, Uksod, it's the only way I can finally get free."

"I understand, Goddess."

"Do you really? Could you imagine being trapped in here this whole time."

"No, I could not."

She paused for a moment, he didn't know if it was to remind him of her plight, or something else.

"There are now four in play, Uksod. I want them all."

"And they are all over Dharatan. Morska, Anderwell and now across the desert, it will take time to get to them all."

"Then get on with it, Uksod. At any cost, throne the boy and get me the rest of the amulets. The rest will show soon too."

107

KARPENMOR

*L*ooking at the city from this distance Karpenmor had mixed emotions. It was good to see his home, knowing he would be back there soon enough, but there was an itch simply being there wouldn't scratch.

With the bridge to Dharatan about to be completed it opened so many more opportunities for him. Much more that he could achieve. He was excited by the option to explore the barbarian realms, hunting down his amulet, the one his father had lost, not back here dealing with petty disputes and administration.

He'd fantasized about what it would be like if he wasn't the High Prince, so he could leave Uksod in charge while he himself was off on the hunt.

The whole idea was ludicrous he knew, and now the barbarians knew he was the heir there would not be any easy roaming through foreign lands. Still, it was a fun daydream while he hurried his way back.

Karpenmor knew that Uksod had spies watching what he was doing. It was why he'd changed how the Vrah around him had operated.

He had set Aika to ensuring that no Vrah messengers were allowed to leave the island. It had caused some problems, clearly they were under different instructions, but she'd stopped them all.

The term spy was probably too harsh, but they weren't working for him, they were sending word back to their previous leader.

That needs to change once and for all. That One has collaborated to help, means he can't stay either.

The leader of the group that had traveled back with him was numbered nine, not quite at the top of the list when it came to rank, but he had proven to be very loyal to Karpenmor.

He was going to need to find the right way to handle replacing One; there had to be a bloodless way for someone to step away from their role and ideally nominate the next leader.

Karpenmor assumed that Two would normally be the logical replacement, otherwise what good were the numbers? But he had not had much to do with the man, nor did he know his allegiances.

I'll need to spend some time on that when I get back.

The gates of the city were open and the Vrah lining the entry all bowed their heads as his party rode through. As their horses led Karpenmor's party toward the palace citizens came out and bowed or waved at him as he passed.

He nodded his head back at many, eventually stopping and focusing instead on the palace they approached. Uksod would be inside, and Karpenmor wondered if he'd still be pretending to be ill.

That he thought he could pretend and keep his own lie to the heir bothered Karpenmor, he just wasn't sure whether he should be calling the old man out about it or keeping it for a later time.

The priest was a cunning and well experienced practitioner of these types of games, and Karpenmor knew he would be wise to not think he could easily outsmart the man.

As it turned out, the priest and an entourage of servants were waiting at the top of the steps in front of the palace as he approached. *Word does travel fast indeed.*

Before anyone could bring the embarrassing steps alongside his horse, he dismounted and left his horse to a servant. Aika quickly followed suit and walked several paces behind him as he climbed the steps to the top.

"Your Highness, welcome home." Uksod's face was all smiles and his voice warm.

"Uksod, you didn't need to greet us. It is good to see you back on your feet and looking in full health."

Karpenmor noticed the old man looked healthier than he had in quite some time.

"How could we not, Highness? Given how quickly you had to rush away, it is our duty to be here for you, now you are back."

An unnecessary statement, a little dig at me not telling him I was going.

"I see you brought Trorn back safely too."

"You thought I wouldn't? He proved very useful I must say."

That will get you thinking. Poor Trorn will be questioned until his ears fall off.

Uksod's eyebrows rose, but he said nothing more about it.

"So much to discuss, Uksod. I am sure you are keen to hear all about it, but I think first a bath then perhaps you and I should share a meal."

"Thank you, Highness, that would be a good way to catch up."

By the time Karpenmor had scrubbed two weeks of grime and dust from himself he was starving but feeling better. He knew he'd sleep well tonight, the first time in a proper bed in more than a week.

He wore a white tunic that reached almost to his knees, with only three buttons from his neck. It was embroidered with brown thread in patterns symbolic of Family One, all squares and rectangles interlinked.

Tan-colored leggings and open sandals were all items he pulled from his vast array of clothes. This top seemed new, certainly he could not remember ever wearing it.

His staff had a habit of replacing items that were old and inserting brand new items into his collection without word. This time he was very pleased with the combination.

Uksod waited in the dining room, stood in his black cassock

holding a silver goblet and looking out the windows toward the city. He turned as the door opened.

"Highness."

"Uksod, sorry for keeping you waiting."

"Not at all, Highness. Feeling better?"

Karpenmor turned to the servant behind him. "You can tell the kitchen we're ready to eat now, but when you're not serving, we can be left alone."

The woman nodded and ducked out of the room, closing the door behind her.

"Shall we sit?"

"Yes, Highness..."

"We're alone, Uksod, please use my name."

"Of course. Forgive me but you did disappear without word."

"Sorry, Uksod, but you seemed poorly disposed and I was set in my mind about going."

"Of course. May I ask what happened?"

"Come now, I am sure you had people sending messages."

Uksod looked at him calmly but intently. "You are changing, Karpenmor, that I can see. I wondered before whether it was too soon, but I think not."

"What's that?"

"The throne. You even sound like a leader now, and yes, I have been told some things, but even that was limited."

"You'd know then that I visited Step Six. The bridges, Uksod, they are better than we even imagined!" Karpenmor could hear the excitement in his own voice.

"Tell me."

He went into detail about what he'd seen and the journey across them. "At times I must admit my stomach lurched and it felt quite threatening, with the wind."

"I doubt you should have been on them; they are not finished."

"Finished enough for single-file horses to travel easily, a bit slower for a wagon, but still our people use them constantly and they are now adding the sides and bracing."

"I see."

"And we were visited by the barbarians."

"This I also heard, but not anything about it."

Karpenmor was happy he had stopped the messengers, otherwise Uksod would already be completely apprised of everything, with his own plans. He explained the emissary's visits and then the other King, and finally the Queen.

"I am surprised she came to the island, that was quite a risk for her. I hear she is very conservative."

"Perhaps our ears over there are not as connected to her as they might have you believe, Uksod."

"Why do you say that?"

"She is stern, I will give you that. The woman doesn't look like she's had any fun in quite some time. But despite her protestations about the city and our temple, she gave in quicker than I expected."

"What do you mean?"

Karpenmor finished explaining the entire negotiations and what he'd settled on. He watched as Uksod sat silently digesting everything he'd just been told.

The door opened and several servants brought in their meal, bowls, and platters, setting up the table for them. Neither man said anything until they had finished and left the room.

"You've done much better than I expected, Karpenmor."

"You thought that little of me?"

"No, but you have done little such negotiation, it is easy to be outplayed by older heads. That you turned your back on them early set a good precedent."

"Thank you."

"Could you not have held out for more though?"

"I considered what mattered and initially I was going to demand more, even part of the city, but then..." He paused and drank some wine before pulling apart some bread.

"What?"

"I kept in mind what it was I wanted, what we needed."

"Which is?"

"The bridges, Uksod, don't treat me like a child. You know darn well what we need, and without the bridges nothing else matters."

"What else?"

"Once we have the bridges, we can take back the city when we're ready."

"You really have come on. I doubt I could have got much more; I would have run with the bridges and them relaxing the numbers of people. I thought they wouldn't buckle when it came to the temple, but our goddess will be extremely pleased with that."

Karpenmor was surprised by the praise. He had been happy enough with what had happened but expected Uksod to be negative about it. There had to be something else, an ulterior motive or something happening he didn't know about. This was too easy.

"When can we place a priest there?"

"Not until the bridge is complete, and they get their first delivery of grains. That was the kicker for them. I think if we'd let them starve into winter, we could have got more."

"But?"

Karpenmor took another drink and looked at his mentor.

I'm glad you're pleased, old man, not that it really matters. I'm in charge now and you just have to get used to it.

The changes in how he felt about ruling had become more pronounced in Karpenmor. He wanted to be in charge now and he needed everyone to know that he was, even if it meant handling things differently than he had.

"I couldn't stay there forever, we have more to do. Now tell me, what exactly have you been up to?"

108

UKSOD

Uksod could see that Karpenmor was ready, or more ready than he had been. The boy had definitely learned some new tricks.

His negotiation with the Ngaherians was admirable, in that he would appear as though he had backed down to them simply by pushing for the unattainable up front.

Setting such a high goal gave him plenty of room to walk back and still get wins, despite the opposition thinking he'd given up everything.

Getting the temple returned to them as well as one priest permanently in it was a master stroke, even if the boy didn't really understand why. His concern for historic significance was good, and Uksod hadn't had to explain why it was such a good result.

Uksod hadn't bothered to tell Karpenmor that once it was open they'd place the four amber stones back in the towers of the temple. It was the one thing his father had done right when he returned from Dharatan.

Grabbing the 'eggs' as they were known were exquisite pieces of amber that acted as beacons for Yantarnaya. Now they could do it again as they had all those years ago.

Had Schevenal left them in place they might have been destroyed by the barbarians, although there was also the possibility that Cumerc might not have been lost so easily.

Uksod smiled. The reach it would give him and their goddess would weaken the city's resolve, and the Queen's armies. It would make the recapture of the city so much easier.

Even better was the extension of the Debrua's reach that it would provide him. When he left Enderk he would be cut off from the power of the Debrua Stone directly, but the temple stones would allow him a stronger connection.

As they were able to place more of them through Dharatan, the connection would become easier.

He would need less life force to speak to her, he could even use an animal if need be. Uksod sneered, he'd never enjoyed using an animal, there was none of the terror in it that came from people. That was the part that stirred him.

Focus.

His energy levels were low because he'd done just that, having to reach out to two people. The first was an agent he'd had in the city of Midderbuilt for years.

That the city was a center of all things related to gems across Dharatan had always seemed such a logical spot for an amulet to turn up.

Do I tell Karpenmor about all these people, or are they my assets only?

He was still undecided on how the complete handover would proceed. One would need to retire from his spot, which Uksod would recommend to the boy.

Give him his own fresh start, or at least that's how it would seem, even though Two and Three were all loyal to Uksod. When Two took the role of leader he would still be accessible to the priest, which would be a bonus.

No, these assets I shall retain, unless we need them for our combined goals.

His man in Midderbuilt was a guard in the fabled city, who he had left alone, reached only by other agents from time to time. Thankfully the man, Tsen, knew where his wealth came from, and the threat to his family that had also been conveyed.

He had been very surprised to have Uksod enter his mind and speak to him, but then that just made it more powerful a threat. Uksod told Tsen of the girl, and what he needed from him.

As much as Yantarnaya wanted the girl back alive, Uksod had left that part optional for Tsen. It was a nice-to-have, but not a necessity, the absolute goal was to retrieve the amulet.

He also connected to a member of the Vrah on Step Six. A delegation had come back to the island and were demanding passage to the capital.

The Vrah had been advised the heir wouldn't allow anyone through until the bridge was completed. Uksod knew that wouldn't do, Yantarnaya had been concerned the boy might delay Ahn's arrival.

He needed to get the heir to agree. As much as he wanted to seek forgiveness and not permission for just approving the request, the boy would question how that happened.

The Vrah had advised him a messenger was already en route to the palace to seek permission from the heir, Uksod would have to wait until then.

Telling the boy that he was able to communicate with those wearing the rings was something the boy didn't need to know about at this time.

Once he was leashed to the amulet he'd understand much more about the Debrua and the powers he could use. It would be too late for him to do anything about it then.

All Uksod needed from him at this time was his help to hunt the amulets down.

Using the bodies like he had made him feel weak and unwell, which meant he'd have to revisit the stone, and soon. First, he wanted to see One and climbed up to ground level, feeling every step.

"Uksod, you look unwell, what is the matter?"

"It's fine, One. When I do that thing, it has this effect."

"You should rest. If the boy sees you, he'll think you unfit for the ceremony."

"Good point, but worry not, I'll fix it after I have finished with you."

"I'm glad you came, I have news."

"What is it?"

"The final two families will make the enthronement ceremony. I have men protecting them at a distance and ensuring no other delays happen."

"Good, and what of the candidates?"

"Both arrived today, with their chaperones. There was some stubbornness from the family heads but the letters from you fixed that."

"Excellent news. Whoever was behind the delays needs to pay, but that will have to come another time. We're going to have our hands full these next few weeks."

The leader of the Vrah didn't respond.

"We will have additional guests for the ceremony, it would seem."

"Who?"

"You'll have a rider coming soon, with news from Step Six, of a barbarian delegation."

"What about them?"

"They wish to come to the capital. For now your men hold them in place on the Step, but they must be allowed to come here."

"May I ask why? We have never let barbarians here before."

"Everything is changing, One, things will never be the same again. The King of Daskare is here to see our mistress. She demands it. He carries one of the amulets."

"I see."

"He also comes with a priest that works for me, despite him being one of them. The rest should all be considered hostile. Especially the Ngaherians and the strange one."

"Strange one?"

"A different type of barbarian. I am unsure exactly what type, but he stands out from them all. His head is huge as are his hands and feet."

"Why are you afraid of him?"

"Afraid may not be the right word, One. Wary, perhaps, might be better. I have not met him, but something about the way Karpenmor described him, struck a warning inside of me."

"Your instinct is normally accurate."

Uksod smiled. "Yes, it has served us very well in the past."

Their mutually beneficial relationship had been formed many years before over such an instinct. One had wished to elevate an ambitious Vrah into the top ten, but something about the man had set Uksod's instincts off.

As it turned out the man had attempted to kill One, accelerated by him being turned down for promotion. One had set a trap for him, despite not believing what Uksod had felt about it.

One had been badly injured in the attack but survived because he was alert to the possible threat. He always listened to the priest's instincts after that, and every time it had paid off.

"Will you tell the Prince?"

"I cannot, One. He has no need to know about that capability."

"Understood."

"Another thing, after the ceremony it would be the perfect time for you to step down."

Despite their previous discussions on the topic, Uksod could see it pained the man. "Now?"

"Yes, him taking on his title makes for a perfect time for change, and we need to go away."

"To where?"

"Dharatan, One. We have amulets to retrieve, and it will not be easy."

"And here I thought I'd be retiring to the south coast to grow fat and idle."

"Far from it, One. Far from it."

109

LANI

As rough as a camp wash was, Lani couldn't believe how good it felt to be able to scrub herself clean. She didn't know yet how long it had been that she'd been lost like that, but it was a month of travel by wagon to get here alone.

She felt as bad for Odajeen who'd had to stay in Lani's company the whole time, a prisoner of her own decision. Lani doubted Tillandra would punish the older woman any further; her journey and guilt was enough.

Despite washing, Lani was already sweating again, from the heat of the middle day desert sun. That was even though they were fully shaded by the rock ledge that jutted out above Traveler's Rest.

While it was separate from Midderbuilt it was still considered part of the city, and most of the rules that ran the city above applied down here.

As she re-joined the motley group that made up her traveling companions, she had to smile. It was such a good feeling to be able to see again.

Lani felt guilty for thinking that way when she knew Odajeen couldn't ever get her sight back. And then her anxiety returned about how to tell the woman her story.

Kooka patted a seat beside him and she sat there, enjoying the feel of it and being able to rest her legs.

"You don't know how good that feels to be able to sit, Kooka."

"What do you mean?"

She told him some of what it had been like to be stuck inside Odajeen's head.

"I don't scare easily but what you're saying gives me chills, girl."

"It does me too now that I am out. Where is she?"

"Odajeen? She's washing too. I paid for a woman to come and help her. Her legs aren't as resilient as yours, she was struggling to hold herself up."

"I'm so sorry."

"Don't be. You and she did what you did. What's right now is that you're free. Tillandra will be pleased."

"Does she know?"

"Not that I am aware of, but then I don't have skills like you lot. Perhaps Leo will know."

"Tell me the whole thing, Kooka, I need to get caught up on what's happened."

Idran and Vefed brought drink and food and Lani filled herself while she listened to Kooka. He had a knack for telling stories and by the end of it everyone but Odajeen was there gripped by the tale, even Carnus.

She looked at the huge warrior when Kooka talked about the attack on death road. Carnus's eyes met hers and she nodded. He blinked his eyes in recognition and that was enough.

Purple had moved next to her, and Lani held the young girl's hand, a connection that she'd missed since leaving her kin. She liked having someone young to care for, even if it was Purple that had done the caring for her.

When the telling was done, parts filled in by each of her companions, her eyes were full of tears that flowed uncontrollably down her cheeks.

"Why so upset, girl?"

It took her a moment before she could reply to Kooka, wiping her face dry with her sleeve. "You… you've all done this to save me, I am so grateful."

"We're family, girl, that's what we do."

She looked at the old man, who'd been the Driver for so many years. Even he, who was meant to be retiring and resting in Anderwell, had come out on this trip.

These ARE my people now, aren't they?

The silence was broken by the entrance of Odajeen, led by a woman of a similar age, into the circle by their camp.

"Odajeen, I hope you feel as good as I do after that?"

"Better, child, but I will kill someone if I don't get a drink soon."

Vefed guided her to sit between him and his brother, handing her a big cup. "Drink this."

The older woman swallowed it in one go before holding it out for more. He tipped more ale into it, and it wasn't until she'd finished the second one that she spoke.

"The only thing better than that will be when my belly is full."

The group chatted as friends while the afternoon slipped away from them. A lightness seemed to surround the group, something Lani sensed hadn't been there since they'd left Anderwell.

"What next then, Lani?"

Odajeen stopped the chatter with her question, everyone turning to look at Lani.

"What do you mean?"

"This was only one part of the journey, girl. Getting you free is great but we came for another reason."

Lani patted her chest. "This."

"Yep."

"I don't know. I should have asked her when I spoke to her."

"You had other things to discuss, none of that mattered until you were free."

Lani turned to Leo. "Can you take us back the same way you did before?"

"I guess, as long as it works like it did before. But can't you just go into the city?"

"How? Don't you need a pass to do that?"

Kooka reached into his coat and pulled out a token from his pocket. "Like this you mean?"

Lani was astonished. "Whose is that?"

"Mother's. She said to give it to you, so for now that's yours."

Lani took it and rolled it in her palm, the silver circle not totally unlike those which the Jester Keepers wore. Carved into this one was what looked like a gate and arch on one side, and a spire on the other.

That must be Mount Qum.

The pass in her hand felt like a massive weight, without it Tillandra could not get inside the city. For her to give it to them, just on a chance, was a massive risk.

Had the attack been successful on them along Death Road, the pass would have been lost. *These people really did want me safe.*

"Then I guess I'll do that and work out what I need to do after that."

Shouting could be heard off across the camp, breaking the peace of their gathering. Kooka stood up and tried to see across the tents, but only shook his head.

"Irdan and I will go and see what it's about."

"Right. Here, Leo, let's tidy up, best we're always ready for anything, we don't need a sloppy camp. Lani, maybe you three should go into your tent for now?"

"What are we, helpless women then?"

"Not at all, but you've got two things on you that would be attractive to robbers, and frankly we've only just got you back. I'll not be the one to lose you again so quickly."

"Alright, but only because you asked nicely." She poked her tongue out at him, wanting to break the mood that had changed. It didn't work and he turned back outward facing.

"Come on, Purple, let's get you inside."

"I can manage, you help Odajeen."

"I can help myself, you lot. Just show me the way."

Lani stood next to her. "Here's my arm, I'll walk us in."

Carnus had moved beside the tent they went into, and the flap closed behind her.

She sat opposite where Odajeen did, and beckoned Purple to crawl closer. "It'll all be nothing, no need to be concerned."

Lani hoped it were true. She'd been feeling so happy since reawakening, the last thing she needed was another drama already. She started stroking Purple's hair to settle the young girl, the action helping her feel better as well.

110

LANI

*K*ooka poked his head through the flap.

"What's happening out there?"

"I'm not sure yet, we're waiting for the brothers to come back. Whatever it is, it's upset a few people in the camp, it sounded like there was a minor clash just before."

"Friend or foe?"

"I don't know, Lani, like I said we'll have to wait for the brothers."

He pulled his head out and the flap closed. Lani felt on edge. She'd only just got free and there was already a threat around them. *It's probably nothing to do with us.*

She struggled to convince herself, and her two companions in the tent showed the same anxiety that she felt. Patting her chest, she felt the amulet tucked away.

Her brooch would be in there too, something she hadn't had to pull out in a long time. Just knowing it was there was a comfort. She looked at Odajeen; it was that brooch that had brought them together.

At some point she'd need to discuss what she had learned with Odajeen/Burgendetta. Lani wasn't sure how she'd explain what had taken her sight to the old woman, even now it made Lani's skin crawl.

Who could be so cruel? Such a monster.

This woman had basically given up her life to protect Lani and asked nothing in return. She had done it again when they'd met in Vidus without even knowing her own truth.

Much of it was controlled by these gods, whether planned or not. The connection that had been made when she was just a young'un with the brooch and Burgendetta was still at work now.

"How are you feeling, Odajeen?"

"Like a new woman." She laughed. "Nothing against you, lass, but being stuck with you for so long was no party."

"I can't imagine at all. You've always been so willing to help me."

"What do you mean?"

"All the way back, you've protected me."

"You learned something then?"

"I did. Not all of it good."

"I doubt it is, Lani. But that doesn't matter, maybe knowing will make sense of it all. What was it like?"

"Being in there?"

"Yes."

"I'd not wish it on anyone, Odajeen. I hate to think what would have happened if this hadn't worked. I would have been..."

The flap opened again, forcefully. "Quick, Lani, bring your things."

She grabbed her satchel and stepped out of the tent. "What's up Kooka?" The brothers were there this time.

"Vefed says there's guards hunting for a girl who supposedly has stolen some gems. It sounds suspiciously like they're looking for you."

"Me? How would anyone know?"

"No idea, lass, but if there's no good coming our way it's best we try to get you out before they find you." He turned to Carnus. "If you have to, she's all yours, okay?"

The Ngaherian nodded.

"Take her up to the city gate, she has a pass." He looked back at her. "When you're inside you need to find a man called Tingfurlew."

"Ting — forlew?"

"Ting -- fur -- lew. Say it."

"Tingfurlew."

"Yep. He's the man that Mother comes to see, he can help you find your way to the stone. Don't come out unless Carnus is at the gate and nods."

"You're scaring me."

"I'm just planning, Lani. This might have nothing to do with you, or us, but I'm not taking chances. After all it took to get you here, we're not letting harm come to you now."

"What about the others?"

"They'll be fine. If someone is after you, then the rest of us don't matter. If it's anything else, then it can't be us. We've only just got here."

Leo rushed into the space in front of their tents. "They're looking for a young woman, sounds a lot like Lani."

"If they are calling you a thief then catching you with anything would be instant death. Make sure your bag has nothing in it Lani, just to be safe."

She did and it only contained her belongings. "Nothing but my things."

"Where's the… stone?"

She patted her chest.

"Good. It's the best place for it. Carnus, you must get her up there now. Whatever this is coming our way, she needs to be well away from it."

Carnus grabbed her by the arm. "Come!"

They weaved away from their tents until they were in a walkway that led toward the gates of Traveler's Rest. It was about fifty paces to go until they reached the token gates, then it wasn't far from there to the path up to the city.

The guards at the gate didn't appear to be letting anyone through, and extra guards were there searching anyone trying to come or go.

"You'll be fine, just remain calm." It was as many words as he'd ever said to her.

Lani felt conspicuous standing in the line wanting to get out. It was the trick your mind played knowing you'd done nothing wrong but feeling guilty anyway.

Some of the people in front of her were getting agitated with the guards.

"What's this all about, we want to be on our way."

"You'll go when we say you can. Now back up or there'll be more trouble."

It took almost an hour before they got to the front. The guards there were not in the mood to be friendly.

"Where you going?"

"Into the city."

"You have a pass?"

"Yes."

"Show me."

Lani was thankful she had it tied on a string around her neck, and not in with the amulet. She pulled it out and let him look at it, but not to touch it.

He turned to his colleague. "She matches the description, and she has a pass."

"Search her!"

"What is going on?"

"You need to show me your bag, girl."

Carnus stepped in on the man. "Careful."

"Best you be careful, big man. You don't want to be causing any trouble here."

"I'll take my chances. Little boys like you taste nice for my lunch."

The guard wasn't a complete idiot. Lani watched him quickly assess what would happen. Even if they were able to best Carnus, he would be the one that suffered most.

"Back down, no one gets out of here without being searched, and if your girl here is the thief, you're both going nowhere."

Lani put her hand on Carnus's arm. "It's okay."

The guard tipped her bag upside down and dumped everything on the sandy ground. He pulled everything apart, shaking clothes and tossing them away before turning the satchel inside out.

He didn't bother to repack it and just turned to her. "Arms up."

She raised her arms out to the side and let him run his hands down her sides and back, up and down each leg. Her skin crawled as his hands felt more than they needed to.

Lani wanted to hit him but gritted her teeth, praying he'd be done soon. He stood up, his eyes staring into hers. She held his gaze making sure to not instinctively look to her chest.

Despite his creeping hands he never touched there. "Nothing." He had turned to his colleague, and two other guards that had moved closer.

"Him then."

"Let them, Carnus."

He grunted back at her, but let the guards run their hands over him, staring at the guard standing closest.

When the guard searching him was done, he shook his head. The others looked disappointed.

"Pick up your stuff and wait there."

"Why can't we go through?"

"No one gets out until the boss says so."

Once she had gathered all her things, shaken them as clean as she could and repacked her satchel, they joined others that had been inspected.

A grizzly-looking guard walked back to the gate accompanied by three others. "And?"

"Nothing, Sergeant."

"I was told it was a girl."

"No one has anything, we've checked them all, maybe they's hiding in a tent or wagon."

The leader looked at the group stood off to the side, his eyes lingering on Lani for longer than she cared. He shook his head and turned back to the gate guards.

"And you've searched this lot thoroughly?"

"There are only two females, but both are clean. That one there has a pass, though."

The sergeant walked toward her.

Carnus stepped closer to her, and half a pace ahead, his eyes on the sergeant, who stopped and looked at him.

"You travel with a strange pet."

She didn't answer but held Carnus's arm firmly. They didn't need any trouble.

"Nothing to say? Where you leaving to?"

"Not leaving, I have a pass, and will be going into the city."

He stared at her. "If you're our thief, girl, you'll get caught. You have a look about you." He looked at the other guards. "Watch her, I want to know everywhere she goes up there."

"Yes, Sergeant."

The leader of the guards turned and walked away back into the camp. Lani felt as though they'd been lucky, and she wasn't sure from what, but it felt very much like their enemies knew they were here.

Her plan to use the amulet had always carried a cost. While she was free, she'd brought trouble closer which not only put the stones at risk but also her friends.

While she was glad to walk through the gates and begin the climb up to the city, she had to look back and worry about what danger the others were in.

111

KARPENMOR

Standing on a stool with the royal tailor moving around him was unnerving Karpenmor. There was a seemingly endless number of things to do leading up to the dance and the ceremony.

"Are we almost done?"

"No, sire, I am sorry, you still have the most important of all the robes to be fitted."

"Now, now, your Highness, he is merely trying to ensure you will look your finest on the big day." Uksod almost seemed to be smiling, he was clearly enjoying it.

"Anyone would think I was getting married with all this fuss."

"That will come next, Highness."

"Unlikely, Uksod, I'll not be ponied up with…" Karpenmor stopped as Uksod had quickly put his finger up to his mouth.

"Why don't you give us a few moments? The Prince and I have a few matters to discuss, and you can finish off once we're done."

"Eminence, Highness." The tailor dipped his head and scurried out of the room.

Uksod walked over and closed the door, checking no one else was lurking in the room.

"You need to be wary about who is in the room when you're about to make political commentary, Karpenmor."

"Political what?"

"Everything you say about your subjects and decisions you make, Karpenmor, are political. Such words can easily get back to others, if not managed carefully. Do you not remember the servant you spoke poorly in front of?"

The scene flashed back into Karpenmor's mind, of the servant whose life he'd ended, simply by them hearing what he had said. While he might not have even given the command, he'd as good as done so by being careless.

"Besides it would be most annoying to have to replace the tailor at such a late stage."

"Why on Enderk are you so happy, Uksod? I think I preferred the sour old priest to this plucky, almost cheerful creature before me."

"I am being serious. You need to watch your tongue around the servants. While they may be here to serve you, we have no certainty about who might be in someone else's pocket."

"You're not making me feel particularly safe in my own palace."

"Good, I don't want you to feel safe and warm. At any point someone could be aiming to do you harm, if not physically, simply by telling another what they might overhear from you."

"To my point, Uksod, I know exactly what Natillian is up to with Bhoomi."

"Bhoomi, is that her name?"

"Yes."

"Your face doesn't seem to agree with your words, Karpenmor."

"What do you mean?"

"The girl appeals to you; it's written in your eyes and the way you almost smile saying her name."

"Pfft."

"It's okay to bed her, Highness, just don't go making her your favored candidate at this time."

"Uksod, that's crass."

"Is it? You've had others, Karpenmor, what's so different about using one for your own advantage?"

"I don't like where this is going."

"Are you in any doubt that she'd tell her grandmother things she might hear in your company?"

Karpenmor thought about what Uksod was saying.

"I..."

A knock on the door stopped him. "Come."

The leader of the Vrah, One, entered the room. "Highness, I have a message from Ponte for you, marked urgent."

Karpenmor caught the man looking out of the corner of his eye at Uksod. *As soon as this darn ceremony is over, I'll have to deal with all of that.*

"Thank you, One." He took the message tube from the Vrah leader and twisted the seal free, pulling out the scroll within.

He read it, before reading it again, and passing it to Uksod.

"I told them no passage until the bridge was finished, which cannot be done yet."

"A sensible point of leverage at the time but does it matter really?"

"You'd have barbarians in the capital now? After all this time?"

"Things are very different now, Highness."

"What of the amulet the King wears, Uksod? Is it..." He looked quickly at One and back at Uksod.

"He knows, Highness, it is his men hunting your amulet, lest you forget."

"Of course. Is it the same as my father's one, that the girl has on Dharatan?"

"It is."

"So, it's connected to Yantarnaya?"

"Yes. I know that our goddess will be pleased to have the amulet in the city."

"What does it matter?"

"They belong to her, that is where they were gifted from. She has been most upset that they have been gone for so long."

Karpenmor was annoyed that the foreigners had disregarded his commands to wait, but then he did want to know more about the amulet the King had. Perhaps he could discuss it with the man and learn more about them.

"You're in favor of letting them come, Uksod?"

"I can see benefits, Highness."

"Such as?"

"We could keep them here, for a while." This time the priest did have a smile on his face. It was a little too creepy for Karpenmor's liking.

"Hostages?"

"Not exactly. They'd be guests for your enthronement, and of course we could tie them up in activities to ensure they are here more than long enough to see the bridge completed as you wish."

"So, hostages, then. It would be additional leverage in the short term. Have there ever been such visits before?"

"Not that I am aware of Highness. If there were, it was long before my time or your father's."

"Then they know nothing of our lands. Are we so sure that it's a good idea to let them travel through?"

"One could ensure there's no room for touring. They'd be brought to the city, and we'd keep them tightly wrapped up so they learn little."

"Agreed. One, send word back that they can come. You heard Uksod, make sure that there's a large escort, and that they know clearly who's in control of their movements without insulting them."

"It will be done, Highness."

He left the room; the tailor poked his head through before it closed. "Not yet." Karpenmor waved him away.

"Is this wise, Uksod?"

"I think you will have two new contacts who will be privileged to attend your enthronement, Karpenmor. That could be valuable moving forward."

"Perhaps. As to all of this nonsense with the dance, and Bhoomi, is this going to be an ongoing thing I have to deal with?"

"I'm afraid so. You will have to have an heir, Karpenmor. While the whole idea might seem of little interest right now, think about how little you cared for the throne not such a long time ago."

Karpenmor could see he paused deliberately to push his point.

"You'll no doubt think similarly soon enough about having a son to carry on after you."

"You're right, I know. While I'm in no hurry, I also don't want to take advantage of these young women."

"Don't lose the new strength you have been showing, Karpenmor. The girl is seeking your favor. Use it as you wish. If that's physical as well as mental, so be it. It's not a new thing, lad, and don't think she hasn't been told to do the same. And you can test them while you're at it."

"What do you mean?"

"A little misinformation spread to see where it ends up could tell you a lot of things about your prospective brides."

"You really do think about all of this as a game, don't you, Uksod?"

"A very deadly game, Highness. It's how I've managed to survive for so long, and if you learn nothing else from me, learn that. It's very much a case of us against everyone else."

Karpenmor looked hard at the old man. Whatever had gone between them before it was now changed. Uksod might not realize it, but it was almost as though he'd already completely shed the burdens of leadership now, and he was much lighter for it.

"Let's get the tailor back in then, can we? You need to get these clothes finished."

112

JUNTHER

*I*t's a stupid name for a town, seriously who comes up with these? Junther trudged his way along the main street from the south gate of Little Big Rock.

His usual humorous side was absent at the moment as the walk through Ngahere had been the least fun of any trip he'd made in a long time. *They have no idea how to smile, those people. It's as if they are always looking for trouble.*

Once King Ahn had arrived in Kuwaha, there'd been no point in him remaining on the south coast. Clannack would watch over what the King was up to.

Instead Tillandra had asked him to check in on their latest addition to the Circuit, before returning south. The idea made sense; he'd travel through the spine of the continent but getting from the coast to here was all forest.

That had meant darkness, damp, and insects. Mosquitoes were the worst thieves in his mind. They stole your humor, your patience and on such a long trip, your sanity.

It's like they don't eat Ngaherians, they were all hungry for me.

Just the thought of it made him itchy and he rubbed his arm against his side. *Thank Thenis for my beard.* Many had died stuck within the hair of his long beard, which had worked wonders. Except for being able to sleep.

At night he'd hear those trapped buzzing, trying to get free, but the sound was easier to become accustomed to than the bites. Junther swapped shoulders for his swag and continued walking. It didn't change the only hand he had to hold it with but at least it eased the rubbing.

Let's hope this Keeper hasn't done anything stupid with the ring.

Tillandra hadn't been sure what to do with it, but the message had said it was contained in a black box, which had a story of its own. Someone had known enough about the ring to lock it away like that.

They'd used what was likely a similar box to block Lani's amulet, which meant the rings must have some form of magic associated with them. *But who would have done such a thing?*

A town guard was stood puffing on a pipe to the side of the road. Junther headed over.

"Day to you."

"And you, stranger. Rough travels?"

"Had to walk, not my favorite way to get around."

"And at your age too."

"Enough of that, you're not the fountain of youth, yourself. Maybe you can point me in the right direction?"

"We'll see."

"Story I heard is there's a new inn in this town, now what was its name..."

"There's only one new inn, they don't pop up very often. Weirdest of names if you ask me."

"What's that?"

"Fool's Bauble."

"Odd but that's the one."

"Keep going the way you were, count out five roads that go left, and take the next. It's down that way halfway to the wall."

"You're a good man... no matter what your wife says about you."

The guard made a mock swing with his free hand, but he had a grin on his face. "After you she had to come back to me, she needed a real man."

Junther laughed and went on his way. *What's the Keeper's name, I can't remember. That's two things that have slipped my mind, surely, it's not going on me.*

He counted out the roads and took the left as the guard had told him to. Soon enough he could see it down on his right, the sign standing out for how new it was compared to anything alongside.

The Fool's Bauble. They've done a good job given it was a burned-out shell by all accounts. He could see the back of the yard was still not rebuilt, stables and store houses were still charred and empty.

Arber, or something like that. That's her name. He headed to the front door and pushed it inward. Not a squeak, or groan, everything about it brand new.

Even the smell of the place was fresh. None of the decades of smoke, sweat and food smells baked into the timbers. This one still had the rawness of fresh wood and stain.

A woman stood at a counter in the reception area, a smile on her face. She wasn't tall but her big smile was like a friendly hug.

"Welcome to the Bauble."

"Good to be here, that's for sure. Arber, isn't it?"

"Almost, Arbery, how do you know me?"

Junther walked right up to the counter and held up his only hand, the ring facing outward. Her eyes startled briefly.

"Oh, one of them." She reached under the tunic at her neck and pulled out her silver token, leaning forward so it was close to the ring; both glowed blue.

Nothing like a new person to follow all the rules. Good to see.

"Sorry, I was told I had to check everyone."

"And good that you did, Arbery."

"You'll be wanting a room then." She gave him a once-over. "And a good wash I'd suspect."

"Look at you, a mind reader as well, they never told me that you were that skilled." He had a friendly smile on his face.

"Ha, and before I make you decent, what do they call you?"

He looked sideways, in mock secrecy, before leaning in. "Those words aren't fit for a lady, so you can call me Junther, that's what my mam called me."

"You're a right one, aren't you? Pleased to meet you, Junther. Come on, let's get you sorted, then you'll be wanting to eat and drink."

"There's another thing we need to discuss as well."

Her face went serious at his words. "What's that?"

This time he dropped his smile too, but stayed close and did speak quietly. "The ring."

"Oh, yes, that. Of course."

He had dumped his swag in his room and asked her to sort through it and get everything cleaned that she could before he went and soaked in his bath.

By the time he was done, he put on the only thing she'd left him, and headed to the main room. The inn was busy, and he could see why — the meal was one of the best he'd eaten in years.

Even the ale was good, and the burly man behind the counter kept everyone peaceful just by his look. Arbery had introduced Junther to him, Dedrick, and told him that he was her husband.

The baker, and a handy bit of muscle as well.

Junther felt like a new man now, full, wetted, and clean. There wasn't much more a man could ask for, but he still had work to do, and he couldn't afford to waste time.

He nodded to Arbery and when she'd left the room, he slowly made his way into the reception area.

"This way."

They went out the back of the kitchen via the hall, before she opened a trap door, and they climbed a ladder down into the basement. It was only half full of barrels and sacks, but Junther could see it too had been recently cleaned out.

Arbery moved several sacks from in front and on top of a chest. She opened it and pulled out the black box that he'd been told about.

On the surface it looked the same as the one Tillandra had put Lani's amulet in.

"Here you go, this is what we dug up."

He took it. "And the only thing inside is the ring?"

"Yes."

Junther sat down on a pile of sacks and placed the box on his lap. He flipped the latch around and lifted the lid. A single ring sat on the inside, much smaller than the size of the box.

The band was a dark muted silver and as he lifted it out, he could see the amber stone within it. It gleamed a little as though it had its own light within.

You're imagining it.

Something felt strange about it, he could almost sense it was reaching outward, but that made no sense to him. *Or does it? Isn't that how Lani explains the amulet?*

He looked on the inside of the ring and saw something carved into the back of the band. It was a symbol, but he couldn't make anything of it.

Junther put the ring back inside and closed the lid. "Exactly like your report said. Good work, Arbery."

"Is it valuable?"

"Not so much for the price, but the knowledge, yes. It's also a little dangerous."

"We kind of figured something wasn't right with how it was in that box and buried down here."

"Who's we?"

"The helpers you sent that built this place, and Dedrick."

"Ah. No one else knows about it?"

"No one, Junther."

"Keep it that way, Arbery, you don't need the attention this would bring."

She looked at him with a concerned look on her face.

"Never mind, I'm going to take it away from here now, you won't be bothered by it again."

"You leaving already?"

"This is important, and there's another thing I might need to do to the south. I'll be gone in the morning."

"You taking a horse?"

"I was just going to ask, there's that mind reading again."

113

CLANNACK

lannack had expected there would be some happiness after the deal had been struck but the Queen was sullen and reserved. King Ahn seemed happy enough, although he had also remained quiet and retired to his rooms with Fuling.

"What is bothering you, Majesty?"

"I don't like being bullied into anything, Clannack, and having given ground to allow them the temple shows us as weak."

"Did he not give up more?"

She looked at him and then at Nikora. "What do you think?"

"I agree with Clannack, Queen Vika. He started demanding the whole city."

"A ruse, no doubt, so he could appear to be letting us win. He might look like his mother only just spat him out, but he's smarter than we might suspect."

"No doubt."

"Why has he so willingly given up so much? That's what bothers me."

Clannack nodded, it was what he struggled to understand as well.

"We cannot assume any part of this will be easy, and we need to be ready for them to try and change things once the bridge is built."

For the better part of an hour, they discussed how to build and secure the marketplace and temple that the Derks could use. As much as Tillandra would hate the connection, at least this created a barrier that could be controlled.

Clannack wondered if he'd need to be stationed up here permanently and how he'd manage that, or would they put someone else who wasn't known?

The King didn't speak to them again until the next morning, but when he did, everything became very tense.

"We are leaving to go back to Step Six and petition to visit the capital."

"What do you mean, the Prince was clear that this wouldn't be until the bridge was built."

"Nonetheless, we're going to try. I cannot sit here for another month or more waiting, we need to try or go back to the capital."

"I control the only steps that grant such access, and you don't appear to be asking for permission."

"You'd try that on us?"

Silence had hung amongst them while the Queen weighed up all her options before she made a decision. "Go if that's what you want, but I'll be sending my emissary as well."

The King shrugged his shoulders. "I'll be bringing the rest of my knights through the city to accompany me; I trust that won't be an issue."

She waved him away and he didn't linger to argue the lack of courtesy she was demonstrating.

Clannack wasn't happy about what she'd just decided but if they were granted access then he'd be the first legitimate one of their court to gain access to Enderk.

No doubt they'd be concerned, but the information they'd get from it had to be worth the risks. At least that's what he tried to tell himself.

The Queen was clear in her brief to him before he left about needing to protect the agreement and watch for anything the King might try to do to undermine her.

She sent him with a patrol of warriors as well, not quite as many as the King's knights but he felt safe enough. When they arrived back across the water, after multiple boat loads, the reception was frosty.

They waited for several weeks camped roughly on the windy island before word came that they would be escorted to the capital. They'd been extended official invitations to the Prince's enthronement.

The trip toward En Carta was slow and steady and they were encircled by hundreds of soldiers wearing all-black outfits. There was no interaction amongst them and the two parties from Dharatan, making it a strange and mildly tense journey.

For his part, Clannack spent the entire time either trying to speak with his Skarian counterparts or watching Fuling.

Once or twice Clannack observed the man aside from his group behaving in a way that seemed familiar. To most people it might appear as though the man was simply lost in thought, simply staring out across the landscape.

But he had a look that seemed more like what he and his colleagues experience when communicating through their masks.

The giveaway for Clannack was seeing his lips move. Knowing he wasn't aware of those around him, Clannack moved in closer, until he could hear what he was saying.

~

"Yes, Uksod, we're here."

"Alright I will ready the King. We have company, the Ngaherians."

"Oh, you know."

"You sure? I could arrange something."

"Alright. His coronation, really? Very interesting. I am pleased we came then."

And then he shook his shoulders out and looked around. Clannack stepped back into the shadow of the tent he was using for cover. Nothing much of what he'd heard made sense except the implied threat to his group.

Who is this Uksod? I am sure I've heard that name before, but where? He can clearly communicate with others, does that mean he has a mask?

Clannack went back to his tent and lay down to think through what his options were. He was heading deep into Enderk territory with a small force of Ngaherians.

He didn't trust the Derks, and he trusted the Skarians less. But it was an opportunity worth taking, he just needed to make sure he survived and got back to Dharatan.

Lying there he watched the sun go down, and with the dark, decided to use his ability to talk to Tillandra through an animal.

He let his senses creep out from the tent and spread around until he found a likely critter. *A rabbit will do perfectly.* Gently he reached into its mind and tied a loop around it.

Then the suggestions began, helping it to locate the spot where he was. As he did so, Clannack sat up and moved to the tent flap, opening it.

His rabbit approached up to him, and his hand wrapped around it as soon as it was within reach. The loop was let go and Clannack swapped from attracting the animal to accessing the rabbit's life force.

He slid himself back and dropped into the Void. Then he pushed out toward his target, hoping she'd be able to join him immediately.

~

"Hello?"

"In All Jest, Mother."

"Hello…"

Clannack could only just make out her voice. The connection was very shaky, as though something was interfering with it.

"Mother, can you hear me, it's Clannack."

"Who… hello?"

Fuzzelbut. What's going on here.

The connection dropped, and Clannack looked at the rabbit in his hand. It was dead already. *That's strange, it shouldn't have been that quick.*

It had to be the ocean or the distance, the creature didn't offer enough for him to reach that far. Either he had to wait for Tillandra to try reaching him, if she could, or he would need to use something bigger.

There was little moonlight and while the Derk guards watched him from a distance, they left him be.

Clannack circled the outside of their camp area before weaving back toward tents and people. He changed direction as though having no direction to head to, passing by the tethered horses.

He stopped and stroked one. His watchers were on the other side of them and couldn't see what he was doing, only where he was, which didn't seem to bother them.

Keeping his eyes open, he left his hand on the horse he'd been stroking. *Sorry, pal.* He reached for its life force and felt the horse shudder a little.

That allowed him into the Void, and he tried again.

~

"In All Jest."

"In All Jest, Mother."

"Clannack, is that you?"

"Yes."

"Was it you not long before?"

"Yes, it was, I'm having trouble with the connection."

"Even now it's very weak, wavering as though you might lose it."

"Very strange. I'm using a big animal so it should be strong."

"Where are you?"

"Enderk."

"That might explain it."

"What?"

"The water. Crossing an ocean takes a much stronger connection and control."

Clannack sought out a stronger connection with the animal and made sure his focus was deep into the Void.

"What did you just do?"

Clannack explained.

"You seem clearer."

"Good."

"Why are you there?"

He told her everything he could, starting with where he was going, and working backward, in case the connection dropped.

"That's very dangerous, Clannack."

"I know. But there was little option." He could sense real concern in Tillandra's voice. "It might be a long time before we can get this close."

"Not at any cost. And if you are struggling to reach me so close, you will be lost to us when you're deep in their lands."

"It's okay, Mother. I want to know what's going on."

"Reach me when you can but be careful. Trying this might give you away. Don't take that risk."

"Okay, but then it might be some time."

"I'll try to be patient."

"What else should I know?" He could sense the connection weakening.

Without saying goodbye, he pulled out of the Void. The horse was wobbling on its feet, and Clannack took his hand off. *Darn. I can't afford him to collapse here with them watching me.*

He walked off casually, circling around the tents before ending up back at his own. He felt weak from what he'd done, and his stomach was not happy at all.

While he'd tried different animals before that was the first time he'd used a horse and he wasn't sure he wanted to do it again. *I'll just have to wait until I'm back on the mainland.*

114

LANI

Carnus walked beside her as they climbed the steep narrow path up to Midderbuilt.

"I'm fine, Carnus, you can go back."

"Not while there's guards following you I won't."

"You can't come into the city."

"Known, you don't have to repeat yourself."

She had been repeating herself. Despite her words she was glad for his company. What had happened down below was strange, as though the guards had been fed information about her.

But by who?

Maybe the man she was going to meet could provide her with answers. Once she was inside the gates, she was going to be on her own which concerned her as well.

There wasn't much choice for now; because of what had happened below, Carnus and she had rushed up here to get her out of harm's way.

Lani was certain that Tillandra went into the city to get to the stone under the mountain. Hopefully this man would help her do the same.

The gates ahead stood out because of their strangeness. While the massive arch and two doors were typical of other entrances to cities, they only had short walls that went no more than a dozen feet either side.

It was more symbolic than anything; the cliff faces, one each side, stopped anyone being able to get into the city via any option but the gates or the gantry.

A guard stood on the outside and held his spear across his body. "Only pass holders can enter."

Lani took out her token and showed it to him. The guard inspected it carefully, before handing it back. He turned and used the spear handle to bang three times on the right gate, which began to open.

"He cannot pass."

Lani nodded, and turned to Carnus. "Don't get into any trouble."

His flat look told her nothing, but he turned to face down the path they'd just climbed. Lani walked into the city and heard the gate close quickly behind her.

Midderbuilt was a town at best, despite everyone referring to it as a city. The Spire of Sand towered over it completely and she couldn't help but stop and stare at it.

This close she could see the sand spinning around it, moving slowly, but constantly. Even this close it made your head wobble to look at it.

"Best you don't stare at it like that."

Lani turned. One of the guards was talking to her.

"Sorry?"

"That wobbling you're doing, happens to anyone that stares, even those that grew up here."

"Right. Yeah, it's just always so fascinating."

"Where you heading?"

"I'm here to see a man called Ting... sorry his name is hard to remember."

"Tingfurlew."

"That's it."

"There's only one Ting in Midderbuilt. Up that way, until the back wall, his is the place backed right up to the spire. Looks like it's part cave, part building."

"Okay, thank you."

Lani hurried off; she didn't want to still be visible when any of the other guards came back. Then she realized she'd just told their colleague where she was going.

Stupid, Lani.

All the buildings in Midderbuilt were one level or close to it, made from stone and solid as the mountains that surrounded the city. Color was limited, everything gray or black, but solid and strong.

There was a busyness to the city, and no one paid her any attention. They all hurried about their business, eyes down, carrying their bags clutched to their bodies as though they carried precious cargo.

They probably do.

Tingfurlew's building was as easy to spot as the guard had said. A strange mix of mountain and building, it was one of only a few connected to the base of the mountain.

A large wooden and steel-braced door faced her and she swung the big knocker on it letting it bang on the surface, the sound echoing around where she stood.

"What?" A high-pitched shriek came from inside. "Busy."

Lani waited but whoever had spoken never came to the door. After her patience had run out, she lifted the knocker again and let it thump against the door.

"What now?" The same voice.

Lani wasn't sure but she thought she heard movement inside and waited. Then she heard a key turning and a bolt being removed on the inside, before the massive door opened.

She was surprised to see such a large door being held open by a man so little. His eyes looked angry, and he snarled up at her.

"Who are you? Why you bother Ting?"

"I'm from Tillandra."

"Who?"

"Tillandra."

"I know who that is, fool, who... are... you?" He spaced it out like he was talking to someone simple.

"I'm Lani."

Suddenly he grabbed her arm and pulled her through the door, slamming it closed. She nearly fell over as she stumbled through.

"Sorry, didn't want you out on the street. I've heard of you. You're the amulet girl."

"I guess."

"You wore the ring!" It wasn't a question.

"Yes."

"How did you do that?"

She smiled.

"Come, come, we drink and talk."

He whisked her past a large work table to some sofas. He patted one. "You sit here."

He went and got a jug and some goblets and put them on the table between the sofas before he clambered up onto his, propping himself up higher with cushions.

"You get to pour."

Lani smiled again. Despite his sharp tone, she already liked the strange man with beady little eyes and a long, twisted moustache. She poured them wine and passed him one.

"Tell me, why are you here?"

She reached into her tunic and pulled out the pouch. Carefully she pushed it out onto the table in front of him.

"Holy Seth! That's the amulet."

"It is."

"Put it away, quickly. Away, we don't want it here."

Lani let the pouch draw it back in, then twisted to open her satchel, lying on the floor. She drew out the box inside and placed the pouch within that.

"My box."

"Your box?"

"I gave that box to Mother; she gave it to you."

"It's the only thing that stops the power of the stone."

"Just leave it in there, don't show it anymore."

"I can't. If it stays in there too long, I get sick."

His face screwed up in confusion.

"It's too hard to explain."

"That stone is much worse than she told me."

"What do you mean?"

"Just from here, I could sense it. It's bad, Lani, very bad, like there's evil inside it."

"No need to tell me, I've felt it. It's bonded to me."

She pulled up the sleeve of her tunic and showed the mark on her underarm.

Tingfurlew shook his head. "You must get rid of it. Bad. Why did you bring it here?"

"To try and get it off me. I have to see the Lady in the Stone."

He nodded. "I see. You know how?"

She shook her head. "Tillandra just told me you'd show me how."

A loud thumping on the door made Tingfurlew jump in his seat.

"Not good, two in one day. Quick, put that away, not in the box."

"Why?"

"Just do it, back where you had it."

Lani fumbled trying to quickly put the amulet back in her tunic before returning the empty box back into her satchel.

"Good. Sit there, have a drink and be calm, let me see who it is." She watched him grab a long nasty-looking dagger from his bench, which was like a sword for him, before he headed to the door.

"What?" The same response she had gotten, in his high-pitched voice. "Busy, leave me."

"Open up, old man. It's the city guards."

"Busy, go away."

"Open up." The thumping continued.

Tingfurlew opened the door. "What do you want?"

"We're here to check on you, Tingfurlew. You have a guest, don't you?"

"So?"

"Just want to check she's not trying to cause you harm. Let us in."

Tingfurlew did as he was asked, and two guards walked into the room toward Lani.

"Well, if it isn't you."

She looked at the guard that had harassed her at Traveler's Rest, and the guard who'd given her directions. *Foolish Lani.* She said nothing.

"What do you want with her? She's my guest, and the mayor will hear of your intrusion."

"Look, Tingfurlew, we're just protecting you. We had some suspicions about this one and needed to make sure you're safe."

Ting brandished the dagger in front of himself. "You think I can't protect myself?"

The guard laughed, the way a young man laughs at an older one who he thinks is easy prey.

"All is good, go now."

"You sure?"

"Already said it, now leave."

The two guards reluctantly walked back out of his building, the main one turning and staring at Lani for a lengthy look before Ting closed the door with a bang.

This time he locked and slid the door bar down.

"Nice friends you've made."

"They tried to set me up down in the camp."

"Then we need to get you to her quickly before someone does something bad."

"What do you mean?"

"You don't want to know."

UKSOD

He'd almost had a bounce in his step as he'd descended to the depths of the mountain, so good was Uksod's mood about how things were going.

Yantarnaya had been a different entity since she'd been able to sense King Ahn's amulet.

Karpenmor had helped seal the deal for the bridges, and soon everything that Uksod and his goddess had planned, for what seemed an eternity, would be in place.

While the boy's enthusiasm had meant the bridges had been built quicker there was still a lot to be cleaned up after him. He was an ideas man, not the ultimate person for delivering a long-term solution.

Each of the islands needed to be built out, supplies put in place, and the capabilities for hosting an army. The barracks would need to be completed and then the soldiers could be rotated in.

Uksod had made sure that more thorough directions were delivered to the Mayor of Ponte about the sizes needed for everything.

He also thought that he would need to suggest to the heir about creating a title for someone just to oversee the Steps. It was going to be a very specific job to manage, and a city mayor was probably not the right one for it.

No other foreigners should be allowed to cross, with all the trading to be done only in Cumerc.

That will be its name soon enough. Once the eggs are in place, they'll have little choice. It will be too late before they understand what the amber will be used for.

~

"You come again; your timing is impeccable."

"Why, mistress?"

"The latest amulet has been leashed."

"Which one?"

"Keep up, Uksod, the third out of the four."

"Four? When did the fourth appear?"

"Recently. It showed up in the desert -- again -- but now it's hidden from me. This other one arrived near the edge of the desert and now it's deep in some forests."

Uksod got better directions from her with some difficult questions.

"Morskan then."

"What?"

"The people in that area, are Morskan."

"Whoever the descendant is there, he has bonded with it."

"A difficult man, their Supreme Commander, that will be a challenge."

"Just do it, Uksod. No time for any more excuses, bring them home to me."

"This one hides away from everyone deep in the forest, in a place called the White City."

"Just get him to come, Uksod. If I could reach out to him, I would."

"I think we'll be able to help with that."

"How?"

"The boy had the barbarian queen agree to let us enter our temple in Cumerc. Once we have someone in there, I will place the stones back."

"I am impressed, Uksod. That might help, this amulet feels very weak, but

maybe when the stones are there, I will be able to reach out. When is that happening?"

There it was, the hint of impatience. Even though everything was going well, she still had little tolerance for everything not happening immediately.

"Not until the bridge is complete, mistress, and the barbarians have their grain."

"Why?"

"It's the deal that was made, just a minor delay. It will come, soon enough."

"No, not soon enough."

Uksod wasn't sure what to say.

"There's another thing. That missing ring, it showed up again."

"Where?"

"The same place as before. Only briefly, but it was there."

"We have people almost there, but it will be like looking for an oyster in the ocean."

"If I knew more, Uksod, I would tell you."

Uksod could sense she was becoming frustrated. "The King is on the move. They are coming this way."

"Yes, I can feel it. I sensed something amongst them."

"What?"

"I didn't get specifics, but there's magic amongst them."

"The priest? Or is it just the amulet?"

"No this was different, it wasn't amber, it wasn't us. There's someone or something amongst them that's with them."

"Them?"

"My siblings, Uksod. I do not like that."

"Do you know who?"

"No, but when they come here, if they use it, I will know."

"Then what? Kill them?"

"That will depend, Uksod, on what it is, or who it is. It might even be to our advantage, don't do anything rash."

Uksod said nothing, simply rolling his eyes. *Rash, as if.*

"When will you go to Dharatan?"

"Karpenmor will be High Prince very soon, mistress, then I will make plans. But not until after King Ahn has come. Perhaps when he returns I will go with him, as you suggested."

"Good. I will be interested to learn more about him when I have his amulet close by."

"You'll need to be careful, we need them alive and well, to be able to use his armies over on Dharatan."

"I know, Uksod. You always slow everything down. Now they are back I can feel it within my grasp. I want it all done now."

"Patience, mistress. We are so far ahead from where we were just a little while ago."

She laughed at him, a sinister sound that made his skin crawl.

"Patience! That's what you think. I've had that much patience with you, with everything. It's been centuries, Uksod. I want it now!"

"Sorry, mistress. I meant…"

"It doesn't matter, Uksod. Just get ready to go when you're done playing kingmaker, I want the eggs in place, and amber spreading where I can reach it. And I want all of the amulets back under my control."

The conversation was over, he didn't need to hear her say it, he knew. *How did all the good end up making her so angry?*

~

The exchange left him flat. He knew it would pass, he'd put it out of his mind, and move forward, but nonetheless each step felt difficult, his mind wanting to take it out on someone else. *No, not today.*

Uksod turned to what she'd told him. The Morskans would be difficult to move. All accounts about their ruler were that he was a maniacal recluse who never left the capital, deep in their jungles.

How will we get him to come here?

That might have to be the first place that Uksod placed some beacons. If Yantarnaya could reach him through a beacon, she could influence his mind and get him to travel.

If.

Uksod needed to find out if the bridge work had started on the Cumerc side. The sooner that bridge was in place the better. Then the eggs would be in the temple.

It is all good, she's just impatient.

Even saying it in his thoughts worried him, as if she sensed them, she'd punish him.

What of this magic she mentioned? Who or what is amongst the delegation?

Uksod thought again about the emissary from the Ngaherians. Everyone's description about him had caused Uksod to be wary of him. Perhaps his instincts had detected what his mistress had found.

Uksod knew he could do nothing about it until he got here, but it was a challenge he looked forward to. It wasn't something he could leave to the boy; this was something he needed to do.

Perhaps he could learn something useful from this plant from the other side. It could not be coincidental that they were showing up now, just as King Ahn arrived.

All in good time.

One thing that could be dealt with was the lost Vrah ring which Yantarnaya had spoken of. Not that Uksod would be the person to solve it, that would be all One's pleasure.

The Vrah leader still carried the scar of that loss as did all the Vrah. They had never left a ring behind or lost one before, and it would be a relief to One that he could put that to rest before he stepped down.

Once the enthronement was done the Vrah could do whatever they needed to find it in that Dharatan city, kill whoever had hidden it from them and bring it home.

And something that Uksod didn't have to worry about. His mind needed to pay attention to these remaining weeks and seeing the boy crowned.

Let's hope the planets align as predicted, I don't think I could go through this for another year.

116

LANI

ingfurlew's home suddenly felt very small. Lani knew they were trapped inside if the guards, or whoever was directing them, wanted to attack them.

He might sound like an angry dog, but she wasn't sure Tingfurlew could defend her if it came to a big fight. The one man she wanted by her side was locked out of the city.

"Eat, you look like a stick!"

The jeweler had laid out a spread of foods on the table between the sofas and darted away to grab a fresh jug. He banged it on the table then picked it up again and poured red wine into her goblet and his own.

Lani picked at the food, her stomach not particularly interested, but she knew he was right. Since she'd been locked in Odajeen's mind, her body had begun wasting away, and her muscles were much weaker than they had been.

"What next?"

"When it's dark I'll take you to your room."

"My room?"

"I have a guest hut; you don't think you're staying here?"

Lani felt foolish by the way he said it, as though she should know better. "I thought you were taking me to the..." Not that anyone was listening, but she didn't want to say it out loud.

"That's exactly why you go there. Inside there is an access."

"Oh."

"She didn't tell you anything, did she?"

"It was very difficult; she couldn't speak to me. I got her instructions through others."

He grunted and stuffed some food into his mouth, chomping away on it loudly, his beady eyes staring at her. Every time he finished eating, he would stroke one side of his moustache or the other, pulling the strands down and twisting.

"Do you still have your brooch?"

She nodded.

"Can I see it?"

Lani was surprised by the request, especially after his reaction with the amulet. She reached back into her tunic and pulled out the jewel, the blue stone shining much brighter than she'd expected.

"It's home."

"What do you mean?"

This time he had a smile on his face. He walked over and held out his hand. Lani surprised herself when she gave it to him without a pause.

"It's from the Citadel Stone, that was cut by the Lapidarist."

"Who?"

"The one who cut the stones."

"All of them?"

"The blue stones, yes. This one, and the one Mother brings, plus its companions in Anderwell."

Lani now understood what he meant. "I didn't know that's what this was."

"Explains why it protects you."

"Why is it shining so?"

"It can sense its own mother. It's feeding off it."

"Feeding?"

"Energy. It is getting energy."

Lani nodded. That's what had happened when she'd been in

Anderwell. Out of everything that had happened recently the thought made her feel happier.

She had a long connection with this stone, and knowing it was stronger again felt good, even if she didn't really understand how it worked.

"Who made the amulet?"

"The Lapidarist."

"The same person?"

"No, like same, but his brother."

"I don't understand."

"She will tell you more, but there were two brothers, one made this," he handed it back to her, "the other those evil things."

Tingfurlew seemed to have nothing else to say, and Lani focused on eating and drinking, until her stomach hurt from having too much. "Can you take me now?"

"Big rush, but okay. If you must be gone, then go, but take the box and don't bring it back."

"I will if I can."

Tingfurlew threw on his coat, which just made him look wider, and slightly comical, before he grabbed his blade again. He gave her a key. "To the hut. Lock it inside and don't open it, no matter who it sounds to be. Even me."

Lani felt concerned by that. "Okay."

"Only open it when you're ready to leave, but never leave the door unlocked, understand?"

"What do I do inside?"

"There's a door, but if you can't find it, I cannot help you. It will either invite you or it won't. If you are there two days without getting in, you should leave."

Lani felt deflated again, it felt like another obstacle that she had no idea on how to get through, when she just wanted to solve the amulet connection once and for all.

"Follow me, stay close, like sticky rice."

He locked his own door as soon as she was out and grabbed her hand, pulling her off to the left. As fast as his little legs would go, they hurried along between other buildings until they came to a smaller hut.

Lani kept checking over her shoulder but saw no one, despite feeling as though they were being watched. The little man stopped outside the door.

"Here you are. Good luck, Lani."

"Thanks." She fumbled with the key getting it in the door and was grateful when it finally unlocked.

She turned to say goodbye, but Tingfurlew had already started off, so she slipped inside and only felt better once the door was locked. Lani removed the key and put it to one side on a small table against one wall.

The room had a lantern burning, which surprised her. Ting had been with her the whole time, and the door was locked, so she had no idea how that would be burning.

Not that she minded, having to do that herself in the dark would have been difficult. Looking around the small hut she tried to see where this special door was.

A bed filled much of the space, then the table with her key on it. She placed her satchel on the bed before sitting beside it. There were only two places that could harbour a door: the wall with the table and the one on the mountain side.

The first would have led back outside, which meant either it was the mountain-facing wall, or the floor. *Don't forget that option.* Nothing about the wall looked like anything other than a solid wall.

What now?

An image of the brooch popped into her mind, and without any better idea, she pulled the jewel back out and looked at it. The stone was still gleaming, possibly even brighter than it had back in Tingfurlew's home.

Lani stood and walked toward the wall, holding the brooch in front of her, letting its light shine onto the surface. The wall looked solid, with no visible doorway in it. She stood clueless about to what to do.

Suddenly the brooch began to pull toward the door on its own, and Lani moved with it. It dragged her arm downward and to her right. A small hole appeared in the wall, and she bent down to look.

Inside she could see the impression of the ring she'd worn before; the one with the Jesters head on it. The brooch tugged in that direction, the stone almost squeezing into the hole.

A loud click sounded, and then the door popped from the wall several inches. Lani jumped back at the movement, only to relax when she saw it stop.

She had to push the bed all the way across the room to open the door enough to fit in. Grabbing her satchel, she slung it over her shoulder and stepped into the dark corridor behind the wall, the brooch in her hand.

A shudder went down her back when she heard the door behind her close. Thankful for the shining brooch, she looked ahead. *In for a toe, in for the whole foot.*

117

TILLANDRA

If the map room was meant to give her solace, it was failing. The darkness felt oppressive to her today, not calming. Tillandra knew it was her mood more than anything else, but the sense of the darkness growing was real for her.

She'd been so used to seeing a cluster of lights above Anderwell on the table with just a few other blue lights floating across the continent that the current one felt very different.

The main reason Tillandra had come down was to see if Clannack showed up on the map. Thankfully he did. Now he was on Enderk and heading east.

What was interesting was that the shape that they knew as Enderk was filling in with detail. Whereas before it had been little more than an outline, with the islands between, the area behind Clannack now had more features.

Fascinating.

She moved around the table closer to it. It showed what looked like the start of a river and mountains or hills. Even the islands now showed the bridges across them. *Imagine how it will look when he gets to their capital.*

Tillandra realized that she had no idea where that might be on their continent.

Back across the bridges she found what had to be Junther, in the middle of Malamig. *Stay safe, old man.* With the ring in the box, Tillandra felt confident he'd not meet anyone on his way back.

What she wasn't sure of was whether he should divert to help Goran or not. She had to give their rogue Jester credit — he had already crossed the mountains between Lletem and Morska and, based on his light, was about to enter the big forests there.

The light that pinpointed Hallendell looked weaker to Tillandra. She didn't want to think about why, especially after the dream she'd had.

Hurry, Goran!

Beantic's was in the centre of the map, still in Callet. As much as Tillandra wanted to help Hallendell, and had considered sending her to help as well, Beantic's role was to stabilise their network, and there was more than Hallendell's situation happening.

Maybe Junther could leave the box and ring with Bea, and head toward Goran? It was an option, especially with Clannack now across the sea.

The last one of theirs that had been on any Enderk soil had been Ashantha, and that had not ended well. She hoped that nothing like that would befall Clannack.

She doubted she could take that again and not want to seek vengeance. Thinking about Ashantha's death did anger her, and she got a sense of the feeling that must have driven Odajeen to do what she had done.

Tillandra doubted she could have done the same, but she did want to find a way to get revenge for Ashantha. Perhaps it was by what they were doing now, trying to stop the wave the prophecy warned about?

She felt better for that, knowing that she didn't have to harm anyone, but by doing her job, their jobs, they could achieve much more. *He served as a martyr to warn us. We'll honor that.*

Over to the far west Tillandra could see Leo's light and wondered what was happening now with Lani. *I'll seek him out shortly.*

That the girl was free from being trapped in Odajeen's mind was a good thing, but unless they could free her from the amulet, she was a problem.

She hoped that Thenis could do something to help with that. Somehow the girl had to get free of it, and it needed to be destroyed.

Gimbden was in the desert south of Watersend. The man seemed to be thriving from the opportunity to organise the armies and building up defences. He'd hated his previous assignment, but since that mayor was now gone, the current one and he were achieving much.

Sinder had to be moved, he was adding no value. Tillandra had the time to sort that now and moving him to Bundok was probably the most logical, or even back here for a bit.

Make a decision and act on it, Tillandra.

Her last scan of the map took her to the far coast of Rohumaa and where Lionel was now based, Okeans. He hadn't seen anything else untoward to report but had said that the compound belonging to Daskare was finished now with a lot less activity around it.

It already had enough men contained within it to be a problem, but without someone close to the Queen in Rohumaa, they had little opportunity to warn her or influence her.

For all they know she could be fully on board with whatever King Ahn, or his priest, were up to. While Junther wasn't near the King, Clannack was, so at least they could keep tabs on him.

It's time to speak to Leo most of all.

She left the map room and slowly climbed the stairs back to her office. Everything felt duller and less vibrant, mostly because all the people who used to keep her busy were gone.

Even Lani had taken up much of her time before she'd gone into Odajeen's head. Tillandra looked at the stack of books they hadn't had the chance to go through.

What would we have learned from those if she was still here?

The Occultation kept unravelling and the one thing Tillandra needed was information. She still had hoped there was more they could learn from the journals, but that opportunity was gone for now.

Lani can head back soon, hopefully, then we can catch up.

Her steps took her out the back of the college and into the gardens.

The late afternoon sky was clear, and a sliver of orange began to mark it as the day closed.

Tillandra folded her long legs and sat awkwardly on the ground, reaching out for the trunk of the tree before her, reflecting briefly on how it had changed since Peka had been with them.

~

"In All Jest, Leo."

"Mother, In All Jest."

"What news?"

"Lani is in Midderbuilt, there's been some trouble."

He explained to her about what had happened and what Carnus had told them of the guards following her into the city.

"Is she safe?"

"As far as we know. We can't get inside to check, but a note came to us from Tingfurlew, to say she was in the hut. Does that make sense to you?"

"Yes. She is safe then."

"Carnus spends every day up outside the gates waiting for her."

"She could be gone longer than you might think."

"What do you mean?"

"Time there is very different."

"I remember."

"I forgot you went in there. You will have to tell me more about that when you get back."

"We're coming back there after this?"

"Yes, I would think so. It's the safest place for her, and you need to learn more."

He had nothing to say to that.

"How is Odajeen?"

"Getting stronger, she was very weak. It took a lot out of her."

"Purple?"

"Quiet, she says very little. I think it's just all overwhelming to her, she spends her time with Odajeen."

"Let me know if anything changes."

~

Leo still intrigued her, but Tillandra knew he was exactly where he needed to be. If he hadn't been there they'd never have gotten Lani to Thenis and got her free.

Things seemed to work out that way, as though an invisible hand was directing things. She wished she knew more about what it had planned, Tillandra much preferred to be in control of events.

What she had to do next made her stomach turn, and she considered putting it off. *I have to know.* She sought out Hallendell, and tried to speak with her, but there was no answer.

Tillandra could feel herself getting upset and had to know how the woman was doing. She changed her approach and used the mask to see things from her perspective and regretted it immediately.

It was just like her dream but instead of seeing it from across the room, Tillandra was seeing it as though in Hallendell's eyes.

She was hanging by her hands, her head drooped toward the floor. The room, or cell, was dark but for a sliver of light, and all Tillandra could see on the floor was blood.

Tears ran down her eyes and she pulled away from the tree and brushed her hands over her face. He fears weren't imagined, Hallendell was in serious trouble and only one person could help her.

Please hurry, Goran!

LANI

When she'd been here a few days earlier it felt quite different to now. Lani felt the same vibration, the hum, through her whole body, but it seemed much closer now that she was herself.

The brooch shone as brightly as any lantern she could have carried, and Lani swore she could feel a slightly different vibration within it. Her fingers seemed to sense it and tingled.

She couldn't tell if it was five minutes or forty, the walk went on for some time, but equally it wasn't difficult. Her expectation was the thing that made it more difficult. Lani knew what she was approaching, and she wanted to see it.

Even the expectation couldn't prepare her for when she turned out of the corridor into the cavern where the Citadel Stone stood. In a way it made the cavern seem small, because of how much of it was filled with the base of the stone.

The closer she got to it the more the space above opened and Lani tipped her head back, unable to see the top of it far up into the mountain.

Amazing.

~

"Welcome."

"Back again. This time is so much better."

"It's good to see you got free. The idea worked, which is good."

"It did, although I had my doubts. Why me?"

"Why you, what, Lani?"

"Why is it me that's in the middle of all this? I never asked for it."

"That's where you are wrong, Lani."

"How?"

"You came into being just for this purpose. As you see yourself now maybe not, but your being was called to it. Your unique combinations given to you by your parents."

"Is that just your way of not answering the question?"

"I did answer it. Do you believe in the prophecy?"

"I have no idea. I have heard only one part of it, and it seemed to describe me, but the words could be taken in any number of ways."

"I think not. But everything that's in them has come to pass, so far. Including you."

"You're saying I had no choice anyway; this was always part of my destiny?"

"So it would seem."

"You're a god, are you not?"

"That's what your kind call us, yes."

"Don't you control everything, what happens?"

Thenis laughed inside Lani's mind. The way she communicated was such a pleasant thing, and so easy, Lani wondered why everyone didn't speak like this.

"It's not the way things work. There are many things we can do, but we do not control the greater worlds or how they unfold. In fact, we operate much like the Jesters do."

"You sneak around?"

Again, she laughed.

"In a manner of words, we do. It's more like we operate behind the scenes and influence the direction things might take. Prepare people for events, make sure those that need to be somewhere make it there."

"Like now?"

"Yes."

"You pushed me into Odajeen's mind?"

"Oh no, Lani, that was all you. We can only nudge and direct, there are few times we can make someone do something that they might have no wish to do. Oftentimes the result of our nudging causes all sorts of complications."

"Like me meeting Odajeen."

"Yes, that wasn't exactly planned, nor that she'd have suffered damage to her head, which opened a doorway for her to see the brooch."

"I am glad she did."

"In the end it worked out okay, but it could have gone wrong several times."

"What now?"

"We're going to attempt to figure out what binds you to the amulet."

"You don't know?"

"No, we do not. This is one of those unintended consequences of people and things. Had the amulet never left the pouch it would never have bonded to you."

Lani felt disappointed. After everything she'd just been through her hope had been that Thenis, or her other gods, would know exactly what to do.

"It's okay, there will be a way that doesn't involve you dying, we just have to figure out what that is."

"I hope so."

"I need to ask you something."

"Okay."

"If there is no way, what does that mean?"

"I thought you just said that there will be a way?"

"I did, this is a separate question. If we can't, then what does that mean for you, for the amulet? What would you do then?"

Lani stood there, the brooch almost jumping up and down in her right hand, soaking in the power of the bright white stone. The more she looked at it the more she could see the blueness within. They were the same stone, just the brooch had taken on more of the blueness.

"Before, I believed that maybe I should go to Enderk, to where this comes from. Simply let them take me, and be done with it, so I can learn what they know."

"And now?"

"Having seen how they kill without a second thought, and who it is they send for me, I don't believe I could ever trust them. If I had no choice, then I'd simply have to live in Anderwell or close by, until..."

"Until?"

"Until I die."

"Would that be such a bad thing, Lani?"

"No, it would not. I wanted to get away from there, but it's my home now. I can see that."

Lani thought about all the people she'd been surrounded by and how they had treated her. Even the party she'd traveled with had all risked much to help her.

They were her family now, her friends, and she was as much a part of them as they were her.

"Then we're ready to begin."

"Did my answer matter?"

"Yes, it did."

"What would have happened if you hadn't liked what I said?"

"That doesn't matter because you answered from your heart, I can see that. And we're not like them, Lani. We don't take lives simply because people don't follow our thinking."

Lani wanted to believe the god, but she still felt a small chill run down her arms.

"You should go to the alcove to your right, set your things down and drink some refreshment. It will help with what we need, and then you must take that... 'thing'... from the shield you're using."

"Won't it show them where it is?"

"Not in here, Lani. The stone will control that, which is why it was so important to do this here."

"Okay."

Lani walked over to the alcove. It was strange she'd thought she would see someone in the stone, the way the voice came to her, but it was simply a massive gem stone radiating light and something else.

It took her a minute or two to get into a calm state of being. Initially her body and mind wanted to jump about, her fingers twitching, her thoughts racing in all directions.

She knew this was as dangerous as anything she'd done so far, despite the warm and loving feelings surrounding her from the stone.

"Now the amulet."

Lani looked at the box on the floor in front of her crossed feet. As she placed her hand onto it, everything inside her was conflicted.

The amulet would take hold of her, she knew that, and expected it, but Thenis had said the Citadel Stone would control it. She hoped so, things didn't always work out as planned when the amulet was involved.

In for a toe, in for the whole foot.

~

"That is the oddest saying, Lani."

"It's just something the man I used to work for would say." She told Thenis about it and heard the goddess laughing just before she was swept into a torrent of white.

LANI

Lani stood in the middle of an immense whiteness and immediately felt scared. The similarities to how she had felt inside Odajeen's head were too much.

Like then she could sense she had a body but there were no actual sensations from it. She couldn't feel her skin, or her breath.

At least she could see this time, which was better than before, but being able to see didn't ease her fears that she'd left one trap for another.

What is this?

"You're within the stone's power, Lani. Don't be scared."

Easy for you to say.

That was when the woman appeared in front of her, or the shimmering version of a woman.

"It is you."

"Yes, or a reasonable likeness to me."

"I know you from the markets in Barnen."

"Yes, you do, you've met me many times, Lani."

"But out there."

"Maybe some other time we will have an opportunity to discuss it, but not now."

"What is this?"

"I told you the truth, we don't know for sure what to do about the amulet bonding, so this is a place to try."

"I had hoped you would be able to fix it."

"We will if we can."

"We?"

That was when another figure appeared, also a shimmering version of a person. And again, Lani recognized him.

"Rainbow?"

"That's what you would call me. How are you, child?"

"So... you're a god?"

"Indeed I am, young lady."

"But... Rainbow, surely that's not your real name." Even here in this place it looked as though his beard was flecked with color.

"No, Lani, it is not, but I like it anyway."

"Can I ask?"

"What?"

"Your real name?"

"Oh that. You can, it's Okicheck."

"Oh."

"Disappointed?"

"No, but I think I like Rainbow better."

"It's more convenient while in your world."

"What now?"

"We are waiting for one more. He's a bit of a tricky one." Rainbow chuckled, which made Lani feel better.

"Tricky, am I? At least I'm not always playing the fool."

The other man appeared on Thenis's left. He was smaller than Rainbow and had long red hair that hung to his waist. It was parted and untied, and he brushed it off his face as he looked between the other too.

"Good of you to show up, Hembleth."

"Some of us have things to do, sister. I fear I'm going to miss the boy's ceremony."

Lani saw Thenis look at him with furrowed brows.

"What's the plan?"

"I've spoken with Okicheck already, and he's none the wiser than I am about it. Do you have any thoughts?"

"I can sense it here now, it's like the other amber I've felt over there. The way it touches you is very different to our stone."

"Has she done something to it?"

"I've not done…"

"Not you, child, Yantarnaya."

Lani felt very foolish, and decided to say nothing unless she was asked directly.

"The only thing that comes close to this behavior are the rings and the masks, but they do it by the process, not by their own selection."

"And both stay with them until the wearer dies."

"Except our girl here."

All three looked at her.

"You wore the ring, and then it came off. How did that occur, Lani?" the God Hembleth asked her.

"It was a man without any eyes, a seer, in Union, that did it."

"A seer took the ring off?"

"Yes."

"Did he say how, or did he do anything specific?"

"He told me he asked it to."

Rainbow laughed. "Of course, he would."

"What's so funny, brother?"

"Have you not met him?"

"I don't think I've had the pleasure."

"You'd like him, he's an old man with an interesting manner."

Thenis spoke. "I'm interested in why it did what he asked."

"He said that it didn't want to be there, as though it had happened accidentally."

"What of your amulet?"

"I asked him to take that too, but he wouldn't even go near it. He said it was a great evil, and they'd all been told to stay away from it."

"By whom?"

"Their leader, I think. It was a while ago."

"The leader of The Eyes being involved, says something. It's not like them to be particularly involved in much to do with the way of people."

"They're on the move."

"What do you mean, brother?" Thenis looked at Hembleth.

"There's a lot of them that have left their island."

"For what reason?"

"I do not know, sister, but one of them was killed by Derks. I've heard they do not take kindly to harm of their kind."

"That is not a rumor, it's a truth. We don't need them interfering at this time."

"It might be too late. If they seek retribution, they might be already planning something."

"I must visit her then."

Lani was completely bewildered by the conversation.

"Shall I ask it?"

"Ask it what, Okicheck?"

"Ask the amulet to release her?"

"If you think it will help."

Without warning the space around them changed and they stood in a circle. Between them floated the amulet, seemingly twice it's normal size.

No one said a word, but Lani could feel pressure around her arm, and around her head. At first she was able to ignore it but it continued to grow until she had to close her eyes and grit her teeth.

"What is it, Lani?" It was Rainbow's voice.

"It's squeezing my head… and my arm."

"Stop it, brother."

And instantly the pain went. Lani opened her eyes to find the amulet floating in front of her, gently spinning around.

"How exactly did you ask it?"

"It didn't respond so I tried something else," Hembleth replied. *"Pulling, twisting, that sort of thing. It didn't budge."*

"And yet, the effort transferred to Lani. Lani, you talk about your arm, what's the relationship to it?"

She explained about the point on her arm where the bond had been made the first time, and that she could feel the connection from there when it was out, like now.

"I want to try something," Rainbow said. *"I'll probe around that area, see what the connection looks like."*

Lani could feel what he was doing. It started like an itch, but then began to burn. She didn't like it, and the amulet liked it even less.

Everything around her began to waver and then she felt herself being pulled into the stone. She had pushed her mind into its power, and she could feel the spot that was being irritated by something.

It was a memory she was meant to understand, a recent memory, but she couldn't. Everything was about her needing to stop that itch... soothe that burn.

What should I remember about it? What is it?

The drive inside of her, inside of the amulet, was too strong and she gathered its power and pushed at the spot that irritated her. The will she pushed at it with felt a resistance, like a barrier pushing back.

Her arm burned more, her anger grew, and she gathered her will again. This time she flung it out with all her intention at the source of the pain forming on her arm.

And with a loud bang she felt the pain disappear. She rushed backward, her mind flying back into her own body, and she dropped to the ground.

"What did she do? What happened? Okicheck, are you okay?"

Lani forced her eyes open. The image of the man she knew as Rainbow lay flat on his back, while the two other gods looked back and forth from him to her.

"What did you do, Lani?"

"I don't know. Is he alright?"

"I don't know. But what just happened was very bad. Very, very bad."

Lani saw the look of almost horror on Thenis's face and cowered back from it. *What have I done?*

LANI

Rainbow came good a few minutes later, standing up and, after looking from side to side as if to find out where he was, he burst into laughter.

"What's so funny, brother?"

"I haven't been bullied about so much in a thousand years."

"Do tell."

Lani was even more confused about what had happened.

"That amulet is much more powerful than it looks. I couldn't help myself once I began trying to pull it away. It resisted fiercely."

"It kicked back like a horse?" Thenis asked.

"No, that was Lani."

"I didn't do anything!"

"Ah but you did, lass. Your connection to that amulet is very strong. As soon as I put my efforts into pulling it free, instinctively your will combined with it and... here I am." Rainbow still had a smile on his face.

"It felt like it was burning up my arm and into my head, I just tried to make that stop."

"She's extremely powerful when combined with that jewel... extremely!"

"We need a more sophisticated approach, brother. You were ever the impatient one."

"Yes, yes, Hembleth, that's your new name today, is it? What do you suggest?"

"Somehow, I think the asking is actually correct. There's something about the connection that isn't quite right."

"What do you mean, Oki?"

To Lani, Thenis seemed the quiet one amongst the two male figures.

"A feeling I got when I was trying to latch onto it. As though she was not quite the right person for it to bond to, but there was a lack of choice."

"Not very helpful."

"I'm just telling you how it felt. I tried asking nicely, but it would appear that our friend the Seer had a more enticing way."

"Or that the amulet is nowhere near as easy. Keep in mind the ring was from our side, this is altogether different."

"It is heavily powered by the Citadel Stone, not that it's replenishing it, but the amulet is able to draw from the stone's power. That gives it much more strength that it would have normally."

"Who is it meant to be connected to?"

All three of them turned to look at her.

"What do you mean?" Thenis asked.

"If it was near to that person, would it let go of me, and go to them?"

"That's an interesting question, Lani. Oki?"

"It didn't say. Or should I say there was no indication. Keep in mind it was a sensation I got, as though it was a key that seemed to fit in the lock, but when you turned it there was a lot of resistance."

"Can we destroy the stone inside it?"

"I thought about that. The effort to do that would be immense. More importantly, I'm not sure what it would do to her."

"Me, you mean?"

"Yes, you, Lani. The bond it had is connected to you in a way I don't really understand. It's deep inside, both your body, but your mind as well."

"Great."

"Don't lose hope just yet, we've only just begun. If it was easy, we'd have already found the solution."

Hembleth had been quiet in this last little exchange, but now he spoke up. *"We should try to probe around that connection. One of them at least. If we can sense how it's connected perhaps we can untie it."*

"I kind of already tried that."

"No, you tried to pull it free. Think about your time on their world, have you ever worked with thread and a knot?"

"I see what you mean, brother. I pulled at it, when that might have made it tighter."

"That's my thought. We are looking for the main thread, or connection, somewhere we might be able to unravel it from. If it's as I'm trying to describe it."

Rainbow looked at Lani. *"Try not to kick me back again."*

"I didn't really do anything."

"In there you did." He pointed toward her head. *"You could sense what I was doing and your inner will fought back using the amulet, with a lot of force."*

"Don't go pulling anything again then, perhaps?"

"Yes, indeed. We'll be back."

Not that the men went anywhere at all, but their talking stopped which was calming all on its own.

"They can be a bit much when they are together."

Lani looked at Thenis. She had been much more in the background than in Lani's previous encounters.

"Are they your older brothers?"

"No, dear, what makes you say that?"

"You seem to let them do all the talking."

"We've been around each other for a very long time, I've learned it's easier to let them do their thing for a while before I get involved. It ends up being a lot easier. Besides, I'm not doing what they are doing, so I can keep an eye on you."

"Why on me? I'm not going anywhere."

"Because if he's doing something that is affecting you, I can stop him. We decided to do that because you weren't in control of what happened earlier."

"But you didn't say anything?"

"We don't have to. This talking thing the way we are with you, that's so you can be involved. But we communicate in other ways also, all at the same time."

Lani suddenly felt a burning in her arm. It came out of nowhere and went from nothing to excruciating in seconds.

"What is it, Lani?"

"My... arm..." Lani had fallen to her knees. She gripped her right arm with her left and squeezed it. "... it's burning."

The intensity of it grew even more, her whole arm felt as though it was on fire, she wanted to scratch at it, to tear whatever was doing it out.

Suddenly it stopped, as abruptly as it had started. She opened her eyes and only Thenis was standing there.

"What happened, Lani?"

"It burned, so much, I couldn't stand it. I wanted to rip my arm away, but then it just stopped. Where are the others?"

"Good question. They were right there, up until that last moment."

By the time she'd finished speaking the two men had shimmered back into view.

"You really don't want to give it up, Lani, do you?"

"What do you mean?"

Hembleth continued. *"You kicked us out of what we were doing as soon as we got our hands on the core strands."*

"Your hands? All I could feel was this burning, as though my whole arm was on fire. And then..."

"What?"

"I got the feeling as though I wanted to tear it out, whatever it was that was burning me, and then it went."

"I think that was us. You wanted to tear us out."

"But it was in there." Lani pointed at the skin of her forearm.

"Where we must have been symbolically. We followed threads from the stone toward you. It was very difficult to go against the amulet, it's quite seductive. But when we got to the place that felt like where it bonded to you, we chose separate threads to tease at."

"Mine felt as though it was part of you, not a separate thread but something that grew out of you, except in one spot."

"Where?"

"Oh, just from the thread, there was like a tiny hole, a gap where it wasn't quite right."

"Similar on the one I had. It's what you described earlier, Rainbow, as though it's almost right, but not quite."

"We both started to poke around at the gap. To see if it could help break the rest of the connection. That's when you threw us out."

"It wasn't me. I didn't do anything."

Rainbow just smiled at her.

"Well, brothers, do you have any other ideas? You can't do that again, or anything like it, she was in a lot of pain just with what you tried."

The two men stayed silent for minutes. Lani guessed they had to be communicating without words, or without speaking. Then Hembleth spoke.

"It needs him."

"Are you sure?"

"Yes, it's more than we can do without harming her. He's the one. He might not have created them, but he'd know how they were."

"Okay."

"What?"

"Perhaps I might discuss it with her. Thank you for your help."

"Not sure we helped, but I do need to get back."

"Don't forget to help with the shield."

"Next time perhaps, there's a lot happening out there."

Lani could see Thenis roll her eyes at Rainbow, but she didn't try to stop him. He waved at Lani then faded away and disappeared.

"I need to be off to the other side. I have enjoyed finally meeting you again, Lani. Stay well, lass, we all need you."

Before Lani could speak, Hembleth had also faded and gone.

"They're like that."

"What, annoying?"

"Very much so."

"What is it you need to tell me?"

"We cannot help you using any of the forces we have -- they are countered by the force that lies within the amulet."

"Why did they say it was me?"

"In a way it was. The amulet is linked to you in a fundamental way, so anything it does is via you, and you via it."

Lani wasn't sure she understood but she did know that the amulet wasn't going to let go easily. The feeling she'd had when they were trying to change it was buried deep within her.

"If you cannot help me, does that mean I'm stuck with it?"

"No. There are two options. The first is that you go back to where they came from."

"Enderk?"

"Yes, and find out what the connection there is."

Lani remembered how the Vrah were originally trying to kill her to free the amulet. The idea of heading back there seemed like a path to her own death.

"The other?"

"To go to the Lapidarist. The man who made them."

"I thought they said he didn't, but he would know."

"Both are true. Originally there were two brothers, twins in fact, both equally as skilled. They have abilities that others do not, which is why Ligriv was able to make the amulets."

"And he's dead."

"Yes, she killed him."

"She?"

Thenis said nothing for a short while.

"Yantarnaya did, or at least that's our belief."

"Why?"

"We have had no contact with her in a long time. We only learned of this through his brother, Nigriv."

"And he's still alive?"

"Yes."

"Why do you think he can help?"

"He will understand how they were made. He carved those you have seen, in Anderwell, and your brooch."

"I see. So, he's on our side."

"Not exactly. He helped us to spite her, and because we begged him. He made the stones in Anderwell, your brooch and a pendant, but he wouldn't make the beacon stones we wanted."

"Beacon stones?"

"We wanted to set the stones in key places around Dharatan to protect and shield everyone. Had we done that then... perhaps the Occultation would

never have become undone."

"Where is he now?"

"A good question. Last we know, far to the west, across the white seas."

"You don't know for sure?"

"We've had no reason to look for him."

"Then how will I find him?"

"We'll help as best we can, now that he's needed."

"And how likely is it he will be able to help?"

"That I don't know either, although my brothers believe if anyone can it would be him."

"My choice, then, is to head to my possible certain death, or on a wild goose chase, that might be a fool's errand in the end?"

"In a way, or you could stay in Anderwell and accept it as it is."

"They won't stop coming for it, though, will they?"

"No. It is part of their prophecy."

"What?"

"They believe possessing them all, they can destroy this stone."

"No one told me that."

"We don't spread that story too far. Besides, while we had them hidden it was of no consequence."

"Until it wasn't. You better tell me everything I need to know about this Lapid..."

"Lapidarist. Nigriv."

KARPENMOR

For the first time in as long as he could remember Karpenmor was very nervous. So much so that he had already vomited once and wasn't sure it wouldn't happen again.

Won't that make a pretty sight for all the guests, the High Prince vomiting on his coronation.

He stood and shook his arms and body out, trying to distract himself. *Soon to be High Prince,* he corrected himself.

The whole process seemed a little silly. Here he was, heir to the throne, and yet he had to go through this whole ceremony just to formalize it.

The leader of all Enderk.

Karpenmor wished that his father and mother were here to witness this, and yet he knew that wasn't how things worked. Even if his family hadn't been broken as it was, typically the heir only took the throne when death befell the father.

Often as not, that might be on a battlefield and not as it was for his father, incapacitated in a bed for years by his madness before he died.

His mother was no longer with him either. Karpenmor wished the story that she was dead wasn't true, but she was gone as well.

He knew nothing of any relatives within Family One until recently, it had been Uksod that had raised him. As much as there was that he disliked about the priest, he was also the only father he had really known, and of late their relationship had taken a new path.

While the older man had taken some time to drop his habits of ordering Karpenmor around, they had become more like peers recently.

The old man had finalized all the plans for the enthronement and helped guide Karpenmor through the cursed Dance of the Brides.

Despite all the delays each of the families presented their candidates and Karpenmor had played his role, spending an equal amount of time with them all, even though he'd have been just as happy to spend it all with Bhoomi.

There'd been little talk between the two men about what would happen after today. Karpenmor had his own plans for what would come next and he doubted Uksod would be particularly happy about them.

Time will tell.

The sound of bugles blowing loudly from the main hall brought his attention back to the area behind a large curtain separating him from everyone else. He could hear Uksod bellowing in the room between each blast.

He'll be loving this, the center of attention and everyone doing his bidding.

A mirror to Karpenmor's left caught his eye again. He'd been preening in front of it for the last two hours, admiring how he looked.

The robe, or long tunic, he wore sat just below his knees and was embroidered with his family patterns in golden threads down both sides and across the bottom.

While the tailor had been from En Carta, the finishing for all his garments had been done by one of his distant aunts, who had swept into the palace and taken over that part of affairs.

Each Imperial Family had their own patterns protected by law and tradition. Only those within each family bestowed with the rights could use them either in sewing, painting or any other form of craft.

This aunt was a domineering older woman, twice his width but much shorter, not that it bothered her. She spoke to him as though he was a child.

At first it had irked him greatly, this woman whom he did not know, telling him what to do, but in the end, he had to accept that this was his part of a tradition and his distant family, and there were things that mattered to them which had to be done.

Now all he could do was to wait. The curtain moved and Trorn slid through it, not opening it enough for anyone outside to see in.

"Any moment now, Highness."

"How do I look, Trorn, is everything in place?"

"Yes, Highness."

It wasn't the first time today he'd asked the very same question to Uksod's number two.

"When the single trumpet sounds seven blasts it will be time."

"Seven?"

"One for each family, Highness."

"Of course."

And then the trumpet sounded, and he counted them, or tried to, stumbling over something so simple, unsure if it was four or five.

Trorn could see his mind spinning and nodded when the seventh sounded, stepping forward and drawing the curtain open. Outside the entire great hall went silent.

It was as though everyone had taken a breath and waited for him to appear, as if they believed at this very moment something could have gone wrong.

He went to move, still out of sight, but his legs wouldn't move. *Come on, Karpenmor.* He moved, almost stumbling, but gathering himself before he turned out through the doorway.

Almost on cue the air returned to the room. He had practiced this several times over the past week, and while it was a short walk toward the dais where the final ceremony would take place it felt like the longest walk he could ever make.

Trorn would be walking behind him, carrying the royal standard, but he couldn't hear him. Karpenmor hardly noticed anything, all he could see was the purple rug that he was following, and Uksod standing on the other side of the dais.

Karpenmor knew there were lots of people all around him and in the hall, as well as a room full of those trying to be quiet, but he could see none of them. Everything was out of focus except for the short distance in front of him

His entire being was just trying to survive this, to not trip and fall, or do anything that would decry bad omens.

When he reached the spot where he would stand, he was able to breathe properly. All he had to do now was to stand still and follow Uksod's prompts.

"Witness all thee present, the arrival of the heir!"

A cheer went up through the hall, and much clapping, which Uksod let subside before he continued.

"Prince Karpenmor Redne, leader of Family One, present here today as heir to the throne of Enderk, son of Schevenal Redne, Yantarnaya rest his soul."

The last four words echoed around the chamber by many voices present.

"Does anyone within this great hall, any citizen of Enderk, have reason to deny this man as heir of the throne?"

Silence again fell across the hall, replaced by a tension that hung there waiting for someone to pierce it. Uksod seemed to wait for an eternity before he raised his staff and banged it seven times on the floor, the cracking of it booming throughout the hall.

"And so, it is now my right as High Priest, to commence the final part of our ceremony."

Karpenmor didn't hear everything said or know how long Uksod spoke for, but slowly he began to relax into what was happening around him. His vision returned and he looked out at his subjects below him.

The front of the hall was divided into seven columns of people, each representing one of the Imperial Families. Left to right, Family One to Seven.

There in the middle sat Lady Natillian, and to her left, Bhoomi. The sight of her was enough to grab his chest and squeeze at it. She was stunning, but he kept his eyes moving along.

Better, Karpenmor, not perfect, but better.

On the sides of the hall there was standing room for a limited number of En Carta citizens that had been allotted a chance to witness this once in a lifetime ceremony.

It had better be a once in a lifetime.

It was his first joke of the last few days, and he almost smiled at it. *That wouldn't do either. Who is that?*

Off to the side in the standing area, a short man with long red hair, who looked somewhat familiar, was tucked in beside a column. *What is it about him that I recognize?*

"Do you honor the tradition of the Imperial Families?"

It was his cue to respond. "I do."

"And do you understand your responsibility to protect and provide for all citizens of Enderk?"

What a load of codswallop that is.

"I do."

"Are you the true son and heir to the throne?"

"I am!"

Once again Uksod banged his staff seven times on the dais, the room again waited for what would come next.

A gasp went up throughout the room and Karpenmor turned to look but there was nothing to see but astonished people looking above him. He went to look up, but Uksod gently shook his head, a thin smile on his face.

He could only just see it, but his crown slowly sank down from above by some magic before it settled on his head.

As it did so he detected the slightest of shifts in how he felt. He wasn't sure what it was exactly, just that something had changed.

~

"High Prince, Karpenmor."

You.

"Who else? Enjoy this moment, Prince, there is much to be done from now on."

Such as?

"Another time, Karpenmor. Enjoy this, I know I am, it's been a very long time coming."

~

And she was gone.

"All hail, High Prince Karpenmor!"

A cry went up through the room, filled with the sound of his name. Emotions flooded through him, most of them good, and he looked out across the mass of people.

He opened his arms wide, he didn't know why, but he felt compelled to do it. Once they were wide open, he bowed before his people, and stood back up.

As he did, he snuck another look at Bhoomi, his heart jumping a little. She saw him, that mattered, then he saw Natillian who had also noticed.

Quickly he brought his eyes back to the room. He stepped backward until he was at the throne and then he sat, while Uksod brought him the imperial staff and sword.

The sword was laid across his lap and the staff placed in his right hand. He sat there on the amber-laden gold throne, crown on his head, staff in hand, and looked across the room.

If anyone expected anything else from him, they wouldn't get it. He waited until it had all died down, before Uksod issued the final decrees to end the ceremony.

He then returned to the room behind the dais where he'd waited and Uksod joined him.

"Well done, Highness."

"And you, Uksod, I do believe you loved every minute of that."

"I'm glad I was able to do it, I would not have been happy had you done it without me."

"I could sleep for a week now."

"Unfortunately, that can't happen, not yet at least. Now it's time for the feast."

"Just the family heads, isn't it?"

"And three guests each."

"I suppose I will have to talk to each." He rolled his eyes.

"It would be a major insult to not. And Karpenmor, you know each will bring their candidate, make sure to give each the same attention."

"I'll do my best."

122

UKSOD

It was all over, after all the years he'd overseen everything in Enderk, now he was no longer the Regent. Uksod had been unable to sleep and sat in his office, being active doing very little.

With Karpenmor distracted by his new duties, it would allow Uksod time to meet properly with Fuling, and to bring King Ahn into the palace.

Yantarnaya needed to check the amulet, to recharge it, and she wanted to discover more about the connection between the man and her jewel.

The Amber Room provided the perfect place for this to occur. A small chamber off the side of it, a place only Uksod knew of, at least for now, would enable this to happen.

Access to it was only available to those bonded to the Debrua, which meant that King Ahn would also be able to come there once he knew of it.

Inside sat the tip of the Debrua, hidden by other amber stones. Had he wanted to, Uksod could access the stone there, except he rarely did.

He'd hated to see Schevenal while he'd lived in the Amber Room, but also because Yantarnaya wanted him to go down and see her, as though her being able to see him in the flesh mattered.

First, he wanted to meet with Fuling face to face for the first time. This man had done well to get King Ahn here and would be very important moving forward.

Uksod still needed to get his measure. He had entrusted many things to the man, but he preferred to look someone in the eyes, to see how much he could rely on them.

He'd sent one of the Vrah to bring Fuling to the above-ground temple, as would be expected for a visiting priest.

The Skarian priest, Fuling, was knelt within the temple, his eyes fixed on the statue of the woman that only Uksod knew was trapped within the Debrua Stone.

No one needed to ever know about the deal she'd made to enhance her powers nor the path they were taking because of it. She hadn't planned to be stuck inside for the length of time she had.

That had happened because the stones had disappeared after the Great Fair incident. Uksod doubted she'd have agreed if she'd known what was going to occur.

She had two choices. The first was to return each of the amulet stones to the Debrua, including the one in Uksod's circlet.

Uksod had no desire for her to choose that option. To do so would kill everyone bonded to their stones, including him.

Which left the other option, to gather all of them together, as they had been intended right at the beginning, and to surround the Citadel Stone.

At that time, she could destroy it using the deep power within the Debrua Stone. She rarely talked about why it mattered so much to her to harm her siblings and their stone, nor did he care.

He could feel her presence in here. She was watching through him and all the amber, wanting to observe this helper in their cause.

"So much beauty in here, the light is quite amazing."

"It's the amber, Fuling. If you think this is impressive, you will be amazed when you see the Amber Room inside the palace."

"I look forward to it."

"I brought you here so you could bring King Ahn with you into the palace this evening. The amulet he wears needs to be reconnected to its source, for a little while."

"And you want this done quietly?"

"This is why you work well with me, Fuling, you understand the subtlety of things."

"It will be done."

~

Uksod hadn't informed Karpenmor that it was happening and all going to plan he'd never find out. He and the High Prince had seen little of each other since the ceremony which had helped Uksod investigate both these Skarian and the Ngaherian visitors.

It was also unusual for anyone other than the High Prince, his family, special servants, and Uksod to be this deep in the palace.

There was nowhere else it could be done; none could go down into the mountain and see her trapped within the stone. The King, Fuling, One and Uksod stood outside the door of the room.

"I must impress on you that this is a one-off opportunity to see this special room. No one else is aware you are coming into this room tonight; I'd like to keep it that way if we can. Do I make myself understood?"

"Yes, Eminence." Fuling spoke up, as King Ahn was in a semi-trance.

Uksod opened the doors to the Amber Room and waved the two guests inside, leaving One to guard the outside. Once inside, he closed the doors, listening to the gasps from both of his guests.

"This one is a little self-consumed."

Which one, mistress?

"The King, he thinks highly of himself."

That is the way of kings and queens.

Uksod didn't want to say *and also of gods* and had to force himself to put the idea far in the back of his mind.

"Uksod, this is unbelievable." Fuling couldn't stop babbling about the room.

"Like I said, it is something very special. Look around while I lead the King to where he needs to be."

Uksod took King Ahn by his arm and walked to the far wall before touching his circlet to a panel about chest high. A much bigger section of the wall popped open slightly and he pushed it wider.

He and the King went in before he closed it behind them. Inside the small room stood a thick glass box encasing the top of the Debrua stone.

Uksod took the King there and stood aside.

"I'll take it from here, Uksod."

Mistress.

The man unpinned his amulet from his chest and held it out in front before moving until it touched the point of the amber spike poking from the top of the glass box.

Uksod could feel the pulse of energy with the small space and the room flooded with orange light. Despite not even touching it he too could feel the power flood through him.

The King's eyes popped open suddenly and a look of horror crossed them. Uksod knew that he was being shown something or feeling something that would cement his loyalty.

The first time the circlet had been connected to his head, he had undergone a series of visions, and changes within himself that he couldn't explain.

After all this time it was difficult to remember the full extent of what he had gone through, but what had been clear was the extent of her power and what she could do to him.

The King shuddered and began to cry.

And then it was over. The light receded and the King removed his hand, pinning the amulet back on his chest.

"And so it begins, Uksod, I am very pleased.

What did you learn?

"Only that they can't be left unguided for too long. You need to get more amber on Dharatan. When the stones all come together, if there's no one to

guide them they will behave like they did all that time ago. You can take him now, he's mine."

Uksod led the King out of the room and took him to Fuling.

"What happened, he looks upset?" Fuling asked, slightly agitated.

"It's all okay, Fuling, what needed to be done has been done."

"I see that one still thinks he is in control."

You will disavow him of that idea, I am sure.

"Did you bring the item I asked?"

I did.

"Good, then we should get it done."

He cannot wear amber anywhere visibly, it's still not allowed on Dharatan.

"We need to change that."

In time it will.

"Have him put on his ring, so he has amber against his skin, then I can work on him more easily."

"You don't wear your ring, Fuling?"

"I forget about it; I'm so used to not being able to back home."

"I think Yantarnaya would prefer you did in her company."

The priest took it from inside a pocket and slid it onto a finger. Immediately Uksod could see his mistress working on him through the amber touching his skin.

At first his face indicated he was fighting against what she was trying to do to him, but slowly his will was broken.

"When he takes off his tunic, slide the bracelet up his arm."

Uksod waited and after another five minutes the priest in front of him began to remove his tunic. Reaching into his pocket, Uksod pulled out the small sliver bracelet with the special piece of Debrua Stone set in it.

"His right arm, up to the top."

Uksod walked to Fuling and slid the bracelet up his arm, forcing it over the man's bicep, hoping it wouldn't snap. Above it the arm was narrower, and the bracelet sat almost perfectly.

The amber stone within the bracelet began to shine, getting brighter and brighter.

"Take his ring off and let go of him."

Uksod did as she asked, stepping back several paces. Fuling's arm seemed to shine like the sun as the amber stone filled with orange light.

As the stone began to dull, the priest shook and wobbled on his feet, his eyes closed before everything stopped and his eyes popped open.

"What happened?" The man rubbed at his upper arm then saw the bracelet on it and tried to pull it off.

"I wouldn't do that."

"Why not?"

"If you actually could, you'd die instantly, but I doubt you could, at least not without the most excruciating pain."

"What has been done?"

"You've been bonded, Fuling. It's much better than the ring, now you're connected all the time."

"But if anyone sees it..."

"You'll just need to make sure they never do. At least until the views on such gems has changed."

Fuling seemed to relax, and replaced his tunic, no doubt still not feeling like he had before. Uksod could tell him he never would, but he needed the man to remain calm, and to get the King back to his accommodation without making any scenes.

"All done, that was very pleasing, Uksod."

I am glad you are happy, mistress. Anything I should be wary of with them?

"Plenty, especially that priest. He thinks far past his station and wishes to be in charge of things. We can control him now, but don't let him far from your awareness."

Understood. The King?

"He's all ours now. The first piece in the game is locked away now, Uksod. With him in place it will only get easier. In time Dharatan will be ours."

123

LANI

*L*ani didn't know if it had been hours or days that she had sat under the mountain trying to make sense of what she needed to do.

Thenis had left her with a choice between three things.

Going west, somewhere over the White Ocean, looking for the remaining Lapidarist, Nigriv; going to Enderk; or back to Anderwell.

Thenis had tried to explain to her how difficult it would be hunting down Nigriv. Firstly, he'd purposefully hidden himself from the world, but also that the lands to the west were vastly different to what she was used to here on Dharatan.

The goddess had also hinted that the path to removing the amulet would not be easy on Lani, but that if anyone could understand how to remove the amulet it would be Nigriv.

The thought of having to travel across a huge ocean frightened Lani. She'd never been on the ocean and the few times she'd been on rough water recently didn't inspire her to take that path.

Yet every time she thought about heading to Enderk, her body reacted negatively. Lani wasn't sure where it originated or if it was the Citadel Stone that was making her feel that way.

In her mind she could see what the Vrah had been attempting to do, replaying the events all the way back including watching Henri sacrifice himself for her.

When she'd heard them in the forest, before she'd escaped, it had been clear they were going to kill her to take the amulet, and she couldn't see why that would have changed.

She was of no value to them; it was the amulet they wanted. *Unless... if their master made these, then would they want to know why I am bonded to it?*

Or do they already know? Do they have answers for me?

They'd killed her mother and what she'd learned from Burgendetta's memory wasn't making her feel any safer. They would kill her it was that simple.

Her mother had come from there, something she struggled to understand, and there was a fleeting mention of a sibling.

A tease from Yantarnaya perhaps, whom Lani didn't feel so good about trusting. Was it enough to draw her that way, to find out about her sibling and her father?

Would it provide the other answers about her family she didn't have? Or was it all about the amulet to them? Why would they want to keep her alive?

Lani knew going back to Anderwell wasn't the right thing to do. It was the easiest thing, Lani knew that, and the little child within her wanted to choose that path.

Or is it the coward?

She knew that back there was a degree of safety, at least partly. Within the city there seemed to be few ways the Vrah could reach her. But whether that would last forever she didn't know.

But there was no guarantee any protection of the stones would last forever which meant everyone there would be in danger. If she went there, she'd be drawing the killers there.

Lani knew she couldn't do that, not now that she considered it her home. She couldn't put those people at risk, too many had already helped her too much.

Even now the group with her were putting themselves at risk for her benefit. These people cared and tried to do the right thing.

She shook her head and reflected on the only two options to choose between. Lani knew her decision was made, she just had to accept it.

Whether or not she liked the option wasn't important, that's what she had to move past. Her responsibility now wasn't just about how she felt, it was about much more than that.

Like it or not, she was in the middle of this chase for the amulets and protecting the Citadel Stone.

And I can't go to Enderk, not now. Maybe when I have the amulet removed and I'm not their target.

Lani laughed. She had no idea how to get from here to the western lands and knew there was no guarantee Nigriv would help or that he could. What she did know was it was the right thing to do, and she just had to do it.

A sense of relief swept over her. That she got to choose about what happened next mattered.

Despite what she'd been told, she hadn't felt like she was making choices early on.

In the beginning she'd simply fled from Ashantha's body and the Vrah. Even heading to Anderwell had been based around what others wanted for her.

Now this was all hers. She got to make the choice, and she was free to do so. While others were influencing her, none of them had told her what she had to do.

She knew she'd figure the how out, that didn't matter as much as the decision she'd made. Now she had a place to go, something to do, it was enough to guide her.

~

"I see you've made up your mind."

I have.

"You are sure?"

I am. But can I ask where to start?

"Of course, child. It's not that much of u guess for you. I said that we didn't know exactly where he was, but we do know where he went, and how to get there."

Lani smiled.

"You will need to make your way to Rocknigh on the western coast. You will need to find a man known only as Dranoll; he will be able to secure you passage."

What about Mother Folly?

"I will tell her of your journey."

Thank you.

Lani picked up her brooch which had been sitting on her lap and held it to use as her light to get back to the small room she'd entered from.

It was difficult to leave the embrace of the stone, you couldn't help but feel full of goodness and light while there. Walking away brought with it the heaviness of the outside world.

When she reached the solid wall at the end of the passage, she had to fumble around to find the lever to open it. The little hut felt tiny in comparison to where she'd been.

After closing the hidden door, Lani reset the bed in the room and made sure everything looked normal. She left and, still feeling light, floated back to Tingfurlew's house.

She almost jumped out of her skin when he flung the door open before she could even knock.

"You're back."

"I am."

"Do you still have it?"

She nodded.

"Then you should go. It's not good to have it here, only bad can come from it."

"I am meant to leave this with you." She held out Tillandra's pass for Midderbuilt.

"What am I meant to do with this? I have my own."

"It's Tillandra's. She will need it next time she comes here."

"Aren't you going back to her?"

"No, Tingfurlew, I am not."

"Where are you going?"

"I'd rather not say, but it's to get rid of the amulet."

He shook his head rapidly as though he could shake what she said free.

"You be safe, Lani."

"I'll try my best, Tingfurlew. Thank you for your help."

"Done nothing. Now go, quick now."

"I just wanted to say goodbye."

"Goodbye." It was said as matter-of-factly as it could be then the funny little man closed the door on her. She could hear the key turning and a bolt sliding across.

"Okay. Thanks again." Lani wasn't quite sure how to take it but turned and headed toward the gates.

I just hope Carnus is still there.

There was no way for her to know for sure until the gates opened, and the looks of the guards didn't help her feel any better.

As she stepped through the left gate which they only just opened, she was relieved to see the large man whom she had to consider a friend stood off to the side.

He said nothing but she could sense him following her as she started down the hill.

124

KARPENMOR

*I*f he thought the world was going to change around him after his enthronement, he was disappointed. The only thing was, his position was now public and permanent.

Karpenmor had made a point of doing a public parade the day after the ceremony. No longer would there be a hidden ruler, nor a Regent who treated the public with contempt.

He wanted everyone to be reminded that it was his word that was the rule of law, leaving no ambiguity for anyone who had served under Uksod's rule as Regent.

Karpenmor knew it would take more than a ceremony or parade to change anyone's perceptions of the role, but it was a start.

As for his Regent, the old man had all but disappeared, retiring from public view, which was both good and a little disconcerting for Karpenmor.

It meant no one to push off tasks to, they all fell onto his shoulders which was already tiresome.

"Aika, is it really that necessary I meet with the delegations?"

"Yes, Highness, although it would appear Eminence Uksod has the attention of the King and his priest at the moment."

So that's where he's been.

"What is he doing?"

"I am unsure, Highness. He met with the priest in the temple, and then went to their accommodation."

"It would seem, Aika, that you've taken to this role like a fish to water."

"I serve as you requested, Highness."

"Better than that, Aika. I am impressed. How do you know your people aren't also talking to Uksod?"

"The people I am using are my closest family members, Highness, cousins that I trust."

"They do not know what you are doing with them?"

"A little, but not all of it. The smarter of them will figure it out in time."

"And they won't sell you out to him for a higher price?"

"Not if they value their eyes and ears." Her eyes looked downward as she said it.

Karpenmor looked at her, she was serious. "You wouldn't?"

"I think it would be best if you didn't ask those questions in future, Highness."

Karpenmor knew that he was being unrealistic if he thought everything could be done without violence. Some things required it. But he had hoped in normal day-to-day business that such things could be avoided. Although he was beginning to doubt even that was possible.

"So then, the Ngaherians?"

"Yes, you should host them here."

"Why are they here?"

"The wallboy..."

"The what?"

"Wallboy. He lives inside their walls, in the spaces where he can hear them."

"Ah."

"He has told me that they are very suspicious of us, and even their traveling companions. They only came because the King came, and the Ngaherian Queen did not want to be left out of any discussions."

"Interesting." Karpenmor could see how vital this spying on everyone would be.

At a guess he assumed Uksod would have employed the Vrah to do such things during his time as Regent, if not still. Karpenmor knew he needed to deal with removing the priests use of them.

"I will need to have a discussion with One shortly as well."

"When shall I arrange it?"

"Tomorrow, though perhaps I should speak to Uksod first. Have you been able to find anything else out about the process for such a change?"

"Nothing, Highness, but I have been too busy to look very far."

Her blushing had come back, it was the thing she needed to drop. She didn't need to be embarrassed for not doing something.

"Enough of that, you don't need to feel bad for that. If it was more important, I would have advised so. Leave that to me."

Sitting at his desk Karpenmor was anxious about the steps he was taking. Yes, he was the High Prince, but it still wasn't second nature to make definitive decisions that everyone followed.

Nine sat before him.

"What do you have to report?"

"His Eminence..."

"When just in my company you can use his name."

"... of course. Uksod and One brought the foreign King and priest into the palace."

Karpenmor sat more upright. "Where did they go?"

"The Amber Room, Highness."

"Really?"

The man carried no emotion in his expression. His face was lean and almost perfectly symmetrical, his jaw as though carved from rock, jutting forward.

"Yes, Highness. The priest and foreigners were in there for almost three hours."

That's a very long time to be in there.

"What about One?"

"He remained on guard outside."

"Did they go anywhere else?"

"No, when they came out, the two men were escorted back to their accommodation by Vrah, and Uksod returned underground."

"Any observations?"

"Uksod had a smile on his face."

"That in itself is unusual."

Nine said nothing about that. "The two barbarians appeared very groggy."

"Explain?"

"They were very unsteady on their feet, as though they had been heavily drinking, and yet they were not drunk. If anything, they appeared confused, or almost stunned."

Now that I can understand. So, she spoke to them.

"Anything else?"

"The other barbarians are up to nothing other than what they are allowed to do. The big-headed one often stands on the rooftop balcony and studies the palace or city."

"That one has strange origins. Do you have any more information on where he is from?"

"Not yet, Highness."

The pair sat in silence while Karpenmor thought about what he had learned, and the other topic.

"You have been very helpful to me, Nine. Do not be offended by what I am about to ask."

The senior Vrah leader's eyes closed briefly as he dipped his head in acknowledgement.

"Why?"

"Why, Highness?"

"Why have you made yourself available to me in this way, outside the chain of command?"

There it was, the primary question that would determine this man's fate. Both he and Karpenmor knew that either he was working with One, or the manner in which he was helping went against One's control.

For the first time, Karpenmor could see a reaction within the man. He was deciding how to respond, which pleased Karpenmor further.

The man knew he had to consider his words and options carefully, not just rushing forward.

"It appeared to me as an opportunity, Highness."

Karpenmor raised his eyebrows but said nothing.

"Things within the Vrah do not appear to be changing as much as outside of it. It became apparent over the time since you came of age that One and the others ahead of me are all very connected to the ex-Regent."

"Go on."

"Many of those between him and myself are all loyal to Uksod."

"All?"

"Not all, but several wouldn't fight against it."

"I see. And?" Karpenmor didn't want to lead this conversation in any direction. He needed it to be entirely of Nine's mind.

"Were One to step down, then the Vrah would still be under his influence, through Two or any of those that followed. His reach would continue. Even when you went to the Stepping Isles, still they tried to get word back here using Vrah messengers. Which means such knowledge would have been gathered for Uksod which bothered me. I could see that the leadership of my own kind was not honoring our position. I sensed an opportunity to change that."

Karpenmor paused. He needed to get inside this man's head, as much as one could, for his plans to work.

"Were One to step down, you're talking about removing seven people ahead of you from contention for the position."

Nine didn't say it in words but he dipped his head in acknowledgement. *Clever, you could always deny this and say it was purely hypothetical, that you never actually said those words.*

"To do such a thing requires blood to be spilled. From all that I can find, there are only three paths to leadership in the Vrah. First is to be handed it by the current leader. Second is if the current leader dies, it automatically passes."

Karpenmor sat back in his chair and stared at Nine.

"And the third is the right of challenge to anyone who fills the seat through the first or second option."

"You are correct, Highness."

Again Karpenmor, studied the man. It was one thing to take on one person and challenge them, but in this he would have to take on seven people, one at a time, until none remained.

"It is unusual for a leader to step down."

"Unusual, but watching One and Uksod, I believe they are planning this."

"For what purpose?"

"I can only suppose from rumor."

"Suppose away."

"Uksod wishes to set up his own protectors. One would move into that position."

That surprised Karpenmor. He hadn't considered Uksod might seek his own protection once he lost control of the Vrah.

"To what purpose?"

"I do not know, Highness. That's purely rumor from those around my leader."

"You are well suited to this role of spying, Nine. If nothing else, you would make an excellent spymaster."

"Thank you, Highness."

"Could you still serve me in this way, Nine, if you were not the leader?"

"I could find a way, Highness, although I could not do much more than spying. If I were ordered to go somewhere by the new One, I would have to obey."

"An interesting discussion, Nine, one that will not leave this room. You have begun to earn my trust by the manner in which you have conducted yourself. I would like to have those unburdened by the past around me for my rule, and I will think more on it."

"Highness." He dipped his head.

"Continue to keep an eye on the barbarians and should Uksod bring any of them into the palace again, make it difficult for him, while someone fetches me; at any time of the day or night. Understood?"

"Yes, Highness."

～

He left his office and walked back to his rooms, heading directly out to his balcony. It was still the place that felt the calmest to him.

And he wasn't particularly calm anymore. Now that the power was all his, he felt an excitement to use it. He wanted to move forward without delay but was trying to check his own decisions.

It's silly, I know what I want to do, and no one can stop me anyway.

Far below, he could see someone standing out on the balcony of the residence where the Ngaherians were staying. *The emissary no doubt. Who are you really? There's something different about you other than your looks, but you give nothing away.*

Uksod and he had originally discussed delaying these delegations for a longer time, but there seemed little point. The sooner that trade began with their people the less threatening they would appear.

No, we need to get all these barbarians out of our capital so I can start working on reclaiming Cumerc.

125

KARPENMOR

*D*espite the outer calm he'd shown to Nine, Karpenmor had been annoyed by what he'd been told, and that was growing into a full-blown anger.

Uksod was still up to his antics even with the crown now Karpenmor's. Staying out of Karpenmor's way these last days had just been a ploy for the priest to carry out his own plans.

Had he held a simple meeting in one of the rooms where visitors came during the day it wouldn't have bothered Karpenmor like this.

But they'd brought a foreigner into the palace at night, Karpenmor's palace, without any acknowledgement or invitation by the ruler. Then they'd taken this barbarian into an inner part of the palace all without his consent. It was a step too far.

It wasn't just any place either, it was the Amber Room. A most significant and personal room that wasn't available to almost anyone, and yet they had taken the King and his priest in there.

Whatever the reason for it, there was someone that would know why.

I wonder if she'll tell me?

In the past he'd have been unlikely to have gone there. He didn't like speaking to her, nor did he like the place, but his mood was sour and he wanted answers.

Karpenmor left his room and walked to the back of the palace where the Amber Room was situated. Standing outside the doors, he readied himself to speak with her directly.

It had never been something he enjoyed, which is why he avoided it. Karpenmor opened the doors and entered the empty room, half expecting to see his father's bed and sitting chair.

None of those were there anymore and the room stood open to walk around. Light shone from every corner, every gem set within the walls and columns, and it took his eyes some minutes to adjust.

He reached the middle and could feel the power of it, coming at him from every angle, touching his skin, probing him.

~

"This is a surprise."

There you are.

"Why are you here, and now, Karpenmor?"

You're up to something.

"I am always UP to something; can you be a little more specific?"

The barbarians, why were they in here?

Karpenmor could sense her chuckling. It didn't help his anger.

"You still have a lot to learn, High Prince, but you show lots of promise; much more than your father did."

Keep him out of it.

"You people have so many foolish emotions about the dead, it is quite interesting."

The barbarians?

"What of them? They needed to be influenced to do my work."

What work is that?

"Whatever I wish them to do, Karpenmor. There's more at play here than you playing Emperor."

And what is at play?

She laughed again.

"Your job right now, Karpenmor, is to get the city back, and your amulet. You've made a good start on the first of those, but I need the amulet."

Is that why the King was here, his amulet?

"Yes, Karpenmor, all the amulets need to come back to me, they're mine, not yours. Anything else Uksod can help me with, for now you've got your hands full."

That's not really an answer.

"You can go now, boy. Come back when you've got something useful to tell me."

Karpenmor left the room, angrier than when he'd gone in. He remembered why he didn't like having her in his head, now he couldn't stand the way she treated him.

What irked him more was that she had Uksod doing her work and he had no idea what it was. While he couldn't stop her, he could control what Uksod did, and he didn't have to have Uksod undermining him in his own palace and realm.

And certainly not with his lapdog, One. If he had harbored any reservations, they were gone now. It was time. He returned to his office and paced about until he felt under control.

When he had his plan, he asked one of his guards to get Aika. While he waited, he drank some wine. His mouth was completely dry and his stomach was flipping over what he was going to do.

"Highness, what can I help you with?"

"Come outside, Aika, this matter is sensitive."

When she was standing next to him, he spoke quietly.

"I want you to get Uksod to come and see me. He's not to refuse."

"Understood."

"Then go to One, and advise him I wish to see him. Tell him he should hurry, that there must be no delays. Clear?"

"Yes, Highness."

"Once that's done, take your time before going to seek Nine. I don't want the others to know. He's to stay out of sight until both Uksod and

One are inside my office. Once they are, he should wait outside the door with the guards until he is called for."

She nodded. "Yes, Highness. Then what?"

"Then stay away until morning. Whatever happens, tomorrow will be a different day and I'll explain it then."

She looked at him without words.

"Okay, go now."

Aika turned and left him. He went back into his office and tidied everything so it looked very organized, before preparing what he needed for the meeting that would happen.

It seemed like forever before there was a knock at the door. "Come."

It was Uksod, which pleased Karpenmor. It meant that the first part was underway.

"Highness, your aide said you wished to speak with me?"

"Yes, Uksod, I haven't seen you since the ceremony and I wanted to catch up. Have a seat." Karpenmor held out his hand pointing at the seat across the desk from him to his left.

The old priest approached it and sat down, his face showing no signs of concern, the typical lack of emotion from the old man.

"So, what's been happening, Uksod? I've been so busy with everything this role requires."

"Little, Highness. I am slowly adjusting to the changes it means for me."

"And you're okay with that?"

Uksod showed a small smirk, it was as much as the man ever showed. "It is taking some adjustment, Karpenmor... may I still call you that?"

"Yes, don't be silly. Nothing has really changed, not that much."

"True in some senses, and not in others. You are the High Prince now; your word is final."

"Indeed."

"I am fine, if that's worrying you. There are many things in the priesthood that I can now focus on, including the restoration of the temple in Cumerc, that you negotiated for us."

Perhaps that's all it was about.

"And what of the guests, Uksod, how are they faring?"

There was a slight pause.

"I don't know much of them, Highness, they are not mine to deal with."

A lie.

"I have been wondering about the King and his companions. What might I offer him as a guest to our city? What should I show them?"

"I think it important to not show them anything at all, Highness. They need not learn anything about what exists in our city, or country."

"Not the countryside, Uksod, but perhaps something impressive here in the city, or even in the palace. Perhaps the Amber Room, that would impress them."

Uksod's eyes narrowed and he took a moment before he replied.

"You are negotiating with them about the trade are you not?"

"With the Ngaherians so far, and then I will hear what the others seek."

"And they witnessed your enthronement, a truly unique experience for foreigners like them. I think you owe them nothing else."

"So you see no value in anything else?"

"No, Highness."

Karpenmor sat patiently thinking about what he had been told. Did it matter? Was it enough?

A knock at the door broke his silence. "Come." Uksod turned to see who it was. Karpenmor caught a slight tremor in his eyes when he saw it was One.

"Highness, I received your summons."

"Thank you for coming so quickly, One. I was hoping to be finished with Uksod before you arrived, but it matters not. Have a seat."

Karpenmor stood and pointed to the seat on Uksod's left. He remained standing.

"Do you still need me, Highness?"

"Perhaps, Uksod, stay for a minute."

He turned back to One who was now sat in his chair and walked around his desk closer to the Vrah leader.

"Tell me, One, you control all of my security including for the palace is that correct?"

"Of course, Highness."

"You'd be fully aware of everyone that comes and goes into it?"

"To a degree, Highness."

"What degree, One? You either do or you do not."

"I am not told every day about servants coming and going, so in those circumstances I do not track changing of guards or servants."

"What is to stop the wrong people from coming in without your awareness?"

"It is only those who are already vetted and approved that I do not get notified of. Anyone that shouldn't be here, or who is new, I am advised of."

"Every day?"

"Yes, Highness."

"You would know, for example, if the emissary of the Ngaherians came to the palace."

"Yes, Highness. As I recall, you met with him yesterday and left him with your chancellor, before he was returned to his accommodation."

"Very good."

Uksod was looking at him curiously. "Am I needed for this, Highness? Surely One's service cannot be questioned?"

Karpenmor looked at the priest. He had no patience for any of them. "You'll stay until I say you can go, is that clear?"

"Of course, Highness." The tone in his reply was careful but still a little sharp.

"So, One, have there been any other visits to the palace that are unusual, or not normal, over these last few days?"

One sat still in his chair. Karpenmor felt as though the man desperately wanted to look at Uksod but couldn't. Out of the corner of Karpenmor's eye he could see Uksod had tightened his grip on his thighs, where his hands sat.

"No, Highness. That is the only one that occurred."

"And you are certain, absolutely certain?"

"Yes, Highness. Without doubt."

"Thank you. One moment."

Karpenmor walked to his door, and opened it, seeing Nine, standing there. "Please come in."

As Karpenmor walked back toward his desk, he could sense the Vrah behind him. Whatever happened next was going to be hard to control. He stopped beside One, whose eyes were focused very much on his peer, and turned back to Nine.

"Nine, thank you for coming. Can you advise me of any comings into the palace over the last few days, including anyone unusual or of note?"

"Yes, Highness. You met with the emissary of Ngahere, who was accompanied into the palace by two guards. They waited outside the meeting room and left with the emissary after his meeting with Chancellor Aika finished."

"Thank you, anyone else?"

"Yes, the Skarian King and his priest came into the palace two nights ago and met with Eminence Uksod in the Amber Room."

"Truly?"

"Yes, Highness."

Karpenmor circled around in front of the two seated men.

Uksod spoke, his eyes very focused on Karpenmor's. "I can explain."

"What is it you can explain, Uksod? That you brought an enemy into the palace, into the inner sanctum of MY palace, without my knowledge, or that you lied about it?"

Uksod's face had flushed bright red and his mouth was clenched closed. Karpenmor doubted that in all his plans for today none had included being called out like this and especially as it was being done in front of others.

"Or perhaps why the head of my security lied to me just now as you witnessed."

"He did so on my command."

Karpenmor stepped around the side of One's chair, standing over him. "Is that true?"

The leader of the Vrah looked up with a serious expression on his face, almost resignation.

"You followed this priest's command to allow foreigners into the palace, without my approval, and then lied to me about it."

"I..."

Karpenmor didn't let him finish. The anger that had been floating around the whole day had changed now into a steely resolve and focus.

"There are many words for those that might seek to undermine a ruler, either by action or word. While it is one thing for a subject to conduct sedition or treason, it is something altogether different for the head of my own security to do so."

The words hung in the room; now spoken they could not be unspoken. The Vrah leader was challenged with either failing in his duties or treason, both of which were unresolvable.

Karpenmor stood, with his hands clasped behind his back, trying to appear as commanding as he could. He glanced at Uksod, who remarkably actually looked pale and said nothing.

"I have failed you, Highness. I will step down immediately."

"You will do only what I say you can do!" His voice rose, causing the door to open and the guards outside to step in.

"Get out! If I need you, I will call."

Both hurried back out. None had seen the Prince behave in this manner before.

Karpenmor looked at Uksod. "You continue to work behind my back, priest. See now what happens when you do so."

"Whatever you're thinking about doing, Highness, don't do it. Let us discuss this in private."

Karpenmor looked at Nine. "Nine, what is the price of treason?"

"No, Highness!"

"Silence, Uksod!" Karpenmor didn't even look at him.

"It is death, Highness."

"So be it."

Everything slowed down for Karpenmor. He was done with not being in control, with others thinking they could operate in their own best interests.

Something else had taken control of him now, and he didn't recoil from it like he believed he would have, not so long ago.

He already had his dagger in his right hand, hidden behind his back. Karpenmor quickly stepped behind One, and holding the man's forehead with his left hand, dragged the sharp knife across the Vrah leader's throat.

Blood spurted forth and the man gurgled. Karpenmor had factored in that due to the man's honor he wouldn't fight back and had been right about that.

"No! Karpenmor what have you done?"

Uksod's face had grayed and his eyes were wide open. Karpenmor hadn't expected to see the priest disturbed by death.

"What did you call me? I am your Highness. Guards!"

The door opened and the two outside stepped in. "Take Eminence Uksod back to his quarters now and keep him under close guard, he is to go nowhere else. Place a guard in his office as well, he is not to leave his rooms until I say so, understood?"

The two guards looked quickly at the scene where their leader was slumped forward, a pool of blood at his feet, and the High Prince.

"Yes, Highness."

"Now!"

"Highness, please let me explain."

"Your time will come, Uksod, but not now."

When the room was empty, Karpenmor turned to Nine who equally seemed very surprised by what had just happened.

"Do you still wish to be my man?"

The soldier looked directly into Karpenmor's eyes. "I do, Highness."

"Then let's go."

"Now?"

"Yes, now. I want this matter resolved by morning."

There was no guarantee about what would happen next and Karpenmor hoped he wouldn't regret what he'd just started. What he felt at that moment wasn't disgust or horror at what he'd just done, it just felt right.

Am I any different to him after all?

126

LANI

$\mathcal{A}$s Lani and Carnus reached the bottom of the road down from Midderbuilt their friends arrived.

"What's going on, Kooka?"

"Been watching for you, for days now. We're ready to get moving, the camp's been tense ever since you left. Guards storming around every day. Doesn't feel right."

"I guess we're leaving then."

"Unless there's any reason not to."

"None. I need to discuss something but here's not the right place."

"Let's get moving. We can stop up the road."

Lani climbed up beside him and sat quietly while they got underway. The whole group kept to themselves as they rode slowly along the edge of the mountains.

Off in the distance the crack of something loud broke the sounds of the wagon wheels.

"What's that?"

Kooka looked across to the east. "Desert storm."

"Coming this way?"

"They always come east to west, but whether it will hit us, too early to say."

"What will we do if it does?"

"Get inside and hold on for dear life."

Lani didn't like the sound of that at all.

"Kooka!" Irdan rode up beside Lani.

"What's up?"

"I think we've got company."

"Who?"

"Riders from the camp. Didn't take them long to set out after us, been watching them to see who they are. They're holding back for now, tracking our pace."

"Which means they aren't on their own mission, or they'd be long past us."

Carnus startled both Lani and Kooka, speaking from their right. "What's that?"

Kooka looked ahead where the Ngaherian was pointing. "More riders. I don't like the feel of any of this."

"Could be coincidence," Lani said, trying to be optimistic.

"Or just trouble."

"Leo!"

The young Jester clambered forward. "What's up, Kooka?"

"Isn't that spot up there the place where you went in?"

The young man peered up ahead where the slopes of the mountain-side were less steep.

"Yeah, it is."

Kooka said nothing for a bit. "My gut tells me we need to get off this road. Not sure about what's ahead but I doubt what's behind us is just following us for protection. We might be able to handle one group but two seems a bit of a stretch. Up there at least we'd have the high ground."

"I agree," Irdan said.

Kooka whipped the reins. "Then let's get everyone up there fast."

It was only a short distance from where they were, and they grabbed what provisions they could, tied the horses and cart up so they wouldn't bolt and began the climb up the hill.

They'd only got three-quarters of the way up when the group

behind them caught up. A dozen men, all armed, surrounding their cart and looking at where they were climbing.

"That confirms they weren't friendly," Kooka said to them all.

Lani looked at Leo. "Can you do it again?"

"I hope so."

"Do we really want them to see us do it?"

"I don't think you can see the actual spot from down there, only roughly where we are. Besides, that storm is coming this way. I think we'll have to take the chance."

"Let's leave him to do his thing, we'll stay here just in case, and he can call out when he's done." Kooka was happy to take charge.

"Okay."

Once Leo had climbed up ahead of them the wagon driver leaned in toward Lani. "He gets a bit of stage fright with people around."

"That's okay, I probably would as well. Who do you think they are?"

"Down there?"

She nodded back at him.

"You tell me. Someone knew we were coming, or that you were in the camp. Whoever that was, it wouldn't take much to buy some men, plenty of money out this way. Probably just soldiers for hire."

They sat there watching the men below and saw the other group ride up, speak to them briefly then ride on toward Midderbuilt. Lani guessed they weren't after her, just other travelers heading in.

Not that it mattered now, the men below were more than an obstacle to her getting to Watersend safely.

"Let's go."

She turned to see Leo calling out to them. Once everyone had made it into the tunnel Lani took out her brooch just before Leo closed the outside door.

It shone like it had before and she led the group back the way she'd come earlier.

～

"What happened?"

We got followed, by men looking for me, and there's a big storm coming, we had to shelter.

"*That's not good. They won't stop waiting for you out there, Lani.*"

What do we do then? There's a lot more of them than us.

"*There's other ways to where you need to go than following that road.*"

Such as?

"*These mountains have many pathways. They aren't easy but they will get you where you need to go.*"

What about the others?

"*They can wait, or they can go with you, either way their paths will not be easy.*"

I had better discuss this with them.

"*It's a long and not easy journey under and over the mountains, Lani. Your brooch will guide you.*"

Thank you.

⁓

When they got to a wider section of the tunnel, Lani stopped and turned to face the group. "This is far enough for now. I need to tell you something."

"That doesn't sound good," Leo replied.

"It's not likely our friends out there are going to leave us alone. It won't be safe going back that way, not for a while at least."

"Can we stay here until the storm's passed at least?"

"Yes. For as long as you have provisions, Kooka."

"That sounds like you're leaving us?"

"I guess now's as good a time as any to tell you."

She told them what she was going to do.

"I'm going with you." Carnus wasn't asking.

"You can't, Carnus. I don't know how long I'll be gone, or if I'll get back."

"I'm going."

She shook her head, there was no reasoning with him.

"Me too."

"Odajeen, it will be dangerous."

"We're all one, you need help, I'll do what I can."

Lani knew that meant the brothers would be with her as well.

"Kooka?" Purple had spoken for the first time.

"What, Purple?"

"Us too!"

He shook his head. "You sure, little one?"

"Yes, Kooka. She'll need us."

"Well, I'm not going to be the odd one out," Leo chirped up. "I guess we're all going."

"What about the wagon and horses?" Lani asked.

"Someone will take care of them, not our problem anymore, lass."

"You know it's going to be dangerous and possibly the biggest fool's errand known to anyone on Dharatan?"

They all nodded.

"Why are you so adamant about coming then?"

"You're one of us, Lani. We're all in this together. When we left Anderwell it was to help you out and keep you safe. Sounds like that job isn't finished." Kooka spoke for them all.

"We better hurry. Supposedly we don't have very long until all the boats will stop for the season."

Lani hoped she'd not regret fighting harder against them, but deep down she was very happy to have them with her. Kooka was right, they were her family now, and she belonged with them.

For the first time in her life, she felt as though there were people who had her back. Despite the situation, and what might happen, she felt better than she had ever felt.

I just hope it stays this way.

127

KARPENMOR

The Vrah compound was more alive than Karpenmor had expected given it had only been half an hour since this all began. Word had traveled about One's death much quicker than he might have imagined. The guards escorting Uksod must have sent word.

When he passed through the open gates, the guards bowed lower than he recalled them ever bowing before. Nine walked behind him, several steps back.

Instead of heading to One's office, Karpenmor stayed in the outer courtyard, where groups of Vrah stood off to the sides. It didn't take long before the man he expected to see came out.

Two was only slightly younger than One had been, plumper and looking like he had not been on the road in many years. *That's one of the problems of leadership, not getting out in the field, you lose touch, and shape.*

"Highness." He bowed deeply before him. *At least you're showing respect. Let's see how long that lasts.*

"You are Two?"

He nodded. "If word is correct, that will change."

Karpenmor could see the happiness under the surface. Despite what had just happened, this man sought the power of the seat he expected to now have.

Inside Karpenmor felt emboldened by what he'd just done as well as sickened. He needed to focus on his drive to get this settled before the anxiety underneath came out.

"Yes, it will change. We will conduct the ceremony right here, and now."

"Now, Highness?" This surprised Two.

"Yes, I think it important. There is no need for pomp and fancy ceremony, Two. Wouldn't you agree?"

"As you wish, Highness."

Karpenmor turned to a Vrah stood close by, one that had come out with Two. "Your number?"

"Fourteen, Highness."

I will need to remember him; he is close to Two. "Fetch the ceremonial swords from the office, Fourteen, and a stand to place them on."

"Yes, Highness."

No one spoke while they all waited for him to return. When he did, he was accompanied by another who carried a tall wooden stand.

"Place it here."

Once the swords were laid on top of the stand, Karpenmor stood beside it and raised his voice to the compound, where now many of the city's Vrah had hurried to gather.

Word really does travel fast; I need to learn more about how they do that.

"Tonight, I executed your previous leader for treason."

A gasp went up across the courtyard, quickly quelled.

"Everyone is aware that I am the High Prince, and that the Vrah serves me, and no one else. Your ex-leader decided that he was still serving the ex-Regent against my wishes and protection. It is unacceptable and has been punished."

Karpenmor let this sink in for a moment.

"If there are others who have dishonored their families and themselves who wish to admit to their treason, step forward and commit the only act that will bring you redemption. There will be only one chance."

Karpenmor paused briefly to make sure everyone heard what he would say next.

"If anyone else is found to have dishonored his family and doesn't come forward, their punishment will be much worse. Every member of his family will be hung from the city gates, one a week, and he will be stockaded there to watch them until it is completed. Then he too will suffer a painful and slow death."

Only one man came forward, from Karpenmor's right. He too was older, with gray hair and a portly build.

"Your number?"

"Three, Highness."

"And?"

"I have sided with the one you have judged and on matters not in honor of my family. Allow me to take my own life."

Karpenmor nodded.

The man knelt, pulled out his own long dagger, and placed it upright on his chest, before falling forward onto it. The blade broke through his chest and deep into his heart. Blood rushed out and he toppled to the side, life leaving him quickly.

"Any others?"

No one stepped forward.

"As per the rules of appointment there are three methods to replace the leader of the Vrah."

Again he paused, letting his eyes roam across the group gathered, finishing on the man who assumed he would be the one.

"The first is that the leader names his own replacement. That has not happened."

Karpenmor took a deep breath. "The next is that the next in line takes the position. This would mean Two would take up the mantle."

The man before him stood as tall as he could be, ready to be anointed.

"And the third option is that any challenge to that role must be accepted but within the rules that apply.

"Whoever throws the challenge must first fight any and all numbers inside the ten that are above them. Only when they have been bested or step aside can the challenger fight the appointed."

Karpenmor took a breath before he continued. "There can only be one challenger. Should more than one person raise a challenge then they must fight until only one remains. That person then must fulfil the challenge of the Vrah above them.

"Once this challenge is over, there can be no more. From that moment forward the person who takes the title One will be obeyed by all."

He wanted to allow the gravity of the situation to sink in to all of those watching the events.

"Thus, I appoint Two to take up the role of the title of One. As explained, I ask you all, is there anyone who does not accept Two to take up this role?"

The courtyard was quiet, only a shuffling of feet. Karpenmor began to get concerned when no one said a word. *Has he played me?*

"I do not!"

Karpenmor's chest relaxed as Nine spoke up.

Two turned with scorn on his face to look at the challenger. "Prepare the circle."

All the Vrah surrounding them stepped back and created a large circle. Karpenmor stood at the southern end of it, a space left around him.

He felt exposed standing there amongst all these assassins, but it was too late to do anything about that now. If he showed any weakness in this moment, it would undermine everything he was trying to do.

One of the other elder leaders took the two ceremonial swords from their sheaths and tossed them to each side of the circle, one landing by Nine's feet.

"Your number?" Karpenmor called out to the challenger.

"Nine."

"Then I call on Eight."

One of the most senior Vrah limped out from the crowd. "Highness."

Karpenmor could see his lame leg was half the thickness of his other. No doubt the man had not expected he would have to fight for his life this evening.

"You are first defender of the challenge, Eight..."

"Highness, I would request to remove myself from the line." The man bowed and held his downward pose.

"You understand this means exile, Eight?"

"Yes, Highness." He stood back up.

Karpenmor looked past Eight and looked around the crowd. To be exiled was in many ways worse than death in Enderk.

No family would take you in, which meant living on the mountains south of En Carta. That was the only place owned by no one unless a family would hide you.

To do so would mean high treason, a whole family would be killed, if found out. Exile was a harsh choice for this older man but he was prepared to choose that over death.

Karpenmor turned to look at Two, who understood that the Prince wasn't sure about the process. The Vrah stepped forward and spoke quietly into his ear.

"He is to be stripped of his Vrah items and sent from here immediately."

Karpenmor nodded and turned back to Eight, pulling out his dagger as he stepped forward. He pulled the man's black tunic toward him and cut it, hacking until it split open, ripping it free of the man.

Thankfully Eight stepped out of his tights saving Karpenmor from having to hack them off. He lifted the older man's right hand and pulled his ring off, pocketing it before dropping the man's hand.

"This man is no longer numbered and is not Vrah. Escort him from the city immediately."

Two Vrah stepped forward, grabbing the man who'd up until then been one of their leaders, and marched him out of the circle toward the gates.

Karpenmor looked back across the crowd. His heart was pounding and he had to remember to breathe.

"Seven, come forth."

No one stepped into the circle.

"Seven, come forth."

Karpenmor turned to face Two.

"He is on the Steps, Highness."

A wrinkle in the process, but not one Karpenmor could control. "Then his role is forfeit. As he cannot be here to defend himself or the challenge, he shall be returned to a number, and no longer holds the title Seven."

If anyone disagreed with his decision no one said a word. Karpenmor found it intoxicating to be standing here amongst these killers all following his every word.

"Six, step forward."

A tall and lean man moved gracefully into the circle. "Highness."

"You are Six?"

"Yes, Highness."

Karpenmor did not ever recall seeing this man before. If his appearance counted for anything, he would be a difficult opponent for Nine.

"You will defend the challenge?"

"I will."

Six wasted no time, spinning around low to the ground, scooping up the free sword at this end and attacking Nine who had to whip down and grab his.

Several times he lunged and swung the sword at Nine, whose movements were incredibly swift, weaving and dipping out of reach. Around they swung, first to the left then back to the right.

Karpenmor could see that Six relied too much on his height and reach, his skill with the blade was cruder than Nine's.

Nine feinted left then right, then left again, drawing a lunge from Six, before he ducked right and tumbled forward in a roll, slashing the hamstring of his opponent's left leg as he came back to his feet.

Six's leg collapsed on him, and he fell to his knee. Nine didn't rush back in but moved rapidly around in a semicircle, forcing the man to twist and turn, unable to use his sword arm easily.

Slowly he pushed his injured leg upright, but he wasn't anywhere as nimble now. Their swords clashed and the taller man was able to keep Nine away for the time being, letting the sword do the work.

Both men were covered in sweat. Nine feinted forward as though to rush Six, who instinctively pushed backward, grimacing as his hamstring wouldn't play along. He found himself off balance and open to attack.

Nine swung in, slicing across Six's stomach, opening it wide, causing the other man to cry out and snarl. His sword arm dropped as he reached for his wound. Nine didn't delay and swung his own blade heavily, severing the wrist carrying the sword.

He spun around and drove his own sword deep into the man's middle, twisting it as he did so, before yanking it out and kicking out to knock the man down.

Six didn't die straight away but there was no doubt who had won. Nine stepped away from the dying man and back to the far edge of the circle, sucking in air.

It would be a difficult task for him to beat everyone ahead of him if they fought like this. Ultimately it didn't really matter to Karpenmor who won, as long as whoever remained was in no doubt about who now ruled Enderk.

Whether by loyalty or fear after tonight he would have their allegiance. Karpenmor would prefer the former but he knew it was all different now than he'd expected.

Things were changing, he'd changed, and the future was going to be different.

"Victory goes to Nine." If he managed to fight his way to the top things were only going to get bloodier from here on in.

"Five, step forward."

No one moved. Eyes began to move sideways amongst everyone. "Five, step forward!" Karpenmor shouted louder. Still, no one moved.

"Where is he?"

Again, no response. A Vrah hurried up behind him, Karpenmor turning on high alert. "What?"

"His body is in his rooms, Highness."

"What happened?"

"He took his own life, Highness."

Karpenmor nodded. "Deal with it." He then turned back to the circle and shouted, "Five has taken his own, another traitor. Clear the body, now!" When it was done, Karpenmor looked around the people on the edges of the circle. None of them would have expected this event to happen this evening, but they all lapped it up like hungry wolves.

He was about to call out the next defender when a squat man stepped out from directly across the circle. Karpenmor saw a pair of hard cold eyes and knew this was the biggest challenge Nine had to face.

"Four?"

The man nodded, "Highness."

There was an anger within the man's eyes directed at Karpenmor, which would mean more problems should he win. There was nothing he could do to change what would happen next, but he could only hope that things turned out the way he wished.

Nine kicked the sword Six had used across the circle, a clear signal that he would not dishonor the code of the fight by denying his opponent a weapon.

A clever move if you win. Everyone will remember your actions; if you win.

While the earlier fights had been dealt with swiftly, this one kept them all transfixed for the next hour. As the earliest threads of dawn light began to reach the courtyard both men stood opposite each other, their spare arms drooping from tiredness and blood loss.

Both had numerous cuts on them. Nine had a gash across his back that had bled a lot, and Karpenmor didn't doubt he must be reaching exhaustion.

Four had only had to fight once but didn't look any fresher for it. His cheek was sliced, as was his chest. Both had bled heavily even though it had slowed.

Again, they stepped together, steel clanging, Nine parrying off the swing from Four, before sliding backward. In again this time lunging, parried by Four.

The sharpness was gone, it was pure survival driving their actions now, coupled with training. The turns were sluggish, and the gap much narrower.

Four lunged, more clashes, and the men came together, each holding the other's sword away and down between them. Words were uttered but whatever was said no one else could hear. As they were about to push off, Nine swung his head forward, cracking his brow across the nose and eyebrow of Four.

Four's head rocked backward such was the force, causing him to stumble back. Were Nine fresh no doubt he could have swung in then, but he seemed stunned from his action as well.

Neither man raised his sword as they tried to clear their heads. Four seemed to recover more quickly but his eyebrow had split, and both his nose and brow were streaming blood.

His breathing interrupted, he tried to take in air through his mouth, spitting out blood to allow him to breathe, while he raised his sword arm to brush his eye clear using the back of his wrist.

As he did so, Nine recovered enough to see what was happening, and lunged, slicing his sword up and under the armpit of the man. Dragging the sword backward he sliced open the skin and in pain Four's hand released, dropping the sword.

Nine stabbed his sword forward and into the chest of his opponent, dropping him instantly, leaving the blade inside. The challenger stood exhausted, his hands on his hips.

Karpenmor began to fear that his choice wasn't going to make it. With Three already dead there was only one person left, the number that Nine had challenged at the start. He'd already been lucky enough that several of his possible opponents hadn't fought but to win he had to defeat Two.

The older man had a distinct advantage, everyone could see that Nine had given his all to defeat Four. Despite that, when Two stepped into the circle he didn't look as confident as he had earlier in the night.

Nine stepped forward and pulled his blade out of the body still lying on the ground. He wiped it as best he could and backed away from it and the other sword.

Karpenmor called out for the last time. "And now the challenge shall be settled." He too backed out of the circle into a gap that formed out of nowhere in the crowd.

As soon as Two had picked up his blade Nine rushed forward, catching his opponent slightly off guard. He managed a slight slice across the man's left thigh, but not enough to take the man down.

It made sense, he wouldn't want this to be a long drawn-out affair, that only favored Two. He needed to weaken the other man as quickly as he could to create an opening.

Two didn't back away from the challenge and the fight began in earnest, the clang of steel echoing around the courtyard. There was no cheering from the men watching, only a growing tension as the battle continued.

Minutes coupled together as each man feinted and lunged, the other parrying or ducking out of the attack, neither landing anything other than occasional minor nicks.

Two backed out of an attack but his feet tripped over each other and he stumbled backward half down to the ground. It was enough, Nine wasn't patient and swept in, slicing the man's leg viciously, causing him to scream out in pain.

Nine stepped in closer and drove his sword through Two's chest, twisting it once it was in, staring at him until his face turned still.

And with that it was all over.

Nine could barely stand and was gasping for breath. The soldiers that filled the area all knew the gravity of what had just occurred. There would be no celebrations.

An eerie silence hung across the circle and no one moved. Karpenmor felt as exhausted from it all as Nine looked, and wanted to be gone from here.

"The decision is made and is final. This challenge is over and from this point forward, this man is your new One. His word is final."

He turned and left the compound, two guards accompanying him back to the palace. His heart only settled when he reached his room.

There was only one place for him and he was grateful for the stiff breeze that greeted him out on the balcony. If ever he wanted any of that amber brandy it was now.

So much had altered since he stopped consuming that, and for a moment, Karpenmor wished for the numbness that he'd felt back then.

Not knowing, not caring, being self-absorbed and uninterested in the ways of things had an appeal. The thoughts only lasted for a brief minute.

Looking out across the city as it woke he stiffened his back and gripped the balustrade. He'd chosen this path, it was what he wanted.

His father's words came back to him: `you can be better than me... watch out for them.`

Karpenmor didn't know who it was he had to watch out for, unless he'd meant Uksod and Yantarnaya. Underneath he thought that was part of the motivation behind what he was doing.

He didn't trust them, they'd used him before and he wasn't sure what they were up to.

From within his pocket he pulled out the pendant, and let his thumb rub over it as had become a habit. Slowly he calmed to a point where he could simply accept all that had happened.

"What's done is done."

Karpenmor knew that he'd drawn a long bow to define One's actions as treason, but then no one would question him about it. He'd ruled on it and already he could feel emboldened by that knowledge.

I'm in charge, and it will be my way.

The Vrah leader had been following the orders of Uksod, as he had for his whole life. His mistake was being unable to adapt to the changes happening around him, and trusting Uksod.

Karpenmor would deal with that one later. He wasn't even sure what that meant. Maybe it was time for the old priest to go away, to be out of the city and somewhere where he couldn't cause problems for Karpenmor.

"Highness."

The voice startled him and he turned, ready to reach for his dagger again.

"I'm sorry for surprising you, Highness." Aika stood there, her face reddening.

"Oh, it's only you."

"Who did you expect, Highness?"

"No one, Aika, it's just been a long night."

"So I hear."

He looked at her. Of course she would already know what had happened. She was going to be very good for him. He began to smile.

"What is it?" She blushed even more.

"I was just happy that it was you, and that you're working with me. Come and stand with me for a while."

She did, and he turned back out to look over the city. Things hadn't worked out how he might have expected months ago, but they were still heading the way they needed to.

While Aika said nothing, he appreciated the company, something else that surprised him. He wanted to look at her again for no real reason, but knew she'd be uncomfortable with it, so he just looked across the city.

His city... and out across the plains. It was all his now, he was the High Prince. He had Aika on his right and Nine on his left.

Soon the final bridge would be completed and he'd be able to set in motion important changes for Enderk. It was going to require more violence, perhaps deep down he'd always known that.

The difference was, he accepted it now. Soon he could finally get revenge for his father.

Everything has come together better than expected.

THE END

ACKNOWLEDGMENTS

A huge thanks to everyone that has read the first two books in the series and have been asking for me to hurry up and get this one done.

The solitary task of writing and editing a manuscript is made easier when you know there are other people just as invested as you are.

Thanks to my editor Fleetwood Robbins and proofing editor Robin Seavill and Jane Dixon-Smith for the cover.

My wife, Gill, is an important part of the process of producing each book and it would be infinitely harder without her.

FROM THE AUTHOR

In All Jest,

Thank you for choosing to read *Spire Of Fools*.

I'd be grateful if you could write a review. It doesn't have to be long, just a few words, but it's the best way for me to help new readers discover the book, and my series, for the first time.

If you'd like to stay up to date with my new releases, as well as exclusive competitions and giveaways, you're welcome to join my Reader Group at my website, www.kingdarryl.com.

You can also contact me via TikTok, Twitter, Facebook, Instagram or by email.

Thanks again for your support.

Best wishes,
Darryl King

A Fool's Errand

Fool Me Twice